The
Book of
Shadows

The Book of Shadows

James Reese

wm

WILLIAM MORROW
An Imprint of HarperCollins*Publishers*

HarperCollins books may be purchased for educational, business, or sales promotional use. For information please write: Special Markets Department, HarperCollins Publishers Inc., 10 East 53rd Street, New York, NY 10022.

FIRST EDITION

Designed by Nicola Ferguson

Printed on acid-free paper

Library of Congress Cataloging-in-Publication Data

Reese, James, 1964–
    The book of shadows / James Reese.—1st ed.
        p.   cm.
    ISBN 0-06-621015-1
    I. Witches—Fiction.   I. Title.
PS3618.E44 B6 2002
813'.6—dc21   2001031275

02 03 04 05 06 RRD 10 9 8 7 6 5 4 3 2 1

To JER, MMR,

PL, MR, and AJL

. . . such things,

though rare in time,

are frequent in eternity.

—Byron, "Cain"

The
Book of
Shadows

Prologue

I VIVIDLY RECALL my mother's blood.

I am at sea now. The ship on which I sail lists badly, despite its ballast: casks once full of whale oil and corn, now empty. The candelabrum by which I write is mounted to this tiny table; its candles burn at odd angles; pools of wax spill over at the wick. There is a full and golden moon tonight, but its light does not enter my cabin, and the weather just now prohibits my going topside. So here I sit, in this dank and dreary hold, my body as troubled by the sea as my mind is by the story to come.

The day it began, all I had was life (some five or six years' worth), language, and a name: Herculine, inherited from a father . . . rather, from a man named Hercule whom my mother did not know well, and whom I knew not at all. For many years to come I would have little else. Life, language, and a name. And always the memory of the blood.

The Day of the Blood dawns green and gold. It is late summer. Sunrays burn the morning mist from the fields that spread all around us, sizzling in the rising heat. A haze like gold dust in the air. Roadside, fields of hay have been harvested into cones twice my height. A distant barn. A brook runs along, mimicking the road. Far away there rises a black wall of forest.

No people. No sounds but the brook.

I am tired. The sun has risen since we left home, *Maman* and me. I don't know where we are going. I struggle to keep pace.

The road beneath our thin-soled shoes is baked golden brown, dry and dusty and cracked as bad bread. My perspiration falls to pock the earth. My mother perspires terribly; my small hand in hers is a wet rag; it would slip from her grip if it were to slacken at all, but she holds so tightly to me, so tightly.

Nearer now, the forest is not black but green, with its underglow of gold. The sun. The golden undersides of all green things. . . . Deeper, I know the forest is still dark, dark as night.

We walk on, beside the brook, which runs red, clogged with clay. Stones in the shallow water, the hunched and armored backs of ancient animals. The water whispers over the stones.

. . . My mother. Her face is a vessel that has been emptied, that has been broken, has spilled. Her eyes are melting ice. Her simple dress is dark at the crook of the arms, a triangle of dark spreads from her throat over her chest. Already the kerchief at her mouth is spotted red. I fear for her. I know she is not well.

I don't know where we are going. We have been on the road for hours. I have never been this far from the cottage. Are we near the place we are going? Somehow I know we are. My mother's gait quickens, then steadies and slows.

Why am I in my one dress, with ribbons wound through my long blond plait? The church shoes hurt my feet. And why does *Maman* carry that satchel full of things drawn hastily from my drawer?

The day has been a secret since its start. She laid me down last night as she woke me this morning, with whispers and a kiss. Prayers, I am sure. Now she says nothing. The last of her strength is in her step. Yet she trips over a stone half-sunk in the road and nearly falls. She stops, stands still, and then regains her sickly pace. Her hand tightens around mine, tighter, tighter.

Maman, what is it? Please talk to me. Are you all right? *Maman,* why don't we rest?

I see her trembling lips moving in muttered prayer. I see her cross herself.

Suddenly she stops beside the brook and kneels. Down on her bony knees, as I have found her every morning of my life. But this is not prayer, no. She sways, her head in her hands; for the first time she lets go my hand. I am afraid she will fall forward, face first into the brook, dashing her head on a stone. Moments, long moments like this.

Finally I kneel beside her. I cup my hands and scoop water from the brook. *Maman,* drink. *Maman?*

Her hands fall heavily to her sides. She turns her face to mine, slowly. Her eyes roll back to show only their whites. She breaks at the waist. The water falls from my hands as I reach fast for her shoulders, to steady her. She grabs my hands, laps at them, her tongue taking the water that is no longer there. She holds to the empty cup of my hands. Then I see, I think I see, a strange shape come into her eyes, a blot of blackness, writhing, taking shape, and . . . And into my hands she spews and spits the upwelling blood.

Her chest heaves. Her nails dig into the flesh on the back of my hands, slickened and red. There rises a sweet acrid stench.

Blood from her nose. From her mouth. She cries out, tries to speak, but chokes on the blood.

Her eyes flutter shut. Still the blood wave comes, forces her sealed lips to split. While the blood wells again, she tries to speak. I cannot understand her. Her eyes are not her eyes; something else is at their center.

I hold to her. She is heavy. She slips from my blood-slick grip. Her dress tears and she falls on her back on the bank, near the brook. In the brook. I hold her head up. If she turns to either side she will drown.

Standing above, knee-deep in the brook, I cast a shadow over her face. Her eyes open. She focuses with the strangeness at the center of her eyes. The pupil transshapes. Twists and turns into a recognizable shape, but still I cannot identify it. Then her eyes roll back to the whiteness and there is nothing.

I am crying. My mother is dying, I know this. She spasms, coughs up a huge clot of blood. Flat on her back, she drowns not in the brook but in her own blood.

I pull at her. Try to pull her from the water. She is heavy, too heavy. To move her, to take hold of her twitching legs, I let go of her head and it sinks into the red water. Still I pull at her legs. She is too heavy. I pull and pull and she does not move. I see her red and wavering profile underwater. Bubbles rise from her mouth, and underwater I see a black skein of blood unravel.

I am in the brook now, standing knee-deep, trying to maneuver beneath my mother. Trying to shove her up onto the bank. Nothing. Then suddenly she turns.

I shove. Harder. She is on the bank now, on her side, spilling blood into the mud we have made, the bloody mud. She revives. It seems so. But everywhere the blood smell.

She spits, coughs. Tries to speak. And then, clearly, I hear, *Go to the Stone. Take this road to the Stone and* . . .

And with the last of her strength she raises her arm. It hangs in the air like a crooked branch, one long twig-like finger pointing down the dirt road. *Go to the Stone.*

I follow her finger. There, on the horizon, I see it. Far away.

Go, I hear her say. A watery, eerie, deafening cry. *Go to the Stone.*

She rolls from the bank to the brook, and I rise up and run. I run and run and run. To the Stone.

Book One

The Night of the Senses

Thou shalt not suffer the
sorceress to live.
—*Exodus 22:18*

1

Early Life, Such
as It Was

Iₙ 1812, I went to "the Stone," the holy house at
C——, a village straddling the ill-drawn borders of
Brittany and Normandy, dependent upon the grace of
the Church. For the next twelve long years, the nuns
who had taken me in made it plain: if I lived cleanly,
devoutly, as they did, I might one day see the face of
God. . . . But no; lately I've seen only Satan. The sweet
girlish faces of Satan. . . . Ah, but I don't mean to self-
dramatize; I mean only to situate you, Reader, and
so . . .

My world was the domain of C——, its sloping
fields bounded by picket fences and, beyond, hedges
and waves of mounded stones. That place was comprised of a series of outbuildings surrounding three
larger, two-story buildings conjoined by galleries,
some shuttered, others open. It was hewn of darkly

mottled stone and gray slate. Surrounded by tall stands of deciduous ever-greens, the place seemed to leech the very light from the sky.

Set loosely at right angles, and forming an inner yard at the center of which rose a statue of the Sacred Heart, the three main buildings were these: St. Ursula's Hall, a large and featureless space sometimes used for assembly, beneath which were the kitchen and dining hall; the dormitory, set above a bank of classrooms, nuns' cells, and offices as well as our Pupil's Parlor, where the girls received their visitors; and the third building, which housed the main chapel, Our Lady of Prompt Succor, as well as the sisters' chapel, the main library, and several lesser libraries. Beyond the chapel sat the dairy and the sta-bles. Beyond the stables was a graveyard, where we buried our dead in private. Too, there was the laundry, a dovecote, a carpenter's shop, a smithy, and the building known as the Annex, which sat empty and unused all my years at C——. White pickets formed our inner borders; and it was within these pick-ets that we girls, twice daily, surrounded the Sacred Heart to take our exercise. The youngest girls formed an inner circle, so near the statue as to see our Lord's incarnadine heart amid the marble folds of His robes. If the weather was fair, it was in the yard, thusly circling our Savior, that we would stand with arms akimbo, bending at the waist, doing this and that, careful always to keep one foot firmly planted on the ground, "as befits a lady." In winter, we would crowd under the galleries and stretch and bend as best we could. My position in these drills was fixed: I had always to stand nearest the kitchen, lest Sister Brigid need me for some duty therein.

Understand: I was the sole scholarship student at C——, and I was made to work for my keep. Usually in the kitchen, sometimes in the laundry or gar-dens. Though Sister Isadore ran the Lower School, and Sister Claire de Sazilly the Upper (both answering to Mother Superior Marie-des-Anges), it was to old, enfeebled Sister Brigid that I reported. I loved her; she was kind. Kind too was the extern I knew from an early age, Marie-Edith, who came to C—— from the village thrice weekly to help with meals; she also did our shopping, as the sisters were suspect of all worldly commerce. Indeed, it was I who lately taught Marie-Edith to read in my room off the kitchen. . . . Yes, I lived apart, at Sister Brigid's request, and I did not mind. The cellarer, Sister Margarethe, however, did mind: not only did I occupy her pantry but I deprived her of the root cellar dug into its floor and covered over with boards. Though it was bar-ren and cold in winter and damp in summer, with its walls in constant sweat, the room suited me. It was private; and it was privacy I craved above all else. No novitiates came to see that my Bible lay beneath my pillow as I slept. No one woke me harshly at first light. Neither did the candles I burned through the night attract attention. And, blessedly, a pump sat just outside the kitchen door, and it was from this that I drew my bath water, bathing alone behind my closed door.

Not only did I have to work for my keep—and countless were the potatoes peeled, the corn shucked, the fish scaled and gutted . . . —I had to succeed academically. If I did not—and this was intimated, if never stated—I might be sent away to an orphanage or some lesser facility of the Ursulines.

And so I became an excellent reader at an early age. In time, no text was beyond me. And the books at C——. . . . So many wondrous works, though I remember too some particularly hateful theology and sheaves of impenetrable poetry. . . . I was perhaps ten when I began to study Greek under the tutelage of Sister Marie de Montmercy. I immersed myself in the language; but only until I discovered Latin, to which my allegiance shifted. Here was the language for me! So sensible, the construction of its sentences as satisfying as a puzzle perfectly done. I don't mean to say that I rambled about C—— with Aeschylus and Cicero tripping off my tongue, but fluency did come in time. Additionally, there were the hours devoted to the perfection of our French, of course— and her sisters, Italian and Spanish. I worked diligently on English and German in private; quite similar, the two, though I loved the myriad exceptions of the former and detested the guttural rattlings of the latter. For this, I relied solely on texts and guesswork, for none of the nuns spoke English and only one spoke German (ancient Sister Gabriella, as likely to nod off as to assist me with the nuances of pronunciation).

Mathematics, penmanship, geography. . . . These were easy and unexciting subjects, which I easily mastered. (Immodest, but true.) Yes, scholastically, I further set myself apart and eventually won access—for one hour each day— to the private library of Mother Marie-des-Anges.

That library! . . . The rich, supple bindings of Cordovan leather. And the thin blue cloud of smoke that seemed always to hang in the air (Mother Marie-des-Anges favored an occasional Spanish cigarette, en vie privée.). Sunlight seeped into the library through two large windows of Bavarian stained glass. That pied light was enrapturing. I would position myself to let the multihued light swim over whatever text I read. . . . Those hours in the library of the Mother Superior are my finest memories of C——; and it pleases me to have them, for all my other memories of C—— are of the Chaos that overtook order there.

Order? Oh yes, life at C—— was well-ordered. Our days were divided into canonical hours, those times appointed for an office of devotion: Matins, followed by Lauds, then Prime, Terce, Sext, None, Vespers, and Compline. After Lauds we studied for one hour, at which time a bell would summon all the girls to a breakfast of white bread (wonderfully warm on Monday and Thursday), thick pats of cold butter, and coffee. We ate in silence, seated on benches before long oak tables. We wore our gray work pinafores, white puffs of tulle at the sleeves (so extravagant that seems now!); our hair was wound into braids or tucked beneath caps of white chamois.

Breakfast lasted a half hour. A Low Mass might follow; typically, classes would commence directly. Then Terce, or High Mass on holy days. Followed by more study. Occasionally, the younger girls would be granted a fifteen-minute recess during which they would receive black bread and water. Thrice daily, at the discretion of the Mother Superior, the Angelus bell would sound and we would gather to commemorate the Incarnation.

We ate our primary meal at Méridienne, or high noon. This meal—dinner, we called it—consisted of vegetables grown in our gardens, perhaps a stew of game, or seafood that Marie-Edith had begged from a fisherman "of the faith" down on the quay. Wine was often poured from the vast store kept by Mother Marie-des-Anges. We ate well, owing, I think, to her presence: she had a taste for . . . for life's finer things. (At our meals, I served, eating only after the other girls, and in the company of various externs and aged, infirm nuns. This did not shame me, though it was often suggested to me that it should.)

Dinner was followed by exercise, rest, or prayer—the decision was not ours. Then None. More study. Vespers. Meditation. Study. Collation: a light meal of fruits or cheeses. Compline. And finally, sleep. Our routine was only slightly more relaxed during summer recess, when the great majority of girls left C——— to vacation with their families; many nuns, too, went on summer retreats of one kind or another.

. . . Regarding my time at C——— . . . I endured. Took refuge in the orderliness of the convent school, the ceaseless tick-tocking of that canonical clock, every day the same, same, same. . . . And I tasked myself with study.

. . . Ah, but of course there is more to say. I do not wish to say it, but I must, and will.

The school at C——— was attended by girls of a particular sort, and it seemed to me that by some cruel act of Providence I'd been cast there to remind them of their many advantages. They were lace to my linen, jewels to my gimcrack. Upon maturation, they would *ascend.* Their fathers had made fortunes in commerce; the daughters of these men, though derided as "common" by the girls of bluer blood, were rich. They spoke of dowries and diamonds and what Papa and Mama were doing with whom and where—polo with a crowned prince, horse racing with the Raj, brunch in Paris with a Swedish baroness, et cetera. It was a language I could not speak.

That no beribboned packages from Paris came for me was fine. True, I would never spend summers where another language was spoken. I would never "take the waters" here or there. No pieces for violin and pianoforte would be commissioned and played to mark my birthday. About this, nothing could be done.

Though shy and unseen by the other girls, I, at an early age, became a favorite of certain nuns. Sometimes the attention accorded me in the classroom was an embarrassment. One nun in particular seemed almost smitten. She would stare at me, every question was asked *of* me, every answer presented *to* me as a gift. These attentions decreased over time; still, I would sometimes stare at my hands (so despicably large!) or at the bank of fir trees beyond the classroom window so as not to meet a sister's gaze. There was one nun in particular... Of course, I'd no idea what this nun sought, if anything; now I might hazard a guess, for I know things about the lives of cloistered women, things I'd no inkling of then.

Perhaps the nuns' small favors encouraged some enmity among the other girls, but I didn't care. Let them say what they will, I thought. Did I revel in their envy? Perhaps. I hadn't their wealth, their graced and easy lives. Let them envy my learning.

Yes, the more attention I received from the nuns, the farther I was distanced from my peers; it was an unfortunate equation. I did not fight this; indeed, I simply studied harder. For me there was nothing but the books. I *lived* in the learning.

Yet, some years after arriving at C——, I began to *sense* ... things. Sense the reason I lived life at a remove, distanced from the other girls, distanced from my true self.... In later years, I began to notice certain changes taking place as regards my body. My appearance began to change in ways that shamed me. The other girls were changing as well: some sprouted early into womanhood. None of the changes I noticed among them mirrored my own, and this alarmed me. I waited vainly for my figure to become fuller; but I remained ... unendowed.

Of course, the majority of the girls must have been simply made; but to me they were perfection. Delicate as dolls in their lacy white dresses; one, I recall, wore a cameo of her mother, deceased in childbirth, on a ribbon of apple-green silk; another, pale and sickly, was sometimes let to wear the pearl earrings sent to her from the Azores by her father—and those adornments, like calcified tears, seem to me now to be emblematic of the girl. It was to her that I was most drawn. (Pride bars me from naming her here. And to deem her a "friend" would be inaccurate.) Frail and often ill, she lived her life at a remove from the sorority. Our physicality set us each apart: she was weak and I was . . . *alors*, I was me. . . . She was kind to me on occasion; unaccustomed to such and ever-wary, I took her kindnesses and tried to spend them in turn. . . . No act of kindness, no matter how small, is ever forgotten; this I believe. It becomes an emotional currency, remaining in constant, universal circulation. As for the opposite of kindness, which I have known well, it deserves no name.

. . . Yes, the girls were the manifestation, the literal embodiment of my dreams. They were what I wanted, impossibly, to be. Understand: I hoped then that I might change. Hoped that I might yet ripen into an approximation of what they were: beautiful girls. But I was . . . indelicate, graceless, and overgrown. In time, I lost that hope and reconciled myself to my fate, to my physical state . . . my particular, my *peculiar* physical state.

I had always been tall, but by thirteen or fourteen I stood a full head taller than any other girl at C——. My form lacked the roundness, the suppleness of the other girls. I was angular where they were curvaceous. I was lean where they were plump. My limbs were embarrassingly long, and I possessed an uncommon strength. (How I would flush with shame when asked by Sister Brigid to reach down a jar from the cupboard, or force a stuck door, or pull a swollen cork from a jug of wine!)

Even the features of my face began to change; imperceptibly, of course, but to me the changes appeared sudden, drastic. My forehead grew more prominent, and the planes of my cheekbones seemed too high and angled. My eyes embarrassed me: they seemed the portals to some secret place, and I was loathe to meet anyone's gaze. (My eyes are well-shaped, and of an uncommon blue-green. . . . I will say that I have recently been told they call to mind the shifting shades of shallow seas.) My nose, which had been pug, slightly upturned, matured to its present shape—Roman, one might say, well-shaped; at the time it seemed to me grotesquely long. My lips grew full to frame an overly large mouth. My skin—unblemished, fast to blush—bore a natural pink tinge; other girls used powders, or pinched their cheeks to achieve a similar effect. As for my neck, it seemed an aberration: spindly, too long and thin. My hair was like straw to me then, unruly, brittle and thick. I wore it in a tight plait that hung down, bisecting my back. I would wear no ribbons. I did nothing to attract attention. . . . My feet? What horror they stirred in me! Laughable now, really, but at the time I strove to conceal them. I, like Cinderella's stepsisters, tortured myself with shoes whole sizes too small. And I wore gloves to hide my hands, which seemed to me those of a giantess.

Enfin, every detail of my physical being embarrassed me. My stomach was in a constant state of upset, so scared was I that someone would tease me, or even talk to me. The nuns and girls had the power to mortify me with a single word, uttered innocently or not. I lived in a state of abject discomfort . . . physical, social, and emotional discomfort. I wanted to disappear, dissolve into imagined worlds, the worlds of which I read.

The nuns at C—— knew where their charges were headed: back into the bourgeois homes from which they'd come—having left one as Daughter, they'd enter another as Wife. And so the requisite skills were taught them. "Parlor skills." I had no aptitude for such. I hated those long hours engaged in inane handicrafts: the spinning and whittling of little masterpieces destined to gather dust in drawing rooms; the making of fabric-covered buttons intended to bedazzle a maiden aunt or adorn the waistcoat of a younger brother. . . . We were schooled in the mending of lace, taught to paint mini-portraits on ovals of ivory with single-bristle brushes (the worst!), and shown how to tie off needlepoint knots so that the back of a canvas was as tidy as the front. Never in my life have I felt more keenly the passage of time, its utter *waste*.

I managed to turn my scholastic success to my advantage; it seemed a matter of my sanity! I petitioned for and was granted time away from those handicrafts to study independently. It was tacitly held that I would have no use for such skills; what parlor talents I'd acquire would never be put to practice, for the wars of my life would not be waged in parlors. I'd need no such arsenal to back my efforts at securing a husband or subordinating a servant.

And so on those afternoons when all the girls strove to acquire the arts requisite to their success as ladies, I wandered the gardens alone. In dire weather I took refuge in the Mother Superior's rooms, at a tiny table inlaid with roseate marble.

I read while the others darned and sketched and sang. In time, I came to long for books physically—the ink-scent of a new book, the musk of an ancient tome. I would finger the threads of the sewn bindings; and how luckless I felt if a favorite book did not have gilt-edged pages. These works transported me; and the leather-bound pages forged a shield behind which I hid.

Such friends I made: Mrs. Radcliffe and the Scotsman for romance. Their novels were read by the light of pilfered candles in my pantry-room, or slipped between the leaves of some more suitable work. They were scandalous, not the proper pastime of a girl. . . . Ah, yes . . . It was in the works of those two novelists that I lost myself, wholly and happily. What a world they conjured, filled with love affairs, sly mistresses, persecuted ladies fainting in lonely country houses, post-riders slayed at every relay, horses ridden to death on every page; there were dark forests, mountain vistas, palpitating hearts, vows, sobs, tears, kisses, skiffs in the moonlight, nightingales in thickets, and gentlemen brave and virtuous as God. In my dreams I was the chatelaine in the low-waisted gown whiling away her days with her dainty elbows at rest upon the casement, chin in hand, attendant upon the white-plumed rider who'd gallop toward her across a windswept moor. Sometimes, too, I was the white-plumed rider. (Of course, I didn't know a skiff from a barge and I'd never set foot upon a moor, windswept or otherwise, but that mattered not at all.)

I had Browning for beauty, Shakespeare for the lot of life. I committed whole soliloquies to memory, treating stands of trees and inquisitive squirrels to my theatrics. I favored Hamlet's indecisiveness, Prospero's pained anger, and Lear's loneliness. I attempted Lady Macbeth's crazed strength, but I could never quite achieve it.

Quieter hours were passed with Pliny and Plutarch. (Nothing rivals the romance of a fallen empire—the intrigues of statesmen and debauched emperors, daggers drawn from cloaks, and poisons tipped from rings into gem-encrusted goblets. . . .) . . . It was Ovid and me. Horace and Homer. Plautus, Pythagoras . . . any philosopher I could get my hands on. I read everything. One long weekend, I recall, I even read a collection of papal bulls!

. . . And through all the reading, I held to a false belief: that this was living. I know now that books are but ashes to the fire that is life. Still, I do not regret a single moment spent reading, not a one. I am thankful for the diversion the written word afforded. I don't know what I would have done otherwise, for my life was horrid. Horrid and unlivable. Yet I lived it, I survived. Granted: I do not speak of cramped quarters, consumptive girls sleeping four to a bed, or meals of chestnut gruel. . . . No; I speak of things far less common than that, and far, far stranger.

. . . I am trying to summon courage here. There are things that must somehow be said. Yet I hesitate. It's not that I grasp for words—the opposite really: I'm afraid that once I start telling this tale I won't be able to stop. No, I know the words will come; it's controlling the rush of recollection that concerns me. But there is a story here to tell, and I have sworn myself to tell it truthfully. To tell it even though the facts are preposterous; they strain credulity and will be, for some readers, beyond belief.

... But please, you must believe me, or I cannot go on. And you, Reader ... well, there is a reason you hold this work in hand, no? Perhaps that reason is clear to you now; if not, trust in this tale of mine and all will come clear in time. I promise you that.

... We return to C——.

Long years passed. I remained apart from the others. Apart from life. No one touched me, and I touched no one; no mother's touch, no sister's touch, and certainly no lover's touch. True, I excelled at my studies, and was eventually let to determine my own course of study. So I would retreat into St. Augustine, or lose myself in the labyrinth of Latin grammar. . . . Books, books, and more books. It was all ash; no fire; and no warmth.

Finally, one morning not long ago, while I was rolling dough in the kitchen, Sister Isadore came to request a moment of my time. We quit the kitchen together. We walked in silence through the gardens near the kitchen, traced with our steps the narrow paths of flagstone; the whole of the garden was bordered by boxhedge, and geometries of box within the garden kept our herbs from overtaking the cellarer's vegetables, kept the tomato stalks from leaning too far into bright batches of begonias, dahlias, fleur-de-lis, oleanders, marigolds, purple ageratum, and gray artemises. . . . Sister Isadore asked how I was progressing with my studies. Well, said I. Did I enjoy my kitchen chores? Yes, I lied; she said she was glad. Silence ensued, and I broke it, as I knew I ought, by expressing yet again my thanks to the Order for taking me in when I, as a child, had run crying to their door. Sister Isadore bowed deeply to accept my thanks.

"Confirmation is fast approaching," said she, finally. She stood straight-backed and tall, weaving her long spiderish fingers into a web. I stared up into her colorless eyes, for already I knew a pronouncement was in the offing.

"Yes," I said. All those younger girls who were set to be confirmed were busy with preparations, as were we in the kitchen. "In July, no?"

"July the sixteenth, to be exact. Mere weeks away. After confirmation, as you know, there is always a . . . a reordering of the girls." Sister Isadore fell silent. I understood when finally she said, absently, more to herself than me, "Of course, there's the slight matter of the exam . . ."

"Yes, Sister," I said.

"But surely *that* will not trouble *you* at all." Sister Isadore congratulated me, assured me that this was in my best interest—which meant, of course, What else was to become of me? I'd come from nowhere, and had nowhere to return to. Evidently, she deemed me unworthy of a sacral marriage to Christ. What else was I to do but teach?

Yes, I was to be sent up. To the Upper School. There I would be trained to teach.

My only thought was this: that I would have to live in the dormitory, among the other girls. Sister Isadore confirmed this, and congratulated me again; she added that less would be expected of me in the kitchen, though I was still to serve at mealtime. She looked at me incredulously when I asked if I might remain in my room. No, said she; clearly the cellarer had succeeded in her long campaign to win back her pantry and root cellar. I begged to remain in my room and Sister Isadore grew impatient. In the end, she walked away.

When next the test was administered, in the week preceding confirmation, I sat for it. I had already filed my birth certificate at the office of the superintendent. (Actually, as I have no birth certificate, I presented a letter from Sister Isadore.) The mayor of C——— endorsed a certificate of good morals on my behalf, though he knew nothing of me, let alone my morals. I more than passed: I answered every question correctly, thus earning for myself the unframed picture of the Virgin that had long hung in the laundry.

The day of confirmation—16 July—came quickly and passed slowly. At day's end, with the greater part of the girls gone, I was to move into the dormitory.

Twenty girls dressed in white formed a procession that wound through the house and yard toward the chapel. They were slick with perspiration beneath their decorative dresses, lace-fringed confections. We older girls, confirmed in years past, sat shoulder to shoulder in the back of the chapel, among mothers, sisters, aunts, and grandmothers busily fluttering fans before their flushed faces. (No men were allowed within our precincts. They waited at the gates.)

The ceremony progressed with all the pomp and severity a holy house can display on such occasions. Afterward, the double-parlor beneath the dormitory was opened to receive the girls and their female relations. There were hugs and kisses and introductions, invitations to meet here or there during the recess. I stood idly by in a corner for nearly an hour, still as the portraits hanging above me, and having no greater role to play in the day's events than they. Finally, unable to bear that society a moment more, I made my way back to my room. It was dark and dank and undecorated, but it was mine, and I was loathe to leave it. From my tiny trunk, I unpacked a simple shift. I slipped from the kitchen through a back door.

I did not know of my destination until I arrived there: a faraway, neglected grotto. This tiny structure built of stone had long ago fallen into disuse and disrepair: it sat too near the dairy and the fetid perfume of our few cows wafted over it when the wind blew just so. I loved the grotto for its seclusion, for its lichen-covered statues, for the pocked and friable faces of its unknown saints standing sentinel beside the Virgin. There was a rusted stand of wrought iron, intended for votives, which stood on bowed legs, brittle and thin. Sundry ferns, seemingly borne on the air, grew from between the mounded stones. There, in the grotto, I had often spread a shawl on the bench beside the Madonna and sat reading for hours. That day, I sat staring at the Blessed Mother and the idling saints. When I began to pray—rather absently, I confess—my prayers fast dissolved to tears, and for a long while I sat crying for reasons I could not have named.

The day had dawned brightly, the summer sun falling down like bolts of golden cloth, the sky cloudless and perfectly blue. But as I fled the high-pitched din issuing from the double-parlor, as I stole away from the house proper that early afternoon, a bank of low clouds slid in, occluding the sun. The clouds were grayish-green, laden with rain. I heard the rolling groan of still-distant thunder. A warm wind rose up; a lone shutter slapped against the casement, crisply.

The skies were darkening. The air, redolent of rain, of turned earth and decay, was cooling quickly as I hurried on to the grotto.

In time the cloud cover settled squarely overhead, infusing the sky with light the color of a new bruise. The wind grew stronger, till the trees spoke for it with rattling green tongues. Though the thunder rolled ever nearer, there was no sign of lightning.

Already I heard the first of the coaches rumbling away from the convent, bearing down the packed-dirt road that passed not far from the grotto and led from C——; the celebrants would hurry away before the coming rain rendered the road impassable.

I remained.

Then the rain came. First a few drops, falling on the thin canopy like nails on tin. When the rain fell faster, harder, the green covering caved. The grotto sat in a recess of lawn, saucer-like; soon, the rain pooled at my feet.

Not long after, the lightning came. Only then did I rise to leave, and I did so unhurriedly.

I was still some distance from the front door when Sister Isadore swooped down upon me, unseen, like a dark and winged thing. How unlike me to leave her wondering and waiting, worrying. Had I lost my mind, dallying beneath a summer storm? Had I forgot that I was to serve our guests? Ahead of us, beside Sister Claire de Sazilly, Head of the Upper School, stood the cellarer Sister Margarethe (who seemed to exist in the Head's shadow) and Mother Marie-des-Anges, beautiful Mother Marie, who'd always been kind to me and with whom I would converse on those occasions when she'd discover me in her library, lost in thought. It was she who welcomed me to the Upper School; and it was she who pointed out a faraway rainbow, its arc complete.

"Rainbow, indeed," dismissed the Head, adding, to me, "You'll find that your trunk and whatever else was yours has been delivered to the dormitory. As for your room," said she, turning to her great and good friend the cellarer, "its restoration to a pantry has already begun."

"Shelves," breathed the cellarer, leaning nearer the Head, "remember, Sister, you promised me shelves."

"And you'll have your shelves," said Sister Claire. Which assurance caused a smile to spread over the pinched face of the cellarer, whose pink cheeks oozed from the tight white wimple she favored.

In the company of Mother Marie, I made my way to the dormitory. She suggested I change from my wet dress, but I declined. She insisted, kindly, and as I was shivering I did draw from my trunk my second shift. Refusing the Mother Superior's help, I slipped behind a screen of white tulle and shed my soaked clothes like a skin; they lay lifeless on the parquet floor. I did not strip off my stockings, and I donned again my sodden shoes.

The dormitory, which I had visited but once or twice when charged with bringing a sandwich or such to a bedridden girl, was barn-like, huge, with no interior walls; its pitched eaves rose up into raw rafters in which small black birds nested. Later, I would see bats hanging head-down in those rafters. I learned quickly to sleep on my stomach—a safeguard against the falling excrement. Set into the angle of the roof were two huge skylights. It was through these panes of thick, yellowed glass that light (and rain) fell into the dormitory. This glass jaundiced the brightest dawn; through it the most perfectly pale and opalescent moon appeared waxen and flat.

At either end of the dormitory, capping the rows of closely spaced and scantily screened cots, were two beds overhung with white linen, each belonging to a novitiate whose job it was to guard the girls in slumber. Beside each of our cots was a small table with one candle (which we burned with care, for one had to petition the Head for another). Above each bed was set a small crucifix of birch. At the foot of our beds sat our trunks, which were left open as (quoting the Head), "Christ's child has nothing to hide." Our sheets were of coarse linen, our blankets of coarser wool, and our pillows were filled (or so it was said) with the down from a single goose.

Mother Marie-des-Anges directed me to my place, and took her leave. I dragged my battered trunk to my cot, near the end of one row, beside two cots whose mattresses were rolled, their tenants already departed.

It was, of course, the lack of privacy in the dormitory that unnerved me. And it was the hour of rising, when that lack of privacy was most pronounced, that I would come to dread. I would hide myself within the sorority as best I could. I *knew* to. I was aware of . . . of *something*, something that shamed me.

Understand: I had been motherless nearly all my life. I was in many ways younger than my years, less mature. (I believe I am seventeen or eighteen now.) I had not known any woman well; no one had become that special someone— for most girls it is their mother, an older sister, an aunt or cousin perhaps. Nuns and girls had been my constant companions, yet among them something had set me apart. The nuns' interest in me was academic, sometimes spiritual; they sought to instruct or save me; none of them taught me what I needed to know. No, there was no one to whom I might address certain questions, questions of a *delicate* nature. . . . Must I be more specific? No; I will trust to your good sense. Think of those things a young girl, a young *woman* should know; and believe me when I tell you I knew none of those things. *None!* I was ignorant, pathetically so. What knowledge I had I'd gleaned from the girls. And often the information proffered by them was deliberately misleading; it was a game played against me, against all the younger girls at times.

That summer we remaining girls rose *en masse* in predawn darkness to dress and see to our toilettes. I can still hear that horrible bell shattering the silence of sleep. I can see the novitiates marching down the rows of cots, ringing that bell, banging it on the beds of the girls who lay in the deepest sleep. Its brass cup would send a shiver through the bed frame, through my very bones. . . . I lay feigning sleep, a sleep so deep I simply could not rouse myself from it. I lay listening to the sibilance of slippers shuffling across the floor, waiting for the novitiate or nun who would come and chide me with bitter breath. How skilled I became at deception! And for this I incurred their wrath, and chores beyond number.

On appointed days, a rotating shift of girls rose early to fill the tubs with tepid water for bathing (heating the water had been my job previously, when I'd been resident in the pantry). These days we were expected to don our thin bathing dresses and dip, two at a time, into the tubs. I could not do this. *I simply could not.* I would sneak into icy baths in the predawn hours, when all the others slept, or I would rise late and slip into a tub of dirt-darkened water.

Invariably, I would arrive late to Lauds. I would slide into a back pew beneath the heated, scornful gaze of the nuns, frequently disrupting the service. But I hadn't a choice: I would suffer what I must in order to keep my secret, a secret unknown even to me.

That first afternoon in the dormitory, Mother Marie had introduced me to several girls gathered around a certain cot. They knew me, and I knew them, but it was as if I'd come from another world. "This is Herculine," said the Mother Superior. "We welcome her to the Upper School, where she will train for the teaching certificate." There was snickering and bitter words; one girl estimated my height in hands, as one does for a horse.

I kept far from that gaggle of girls, walked toward the dormitory's far end. There was a broad window, giving out to the sea. Through it, I saw that same rainbow. A great arc of pure color, its bands distinct. Earlier, outside, before Sister Claire had dismissed it, Mother Marie had averred that the rainbow was a gift from God and, in a whisper, she'd added to me how lucky I was to be in receipt of such, on "this of all days."

That afternoon, with the girls milling about behind me, I stood staring at the rainbow a long while. It was beautiful, yes, arching over the summer fields of hay cones and crops, the sky a deepening blue behind it, its colors as elemental and pure as the storm it trailed. But I closed my eyes, clenched them tight as fists so as not to see, so as not to cry. For this is what I knew to be true: the rainbow was no gift from God. It was a promise He could never keep.

2

Peronette
Gaudillon

NOT LONG AFTER my "ascension" to the Upper School—it was 21 July, to be exact—as I sat on a stony bench in the shade of a tall chestnut, reading some ill-gotten novel, a girl came up behind me, unheard, and startled me terribly by asking: "What book is that?" (It was, I recall, Mathew Lewis's *The Monk*—its utter and wonderful depravity cheered me.)

The book slipped from my hands. It seemed my heart might pop. I stood and turned to the girl. Finally, when I was able, I said, "You gave me quite a fright." I retrieved the book from where it had fallen. I showed the girl its imprinted spine; she shook her head, shrugged her shoulders. She did not know the book, and neither did she ask about it.

The girl was Peronette. Peronette Gaudillon. With whom I fell instantly in love. My association with Peronette, lasting but a few short weeks, would very nearly cost me my life.

She was beautiful. Tiny. Fine as a doll. Dark-complected. With long hair, black as jet, which she wound into a braid as smooth and sleek as a whip. But what distinguished Peronette was something ineffable at her core that roused or riled one; no one was indifferent to Peronette Gaudillon.

I would learn that Peronette had come to C—— just two days prior. I remember thinking, how strange that one should arrive during recess. "Family circumstance," it seemed, had dictated that Peronette be consigned to the care of her aunt.

"Who is your aunt?" I asked.

"My aunt," said she, "is Mother Marie-des-Anges. . . . Of course, I have never known her by that name; it will take some getting used to."

I had naively taken the Mother Superior to be alone in the world. I believed this of every nun, that her marriage to Christ was her sole attachment. Yet the fact that Peronette and Mother Marie-des-Anges shared blood seemed to me somehow . . . *right*, for weren't they both extraordinary?

That first afternoon we slipped away from C—— during the hours of private study. (This was at Peronette's suggestion. I simply did not do such things, did not *disobey*.) We toured the farthest reaches of the grounds. When I turned to hurry back to the chapel at the sounding of the Angelus bell, Peronette grabbed my arm, looked deep into my eyes, and said, "We did not hear that."

"But we'll be in trouble," I countered. "We'll be scraping plates for a week."

"No, we won't. Who am I?" asked Peronette. "Answer aloud."

"You are Peronette," said I.

"More," said she. "Go on."

"You are the niece of Mother Marie-des-Anges."

And so we continued our tour, Peronette taking my hand in hers.

I was nervous: I overspoke. I believe I proffered the Latin name for every animate and inanimate thing we saw. Finally, after I'd mumbled the name of a certain thin, barkless tree, as well as that of the mushrooms clustered at its base, Peronette let go my hand, turned toward me, and said, "Really, dear. *Do* tell me you're this boring because you're nervous."

I affirmed that that was indeed the case.

"*Arrête!* Your nervousness is unnecessary. And boring me further will cause me to cuff you." She raised her hand. I thought I might cry. She started laughing and did, indeed, slap me—a quick slip of her hand across my cheek, which left a light, thrilling sting. I felt the heat in my cheek, the blood rise up. I held my hand over it for moments, until the skin cooled. I blinked back tears, cleared my vision. It seemed I had never been so exhilarated, so excited . . . so *alive.*

Peronette soon had my hand again and we were off, weaving through a copse of tall trees toward the shore. I could smell the shore; then I heard the sea, the grate of the stones in the surf. Suddenly we stood atop a dune; from it, sculpted sand sloped down to the shore.

Feeling wonderfully naughty, I followed Peronette down the dune; our descent was made on our buttocks, crab-style. She ran out upon the strand. I followed her over slippery, moss-covered stones, huge stones strewn about by the surf. Peronette perched on the largest. She took off her shoes and bade me do the same. She didn't give a thought to this act but, of course, I did. I was as ashamed of my feet as I was of the rest of my body. I did not think I could do it. I *knew* I couldn't. But I did. Again, Peronette had about her a . . . a *power.* That Peronette made me comfortable enough to do this is something for which I will remain forever grateful, despite all that came to pass. She thought nothing of baring her ankles before me, before "God and man." How scandalized the sisters would have been!

We sat on that rock a long while, squinting into the high sun, letting the sea air settle its briny, sweet perfume over us. Gulls rode the wind; their chatter ricocheted rock to rock. The water itself was still quite distant: low tide. I'd often heard Marie-Edith refer to the powerful tides along our coastline; it was said they returned at a gallop. Each summer a traveler or two would drown: caught too far from the true shore, sunbathing or gathering shells, they'd be outrun, overtaken by the inrushing tide.

That afternoon, as we lounged on the rock, Peronette spoke of her family. Her father was Breton; Madame Gaudillon, sister to Mother Marie-des-Anges—whose real name I would never learn—was of wealthy Norman stock. "We are rich," said Peronette. "Fabulously so. . . . But it has not helped at all." I did not ask what she meant; indeed, I said nothing. I listened. I did, however, see things differently all of a sudden: the gold-leafed prie-dieu, carved with scenes from the lives of the saints, which sat in the Mother Superior's rooms; her night robe of silk, embroidered with crosses, sacred hearts, and nails-of-the-cross; and, of course, there were those books that arrived from London and Paris, and the cigarettes sent up from Madrid.

"We are religious refugees, my aunt and I," said Peronette at one point. When I questioned her, she asked, "Do you think your Mother Superior was born to that role? No, indeed." And she proceeded to explain to me things of which I'd no idea, though they'd happened while I was at C——. Yes, I vaguely recollected some hullabaloo surrounding the arrival of the new Mother Superior, several years back, but... "My aunt," said Peronette, "was set to be allied to the finest family of Ireland. Specifically, its eldest son, a Kerry man whose name I cannot recall. There was a vast estate in the mountains near Cahirciveen, which is beautiful land. Have you been?"

I said I had not.

Peronette shrugged. "There was the estate, and there were plans made and invitations passed about and... and suddenly there were developments that all strove to keep from my young ears. With success, unfortunately. But I do know this: the engagement was canceled, the Kerry man sailed for London, and my aunt was sent here. The same relation who's arranged my captivity bought this House for her."

"Bought?" I asked.

"Essentially, yes," said Peronette. "That is, with the bishop's intervention, my aunt—or the Second Coming of that person, this *new* Mother Marie-des-Anges—was given the rule of this House.... You didn't know as much?" asked Peronette, incredulously. "You don't *see* the story carved like scrimshaw into the hard eyes of that *dreadful* Sister Claire? It was she who was cast aside, for coin and favors." Indeed, though I knew nothing of its genesis, there *was* something between Mother Marie and the Head, something cold and sharp, blade-like; rarely had I seen them together; neither could I recall overhearing any conversations of theirs.

Peronette spoke too of her brother, who had died two summers prior. Deaf, he'd been gored from behind by a bull as he'd gathered flowers in a field. His neck had been broken; he lay suffocating beneath a blazing sun for hours. Jean-Pierre, the brother, nearly dead from the loss of blood, was found by Peronette. He held still to the flowers he'd gathered, a withering red gift in his fist, expiring in time with his heart. He'd somehow managed to give the bouquet to Peronette. A dying gesture. Or so she said.

As for Papa, he kept a mistress in Rouen and was hardly ever at home. He made a fortune as a merchant—textiles, if I recall—but spent twice what he earned; he'd been saved from his creditors more than once by his unloved wife's considerable inheritance. That he worked at all was to his credit, said Peronette. And who could blame him for taking a mistress? "*Ma mère,... elle est folle.*" Peronette, with a forefinger, made a winding gesture beside her head; she whistled too, whistled in imitation of those mechanical birds that pop from Germanic clocks. Apparently, Madame Gaudillon needed constant care. If left alone she would turn to self-abuse; as a child, Peronette had come upon her mother often in the throes of such, once with chimney tools, once with the long wooden spoon that the cook had reported missing. It had gotten so that the servants had to hide the tapers when the family chapel was not in use. Not to mention the scenario she'd forced the dim-witted stable boy into; the only remedy for which was the boy's quick removal to an asylum just outside Lucerne.

I sat stupefied. I had never heard anyone talk so freely, so frankly. (So . . . *crazily*—I think perhaps Peronette took after her mad mother in many ways.)

"We ought to be getting back, don't you think?" I asked finally; hours of the afternoon had quickly passed. "Don't you agree?" I prompted.

"Doesn't the sun feel sublime?" This, after a long silence, was Peronette's response. With it, she loosened her dress at the collar and bared her throat to the sun. She lay back upon the rock. I stared at her, pleasuring in her presence and growing ever more conscious of my laboring heart and lungs; yes, her effect on me was bodily.

I had always shied from the sun, as from so much else. But how glorious it felt to bare oneself to its rays! Of course, I did not loosen my collar, did not raise my skirts to the knee as Peronette had, but still . . . I lay down beside her. . . . And dreamed, wakefully; I may have nodded off.

Then, I sensed . . . *something*. A change. I sat straight up. The sound . . . the rush. . . . The tide was coming in! The rocks that had led to our perch were already underwater, or nearly so, and the sea was rising up the rock on which we sat, stranded!

I shook Peronette, frantically. "Wake up!" I cried. "Wake up, *please*. The tide—!"

Peronette rose up leisurely onto her elbows, looked this way and that, and, to my astonishment, lay back down.

"Peronette! We will drown!"

"Don't be silly. The tide will not rise as high as this rock," said she, quite calmly. "Or at least, it won't *cover* this rock."

"But it has already risen over the rocks behind us! . . . Hurry, please!"

She rolled her skirts higher. "But wouldn't you rather wait and see what happens? Watch the water rise?"

"*I would not!*" Once the tide returned, fully, we would be a watery distance from the shore, from safety. I *knew* I would die that very day, my head dashed upon the rocks as I tried to swim ashore! Trying to put my boots back on, I worried the laces into knots; finally, I could but sling the pair over my shoulder.

"We can always swim in," said Peronette. "If we must."

"*I cannot swim!*" I began to cry. It was a child's sobbing, graceless, complete with heaving shoulders and contorted features, and it seemed to amuse my companion.

"Ah, well then," said Peronette, reaching for her shoes and smiling, "in that case we ought to go, no?" She held my hand and uttered through her laughter a thousand hollow assurances. I followed her over the rocks, some of which were indeed submerged, more slippery and sharper than they'd been before.

When finally we'd made it ashore, scrambling up the dune, I was fairly hysterical. I stopped crying only when I *determined* to do so. However, no strength of will could arrest my shaking and shivering.

When I sat in the tall grass to tackle the knots in my laces, I saw how badly I'd cut my feet. Our footing had been so unsure on those shell-encrusted rocks. Blood seeped through the sand that covered my legs to the shin. It was then the pain began. Peronette was smiling still: I assumed she had not cut herself. But I was wrong; she had. And I might have begun to think her *too* strange had she not then knelt to take my feet in her hands and, with the sea-wet edge of her shift, clean my wounds.

"Nothing too serious," was her assessment. She pulled that fabric through the deepest gashes; the pain was indescribable. She set my ruined feet upon her knees. "We'll let the air get at these scrapes a moment. They say the sea air is a curative. . . . That's why I was sent here, I think." And she kissed lightly my sandy instep.

Further unnerved by seeing that the tide had slipped over our rock, had covered it completely, I wanted to leave the shore. I said so; and surprisingly, Peronette obliged.

I would have liked to run, but pain prevented it. My feet were sore inside my boots. Peronette had replaced her shoes without caring for her own cuts; when I offered to tend her wounds, she declined and . . . and expressed a fondness for pain. "Stare at the pain," she counseled, "stare at it as though it were the sun, and something *magical* happens."

"Indeed," said I, "you go blind. What's magical in *that?*" I had already set to wondering how I'd secure the salve and bandages I'd need to tend properly to my wounds without having to undergo an examination from the infirmarian.

As we walked, the pain did lessen. Rather, it was replaced by all that I would feel in the weeks to come when Peronette would overwhelm me similarly, cause me to feel things I could not name, cause me to forget things easily named: prudence, pride, discretion . . . the list is long.

It had grown late; the sun had begun its descent. The clouds ran quick and thin. Striate bands of orange and red spread across the sky.

Fortunately, no one had remarked our long absence. Peronette and I entered C—— through separate entrances. Her parting words were these: "I shall ask for you." And in a shadowed doorway, she, on tiptoe, leaned in to kiss me on the lips; and then she was gone. I stood stunned. It was as though I'd been . . . as though I'd been beaten. Some months earlier, not wanting to peel, dice, boil, and mash yet another bowl of turnips, I'd stashed them in a cupboard; had Sister Brigid discovered them, I'd have been chastised, sent off to ask forgiveness of the Virgin. But it was the cellarer who found me out, and she went straight to Sister Claire, who deemed my crime worthy of punishment involving my palms and a thin whip carved of birch. Yes, stunned I was by Peronette's kiss, stunned as I'd been beneath that birch rod. And stunned I would be each time she kissed me.

That night I sat alone in the small library above the sisters' chapel, trying to study but unable to concentrate. The wounds to my feet were reminders that the day *had* happened, that I had not descended into a dream world. And Peronette's mysterious good-bye resounded in my head, overwhelmed every word I read.

I was roused by a rap at the library door. One of the sisters—no matter which—came into the library, chided me for "secreting" myself behind a closed door, said she'd searched for me everywhere. Mother Marie-des-Anges wished to see me in her chambers, immediately.

I rose and followed the nun. I was certain Peronette and I had been found out, and that I was headed toward punishment: a month's chores, perhaps two. Always, too, there was the threat of banishment: I could be sent from C—— as quietly and unceremoniously as I'd arrived. I was resigned; still, I wished it were not Mother Marie who'd mete out my punishment. Why couldn't it be Sister Claire, the Head, or another nun who meant nothing to me? Not far from Mother Marie's rooms, near our dormitory, with windows giving out on to the yard, my escort gestured that I should go on alone. She handed me her stub of candle, and I proceeded, guided by its weak light.

"Yes, come in," was the response to my tapping at the door. "Come in, Herculine."

Mother Marie-des-Anges stood as I entered. She was dressed in her embroidered robe and her hair hung down such as I'd never seen it, beautifully full and freshly brushed. That familiar blue cloud was in the air, quite strong now; a curl of smoke rose from the cigarette at rest in the bowl of a large scallop shell. On the table beside her favored chair was a book that was not the Bible.

She beckoned me to join her at her table; we sat. There were ripened fruits and a wedge of white cheese in a pale porcelain bowl. There were two goblets of a deep red wine. She slid one toward me. "You will share collation with me tonight. Does that suit you?"

As reply I lifted the goblet and drank. Mother Marie stared at me; I stared deep into the wine, and drank till it was gone. Finally:

"Herculine, dear, Christ needs a favor of you." Pause. "You have met my niece, Peronette?"

I could not respond. Mother Marie poured more wine; she pushed the porcelain bowl toward me. I took another long draught. I nibbled at a sweet, white pear.

"Peronette is joining us at an odd time. I fear she may fall behind when our regular course of study resumes." The Mother Superior turned her eyes from mine. She fingered a cluster of crimson grapes. "A family situation has occurred, one which could not be helped." She looked up at me. "What I'm saying is this: she needs a tutor, and she has chosen you."

I shall ask for you.

Mother Marie waited for me to speak. I could not. Instead, I drank. I must have been smiling, for a red rivulet ran from the corner of my mouth. This, apparently, was all the answer I needed to give, for the Mother Superior smiled herself and said, "It is settled then. I shall set a schedule for you both. You shall begin tomorrow."

Immediately, I stood to leave.

"Not so fast, dear Herculine," said she. "I do not intend to have you fall behind in your own studies." I saw that she worked her rosary, absently, beneath the lip of the table. "Perhaps that fear is unfounded. You are, after all, the finest student we have known here." At this I hung my head. "In any event, I'll be watching."

Mother Marie-des-Anges led me to her bookshelves, which I already knew well. She asked me questions about my studies in general, about certain works in particular. Had I made it around to the Aquinas yet? I had indeed. And surely I would set time aside for St. Teresa, if I had not already? I would, yes. I stood impatiently beside her, speaking only as was necessary: I wanted to find Peronette and tell her the good news. But of course, she already knew; after all, she had requested me as her tutor. *Me!*

I was shaken from this reverie by Mother Marie. "It is time you started your own library, Herculine." She gestured grandly to her shelves, which spread over an entire wall. "And the best books are the ones that have been lovingly read. Choose." I demurred, said I could not accept such generosity. It was insincere politeness; Mother Marie would have none of it: "Nonsense," said she. "Choose." She ran her finger along my jaw, tilted my face back at the chin; she looked at me a long moment. "Peronette is very special," said she. Our eyes locked, and she went on: "But mark my words: it is dangerous to indulge her." And with that the Mother Superior set to drawing down books and piling them into my arms.

"Let us see. . . . If you've already read the Aquinas then you should have it, no? A trophy of sorts." She smiled. "Oh yes, Plutarch. And Petrarch. . . . Have you read Shakespeare's sonnets? No! Well then," and she loaded me with the Bard's complete works, quarto-sized and bound in red kid, quoting as she did, " 'Two loves I have of comfort and despair,/Which like two spirits do suggest me still.' " I knew she might have finished the sonnet, but chose not to; a sadness overcame her then, and hastily she drew down the rest of my gifts. *The Lives of the Saints*. Texts in Latin and Greek. Writers I knew and others I didn't. Poets. Obscure theologians like Busenbaum, Ribadeneira and Sánchez. Here was even the latest novel by Mrs. Radcliffe! She stopped, smiling, when I could carry no more; and wordlessly she showed me from her rooms.

Ironic, that I should be given a store of books that were to teach me of the world, of life, when all that would soon transpire at C—— would make plain but one overarching lesson: *I knew nothing*. I held to a dream of friendship, as the Faithful hold to the dream of Redemption; but I knew nothing of friendship, nothing of love, certainly nothing of lust. Likewise, I was unacquainted with Evil, then.

3

The Devil's
Dance

PERONETTE, AS THE niece of the Mother Superior, the daughter of that woman's beloved, afflicted sister, enjoyed privileges the other girls at C—— did not. If this was to be expected, so too was the envy it incited.

Peronette, more accurately, might be said to have *assumed* such privileges; they were not all accorded her by Mother Marie, whose heart beat weakly before her niece. Peronette came to C—— quite spoiled. Once arrived, she remained so. Living among girls who sensed this favoritism and some nuns who, one assumes, did sometimes struggle against their vows of poverty, chastity, and obedience, all of which Peronette mocked, it would have been wise for Peronette, with her gaily-wrapped boxes arriving almost daily, chock-full of perfumes and candies and clothes, to have shown some discretion. She showed none. These parcels—sent by her father, who thus relieved himself of the duty of visiting his daughter—came from Paris, Vienna, Brussels, London; they came too from smaller cities where a certain craft was practiced perfectly: lengths of lace from Alençon, for example. Peronette would receive these parcels with utter equanimity. Often, I would be asked to open them. And often Peronette would let the contents lie wherever it was we'd laid them bare; and so some wanderer at C—— may have come upon pink scallops of soap at the shore, candied fruits strewn through the woods.

Yes, with her wild heart and untamed tongue, it would have been wise for Peronette to have exercised a little discretion, but no. . . . And the least hint of ill-will or censure simply encouraged her. She would wear a new and blindingly exquisite brooch to mass. She would pull an atomizer from the folds of her dress and spray lavender- or orange-water on a passing nun. And, as she enjoyed the protection of the Mother Superior, no one, not even Sister Claire de Sazilly, who ruled the Upper School with a simple and unwavering will, dared to discipline Peronette.

To the private rooms of Mother Marie, Peronette enjoyed absolute rights of in- and egress. She spent more time there than in the dormitory. Any hour of the day she might slip away to those well-appointed rooms, forbidden to everyone else (I was fortunate, indeed, to have enjoyed library privileges there), and while away the hours; in the heat of the day she would strip down to her "inexpressibles" and take to the cool stone of the windowsill. Meanwhile, everyone else kept to the strict routine at C——, only slightly more relaxed during summer recess.

I cannot say for certain that Mother Marie knew of her niece's behavior. Someone would have had to alert Mother Marie to Peronette's absence from services or class, or some other activity. And Mother Marie, who was the soul of sweetness to me, was feared by her sisters; more accurately, she intimidated them, with her beauty and extravagant ways.

But surely the Mother Superior noticed the dwindling supply of wine in her cellar, the aroma of freshly smoked cigarettes in the still air of her chambers, the missing articles of clothing, et cetera. If she did, she said nothing; and Peronette went undisciplined. This went on through late July and the first weeks of August; and all the while I was Peronette's constant companion—ostensibly, her tutor.

Of course, our tutorials were a sham. "Peronette," I would say, "your aunt worries that you may fall behind in September, when regular study resumes."

"September?" she would adjoin. "God help me . . . God help us *all* if I'm here come September!"

And though I tried in earnest, for a short while at least, I could not discipline Peronette's mind. Let alone her behavior. Often in the course of a lesson—held outside, weather permitting—it would occur to me that I might address a squirrel or stone with equal effect.

She had no use for history: "the mere exploits of the long dead." Regarding penmanship: "I never wrote a word *I* could not read." Mathematics, she said, was for merchants. Greek and Latin hurt her head; and German rendered the tongue obscene. Her written French was passable, almost good; her spoken French was crisp, elegant, and correct, and her voice mellifluous.

The tutoring went on with little progress. Mid-exercise, she'd up and run toward the shore or someplace, anyplace, leaving her books open to the elements. A session in which I held her attention for a half hour was a raging success, after which I too would be tempted to retire for the day. Miraculously, Peronette often performed well on examinations. Perhaps she listened more intently than she let on; perhaps she studied. More likely she cheated. Regardless, I would be quite relieved at these occasional successes, for I feared constantly that I would be summoned yet again by the Mother Superior, who'd relieve me of my charge. This, of course, never happened. Would that it had.

I should say that I *knew* Peronette offended, was disliked and envied. I *knew* she was willful, rude, grossly inconsiderate of others. She had a talent for such. Still, as she seemed to like me, I loved her.

Enfin, I was helpless before Peronette. I did as I was told. Often, after a day in her company, under her command, I would burn with shame at what I'd done. Never the truest of believers, I would then spend hours in the chapel begging forgiveness, for Peronette as well as myself, for all that we had indulged in. As is always the case, the progression from bad to worse was quick. I too entered Mother Marie's rooms, lounged about there without permission. I too smoked Spanish cigarettes and drank cognac—discovered beneath layers of bed linens, buried deep in a trunk whose lock we broke—until I was light-headed. I too rummaged through the splendid, secular wardrobe Mother Marie kept.

The end began on a beautiful late-summer day. Peronette had been at C—— but a few weeks. Bees droned about the convent grounds in pursuit of their queen; so too did the girls move in their constant, ordered allegiance to Sister Claire de Sazilly. The clouds hung low and seemingly motionless in the sky that day, the day I followed Peronette into her aunt's rooms, as I had countless times before. This was the time of year when rain showers come quickly at midday; a quarter hour of rainfall, often less, and all the while the sun continues to shine. Such a storm was expected that day: the heat of the day simply had to break.

Peronette and I had repaired to the Mother Superior's rooms. Such was the routine we'd established—no more than a half hour of study couched in two or more hours of idleness, during which we'd often hie to the Mother Superior's rooms while she, in her office, saw to the secular affairs of the house, such as they were. In recent days, I'd realized that Peronette was bored; it seemed she was begging to be caught, leaving the door to our refuge ajar, wearing the Mother Superior's rings to mass, unmaking her bed. . . . The games we played in the room had been fun enough for me, and indeed they still were— just being in Peronette's presence was enough for me—but it was the danger of detection that thrilled Peronette. Consequently, she grew ever more bold. I waited, worriedly, for what was next. . . . And then, that day, as we lay across Mother Marie's bed, sated, smoking, giddy from an imagined excess of liquor, listless in the late-day heat, attendant upon the rain, Peronette had an idea.

"Get up," said she. "Quickly."

I jumped to my feet. "What is it? Is someone coming?" I ran about the room fanning away the telltale cloud of blue smoke, throwing back the last of the wine in our glasses. . . . But I stopped when I saw that Peronette was taking off her clothes.

Her back was toward me. I watched in absolute wonderment. My jaw was slack; so too were my arms at my sides. I had never seen anyone naked before. *Never.* All those years of avoiding the crowded washroom and bathing in the night-stilled kitchen, or in the pantry proper. It was then, at that very moment, that I realized I did not know what a woman looked like. I knew even less of men, of course. And there before me stood a beautiful near-naked woman, for Peronette was no longer a girl.

She stripped down to nothing; she let her simple day uniform fall at her feet and stepped from the gray puddle of wool and tulle. She giggled, amused by whatever idea she had, but she did not speak. I stood staring as she moved to the huge armoire.

"Is the rain falling yet?" Peronette asked. "Look and see. *Go!*" I did not turn from her; I could not. Instead, I looked her over top to toe. It's a wonder I remained upright. I said, "Yes. It is." It might have been raining holy water and hosts, the pope might have been dancing with the Devil in the garden, I had no idea what the weather was.

Peronette ran to the window. Clearly, her plan, whatever it was, hinged on the weather. "Splendid," said she. "It's falling fast now." I watched as she leaned over the casement. I saw her small conical breasts; I marveled at their rosy tips. I drank in the smooth and supple curves that spread down the entire length of her body, from her beautiful brow to her delicate instep.

"What is it?" I managed, my heart skipping like a stone thrown across a still and shallow pond. "What will you do?"

"Just a little fun," said Peronette, tripping lightly across the room. The armoire to which she returned was so large she could have crawled inside it. Instead, she bent at the waist and riffled through its store. Muffled, her voice came back to me: "This will be *great* fun. Get ready. And watch the rain."

"I am," I said. "I will. . . . But what for?"

Peronette did not respond. I watched as she bent deeper into the armoire. I stood directly behind her. I grew weak, *physically* weak; I sat down heavily on the edge of the bed. I was still behind Peronette, but now I saw her from a lower angle, an even more revealing angle. I learned then what I had always, somehow, known: I was different. For as I looked at the naked woman before me, as she bent over, distracted by her plan and the contents of the armoire, I saw the wide curves of her hips, her weighty, shapely buttocks, and . . . and the darkly furred cleft of her sex, there, *there*, and nestled within the darkness I saw the easy folds of her lips.

But I . . . I am different. I don't look . . . My . . . I could not think. It was as though the breath had been sucked from my lungs. I began to cry. Tears of confusion. Tears for the kernel of knowledge ripening, ever faster, at the core of that confusion.

And then Peronette turned around to face me. I could not look at her: I was afraid. She held up a dress, not from modesty but rather as an introduction to her plan. "What do you think?" she asked breathlessly. And then she realized I was crying.

She let fall the dress—it was then I saw, *saw* the truth I already knew: just how different I was—and she came to me, knelt before me. "Silly, don't cry. This is all harmless, just a bit of fun." Her nipples were erect. Her skin was flushed. Her hands on mine were hot.

I was thankful she'd misunderstood my tears.

"And we won't get caught, if that is what's worrying you." She stood again, picked up the dress, which was in fact one of her aunt's habits—a simple shift of brown wool favored by the sisters in winter—and went to the window. "Splendid! The rain is letting up. Soon they'll venture out for a bit of sun. *Splendid!*"

Still I'd no idea what Peronette's plan was. Neither did I ask. Rather, I watched as the pieces of the puzzle came quickly together.

Peronette dressed in the shift. She took from the wall a large crucifix and threw it on the bed. She powdered her face. A red woolen skirt, drawn from the depths of the armoire, was wrapped around her head: hair, of a sort. And then she handed me her aunt's violin, swathed in blue velvet; she drew it from its snug fit within a specially-carved case, which she then set atop the table in the center of the room. The burnished wood shone; the dried bow was bent.

I protested, said I hadn't the requisite skill, that I knew nothing of the violin.

"All the better," said she. And here she turned back from the window, where she stood sentinel over the courtyard below. "This is no recital we are preparing for."

"What is it then?" I asked. "What *are* we preparing for?"

"We are preparing for the arrival of Satan. We are preparing to dance Satan's Dance upon this sill!"

"Peronette, no," I said. "You mustn't." I don't know if she heard me; certainly, she did not heed me. She hung out over the casement, gazing three stories down into the courtyard, waiting for the first of the girls to arrive outside. "It's always the youngest ones who scurry out first after the rain," said she. "The little puddle-hunters."

I was still stunned by what I'd seen of her . . . undressed; and, in truth, it did not matter what she had planned. Whatever she did, I would follow. We each of us knew it.

"There!" said Peronette, excitedly; the word came quiet and quick as an exhalation. "They are outside, the first of them. . . ." She smiled broadly at me, and gestured to where I should stand, violin in hand. She scampered up onto the wide sill. She edged out, out . . . dangerously far. Beyond her I could see the tops of the distant trees; through their thinnest branches, I saw the deep green of the sea marry the summer sky. I hurried to grab a fistful of the shift; I held to it as tightly as I could. I asked her, *begged* her to reconsider. She wheeled around, yanking the fistful of material from me. "Get ready, fool! . . . *Now stand back!*" Her face was contorted; whatever it was that came over her in that moment masked her beauty. She scared me. I recoiled. . . . Moments later I stood sawing a dissonant song on that violin; one to which Peronette—with the aspect of a snake charmed from its basket—danced, lasciviously.

"Faster! *Faster!*" she said; and I played on though the dried horsehair of the bow snapped, strand after strand.

Peronette had the crucifix in her left hand. "Play," I heard her say. *"Play!"* I brought that warped bow down upon the strings again and again. I held so tightly to the violin I feared I might snap its thin neck. *"Louder!"* The bow scratched and slid over the strings. A *horrible* sound, well suited to a devil's jig! *"Yes! Yes!*... Louder, and again!" Peronette gyrated upon the sill, swayed to the infernal tune. All the while I remained hidden behind a heavy drape. Her movements were so broad, so lewd, I was certain she'd fall from the sill. Frenzied, she swung her wig of red wool around and around. I flushed with shame at what she did with the crucifix, using it as an instrument of self-abuse; she held its bottom and, through the shift, verily *throttled* her sex with it. It was all I could do to keep the bow upon the strings! But I dared not stop. I dared not disobey.

Rising above the din, there came a scream. Sharp and shrill, it clawed its way up the stone walls to our ears. Peronette leapt down from the window and snatched the bow from my hands. "That'll do," said she, smiling; and then she added, rather ominously, "I got one."

Moments later, the crucifix was back upon the wall, the violin was returned to its case atop the table, and the rooms were back in order. Peronette scrubbed the powder from her cheeks, and quickly lifted the shift over her head; once again, she stood before me naked. She stuffed the shift and the red skirt into the armoire. She dressed, not bothering with her undergarments, which she kicked under the bed; their buttons and laces would take far too long, and we hadn't the time. We had to hurry—to where, or from what? I'd no idea.

"*Go!*" directed Peronette, pointing to the casement. "See what is happening down there?" I moved too quickly toward the window; I would have stuck my head out had she not stopped me with a hiss. "*Arrête*, fool! From behind the drape. You mustn't be seen."

"Yes, of course," I muttered. "Of course... mustn't be seen..." And I slipped behind the dark drape to peer down into the courtyard. Only later was I able to describe what I saw; at that moment, as I pulled back from within the folds of the drape, Peronette had but my horrified expression as testament to her success. She surveyed the room a final time. Deeming the scene satisfactory, she said, "Come, and quickly!" I obeyed.

This is what I had witnessed, down in the unpaved courtyard, puddled, muddied by the just-passed storm:

A group of girls, most of them young, encircled a figure prostrated on the ground. It was a girl, of course, lying motionless; she looked so small and lifeless, I wondered if she might be dead. Absurd, of course. A nun—Sister

Claire, I think, though I cannot be sure—tended to the fallen girl. Someone had quickly produced salts and Sister Claire (it *must* have been Sister Claire) was trying to revive the girl. The girl had merely fainted. I would soon learn that it was young Elizaveta, of whom we knew nothing. Then, as I spied from the folds of the drape, Elizaveta, shocked or startled—no doubt they were very strong salts—Elizaveta sat straight up, screamed, and pointed to the very window at which I stood! I fell back, quick as I could. Had I been seen? Had any of the girls followed Elizaveta's accusing finger? I dared not look out again. But I had an answer when there came a chorus of screams from below. I heard then one distinct word: "Satan." It was repeated, passed from girl to girl. It was then I heard Peronette speak: "Come, and quickly!"

Had it not been for Peronette's command I would have stayed in that very spot, would have been standing there, dumbstruck, in that drape, when the crowd—surely rushing up the main stairs at that very moment!—arrived at Mother Marie's rooms.

Peronette took me by the hand, as one does a child. She opened the door to the corridor; immediately we heard the scuffling and shuffling of a corps of girls ascending the stairs. Others were coming fast from the dormitory.

Peronette shut and locked the door.

"They'll send me away for sure, and I'll—"

"*Stop!*" said Peronette. "And let me think." She cupped her hands over her face. Was she crying? Would she admit that her charade had gone too far, and . . . No. When those hands fell a moment later it was to show a broad smile. "Yes," she said, rather dreamily, "yes, of course."

She directed me to retrieve the violin from its case atop the table. This I did. "What now?" I asked, turning to see that Peronette was gone and that the door to the hall now stood open; through it I could hear the oncoming girls.

I crossed quickly to the armoire, but I could not open it. Then I heard that familiar laughter, muffled, and knew: Peronette held the door fast from within.

A voice. "What is happening here?" I turned and watched with relief as Mother Marie slipped into the room, shutting the door behind her. She locked it against the girls massed on the landing, awaiting Sister Claire, no doubt, and against the braver girls who'd soon arrive from the dormitory to rap on the oaken door. "*What is happening here?*" repeated the Mother Superior, in hurried yet hushed tones.

"I . . . We . . ." I stood stupefied, both violin and bow in hand. "I . . . We . . ."

"Where is she?" asked Mother Marie; and in involuntary response I must have cast my gaze upon the armoire, for she moved to try its door, without success.

More rapping at the door. Ten, perhaps twenty girls buzzing hive-like behind it. And then the command of Sister Claire de Sazilly: "In Christ's name, open this door!"

Mother Marie took me roughly by the shoulders. "Did I not warn you?" she asked. And she said that we knew not what we'd done. Finally, she called over her shoulder: "Coming! One moment, Sister."

"Sister Claire!" said I. "Please, Mother, no!" I shook my head in supplication. "Please, no."

Mother Marie let go my shoulders. "Go then," said she, "into the folds of the drape. There! And not a breath from you!"

It was from within those drapes, those folds of chocolate damask—not nearly as prime a hiding spot as my companion had secured—that I heard Mother Marie open her door to the sorority. The rush of bodies into the room warmed it and set the heavy drapes to rustling. Quickly, bodies gathered near me; they leaned over the sill; one girl pressed into me but mistook the mass of my body for pleated fabric. I stood flush against the cold stone wall, certain I'd be discovered.

"What is happening here?" asked the Mother Superior, feigning indignation. "I am passing by my rooms when suddenly I see a rush of pupils to my door. Who can explain? Can *you?*"

I marveled at what I heard: "It's Elizaveta," said the questioned girl. "She's had a vision."

"A *vision?*" mocked the Mother Superior. "And what of?"

"Satan Himself," said another girl. She spat the salinized words.

The girls were afire with tales, growing ever taller, of what Elizaveta had seen. *The Prince of Darkness . . . One of his minions. . . . The Devil dancing with a possessed sister . . . Sex acts. The Dance of Death. Horrible curses . . . against the house, against Christ and the good people of C——— . . . The music of the Dark One's fiddle.* Mother Marie dismissed every claim.

It was then, judging from the sudden silence, that I knew Sister Claire de Sazilly had come forward. I knew too—for it was just like her—that she had Elizaveta in her arms; yes, Sister Claire would have climbed the stairs with the stricken, the "sighted" Elizaveta in her arms. I heard the mention of salts; and soon Elizaveta spoke, incessantly, nonsensically. The other girls cried out at her words, her testimony. When she fainted away, the Head ordered another wave of those salts, and Elizaveta burst back into consciousness, screaming, her horror bright and fresh.

Poor Elizaveta. Not nine years old, and she'd believe in the bad—her sighting of Satan—as ardently as she believed in the good, perhaps more so.

"What do you, Claire, make of this? Surely—"

"No untaught child lies, Mother."

"Do you mean to affirm this child's vision?"

"Do you mean to deny it?" Sister Claire must have turned to the girls, for it was then that one asked of Mother Marie:

"Is she lying, Mother? Or was it Dark Work that she witnessed?"

"I do not say she is lying, no."

"What then? If it was not—"

That the girls would question the Mother Superior so, that they would shout out in her presence . . . these were peculiar circumstances indeed. And all the while Sister Claire stood silently, ominously by.

"I say only that this child, after some orange water and rum, will rest through the night and wake in fine shape, no worse for her . . . her 'vision.' " Clearly, to use the word pained the Mother Superior. "And you, especially the senior among you, will apply your faith and maturity and conclude that certainly no such thing has occurred."

"She *is* lying then!"

"But I saw the fire-haired fiddler, too. I swear it!" And all eyes were thus directed to the violin case, empty now atop the table.

"Girls, girls," began the Mother Superior; but she was interrupted by Sister Claire, who said simply:

"We must pray. We must pray against this." And tens of voices set to rumbling in fervid prayer. That the Head would interrupt the Mother Superior, and to direct the girls to action no less: this did not bode well. Sister Claire, in leading these prayers, invoked the "Darkness"; and at this a second girl fainted away. Now the prayers grew more fervid; and I was distressed to recognize the voices of several of the most senior girls. In the confusion a vial of holy water slipped from its holder near the door, cracking on the floor: proof positive of Satan's presence. And it was this shattering glass that set the flock of girls to rising up, noisily, and flying from the room—no doubt to spread their devilish stories. It seemed the room was suddenly empty, save for Sister Claire, the lifeless Elizaveta, and Mother Marie; and yes, my coconspirator.

Sister Claire came dangerously near the drape. I could feel her heat. "Are those not scuff marks upon the sill?" she asked of Mother Marie. "And what, among your *worldly* goods, is missing, if not your violin?"

"Take that child to the infirmarian," replied Mother Marie. "And put a stop to this madness."

"Madness, is it?" asked the Head. "Madness is your ruling over a House of one hundred girls when you cannot control that one, your pet."

"Do you threaten me, Sister?"

"I do, yes. . . . Indeed, I have long been attendant upon your ruin." With these words—and a whispered *"Adieu, ma mère"*—Sister Claire turned to leave, Elizaveta in her arms; and in so doing, the girl's slippered foot—like a hook at the end of her lifeless, lank leg—caught the drape and pulled it back just enough to show the very end of the bow I held.

Sister Claire, fast handing off the unconscious child to Mother Marie, pulled back the dark folds of fabric, its rings screeching along their iron rod. There I stood, bow and violin in hand.

"Of course," said Sister Claire, snatching the instrument from me. "I should have known. The accomplice." She slammed the violin down on the table. She brandished the bow. I raised my hands to my face as a shield: she would slash me as though the bow were a riding crop and I the slow or stubborn beast.

"Stop!" shouted Mother Marie; and she stepped between the Head and myself. "Go from here, you . . . you *animal!* . . . Go from my sight."

There was silence. In the Mother Superior's arms the girl groaned; she was coming around. "I will go," said Sister Claire; "but this one," and she pulled me to her, roughly, "this one comes with me."

4

The Passion

I PASSED THAT long, punitive afternoon in the smithy, planing the boards of rough-hewn pine that were to be installed in the pantry, my former room. Shortly after being discovered, and after being dragged rather indelicately to my sentence by a seething Sister Claire, a storm settled over C——, persistent and at times severe.

The work was difficult, as it involved heavy planks and chisels and blades of varying thickness. The slow-burning fire of the smithy and the heavy humidity occasioned by the storm made the tiny outbuilding grossly uncomfortable. Yet I remained; I had to. I grew slick with sweat; droplets fell from the tip of my nose onto the pine, as if to mock the rain slanting down in silver cords beyond the open half-door, falling from a leaden sky hanging suffocatingly low.

Those hours I had but two visitors; three, if one

counts Sister Claire, who came twice to threaten me with more and varied labor. Marie-Edith came, at great risk, to offer me an apple—unaccountably delicious, it was—and a dry shift. And Mother Marie came, very late in the day; it seemed she'd come to apologize, though of course I did not yet know what for.

"It was unwise," said she, "to indulge my niece. Did I not warn you?"

"You did," said I. Where was Peronette? Was she among the girls? Did she too stand accused? Was our ruse known? Had Sister Claire meted out to her punishment such as I . . . But the Mother Superior answered none of my questions. Finally she raised her hand to still me, saying only, "I fear things may not, cannot be as they were. The balance of the House is upset."

"What do you mean?" I asked, though I understood her too well.

"Claire is the Head, and it is within her purview to do so. . . . Sister Claire has declared the Great Silence, and I dare not rescind it." Mother Marie added, absently, "Perhaps it is wise. Perhaps order and discipline are our only hope." (Only twice in my years at C—— had the Great Silence been declared: once when a group of monks came to us for shelter, and once to quell the hysteria occasioned by three girls suffering the simultaneous onset of their first blood.) "But what scares me," continued the Mother Superior, "is that she is using the Silence to stir the girls, to rile them and win them to her ways."

"What are 'her ways'?" I asked.

Mother Marie looked at me. "You were there, were you not? You heard her: she has long coveted the rule of this House. How did she put it? Oh yes— she is 'attendant upon my ruin.' "

"But can you not . . . ?"

"I cannot order the girls *not* to pray; neither can I order Claire to desist from her prayerful talk of Darkness and such."

"Then they do not know? They do not know that it was Peronette upon the sill, that it was I who—"

Mother Marie fairly shouted at me then: "Did I not tell you," she asked, "that she was wild, that it was dangerous to indulge her? I did. *I did!* Silly of me to have thought you might control her. No one can control her. And now, the danger has come. I could lose this House! What then for me? Indeed, mark my words: danger has come."

Mother Marie then directed me to follow her back to the house proper. "You must not remain apart. Go among them as though nothing has happened," she advised, or commanded. I said I would—did I not owe her that much?—and the two of us, huddling beneath her umbrella, made our way back to the house with nothing but a cloud-occluded moon to light the muddy way.

It was in the kitchen gardens that my resolve began to break, and by the time I stood inside I wondered how, *how* would I find the strength to go among the girls in the dining hall beyond?

All was silent, as Sister Claire had decreed. Marie-Edith and, as best she was able, Sister Brigid, had just laid out collation. Mother Marie led me on.

There we stood, in the service doorway. At first unseen, hisses and whispers built within the Silence till all turned; none stood, as they ought to have in the presence of the Mother Superior, but I made nothing of this, so distracted was I by my own discomfort. There I stood before the assembled girls, bedraggled and scared, yet trying to act as though nothing untoward had taken place. What a sight I must have been! Like some creation of the Shelley girl, sister to her sad, sad monster.

"Perhaps this is not a good idea," said I to Mother Marie, as I tried to circle behind her, back into the kitchen.

Mother Marie held fast behind me. "Go," said she, shoving me forward. And I'd not taken two steps into the hall when I heard behind me the door's rusted hinge: Mother Marie had gone, and I was alone. This I had not anticipated.

As I walked between the tables, the girls on their benches spoke curses, and prayers that sounded like curses. Someone invoked the Prince of Peace. Others—much to my astonishment—railed against the Prince of This World. Sister Paulien, wordlessly, with the rapping of a wooden spoon, reminded the girls of the Silence. A group of younger girls sat before their chilling stew, reading their rosaries so fast it seemed the small wooden beads might burst into flame. I moved as though deaf and blind, guided to my seat by something unseen. It was as though I walked through water: every step slow, deliberate, difficult.

A small medallion of hammered gold was thrown; it landed at my feet and skidded across the smooth floor. Of course, this—the sacred thing's revulsion, its sliding away—was proof of the devils resident within me. At this there were audible gasps; and someone begged Salvation in nearly unintelligible Latin.

Nearing my usual seat, I noticed two things: no one, not even the old mumbling nuns with whom I usually dined—and certainly not Peronette—was seated at the table; and a book—a black leather-bound tome, its pages yellow with age—had been spread open on my seat. The Silence then was deafening! Every eye was upon me. What to do? I swallowed my tears. And then . . . and then I did something quite . . . regrettable. Irresolute, confused, I simply sat down at my usual place as though the book weren't there. Why I did this I have *no* idea—I might have closed it and set it aside, swept it onto the floor—but no. It was as though Satan Himself had appeared at my side.

One girl—beautiful, quite tall, whose grace I'd always admired—stood on her bench, pointed down at me, and asked of all present what further proof was needed of the pact I'd signed with Satan. Hadn't I sat upon the sacred text? (It was the writings of an obscure theologian, opened to a passage on tribadism.) And hadn't every eye seen me shamelessly kiss the sacred text with my nether mouth?

This girl's witnessing was met with fearsome cries and prayer. The nuns, with pinches and pulled hair and rapping rods, succeeded in restoring a modicum of calm.

I dared not move, dared not slide the book out from under me. Shaking, shivering, I tried to choke back my tears. I even tried to eat the bowl of now-cold stew that was slid before me by . . . I don't know who. The stew—rabbit? venison?—was gamey and slick, a heartier collation than usual. I could not eat, even if I'd wanted to: my hands shook too badly to use a spoon.

I did not look up. I stared down into the enameled bowl. Tears fell onto the skin of fat covering the stew like a caul.

I prayed. Prayed for *release,* for something—god or demon—to deliver me. I would do anything. Sign any blood pact, agree to anything.

Just then the far doors of the hall opened, and a group of older girls nearest the doors stood, with slight hesitation; soon all the girls rose, and I stood too, so great was my relief that Mother Marie had returned to . . .

. . . But with a sickening twist deep within, I saw Sister Claire de Sazilly enter the dining hall and scan the room. She was looking for me; I knew it. The others knew it too, and when their quick glances betrayed me I found myself staring across the hall at Sister Claire.

That Sister Claire had come in search of me was bad fortune; that the girls had risen in her presence was something else altogether.

Yes, it was clear, and irrefutable: there stood Sister Claire de Sazilly, ascendant.

After surveying the girls, quite contentedly, and nodding that they should resume their seats, Sister Claire made her way to her seat. From over the trembling rim of my cup, I spied Sister Claire talking to Sister St. Eustace and a group of the older girls. Sister St. Eustace—insipid, rail-thin Sister St.

Eustace, who suffered an unnamed disorder of the skin and was ever scabrous, like a half-flayed deer—Sister St. Eustace sat nodding her head. This conference, held in defiance of the Silence, did not bode well. The girls attended a pronouncement, and finally it came:

Sister St. Eustace rose to announce with tremulous voice a work plan: flooding of the grounds threatened the first-floor rooms of the house. The sandbagging drill was familiar to us all. At the expected groanings, the audible laziness of several of the girls—they were, of course, less than fond of such labor—Sister St. Eustace reminded one and all that the Great Silence was still in effect, would remain in effect until we retired. Silence only descended in full when Sister Claire stood; she bade the girls follow suit and join her in prayer. I stood as well, but knew not to join in the prayer; and indeed it ended with: ". . . keep us safe, Lord . . . safe from the Darkness that has come." By which, of course, she meant *me;* lest any doubt it, with a nod she led all eyes my way. I was the first to sit.

Order, and silence, reigned, though Chaos threatened: several girls rose and ran from the hall. Others clung to their neighbors as though they were being led sightless through the deepest night. There were the requisite tears and prayers. Most disconcertingly, every girl, as she filed from the hall, passed Sister Claire and was informally "received" with a nod or a word; in this way, pledges of loyalty were sworn and accepted.

Where, I wondered, was Mother Marie-des-Anges? Had she willfully ceded the rule of C—— to Sister Claire? If so, why had she not told me? When would she come among us to set things right?

Forbidden to speak through the afternoon, the girls had been unable to calm or comfort one another, had been unable to relieve their fears, unfounded or not, by giving them voice. Sister Claire, the strategist, knew the Silence would only stir the girls, make them more impressionable. They were further agitated by the break in our well-ordered day, the strangeness of the declared Silence; and later by the steady rains that had begun to fall, rains that came now to the accompaniment of thunder and ragged seams of light that showed the girls pressed into service.

We were made to stand at arm's length from one another and form a loose chain that wended up from the mud-floored basement to the kitchen, where it branched in three, each line ending at an exterior door of the house, under which a sort of primordial slime oozed. The youngest girls worked below-stairs, filling the canvas bags with sand shoveled from several mounds kept for this purpose; older girls tied off the bags and passed them upstairs and along the lines to us, the oldest girls, who secured them around the doors. I was stationed at the kitchen door. We succeeded in stanching the slow flow; and we did so in silence. I was grateful for the quiet, and the distraction of a duty.

Two branches had been disbanded, and I stood at the end of the third line when the youngest girls were dispatched, told to wash and ready for Compline—the seventh and last of the canonical hours—and then, blessedly, sleep. Finally, I was released by Sister Claire: the last to leave the kitchen.

When next I saw Peronette it was in the dormitory, where she waved to me from her cot with red-tinged fingers. As Sister Claire eyed us both, continually, I dared not speak to Peronette; but she, tripping lightly past my cot as she came from the washroom, whispered, wickedly, "*Bad* girl! See what it is you've done?"

In concession to the storm, and to the strange events of the day, the novitiates let the younger girls burn their candles down; this, and a faint moon, lit the dormitory, but still I fell fast asleep. I was exhausted—emotionally, yes, but more plainly from my labor in the smithy and on the work line.

Attendant upon sleep, I listened to the rain fall from the roof into buckets and bowls placed among the disarrayed cots, and I tried not to cry. The storm raged on, and the crash and spark, the great show, gave rise to something akin to the call and response of the mass: one girl would whimper and another would cry out to comfort her, and so on till a high-pitched keening filled the room. Scattered here and there were appeals to the Higher Powers.

My neighbor, a bovine little blot named Constance, whimpered terribly. When she'd woken me a second time, I leaned from my cot and threatened to cuff her if she did not desist. I was terribly tired, and hopeful of sleeping away my fears.

It was later that night—how much later I cannot say—when I was woken by the movement of my cot, and a warmth beside me: Peronette.

Though I'd begun to consider her careless and dangerous, though I had begun to see her as willful and wrong, irresponsible, all she had to do was come near me and I forgave her all and everything. Fool that I was. What's more, finding her beside me, I opened to her comfort.

Of course, we girls were not to sleep together; this was plain, so plain as to have never been openly stated. Still, it sometimes happened, for myriad reasons. It was a punishable offense, yes, but we slept unpoliced—rarely did the novitiates dare to walk those dark and quiet floors at night, for fear of mice, or worse. And that night—that night of all nights!—I gave not a thought to breaking the rule, gave not a thought to the day's hysteria and the heightened . . . *feelings* to which it had given rise. All I thought about was . . . In truth, to say that I *thought* at all is to overstate things; all I would do that night is better described as *instinctual*.

Peronette was shivering, no doubt from stealing barefoot across the stony floor, amid the scattered cots. I folded back my blanket, slid the single sheet down, and as she slid in beside me the mattress sank, and the thin strips of hammered iron stretched across its frame gave with an eerie song. Her white nightgown was buttoned up to the base of her neck; a thin band of throat showed like a collar beneath her chin. Her loose, dark hair was afloat on the pillow, wavering in the inconstant light.

This memory is muted, like a dream forgotten too fast.

Did Peronette take my hand in hers? Did I drape my arm over her, forming of it the soft harness by which I would bind her to me forever? . . . Let me say only that I pulled the sheet up over us both that stormy night; and therein contained the world entire.

Her gown of white flannel, worn and soft, smelled like water. She bore too the scent of lavender. Her unbound hair had a scent all its own; pure, clean, and natural, perfumed, it seemed, by herbs or wildflowers or fruit. *That* is the scent I recall . . . can verily *smell* if I close my eyes and put myself there, in that bed, that unquiet night, beside Peronette.

Peronette curled into me, into my arms. Her eyes were shut, but was she asleep? Was I? Was this supreme wakefulness in the guise of sleep?

If only I'd had the good sense to hold Peronette awhile, calm her, steal a kiss or two, and send her back to her cot. If only . . . But no. . . . I liken myself, at that moment, to those mathematicians whom I have always envied and never understood; looking upon complicated arithmetic, they see answers where I would see mere symbols, signifying nothing. But that night, I saw the answer; and so set to work upon the equation:

Her forehead at rest in the crook of my neck. I kiss the crown of her head, and then . . .

. . . This is difficult. I cannot be sure what was dreamed and what was real that night. I do know that I . . . I did things for the first time. Did things to myself and to the sleeping Peronette. (*Was* she asleep? I will never know.)

. . . At first I kissed her innocently, but then something overtook me. The first of those kisses is the one I remember—the one I placed on Peronette's head, the one I set there as sweetly as a priest places the Body of Christ on a celebrant's tongue. As for the others . . .

Alors, I knew from recent and fevered dreams just where to place the kisses, and so I set to preparing each spot. I caressed, smoothed, and heated the skin with my fingers. I have the faintest recollection of *doing* this, of feeling the shame yet not being able to stop, of hearing my heartbeat and doing what I did despite that deafening drumming. . . . I was rushed by lust, perhaps asleep yet never more *alive*. . . .

First her neck. Then her cheek, and her lips. The lips again, and again. . . . And then my hands sank to raise her nightshirt and—with my eyes, with my hands?—I *saw* her, all of her. I cupped her breasts and their supple weight surprised me. I kissed her breasts; their dark tips flared at the touch of my tongue. I slid daringly down the smooth slope of her stomach to her navel. Another kiss there. Downward still. To the secret of her sex. I heated her thighs with my hands, and kissed her there. She opened to me. I kissed that mouth. I drew her wetness. I took her with my tongue.

I explored. And I discovered again that Peronette was . . . *different* from me, very different indeed. . . . But it was all so confused. Wakefulness and sleep. Desire and dream. And I was so unsure—so very content, yes, but still so unsure of it all.

I lay atop her. That much I know. I know I pulled Peronette up toward me, my hands beneath her buttocks. I know that I pushed down upon her. Drove down. Into her. I know that what I did caused her some measure of pain, but I know this too: she did not resist.

I do not remember the nightsalt coming. But it did. And it, mixed with Peronette's blood, would be the viscid proof of my devilry.

Only when I woke, suddenly, Peronette asleep beside me, in my arms, only upon waking did I realize that the screams I heard were not my own. My heart blew apart like a bomb, and so rattled was I it seemed my skin might slip from my skeleton! I was not screaming in dreams of my own device, no . . . These were the real and wakeful screams of others . . .

The very first came concomitant with a stroke of thunder, and I mistook it for same. But the rest, coming in quick succession, were unmistakable. Screams. Coming ever nearer, in the company of their source:

Agnes, a novitiate, a stolid girl of good faith, from St. Malo, ran from cot to cot, screaming, nonsensically. It seemed the novitiate, for whatever reason, had determined to check on the sleeping Elizaveta. And in the infirmary, by lantern light, Agnes saw upon the girl the "marks of our Lord's Passion." The stigmata.

What had been the Great Silence ceded now to far greater Chaos.

My heart raced from the nearness of the screams, but my head . . . My eyes

adjusted slowly to the darkness. . . . How was it I'd come to be outside, for
surely those were stars shining all about me, a ring of bright stars surrounding
me? Pale moons too? . . . But no: the stars were the sizzling wicks of candles
and the moons were the faces of the screaming girls who now surrounded my
cot. Scream after scream unraveled like black pennants; and Agnes's voice was
overtaken by those so near, speaking of Satan and his dolls and such.

It was then I sat suddenly upright. And I knew: those whom Agnes had
woken had discovered us together, Peronette and I.

"Certainly *he's* come. *He is here now!*"

"Look at them! He is within her, and he's claimed the other!"

"No," I said. "Stop it! Go away! We only . . ."

Something flew at me, end over end. It struck me on the cheek. I felt the
skin split and the pain flare; soon the blood flow seeped into my mouth. The
biting *thing* had fallen into my lap. It was a small crucifix of wrought silver.

The blanket and sheet were pulled back. My smock had settled up around
my hips. I struggled now to pull it down, lest it . . . lest I be . . .

The screams were deafening. Agnes's and all the others. They prevented
thought: *I could not think.* I saw, *I sensed* that nearly the whole sorority surrounded
my cot. Spit landed on my leg. A bowl of cold water—holy water—was
thrown.

And there I sat cowering at the center of all this, my knees drawn to my
chest, holding my shift down against those hands that sought to raise it. ("See
it? Did you see it?") Other hands pulled at my hair. Scratched at my bare
hands, my forearms.

I turned to Peronette and . . .

She was gone. How had she slipped from the cot? Where was she? And
then I saw her standing at the side of the bed in her rumpled and . . . and
bloodstained shift. Her stance puzzled me: she stood slightly hunched, with
her hands pressed into her groin, where a roseate stain had spread. She raised
her red fingers up.

She would not look at me. I saw her face in profile—a hideous mask it
seemed—and wondered were her tears real or part of a plan quickly hatched.

Look at me, I wanted to scream. *Look at me!* But I could not speak. And then
suddenly someone—Sister Catherine of the Holy Child, I believe—wheeled
on Peronette, asking. . . . I cannot recall the question; but I remember the
response:

In a gesture that stopped my heart, Peronette slowly raised her hand—to
help me? to pull me away? But then her first finger crawled from her fist like a

worm from an apple. To point. At me. And in so doing, accuse. Turning to face me full on, and grinding her fists deeper into her groin, against her sex, Peronette said, tearfully, angrily, grotesquely:

"You . . . you are *unnatural!*" She turned from me disgustedly, and disappeared.

The breath flew from me like a bird from its cage.

And so it was decided: *I* was the Devil. I was the Darkness that had been visited upon C——. The storm, Elizaveta's fire-haired dancer, her stigmata— it had all been my doing.

I sat trapped on my cot. Too shocked to cry. Too confused to scream. I realize now that my silence, my impassivity, only spurred the girls on. For what seemed an eternity, for what *was* an eternity, spit and holy water and statuary and crucifixes and bibles and strings of rosary beads . . . all manner of talismans, sacred and profane, were rained down upon me. Trying to rise from the cot, I was thrown back upon it, time and again.

No escape. No defense.

Suddenly, finally, the sorority parted at the foot of my cot, and there appeared Sister Claire de Sazilly. Surely she'd come to restore order, to end all this, to ease my shame and save me. Surely . . . But no: her smile had already opened into horrible bloom.

5

Attack

SISTER CLAIRE DE SAZILLY. Where to begin? I never knew her well, no one did. Christ and the cellarer were her sole companions. I know nothing of her beginnings. Her speech was flat, unaccented; from it one could infer nothing. By now, I'd learned that she coveted the place of the Mother Superior. She was ambitious and simple—in a word: *dangerous*.

Sister Claire was not old—perhaps in her late thirties, several years older than Mother Marie—yet for years she'd calculated, counted every step of her slow and steady ascent, only to be bested by "the Actress's" wealth and connections. Years more she'd had to plot; and this effort of patience showed on her plain face.

I stood a full two heads taller than Sister Claire. Squat and strong, she was as useful in the field as any farm animal. She pleasured in manual labor, and could often be seen digging in the dirt; she contentedly tore vegetables, flowers, plants, and weeds from the earth by their roots. With the agility of a mountain goat, she'd scramble out onto the roof to secure loose slates or shoo nesting birds from the chimneys. She seemed happiest when sweating in her makeshift smithy, pounding white-hot nails into shape.

I never saw Sister Claire smile, but when she spoke, or prayed—and she would sometimes close her eyes tightly, tilt back her head, and pray quite *violently*—she showed a whitish bank of gums on the left side of her mouth, and stuck into this like sticks in snow were several mud-colored teeth. Her eyes were closely spaced, dark as night; and their lids seemed always moist, set off as they were by the scaly, sere skin of her cheeks, which would, in winter, crack and bleed. Her lips were a bitter red twist, and a long thin nose rambled down crookedly above them. She was . . . *severe*.

If, when walking down the corridors of C—— at daylight, or better, with a torch in hand, one were to stoop to inspect those cold walls of carved stone, there, waist-high, one would see faint red marks scattered about. Traces of blood; flecks of flesh. Sister Claire, while making her rounds, deep in reflection or intent on some disciplinary mission, was wont to drag the backs of her hands along these walls. It was a means of mortification, and a habit; and an act that perhaps pleasured her. Her knuckles were constantly red, raw; like meat fresh from the knife. Her every step was penitential, her every act contrite. She schemed always, and artfully. And in the manner of a true zealot, she could convince herself of anything; and indeed she'd long ago convinced herself that her faith was true.

Sister Claire slept on a thin pallet, beneath one worn blanket. Often, she deprived herself of the pallet and slept on the stone floor of her cell. That she slept at all is a wonder, for sewn into the sides of her burlap shift were nettles and rose stems, their thorns large and hard and dark with her dried blood. They would stick her as she turned in her sleep. Wounds along her sides were opened anew every night. Scars—and I would be told this soon by one who'd seen them—attested to the fact that Sister Claire had been sleeping like this for years; the scars, it was said, resembled the work of a blind seamstress. When her wounds became infected, Sister Claire would wash them herself with holy water and seal them with hog's lard; or, ecstatically, she'd suffer their suppuration.

Such was the character of Sister Claire, the woman who would serve as my introduction to hatred: both hers and mine.

Now here stood the infirmarian, Sister Clothilde, alongside Sister Catherine of the Holy Child. I saw these two look at each other, questioningly. I saw

Sister Catherine—not two years into her vows—fall to staring at Sister Claire; unknowingly, it seemed, she shook her head as Sister Claire extricated testimony from the hysterical Agnes before that girl was led away. With this nodding she seemed to ask of the senior nun, *What now? What scheme might this be?* Soon she, Sister Catherine, set to soothing the youngest girls, with little success.

Sister Margarethe came too, of course; arriving late, the cellarer clamped her fat hands to her fatter cheeks when told of Agnes's claims. *"A miracle!"* said she. *"It's a true miracle!"* And it was she—that stupid, *stupid* woman—who invoked the name of Maria de Moerl, causing those girls who were doubtful still to suddenly call out for their salvation, and to join in the fight against the Holy Darkness, against me. (Not long ago, at a sister House somewhere in the Tyrol, three girls had suffered "Visitations," shown stigmatic symptoms. Maria de Moerl—whose name was known to all of us, as we'd been made to pray for her—had shown signs of the Five Wounds on the very day of the Corpus Christi procession.)

There stood Sister Claire in her bloodstained burlap shift, at the foot of my cot in the company of my captors.

I reached out to her. I implored her. I don't know if I spoke; if I did it was to say, *Save me. Help me.* In a near fetal curl, I sat cowering against the thin rails of the low headboard that rose from my cot like a prison grate.

All around me I heard the girls in accusatory chorus:

"We woke to find her atop Peronette . . ."

"And where has Peronette gone?" asked Sister Claire. "I want her as well."

"She slipped away, and we thought it best to let her go in case—"

"Find her!" commanded Sister Claire.

"And if she's gone to Mother Marie?"

"Find her!"

"Oui, ma mère," came the ominous response.

"Say it again," commanded Sister Claire of another girl, "you found them *how?* In what state? Naked before you? Entwined in shame and—"

"Yes. . . . No. . . . Not naked," said one of the girls, "but Hélène swears she saw . . ." and here poor Hélène, to whom all turned, struggled for words; other voices rose to bolster her testimony: "Hélène says when this one's nightshirt rode up on her hips . . ." ". . . that she saw . . . that *she* had *la partie honteuse d'un vrai démon!*" What were they saying? I didn't know who spoke. The voices were as one. ". . . And the sheet that covered them . . . we stripped them of it: we knew you would want to see it, for it is proof of—"

"Proof of what?" demanded Sister Claire. Before any girl dared answer, the Head screamed her question a second time: "*Proof of what?* Say what you mean to say!" Several of the girls began to cry. Others ran from the dormitory. Did I stand a chance yet? Was Sister Claire going to deny these lies, punish their tellers?

Another girl spoke, an older girl: "Here then is all the proof needed." Girls parted to let this witness approach Sister Claire. She did so, bearing the sheet they'd stripped from us, holding it far from her body. . . . Instantly, shamefully, I understood.

The white bundle fell to the floor at Sister Claire's bare feet. Extending her arms cross-vigil, in imitation of Christ's on the cross, the Head began to pray, loudly, ecstatically, in Latin. She bade the others join her, and the majority did. All the while she glared at me with those horrible dark eyes, a trace of a smile at play on her bitter lips.

. . . Let me now say what I must about the sheets:

In the long months leading up to . . . up to my identification as *Satan* Himself, strange things had been happening in the night. To my body. I had never led much of a dream life; yet within those few months my dreams grew increasingly vivid, and sexual. I could recall them in titillating detail the next day, but I would not: the recollection shamed me. Rather, I *tried* to resist the recollection. How better to say it than this: my *body* began to dream.

And in the morning, on sheets stale with sweat, I would wake to find the dream distilled to nightsalt. A discharge. The viscid milk of the dream.

When first I woke with this wetness beneath me, I'd no idea what it was, or where it had come from. I looked up at the ceiling to see if a skylight or some part of the roof had given way. I did not think that *I* had produced it. I did not know that the body, let alone *my* body, was capable of such. No, this thought did not occur to me until the second discovery, several mornings later, and the subsequent recollection of the preceding night's dream, which produced in me that now familiar shame. . . . These dreams were exciting, confusing, and, when recollected, deeply shameful. They showed me things I did not know from life. . . . *Enfin*, it was some time before I realized, *understood*, that it was the dreams that brought the nightsalt, brought it forth from me.

I knew to hide this, and to pray against it. I knew, *knew* this to be the manifestation of the strangeness, the differentness I felt. Surely I was impure—what proof did I need besides *this*, my own body's betrayal? I would be punished if these emissions were discovered. For a long while I believed I *should* be punished; still, I kept my secret.

Thankfully, I would wake early those mornings when the nightsalt had come. I would rise before the others, strip my cot in the darkness, dress, and slip from the dormitory. Then I would quit the house, steal in absolute darkness along the cold dark corridors and shuttered galleries, perfectly silent. I would be slipperless, lest those satiny soles be heard sliding along the stone floors. Whatever the weather, I would exit through the kitchen door—only then did I dare light a lamp—and make my way through the cellarer's garden, along the rutted rows of tomatoes, seeming to beat like black hearts in the dark, tied with twine to their spinal stakes; it seemed too that the pumpkins in autumn would tilt their plump and dumb heads quizzically up to stare at me as I passed, and that the summer corn, tall in its resplendent dress, mocked my ugliness and shame. I would pass fast through the garden and continue on to the dovecote, some distance beyond the laundry, far from the main house. No one ever went to that small stone outbuilding, which sat in disrepair, unused but by the bats, which hung head-down in its eaves. There, behind the building, I kept a bucket. I changed its water twice weekly; and no one looked askance if I were spied carrying buckets of water toward the laundry, or from the kitchen. Often I'd have to shove the soiled sheet down into the bucket through a thin layer of ice that had formed overnight. By moon- or starlight I would scrub the nightsalt from the sheets in the iced water. My hands would freeze, turn red and raw. I would scrub till my nails bled: this was *my* mortification. I would squat before that bucket, shivering, never far from tears, and all the while I would pray. My prayers consisted of questions. *Was this nightsalt proof I was bad? Evil? Was there meaning in this? What had I done? When would I live at ease in the world?* Such questions came to me, and I would offer them up as prayer. My final prayer, just before I'd trace the cross over my face and chest with numb and bloodied fingers—*in nomine Patris, Filius et Spiritus Sanctus*—my final prayer was always the same: I'd ask for answers.

I would hang the sheets to dry. I'd strung a line, stretched it hook-to-hook across the dovecote's back wall; I would weight the hem of the sheet with rocks so it lay flush and unseen against that wall, no matter how strong a breeze blew. Over these months of shame, I'd managed to steal extra sheets from the infirmary—which crime, had it been discovered, would have been punishable by a half-year's worth of stable duty, or worse. I didn't care. I'd shovel waste till Christ came again if it meant I could keep my secrets. Eventually, I had four sheets in rotation. One would always be hung out behind the dovecote. Another I kept wrapped in paper and hidden behind a statue of the Blessed Mother, which sat in an alcove on the second-floor landing. The third I hid in the sacristy, at the bottom of the pile of white sheets used to cover the altar. A fourth, of course, was always in use.

In this way the secret of the nightsalt went untold. Until *that* morning. The morning I woke with Peronette in my arms. The morning after that active and wondrous night when I . . .

. . . Sister Claire, yes.

. . . Daring finally to lift the sheet from the floor beside my cot, Sister Claire de Sazilly examined it, and, in a manner worthy of the Inquisitor she would soon become, pronounced:

"It is icy cold, this . . . this ejaculate. *This demon seed!*" She fell so hard, so fast to her knees, that I heard the meeting of bone and stone. She fairly *screamed* a prayer. Several girls did the same; others shied from Sister Claire's pronouncement, from that theatrical dropping-down onto her knees.

I lay prostrate, perfectly still; the slightest movement, or a single word, could only further condemn me. Sister Claire rose and came around the side of the cot; the sea of girls parted for her. She retrieved the crucifix from the floor beside the cot. She held it . . . she *brandished* it. She took up her prayers, reciting them in Latin; though she mumbled, unintelligibly, I was certain I had never heard these prayers before. Finally, she stopped speaking; she could not have been any nearer to me. I felt her weight against the thin frame of the cot. The remaining girls—fifteen, twenty?—were silent; they stared at Sister Claire. "Step back!" she warned. "Take to prayer!" And indeed they all fell back and cried out in chorus as Sister Claire de Sazilly leapt up cat-like upon the cot! Fast, so *very* fast, she fell to kneel on my chest, crowding the air from my lungs. I swung blindly at the nun, thrashed at her, but quickly she pinned my arms to my sides with her legs. Her knees would leave bruises where they ground against the cage of my ribs.

Again, the incantatory Latin. Sister Claire lowered her face to mine. *Her face!* That hideous mask, that contorted mass of blood-flushed flesh and bone! Silver and gold spurs shone at the center of her pitch-filled pupils. The whites of her eyes were yellowed, mottled as eggshells are. Her cracked and colorless lips bled where she'd bit down into them. Her horrible teeth were clenched so that her jaw pulsed, her nostrils flared; from her came breath reeking of rot. She breathed thickly, like an animal, with an effort that belied her still stance atop me. At one point—this comes back to me with such revulsion, I shiver— at one point, as she lowered her face to mine, the oily wheels of her mind already at work, she said, with sinister glee, and so only I could hear her, "The *stigmata*, you fools? . . . Will it be *that* easy? You must thank your delicate friend for me," and spittle slid down from her mouth into mine.

I spat and gasped for air. I begged for release.

Sister Claire leaned back, shifted her weight just slightly—I drew a deep breath—and just when it seemed she might release me, quickly she brought that silver crucifix up to my face. She held it before me and seemed to bless it before bringing it down, *grinding* it down against, *into* my forehead. *The pain was blinding!* Tears slid from my wide-open eyes. Trying to turn away only worsened the pain. I held as still as I could. Sister Claire *leaned* down into me, held the crucifix fast against my forehead till the tiny figure of Christ cut into my flesh. With all her weight she pressed her Savior against me, praying all the while, cursing the devils I harbored, the devil I *was*. This was pain of a kind I'd never known. Defending myself, I suffered cuts all over my hands and wrists. Then I let fall my arms: I would surrender, take what punishment the Head had to give.

When finally she lifted the crucifix from me I saw by candlelight, or by the light of the moon or the rising sun, by whatever light shone faintly in the dormitory, that the silvered body of Christ was slick, dark with my blood. "Ah!" proclaimed Sister Claire to those assembled, "See how the Lord's Cross marks her forehead, as it does all demons in league with Lucifer!" Blood stung my eyes. The wound itself was oddly cold. Satisfied, Sister Claire regained her breath, steadied herself from the exertion; still, she did not relax her hold on me . . . not yet.

Sister Claire came at me again with that cross. I felt it strike the side of my head, cutting me near the ear. And again, like a hammer just under my right eye. Had she brought the crucifix down an inch higher, surely she'd have blinded that eye. As it was, a gash opened in the soft flesh there and blood ran from both wounds to pool in the crook of my ear.

I gave in then to a simple impulse: I screamed with all my soul. Screamed for Peronette, for Mother Marie-des-Anges, for Christ Himself to come save me; of course, I named none of them; I simply screamed and screamed until . . . Until I saw a way open before me.

When Sister Claire shifted, and the vise of her knees went slack, I reacted, reflexively. I wriggled an arm out from under the nun, and I fairly *flew* up at her, striking her full and hard across the face. It was a backhanded slap that sent her reeling.

One shove and Sister Claire de Sazilly toppled from the cot, fell to the

floor. I could sit up; doing so, I saw her prostrated at the slippered feet of her lieutenants, who stood staring down at her. I rose and broke that human chain at
its weakest link: two younger girls who fell back easily; from one of them I took,
roughly, the large (*very* large!) cypress crucifix that she or someone else had
drawn down from above the novitiate's bed at the end of the dormitory. She'd
had to hold it with both hands, her tiny fists wound tightly round its base.

With a resolve that came from I don't know where, I threw back my broad
shoulders, squared them to the doors, sucked up my breath, and, raising up the
cross before me—the bastard child of Jeanne d'Arc and Moses!—I parted the
mob. I did not want to hurt anyone else, though I would if need be; I let this
be known with a few strategic and well-swung arcs of the cross. There was
spittle and prayer and screams. Some of the more industrious and superstitious girls must have harvested branches of hazel and elm the afternoon prior;
these they worked like whips; one of them caught my face. Still I walked on,
resolute; I wanted to run, but didn't. And then, as though that gash from the
witches' whip (hazel and elm ward off witches, or so it is said) . . . as though
that witches' whip had cut the bloody question into my flesh, I wondered
where I was going. I'd best decide quickly, for Sister Claire would soon rise,
and already the girls were coming together in my wake.

Outside. I would go outside. Out into the corridor and down the central
stairway, down to the door giving on to the bricked gallery and . . .

Only when the low but rising sun fell on me, only when the rain- and sea-
scented air washed over me, only then did I break my steely stride and run. Yes,
I ran. Through the yard, past the pedestaled Christ with His outstretched
arms, around the kitchen gardens and up the drive: away. I could not see clearly
for the tears; and again, I tasted blood. (The witch's whip had caught that soft
flesh above the lip and below the nose, which bleeds and bleeds and bleeds!)

. . . I turned back to see a ragged band of girls coming on. This lot was
comprised of the very youngest girls, those too young to grasp the scene's
severity, those who'd not yet had the pure fun of running bred out of them. As
I rounded St. Ursula's Hall and the kitchen door, as I disappeared around the
building's edge, I heard these girls recalled by my peers, whose terrible, high-
pitched cries roused rooks from their nests and sent squirrels scampering,
causing nuts and twigs to fall clatteringly down through the tall dark trees.

I ran up the drive, along a line of hedges that bordered our neighboring
fields. I bore through a narrow opening, into the hedge, full and green in its
summer dress. I pushed thorned branches aside, incurring more scrapes and
cuts, like those from a cat. . . . Ah, but what of a bit more spilled blood?

I sank into the lower branches of the hedge. A sort of rude pallet was formed of an exposed web of roots, the muddy soil, the matted leaves blown there by the winds. I'd disturbed the soil: pale and belted worms writhed blindly up from the coffee-dark earth. A branch too near my face bore the slick, sticky trail of a snail.

It was then, hidden—safe?—that tears truly overtook me. I trembled. And panic settled over me like a cloak. Panic and other strange desires—to fight, to flee, to die, to kill.

Eventually, reason prevailed:

What would I do? I could not run away. I hadn't the means. . . . Ah, but there was money in my trunk, was there not? (Enough to hire a horse and driver? Enough to buy a crust of bread? I did not know.) Perhaps, if only. . . .

Pushing branches aside with the cross, I opened a window in the far side of the hedge. There sat our tenanted fields of harvested wheat sloping away toward the sea. The sun gilded the thick cones of hay. The storm had passed; the sky was cloudless and pale. A large raven wheeled overhead, claimed the sky with its scrawled black X. Alert as I was, I took in the greens and golds of the trees and the leaves, the browns of the branches, and the textures of it all. And this stilled me. Calmed me. For a short, very short while, till reason again demanded, *What will you do?*

I slipped from the hedge, cross in hand. Moving along its far side, I'd be obscured from sight. My wounds, certain of them, still ran red. To anyone seeing me, I would have appeared a terrible, feral thing crawling from the scene of a fresh kill. Or my own birth. Keeping close to the hedgerow, pulling myself along by its heartier branches, I made slow, *very* slow progress. Back to the house.

Then a seed of . . . of *stupidity* bloomed suddenly, a horrid black-petaled flower in my mind, and yes, I resolved to make my way back to the house. To gather my things and go. Escape.

Whatever was I thinking? Was I *thinking* at all?

6

Maluenda

My reasoning, as best I can recollect it, was this: I would wait for the girls to gather, in the chapel or elsewhere, allowing me to move through the house unmolested, gather my things, and somehow effect an escape. I had that stash of money in my trunk, for Marie-Edith had insisted on paying me for our months of clandestine tutorials. I knew not how much money I had; for, embarassed to accept it, afraid to be caught with it, I stuffed it away without further thought. Too, I'd no idea of its value. What was money to me, then? With this money and my very few effects, including a change of clothes, I might make my way to the cross-roads on the far side of the village of C——, where the southbound *hirondelle* stopped on alternate days. Perhaps I'd go to Mother Marie? . . . *Thought? Planned?* No; to say I did either of those things is inaccurate. I merely *moved*, fearing that an excess of stillness might cause my fears to rise up, strong as the Breton tides, and overtake me.

I sprang from the bank of hedges to the kitchen door, and there saw that room empty—blessed be!—save for the turned back of Sister Brigid. Two quick corners and I gained my former room, the pantry, where the pine I'd worked stood against the wall and tools lay scattered on the packed-dirt floor. My cot had been disassembled, the thin mattress rolled. There I would wait: I had no plan.

It was not long before I heard the outer door open—my breath caught!—and then there came the welcome voice of Marie-Edith. *"Bonjour,"* said she, quite happily, to Sister Brigid, whose face must have been set with deep concern. *"Mais,* what is it, *ma soeur?"* asked Marie-Edith. "Are the geese still aflutter?" (She referred to the girls thusly.) "All because of that innocent prank of yesterday? *C'est fou!"*

"Things turned worse in the night," said Sister Brigid; and I heard the two take their habitual spots at the table, with their blue and white bowls of coffee, no doubt. "I fear for our friend."

"Herculine? *No!* What has happened? Tell me!" And I might have stepped from the pantry then to go among these friends, to solicit their help—surely *they* would have helped me; but just then I heard the pinched voice of the cellarer, and I retreated deeper into the pantry's shadows.

"Whatever might *these* be?" asked the cellarer, referring to I knew not what.

"You do not know an oyster when you see it?" asked Marie-Edith, rather sourly.

"Indeed I do," replied the cellarer, hearing no insult in the extern's words. "But this *bushel* comes here at what cost? Whose coin has—"

"You have no memory for kindnesses, Sister," interrupted Sister Brigid. "Marie-Edith's brother tends the beds at Cancale, and for months now we have profited from his generosity."

"Hmph!" came the snorted reply; and in the ensuing silence Sister Margarethe took her leave, freeing Sister Brigid to speak:

"I tell you it's profane and absurd, if innocent. Someone—and we need not wonder who, I think—has graced the stricken Elizaveta with . . . with signs of the stigmata."

"Mais non! Ce n'est pas possible!"

"Well," said Sister Brigid, "it may be possible—or so say the Church Fathers—but it is unlikely. Indeed, I've seen these 'signs' on the child, and they are but a poor imitation of blood; and there is no wound proper."

"A prank? . . . Not another, *non!"*

Presumably the older woman nodded in assent. "But Sister Claire stokes the hysteria with her fiery talk, and she is intent on putting it to purpose. What started in mischievous innocence will end we know not where.... Oh! that one, I've never known the like; and I say she knows *nothing* of our Lord but his ambition."

"But, Mother Marie," said the extern, "surely she—"

"Blood and water, my dear; blood and water," said the nun. "She has retreated to her rooms with that niece of hers. I'm afraid the Head's hour has come, for it seems she has won the girls. Oh, patient as the serpent she's been, and now she's arranged these silly circumstances to suit her end! I fear for our friend."

"This ... this cannot be!" said Marie-Edith. "Where is Elizaveta? The infirmary? And where is Herculine?" When Sister Brigid made no reply, the extern went on: "I must see this ... must see this foolishness for myself," and she quit the kitchen, leaving Sister Brigid to fall into the mumbled reading of her rosary beads. And as the door to the dining hall opened, I could hear the barely bridled hysteria of the girls. No Silence had been declared this morning.

I dared not risk discovery. I would hide; to stand in the pantry's shadows would not do.

And so, with great reluctance, I lifted the rug sewn of rags, which sat on the pantry floor, uncovering the trap that led down to the shallow cellar. There, amid sweaty and cobwebbed jugs of fermented cider and wine, long-forgotten, I settled myself on the cold dirt of the cellar's bottom step; and discovered that I could, quietly, carefully, lift the trap, just so, and spy a sliver of the kitchen.

There, in that dank and muddied hole, I waited. And waited. Growing ever more certain that the distant hysteria of the house—surely they were searching for me—and the stillness of the kitchen did not bode well.

Finally—and I was crying when I heard this, for I had been utterly reduced by recent events, reduced to tears and abject fear and ... Finally I heard the sound of oncoming thunder. But no—the skies had cleared, the storm had passed. This I'd seen.

If not quick-coming thunder, then what? Instantly I knew: what I heard were the wheels of a carriage. A cry rose up from the house. One voice, then many. The carriage came closer, closer still, rounding out past the kitchen toward the drive down which I'd crept. I could not see it, of course, but through the earth I could *feel* the horse's hooves. Two horses. The earth trembled at their approach. The stoneware jugs at my feet chattered like teeth. Only one conveyance at C——— harnessed two horses, and that was the barouche kept by the Mother Superior.

My heart stopped, was mocked by the beating-on of the horses' hooves. I listened to that carriage, listened to the sound of escape. It faded fast; and there was silence, and nothing to see. I let fall the trap, and I sank into the dark cellar. Earlier tears were nothing to what fell now.

Surely it was she and Peronette, flying fast from the house at C———.

I wanted to die, but what would take me? I thought to pray, but who would hear me?

I was drawn from this dark reverie by the voice of Sister Claire de Sazilly, in argument with Marie-Edith; so heated was their exchange, neither seemed to have heard the running coach. "I'll wager there's proof here in this very kitchen of that godly blood!" Marie-Edith spoke to the Head as no one else dared. Now she further challenged her. "I'm no idiot, woman!" (Marie-Edith was a nonbeliever.) "And I'm no longer an impressionable girl," she added with a great and almost bawdy laugh, "so you'll not convince *me* that some devil has sent this sign to us."

I could not believe what I heard! To judge by her great exhalation and uttered cries to God, neither could Sister Brigid, no doubt as shocked as I by the arguing party that tumbled then into the kitchen, comprised of the extern, the cellarer, and the Head—or presumptive Mother Superior—who now warned Marie-Edith, hissing, "Scullion, your words will see you shown from this house if you do not—"

"*Ach!*" Marie-Edith dismissed the threat. "You've finally spoiled, turned like bad cream, you have. Well, I'm not afraid. . . . It's you, *you* who should be afraid, for you're not fooling me, and you're not fooling that God you claim to believe in, that God you torture yourself for." I heard, *heard* the tacit shock that came from those present when Marie-Edith spoke thusly.

"Marie-Edith, *stop*," counseled Sister Brigid; for she knew, as did I, that the widowed, red-tempered Marie-Edith, with her dim-witted daughter with child for a second time, was in dire need of work. But the extern ignored her, and I saw her push past Sister Claire to the washbasin. "I knew it. . . . And so here it is," and she raised from the cold suds of the large basin a mortar and pestle, the smooth wood of which still showed a deep red stain. Having shown the pestle, she then touched it to her tongue. "Ground cranberry, I suspect," came the verdict. "Mixed with molasses. . . . As well-suited to white bread as to the imitation of your Lord's Passion." I could see her staring at the Head. Finally, she let the heavy evidence sink back into the tub.

"Ah, but the passion at issue here is not passion as *you* know it," said Sister Claire, leaning nearer the extern to add in a whispered hiss, "nor as your *daughter* knows it."

"Foul woman," said the extern, shaking her head in scornful disbelief. "It is your evildoing that will see me quit this place, not my words!"

"But what does that prove?" asked the cellarer, still mulling over the cold contents of the sink. "Perhaps our Lord in His infinite—"

"Hold your tongue!" said Sister Claire, turning on Sister Margarethe, whose wimpled face went pale. And she paced once around the large table, lost in thought. No one spoke. As Sister Claire passed the crying cellarer I heard her say, *"Calm yourself, dear,"* and coming around again to face Marie-Edith, who would not meet the nun's gaze, I heard what it was I'd dreaded: "Go," said Sister Claire.

"No!" said Sister Brigid. "Forgive her, Sister, for she has only spoken her mind in a moment of—"

"Ah," said Sister Claire, turning now to the older sister, seated out of my sight, "speak if you will in her defense, please do. But remember, my Sister," and her voice fell, menacingly, "you are an old woman, and when I rise here— as I will—it is I who will determine how your days are passed. But please, go ahead: speak. *Speak!*"

"I am an old woman, it is true; and perhaps I cannot interfere in your plans. But heed this: the Lord marks well your depravity, and it is His interference that you should fear." This set Sister Margarethe to verily blubbering; but Sister Claire silenced her with a single look, and said to Sister Brigid, "Read your beads, and know that your silence will keep you safe."

"Wretch!" said Marie-Edith, who, burning with indignation and shame and anger, set to gathering up her overcoat and bag; she would take with her too the bushel of oysters. "I've spoken my mind today, yes; and I'll speak my mind to the bishop too when I—"

"*Do!* Oh yes, do!" Sister Claire let go a great laugh. "And when you," said she, leaning so near the extern she'd only to whisper, ". . . and when you, a heathen, an impoverished and illiterate whore's mother—when you win your audience with His Holiness, as *surely* you will, give him my best. Ah, but I beg pardon: you are *not* illiterate, are you? Not wholly, no; for you've had your little lessons with our resident . . ." and Sister Claire hesitated, not knowing what to call me, not deigning to use my name. "But tell me," she went on, for all to hear, "for I've long wondered, just how have you managed to pay for your tutorials? . . . Quite coincidental, it has seemed to me, that money goes missing weekly from the cellarer's account. Perhaps you'll tell the biship *that*, should he allow such filth as you to see the inside of his confessional. I say again: Go."

And I heard not long after the slamming of the door, and then the distant song of our hinged gate as Marie-Edith crossed the yard and disappeared from our precincts with not another word. I knew she'd not come again; and neither would she seek out the bishop. Had she truly stolen to pay me for our lessons? And this when I tried, repeatedly, to refuse her coin? I heard the familiar shuffling away of Sister Brigid; and now only the two, Sisters Claire and Margarethe, remained, standing quite near the pantry door.

They came nearer the pantry. They were not three paces from me. Sister Claire leaned on the door's jamb, and said to the cellarer, "You shall have your pantry, my dear. And I . . . I shall have my House."

"Yes," said the cellarer, very near tears, "but . . . but . . ."

"Calm yourself, Marta, and answer me this: are you clear? Do you understand what will happen?"

"I do," said the cellarer, excitedly. "But . . . hammer and nail to mock our Lord's Passion?"

"Tell me," insisted Sister Claire, "tell me how—if that child learns something of her Savior's sacrifice and suffering—tell me how she'll be the worse for it. *Tell me!* And answer me this: have we not suffered long enough that woman's lenity? Have the girls themselves not suffered from the laxity of her rule? . . . That . . . that *Actress!*"

"Yes, but the little one . . . That girl, Elizaveta, will her wounds . . . ?"

"Fool, of course she will recover," whispered Sister Claire. "I will only tap at the nails, tap them into the top of the hands, not *drive* them through the thick of the wrists! And with enough of Clothilde's soothing syrup she'll hardly feel anything. What good would a *dead* girl do us, my dear? And what is her passing pain if it brings about the restoration of this House? If it allows me to drive the Actress away, with her niece and her . . . her *amphibious* friend. By the way, how many shelves did you request, eh?"

"Six," said the cellarer.

"Then it's six you shall have." And the two stepped from the pantry's doorway. Sister Margarethe was calmer now, but still she teetered on the brink of tears. Sister Claire further assuaged her, and I heard then the kiss of dry, lifeless lips. "In time, if you wish, I will line this whole kitchen with shelves. . . . Now go, go stir the girls as we discussed. No one, *no one* but Elizaveta must be in the infirmary. And avoid the Actress, leave her to me. Seize the accomplice if you see her, detain her if she's been found. And, Sister," said the Head, calling after the cellarer, "we shall keep each other's secrets, no?" The cellarer made no response, and was gone: I heard the closing door.

Too, I heard Sister Claire sit: the scratching of chair legs over the stony kitchen floor. And I heard her set a thing of heft upon the table; this was followed by a sound—a steady grating—the cause of which I could not define. Long, long minutes passed as Sister Claire allowed the cellarer to play her part in the dormitory.

Finally, movement. Sister Claire rose to leave the kitchen. In so doing, she darkened the pantry doorway; she remained but an instant, long enough to toss all but one filed nail into the room, where they sprayed like shot, fell to lie strewn amid chisels and planes and the soft planks of pine. I saw in Sister Claire's hand a hammer; and my worst fears were confirmed: she would finish Peronette's prank in a wicked way all her own.

Sister Claire left the kitchen. It was empty. Stunned and scared as I was, I could not move. Not to save Elizaveta. Not to save myself.

It was sometime later—a half hour, two hours?—that the Angelus rang, summoning the girls to chapel, and I knew that I must move. I pushed open the trap, just so, and listened. Sister Brigid had returned: I knew her by her hushed and steady movement. I waited. All was quiet then, quiet save for the murmur of her Rosary, more breath than discernible prayer. She'd settled into her chair. I could see her at table's end, reading the blue crystals with her gnarled and near-useless fingers, their knuckles large and hard as rocks.

I crawled from the cellar.

Could I slip past Sister Brigid, to the dark twist of a stairway that led up to her rooms, that stairway she could no longer navigate with safety? From there I could take to the second-floor corridor, steal along it to the window at its end; then through that window, onto the terrace above the gallery, and over to the vacated dormitory. Could I . . . ? Ah, but what choice did I have?

And so I slid from the pantry, quiet as air, keeping to the kitchen's wall, far from the mumbling nun. But I'd need to pass her, for she sat not far from the stairwell, her back flush against her throne-like chair; her head hung low, chin to chest, deep in prayer or sleep. And as I did so, as I slipped beside the nun, she, without looking up, shot her useless hand out at me; with it she seized my hand, and held me fast. But before I could speak, she raised her rheumy eyes to me—tears dampened her sunken and papery cheeks—and from her hands to mine she passed her Rosary; and told me, "Go with God, my child. Go from this place as fast as you can!"

So dark was the stairwell, I had to pull myself up by the rope banister, which threatened to slip from the wall, rusted rings and all, at any moment. I thought of hiding forever in the safe dark. Here was my last chance to change my mind. Did I *truly* wish to steal along the convent corridors and galleries, risk everything to sneak back into the dormitory? And why? To gather my few possessions? I could wait in the stairwell and later slip back into the night unseen. But what then? Where would I go? What would I do? Curl up under a bush, fight foraging squirrels for nuts and berries? . . . Yes, I would go on: if for no better reason than I needed that money. And clothes.

And so, slowly, I pushed open the door and spied into Sister Brigid's room. The door to the corridor was closed. I pushed the stairwell door wide—it gave with a deafening croak—and I slipped sideways into the room, like a cat. The sun came in through the wavy panes of the lone window. No one. Nothing. Just the cell-like white room: the bed with its thin spread, the bowed legs of the nightstand, a bureau with an unpainted porcelain washbasin—I didn't dare look at myself in the small mirror attached to it—and, of course, the requisite crucifix on the wall above the bed—

"*Merde!*" I said it aloud, for I realized then that I'd left the cypress cross behind me in the cellar. My only weapon! What to do? I couldn't retrieve it, not now. But how would I get by without that cross, without its rock-solid cypress arms to hold to? I told myself it would be there when I could get back to the cellar to claim it, if ever I made it back.

I listened through the oak door a long while. Silence in the corridor. I opened the door slowly, so slowly. I heard again Sister Brigid's admonition: Go! I told myself. *Go!*

Out into the corridor, to the window at its end. I forced it open, grateful, for once, for my God-given strength. Over the terrace, moving low behind its trellised vines of pale blue morning glories, withered now by the noonday heat, and onto the dormitory. Through a window I saw the well-ordered cots. No one was about; as hoped, they'd proceeded to chapel as a pack. Certainly, with Satan among them, none would stray. It was their fear that allowed me to move among them unseen. It came to me then: *Use their fear.*

The corridor, and the terrace too, though seemingly empty, felt somehow . . . *alive.* Stealing along them, I felt a presence. I kept turning around, looking every which way, expecting to see someone, some*thing.* But there was nothing, just that . . . that *presence.*

Soon I found myself standing before my cot. My trunk lay empty. Everything had been taken from it. The ragtag trunk—when I'd been given it, it held still the effects of the deceased nun who'd owned it previously—held only

Sister Claire de Sazilly's silver and bloodied crucifix. How angry I was then! That trunk, with its split canvas strapping and busted lock, had held everything in the world that was mine; true, it hadn't held much, but it had all been mine. Not only what money I'd secreted away, but the books given to me by Mother Marie, a pair of earrings discarded by Peronette, which I had not yet dared to wear, fearing, *knowing* that any attempt at self-adornment would be ridiculous, and ridiculed. My clothes, shoes, everything was gone. *Gone!* I took the cross from the trunk and hurled it down the length of the dormitory floor; it clanged off bedposts and skidded along the stone floor till finally it stopped in the center of the aisle, shining and defiant.

The sheets of course were gone. *The cold demon seed!* I heard again the screams of that morning and I wondered what stoked my anger more, the accusation itself or the absurdity of it. My thin mattress was bare but for branches, twigs cut from the elm and the ash, from sweet briar and thorn. Superstitious bitches! The anger welled within me. Yes, *yes!* So *absurd*—to believe in this Darkness, to believe that twigs spread on a bed might stop Satan's Work! I swept the branches from the bed and sat on its edge. I fell back, crying tears of anger and frustration and pain. Yes, pain, for the fast-flowing tears stung my cut face! And I discovered that the bed was wet. I knew instantly they'd doused it with holy water.

My pillow, linen-covered, dry, seemed to have escaped their base rituals. Quickly, to take what comfort I could, I pulled it to me. I buried my face in it and *yes!* . . . there was the lingering scent of Peronette, departed Peronette, for surely it was she who'd sped away beside her aunt. That lavender scent was overtaken by another smell, much stronger. Iron? The pillow was odorous of iron, or rust. Of course: the iron-frame bed had been splashed with holy water. But as I reached to touch the bed frame I saw that my hand was darkly wet. Looking down, I saw red flecks on the pillow's white cover; and my hand on its underside moved into . . . I flipped the pillow over. A crimson stain spread in the center of the pillow. A stain the size of a heart, or fist.

But whose fresh blood was this?

A noise. An inhuman noise nearby. A mewling. Beneath the cot.

I bent over, beckoned out from under my cot with curling fingers a pitch-dark cat, one I'd never seen before at C——. It came to sniff at my bloodied hand. Its ears had been cut, recently and crudely, as though with dull shears or a single blade. I took the cat up in my arms. What had they done to it? I petted the poor mutilated creature, and begged its forgiveness, for I knew I was the reason it had been hurt. (The only way to prevent a cat's being adopted as a witch's familiar is to cut off its ears; or so they hold in the North.)

Those bitches, those butchers! So, I'd devolved from devil to witch? Where would this all end? How much more blood would be shed, and whose blood would it be? Not mine; of that I was certain, and newly determined. Their malice, their ignorance, their cruelty, their stupidity, and their superstition were deciding my course.

I hugged the cat close. Poor thing. It passed its forepaws again and again over the stumps, the bloodied tags of fur that had been its ears. It purred and mewled till I grew *convinced* that it questioned me, asking the how and the why of all that was happening. Of course now I wonder if the cat didn't somehow *direct* me.

It rubbed against me, it burrowed into the crook of my arm. A *familiar,* eh? Here was an idea. I thought then of Prospero, Shakespeare's deposed Duke, the would-be Conjurer-King, who, speaking of the creature Caliban, says, "This thing of Darkness I acknowledge mine." But what to call such a dark and damaged thing, my familiar? . . . *The Tempest.* Miranda, Prospero's daughter. Ah, but that name was not *dark* enough . . . still, I liked the sound of it. I thought a moment more. Maluenda. Yes, that would do. That would do nicely. *Maluenda.* Equally magical and mean.

I sat on the edge of the ill-blessed bed, sprigs from the witch-defying trees spread all around me, and I held to my Maluenda. I'd never had a pet, let alone a *familiar!* It's likely I laughed out loud at the thought: a *familiar!* Suddenly I cared not a whit if I were caught, found, discovered on that bed clad as I was, filthy, defying the holy water—which ought to have burned me, of course— tickling my familiar. . . . Why? I cannot say.

I sat thinking how wonderful it would be if I *were* what the sorority believed me to be. I *wished* I was such a thing. *Willed* it. Would that I had Dark Powers, demons to do my bidding! Would that I knew spells to cast, dark prayers to pray. Only later would I learn that the wishing, the willing was prayer enough. And that those prayers were being heard, and would be answered. But I forge too fast ahead. . . .

So, the sorority of C—— had given me my familiar. How kind of them. What other powers did they attribute to me? Wasn't I as strong as their skewed convictions, as strong as their false faith and superstitions? *Use their fear.* Cradling the cat, I felt my strength increase, as though somehow I drew it from the animal.

I was still in pain, yes, but I was *unafraid!* And gaining strength. Indeed, I was stronger than I'd ever been; strong in every sense. And yes, fearless; for, having so little to lose, I had no fear of loss.

Still, I would escape.

7

The Franciscan Way

BUT FIRST I'd bathe. *Extraordinary!* Here I was—
me, who'd never dared expose my body—stealing
naked down the dormitory to the washroom, Maluenda tripping lightly at my heel.

In the washroom I found several tubs half-filled,
their stagnant cold water dark with . . . was it the faint
light, filtering through the skylights, sliding into the
dented copper tubs, that gave the water its leaden cast?
Or was it merely the girls' gathered dirt? Maluenda led
me to a tub whose water was by far the cleanest, perhaps even unused; and its cold water was calming. A
salve, it was, as I took up a clean cloth and began to
wash, hunched over the tub.

Maluenda perched on the tub's side, pawed at the
water and cleaned herself. She seemed to revel in
her dark reflection; her orange eyes glimmered on the
dim water, the color of old coin. Heartrending, it

was, to see her tending to the tattered flesh, the *tags* of flesh that had been her ears. Had they *torn* her ears from her? Cleaned, her wounds looked worse.

I walked back to my cot, clad again in that soiled nightshirt; only when I stood before my cot did I remember that I had nothing: all my things were gone from my trunk. Angrily, I began rifling through the trunks within easy reach, but no, this wouldn't do. Nearly all the girls were much smaller than I: their clothes would not fit. Which cots, which trunks belonged to the older girls? I hurried along, wondering who was it slept here, who was it slept there?

I came to a cold stop at Peronette's trunk. She certainly *had* left in a hurry: she'd abandoned her precious dresses. It was then I remembered: days earlier, Peronette had received a package—wrapped in pink paper, with the requisite red bow—that she'd torn into, quite curious as it came from an unknown atelier in Paris. Courtesy of Monsieur Gaudillon, of course. But the untried seamstress had erred, and the dress did not fit. It was much too large. Peronette had verily *raged.* . . . Sure enough, here it was, that dress, stuffed deep inside the trunk.

I dressed, not bothering with undergarments, in this confection of pale pink tulle with an underdress of softer pink silk—quite fancy, far too fancy for me with its full sleeves puffed at the shoulders and rows of opalescent buttons sewn from elbow to wrist. It fell a bit short, and was tight across the shoulders, but it would do.

I dug deeper in the trunk. Who knew what I might find? There were dresses Peronette had never worn, some still in their fancy wrappings. The cards from her father were torn in two and piled in a corner of the trunk, as though blown there by the hot wind of her contempt. There were letters from her mother; the thick pile of pale blue envelopes tied with a ribbon of purple silk. I unwrapped this package and read the topmost letter, dated some months earlier. Rather, I *would* have read it, had it not been perfectly illegible. The scratchings of a quill pen, nothing more; as though a doddering hen with inked talons had skittered across the thin and faintly scented paper. Here and there a word or phrase was discernible; but the letters were nonsensical. So Peronette hadn't lied about her mother. She was indeed crazy. I shuffled a few of the envelopes and saw that many were unopened; all of them were addressed (clearly *not* by Madame Gaudillon) to Peronette. Who continued to post these letters to the girl, so cruelly?

Ah, but this was wrong. I knew I ought not to look through Peronette's things, even if she was already far away. And, though the dormitory was silent, and the girls were assembled at chapel for the Angelus, one or more strays might return at any moment.

As I was about to lower the lid of Peronette's trunk, I spied something sticking up among the layers of linen and lace. It looked to be the thin snout of an animal; at first, taking it to be just that, I stepped back from the trunk. Ridiculous, I know—did I think Peronette had harbored some species of possum? Then again, it was ridiculous that I'd discovered the mangled cat beneath a cot, ridiculous too that I stood accused of congress with Lucifer and... *Alors*, it was a cork, pushed deep into the mouth of a blue bottle. I reached into the trunk, reached for the base of the bottle, and pulled it up. It was wine; and surely it was fine wine: only the best for Peronette. And she had hardly drunk any of it. Strange, that she'd never shared this with me; if not the wine, then the secret: it would have been just like Peronette to boast, slyly, of a bottle of Burgundy secreted in her trunk. I pulled the cork. So rich, so deep it was...a sip. And another.

Bottle in hand, I sought out the trunk of the second tallest girl at C——, a gangly thing known as Spider. Tall as she was, Spider's boots, well-worn, and of a fine white kid, barely fit me. Lacing them up, I earned for myself another draft of wine.

Quickly I twisted my hair into a tight bun, stuck a pearl-ended pin through it. Around my neck I hung Sister Brigid's blue crystal rosary. And, as another girl who remained in residence that summer had the sweetest-smelling scent, I...Suffice to say that I was soon damp at the neck, elbows, and knees with gardenia water.... And dressed as I'd never dressed before, still poor as a pauper—indeed, I thought rather ominously of how the poor, the peasantry, wake their dead in fancy dress—dressed, I walked from the dormitory out into the corridor, Maluenda curled in my left arm, the bottle of Burgundy in my right, and fast gained the shuttered gallery that crossed to the chapel.

From there I might slip down the outer stairwell toward the stables, where perhaps I'd saddle a nag—please, I thought, *please* let there be a beast in the stable besides the dappled dray horse used and abused by the cellarer these long years—and I'd ride away to safety. What was I thinking? Maybe it was the wine; after all, I had little experience of drunkenness, having but tipped Mother Marie's bottles shyly beside Peronette, and here I was partaking freely. Or was this—my moving blindly on—was this what is meant by the Mystery of Faith? Certainly, I *trusted*. Trusted in something unseen, something of which I had no proof. Not then. Not yet.

And suddenly, there it was again. That *presence*. Somewhere in the banded, broken light of the gallery. There and gone. Walking along the gallery on tip-

toe, lest the low heels of the pilfered boots betray me, I found myself following . . . something. Nothing I could see or name, but . . . No, I was being led.
And it was with difficulty that I stopped and settled myself.

The gallery led to the lesser library, so-called as it was a smallish room
walled with shelves burdened by the records of the Order. It was situated above
the chapel, and was commonly accessed by a stairwell on its far side, rising up
from beside the *ex voto*, near the altar proper. I was familiar with this near-pur-
poseless gallery, with its three large windows, arched, their sills deep enough to
sit in, which gave out onto the yard, the gardens, and, beyond, the sea. These
windows were the sole breaks in the gallery's interior, shuttered wall; the opposite wall had long ago been bricked over, for the northern winds were ruinous.

I took my favored seat in the third window, the one farthest from the dormitory and some twenty, perhaps thirty paces from the library. I found no reason to proceed—discounting, of course, the imminent danger to my person
should I be discovered! In truth, I think I was resisting the *presence*, or perhaps
waiting for its return. Too, I was waiting for the girls to move, *en masse*; under
cover of their distraction, I would effect my escape. I sat on the sill, closed my
eyes and offered my bruised face to the sun. Maluenda nuzzled at my neck.
Her weight on my chest was welcome. The bottle of wine sat beside me, its
blue glass reflecting sunlight as does the sea.

Silence save for the distant din, the droning of the girls in the chapel below.
But then I wondered: could they still be gathered in commemoration of the
Incarnation? Surely not. Had I lost track of time, or had the orderly clocks of
C—— ticked to a stop, stilled by all the strangeness?

I expected the first of the girls to come from the chapel at any moment; the
line of them would then pass beneath me, along the crosshatched bricks of the
open gallery below. They'd crowd into the dormitory's first floor, with its hive-
like cells belonging to the oldest nuns—the dying, the addle-brained—and its
cramped classrooms. They'd crawl down the airless cold corridor, its windowless walls hung with dark art in ornate frames, or set deep with undusted statuary of a plaster so white it glowed. . . . Or perhaps—for I didn't know the
hour—they'd cross the interior yard on a diagonal and move toward St.
Ursula's, into the dining hall beyond the kitchen. Lest they take the latter
route, I was ready to slip from the sill and hide, spy them from behind the
bank of cracked shutters further on.

No sign of that *presence*. . . . Had it simply been my fear, manifested?

Maluenda looked up at me with eyes orange and large as harvest moons;

she stretched, the picture of indolence, and settled fat and happy in my lap. I took another drink from the bottle whose wine seemed to issue up from a well, a deep, deep well.

Waiting to escape—that *was* what I waited for, no?—waiting, I watched the cat curled in my lap and I saw . . . No. *Impossible!* Had I looked too directly at the sun, were sunspots spinning in my eyes? I blinked, kept my eyes closed; but when I opened them again, there was no denying it:

The black slits, the pupils at the center of the cat's orange eyes, were twisting. Transshaping. At first their mere *motion* stunned me, but now . . . were they truly taking shape? I couldn't be sure. It seemed that yes, yes they were. But what shapes? I couldn't have said, not then. Distinct shapes they were; moving, each pupil in time with the other. They'd go still, and then the twisting would begin again and the eyes would take another, different shape.

I quickly stood, nearly sending the bottle tumbling down into the yard. Maluenda leapt from my lap. I watched her pass through the shafting sunlight into the shadows nearer the gallery's end. I snatched the bottle off the sill— one sip, two—and followed her.

My eyes adjusted to the deeper darkness and I saw Maluenda, or what I assumed was she: the sole mobile shadow, the gray within the black. I moved farther down the hallway to where there hung a triptych of threadbare tapestries, all but discarded, left to the play of the seasons and the ravenous mouths of moths. Every girl at C——— had been reminded more than once that our tapestries—excepting, apparently, these of the chapel gallery—were not playthings to be hidden behind. The largest and most valuable of the lot at C——— hung in the dining hall, insulating the coldest room, dampening the sound in the loudest. This was Boucher's "The Audience of the Emperor of China," from the works at Beauvais. Its cartoon—the oil painting on which it was based—had hung in the Pupil's Parlor until Mother Marie had arrived and ordered it removed to her rooms—and now that I recall, that *had* caused something of a stir among the sisters. . . .

My favorite of the three tapestries—and again, I knew them well; this was *my* gallery, as surely as the pantry had been my home—my favorite of the tapestries, each depicting a saint in ecstasy, was that of St. Francis. It hung farthest down the hall. I'd often come with a torch or oil lamp to study the stupefied face of the Saint, who knelt in receipt of Christ's Five Wounds, shooting as golden threads from the heart of a hovering angel to Francis's hands, feet, and bared torso. So skilled was the workmanship that the Saint's flesh seemed to pucker around the wounds. Indeed, so skillfully was the carnality of the Saint rendered in thread, the artist had earned the work's banishment to that far and dark corner of the house.

I caught up to Maluenda at the base of the Franciscan tapestry. I could not see her eyes, yet somehow I *knew* they were still. And I knew too that she stared up at me: she wanted me to see something, she wanted me to know something.

I wasn't at all sure I wanted to see or know anything more.

The bottle. *Yes.* Two quick sips.

Faint sunlight floated over my shoulder from the bank of windows behind me. Light slid charily through the cracks in the closed shutters nearer the Saint. The silken threads shimmered in the inadequate light as the tapestry, draped from an iron rod, moved on a breeze I could not feel.

And again, just then, that *presence*: I was not alone. I looked long and hard into the striate shadows, plumbed their depths ahead. "Who is it? Show yourself. *Be seen!*" Nothing. No one.

A votive candle sat on the floor at the foot of the tapestried Saint. Who, I thought, who would have lit such a thing, and in this untrafficked place? The white stub of wax lit the *whole* tapestry, impossibly. Its blue flame rose several times higher than the candle itself and threatened to catch the corner of the canvas frame. The flame was steady, did not waver as a *natural* flame will. It was by the blue light of that votive that I saw the tapestry. Seemingly for the first time.

Maluenda sat beneath the canvas, beside the uncanny flame. She nuzzled its frame. She mewled, plaintively. I knelt down beside her—one knee: a genuflection—and I chucked the point of her chin. "What is it?" I asked in a whisper.

Maluenda rose on her hind legs and pushed with her forepaws against the tapestry and . . .

. . . I've come this far, and there is much farther to go. I will simply say it:

The tapestry bled, plain as day. Blood rose from the wounds in Francis's feet, blood pooled in his open palms, and trickled from his palms down his thin wrists. Not for an instant did I doubt it was blood I saw. It was of a different texture than the threadwork; indeed, its liquescence obscured the very texture of the tapestry.

I *saw* this! I swear it now as I would have sworn it then.

I stood, fell back from the tapestry against the shuttered wall. What was happening here? Who or what was showing me this, and why? Was it to make known the truth of the Franciscan stigmata, and in so doing mock Sister Claire's dark charade? Or was this the work of the wine? I held the heavy bottle up to the votive's flame and saw that it was nearly full, fuller than when last

I'd looked. But of course *that* was impossible, no? I drank again. Perhaps my mind, perhaps my *senses* had been loosed by the beating I'd suffered under Sister Claire. Too, I had never drunk so much wine; and surely I'd never drunk wine as rich and delicious as this.

But I knew that what I saw was real. This was no illusion. No trick of shadow and light.

The flow of blood was steady, yet it did not run from the sewn frame, did not drip. Maluenda wound herself around my ankles. As I bent to her she sprang up into my arms. I cupped her belly in my left hand; her heart beat so strongly it was as though I held it directly, as though I'd slipped my hand inside her, between the fur and flesh.

I stood staring into the Saint's pale face, half-expecting the wide-open eyes to turn toward me, the thin lips to twist with speech. . . . Yes, the sewn Saint seemed real enough to speak.

It was all I could do to hold the straining, stretching cat from the tapestry. When finally she succeeded in slipping my grip, I let her fall and brought the bottle to my lips.

But I could not avert my eyes. Beautiful St. Francis. And with the strange grace of the somnambulist, slowly, deliberately, I raised my arm. There were my splayed fingers before me. My hand glowed impossibly white in the blue light, as though gloved. Something urged me on. Yes, it was that: an *urge*. Maluenda? That *presence*?

Mine was the long Sistine finger of life, reaching, reaching. . . . I touched . . . I touched the tapestry. The Saint's open palm. His wound. His blood.

Nothing. I could *see* the blood, flowing from the wounds, but I could not *feel* it. My finger came away clean. Again, I touched it: the other hand, each foot, the lash marks and spear wounds in his side. I scratched at the threaded wounds with my thumbnail. Nothing.

As though struck, I fell to my knees. Prayer flowed from me, as surely as blood flowed from the Saint. I do not know how long I held that familiar stance; nor can I say definitively that it was prayer I offered. Questions, perhaps. Or did I simply open to the indisputable, strange truth before me? All that's certain is that I would have kept on had it not been for the voices.

Yes, voices.

I rose fast to my feet. My breath was ragged, my heart wild. At first it seemed I'd heard a lone voice. Faraway, yet nearing. "Show yourself!" I said again. But no. There were many voices, speaking as one, a chorus, growing ever louder.

Spinning to scan the shadows, I kicked the votive over. As I moved to right it, I saw that the blue flame shot straight out from the fallen candle, pointed *down* along the floor into the deeper darkness, sure as a finger, when it ought to have reached *up*, as any flame will. It spilled an excess of wax in that same direction, wax that flowed fast, and as sure as the Saint's blood, toward the door of the lesser library.

Maluenda had already moved into the darkness nearer the door. I followed, followed the directives of the candle and cat.

The voices, again.... They were real, quite real; and coming from within the library.

I stole nearer the gallery's end, nearer the voices. There, to my left, was the arched and covered stairwell that gave on to a path leading to the stables. So *that* was how Peronette and Mother Marie escaped. Another door, straight ahead, opened directly into the lesser library. This secondary door was rarely used. I myself had used this door but once, and recently: I'd slipped from it to escape a tutorial on Horace, which seems now to have taken place in another life. As indeed it did.

The voices grew more distinct as I neared the door. A mix of voices, some panicked (the girls, perhaps) and others deeper, demanding (Sister Claire?). I might have run then, down the outer stairwell to the stables. But I did not. Instead, I crept up to the library's thick oak door and listened. And what I heard astounded me: *men!* The voices of men. And then, stranger still, I heard the voice of Mother Marie-des-Anges; and it was my name she spoke!

8

My Accusers, Convened

THERE'D BEEN SOME commotion moments earlier; this accounted for the raised voices I'd heard. A man was struggling still to restore order. From his voice, frail but full, self-important, bloated with bombast, I concluded that he was a man of some position. Perhaps a priest of a higher rank, for it seemed everyone quieted when he spoke; but few such men ever came to C——. Who could it be? Nearing, I listened to the words that fell so slowly, so deliberately from his mouth; and I observed that his speech was flabby with tautologies—that is, he said everything twice, thus gaining time for the slow wheels of his mind to grind. I could not clearly hear his questions, for Monsieur Le Maire (it was, of course, the Mayor of C——) stood far across the crowded library.

How many people were crowded into the lesser library? It was not a large room; indeed, it had but one bank of windows, a single large table, several chairs, and not many books besides those unread histories of the Order. I assumed many of those gathered with the girls and nuns had come from the village of C—— in the company of Monsieur Le Maire; surely they'd all been summoned in the hours just passed. How had they all descended on C—— without my hearing them? Perhaps they'd come up the back path from the village, warned away from the main drive where I'd last been seen. Or perhaps they'd climbed to the lesser library from the chapel while I lay secreted in the cellar, or busied myself in the dormitory, bathing and dressing. I wondered, had the sorority even observed the Angelus, or had the bell I'd heard been a call to assembly? . . . Regardless, here they were. Men, *men* had come to C——. Their voices, the more familiar female voices too, they all bore tones of excess: hysteria or flat, spiritless inquiry. A council, a jury of sorts; this *proceeding* was a trial.

But who stood accused? Peronette? Was she even present? Mother Marie? *Me?* At that thought I very nearly took to the outer stairwell, but I *had* to hear what was going on, for I suspected—rightly—that whatever happened in that room would decide my fate.

I spied slivers of the room through the door where its wood had warped over time. I could not see much in this way, just the bustling of bodies, many bodies, gathered in groups. I squatted, rose on my toes, bobbed left and right. But I'd learn more from listening.

I was so close to the door I feared detection. Like all the doors at C——, that of the lesser library was constructed of thick boards of oak banded by hammered iron. I practically pressed myself against that door. Maluenda sat at my foot, perfectly still, as intent as I on the words we heard.

A question. I couldn't quite make it out . . . something about the Prince of This World . . . something about a pact. . . . A pause, and then the tremulous response of—

—of Mother Marie! It was *she* who stood accused. How I felt for her! What I wouldn't have done to rescue her, save her.

And then I heard her say my name, again.

By the tone of her response, which I could hear quite clearly, as she was separated from me by the door and fewer than five paces, I knew her to be defeated, and resignedly so.

Mother Marie repeated my name when the Mayor repeated his question, which I heard all too well. "Who is the seducer here?" he asked. "Who has brought all this about?"

I had. So said Mother Marie-des-Anges. It was I who'd set all this in motion. I clasped my hand to my mouth and fell back from the door. Maluenda rose up to pull with bared claws at the lacy hem of the dress.

Absurd, to think that I was then capable of seduction. I knew nothing of . . .
of *sex*, let alone seduction. I was completely without wiles, guileless. Yes, there'd
been the milk of the dreams, but I had never initiated that, not consciously. In
waking life I knew *nothing* of my own body, neither its nature nor its ways nor
its . . . its *name*. Had you asked me about mystical theology or Trajan's legacy,
had you asked me to decline a noun in any of the languages I'd learned, yes, but
I avow it: I knew nothing, *nothing*, of self-satisfaction or sex. Or seduction.

I heard the Mayor ask where Peronette had gone—it *was* she who'd ridden
away—but Mother Marie swore she'd known nothing of her niece's plans;
Peronette had harnessed the horses and effected her escape alone. At this the
sorority dissented as one. And even *I* knew Mother Marie was lying; bedeviled
as she was by her niece, there was nothing she would not have done for her.
The loudest of the protesters was, of course, Sister Claire de Sazilly:

"Liar!" said she. "How then do you explain your niece's absence when all
the Order searched for her? You hid her away, till such time as she could
descend to the stables, to your *fine* carriage and two steeds and—"

"I do not know," mumbled Mother Marie.

"Answer!" countered Sister Claire, whose cry overrode some words of the
Mayor's. "Do not lie before your Christ!"

"I do not know!" said Mother Marie; these words she would repeat often in
the course of her interrogation. "Surely you, Sister, believe my niece capable of
executing her escape from *you* and your scheming ways!"

Sister Claire appealed to the Mayor, for it served her ends to do so. "Can
you not silence the accused, Monsieur Le Maire?" she asked.

But Mother Marie spoke on: "Why," she asked of Sister Claire, "why
wouldn't I have gone with her? Why wouldn't I have joined her in the
barouche and escaped if I'd known of her plans, for I've long known of *yours*,
you godless, usurping—?" Mother Marie hesitated; and then, her voice
cracking like thin ice, added, "She has forsaken me." Here was the painful
admission.

"You admit it then," chimed in the cellarer. "You admit it: the accused *has*
escaped. She's escaped."

"No!" said Mother Marie. "She is gone, yes. It is true. But she had no reason 'to escape,' as you say." Mother Marie appealed then to the Mayor, in whom
resided the Law: "I remind you, Monsieur Le Maire, neither my niece nor I
stand accused of any crime."

"Witch!" came the cry, echoed by others. A townswoman observed that as Satan did not stand on formalities, neither should the Soldiers of Christ. Others assented, roundly.

Above the accusatory din rose Mother Marie's voice: "What am I accused of? *Speak!* If this is a trial there must be a crime as well as a criminal."

The Mayor averred that this was not a *formal* trial. "My good man," countered Mother Marie, "formal or no, this *is* a trial. You and all present know it."

The Mayor somehow quieted the girls. "Mother," said he, his words at a low simmer, "indeed you are not accused, at present, of any crime." *At present.*

There came, as though by prearrangement, more crazed accusations from Sister Claire's disciples. Maniacal and nonsensical testimony, every word of it unbidden. "She's loosed devils among us!" This from Sister Claire. "Is that not crime enough among Christians?" Appealing to the Mayor in a more reasoned tone, the Head asked again, "Is *that* not crime enough?"

"You," seethed the Mother Superior. "You with your tools! Your hammer and nail! You who would *use* Elizaveta, who would have beaten down poor Herculine as though she were your own unchaste desires. You . . . you *vulgarian!*"

Only then did I recall Sister Claire's plan. I'd forgotten it during my escape from the cellar, forgotten it as I'd so busily determined to escape C———. Such guilt I felt then! I'd left young Elizaveta to that evil, scheming nun, who'd carried out perfectly her horrific plan to take up Peronette's prank and turn it to her advantage, rile the gullible girls, and finally win the House from Mother Marie. And then I wondered how Mother Marie had learned of Sister Claire's unholy charade. Doubtless the same way that Sister Claire had learned of my tutoring of Marie-Edith—through the nuns' quiet and ever-shifting alliances, a spider's web spun of favors and enmity and secret affections.

"Every devil should die!" came Sister Claire's retort. "That beastly child is among us now due to your intervention. See what she's brought down on my Elizaveta!"

The girls moaned in choral hysteria. They screamed of their own safety; one wondered Whose touch she'd receive: that of her Lord or His enemies.

"Stop your theatrics!" said a scornful Sister Catherine. The faux stigmata, the tomfoolery, she was having none of it. Who among the nuns believed? Who doubted? And of the doubters, who would dare challenge Sister Claire?

Sister Claire must have turned on the Mayor then, for I heard her command the man, "Take this House from her! This blessed House that was hers to keep!"

"*Is* mine to keep," corrected Mother Marie; and to the Mayor, she added,

"She has coveted the rule of this House since it was awarded to me.... And I remind you, Monsieur Le Maire, with due respect, you are the possessor of a *secular* authority, and these are matters—"

"Since you *bought* this House with the Devil's Coin!" Sister Claire must then have lunged at the Mother Superior, for I heard chairs overturn and loud and fast came the prayers of those assembled, their voices ragged, fraught with fear.

How had things devolved, so quickly, to this? I was truly frightened, for if the Mother Superior could be thus abused, what would they do to me? It was then I should have fled. But I stayed, for I heard Mother Marie begin to sob. Soon she'd lost all composure, all grace. Only then, weakened, ruined, was she invited to speak in her defense. She couldn't.

I stood by the library door, trails of salt drying on either cheek, listening. I pressed my ear to it. My hand was flat against it, my fingertips reading, absently, the grooves, the grain of the oak. I was careful to stand far enough back from the door: the shuffle of my feet or some slight shadow I'd cast might betray my presence. With the toe of those white boots I had to nudge Maluenda back from the door time and again; she pawed under it, sniffed at the stale air heated by so many bodies gathered together.

After more questions about Peronette and her whereabouts, which Mother Marie did not, perhaps *could* not answer—thankfully, not a word more was said about me; not then—the Mayor was ready to "pronounce sentence." The *gall!* He would *sentence* the Mother Superior of C——? "Monsieur," asked Sister Catherine of the Holy Child, "excuse me, Monsieur Le Maire, but is that not for the bishop to—"

"*Proof?* Is it further proof you want?" cried out Sister Claire, silencing young Sister Catherine. "Very well. More proof before the pronouncement! Let us *see* the devilry of this one! Let her tongue betray the touch of her Fallen Lord!"

After a quick conference with Sister Claire, the Mayor said he would hear the Mother Superior recite one Mater Dei and one Pater Nostrum, both in French and Latin. "Let her tongue save her," said the Mayor, adopting the condemnatory tone of Sister Claire, "or let it speak of her unholiness; of her unholiness and any infernal alliance she's made. Let her—"

"Let her speak, Monsieur Le Maire," barked Sister Claire. It has long been held that the unholy cannot recite, completely, the Lord's Prayer. The Hail Mary, which is not believed to trouble the Devil's Own, must have been ordered by the Mayor for show; what authority he had was secular in nature: he was easily led by Sister Claire.

Mother Marie—and what choice did she have?—began her recital. The French first; flawless. Everyone knew it was the Latin, the lordly language, over which she'd stumble. Indeed, who, in the heated atmosphere of that room, might have managed the Mater Dei in unblemished Latin?

"*Ave Maria, gratia plena, dominus tecum . . .*" No sound but her voice, slow and sure. One misstep and . . . I feared for her, feared she'd not make it through the prayer in one seamless pass. Ah, but how many times had she uttered it in her life? Of course, this was different.

Mother Marie finished. Both prayers, both languages: flawless. And for naught.

Sister Claire protested—doubtless she feared Mother Marie's acquittal—and quieted only when the Mayor announced the sentence he'd already decided on: Mother Marie would leave C—— immediately. She would stay, under guard, in the Meeting House of the village until such time as her passage could be arranged.

"Passage where?" came the cry, tens of voices in unison. They were scared, said the girls, that the devil-abiding nun might not be sent far enough away. The Mayor made clear his intent: he would arrange for Mother Marie to take up the long-vacant position at the jail in D——, in La Vendée, where she would serve as a confessor to the criminally insane. "Of course," he equivocated, "I'll have to speak with the elders of your Order and—"

"*Pas du tout!*" stated Sister Claire. "Am I not the Mother Superior in the absence of *that* one?" All present, save Monsieur Le Maire, knew this was not necessarily so: the bishop ought to be consulted; but no one dared challenge Sister Claire de Sazilly, who had already ascended, by force if not by right. "I am, yes," continued Sister Claire, "and it is on *my* authority that you will send the woman hence."

Quiet, utter and complete quiet as they stood watching Mother Marie.

With my eye to the door, I saw the crowd part and there, prostrate on the ground, in the center of her circled accusers, lay Mother Marie. She'd fainted. No one dared revive her, and so there she lay, till finally the Mayor directed some of the assembled townsmen to take the nun up to her chambers, stand guard over her till she came to; then they were to gather up a few of her things—"what a woman needs," said he—and bring her to his home, where they were to secure her in a windowless, second-story room till the Meeting House could be prepared. One of the townsmen demurred; how were they to avoid bewitchment? The Mayor had no response; but Sister Claire de Sazilly did. I saw her undo the hasp of the chain she wore around her thick waist;

from it she slid a gold cross and passed it to the townsman. This, apparently, was good enough for that faithful servant; thus protected, he and his fellows turned to their task, each taking hold of one of Mother Marie's limbs. I saw them. It was as though they shared the burden of a sack of potatoes! *"Bastards!"* I breathed aloud. "Let your hour be near!" Maluenda scratched at the base of the door; her claws gouged the oak.

It was then, finally, that I determined to leave; but as I bent to take up the cat I heard again my name. Spoken by Sister Claire de Sazilly, who stood now just on the other side of the door. "You cannot leave us to that witch's ways!" said she to the Mayor.

"No," enjoined her disciples, "you cannot! You cannot leave with *her* among us!" The Mayor had pronounced upon Mother Marie, which was all well and good, but what about *me*, what about the witch who walked among them still?

More accusations. *I* was the devil who'd ridden the girls in frenzied dreams. It was I who'd stirred the storm. I who'd won Peronette and the Mother Superior to my ways. And so on, till finally I was the witch who'd brought a plague of mice into C—— three years prior, who'd blasted the cellarer's tomato crop, who'd killed off the entire farrow when our prized sow had finally pigged.

I raised the blue bottle high, threw my head back, and drank.

Maluenda stirred at my foot. She sniffed under the door, scratched at it, turned herself around and around in tight circles. I worried that she'd give us away. I took her up into my arms to calm her. No wonder she grew wild at the sound of Sister Claire's voice, for if *she* hadn't shorn the cat's ears herself, surely she'd been present when the deed had been done. Every time Sister Claire spoke the cat seemed newly crazed. She verily shredded the pink net of tulle I wore; the satin underdress too was torn. It was all I could do to hold onto Maluenda *and* the wine *and* listen to the hateful sister speak.

She was going on about how I'd come to her in dreams, how I'd taken different shapes to tease and torment her, to urge her to "impurity of thought and deed." Two of the older girls, when questioned by Sister Claire, averred I'd done the same to them.

The Mayor, ruffled by the nature of all he'd already heard, would brook no further testimony. Far easier for him to curse the Darkness in certain terms and vow to see the nuns and girls returned to the care of the Prince of Peace. Just how, I wondered, would the old fool accomplish this? When next he spoke, his plan came clear:

"Where then," he asked, "is this Herculine?" At this the assembled rose to fever pitch:

"We ran her from the hall," said one, "and we've searched for her all afternoon."

"I watched as she ran, fast as a man, up the drive, on and on."

"She lay down upon the dirt and had relations with it."

"Surely she jumped astride the horses pulling her sister-witch Peronette——"

"No," said Sister Claire. "She remains among us, for the Devil's work is
never done."

And so on and so on, till all and sundry impossibilities were addressed.

It was the Mayor finally who broke this chain of accusation, which had
rendered me still when I ought to have run. "We must find her," said he, his
words all afumble, "and find her we will. She can't have gone far. She can't have
gone far and we must find her. We will get from her the answers we need.
Answers, indeed." He directed all present to break into smaller groups; by his
calculation there were some forty people in the library. Each group, led by a
townsman, would search a part of the convent and grounds. Though long minutes were spent debating the plan's finer points, it was finally adopted by all,
and bore the sanction of Sister Claire.

Meanwhile, I stood listening, dumbstruck, Maluenda growing ever wilder
in my arms. Still I did not leave. I could not leave. I could not even reason that
it was the wisest course of action. My sole thought was, *How* can this be happening? Here was a drama from the Burning Days! Had I truly seen what I'd
seen, heard what I'd heard?

Screams within the library. Louder than any I'd heard earlier. And seemingly directed at the door behind which I stood! I peered between the warped
boards but saw nothing, nothing save for the all-obscuring rush toward the
door behind which I——

It happened in an instant. Apparently, in my effort to calm the cat, I'd *shown*
myself. Perhaps I'd let my booted foot get too close to the door, and someone,
one of the girls, spied it there, no doubt the same girl who shouted: "She's
come! There! *There!*"

Moving too suddenly back from the door, three things happened in quick
succession: I dropped the bottle of burgundy and saw it shatter on the stone
floor; Maluenda leapt from my arms; and the back door of the lesser library
opened inward and . . . and there I stood. *There.* Staring back at the council, at
all assembled. Looking foolish—not to say *hellish*—in that ill-fitting torn
pink finery. A blue stone rosary hanging round my neck. My familiar at my
side.

All I remember is a panicky dance—as on a listing ship—for the girls and townspeople pushed toward the library's primary door. Trying to flee. From *me!* The Mayor and an elderly townsman clung to each other like widowed sisters. Only Sister Claire dared approach me.

"You," she spat. "You who dare to—" But Sister Claire de Sazilly would never finish that sentence; for, with preternatural speed, the speed and strength of a thousand cats, *ten* thousand cats, Maluenda sprang at the nun, her claws splayed like sets of knives.

All save the cat and Sister Claire were still, staring down at the scene. Sister Claire had fallen to the floor when struck by the springing cat's weight. She struggled beneath Maluenda, who'd fast taken hold of the nun's flesh with her foreclaws. With her hind legs she scratched furiously at the nun's torso, shredding that rough tunic and the hair shirt she wore beneath it. On the pale plane of Sister Claire's stomach I saw the scars of her decades-long mortification, the thorns' work, matched now by the work of the cat's claws.

Sister Claire's disciples suffered fits, hopping and stomping and screaming, but not a one came to her aid. "I'm going to be sick!" promised one, who promptly was, distracting no one. And indeed my stomach was unsettled, too; as it had been years back, when I'd witnessed an extern cleave from her hand the tips of two fingers, which lay twitching beside the roast that she'd been working.

When finally Maluenda leapt from Sister Claire, she left the nun a bloodied mass on the stone floor, rigid with shock, staring wide-eyed at nothing at all. Maluenda, seemingly loathe to leave the nun, bounded up easily onto the windowsill and, after turning to look back at me, to purr, to pass a paw over her torn-away ears, she leapt from the window, two tall stories above the ground.

"*No!*" I shouted, stepping into the room. "Maluenda!" But to cross the room, to go to the sill, I'd have had to step over the seizing body of Sister Claire de Sazilly; and that I found I could not do. I stared down with revulsion. I hated the woman, yes; but had I ever wished for it to come to this? Sister Claire was . . . unrecognizable. It might have been any woman's or man's face there under cover of all that blood. I saw that the cat had torn away the lobe of one ear.

As I stood staring down at the nun, prostrate at my booted feet, as I stood marveling at the wounds my Maluenda had inflicted, I was grabbed by two, perhaps four townsmen. They'd come up behind me at the Mayor's silent direction. Brave souls, they were. Remember what it was they believed me to be. Surely, if I'd had my wits about me, I might have used their belief against them—*Use their fear!*—scared them so badly they'd have refused to restrain me. If I'd spun around like a dervish or swung at them or sputtered something in a foreign tongue, perhaps I'd have walked from that room, from C———, that very evening. As it was, I offered no resistance at all.

9

I Am Jailed; or,
I Determine to Die

THE MAYOR STEPPED forward to stand between the still-prone Sister Claire and myself. With whispers he directed two boys of the village; they then made their way shyly, hurriedly, through the girl-thick crowd, and disappeared. Shaking from infirmity or fright, and not daring to look directly at me, the Mayor puffed himself up to offer the following by way of pronouncement:

"This child," said he, grandly, raising his ringed fist at me, that fist from which a gouty finger sprouted, its long nail buffed to a sheen. "This child—"

"Guilty!" rose the cry. The townsman holding fast to my left arm cried out. I tried to break free of his hold; this of course set the assembly off—some among them cried, *screamed* that I would free myself and in league with Satan whisk them all away to some black rapture.

The Mayor insisted on silence, without result. He asked for silence. He *begged* for silence. But only when Sister Claire stood, unsteadily, having been revived by Sister Clothilde's fistful of salts, did silence come. And the Mayor spoke on:

"This child shall be held here, secured overnight. At sunrise this council will reconvene to decide her fate and—"

It was then both Sisters Catherine and Clothilde tried to ask again about the bishop. Sister Margarethe stood idly by throughout. Sister Claire wrested her arm from the infirmarian, who stepped warily away from the Head, and said that these were "civil" concerns, to be decided within the House; no need to bother the bishop, who'd surely agree with Monsieur Le Maire. At this the old man demurred, slyly deeming himself unworthy of any alliance with the bishop; but before he could conclude his sentencing—his posture now perfect, his pointed chin protuberant—the girls handed down sentences of their own: I should be burned, banished, pressed beneath boards piled with twice my weight in stones. I stood silent before them, stunned by their *savagery*. By their anachronistic sentencing—burning? suffocation?

When finally the Mayor was let to speak, it was decided: I would be held overnight and tried at dawn. As for Sister Claire de Sazilly, who stood staring at me, her ruined face still horrid with shock, the same sunrise would greet her as the new Mother Superior of C——.

The assembly cheered. The Mayor, as though he *were* the bishop, offered a prayer for Sister Claire's quick recovery, and he blessed her coming rule. With that Sister Claire was led from the library by her lieutenants, with the infirmarian, the cellarer, and an abashed Sister Catherine of the Holy Child following.

Sister Claire had barely passed from sight when I heard behind me the rattle and clank of chains. I turned—as best I could with those townsmen holding tightly to me—and I saw those boys who'd been dispatched by the Mayor. Their mission, having been accomplished, was clear: they'd been sent down the back stairwell to the stables in search of something to restrain me, something to secure me overnight. They had in hand those chains—ancient, thick-linked, crusted with rust and mud—that were used when the horses were bled or otherwise worked upon; at the ends of the chains were the cuffs that were clamped around the horses' legs, just above the fetlock. Instantly, accurately, I gauged that there'd be no slipping from them in the night.

The Mayor, worn, exhausted, announced that the specifics of my imprisonment would be seen to by the townsmen; and he issued from the lesser library the remaining townspeople and girls.

Within the hour Mother Marie and the one trunk allowed her—all those

beautiful things! all those books left behind in her rooms!—would be thrown
onto a dray hitched to the back of the Mayor's carriage. In this fashion would
the former Mother Superior of C—— be led away, bouncing along the rough
roads with nothing but her hands to shield her from the villagers, prone to
lobbing offal and overripe produce at such a one as she.

I stood in the library with four men, three women, and two boys of the village of C——. Two of the men held me fast while the others shoved chairs
against the library's walls, leaving nothing but the large rectangular table of oak
in the center of the room, one chair at its head. The women, ragged and fat,
huddled coven-like in a far corner. As for the boys, they stood untangling the
chains, working wrought-iron keys the size of shinbones.

Finally, my prison was prepared. The chains lay on the floor beside me; it
looked as though someone far luckier than I had recently broken from them.
The women left the library, returning moments later with a jug of water, a
goblet, a loaf of hard black bread (which would prove as impenetrable as a forest turtle), and the small pail into which I was to relieve myself. They set the
jug, the goblet, and the bread on the table; the pail was placed beneath the
chair. Someone, I didn't see who, brought in a straw pallet and arranged it
beside the chair; the townsmen had calculated just how far I'd be able to move
once chained to the table. My world, perhaps five paces in circumference, must
contain all these things. I stood watching the pathetic show as one of the men
sat in the chair and another circled him, holding the chain extended while a
third man tried to figure it all on a scrap of paper torn, without a thought,
from one of the library's volumes, scribbling furiously with a stub of pencil,
which he'd brought to a fresh point on his right incisor. Finally, in exaspera-
tion, the calculations were abandoned. No less self-satisfied, these three men
then placed the shackles on me while the fourth stood by.

I suffered the clamps being fastened around my ankles, heard the grinding bite
of iron into iron. The women were made to see to the finer adjustments, which
they did politely, expediently, while the men and boys huddled near the door.

"Please to place your ankle here, miss."

"Settle yourself here, if you would; in this chair."

When the boys sniggered at some humorless thing, the father of one, to
judge by the resemblance—though, by that same criterion, I might have as
readily concluded that both boys had been borne of any heifer and its idiot
tender—smacked both boys. Hard. And in so doing sought to impress upon
them not only the mark of his hand but a sense of the occasion. *"Elle est le vrai
malin!"* said he. I was the one and true Devil.

Use their fear. But I'd have to do something scary enough, *fearsome* enough to drive all nine of them from the room. What could I do? Enervated, wanting only to be left alone, I did nothing.

Three of the men struggled to lift the oak table a finger's-width off the floor; the fourth man slipped the loop of the chain under the table leg and secured it with a padlock. Two short chains ran from my ankle-cuffs to a third chain secured to the table. They bade me walk a bit, to ensure that my chains would reach as far as the pallet but not as far as the door. Such was the case. They'd done well, and told each other so. And so, they were all of them free to leave the library; this they quickly did.

I heard the long iron key turn in the lock. I heard the rasping slide of iron into stone as the bolt was thrown.

Alone, the first thing I did was take up those chains and pull as hard as I could. This was futile, and I knew it: I'd *seen* the townspeople secure me; and the links on the chains were as thick as my fingers.

I took a quick survey of the library. The earthenware pitcher was full of water. The goblet was chipped and grimy. The bread was old. No knife, no butter. They'd left a candlestick on the table, its white candle burnt halfway down; it wouldn't last through the night. As for the pail, it had come from the stable along with the filthy straw for my pallet.

From where I sat, the locked, main door was straight ahead. Indeed, it *was* out of reach, as the townsmen had so carefully calculated. At my back was the door behind which I'd hidden. That door too had been locked—I'd heard the rattle of chains on its far side. Beginning just to the right of the main door were the shelves that covered that wall and the one adjoining, the wall to my right. The wall to my left was cut with a bank of three tall, arched windows; before them ran a wide sill. As for the windows, they were tall enough to stand in, deep enough to sit in, and far enough away to be of no use at all. The glass of each window's two wings was beveled; and their mullioned panes glistened with the last of the sunlight, the first of the moonlight. The center window was open, slightly (wide enough for my Maluenda to have leapt from its . . . But I would *not* think of that, no. *Madness!*). What use might I make of the opened window? My shouts might be heard by a passerby. I might toss a note from the sill. . . . But no. What passerby would show sympathy for the witch at the window? And what would I write the note on? What would I write it with? To whom would I address it? Marie-Edith? To the bishop? Why not God Himself?

As for the shelves, they too were out of reach. They rose from floor to

ceiling, each crammed with the centuries-long history of the Ursulines. Many
of the volumes looked like they'd crumble at a touch; indeed, I *knew* they
would, for I'd spent long hours studying in this library, and had considered and
dismissed all its volumes. There were sheaves of loose parchment and large
books bound in black leather, their spines gold-engraved. In the dimming light,
I could not read the titles from where I sat. Nor would my length of chain allow
me to take them down from the shelves. This seemed especially harsh: the last
night of my life—I was *certain* of it!—and I would be deprived the solace of
books, however bloodless they might be—papal bulls, vulgates, and the like.

And so it had come to this.

Silence. The library was silent but for the rattle of my chains as I shifted in
that chair. At first there'd been voices on the far sides of both doors, and voices
outside, cursing up at me from the yard. Soon they went away, and silence settled over all and everything.

How sad I was then. . . . Sad enough to die. I *wanted* to die! I sat waiting for
the dawn, and death. I *attended* death, with ever-lessening patience. And indeed,
later that night, while staring deep into the flickering white candlelight, I
determined to die by my own hand.

I searched the room for the means: I had flame: the few phosphorous
matches my jailers had left me, but what was there that would burn bright
enough to take me up? The straw pallet: I could set *that* aflame. No; there was
not straw enough to fuel a funeral pyre. They hadn't left me a knife with the
loaf of black bread. No shears, no keys, no tools—nothing sharp within my
reach. The chains precluded a fall from the window. I'm ashamed to say that,
thinking of Maluenda, I wondered what savage damage I might inflict upon
myself with my teeth, my nails . . . but no, I could not; and such thoughts I
quickly dismissed.

I was exhausted, yet my pulse drummed on at double-time, my chest grew
tight; it was difficult to breathe. I *willed* my blood to slow in its course, I *willed* my
breathing to deepen. And in so doing I rendered myself ever more exhausted.

I laid my head on the table, intending to sleep; instead, tears overtook me.
The force of the tears, the *flood* of tears surprised me. This went on for some
time; the muscles of my face and shoulders and belly grew sore. Such hysteria
is strangely intoxicating. I thought that, I did: *intoxicating*; and in turn I thought
of the wine, the broken blue bottle and, angrily, missing it, longing for its
sweet relief, I swept that squat stoneware pitcher of water from the table. Rather,
I *tried* to sweep it away; as I sat too far from it, the pitcher rolled clumsily to the
side of the table and lay there, spewing its contents over the table's edge. I

sat watching the gurgling spill till it stopped, sat watching the spreading stain.

And all the while I could not spare myself thoughts of Sister Claire de Sazilly. She *infected* my mind. I would cry, hopelessly; alternately I would endure a *raging* anger. My Christian soul sought to assert itself. I wondered, did there burn deep within me a bit of forgiveness, a single ember smothering under an ash mound of anger? If so, and if that ember burned itself out, what would happen to me then? Would I be reduced to one of *them*? And who were *they* anyway, these simple and faithful people, this breed of Christian for whom the Devil is much more exciting, more enticing than God? Their small dark minds dwell on evil; and they create occasions for its manifestation. They see the print of cloven hoofs on everything, all the odd, disastrous, and (if they are truly *good* Christians) too pleasurable events of life. Alone, they are worthless; together they cannot be stopped. It is they who tossed Christians into the pit, speared "infidel" children through on the Crusades, stoned supposed witches—

And it came to me clearly: I was that witch. I was the Radical Evil they'd long awaited.

Dawn crept ever closer. Death crept ever closer. I bemoaned not my certain fate, but rather the long hours that had to pass before its enactment.

I snuffed the candle flame. I would save it, relight it later perhaps. For now I'd welcome the moonlit, the starlit dark; look to lose myself in the shadowed depths of the library. I closed my eyes. I sought a deeper darkness.

Disinclined to slip from the chair and take to the straw pallet, I set my head on the table again. Blessedly, unexpectedly, sleep came. I slept soundly, though for how long I cannot say. Hours? Minutes? I'd no clock, and the arc of the moon is imprecise, or so it is to my eye.

It was the sound of water that "woke" me, water being poured. Waves on the distant shore? The play of a fountain? There was no fountain at C——. Rain. Was it raining? No....I listened. It was, unmistakably, the transfer of water, or *liquid*, from one vessel to another. I could see little by the moon's light, but there ...In the library's far corner...In the shadows.

I watched, waiting for my waking eyes to overtake the dark. Were they *moving*, the shadows? Yes; but only as settling shadows do, in imitation of their source. They were simple shadows, I told myself. Ordinary. Not that species of shadow I'd seen in the shuttered gallery. *Those* shadows, I'd been certain, had harbored the *presence*. These shadows were not *alive*, as those others had seemed. I dismissed it all, told myself it was but some trick of the moon's.

The moon. I could see it, a perfect, prized pearl set in the indigo night, dim now behind a scrim of cloud. Staring at the moon, I thought not only of that stranger species of shadow but of the sourceless blood and the blue-smoking taper and the rich red wine. All the strangeness came back to me then. I shoved it from my mind, rudely; a bad dream.

I fumbled over the table for the candleholder. The matches should be . . . yes, there they were. I struck one against the table leg and it sparked to life.

Where was I? This was not the library as I'd left it, as it'd been when I'd surrendered to the darkness. Yes, there were the four walls, certainly, and the doors, the shelves, and the open window. But the table—what had happened to the table? Before there'd been the tipped and empty jug, the chipped goblet, the leathery bread, and the stub of candle.

Someone had crept into the room and left a plate at the center of which sat two stuffed and roasted squab, still warm and redolent of . . . yes, of a thyme and cherry glaze! Herbed potatoes ringed the huge platter! And asparagus spears. Miraculous, yes; though infinitely more tasty than manna and baskets full of fish.

Even as the strangeness of the discovery struck me, I set to eating. I was hungry, and there it sat.

I ate greedily. Silver had been set before me. The fork was heavy as stone; in its flattened end was carved something ornate, an insignia of some kind.

Well into my meal, as I cut into the fleshy breast of the second squab (sausage in the stuffing, was it?) I thought, absently—so absently I cannot explain it—how sweet it would be to have a glass of the wine I'd found in Peronette's trunk. That wine; yes, if only I could slip into some drunken state, any state other than the state of *self*. But there was no wine. No water, even, now that I'd wasted it. But when I took up that ugly jug—righted now and within easy reach—it was heavy: full. The goblet was overturned; beside it sat a larger, finer one, glistening in the candlelight. I poured . . . not water; wine!

Still I was not *thinking*, not really, so busy was I with the satisfaction of my urges. Surprise had ceded fast to satisfaction; and satisfaction to . . . to *appreciation* as I took in all that someone, or some*thing* had spread before me.

Gracelessly, I picked the meat from the bones. The potatoes went one after another, as did the well-crisped asparagus spears. Only when I'd cleared its surface of food did I see that the platter was painted. With the same design that was carved into the fork's end. Yes, at the platter's center was a large, exquisite blue *S*, and in the lower curve of the *S* sat a fat and contented toad. Strange, I thought. But what was strangeness now?

Finally, my rational mind set to work. As for the food, I reminded myself of the custom of granting the condemned a last meal, if rarely a feast the likes of which I'd discovered. Perhaps it all made sense. Indeed, I might have expected it. I wondered if Marie-Edith had returned, for she alone at C——— was capable of such delicacies. If so, surely she'd alert someone beyond C——— to my plight and . . . But even as I thought this, *hoped* it, I knew it to be fantastical, and untrue.

I sat contemplating all the strangeness, the shadows, the sudden and silent appearance of everything—when I saw that, at the table's end, beyond the candle's brightest band of light, there were piled . . . *books.* Tens of books. They'd not been there earlier. Or had they? I was not sure of anything. Perhaps they had been brought down from the shelves by the same kind jailer who'd brought the meal?

I noticed too that the candle that had been in the candleholder, stunted and half-burned, had been replaced. A taller one rose up in its stead, its flame constant and high. It was by this light that I *saw* again the shadows in the library's dark corner. I waited for them to take on that life, that animate quality I'd seen earlier in the company of the cat. Nothing. Then: a rustling in the dark, down low. Movement. Nails or claws scratching over the stone floor.

I convinced myself it was a rat; we were at times overrun with rats—no girl ever walked alone at night without a candle and a stick of considerable heft— and my attention returned to the books.

They were piled too far away: I could not read their spines, a few of which faced me. And so I looked to the strictly ordered shelves to see where they'd been drawn down from. Please, I thought, *please* let them not be from the shelves of the Order's history. I cannot pass this night with nothing but sheaves of death certificates and the brittle, eczematous lists of the forgotten dead. No; *that* shelf seemed intact. I looked hopefully to the lowest shelf, where certain novels were secreted, their pages well-thumbed by many a girl and nun. Neither had that shelf been disturbed. All the shelves, in fact, showed their shimmering, thick skins of dust unbroken. I could not find a single space from which a book had been removed, but this inventory was taken by the light of one candle, and the shelves sat far across a dark room.

I stood; and, suffering the bite of the cuff—and fearing for a moment that the rat had set to on my ankle—I reached for the nearest book.

The Cheats and Illusions of Romish Priests and Exorcists Discovered in the History of the Devils of Loudun and Louviers. I had never noticed this book before. Certainly not typical fare at C———, though it *would* deal with the Ursulines, and so qualify as part of the Order's long history. But I *knew* the libraries at C———, each one, including that of the Mother Superior, the *former* Mother Superior, and this particular volume was in none of them. Odd enough. Odder still was the book itself. Its cover was of red morocco—much too fine, too extravagant for the nuns. I opened it and there, as the frontispiece, was the same illustration as appeared on the silver and platter. The large *S*, and its accompanying toad. Who would mark their volumes with so strange an *ex libris*? And further, who—and here I tilted the page into the light—who has the means to paint, by hand, such a symbol in each of what I presumed to be many volumes? This was fine work, like that of some monk-adorned medieval manuscript.

Another volume. *Malleus Maleficarum.* I knew this book: its authors had been Dominicans and for two centuries theirs had been the text of choice of all witch hunters, Lutheran, Calvinist, and Catholic. The pages were old, the corners ragged and worn. Again, the red morocco cover. Again, the ornate *S*.

Supplanting one mystery with another, I shoved aside what little remained of my meal and gathered the books to me. Each elegant volume bore the *S* and its recumbent toad. In several languages, they were titled thusly:

The Apprehension and Confession of Three Notorious Witches Arraigned and by Justice Condemned in the County of Essex. Histoire du couvent de Saint-Louis de Louviers. The Trial of Master Darrell, or a Collection of Defenses Against Allegations Not Yet Suffered to Receive Convenient Answers. Procès verbal fait pour délivrer une fille possédée par le malin esprit à Louviers. De Divinatione et Magicis Praestigis. A True Narration of the Strange and Grievous Vexation by the Devil of Seven Persons in Lancashire and William Summers of Nottingham. Ritualis Romani Documenta de Exorcizandis Obsessis a Daemonio.

There were others, all studies of the Burning Days, when supposed witches had been sent to the stake by the thousands, by the *tens* of thousands.

I pulled the candle nearer. I made free with the wine. Taking up a book, I settled as comfortably as I could into that chair and I began to read. (Books in German I had set off to one side; after all, this *was* the last night of my life.)

Here was the drunkenness, the escape I'd sought.

10

Compendium
Maleficarum

As I TOOK up the books in no order of which I was conscious, I struggled still to explain the things I'd recently seen. *Inexplicable* things. The mysterious S-marked books, I told myself, had simply come from some library I had not visited, perhaps in the village; and as for . . . Ah, but I did not dwell on those mysteries, preferring the explicable, *clinging* to it. Still.

The books, the very *real* books. I fingered their identical covers and the golden lettering on their chests and spines. I *knew* them, it seemed, even before I'd opened a single one.

These books were different from any I'd ever seen. They lay before me, *communicating* in a way I cannot describe. Somehow, I *knew* what I was supposed to read, where I was to skim, and where I ought to slow and settle into an understanding of the words. I was conscious of learning *beyond* the page, beyond the written word. It was as though there were two sets of words—the words I read off the page, and the words I came to know as the truth. And so I'd read the writings of X and *know* that he'd been a conniver and a cheat though certainly his autobiography said no such thing. I'd read testimony from trials and I'd *know* who lied and who spoke the truth. It was so *clear*: it was as though the truth were written in red ink.

This *knowing*, eerily, progressed to hearing and feeling. Yes, it seemed I could *hear* the accused witches' testimony in their own voices. These voices rose within me, echoes of the words I read. This did not frighten me. Indeed, I welcomed the voices, welcomed them from the moment I first heard them. Odder still, I *understood* languages I'd never studied, never even heard spoken. Portuguese, for example. And Provençal. I was *alive* in the books. And learning all the while.

I read of Benedict Carpzov, "the Lawgiver of Saxony," the seventeenth-century signatory to twenty-five thousand death warrants.

I read of Marie-Catherine Cadiere, tried as a witch in Toulon in 1731—less than a hundred years ago! She would be remembered by certain townsmen of C——. Doubtless they believed the stories they'd been told as children seated at someone's knee, doubtless they told those stories in their turn.

It was quite cold now in the library—the open window had been pushed wider, and so perhaps there *was* a breeze? It was cold within the library, yes; but I was not cold. I breathed in the moist salted air. I thirsted for the warming wine, the wine that somehow led me back to the books.

It was some time later, as I read, or *heard*, the transcript of a trial held in Scotland—the year was 1704 and the accused, Beatrix Laing, the Pittenweem Witch, would be convicted and crushed beneath planks over which a weighted sleigh was driven five times—yes, intent on the testimony of Mrs. Laing's ten-year-old accuser, I heard a voice that was no echo off the page. This—I *knew* it as soon as I heard it—this was the *presence*. What it said, in whispered Latin, was this:

Trust and learn. Trust and learn.

I did. And I would. I had a mission: *to learn*. I was studying to save my life. This I knew.

At that urging on from the *presence*, I dove deeper into the works before me and gave no due to the real and fast-receding world.

The book nearest to hand was by an Ambrosian monk, Francesco Maria Guazzo. *Compendium Maleficarum*. Its title page bore the date 1608, as well as the *S*-mark.

From chapter 7, "By Their Terrible Deeds and Imprecations Witches Produce Rain and Hail, et cetera":

It is most clearly proved by experience that witches can control not only the rain and the hail and the wind, but even the lightning. They can evoke darkness, cause it when and where they will.... They can cause rivers to stop flowing, and springs to dry up; they can make the waters of a river flow backwards to its source, a thing which Pliny says happened in his time ...

So it was that *I* was supposed to have brought a storm down upon C——. Interesting.

And I read this from chapter 4, "Witches Effect Their Marvels with the Help of the Devil":

Let it be known that the devil deceives us in many different ways.... The demon can effect the most rapid local movement of bodies, so that he can withdraw an object from sight and substitute another so quickly that he deludes the eyes and understanding of an onlooker, who believes that the first object has been changed into the second.... Likewise can the demon seem to raise the dead; in such there is always some glamour and deception.

And this, from chapter 13, "Whether Witches Can Transmute Bodies from One Form to Another":

No one can doubt but that all the arts and metamorphoses by which witches change the shape of men are deceptive illusions, opposed to all nature.... William of Paris tells how a certain Holy Man could surround a witch with an aerial effigy, the likeness of another being, each part of which fit to the correspondent part of the witch, or vice versa; head to head, mouth to mouth, belly to belly, foot to foot, and arm to arm; but this could only be effected with the use of ointments and words, the proper combination of which the Holy Man, it is said, took to his grave ...

From the Guazzo I turned to a pamphlet folded into the *Malleus Malefi-carum*. It was a contemporaneous account of how, in the summer of 1644, after a violent and destructive hailstorm, the inhabitants of several villages near Beaune banded together to hunt the incarnate fiends who'd thus blasted their crops. Sixteen women were sentenced to be beaten with red-hot shovels. Their broken bodies were shoved into kilns. Oiled toads were stuffed into the mouths of those few who'd survived the beating so as to muffle their screams and prevent their summoning their devils. Only one woman was acquitted— mother of the lead witness, a boy of seventeen, said to be able to spot a witch at one hundred paces—and even she, on the night of the sentencing, was stolen from her home; bound hand and foot, weights pendant from her neck, she was pushed from the height of a castle tower, let to fall headfirst to the earth.

It was here I began to empathize, *bodily*, with those whose stories I discovered. I recall too well the writhing, slick weight of the toads on *my* tongue. I *taste* still the scorching ascent of vomit, upwelling vomit.

Yes, it was with labored breath that I read of Giles Cory of Salem, who, in the winter of 1692, at the age of eight, was pressed to death beneath iron weights. The boy lay naked beneath the weights for two days, suffocating. *"In the pressing his tongue swelled and bloated from his mouth and the sheriff, with his cane, forced it back in again and again . . ."*

I read of the Newbury Witch. The English Civil War—1643. Men of Cromwell's army, under the command of the Earl of Essex, while passing through Newbury, saw an old peasant woman walk on water. So they averred. They caught and had their way with this "witch." Sated, they set her up on a barge and took turns firing at her from the shore. *"With deriding and loud laughter she caught their bullets in her hand and chewed them; until such time as the smallest man of the lot, gaining the barge by raft, slashed her forehead and discharged his pistol underneath her ear, at which the Devil's Whore fell straight down and died."* . . . And with this there came a pain to my forehead like that I'd suffered earlier when cut beneath the nose by the witch's whip; and, too, I knew a thudding ache beneath my right ear, as though I'd been hammer-struck.

Could I go on? *Should* I go on, and to what end? . . . *Trust and learn*. Yes; but I was horrified. Sick at the stomach. And scared: would I share the fate of these witches at sunrise?

I looked out the window. Were the tips of the distant trees afire with the first light of dawn? How I *refused* then all thoughts of dawn! Regardless, the dawn would come. And then—

What was that? I searched the shadowed floor, certain I'd seen a rat scamper by. Movement, low in a shadowed corner. Scratching. And then a terrible squeal, as though the rat had met a bad and sudden end at the claws of a cat. (My Maluenda? No, it could not be! Still, nine lives, et cetera.) I sat listening. I heard nothing more. But there, at the height of a man's head, hung the jellied white eyes of . . . No, no, no. I was imagining this, surely; for fast as those eyes had appeared, they were gone.

The candle flame burned a bright violet-blue, then. I reached past it to the wine.

Trust and learn. That voice again. Male or female? I couldn't tell. Such urgency in it. The *presence* urging me on. To what? Did I actually hear its voice? Did it speak? Were its words audible, or merely *known?* . . . I cannot say. I did not allow myself to consider these or other questions, not then. I *knew* I was not alone, but again, and wisely, I did not allow myself to *consider* that truth.

More wine. And more books.

Silence, stillness; and the candle burning blue, its light steady, true.

Trust and learn.

It was then I came across a broadside folded into eight panels. Its parchment was yellowed, chitinous, its type smudged and replete with setting errors: an amateur's hurried work. The thin cover promised *L'histoire illustré du diable de la ville de Q——*. It fit into my right hand as would another's, proffered in greeting. Unfolding the single sheet, broad as a map when I smoothed it over the table, I began to read:

"*There came to the prospering city of Q——, in the Lord's Year 16——, a devil in the guise of Priest, a fiend hell-bent on the ruination of Faith and females. This devil, name of . . .*"

And as I read the devil-priest's name, I heard from the shadows a derisive sound, an anguished laugh. *Prospering, was it?* came the rhetorical question. *I think not,* the reply.

The *presence.* I looked this way and that: nothing, no one. I read on, and twice more came the seemingly sourceless commentary. I read of the Dark Work done in Q——, of deflowered maidens and devils ascendant. But I had not progressed far when suddenly I felt a near, biting coldness, a coldness not in keeping with the season, the summer night; and I saw my right arm rise— the coldness like a vise gripping my elbow—and I watched as I, guided by a thing unseen, fed to the candle flame a dried corner of the pamphlet. It took; cinders swirled, sputtering in the sea-dank air. Flames raced to nip at my fingertips; and I fell back into that heavy chair to the accompaniment of rattling chains.

Yes, it was by the candle's leaping sapphire light that I first saw him. *It.*

It was there with me in the library, the *presence.* I'd known that. But now the shadows started to shift, seemed to take shape: the dark shape of a man. Coalescing, as though it were of equal parts air, darkness, and dream. Standing table-side, he lifted the candlestick—its flame burst up blazingly blue—and I saw him clearly. "It was not like that at all," said he, the voice full now. "Not at all."

It was the devil-priest of Q——, Father Louis M—— by name. Dead these two hundred years.

Surely this was impossible! But I could not deny it. Neither can I deny it now, for it is the truth. *This happened!*

There he stood in his simple black shift. He smiled, slowly, slyly; it seemed I *drew* his smile, as the moon draws the tide. He moved around behind the chair and slipped his hands over my shoulders and throat, onto my chest. His touch was cold, cold as ice. He stroked my hair, my neck. Then he bent at the waist to whisper in my ear; and I shivered to hear his words:

"We know what you are," said he.

I stood—the horrible clanking, the restraint of those shackles!—and turned to the priest.

We stood before each other, he in his black robe, me in that ridiculous pink dress, that silken confection I'd stolen. He stood a bit taller than I.

Then he stepped back from me and—did I *will* it?—his mantle slid down from his shoulders to show him naked. It crumbled from his body, fell to his bare feet as though it were made of ash.

Dare I look at him, standing there?

"Yes," said he. "Look at me."

Could he hear my thoughts? Did he know my mind? Who, *what* was he?

"*Regarde-moi!*" And, smiling, he stepped back farther to show himself.

He raised his long muscular arms over his head, placing his palms together as if in prayer. He started to turn, slowly. Revolve. A sort of dance. A show of such beauty. I saw him full-length from the front; I saw him from behind. He smiled at my awe, my adoration; and my ignorance. He reveled in my straight-on stare.

Tufted black hair in the crooks of his raised arms. His lightly furred chest with its rosebud nipples. The broad, muscled fan of his back. His waist tapering to slender, strong hips and sculpted legs. The full, firm flesh of his buttocks. The supple length of his sex. The curves of his calves. The richly veined arch of his foot...

Here was beauty I had never known, never seen.

Tears stung my eyes. Why was I crying? Was it then I knew the truth? Had the secret of my life been told to me?

... The priest neared my body. With his weightless fingers he took away my tears; they went solid at his touch, solidified from tears to crystals, crystals that he crushed between forefinger and thumb. And then his hands moved, so slowly, over my shoulders to the back of my neck, to the clasp of the dress. He undid it. I stood waiting for the warm breath that never issued from his lips. Slowly, he pushed the dress down from my shoulders, and revealed me naked to the waist.

We know what you are.

There I stood, half-naked before this ... *entity*. He looked like a mortal man, it's true, but he'd been dead these two centuries, no? And his touch was ... he was *cold* and—

"I am the incubus of lore, my dear," said he. "Do not fear." Those were his exact words, accompanied by the broadest of smiles, the deepest of stares. I shut my eyes against his stare. He placed his hands upon my breasts. My skin contracted. His touch, so terrifically cold, somehow *heated* my blood. The porcelain white skin of my throat and breasts flushed. He teased my body with his fingers, he teased my soul with his smile.

When he bent to touch my shackles they sprang open with a rusted pop. Perhaps the old iron teeth of the lock cracked at his touch? Again, I cannot explain; and it matters not at all now.

I stood before the priest and did as he commanded. He did not always speak, yet his directives were clear.

I stepped free of the chains. I let the pink dress fall to the floor; it pooled at my feet and I stepped from it as I had from the chains, left a spill of silk there atop the rusted chains. Father Louis, the flatterer, said, "As Venus stepped from the foam," naming the strange tableau before him. Was he mocking me? He shook his head to say no, he was not.

With every compliment, with every kind word, every sudden thrill, I was more and more his. Soon the seduction was complete. I would do anything he asked.

He bent and took up the dress. He ripped it, effortlessly, along a seam sewn from neckline to hem and, pushing the books back, spread the pink cloth over the oak of the table. With his hands on my hips, he lifted me and set me down upon the edge of the table, upon the pink silk. His strength was supernatural: he lifted me without effort, and it seemed he barely touched the heavy chair yet it skidded fast across the library floor. What *was* he? An incubus? Impossible! And then came this tacit question: friend or foe?

"Why, friend, *bien sûr*," said he.

I was naked but for Spider's boots, the too-small pair of scuffed and worn white leather. Then I lay back on the table, for he asked me to. *Told* me to. He may even have shoved me gently backward, I cannot recall.

Standing between my legs, he reached up over my head—so that I felt his now rigid sex brush against my thigh; it too was cold, and I saw it like a great tusk, or horn; it scared me—and he took up the goblet and the wine.

He braced my head with his left hand so that I might drink; with his right, he held the goblet to my lips. I dared to stare into the ice of his eyes. He tipped the crystal and thin rivulets of red ran from the corners of my mouth; he took them up with his tongue. He lowered his lips to mine; from them I took more of the wine, drop by chilled drop. "Seems a shame to waste it," said he, "precious as it is."

I lay back. The priest set the decanter to the side, near my hip.

He took up first my right foot, then my left. He unlaced and removed the white boots, slowly. Everywhere he touched me I turned cold, but soon the icy shock would cede to . . . to *fire*; truly, it was as though my skin were being singed, but wonderfully so.

The priest held both ankles in his left hand now, balanced them there. I could not move; neither did I want to. With his right hand he reached for the wine. He poured it slowly over my feet, my ankles. He held my legs higher, poured more wine, and watched in obvious delight as the redness ran down my legs, stained its way over the shins to the calves, the knees, the thighs, and beyond.

Father Louis proceeded to pour the wine all over my thighs, my belly, where it pooled in a slight concavity, and my chest. At his touch the wine gelled, turned to a cold salve, which he smoothed over my skin. He covered me with it. I did not shiver, though I was chilled to the bone. I felt my nipples flood with blood, grow indelicate, hard, as the priest smoothed the salve over my breasts.

Soon I was completely covered, coated like a foal just-slid from the womb. Red-stained, as though my own blood coursed *atop* my skin. Father Louis knelt at the end of the table as though at an altar. I sat above him, propped back on my elbows, for he bade me watch. "Watch me work," said he. His head was between my spread legs. He held the red goblet and the white candle, still burning blue. Smiling, his eyes locked on mine, he leaned in to kiss me. I felt the approach of his coldness. His kiss. . . . There. On the inner thigh. He took a deep draft of the wine, holding the candle flame too near my flesh.

It seemed I might faint. "Relax," said the priest. "Breathe. Look into my eyes. *Feel* me." I heard all this from him, but I don't know how much of it he actually spoke.

Only then did I realize that I was not in pain. Rather, what pain there was—the candle flame so near my skin, his cold weight and probing fingers, his tongue—what pain there was was delicious, sublime. I surrendered and I suffered it well. Quite well.

What felt like flame steadied to a sufferable fever.

But then, with his lips just slightly parted, their ends twisting in that sly and ever-present smile, I saw his tongue slide from the cage of his mouth. It came and came: it was too long. *Impossibly* long. It hung from his lip like red meat. He let it hang, let it hang heavily so that I might see it.

My head fell audibly back onto the oak table. With his fingertips, the priest closed my wide-open eyes, as one does with the dead.

The wine went thick, viscid, and cold at the touch of his tongue. It became a balm, an unguent; and he took to it hungrily. From the ankle he followed the flow of the wine . . . down, down, up over my body. . . . And when he kissed my face, ranged his tongue over my cuts, I knew he was healing me. The faintest of bruises would show in the days to come, a dingy gray-green where blood pooled beneath the skin; there would be no scarring at all.

I opened my eyes. My body was red from the wine, as though I bled from wounds I'd not sustained. And there he was, moving over me in the uneven flickering light of that blue-burning candle.

Finally, with his hands on my hips, and my legs hanging slack, the priest went down onto bended knee before me—a prayerful stance. He lifted my legs and placed them over his shoulders. His smile widened as he spread my legs and . . .

"My, my," said he. "What *have* we here?"

The priest's cold hands rested on my inner thighs. He pushed my legs apart. Farther. I felt then the icy tip of his tongue.

We will show you what you are. Words sounding so like a promise.

. . . Then, from the far dark corner of the library, beyond the meager light cast by the moon and the strange candle flame . . . there, deep in the shadows from which Father Louis had come, I saw something. Movement. A dark writhing . . . shape. What was it?

"Stay," said Father Louis, sternly. He wasn't speaking to me, not then. But he was when, a moment later, he whispered:

"We will show you what you are."

We? . . . I sensed that same *presence*, had the same feeling I'd had before Father

Louis had stepped from the shadows. I stared into the dark. Perhaps the moon slipped then from behind a cloud, perhaps the candle flame flared up suddenly . . . whatever it was, I saw a face take shape in the shadows. Beneath it the vague outline of a figure. Male or female, real or revenant . . . I couldn't tell.

Then it spoke. Though, in truth, to call it *speech* is too generous. Its words were unintelligible. Animal sounds, it seemed. The rasping grunt of something caught in a trap. It repeated itself, again and again, till finally I heard the words it whispered, madly. *The most beautiful rose.* It must have known I'd finally understood, for it stopped speaking. Still, I could sense it, could *almost* see it standing there in the dark. How long had Father Louis and I, lying on that oak table, been watched by this . . . this shadowed *thing*?

Just then Father Louis did something to me with the longest finger of his right hand and I forgot all about the shadows. For a moment. . . . I wonder, was I still reluctant to see what he was showing me? Was it the mystery of the shadows I wanted to solve, rather than my own mysteries?

"We know what you are. We will show you what you are."

His words might have seemed a threat, had I not been looking into his face. . . . So beautiful, he was! All strength and sinew, sex and shadow. . . . I believe I returned his smile then.

Stop it. That death rattle coming from the dark. That voice. *Stop your games!*

"Be still, *ma mariée*," said the priest. "This one is alive, and she likes my games."

Hurry, Louis! The others . . .

"*D'accord, tais-toi!*"

But while you play your . . . your games, the others arrive and—

"Oh, all right. Damn you!"

Too late for that, mon prêtre.

"Then damn them!"

Oui. Tous et tout, came the reply.

Father Louis took the candle from its holder. It was thick in his fist. Thick as his wrist. The light in the library suddenly shifted, and I saw something in the shadows. *It* was still there, whatever it was; and it spoke again:

Vite, *Louis! Hurry. Make it known!*

Father Louis lowered the candle, held it so near my face I felt the heat of the steady flame on the softness of my eye, blinding me, burning me. Please, no . . .

"I won't hurt you," he breathed, and, smiling wide, added, "Not like that anyway."

He stood over me. Leaned into me. His weight, so cold. . . . He had form but no density, no mass; rather he felt like the figure of a man made from papier-mâché, yet supple. Something held me to him. I could not move, not even if I'd wanted to. I was as bound by him—by his will, by his strange alchemy—as I'd been by the chains.

Father Louis kissed me. He licked my lips; I felt him spreading them, prying them apart with his tongue, working his way into my mouth. Again, the ice and the fire of his entry. He was filling me. My mouth went wide to receive him. My eyes were tightly shut; first in fear, soon in stupefaction and ecstasy. . . . His hands, no less cold than his tongue, settled on either side of my neck; he held me as a strangler would; he pulled me up toward him, *into* him. His tongue went deep into my throat. Impossibly deep. Was it growing? It seemed to be *expanding* within me. My mouth and throat were verily *clogged* with his tongue and I couldn't breathe and as I started to choke he . . .

He withdrew and . . .

Laughter in his bright eyes, so near mine.

My soul shuddered as my eyes went wide, wider.

That voice, again, from the dark: *Slowly, Louis. The uninitiated* . . .

Then, slackening the muscles of my body's chilled throat, I rose; striking like a cobra, I took the priest's tongue deeply down.

He tried to pull his trick-of-a-tongue from my mouth. (I'd surprised us both with my avidity.) I held as best I could to the icy root. But then I felt its thickness dissolve in our mouths, devolve to a mere man's tongue, which still I worked with mine. When finally he wrested his tongue free of my mouth, Father Louis said, "Know it or not, these are the tricks you want."

Was that possible? Had I the *will* to want, the presence of mind to. . . . Indeed, I was *mindless* though my senses were heightened now to the point of pain; the pain, and the accompanying pleasure. . . . My resistance grew weaker and weaker; through all that followed I did not, *could* not resist the priest. "Yes," he said again, "these are the tricks . . ."

And with that he dipped the candle flame into the wine. It sizzled and hissed, but the blue flame did not die; it simply lit the cut crystal of the goblet. The priest's hands were aglow; it seemed I could see through his lit flesh. Yes, I could! No bones. His flesh as plain, as supple as gloves of kid. He twisted the candle, nearly as round as the goblet, and it seemed to take shape. Turn from a taper into . . . into a member, a member to mock the priest's own, which rose full and hard.

He drew the wax phallus from the goblet. He kissed me, *there*; . . . the icy tip of his tongue and its trail of fire . . .

My lips. *There.* Curved and pink and wet as a shell freshly drawn from the sea, or so he said. . . . How he teased me!

Up, up a bit farther and he swallowed *me,* swallowed my sex as I had his tongue. I was in his mouth. Growing. The bloodrush! I felt the tug of his lips on my . . . flesh. His tongue tripping over the tip.

"Never," he said. "Never before." He spoke admiringly. Appreciatively.

They are coming! Be done with it!

Louis lifted my legs higher. He flicked a kiss at my wine-wet anus, laughed, and said, "The Osculum Obscenum! They call this the Devil's Kiss." . . . How he worked upon me! My nether mouths. My flesh, my sex. With his fingers, icicles all . . .

I writhed in pleasure and pain. The two were one, fused.

He teased both my lower mouths with the warm, thick, wine-red candle.

He stood. He held the candle . . . he brought its waxen head up to my mouth. I opened my mouth to take it, but the priest deprived me. I could not help but smile.

He worked against my reluctant flesh. Prying. He dipped his fingers in the wine, sucked them and slipped them, one by one, inside me. I opened. Slowly. He pushed and I opened wider. I opened to him and to the candle. I opened to the pain and to the pleasure.

The sun was rising. Dawn. The indigo deep of the night grew ever more shallow, and soon the sun would fade it full away. The mullioned panes of the open window drew the day's earliest light; I watched the glass—glistening, glinting, set with small gems—from where I lay I watched the glass give back the light.

And I thought, Let it come! Let dawn come. Let *them* come!

The second *presence,* the . . . the *thing* in the shadows watched us, described tighter and tighter circles around us. Still I could not see into the dark corners of the room, and it was to these that the thing retreated time and again. Its voice came more often, warning, commanding, pleasing, teasing. I understood it, though its words came as a rattling breath, an exhalation somehow strung through with meaning. It seemed sometimes I understood its voice before I'd even heard it speak. It—that voice—seemed to enter me directly. Was more *felt* than heard; like a vibration, the "sound" that issues from struck iron. It said: *My most beautiful rose. . . . My most beautiful rose.*

"Ah," breathed the priest, "see how my words return to *haunt* me?" He laughed and came closer to me, ever closer.

He stood between my bent legs, holding high my heels. I lay back on the table. His sex stood rigid over my abdomen. He placed his hand onto my extended, engorged sex. And he tugged—almost too hard, not quite—at my lips, so slick and eager. *"This,"* he said, "is the most beautiful rose. *My* most beautiful rose."

. . . Ah, what *words* to use? How to tell the truth?

. . . *Alors,* this *was* the truth. Like I had never known it. The beginning of the end of my mysteries.

He spread me wide. Opened me. He fisted his rigid sex, so thick and ugly; beautiful too. He teased me. Wouldn't take me. Not at first. And so how I thrilled when that icy crown of his spread my slickened lips, so slightly. How I thrilled as he started to push, slowly, steadily, and my muscles constricted around him, at once stretching to accommodate him and recoiling from his cold, cold flesh. To even call it "flesh" seems . . . Ah, but then, as had happened with his fingers and tongue, I went warm, *hot* where he touched me. Heat now. Inside me. Flooding me with that sweet fever.

How heavy he suddenly was! Full-bodied as he had not been before. Yes, he was somehow fuller now, his flesh colder. A wonder that I remarked any of this as he leaned down to kiss me on the mouth, to tease my nipples with his teeth. All the while smiling.

The priest stood. Father Louis stood. The incubus stood. . . . *Enfin, he* stood and took me then. Thrusted, slowly at first and then faster. Faster. He rocked into me, rhythmically. Deeply. Pain; pleasure. And the purest delight I had ever known.

Trust and learn.

The first-time kiss. The rending of flesh. The whispering rip of entry. Sublime!

. . . Father Louis withdrew. I felt the ache of his absence. I saw him lift his bloodstained fingers to his mouth. Lick them. Savor the blood. "The most beautiful—"

Louis, came the voice, *stop, now!* This was the loudest and clearest I'd heard that voice. *Stop it. Be done with it, Louis! What heart I have is beyond all this now.*

Her words spurred the priest. His kisses now were quick; and, roughly, he turned me over onto my stomach. He pulled me down fast to the table's end. I held to either side of the thick oak, laid my face in the pillow of bunched pink silk.

The dawn! And the others are coming. Who was coming, my accusers? Was *she* coming forward? Was that her pale, opalescent face there in the dark?

. . . It was then the priest repeated his ritual:

He poured more wine onto my back, spread it down into the cleft of my buttocks and beyond, licking and sucking, with his touch turning the wine to a gel. It was exquisite, and I heard sounds issue from my mouth as though it were a stranger's.

The priest went down onto his knees. Again and again the Devil's Kiss. How I wriggled, writhed against his mouth, into that kiss! Shamelessly. More. *More!* Fingers, his cold fingers prying, prodding, pushing. And I opened to it. Took it into me. Felt it rend me wide, deep.

"Hold yourself," he said. "*Here*, like this." Reaching around me to the front, he took my hand in his and . . . and he led my hand to my own sex. Ah, the fast movement of my hand in his! I had never done this, for self-satisfaction was a sin, no? I had never even known that I could bring myself to . . . Only in those night dreams . . . the salt, the milk of the dream . . . I'd no idea . . .

Enfin, the priest withdrew the candle, slowly. And then he entered me. I took him to the hilt and . . .

Oh! the tastes, the textures, the strange acrobatics of it all! . . . *Enfin*, the *truth* of it all!

Soon—my breath caught, my heart having slipped from its place—I found my hand full of a whiteness like liquescent pearl. I had worked it from myself.

It was then the priest whispered the truth I had never wanted to know:

"You are a woman. You are a man."

And at this, she stepped from the shadows ragged and blue, and was made known to me by name: Madeleine de la Mettrie.

I stood bent over the table, my hands clamped to either side. What had he said? Did I dare *hear* his words again, repeat them to myself till their true meaning came? No; I dared not. Thankfully, there was the sudden distraction of . . . of *her.*

She came out of the shadows, the demon-girl. She seemed *made* of shadows, as had the priest. As she neared she passed from black through gray to blue; the darkness seemed to cling to her, weighting her as water weights the drowned.

That hideous voice was hers, and I heard it again as she neared. *Yes*, she said, in that guttural rasp, *You are a woman. You are a man*. Still the sense of the words did not come.

"Closer," said Father Louis. "Show yourself."

Were those rags she wore? Cerements? And what was that scent? It was neither good nor bad; it was like soil newly turned. A natural smell. Redolent of a forest or woodland; redolent too of rain and salted air. Another step—she moved effortlessly, as though borne on the air—and I saw her long black hair, tangled and filthy, falling to frame her pale and perfect face. Wide-set brown eyes, the high bones of her cheeks, a thin nose and full red mouth. That mouth . . .

. . . It is difficult to describe what it was I saw then.

Never had I seen such a sight. Nothing could have prepared me for it, for *her*. Nothing. Surely she was in pain. Real or not, revenant, specter or succubus, how could she suffer such wounds?

Yes, her very throat was torn away! From chin to chest she was nothing but caked gore, over which trickled a stream of blood that seeped from the black cavity. Blood all over her. The flesh was torn, split wide. The lips of the wound were red and fresh, quivering like the gills of a landed fish.

Don't be afraid, said Madeleine, and I saw that the death rattle came not from her mouth—indeed, her mouth did not open; the lips did not move—but from her throat. She spoke through her throat!

Still, I wasn't afraid. Despite the blood and gore and torn-open throat, Madeleine was *still* beautiful. Her voice too, horrible as it was, assuaged me, calmed me. I could understand her.

We've come for you, said she.

"Yes," echoed the priest, "to educate and save you; and to ask a favor of you."

Not now, Louis! . . . Mon Dieu, *how graceless you are.*

"Graceless? Indeed I am; it's true."

Now is not the time, said Madeleine. *You know what we must do. We must do it quickly, too. The dawn* . . . She raised a long thin arm toward the window. The sleeve of her simple, coarse shift was dirty. It fell back to her elbow as she lifted her arm and revealed her wrist and forearm white and smooth and thin. Her long fingers seemed fleshless. They tapered to cracked nails caked with dirt. Had she dug her way up out of the earth?

No questions, said she. *We haven't much time.*

Louis stood behind me still. He pulled me closer. I stood tall and naked in his arms, in his cold arms, which he twined around my waist.

"I've done my part," said he, cupping my breasts. "And quite well, I think. Education by seduction, one might say." He turned his back to the succubus, saying, dismissively, "The floor is yours, demoness," and asking, "Will you tell our story true?"

11

Creatura Ignis:
The Accused

Daemoni, etiam vera dicenti, non est credendum.
The Devil must not be believed, even when he speaks the
truth. —St. Thomas (Book 22, Question 9, Article 22)

PROSPERING? REPEATED Madeleine. *Far from it.
The village of Q—— was walled and airless, stifling.*

"...Filthy, offal-choked streets," adjoined the
priest. "And wood smoke, wood smoke forever
swirling in bitter blue plumes....Excrement running in thick rivulets, bearing the feeding maggots
that would burst forth as flies....Geese and other
living things at slaughter let go a vaguely tidal gas,
and..."

Louis, please, said Madeleine. *The floor is mine, or so you
say.* And she went on, describing the place of her birth
in apologetic tones: *We tried burning incense against all this,
but to slight effect.*

"Slight, indeed," said the priest. "...horseflesh, burnt bread, swilling swine...And the one unmistakable stench that permeated everything: the acrid, soil-like smell of massed, unwashed humanity."

You speak as though you came to us from the Vatican, or some other gilded place.

The priest walked silently to the windowsill; sitting, he added, ruefully, "Would that I had never gone to that place at all." Only then did he turn the tale over to Madeleine, promising silence save for commentary "as appropriate."

Father Louis, I learned, first came to Q—— to serve as parish priest. Curé of the Church of St. Pierre, by title.

The scion of a respected bourgeois family, he'd hoped for a chaplaincy to a nobleman, perhaps a position as tutor to a future marshal or cardinal. If only he'd been born noble, was his frequent lament: surely then he'd have been able to secure a bishopric, an office to gild and gladden his days. But he was not noble, neither by birth nor disposition. And, as competition among priests was fierce, he resigned himself to the role of curé at the Church of St. Pierre in Q——. Not Paris. Not Marseilles. Not even Avignon. Q——.

Early in his third decade, standing tall and strong, Father Louis was remarkably handsome, with large dark eyes, fine features, and an abundance of black curls spilling out from under his black biretta. He wore his beard groomed in the Van Dyck style. He possessed uncommon confidence, carried himself with a swagger; he was—this was Madeleine's word—cocksure.

The priest's arrival did not go unnoticed, for his predecessor, recently deceased, had been bloodless and devout; unpopular, that is. And so Louis was welcomed to Q——. His affability, his learning, his looks—suffice to say he was soon the dinner guest of choice among the privileged of Q——. And as easily as he'd accessed the finest dining rooms of Q——, so too did he win his way into the finest boudoirs. Thus did his troubles begin.

For the priest was a man of appetites and particular tastes. A man "proud to have the courage of his own perversions," as he was wont to say. True, he'd taken a vow of celibacy, but what of it? No self-respecting cleric gave the vow a second thought once uttered. As Louis said to a mistress on the eve of his ordination, "a promise to perform the impossible is not binding." Besides, didn't the Church have troubles enough—the Huguenot rebels, ever-increasing corruption, et cetera? Louis had no fear of the zealots of the Society of Jesus and the Congregation of the Oratory, for he knew much of their own depredations. Why, he reasoned, would the Church bother to delve into the doings, into the metaphorical breaches—or britches—of a simple parish priest? And hadn't he gotten *this* far without depriving himself?

At the age of fourteen he'd been sent off to the Jesuit College of B——.
The brothers—famous disciplinarians—taught an elegant Latin, and the latest in optics, geography, mathematics, dramatics, and manners. There, Louis had been caught engaging in "private entertainment." Threatened that a second offense would lead to expulsion, Louis tried to behave. For a period spanning the four great feasts of the Church, he did not indulge himself. Not *overly* so. Unreasonable, thought he, for God or man to expect more of him.

His seventeenth summer was passed at the shore in the company of a bachelor uncle, whose maid, for a halfpenny per lesson, continued the boy's "education." With the discovery of women, Louis happily saw the number of his suitors double.

Sexually, no need of the boy's went unmet. Spiritually, he believed in his god; less so in the Church proper. Self-satisfaction was his sole creed.

His contentment, his charms, and his successes bred in the boy a measure of arrogance and he heeded not at all those who warned that such conceit would one day pose a problem. Said he, in later years: "What finer tribute might a man know than to be mistrusted by the stupid for being clever, envied by the inept for making good, loathed by the dull for his wit, by the boors for his breeding, and by the ugly for his successes?"

. . . As word spread of the new confessor, the women of Q—— discovered sins heretofore unheard of. They grew *desperate* for pardon. Had he not arrived, these women (and some men, too) would have one day clogged the very Gates of Hell if they'd in fact done *half* of what they confessed to. Within weeks of his arrival, Father Louis was overworked, satisfied, and very tired.

Suspicions rose, giving rise in turn to rumors. The seeds of enmity were sown.

Still, Father Louis carried on. Every Sunday the aisles of St. Pierre were crowded with the desirous and newly devout. And there, in the center of the first pew, sat the Prosecutor of Q—— with his wife and child, a girl of fourteen named Madeleine.

In Q—— the seasons turned. It was six, nearly seven months after his arrival in Q—— that Father Louis first heard the confession of the Prosecutor's wife. The Prosecutor had denied his wife at first. Warned by men of his acquaintance, he forbore; finally, in proportion too direct to withstand, his wife withdrew from him. Went cold. The Prosecutor relented: his wife was scheduled for Wednesdays, in the early afternoon.

One such afternoon, as the confessor came from the Prosecutor's parlor, closing the double doors behind him while tackling too the brass buttons of his waistcoat, he literally stumbled upon young Madeleine.

The picture of grace. Long and lithe, with a plait of black hair, pale skin, and warm brown eyes. "Marriageable," as is said; ripe.

Louis struck with every weapon in his arsenal. He worked upon Madeleine's mother, who finally agreed to speak to her husband. Father Louis was right, said she: the girl needed a tutor. Yet again, the Prosecutor relented, and Father Louis began to tutor Madeleine.

Madeleine de la Mettrie—for that was the girl's full name, the noble *particule, de,* purchased long ago, by her father's father—fell in love. Deeply, as a girl will but once or twice. She lost all sense of self. In her mind, she was one with her lover. Yes, Father Louis became her lover. (Madeleine confessed this as the priest sat silently on the sill.)

But first there'd been that strange courtship, those first few Friday afternoons sitting side by side in the Prosecutor's study. It had taken some time, but Louis succeeded in convincing Madame that a chaperone was unnecessary.

And at first, they did study.

How Madeleine thrilled at Louis's threats! He balanced a small riding crop across his knees, slapped it against his thigh each time the girl stumbled over her Ovid. They each of them reveled in the tension. Finally, one day, after Madeleine willfully translated "to stick" as "to prick," Louis told her to stand and raise high her skirts. She cried. He insisted. She begged, and did as she was told. He slapped the crop, once, crisply, against the upper, inner part of her thigh. Though she'd been wearing stockings (a mistake she'd not make twice), the welt lasted three days. Madeleine cherished it. After that, her Ovid only got worse.

Their Fridays became Saturdays too, then Mondays, and so on. The Prosecutor protested. His wife began to wonder. Madeleine, for her part, learned Latin and much, much more.

Soon there was a secret in Q——. A secret that would be nine months in the keeping.

Madeleine was no longer seen in the streets. Louis, with the cooperation of the family's cook, passed letters to Madeleine, tiny missives she'd find beneath her morning bowl of porridge or tucked among a basket of plums. He wrote not of love but of need; and he promised to win her release. The priest had to pick through the family's refuse for Madeleine's responses, for the cook dared not pass them on more directly than that. Madeleine's letters told how her father beat her, how he'd made her soak for hours in a bath that was two parts water and one part mustard, a concoction reputed to loose a man's seed from the womb. Worse was suffered by her mother, whom the Prosecutor accused of the most vile complicity and faithlessness. The letters told how each woman was confined to her room, the windows of which—shuttered from the out-side—were chained within. They told how Madeleine's body was changing, and spoke of her undeniable delight in the growing manifestation of their love. Too, she begged for rescue.

Publicly, the Prosecutor denied everything. His wife and child had gone to care for a sick relation, said he; he denied their very presence in his house. One night, not long into her captivity, Madeleine's mother fled, fearing her husband and hating her daughter.

Then one morning there appeared tacked to the Prosecutor's door, as to the doors of many shops on the square, and even the church, an "Ode to the Public Prosecutor's Bastard Grandchild," to be sung (as it was in all the less reputable pubs) to the tune of *"J'ai rencontré un allemend."*

Something had to be done, and something was.

The cook was sent away, for the Prosecutor sensed her sympathies; in her stead came an elderly zealot best described as Madeleine's Keeper, or Wrangler, for she tended to the girl as though she were an unruly animal. She communi-cated corporally, refusing to speak to "the expectant." She tugged at Madeleine's braid if the girl was slow in responding to a directive, issued tersely or with a pointed finger, and she'd stamp her foot to summon the girl, or rap at the kitchen ceiling with a broom when Madeleine was to descend to her daily meal. Yes, one meal daily: of bitter herbs boiled down to gruel; into which went antimony pellets—these, when passed whole, were retrieved from Madeleine's waste bucket, rinsed, and returned to her gruel in the hope that the resultant purging might loose "the item within" from its hold. Ants' eggs, too, were stirred into the gruel, for it was known to her that ants' eggs, if ingested, would undo a devil pregnancy. And Madeleine was made to soak *twice* daily in her mustard bath.

Madeleine wrote letters; but when a passel was discovered by the Prosecu-tor and returned to her, whole paragraphs drowned in spills of wine-dark ink, she desisted. (In truth, she kept on: she wrote at night, when it was thought she slept, and slipped the letters to priest and progeny into an envelope glued to the bottom of her bureau.)

As for Father Louis, he'd last seen Madeleine three days before her sudden "disappearance." Save for the sole time he dared knock at the Prosecutor's door, he'd not tried to contact the girl. And with the cook's dismissal, he'd no avenue. So he went about his life. Yes, he heard his private confessions with less ardor than before; and it was whispered that some wind had gone from the priest's sail, but what was he to do? This he asked of himself and God; receiving no reply, he did nothing.

Then, five Sundays into Madeleine's sequestration, Father Louis was attacked as he entered St. Pierre. The Prosecutor paid a laborer ten sous to strike the cleric with a brass-handled cane as he took the first step leading up to the church. Father Louis, cracked across the back of the neck, fell to his knees. The laborer walked away, unpursued.

This was but the latest and most public offense. There'd been others, quite petty—one involved the dung of the priest's stolen horse, another featured scrolled scripture tied to thrown rocks—but this was the first assault upon the priest's person.

Of course, Father Louis and all of Q—— knew the Prosecutor was behind these attacks. What was the priest to do? What would the Prosecutor and his accomplices do next? What were they capable of? Angered by his three-week-long inability to turn his head to the left, the priest struck upon a plan:

Violence against the person of a priest was sacrilege, blasphemy in action! He would go to the Parliament of Paris, the chancellor, to Louis XIII himself if need be! He would demand justice! Demand that his enemies—and weren't they, by association, enemies of the Church?—be sought and dealt with severely.

What's more, he'd not been to Paris in some time. The change would do him good, he reasoned. True, the trip was long. But Paris held the promise of old friends and new acquaintances, distractions; indeed, he'd heard tell of a woman there, a former circus dancer living near the Pont Neuf, who could, with her tongue, tie . . .

So, Louis, having foolishly stated his intentions to too many people, left for Paris.

The curé's departure for Paris was just what the Prosecutor and his cabal of coconspirators had hoped for. Their initial attacks against the priest were nothing compared to the counterattack they now launched. And so, as the priest left for Paris, the Prosecutor undertook the much shorter trip to P—— to see the bishop.

The documentation had been prepared weeks prior. Now, with the priest beginning his own legal proceedings in Paris, the Prosecutor could make his case, or rather the village's case, against the curé. In defense. It was a brilliant plan, and the cabal was proud. Papers were presented to the Promoter of the Officiality, the bishop's legal representative. Father Louis, pleading his case before the Parliament of Paris, would return to Q—— to find himself accused of "having debauched innumerable married women, having ruined five young women of Q——, of being profane and impious, of never reading his breviary, and of fornicating within the precincts of the church." A lesser priest of St. Pierre was prepared to swear to the truth of the last charge, for he'd seen his superior sporting with a woman on the stony floor of the sacristy, not fifteen paces from the blessed sacrament.

Father Louis, in resorting to justice, ensured that it would not be served.

Though his hours in the pulpit had honed his speech, rendered him eloquent, Father Louis failed to make his case before the Parliament of Paris. His charms were nothing against the law, and the assembly was unmoved by his tale of calumnies and conspiracy.

The Prosecutor fared far better. From his friend the bishop he won the following sentence: the curé was condemned to fast on bread and water every Friday for three months and was forbidden to exercise the sacerdotal functions for five years.

Louis returned from Paris to learn of the sentence. Nonsense! An outrage! Condemned? In his absence? He would appeal.

But he soon discovered that he could not appeal, for the Prosecutor had *already* appealed the sentence: as the bishop and his ecclesiastical judges could only mete out *spiritual* punishment for such crimes, the Prosecutor had also petitioned the Parliament of Paris, asking the civil magistrates to consider *corporal* punishment. The appeal—presented at Parliament two days *after* Father Louis's failed plea—bore the weighty signature of the Bishop of P——; it asked Parliament to consider "hanging, maiming, branding, or condemnation to the gallows." (The bishop had been swayed toward severity by the Prosecutor, to whom he owed a favor or two relating to certain indiscretions within his See.)

The bishop's sentence stood while the matter went before the Parliament of Paris.

Louis canceled all confessions and took to his rooms. His thoughts were not of Madeleine but of his friend René Sophier, the Curé of T——, who, just six years prior, had been burned alive, guilty of "spiritual incests and sacrilegious impudicities." To him, René had been a trusted friend; and indeed, the older man had taught Louis a thing or two. Could it be that the same fate lay in store for him? Impossible! Weren't the men considering his case—men of the Church and courts—righteous and smart, principled and learned? And hadn't countless clerics committed acts far worse than his? For what had he done but love as every man should?

Ten days passed with no word from the Parliament. The good men and women of Q—— went unconfessed. It was rumored that the omnipotent Richelieu had taken an interest in the case. Louis thought about leaving Q——. Several of his friends and lovers advised, even begged him to do so, offering to slip him unseen into the Italian hillside, or place him among the peaceable Swiss. . . . No. He would stay. He would fight.

Finally, word arrived from Paris: the Parliament wanted proof of the priest's infidelities.

The Prosecutor, despite the cabal's efforts to dissuade him, continued to deny the presence in his home of the pregnant Madeleine. The coming bastard would *not* be proof. And so, lest the door to his good home be opened, and infamy let in, the Prosecutor dropped his case and the inquiry was ended.

Without proof, the appeal and all outstanding charges against Father Louis were dismissed and the bishop's sentence was rescinded. The curé was restored to his office and full duties.

Ever more impudent, Father Louis returned to the sins of the willing women and men of Q——.

As for the Prosecutor and the cabal, they would watch, and wait.

12

Creatura Ignis: The Cabal

IT WAS one month later that the Prosecutor duly served notice to the bishop that the case against the curé was to be reopened. A petition bearing the signatures of the fine men and women of Q—— (many of whom were dead) was sent to P——. This was not evidentiary; but it was effective. The bishop was bound to respond to the town's plea in some way. He could not ignore their request, which was for permission to receive the sacrament "from hands other than those, so notoriously impure, of our parish priest."

The bishop, deeming his debts to the Prosecutor paid, followed Parliament's lead: he would do nothing without proof of some sort. And in private correspondence, the bishop stated plainly that "the bastard spawn of a cleric" would not suffice. The bishop would have true proof of the priest's perfidy—of sacrilege, of devilry, of bewitching, of possession—and he'd have it soon, for he'd not suffer much longer "the distractions of Q——."

The cabal accepted the bishop's challenge, and acted quickly.

Off the main square of Q——, over the glass-paned door of a large shop, there hung a sign. Into the wood, cut to resemble a pestle, were carved the words *M. Adam, Apothecary*. Sagging shelves, heavy with jars, lined the walls. Jars full of dark, viscid . . . *things*. Fetal shapes peered out from within the jars, pale, pickled, seemingly suspended between life and death. Other jars held powders and berries and extracts, all labeled in Latin. Hundred of herbs, some dried and others fresh. Three flying fish had been pinned to a thin sheet of cork; afternoon sunlight shone on the webs of their outstretched wings, dry and thin as parchment. An alligator, tall as a man, hung upright on a wall. Tortoise shells of sundry size were displayed like armor. There were dried vipers, horses' hooves, and human bones, either whole or powdered. A sign announced that powdered sapphire and pearl were available, payment due in advance if you please.

Behind a half-wall at the back of the shop could often be found four men at a round table.

Present would be the old pharmacist, Monsieur Adam; his nephew, the Public Prosecutor (and Madeleine's father), tall and bald and stoop-shouldered, with a horrible hook of a nose; dressed in full robes despite the heat would be Canon Mignon, oldest of the men, dry as dust, with tiny ice-blue eyes; and the quietest of the men, Mannoury, the surgeon, would be known by the rings he sported on the small finger of each hand—bands of white gold, inlaid with gems.

"Mademoiselle Dampierres was in not one week ago," said Monsieur Adam, the shopkeeper. "She came, as always, in the company of her nurse, and she complained, as always, of the *female* problem, for which I sold her mugwort."

"What is your point, Uncle?"

"Just this," came the reply. "The nurse tells me the new confessor takes to the back parlor of Madame de Brou's, with the lady herself, each Tuesday in the afternoon, and for no less than one hour."

"Can the good lady have so much to confess? What crimes could the magistrate's widow be committing that she needs—?"

"Don't be a fool, man! The worst criminal need not see his confessor as often and as long as that!"

"There it is then!" fumed the Prosecutor. "Another victory for the cassocked pig!"

The Canon counseled patience: "Take your ease, man," said he. "As you all know, I am confessor to Mademoiselle Sabine Capeau—"

"The hunchback child?"

"The same; but she is hardly a child. Indeed, she speaks to me of . . . of certain *things*. . . . Let me simply say she has strong, *very* strong feelings for the priest."

"As do they all. . . . As do they all."

The Canon continued, "*Oui*, but this Capeau is different, I tell you. She is," and here he paused, sought just the right word, "desperate. She is *desperate*. The things she says I have never heard before—not from a woman, certainly, but neither from a man; not even, I swear it, from a criminal about to swing at the city gates! She talks of crimes, of carnality! She has thoughts that would shame the Devil's maids! And all her thoughts feature the curé. . . . Oh, how she *hates* that man!"

"But what of it? What does the crooked little cuss have to do with us, with our plan?" The plan, of course, was the ruin of Father Louis.

The Prosecutor said what they were all thinking: that perhaps they'd found the bishop's witness.

It took but a few short weeks for the cabal to convince Sabine Capeau that she was possessed.

At twenty-two years of age, Sabine Capeau was an old maid of Q——. Her mother long dead, the girl lived alone with her father, a rich and disreputable ship's chandler, in the finest home of Q——, just off the square. In fact, Monsieur Capeau was rarely at home—his business and a favorite whore kept him in Marseilles many a night—and when he was in residence he and Sabine hardly spoke. They took their meals at opposite ends of a long table, the wrought-silver screen of a branched candelabra rising up between them. Once a year they rode in ritualized silence to Madame Capeau's grave.

Monsieur Capeau had found himself unable to love his deformed daughter; to assuage his guilt at this, he spoiled her. Sabine had a maid and a cook. She had the finest dresses, tailored with some difficulty. She had money of her own to spend in the square and at market, when on rare occasions she ventured out, and she was accountable to no one. Monsieur Capeau was a bankroll and nothing more to his daughter; this was as he wished it. Sabine had even managed to save a great deal of money over the years; for, in addition to an ample allowance, she stole from her father. It was a hobby of sorts. Had she been "normal," these monies might have been added to a dowry, something to sweeten a marriage deal; but Sabine was not "normal," and no dowry, no matter how great, would render her marriageable. This her father told her.

Sabine, at the age of seven, with her mother not six months in the grave, had been packed off to live at an abbey on the River L——. Though the prioress was well-paid to keep her, some months later Sabine returned home with a kind yet emphatic note recommending a regime of prayer and regular blood-letting, "to loose the dark humors from the child."

As her father had been assured that young, misshapen Sabine would not attain the age of ten, the party marking said occasion was a grand affair, a feast for all the village held in the square. Free food and drink drew nearly all the villagers (if not their children), few of whom addressed Sabine.

First from the nuns, and then from a series of tutors, Sabine received the rudimentary education offered to girls. She was smart, and supplemented her schooling by reading on her own. However, Monsieur Capeau would allow only theology texts in his library; and so it was Sabine grew devout by default. Sadly, at a most impressionable time, she discovered the Old Testament.

Due to her unnamed affliction, she grew increasingly misshapen over the years till, at twenty-two, with her outsized features and humped back, she had the appearance of a gnome. Or—more accurately, if less kindly—a troll. This might have made the girl the focus of sympathy had it not been for her disposition.

She was by nature melancholic; the events of her life rendered her first sad, then bitter; and in time she'd turned sour, if not acidic. In town it was joked that she'd once bled venom when cut. A shepherd, misused by her father, held that one look from "la petite Capeau" could kill a lamb, and cross words could ruin a flock.

Sabine had withdrawn from the world, was already living as a recluse—friendless, loveless, without family, she had no one to see, nowhere to go—when the new confessor came to Q——. She spied him from the parlor window one Sunday morning, dressed in full canonicals, making his way through the square to the doors of St. Pierre. That afternoon Sabine's maid had two errands: deliver her mistress's card to Father Louis and inform old Canon Mignon that his services as confessor were no longer needed.

Sabine waited patiently for the priest to arrive. Finally he came, unprepared; and the look on his handsome face when he was led into the parlor to meet Sabine seared itself into the girl's brain like a brand. Father Louis agreed to hear the girl's confession but, despite the sum offered, then doubled, he would not come but once a month. Nor would he stay for supper, not even when Sabine had gone so far as to have the table set with linen and silver and china, and laid with fruits and sundry viands; still the priest excused himself with fast politesse.

After three months Father Louis stopped going to the Capeaus' altogether. A two-line note said his schedule did not allow it. As apology, he promised to pray for Sabine. Her gift of an ivory cross inlaid with small emeralds was returned.

Of course, Canon Mignon returned to hear the girl's confession, but not without feigning hurt at having been dismissed. Sabine apologized, and the Canon accepted and sold the ivory and emerald cross. And so each Friday the Canon sat beside Sabine in the parlor, blushing at the changed content of her confessions.

In the following weeks, the cabal's plan in place, no one noticed that Canon Mignon spent his days at the Capeau house. Monsieur Capeau stayed happily away. The servants did not care what their mistress did, so long as she left them alone. As for the neighbors . . . well, so disliked were father and daughter that their neighbors had stopped gossiping long ago. So barren were their lives, especially that of the humpbacked girl, that no one begrudged them their finery, their furnishings, their three-story home dominating the square.

Sabine and the Canon met in the library. They sat knee to knee, with the Canon whispering. It was quite warm, with spring quickly ceding to summer, but the Canon insisted on keeping all the doors and windows shut. He told Sabine he feared the spirits; in truth, he feared the servants, or anyone else who might overhear and one day testify to the content of these sessions. They prayed, but only as much as necessary, which is to say not much at all. Mostly Canon Mignon asked questions of Sabine, leading the girl like a beast on a leash. Wasn't it true that the curé came to the girl in dreams? He did indeed. And wasn't it true that he committed unspeakable crimes in the course of those dreams? He did. And hadn't she, when first she'd seen the curé, been seized by a *violence* the likes of which she'd never known, one that began with the deepest of thrills and localized to a . . . wetness, to contractions of certain muscles . . . ? Hadn't she wanted then and there to offer her womanhood? Yes! Yes it was true, every word. And wasn't it true that the man was a devil? Yes! A thousand times yes!

On and on it went. With the Canon telling tales of mystics and saints, of Satan and his ways, of the Five Sorrowful Mysteries, of wrongdoers and the Wrath of God, et cetera. He brought in books on devilry for Sabine to read.

They reviewed the transcripts of countless trials. They read the testimony aloud, with Sabine taking the role of the possessed, the witness, the witch; the Canon, of course, was the Inquisitor.

Summer came, and their sweat-drenched sessions continued in the library, which wore now its summer dress, as did the whole house—woven mats where thick carpets had lain, damask panels in place of the velvet curtains. The shut-up room was airless and powerfully hot. The Canon went through countless collars. Sabine lay on the daybed (on her stomach, of course: pressure on her hump pained her) and pulled at the string that made a fan of a large palm leaf. Periodically, the Canon would calm her with a concoction of Monsieur Adam's. Sabine, tired by the heat and lessons, would doze and dream. Upon waking she'd call for the Canon, who was always there, waiting to record her words. Such dreams she spoke of!

After one particularly successful session, during which Sabine put a gilded candlestick to abominable use, the Canon reported to the cabal that their witness was ready. Ready to go before the baron, the bishop, and God's good people. She was all the proof anyone would need to condemn the curé.

That very day, Father Louis was formally accused of having had commerce with the Devil and of bewitching Sabine Capeau.

As for the bishop, he sent his promoter to Q—— to meet with Sabine, to hear her testimony. And so the company—including the promoter, his lieutenant, two magistrates, one clerk, the baron, and, of course, the cabal—crowded into the Capeaus' library on a steamy afternoon in early August.

The Prosecutor produced two pacts, which, he said, were proof that Sabine had sworn herself to the Devil: bunched hawthorn prickles, which he said she'd vomited up, and a witch's ladder—a cord tied with nine knots—which Sabine woke one afternoon to find pendant from her belt. To her visitors, and in response to no particular question, Sabine averred that "men such as I have never seen come to me in my dreams; they come from the Darkness and each one, speaking words of devilled Latin, changes his shape and speech till each becomes the Curé of St. Pierre; and then I know that *he* is with me, to tell of the Devil's amours, to ply me with caresses, to work my own hands upon me in self-abuse, which sometimes lasts the night long and leaves me swollen, and to ask me with words insolent and unchaste to offer up to the Devil my womanhood . . ." Et cetera.

Such talk, accompanied by minor acrobatics, convinced the bishop's party. They returned to P—— without meeting the accused, imprisoned in an attic across the square. They advised the bishop to proceed. In haste.

Which he did. He issued a monitory against Father Louis, denouncing him, inviting the faithful to inform against him. The monitory, fixed to doors throughout Q——, quoted the *Malleus Maleficarum*: "... for witchcraft is high treason against God's majesty. And so the accused must be put to the torture to make them confess. Any person, whatever his rank or position, upon such an accusation may be put to torture. This is the right of the Church, thus decreed. And he who is found guilty, even if he confesses his crimes, let him be racked, let him suffer the tortures prescribed by law in order that he may be punished in proportion to his crimes, in order that the faithful may triumph over the Prince of This World in the good and great name of the Prince of Peace ..."

At the bishop's order, a Dr. Lucien Epernon was dispatched to Q—— to examine the bewitched. He determined that Sabine showed no signs of possession, that no war was being waged for her soul; rather, he reported that "the girl suffers from a species of uterine fury, whose symptoms are an excessive heat on the body, an inextinguishable appetite for venery, and an inability to talk about anything but the body and the veneric act." He opined that she was "highly impressionable, for she felt pain when I told her she ought, though no source of said pain existed." The doctor's report, a simple inquiry, more a matter of custom than law, according to the bishop, was filed deep in the bowels of the bishopric. Dr. Epernon himself was dispatched to the Auvergne on six-month assignment.

As for the cabal, its members took turns coaching Sabine. Canon Mignon continued his daily tutorials, of course. Mannoury arranged to keep Monsieur Capeau in Marseilles, dumb and disinterested. The Prosecutor and Monsieur Adam, with calisthenics, pills, and potions, put Sabine through her paces. Acrobatics had so impressed judges at trials in the past—no better show than a nun or good girl suddenly taken with an urge to do the splits in open court! But little Sabine was brittle-boned and stiff. Still, she progressed. Soon she could, if seated, raise each foot to touch the opposite shoulder. And, with a literal blast of good fortune, it was discovered that this pose rendered the girl flatulent. Further testimony.

When finally Sabine was ready to show, and with the curé chained away in a sweltering attic, the cabal recruited the bit players. Willing witnesses were auditioned, hired, and readied for the trial. A jury of thirteen magistrates was assembled by means of blackmail and cash.

Though the arrogant and too pretty priest had grown less popular, still many people of Q—— doubted the charges and pitied him. The curé's lovers of both sexes were all tears and stifled support. They smuggled unsigned letters of support into his attic via the boy who emptied his bucket, but these were slight consolation; still no one spoke publicly in his defense. He'd gotten word to his family to stay away, lest they be implicated. So, denied counsel, Father Louis waited patiently to speak in his own defense; that opportunity, if it came at all, would come at trial and not before.

No. Neither his lovers nor his family nor his friends could counter the opposition—the Prosecutor, the bishop, the cardinal, and, by extension, the king. Only a fool would have spoken in the curé's defense. A fool, or someone in love.

And lest such a one come forward, it was decreed that any person speaking against the proceedings would be fined ten thousand livres; further, any group of three or more unrelated persons meeting without permission and for unclear purposes, would be liable to a fine of fifty thousand livres. And as no man relished the prospect of a stay in debtor's prison, no one spoke against the proceedings. Indeed, many good and just people of Q—— saw fit to travel; the time was opportune.

The prosecution progressed quickly that horrible hot summer. But not too quickly . . .

For, as word of the curé's certain condemnation spread, a tide of tourists flooded Q——. The town happily suffered twice its normal number of inhabitants. Innkeepers tripled their rates and still turned people away. Strangers walked door to door in search of a cot and some ale. Business had never been better. Bakers fired their ovens both day and night. Many men and all the whores of Q—— became rich that long summer. Monsieur Adam convinced his fellow merchants to pay for the printing of broadsides detailing the charges against the curé, each more exaggerated than the last; men and boys were hired to spread these sheets through every village less than two days travel from Q——. Not since a troupe of acrobats had come from Paris, with dwarfs and dancing bears, had Q—— seen such a show as this!

Father Louis could see the crowded square through the slats of his attic cell. The noise kept the priest awake at night; rooms, crammed with cots, were rented in shifts and so scores of tourists drank and danced; fighting, fornicating, roasting bothersome mutts on pits set up for boar, they awaited their turn to sleep. Friends traveling separately from Marseilles and lesser cities made plans to meet in the square at Q——, beneath the Bourbon standard. The priest knew that this did not bode well: no one traveled to witness a trial; only an execution.

Words of the bewitching in Q——, of the capture and killing (premature, of course) of a devil, spread wide and fast. Few peasants could read and so, traveling by tongue, the tale grew ever more fantastical; and Madeleine heard enough to puzzle out the cabal's progress as she sat beside her shuttered window, listening to talk in the narrow street below. And lest she harbor hopes of reunion, her Keeper cruelly slipped beneath her door the merchants' broadside, detailing in words and sketches the many misdeeds of the Devil-Priest of Q——.

Madeleine knew she must do something. In two days' time she had a plan:

She would testify against Louis. Wasn't it widely rumored that he had ruined her? She was the *perfect* witness. She'd show little Capeau, the vicious bitch! For wasn't seduction—and all of Q—— knew she'd been seduced—wasn't seduction just below bewitchment on the Devil's agenda? Yes, she'd say or do anything to be at that trial. Anything to see Louis again.

Surely she knew enough about other trials, about testimony and false religion, to appear *afflicted*. She knew enough about witchcraft and such. She could do it. She *had* to.

And when she saw Louis, as soon as she stood before him in open court, she would recant. Recant, recant, recant! Take back every word. And save him! Say that she loved him and that he loved her. That yes, he was the father of her child. Yes, they were going to spend the rest of their lives together, for they were married . . . more or less.

Madeleine held to the sweet memory as she lay plotting in her airless cell. The memory of their midnight marriage. The night she'd slipped from her home to meet the priest at St. Pierre. It was a cool night in early spring, with a quarter moon high in the sky, sharp as a sickle. The night had been so quiet! A lone raven far away. The lazy turn of wagon wheels on cobblestoned streets. A fecund wind, not unpleasant, swirled within the village walls. Careful lest she be discovered, she'd slipped into the shadows at the slightest noise; and slipped finally into the great church on the square, its spires rising up sharp and high enough to tear the black fabric of the night.

Louis was waiting for her. As he'd promised. In his arms were thirteen red roses. "For my most beautiful rose," he whispered.

Their footsteps echoed in the cold and empty church. He'd met her at the front door, answering to her three light raps. She'd stepped quickly through the small door cut into the larger. He took her hand and they walked, wordlessly, down the length of the nave to the altar, which he'd illumined with white votives. Hundreds of candles, it seemed; she was deeply moved. The candles lit the carved Christ on His cross above the altar, and for a moment Madeleine was scared. She'd never been in an empty church. Strange, since she'd been coming to St. Pierre all her life, that she was just now noticing its details: how the stained glass windows, twice as tall as she, depicted the Fifteen Mysteries of the Rosary; how the moonlight lit the glass faces of the saints; and how the blue and gray panes of the Virgin's robe fit together so well, looking as though they might move on the slightest wind; the lingering incense; the worn wood of the pews, as cold and smooth as the attendant statues . . . and the glistening altar, all gold and bright white cloth.

As priest, Father Louis asked himself did he take Madeleine to be his wife; as bridegroom he answered in the affirmative and slipped a thin band of ivory onto her finger. As priest he invoked a blessing; as groom he knelt to receive it.

Madeleine giggled and cried through the ceremony, said in defiance of law and custom, Church and state. She was scared, and excited.

Yes, in her heart and mind she was married.

Sweeter still the memory of how, the ceremony said, the impassive faces of the glass saints staring, he had carried her into the sacristy and taken her for the first time, slowly, smoothly, on the stony floor, not fifteen paces from the sacrament. . . . How it had hurt . . . How Louis had held her, whispered words about *her* most beautiful rose . . . How she'd bled onto the stones, and how he'd wiped up her blood with the whitest cloth . . .

Yes, she must save him. Do whatever she had to do to save him.

And so, when her Keeper came to her one morning shortly thereafter, to lead her to that putrid bath, Madeleine took the woman's hand and sucked hungrily, wildly at her fleshy fingers—"as my devils suck at my teats," said she—and averred, *sotto voce*, that she was indeed bedeviled, and that her devils had turned against their brother and instrument, the parish priest of Q——, "that goat in a biretta, that cassocked Priapus."

By midday, Madeleine had had an audience with the cabal—all save her father; and that night she was slipped unseen into the Capeau home.

The cabal convinced the Prosecutor to let Madeleine testify. She was the perfect witness, they said. She'd rid them of the confessor once and for all, and wasn't that their goal? It was indeed. She, the Prosecutor's daughter, could help them achieve it, especially if her Keeper would attest to what she'd seen the girl do, especially if Madeleine's resident devils could be coaxed into a second appearance. Yes, said the cabal, the girl ought to be brought in to testify. To be *trained* to testify. Clearly she was willing. And vengeful. The Prosecutor relented. Madeleine would testify, but he would not see her outside of court, and at the conclusion of the trial she would be "dealt with," sent away. Some-where. He didn't care where. The cabal swore they would see to it.

Canon Mignon was, at first, careful with Madeleine. He knew what he'd achieved with Sabine—though just *how* he'd achieved it he could not have said—but what had he here, in Madeleine? Her state—she was *enceinte*, seven months into her term—added to the priest's fear. Still, he played his part: tutor to the possessed.

They sat sequestered in the Capeaus' library. They read aloud accounts of other trials—the testimony and detailed descriptions of how the possessed had behaved. They prayed aloud that they would be able to prove what the curé and his demons had done to them.

Of course, this was all more than Madeleine had expected. The crowds. The court already in session, she carried on: she had no choice. She did what the Canon said, and he was pleased. Yes, everything he said was true. Yes, she would swear to it. The descriptions of the possessed might have been written of her. Yes, yes, and yes again. Her tongue was slick with lies, and her limbs grew slack from the acrobatics. She was ready to spout the cabal's truths, ready to scamper about the court as they wished. Ready, indeed. She begged to speak against the Devil. She *begged* to be taken to the trial.

While Madeleine made of herself the perfect pawn, Sabine grew ever more difficult:

She ended each session by falling into fits, by demanding in top-voice that her demons take their leave, by condemning the Devil-devout curé to an eter-nity in heaven. The Canon pleaded with the girl: wouldn't she do better to save her strength for the trial? She said the decision was not hers. Her demons had her.

Canon Mignon reported to the cabal that Sabine had become too much for him. He was aging at double-speed. She'd even knocked him over once as he'd tried to calm her, and he'd fallen head first onto the hearth. Had badly cut his head. He worried that the girl would be the death of him. He needed help.

But the cabal, knowing well the Canon's vanity, only commended him on a job well done; this worked: the Canon returned to the Capeaus' the very next afternoon. "Ah, but I'm afraid all credit goes to the child," he demurred. "She took over some time ago," adding in a whisper, "now she *believes* herself!"

Monsieur Adam mixed some more of Sabine's soporific. He'd concocted so many variations of the original that there was no longer a recipe. Still, Sabine would not sleep, and so the apothecary threw in a little of this; she grew constipated, and so in went a little of that. She began to rave. Mannoury bled the girl, to no effect. The Canon kept a store of dried blood gathered by the Visitandines of Annecy from the tomb of St. Francis de Sales; he gave up a cherished clot for the girl to eat. Nothing. No improvement at all. The Canon was at a loss. Monsieur Adam had mixed his best. Mannoury reported that there was nothing in Aristotle or Augustine, nothing in Gallen or the Arabians that might explain away Sabine's behavior. They knew not what to do.

The trial of the Curé of St. Pierre of Q—— convened on 2 September, 16—.

The monitory had ensured that there would be no shortage of testimony. The townspeople of Q—— vied for a chance to speak against the curé; for them, the trial was a mere extension of the games they'd been playing all summer long in the pubs, over tankards of rotgut and ale. Their testimony—lies and tales—was reported to the thousands who gathered in the square, too poor to pay their way into court.

Of course, some few told the truth. Far less damning, and wholly believable. In this number were the curé's spurned lovers and their spouses.

The secondary priest of St. Pierre was all cooperation. Throughout the testimony he sat in the front row, in full view of the magistrates, and watched Canon Mignon; when the Canon rubbed the cross pendant from his neck with his left hand (the agreed-upon sign), the aspirant would rise and vehemently affirm the testimony. After all, as second in command at St. Pierre, who'd know better than he what atrocities Father Louis had committed? Meanwhile, in a locked box beneath his bed, the priest kept a postdated letter appointing him curé upon the condemnation of the accused.

More witnesses, one after another.

Old Madame Épouse, widow of the cooper, attributed her infestation with lice "big as your fist" to Father Louis, whom she'd never met. A young wife brought her dim-witted husband before the court, complaining that he had been "unhusbandly" since their wedding night. Father Louis was accused of ligature, and was ordered to tell the court where he'd hidden the leather strip that he'd tied into knots to thus afflict the oaf. Louis, stupefied, could not speak. And so his Second rose to say that he'd seen such a knotted cord in the sacristy. (The next day it was introduced as evidence; at day's end it was untied and returned to the boot of the priest's younger brother.) The wife, hell-bent on satisfaction, led her mate from the courtroom by the ear, much to the amusement of all assembled—

"He'd best come up with another excuse . . ."

"He'd best *come up* with something!"

"And quickly too, as that bitch of his looks ready to ride!" Et cetera.

There were days and days of such testimony, till it seemed that every petty grievance of Q—— had been aired in open court.

The Prosecutor had, upon his daughter's "return" to Q——, thrown himself even deeper into the trial. He neither saw nor mentioned Madeleine. He'd consigned her to the care of the Canon, the Apothecary, and the Surgeon. But it was he who finally decided on the cabal's course of action: they would hurry both girls to trial.

13

Creatura Ignis: The Condemned

WHO HAS done this to you?"

Sabine and Madeleine sat side by side on a bench in the witness box. The question was posed by Father Tranquille, the ancient exorcist sent by the bishop, and each girl answered in turn, in Latin as was the custom, and pointed at the accused.

"*Dic qualitatem,*" commanded the Exorcist. *Tell his rank.*

"*Sacerdos.*" Priest.

"*Cujus ecclesiae?*" *Of what church?*

The Church of St. Pierre, they said.

These were the first questions asked of Sabine and Madeleine at the trial of Father Louis. Sabine responded well, and the cabal was relieved. As for Madeleine, when first she'd been ushered into court to see her Louis, her lover . . . *Mon Dieu*, what they'd done to her beloved Louis.

As a matter of law, Father Louis had been searched for signs of dark commerce; for all fiends, it is said, betray the touch of their Prince. The Dark Touch leaves either a visible mark, or invisible spots on the flesh that are impervious to pain.

The Prosecutor and Mannoury, the Surgeon, went to the prisoner's attic cell one afternoon early in the trial. The curé was stripped and restrained by three convicts freed for this mission by the Prosecutor. His rich black curls were shorn, and it was with little care that the curled hairs on his sex and scrotum were scissored away. The Surgeon passed a razor carelessly over the curé's soaped skin, and in no time the priest was hairless and bleeding.

"The eyebrows as well," directed the Prosecutor, and the Surgeon complied. Both men, in shirtsleeves, stood over the accused as he, naked, struggled vainly against the three men who held him—a murderer and two cattle thieves.

Father Louis was bound to a large board held by the convicts. The ropes that restrained him must have come from Marseilles: they were thick and rough, stained with seawater and oil, and looked as though they'd been gnawed by rats; the ropes tore the priest's flesh each time he moved, so he kept as still as possible, praying, feeling his blood pulse, feeling the sting of his sweat as it slid between the fresh red lips of the razor cuts.

As no Devil's Mark was found, it stood to reason that the priest had been favored with spots insensible to pain, fleshy portals for the passage of his demons. The Canon had asked Sabine where they should search for the priest's devil-spots. The curé bore one such spot on his shoulder, said she; prodded by the Canon, she added that there were two spots on his buttocks, very near the fundament, and yes, one on either testicle.

"This may take some time," said the Surgeon.

"Good," replied the Prosecutor, taking to a three-legged milking stool in the attic's corner. He rolled his sleeves higher and cooled himself with a fan sewn of sea grape leaves.

The Surgeon spread his tools on a low bench. A worn leather kit contained all the needles he'd need. On the dark wood of the bench, each silver needle shone in its place; they glinted in the sunlight shafting into the attic through the same openings in the warped boards used by the bats, rats, and swarming insects that plagued the curé night and day. "Yes, this may take some time," mused the Surgeon, arranging the needles—short and thick to his left, longer ones to his right. Some were as short as his thumb, others were as long as his arm from elbow to wrist.

The Prosecutor sent one of the cattle thieves down to a tavern off the square for two tankards of ale. "And if you so much as sip from the bucket," cautioned the Prosecutor, "I will see you swing."

In the still, stifling air of the attic, stinking of waste, hay, and sweat, the Surgeon began.

The shortest and sharpest needles were used on the scalp, the back of the hands, the top of the feet, and around the joints of the arms and legs. Mid-length needles were used on the chest, the upper- and forearms, and the back. The fleshier parts of the priest—the legs, buttocks, et cetera—called for the longest needles. The very longest pierced the tough muscle of the priest's left leg; the Surgeon, with some difficulty, shoved it through.

It was not until the fourth needle that Louis screamed: of medium length and width, the Surgeon shoved it up into the arch of his left foot. Pain shot like a spark up his spine, seemed to set the back of his neck ablaze. Yes, only then did the first scream tear itself from his throat, despite his prayers and all his summoned will. As the shortest needles were slipped sideways into his scalp—*blinding pain!*—Louis let loose scream after scream till finally the littered square was loud with applause.

On and on it went. Twice the cattle thief descended for more ale; he also briefed the crowd in exchange for coin. He returned to the attic the final time bearing a tray of cheeses sent up courtesy of Monsieur Colombel, owner of the aforementioned tavern.

The Surgeon worked himself to near exhaustion. The criminals lazed in the shadows, for Father Louis no longer struggled. And the Prosecutor came to the side of the accused, directing the Surgeon. Here. There. Deeper.

Each time Father Louis fainted he was subjected to salts, or had slaps dealt him by the Prosecutor. He couldn't speak. Couldn't think. There was only pain; and the blood that seeped from a hundred holes in his flesh.

Finally the Surgeon stopped. Those in the square who'd bet that the session would last one and one-quarter hours gathered in their winnings. The Surgeon was drenched with sweat, too tired to continue. He passed the salts under his own nose, once, quickly.

The Surgeon reported to the court that he'd only found two insensible spots, and they'd been two of the five described by Sabine Capeau—on the left testicle and lower right buttock, the rim of the anus. He had tried ninety-one spots in all, from scalp to sole, and all but these two had brought pain. (The priest was, of course, unconscious when the two spots in question were tried.) "Such a clever devil," opined the Prosecutor in open court. "Able to hide his spots so well."

Upon quitting the attic, the Prosecutor and Surgeon were hailed in the square. Moments earlier, the Prosecutor had handed a small bag of sea salt to the murderer—along with a fistful of coin—directing the man to work the coarse salt into the priest's wounds. He said too that he'd send up some ale for the three men.

The Prosecutor waited half an hour before sending seven jailers into the attic with shackles and orders to seize the criminals and recover his coin. He'd never intended to set the men free, as agreed. He'd only needed their services for a short while; now he signed warrants for their execution. He prided himself on the plan: he could clear Q—— of three renowned criminals, do away with three witnesses to the surgeon's work, and slake the crowd's bloodthirst all at once. Brilliant.

And so by sunset, the three men swung above the city gates. That night they were the talk of every tavern; for days after they were the sport of birds.

Three days after the search for the Devil's Mark—it was the thirteenth of September, though Father Louis had grown uncertain of the date—two men came to the attic at dawn to ready the curé for trial.

Father Louis was fevered. He still bled from a puncture in his side: the Surgeon had pierced an organ. Infections sprouted and began to spread. Other wounds had begun to heal. The salt, despite the sizzling pain it had caused, stanched the bleeding.

Dressed in a long soiled nightshirt and worn slippers, the curé was led down from the attic. He was placed in a trundle cart, thrown over with a tarp to keep him from the mob, and led through the crowded square to the courthouse.

Only the rich or otherwise favored had been able to secure a seat in court. The first benches were filled with officials of the Church and state, men of rank, various nobles, and well-connected cardinalists. Silks rustled in the gallery. There was a rich glow of velvet. The ladies wore summery pastels of every shade. In the heat, beads of sweat vied with gems for position on every bosom. Fans of bamboo and lace were in constant motion. The air was thick with civet and ambergris, as well as the very human odors those scents could not conceal. The finest families had their servants in tow.

The magistrates had been the first to file into court, sitting shoulder to shoulder in two tiers near the witness stand, their full red robes spreading one into another like seeping blood. Next came the exorcist: Father Tranquille, nearly three times the age of the accused, thickly spectacled and nearly deaf, dressed in black robes of worsted wool, took up his consecrated whisk and scattered holy water over the court and the crowd. There followed the Prosecutor and the Canon, and (for no official reason) Messieurs Adam and Mannoury. Various and sundry officials came quite socially into court, taking their seats with great show. Finally, Father Louis was escorted to the high and backless stool by two clerks of the court.

The curé, a skullcap on his shaven, scabbed head, was made to kneel before the magistrates as the exorcist sprinkled the stool. With his hands tied, Father Louis could not bare his head as directed. At a sign from the Prosecutor, a clerk snatched the skullcap off. Some in the gallery giggled, others sneered or fell silent at the sight of the abused priest on his knees. A few women betrayed themselves with tears. Ushers in the gallery called for silence.

Charges were read. Prayers said.

It was on the fifth day of the second week of the trial that the Prosecutor presented the possessed: Sabine Capeau and Madeleine de la Mettrie. It was shortly thereafter that the exorcist's voice rang out, rhythmic and brittle, clogged with the cadence of the Church: "Who has done this to you?" And the girls began to testify. One desperate with hate, the other with love.

Madeleine, overwhelmed with grief, futility, anger, and remorse, and still plotting to save her Louis, found herself party to his certain condemnation. No one would listen to her, not to her *truths*—they wanted only to hear the lies she continued to tell in court, biding her time, waiting for a way to open before her.

But that never happened.

With the exorcist at the ready, the Prosecutor and Canon Mignon began to offer proof that Sabine and Madeleine were riddled with demons, each and every one introduced to them by the accused, the Curé of St. Pierre. The bishop sent word that he awaited proof of possession, and that the inquisitors were to apply, in open court, tests in the four areas long ago set forth by the Church: tests of language—or the ability of the possessed to speak and understand tongues unknown to them; tests of preternatural strength; tests of levitation; and tests of clairvoyance, or prevision.

Levitation would be difficult. So it was determined during the cabal's daily meeting in the apothecary to begin with the easiest proofs: those of language. As for levitation and the rest? Well, all in due time.

And so the Canon set to work, as best he could, teaching Greek to Sabine and Hebrew to Madeleine. He read aloud from ancient texts, the words rattling off his rusted tongue. He understood little of the Greek he recited, none of the Hebrew. The Canon had the girls read aloud, hours each day; they approximated what appeared on the page or they simply parroted the Canon. Birch rod in hand, he ensured that the two languages did not sound alike, for that was all that mattered.

Sabine was tested first, with Madeleine directed to follow her lead. The cabal did not expect a show from Madeleine; obedience was all they asked for, *demanded;* and obedience they received, for it was during these sessions that the Canon said, "Perhaps, Madeleine, you will be let to keep that child of yours, if our end is achieved." As for the crazed Capeau girl, well who knew what she might do?

A table had been brought into the court and on it was spread an odd collection of objects from the church, the market, and Monsieur Adam's shop. A small iron crucifix, identical bottles—one filled with oil, the other holy water; an ear of corn; spices; a sow's ear; metal bracelets; several hard cheeses, et cetera. Speaking in Greek, the Canon told Sabine to approach the table, say an Ave Maria, and pick up the star anise. They'd rehearsed this; nevertheless, Sabine chose a pin and a clod of dirt, and did not even essay the prayer.

Madeleine, truly deviled by thoughts of Louis and her child, did as she was told. In Hebrew, or a perversion thereof.

It was the Canon who excused Sabine's error by stating, simply, that the girl was host to uneducated devils. Devils who had not traveled, and thus had never heard the tongue of Greece. Of course they'd misunderstood the Canon's command. The magistrates nodded solemnly at the Canon's logic, though giggles rose like breaking bubbles from the gallery.

That very night, Mannoury and Adam came to the girls' room. Madeleine woke to rattling chains and whispers. She feigned sleep, hoping that the men had not come for her. She listened with horror as the Surgeon held Sabine down and Monsieur Adam daubed her lips with sulfur. Maybe now, said he, she would speak as instructed.

Sabine said not a word through burning lips that night, shed not a tear. As soon as the men had left, she got out of bed, walked to her bureau, smashed a bottle of perfume on the floor and knelt cross-vigil on the shards of glass. She was like that still when Madeleine woke, four hours later.

Madeleine worried that she too might lose her mind. Her only hope was escape. But how? Every door was locked behind her. Her Keeper and Sabine's nurse were ever near. Even if she were to somehow open the bedroom window, it was a three-story fall to the courtyard below, too far to jump certainly, and too far for a rope tied of the two girls' bedclothes. And if she freed herself, how would she free Louis? No. She'd have to wait. Testify, and somehow effect her plan.

When Sabine was seen in court with deep orange sores on her lips and chin, she testified that such sores had recurred since first she'd given the Devil his Kiss. The gray and blood-black bruises blossoming on her hands and forearms she attributed to the Devil's grasp. This said, she redoubled her efforts to please:

She put on such a show of possession that the bishop's dictates of proof were forgotten. The exorcist said in all his years he'd never come across a case like this strange Mademoiselle Capeau. The square was abuzz with bloodlust, for a pamphlet printed the night of her testimony gave this summary:

> . . . the little hunchback, her lips dripping blood, fell on the floor; she spat and vomited such as we have never seen. She passed her left foot over her shoulder to her cheek. She passed her feet over her head till the big toes touched the nose, and then let come a black gas from her bottom side, such that the ladies of the assembly held kerchiefs to their faces. She stretched her legs so far to the left and to the right that she sat flat on the ground, with no space visible beneath her, and bounced, as if to copulate. She stretched her legs to a length well nigh seven feet, though she herself stands but four, bent as she is . . .

Indeed, Sabine did vomit. Monsieur Adam had seen to that, giving the girl's nurse "medication," which was to be mixed into her breakfast each morning. Sabine's medicine rendered her vomit a bright, crowd-pleasing blue. Additionally, the apothecary had crafted other items which the Prosecutor produced as evidence, saying that Sabine had expelled them in the night. One was a wad of paper, stained with three drops of blood and containing three orange seeds. Another was a bundle of straw and pieces of rag that were "wet with woman's waste." A third was made of dried mud with cinders, hair and nail parings pressed into it alongside purple pieces of worm. These were quickly passed among the magistrates. According to Dog's Tail, one of Sabine's demons, who spoke through the girl in a horrible high-pitched voice, the favorite pact of the court contained a piece of the heart of a child boiled at a Sabbat in Orleans as well as the ashes of a consecrated wafer, all of which was seasoned with the curé's semen. Sabine swore that she'd swallowed these pacts some time ago, when first she'd consigned herself to the curé and His Prince.

Some members of the gallery were greatly amused; others sighed; some went sick at the stomach and had to excuse themselves. Those in the square loved it. Monsieur Adam joked privately that not only had the question of levitation been forgotten, it was as though it had never been raised.

The trial proceeded just as the cabal had hoped.

In the days that followed her vomiting, Sabine identified her devils for the court. In addition to Dog's Tail of the Order of the Archangels, Sabine hosted Leviathan in the center of her forehead and Beherit in her stomach. Balaam was resident under the second rib on the left side. Isacaaron lived in her heart. As Madeleine sat silently by, Sabine deigned to identify hers as well: she kept the Enemy of the Virgin in her neck, Verrine in her left temple, and Concupiscence, of the Order of Cherubim, in her right. Asmodeus had her heart.

Someone in the gallery called out, wanting to know what lucky devil had Sabine's hump. The court erupted with laughter. Old Father Tranquille rose to restore order with prayer. To no avail. He invoked the bishop's name. The king's as well. Still nothing. It was Sabine who silenced the assembly, rising to deliver more testimony of her own authoring.

Soon it was Madeleine's turn to take the birch rod. She was, it was said, insubordinate. No member of the cabal dared strike the girl—respecting not her condition, but her father's changeable wrath—and so the Surgeon hired a boy out of the square for three sous. One night in the quiet of the Capeau house, the boy brought the rod down again and again on Madeleine's bared lower back as the Canon demanded to know why, if she'd put on such a show for her Keeper, and if she'd sworn to him her hatred of the curé, *why* did she not do so now in court? She tried to say that she'd been lying. She tried to tell the Canon the truth, but he refuted her with shouted scripture.

Her plan having failed, broken in body and spirit, Madeleine sat silently by as Sabine carried on, contorting her misshapen self and spouting her untruths. When next she tried to tell the truth she was delivered back to the village boy and his birch rod. She was beaten at night, with no member of the cabal present; her hands were tied to a tether, which was passed over an open door, so that she hung like a side of meat. Sabine watched from her bed, bouncing about on all fours begging for the rod.

How Madeleine *hated* Sabine! Hatred too for her father and his plotting friends, for the magistrates who'd sold their souls, for the assembly with its silks and basket lunches, for the rabble that lived as one multilimbed, foulbreathed beast in the squalor of the square . . . but yes, hatred above all for Sabine. Sabine, who cheered her beatings. Sabine, who would slaughter Father Louis with her words. Ugly, mad, evil Sabine. Sabine, who yammered all night in a dozen different voices, and who cried out for the Canon each day at dawn. Sabine, who convulsed and contorted in court. Grotesque Sabine. Heroic Sabine, fending off Satan in the name of Christ and His Church. Crazed Sabine Capeau, the cabal's toy and martyr to the mob. Martyr, indeed. Sabine would find her fate, as surely as she was sending the curé to his. Madeleine would see to it.

Finally, the trial ended and the matter was turned over to the magistrates.

But first Louis, who'd been denied a doctor (he had the Surgeon, after all), a confessor (Canon Mignon was available to him, of course), and a counselor (the Prosecutor . . .), at last, before the trial's end, Father Louis was allowed to speak in his own defense. This was no concession to the law, to the principles of justice; no, the mob simply wanted the devil-priest to speak, *demanded* that he speak.

Father Louis could barely stand. He was thin and weak and fevered. He'd not slept for some time: the day-and-night din of the square, the curses hurled up at him by a thousand voices as he lay in the attic . . . Still, he rose to speak and the court fell quiet.

"I call God the Father, God the Son, and God the Holy Ghost, together with the Virgin, my sole advocate, to say that I have never been a sorcerer, have never known Satan, have never committed sacrilege, and have never acknowledged any magic other than that of Holy Scripture, the which I have faithfully preached. I adore my Savior and pray that I may partake in the merit of the blood of His Passion."

The curé then fell back heavily onto his stool. Silence in the court. Quiet outside in the square. Tears were shed in the gallery.

Now, thought Madeleine. *Now!* And she shot up from her seat to speak, to recant, to save her Louis, to—

She was not heard. For just as she rose to speak, so too did Sabine.

Madeleine was led struggling from court by three clerks. Sabine was left standing on the table, where she lifted her skirts high over her head and howled that Isacaaron, on orders of the curé, was taking her then and there. She gyrated and ground her hips lasciviously. She worked the cleft of her sex with her fingers. She spouted such obscenities that it was the duty of the finer ladies of the assembly to faint away.

Within an hour the verdict was returned and read:

Thirteen counts of guilt. On the morrow Father Louis was to be subjected to the Question, both ordinary and extraordinary (the former as punishment, the latter to elicit a confession and the names of accomplices). He was to kneel at the doors of St. Pierre and beg forgiveness of God, the king, and Justice. Then he was to be led across the square, tied to the stake, and burned. Alive. After which his ashes were to be scattered to the four winds. The clerk concluded the reading of the sentence by saying that a plaque, commemorating the event, was to be placed on the door of St. Pierre at the cost of one hundred and fifty livres, chargeable to the condemned's confiscated estate.

Court was dismissed.

Sabine was led into the square, where a makeshift stage was set up for her. As her testimony had not yet rid her of her devils, she was able to oblige the crowd: she spat and twisted and grimaced and brayed like an ass till a soft but persistent rain drove her audience into the taverns ringing the square.

Father Louis was being held in a back chamber of the courthouse. It was considered too dangerous to return him to his attic cell; the mob might feel free to steal the curé and exact their own rough justice. Far better he be burned by the Church. But before that happened, there remained one small detail:

A confession. The curé's signature on a single piece of paper absolving the Prosecutor and the Canon, and by extension the bishop, the cardinal, and the king, from all guilt, from any charges of wrongdoing that might be brought before the Parliament of Paris or some such body.

Father Louis, wholly broken, body and soul, said that he could not confess to crimes he had not committed. Neither could he identify accomplices he had never known.

But that wouldn't do. Not at all. He *must* sign. Only a signed confession would silence the skeptics, the anti-cardinalists or other critics of the proceedings who might speak up despite the fines. No, the facts of the trial would not, *could* not be called into question, and so a confession was all-important. Of course, such a document could easily be forged, but the bishop had warned the cabal against this, expressly.

Father Louis refused. Once, twice ... twenty times. The cabal conferred. What to do? Perhaps the priest would change his mind under the Question; after all, hadn't that device drawn its share of confessions? "Still," said the Prosecutor, "let us put the screws to the goat, tonight," and so the executioner was sent for. Found at his dinner table, the family gathered to dine on celebratory duck (for the executioner had been paid in advance for the next day's work), the executioner excused himself and his eldest son who, at sixteen, six months into his apprenticeship, had not yet mastered the screws, and the two set off for the courthouse.

Just as the executioner (Monsieur Martin Boileau by name, who'd learned his trade at his father's side and was now first in his field, having hanged and tortured hundreds, from Marseilles to Poitiers) and his son (Boileau *fils*, named Jacques) arrived at court, a clerk announced that Madeleine de la Mettrie wished to be heard.

"Pardon me, sir, if you will," said the red-faced clerk.

"What is it? Speak," said the Prosecutor.

"The witch, sir . . . I mean, the girl . . . your daughter is here. At the back door, sir."

The Prosecutor refused her, said that the proceedings had been concluded. Court had been dismissed. The thirteen magistrates were disbanded, were scattered about in as many taverns taking their supper. No. Deny her. Send the girl away. He then ordered the executioner to set the screws on the priest's left hand. "Leave the right free to sign the confession—but tear the nails off if need be."

But as the clerk turned to leave the chamber and return to Madeleine, the exorcist raised his tubular device of carved elm and enameled tortoise shell to his ear and asked what the matter was. When told, he said that he would hear the girl.

The Prosecutor seethed. He asked, *begged* the exorcist to reconsider. When he would not, the Prosecutor directed the executioner to turn the thumbscrew, and so it was that Madeleine entered the antechamber to the accompaniment of her beloved's screams.

Madeleine saw again the wraith, the man who had once been the handsome and prideful Curé of St. Pierre. She stood before him now as the blood pulsed from his thumb, spurted up into the air, higher with each turn of the screw. She could not look away. Neither could she speak.

After the verdict, she'd returned unguarded to the Capeau home, for she'd nowhere else to go. There, she listened to Sabine being cheered in the square, asking herself how it had come to this. The sounds of the square resounded in her head. Then there came the blessed rain, and the square quieted. She could think. She could hate herself for the foolish plan she'd had. How could she have been so naive? Now Louis would burn, and she was as much to blame as crooked, conniving, crazed Sabine. Yes, she and her coming child would be marked forever by the blood of the priest, blood that would boil on the morrow.

Moments before Sabine returned home (drunk for the first time, having happily agreed to dine with the rich cardinalist, Monsieur de Sourdis and his family), Madeleine came to understand that she was unguarded, after long months of captivity. Of course: what did they care for her now that the trial was over? She'd come back to this prison of her own accord.

Quickly, she gathered up a cloak belonging to Monsieur Capeau. She found an oil lantern. She fashioned a noose from the leather tether that fell down through the house's three stories and was tied to the servant's bell in the kitchen. Then she slipped from the kitchen into a back alley. Alley to alley in the cold rain, shadow to shadow through the darkest parts of the night, she made her way to the courthouse. Did she think that her Louis would be there alone? That she'd finally be able to tell him what she'd done, beg his forgiveness for having failed him? Effect a rescue? Or had she known that the core of the court, minus the magistrates, would still be convened? Had she hoped to be heard as, now, she was?

Madeleine was led by the clerk into that antechamber of the courthouse, its stone walls ringing with the screams of the man she'd come to save.

Then: "Speak, child." It was the exorcist.

The executioner's son stopped turning the screws. Louis, his drawn face and chest awash with blood, was conscious, barely so. His head lolled about on his shoulders, rolled right to left, forward and back, as though his neck had been broken.

Her father stood far across the room staring out a high window at the starless dark, his arms folded across his chest. Canon Mignon glared at her through tiny reptilian eyes, beads of sweat slipping over his high freckled forehead, over his razor-thin upper lip. As Madeleine spoke, all present turned from her. All save the exorcist.

Madeleine explained every part of her plan and how it had failed. She said she had lied. She was *not* lying now as she told of the midnight marriage, the child to come, and the love she bore for the priest. The love he had shown her. She was let to speak the truth; and the priest's condemnation was complete.

For, learning of that sacrilegious ceremony and its satanic issue, staring at its living proof, the exorcist averred that he'd heard the most damning and damaging words of all. On behalf of the bishop, the cardinal, and the king, he ordered the "whore-child" out of the courthouse.

Madeleine screamed, started to scream and could not stop. The clerk could not control her. The executioner's son laid his bloodied hands on her. She managed to show the noose (only then did she know why she'd crafted it, expertly, as she'd seen her father do countless times; it was a hobby of his: nooses of rope, twine, licorice . . .). "If you kill him," said she, swinging the noose toward the priest, who'd come to full consciousness, "you kill us! You will all stew an eternity in our innocent blood!" She damned them all. She taunted her father with her swelled stomach.

Somehow she broke from the clerk and the executioner's son, whose grip was slick with blood, and ran to Louis. She fell to her knees and kissed his broken hands. The clerk tore her away, controlled her: her arms were breaking behind her. Only then did the Prosecutor train his eyes on his daughter; and he strode to the barely conscious curé and with one quick twist turned the screws himself. Blood. Clots of it falling onto the curé's forearms. Father Louis screamed. Again the exorcist ordered Madeleine cast from the court; but first, slowly, he bent to retrieve the noose from where it had fallen in the fray; solemnly, ceremoniously, he slipped it over Madeleine's head, and with his thick thumb he forged a cross on her forehead.

Madeleine landed in the alley on her back. A sharp slipping pain stabbed her abdomen. Rats scattered over the crooked cobbles. Rain fell, gathered in pitch-black pools. She was ashen; bloodless. Drained by rage. As she lay in the alley her screams devolved to crying. An instant or an eternity; it might have been either. The rats grew brave and crept ever closer. Then the door to the courthouse opened and she saw a man in silhouette. Louis! It was Louis! She scrambled onto her knees (the slipping, the *ripping* pain!) and began to beg his forgiveness, swear her love and vow that they three would—

Then the silhouette turned, just so, and she saw the man in profile. That horrible hook of a nose. Not Louis. Her father, who raised the small lantern Madeleine had carried with her from the Capeaus'. Madeleine hadn't time to think, let alone speak or act before she saw the lantern coming at her end over end through the darkness to burst at her knee. Glass flew up into her face. The scurrying rats were a gray-black wave breaking over the stones. Hundreds of them, it seemed. Moving in a rippling motion away from the explosion, the fire. . . . The flame had caught the hem of the cloak she wore. It was on fire. *She* was on fire. Still she sat, as the flames twisted deeper into the cloak. She felt fire on her hands, fire on her arms and shoulders, fire on the drum-tight skin of her belly. . . .

She stood up hurriedly, stripped herself of the burning cloak and cast it like a red net over the stones. The burning oil was smothered; it expired with a hiss.

Madeleine, newly purposed, walked calmly from the alley in her shift, the rough, wet fabric of which clung to her every curve. Still she wore the noose. Blood at her knees, blood pooling with rain in the heels of her slippers, she walked back to the house that had been her prison, the house where a drunken Sabine lay sleeping. A quarter-moon shone through wisps of blue cloud.

Shadows fell thickly at the feet of the stone-and-timber homes that leaned over the streets. In the square, people peered out from under their tarps and men called to her. Sums of money were mentioned. Two men approached her directly; upon seeing her state and her vacant stare, they let her pass. Whores danced in dark corners, staring out over the hunched shoulders of the men who bucked against them. A carriage nearly ran her over, the horses rearing wildly at the last moment and the driver cursing down, brandishing his crop. Madeleine was oblivious to everything but her purpose. The world as it was fell away.

The next morning, dawn showed the square of Q—— already crowded. Every window had been let. Spectators sat on the peaks of slate roofs. Boys straddled the gargoyles that jutted out from the high corners of the church. A grandstand had been set up for the cabal, the magistrates, and their guests, but the rabble had taken every seat and had to be dislodged by guards at the point of pike and halberd. Blood was shed. Two tourists and one guard were killed.

With the sun not yet high in the sky, the condemned was sent for.

In their excitement, the cabal forgot to force the curé to make his amends, to beg forgiveness of God, the king and Justice. Instead the Prosecutor ordered Father Louis led directly to the Question.

A second platform had been hammered together hurriedly in the night. It stood across from the grandstand. Set before the church doors, it resembled those stages wheeled from village to village by traveling players; its boards were pitched so as to afford the assembled a better view. The crowd would riot for certain if they could not see the executioner at work.

Across the square stood the high stake, sticks and loose straw piled at its base.

The bells of St. Pierre struck nine.

The privileged took their seats. An uncommon quiet settled over the crowd. The executioner and his assistant, clad in black from head to toe, hidden—though many present knew the men by name—climbed atop the platform to a chorus of cheers. There followed the Prosecutor, the Canon, the exorcist, and the condemned.

The mob pressed forward.

The Prosecutor spoke to the curé. His words were heard by those nearest the platform, who turned and whispered behind them, and so on and so on, a sibilance snaking its way through the entire square.

"You are a magician," said the Prosecutor, "and have had commerce with the Devil! *Answer!*"

The curé responded, "I have been a man, and have loved as a man must." His words spread through the square. Random cheers rose up.

The Canon: "You admit it then, demon! You have broken every vow!"

"A promise to perform the impossible is not binding." Those words would appear on many a souvenir. The crowd grew frenzied. As it was some time before they fell quiet again, no one heard the curé say, as he stared across the square at the stake, "Such vows are as straw to the fire in the blood." But many people saw him summon his remaining strength and spit into the face of the Canon.

The crowd was verily crazed. Men and women nearest the platform spat upon it.

Father Tranquille stepped forward to exorcise the ropes, boards, wedges, and mallets of the Question. He sprinkled these tools with holy water, lest the Devil work some infernal art and render them useless. Then he heard a quick confession from the executioner and his son, who set to work in haste.

They tied the curé to a thick board, twice as wide as himself, and tilted it toward the crowd. They enclosed his legs, from knee to foot, between four oak boards; the outer pair were fixed, and the two inner movable. The son readied the wedges, which the father would drive between the two movable boards, crushing the curé's legs against the outer boards. This was the ordinary Question; the extraordinary involved wider wedges and would come later.

The Prosecutor, against all custom, came forward and took for himself the task of placing the first wedge. Between the knees of the priest. The executioner raised the mallet high, higher, both hands on the long worn handle . . .

The wedge drove the boards beside the priest's knees a finger's-width closer, just enough to split the sturdy bone of the kneecaps.

The crowd cheered and ordered more, *more!*

Father Louis, tied to the board and tilted forward, saw through his tears the thousands who mocked his murder. He tried to pray, but could not. What god, he wondered, would leave him alone beneath a blue and cloudless sky to die? To be tortured. Burned. He was guilty of love, perhaps an excess of its practice. But he'd had faith, and had served his god well. Now this.

Father Louis tried to hide his pain, tried to deprive his torturers of the joy of his pain. Something quick and hot shot up his legs from the burst bones of his knees to settle in the small of his back. Do not *show* them, he thought. Do not let them see. Do not fear the falling mallet. He began counting backward from one thousand. He closed his eyes and recalled the faces and bodies of his lovers. None more readily than Madeleine's. Madeleine. Hadn't he heard her yesterday, between turns of those screws that had wrenched the nails from his fingers and ruined his hands till they now hung like tattered pennants? Hadn't he heard her confess her failed plan, and say she loved him? Say she'd only come to save him? He thought so, yes.

A cry rose from the crowd as the second wedge was shown them. Father Louis felt the hot breath—scented with ginger beer—of the executioner's son, standing so close beside him, watching his lips, waiting for them to twist into the shape of a confession. They would not. The boy held the written confession. Five times the priest let the quill fall to the boards. He would not sign. Never. No pain could make him. No pain . . .

Father Louis realized that within the hour, when the mallets' work was done, he would be trundled across the square, tied to the stake, and set afire. He would burn. Die.

Count! Count against the coming flames! But here was the Canon, standing over him, the rubies and hammered gold of his cross glistening in the sun. Father Louis refused to sign a sixth and final time.

The second wedge then. At the feet, snapping and smashing the small bones like so many twigs. And the third, placed near the first: the bones of the knee broke the skin; marrow oozed.

The curé's world was alternately lit and extinguished, loud and silenced as he drifted in and out of consciousness. Always those damnable salts brought him back to life, only to die again.

He damned his torturers, but the crowd was crazed now, with the mallet falling fast, and no one but young Jacques, the executioner's son and assistant, heard his words.

A fourth, very wide wedge broke the curé's ankles. They gave with a pop that resounded in the square.

Then the fifth, sixth, and seventh wedges. The shins and thighs. More for the ankles and feet. Bone shattered, splintering the red and gray flesh. The trays that held the legs in place were sluiceways; blood, marrow, and splintered bone ran from them at the curé's heels. (The executioner's son gathered the red stew in buckets; later the family would join the tourist trade, selling vials of it, cut with two parts river water, as relics.)

Father Louis wanted to die. Tried to die; willed it. But neither the cabal nor the crowd would be deprived.

A chant began: *Burn him! Burn the holy devil!*

The Canon summoned the Surgeon, who ascended the platform. Did he think the curé could survive another wedge, perhaps two? Mannoury opined that yes, the priest might survive several wedges more; but, he said, it was best not to risk it. The crowd would not look kindly upon a burning corpse. Keep the curé alive. Stop the Question and start the burning. The Prosecutor wanted to drive more wedges, though the executioner said the Question was already well past the extraordinary stage; if they were to keep on, his boy would have to run home for wider wedges. The exorcist convinced the Prosecutor to stop. It was clear, said he, that the curé had invoked his Dark God, that Satan had rendered the priest insensible to pain. They might drive wedge after wedge, even work the arms, but all to no avail, for Satan had surely interceded.

The Prosecutor ordered the Question dismantled. The crowd clapped in a ritualized rhythm.

The curé received the strongest of the salts and was made to swallow vinegar and oil from a deerskin bladder. Lime juice was rubbed into his cracked lips. Then the executioners stripped the priest (careful to save the stained shift for resale) and slipped a nightshirt, stinking of sulfur, over his head. A rope was wound twice around his waist and tied off. They then carried him down to a cart that stood at the ready, harnessed to two mules. He was hoisted up and set on a bench. His legs hung shapeless before him. The executioner's son knelt at the priest's side, balancing him, salting him to consciousness time and again. Young Jacques must have been thankful then for his thick hood and half-mask, for the crowd rained stones, sticks, and overripe fruit upon the slow-moving cart.

The driver whipped the confused beasts till their hides split. Finally, preceded by a company of archers who divided the crowd, the cabal, the thirteen magistrates, the exorcist, and assorted cardinalists all made their way across the square to the stake. The cart came behind them.

The crowd closed in on the cart. Rocked it side to side. At one point the priest fell from the bench and, having no knees left to break his fall, fell flat onto his chest and face. The boy quickly lifted the now-conscious curé up by the rope tied round his waist and set the much larger man on his lap, like a doll sewn of rags. He held tightly to him, *showed* him, for his safety depended on it.

The curé spoke. A ragged, stertorous whisper. "Searcher of Hearts, know that I am not guilty of these crimes imputed to me, and that the fire in which I will die is but punishment for my concupiscence." He looked at the boy who held him, at the wide-set pale blue eyes peering out through the half-mask. "Redeemer of Man, do not forgive my enemies. Punish them, as I cannot." Tears, fearful tears slid from the boy's eyes, ran down over the cracked hide of the mask. Just then the cart halted at the stake and his father relieved young Jacques of his charge.

A small iron seat had been nailed to the stake, just above the straw and stacked wood. Father Louis was lifted from the cart and placed on this seat. The rope at his waist was used to tie him to the stake; it was wound once around his waist and once around his neck to keep him upright; a second rope was used to bind his hands behind him.

Father Tranquille exorcised the stake and sprinkled holy water on the wood, the straw, the executioner, the crowd, and the condemned. He prayed against those demons waiting to deny justice, who would somehow prevent the priest from the suffering that was his due.

The Prosecutor and the Canon approached Father Louis, confession and quill in hand. More salts and a mouthful of lime juice forced on him from a wooden cup. "I have nothing to confess," managed Father Louis. "Give me the Kiss of Peace and let me die." The Canon refused him. Those spectators at the fore of the crowd who knew what the condemned man had requested chanted against the Canon and so un-Christian an act as his refusal of the Kiss. And so the Canon kissed the curé's cheek. The crowd jeered. A woman, safe in the anonymity of the mob, shouted that the Canon owed the curé the Devil's Kiss, and a new chant was taken up, one that shamed and angered the Canon.

Strangulation at the stake was customary, but the Prosecutor had seen that this was left from the curé's sentence. He was to be burned alive. The crowd, very few of whom had bothered to read the verdict against the curé, posted all over Q—— the previous night, did not know this. And so, when the Prosecutor and Canon Mignon gathered fistfuls of flaming straw, lit at the lantern swinging stake-side for this purpose, the crowd stopped chanting of the Devil's Kiss and took up a new, one-word cry: *Strangle! Strangle! Strangle!*

The Prosecutor set the straw aflame and, quick as the flames took hold, the crowd fell silent. The Canon lit the sulfured hem of the curé's nightshirt.

And Father Louis began to burn.

Silence. Soon the sound of sizzling flesh. The stench. The priest's screams— no, it was not a scream; he hadn't the strength to scream. It was an even more pitiable sound, high-pitched and hurried, like that of a rabbit caught in a trap.

A radiant pulsing among the assembled. A rush like lust. And the twigs and straw and chunks of wood catching fast, crackling, snapping.

Smoke. Swirling white smoke. Pure white. Obscuring sight.

And then from the center of the white smoke came the sound of coughing, choking.

"No!" cried the Prosecutor.

"It cannot be!" said the exorcist. The condemned, aided by his devils, would *indeed* deprive Justice. He would choke on the smoke, suffocate before the pure tongue of flame had licked him clean. Someone, over-eager, had set the straw and kindling and wood out too early; it was wet from the last night's rain; and so it smoked to excess.

The exorcist and Canon Mignon cast holy water on the flames, inveighed against the unseen devils that circled the stake. *Exorciso te, creatura ignis* . . . And more prayer: *Ecce crucem Domini, fugite partes adversae, vicit leo de tribu Juda, radis David . . . in nomine Dei patris omnipotentis, et in nomine Jesu Christi filii ejus Domini nostri, et in virtute Spiritus Sancti* . . . They ran around the stake, the trains of their black robes tracing the circle of flame. They swung crucifixes and thurifers of frankincense. The executioner fell back, staring at the two old men who danced around the stake looking more demonic than anyone or anything he'd ever seen.

Father Louis slipped from light to darkness, from screams to silence.

Conscious, he felt the flames lick at his crushed feet. Rising up the torn, tattered flesh of his legs. He could not move his legs. He was stuck like meat on a spit. Roasting. The sulfur of his nightshirt caught the flames and spread them over his back, chest, and arms. The flames on the flanks of his back and buttocks were the worst. He looked down through the choking smoke to see the skin of his feet burning away from the bone. He could not feel it. His eyes fell shut. Darkness.

Light.

He heard strange rites being read. He fell again into the pain, descended. Darkness. Light. . . . Finally, he had the answer to a prayer: he knew that neither heaven nor hell would open for him.

The executioner, seized by something, a spirit of sorts, stepped into the flames. He reached around the screaming curé's head from behind and snapped his neck. One quick twist.

And Father Louis died. The living Father Louis died.

And, as though summoned by the snap of the spine, there descended into the square a flock of bright birds. Flying noiselessly down from every tree, turret, and spire off the square. Pigeons and doves. Whirling silver and white wings like blades. Hundreds. Thousands. Cutting through the bright white smoke, which itself took on the scent of violets, the deeply sweet scent of violets. Dipping, diving, wheeling down around the stake and through the flames, singeing their wings.

The exorcist stood as the birds circled low. His lips moved in mumbled prayer. He gagged against the sweet perfume, knew it to be the Odor of Sanctity. His thoughts were of the Apocalyptic Moment. Henceforth, he'd speak only nonsense.

Canon Mignon fell prayerfully to his knees. Here was the miracle of evil he had waited a lifetime to see! Demons! Come to carry the curé home! He rose to stand in the flames and begged deliverance of Satan. Canon Mignon never uttered another word save prayers to Satan. The burns on his feet, legs, and hands, and their resultant infections, would be recorded as the cause of his death, which came one month to the day.

Panic ensued in the square. Some in the crowd fell to the ground beneath the birds. Hundreds ran choking from the square. Fifteen people were trampled to death, their names to be published in a memorial broadside bearing the title, "The Innocent Dead."

The executioner slipped from the square into the Church of St. Pierre to pray. The Prosecutor, the Surgeon, and Monsieur Adam remained in the square, cowering beneath the grandstand. Within the year they would all be dead: Monsieur Adam would choke on a potion taken against impotence; the Surgeon was waylaid on the Marseilles Road and stabbed thirteen times by thieves; as for the Prosecutor, he would start to hear voices that very night and, on the first anniversary of the burning, he would do as they bade him and climb up the bell tower of St. Pierre to hang himself.

Of course, none of these deaths were quite what they appeared to be. No poisoning. No robbery. No suicidal urges. Father Louis and Madeleine returned to haunt these men, kill them each and every one in turn; and each man, at the moment of his death, knew it. Saw the faces of the priest and girl and knew, *knew* their fates to be in the hands of devils.

As for Father Louis, he burned down to ash.

The smoke eventually cleared, the scent lifted. The silver and white birds stopped circling, though for days they could be seen ringing the square, in the trees, in eaves, and on statues. Indeed, in Q——, for long years to come, those present at the burning swore they could see the birds, swore they could smell the violets.

The curé's ashes were never scattered, at least not in the manner set forth in the sentence. Rather, late that night, when the flames had died, a few of the faithful and many tourists returned to sift through the warm, unguarded ashes. They hunted the warm dust for pieces of charred flesh, bones, or still-hot teeth. Some searched for relics. Some for souvenirs. Still others sought simple charms that might bring luck or compel love.

What no one knew that day was this: that as the flames and white smoke rose up, as the executioner broke the neck of the curé and the birds and floral stench descended, a thief, under cover of the ceremony in the square, broke into the home of Monsieur Capeau, knowing only that it was the finest on the square. What the thief found, in addition to silver and money enough to sail fast from Marseilles, lest he be implicated in his bloody discovery, was this: the bodies of two young women.

For Madeleine had beaten Sabine to death. Had gone up the back stairs slowly from the kitchen, in her hand an iron of cast steel. With the iron she crushed the skull of the sleeping Sabine. She then descended to the library, the same library in which she'd been coached by Canon Mignon, and there she passed dark hours in a state resembling prayer, suffering extraordinary pains she did not understand. She had her letters. She untied the ribbons that held all the letters she'd never sent to her lover and unborn child. She fanned the letters out around her. She lit a fire and consigned the letters, slowly, one at a time, to the flames. (The ever-increasing pain!) She listened to the commotion in the square that night, heard the hammering together of the second scaffold. The night passed; dawn came. So too did the child, poisoned and abused to an early birth; and death. Madeleine waited. And just as the crowd's cheers told her that the Question was about to begin, she took up the small forked tool used to take coals from the brazier and with what strength remained to her she raked its three blackened tines down the length of her throat. She tore out her tongue. Wrested it from her neck. She choked fast on the upwelling blood.

The thief entered the library last. He'd moved fast through the upper rooms, and had seen only Sabine's stunted left leg, for in her death throes she'd slid from her bed and lay between it and the wall. Still, it was evident a crime had been committed. Blood on the pillows, blood splattered across the silk moiré wallpaper. Then, discovering a second body in the library, one in so gruesome a state, and with the stillborn child blue in the cradle of her legs . . . seeing this, and realizing too that he already had more than he could carry in the way of wares, the thief left the house as he'd entered it, quickly, and through a kitchen window.

That night Monsieur Capeau returned to Q——, and a burgled and bloodied house from which he'd long been absent. Within the month he'd sell it at considerable profit.

Sabine, one bright morning in mid-October, was buried in sacred ground. It was a grand funeral. Only tourists and the truly curious were in attendance.

The child, a girl, was cut from its mother and burned in the ovens of the Foundling Hospital. Madeleine, as a suicide, was interred at a crossroads well beyond the city walls. Scant rites were read.

14

Escape

Not long after the tale was told, Father Louis, seated at the window, broke the silence with, "She's come," and I watched as he waved to one below.

She comes! said Madeleine. It was as though her sad fate, so recently recounted, was that of another. *Sebastiana comes!* She said it thrice more. Excited, the red-black lips of her wound verily pulsed; clotted blood fell from its edges, and from its center blood spurted as though from an opened vein. Her *speech*—what else to call it?—loosed a torrent of blood to run down the sides of her split-open throat.

Gently, but with preternatural strength and speed, Father Louis came to lift me from atop the table, where I'd remained all through the tale. He was laughing, and smiling at the succubus. As though he stood before a misbehaving and well-loved child whom he could not scold and must indulge. "I must apologize for my companion," said he. "She is excited: she has waited centuries for this day."

Madeleine had made her way to the windowsill. I heard her say again that name that was new to me. I looked to Father Louis.

"She says Sebastiana has come. Sebastiana d'Azur." And then, suddenly, he returned to the window, signaling to someone out there in the late dark, in the early dawn.

Blood betrayed Madeleine's fast path from the table to the sill. And now blood formed a red ring, a spreading nimbus around her feet, slick on the stony floor.

"Sebastiana comes," repeated Father Louis.

As does the dawn. This from Madeleine. *We must hurry if we are to*—I didn't understand the rest of her words. I was, it is fair to say, stunned; exhausted and awestruck. And I was sore, terribly sore where the incubus had had his way. "What . . ." I began, "what is happening here?"

"Hush," said Father Louis. He came so quickly toward me that I stepped back and stumbled, nearly fell. "Don't be afraid," he said, steadying me. "And don't ask for explanations. Now is not the time. Indeed, we've not much time at all." *There exists the inexplicable;* this I told myself.

The priest placed his cold, vise-like hands atop my shoulders. "The soreness," he said, pride in his tone, "*that* soreness will be with you awhile. But you enjoyed yourself, no?" I didn't respond. Or perhaps I smiled. It was then I realized that the soreness I was regretting was not the soreness the incubus had caused; rather, it was the soreness that Sister Claire had inflicted.

Sister Claire de Sazilly. I'd nearly forgotten her, for I had not felt the effects of that beating all through the tale of Q——; and afterward, I'd been fast overwhelmed by . . . *Alors,* here it came again: the blue skin, no longer broken but still tender to the touch, and the blood crusted in the angles of my ear, and the swollen lip still aching where it had been split. With this slight pain—it was slight, yes—there came again the anger, the wild red anger. As for that other soreness, Father Louis's, it was easily suffered. "Ah, yes," said he. "Savor it. Savor that soreness while it lasts."

Look! said Madeleine then; and I moved to join her and the incubus at the library window, the mullioned panes of which were coated with the slightest rime, like the shavings of diamonds. I saw no one, nothing beneath the pale and cloudless sky. Yes, I saw only the first of the sun, and spoke the dreaded word: "Dawn."

A rustling in the gallery beyond the lesser library's back door, or was it in the corridor? Had the others heard it? I looked to Father Louis, who said, with a sigh, "Yes, I know. They're all about, already; like mice in the night." And then he sat cross-legged on the table's edge, his arms folded across his broad chest. He shrugged his shoulders, as if to say, *Sorry*, and said, "Tell me while we wait: do you know who we are?"

"While we wait for what?" I asked. I was all atremble. I was naked and cold and certain I'd die within the hour. I considered trying the doors. I was ready to run.

Madeleine and Louis looked me up and down, appraisingly. I felt no shame; I didn't recoil from their sight. This surprised me. It surprises me still.

Madeleine came to me from the window—again, she moved as fast as light; she had the torn pink dress in hand and though it was horribly, grossly red-stained, I welcomed its warmth on my shoulders. An instant later I saw the succubus sitting atop the table beside the priest, who asked again: "Do you know who we are?"

"I know who you *were*." I whispered it: my throat was sore from ill-use.

"Ah, very good," said Father Louis. "But do you know who, or *what* we are now?"

I could only nod in weak assent. What words might I have offered then to explain what I'd learned? *Trust and learn.*

"All right," said the priest, "we'll get to that later. Tell me, do you know who *you* are?"

I said my name in full.

"Of course," said Father Louis lightly. He looked at Madeleine. "What I mean is, well . . . can you tell us *what* you are?"

I heard those words again. *You are a woman. You are a man.* But I could not repeat them. How could they be true? Yet didn't I *know* them to be true? *What*, in fact, was I? Am I?

(Yes, yes, there are words to describe what I am, my *state* if you will, my physiology. But I choose not to use such words; for all their Latinate elegance, they are ugly, and *I* am not ugly. I know that now; and so those words do not suffice.)

I said nothing. And when Father Louis started to say again, "You are a—"

He was interrupted. By a voice I'd never heard before. Coming from behind me, near the library's secondary door. "You, dear one," it said—a woman's voice, smooth, warm, and mellifluous—"you are a witch. And you, *mon prêtre*, ought not to tease." I *longed* to turn toward that voice—how did I resist?—but something stilled me.

Father Louis offered a baldly insincere apology. To me? To this Sebastiana? (For surely it was she who'd come.) It didn't much matter. Only then did I turn to see her standing there beside the now open gallery door. I hadn't heard the door open, and I knew my jailers had locked it when they'd left: I'd heard the rattling chains. Surely she hadn't been in the library all night, in the same shadows from which the others had stepped. But how then had she entered the library?

"Did you hear me, heart?" she asked. "Did you hear what I said?"

I shook my head. She said it a second time:

"You are a witch."

I said nothing. Had no reaction at all. I simply stared at this . . . this *apparition*:

A tall thin beautiful woman. Older. She wore diaphanous robes whose blue rivaled that of her eyes. Such extraordinary eyes! "Azur, dear," said she. "Sebastiana d'Azur." Indeed her eyes *were* azure blue. Part sapphire, part sea. Her long black hair fell forward over her shoulder in a thick plait. Her skin was the whitest I'd ever seen. A near deathlike pallor. But this woman, I knew, was *alive*. And this—need I say it?—was a great relief!

She—this Sebastiana d'Azur—came toward me. As she moved, slowly, deliberately, she undid the hasp of a huge bloodstone broach at her shoulder, freeing one of the robes she wore. Panels of fabric, they were—silk and satin. She took the pink dress from my shoulders, said something about needing it to "effect the trick." She then stepped back from my nakedness to look me up and down; she did this without comment. She came closer and wrapped me in that bolt of blue. Her arms around me . . . Ah, the rush I felt then of her warmth, so different from the deathly touch of the incubus. She stood so close she had only to whisper, and as she dressed me she did so, saying: "Not because you are naked, but because you are cold." And she knotted the robe at my shoulder.

I asked her who she was.

It was Madeleine who replied in hurried tones. *Know that she is the only one who can save you, and ask no more questions.*

Sebastiana looked to Madeleine—not at all kindly, it seemed to me—and said, "I am the only one who can save her, yes. But she is the only one who can save *you*. . . . So mind your tongue, Madeleine." These last words were rather cruel, of course. And I'd no idea what Sebastiana meant. *Me* save Madeleine?

My wonderment must have shown on my face, for Sebastiana said, "Ah yes, dear, all in due time." She moved toward the window. "But time, I'm afraid, is what we've precious little of. For the dawn—"

The dawn, said Madeleine to me, in a crazed rush, *will see you dead unless you do as you are told!*

(I know now that Madeleine was not mad; she was eager, exceedingly so, and scared lest we fail at what we, at what *they* had come to do.)

Sebastiana turned back from the window. She smiled at me and, moving to where the succubus sat beside the priest, said, looking disdainfully down at the stained table, the stained stone floor, "Madeleine, can't you do something about that . . . that *damned* blood. It really is so unsightly."

Father Louis could not help but laugh. As for Madeleine, she turned from Sebastiana, who, loosing her gaze from the chastened succubus, was reminded by Father Louis that Madeleine's blood flow could not be helped; what's more, said he, there was little point in cleaning it up: one had only to wait seven hours for it to fade away.

"Yes, yes, I know," said Sebastiana. "But I've always found that to be seven hours too long."

Madeleine slipped from beside the incubus. I nearly succeeded in tracing her movement to the window.

"Well," said Sebastiana, summarily, "would that we had seven hours to effect an escape from this cell, but we do not," and I saw that she was looking beyond Madeleine, gauging the brightening sky; already the coming sun had begun to light the shadowed corners of the library. Sebastiana began to pace, and this same faint light showed her to be naked beneath her thin robes. As for the priest, he sat perched on the table. Finally, from Sebastiana: "You, Madeleine. Did you do as planned?"

I did. . . . Of course, I did.

"Good. Then we have only to wait—"

Just then we all of us turned toward the corridor. From it came the sound of voices. How many voices I could not say. But one voice I knew, heard distinctly: that of Sister Claire de Sazilly.

I stepped back from that door. Retreated. Nearer Sebastiana.

"They come, yes," said Sebastiana, smiling at me. "Good, good, good."

"But Sister Claire, she—" I stammered.

"A handful, that one, eh?" And I watched as Sebastiana squared her shoulders, turned to face the main door full on.

"They are coming," I said, panicked. "Should we not run and—"

"Indeed not, dear." She dismissed the idea.

I shot quick looks all around the library—at the main door, still locked and bolted no doubt; at Louis and Madeleine, standing in the last of the library's shadows; at the open window, the open gallery door. Where could I hide? Should I run? Why was no one bothered by this, the advent of my accusers, of Sister Claire? So calm, they were! "Shouldn't we at least—"

"You are safe, dearest," said Sebastiana. She then raised her arm and I stood so near I had only to take a half-step more for her to settle that arm around my shoulder. She turned just so to kiss my forehead. "We haven't much time, it is true, and there remain a great many details . . . but you are safe." Sebastiana was warm to the touch: *she* was alive; and this only served to remind me that my other two saviors were not.

I leaned into Sebastiana. I felt the comforting weight of her breast, the curve of her hip. My arms hung slack at my sides; I dared not touch this woman, not directly, but how I reveled in her warmth, sank into the warmth and safety of her embrace.

I looked at her beautiful face: it bore the traces of her age—shallow creases, thread-thin wrinkles—yet the skin was smooth and pale, and the cheeks were rouged. I saw too that she'd painted her lips red. Her lashes were long and black; they were straight, and so gave to her eyes an ease, an indolence. . . . Those eyes . . . I noticed too a scent, what was it? Lime water? No. *Roses.* Ah, yes . . . roses. Unmistakably. She wore one in her hair, tucked into the first strands of that long black braid. Fresh, its petals red. Red too the coral combs in her hair. And red the stones in the silver earrings that hung low, tossing off the rising light of day.

She stepped from me then, left me standing alone. "But, but . . ." I stammered, pointing toward the library's main door. Sebastiana made no response; instead she moved to the table on which sat the empty platter, not long ago loaded with roasted squab and such. She traced the painted *S* at the platter's center with a long thin finger, its nail red-lacquered; she sucked at her fingertip and asked, "It was good, no?" I nodded that yes, it was.

"*S* for Sebastiana," I said.

"Indeed," said she; and she took a seat on the table's edge. The platter was hers. As were all the *S*-marked books I'd read.

With that commotion in the corridor coming ever nearer—it was Sister Claire, certainly, but in whose company?—Sebastiana, nearly as tall as I, tilted her head just slightly. Somehow she drew my eyes to hers. She stood a few steps from me, in the still-dim library, but I was certain I saw her eyes. . . .

Oh, those *eyes!* Yes, that was when she first showed me *l'oeil de crapaud.* The witches' eye. And I saw that those blue eyes of hers, like Maluenda's, had at their center—

Attendons. Wait. I will speak of those eyes—I swear it—but just then, as I stood staring into Sebastiana's shape-shifting eyes, I heard those voices—mere steps from the door!—or rather that *single* voice break into a stream of invective and prayer. This I could not conceive; who or what could frighten Sister Claire so? Then, from deep within her cries there rose up two words of Latin:

"*Dis Pater*," said she, repeatedly. *Father of the Night*.

She spoke those words not to, but rather *at* someone. The nun was not alone. I heard a man's voice. But whose? I heard the breaking of the chain, the sliding back of the bolt. And the library's primary door was thrown open to show Sister Claire de Sazilly trapped half-naked in the arms of a man.

The largest man I had ever seen. Tall and broad and blond, with thick arms that seemed to wrap twice around the struggling nun. He filled the doorway. Then, as a child lets go a toy top, he spun the nun from his hold and sent her reeling into the library proper, where she landed dizzily on the stone floor at Sebastiana's feet. He stepped through the door behind her—stooping to do so—and running his hand through the curls of gold that hung to his shoulders, he hissed, "*Damnable bitch!*" and kicked the length of broken chain toward the nun. (How he broke the chain, I've no idea.) "She *bit* me!" He pushed up the full sleeve of his white blouse to show the marks on his thick wrist. Sebastiana said nothing, but it seemed the corners of her lips rose ever so slightly. As for Father Louis, he laughed aloud. At that the man slammed shut the library door.

"Quiet!" chided Sebastiana. "They will come soon enough without us drawing them here."

"Tell that to this screaming . . . *thing!*" said the man, bending over Sister Claire and taking up a length of broken chain to wind around his fist. All the while he glared at Sister Claire, who continued her litany of curses and prayers. "Yes, yes, prattle on, you scheming, sanctimonious Christ-whore!"

This man was Sebastiana's age, perhaps a bit younger. Remarkably strong, the muscles of his forearms moved like snakes in a sack as he worked that chain. Indeed, it seemed he might pulverize the chain, grind it down to a silver powder. It seemed too that he might at any moment *work* the chain upon Sister Claire. With a single strike of his chain-wrapped fist he could split her head and . . . But all he did was speak, mocking Sister Claire, in simpering tones: " '*Dis Pater!* Satan!' Keep on! But be warned: flattery will not save you." His wide, full mouth was twisted into a sneer, and his squared jaw, covered with some days' growth of beard, was fiercely set. His eyes were a green to rival the blue of Sebastiana's, and they shone out coolly from under his brow.

As I admired him—not knowing I did so, at first—he turned and faced me for the first time. He took me in without comment, without expression. I felt my heart stop. I did not, *could* not draw a breath. Finally, thankfully, he looked away. Turning back to Sebastiana he said, flatly, "Let me kill her. Here and now." I thought for a moment he meant me, and I—But no. He meant, of course, Sister Claire.

Sebastiana rolled her eyes—those eyes!—and sighed. "Patience, patience." And then she tried to calm the man with a question: "Besides," she asked, "won't our plan be more fun than simple, *mere* murder?"

"*Bah!* I want her now!" And with that the man fell to one knee—his black leather boots rose high, over the knee and almost to the thigh; I could not tell where the soft hide ended and his black tights began—and he grabbed Sister Claire by the hair. He cocked his arm, his chain-wrapped fist poised to strike. "Yes," he said, dreamily, "one blow to the face to break the bones of the cheeks. Or perhaps I should slap her into unconsciousness first. Show that much mercy at least. . . . Or should I wring her neck till the skull pops from the spine. *Pop!*" He laughed close in Sister Claire's face. Hers was the face of a corpse dead of fright—the fixed expression of fear. Now he leaned even nearer; his lips fairly touched Sister Claire's as he whispered, "I could kill you forever, and in *infinite* ways." He then let the nun drop back onto the stone— her skull met it with a horrible crack—and he said, "but I won't."

He stood. A full head taller than me. I could not look away from him. Who was he? Clearly he knew Sebastiana and, I assumed, the specters standing silently in the shadowed corner. How many more saviors would come? Yes, strange as they were I knew now that they'd all come to save me. *You are safe. . . .* But all thought withered away as I stood admiring the man. Such strength and beauty. Father Louis was a beautiful man, in life and after; but this being was different, more *animal* than man it seemed. His skin was tanned, bronzed by the sun, but still I could see that his excited blood had risen up the sides of his thick neck, risen to the surface of the thin skin under his eyes. He'd been enraged and was only now growing calmer. I was, at once, afraid and awed. He stood over Sister Claire, and his thinking was plain.

"Asmodei, enough." Sebastiana went to him, placing a hand on his rock-like shoulder to soothe and distract him; it seemed neither the gesture of a sister nor a lover—or was it both at once?—and again I wondered who and what my saviors were, what were they to one another?

"Do you have the case?" asked Sebastiana. "The needles, the things we need?"

The man—Asmodei—nodded; he could not pry his eyes from Sister

Claire, who might have succeeded in crawling from him had he not brought his foot down on her ankle just then, pinning her in place. She screamed and he bent to slap her with the chained fist. "No, no," said Sebastiana. "Behave. . . . Now, do you have the—"

"Yes, yes, I have it," he said. "I have the case." He lifted his shirt and drew from his waistband a thick pouch. A square of black velvet. He handed it to Sebastiana. He looked at her, looked at me (*my heart!*) and, sighing, he walked to the window. "Yes, yes," said Sebastiana; what she meant was, *Yes, go, calm yourself.*

Though her tormentor had left her, Sister Claire knew better than to move. She lay crying on the floor. Her shift of worn burlap had risen over her hips to reveal her sex and the sets of stitch-like scars on either side of her stomach.

Madeleine warned of passing time. She said that the others were gathering downstairs, that indeed they had heard the struggle between Asmodei and Sister Claire, the rattling chains, the slamming door. *They attribute it to the advent of her devils.*

"For once they're right," opined the priest.

Asmodei turned to look at Madeleine, who moved nearer Father Louis. "So be it," said he, emphatically. "Let them come to die one by one! All their spilled blood will not sate me!"

"Mon Dieu," said Sebastiana, "such drama!" She was busy with the contents of that black pouch. "You send me back to the high days *de l'opera!*"

Father Louis's laughter incited the man more.

"I won't have *her,*" said Asmodei, pointing at the succubus, "telling me what to do when—"

"Take your ease, friend," interrupted Father Louis. "All she says is that we must hurry if we are to save the witch."

Save the witch, echoed Madeleine. It was a plea, one she repeated twice more. I assumed she meant me. *I* was the witch to be saved. I concluded this not from what Sebastiana had said earlier. Rather, *I* was the one who needed saving. And quickly.

It did not occur to me to wonder how it was Madeleine tracked the goings-on in the convent that morning. I'd later learn that while we'd all watched Asmodei grapple with the nun, she'd slipped away for the first time, unseen, to speed through the halls of the house. Before we even realized she had left, she returned. She would do this time and again, returning to offer her report.

"All right. Let us start," said Sebastiana.

"Start what?" I asked.

"Hush, dear heart. Do as I say; and ask no questions now." And so when Sebastiana directed me to lie atop the library table, I did. And it was from there—supine and still—that I watched my saviors set to work.

Father Louis cleared the table around me, piling the S-marked books on the windowsill, setting the painted platter and silverware aside and gathering up the torn dress, stained with blood and wine. Madeleine had taken the loaf of hardened black bread; softening it with wine, she fed pieces of it to Maluenda, who seethed audibly at Sister Claire from the library's darkest corner. Indeed, my familiar had returned. (Surely it was she who'd snacked on that rat earlier.) I'd missed her! There she sat now, seemingly fine, her ears cut as they'd been, but she looked no worse for having *flown* from the library's sill. I was so relieved to see that cat again, *so* relieved.

While Sebastiana busied herself with the velvet case and its contents, Asmodei moved to stand over Sister Claire. I watched from where I lay on the long table. I expected him to attack. And judging from Sister Claire's crab-like scampering away at his approach, so too did she. Asmodei, with one lunge, overtook her. He towered over the cowering nun, whose threadbare shift now revealed even more of her body. I saw then the scratches on her neck and face that Maluenda had left; apparently, in the struggle with Asmodei, the clotted wounds had opened and begun to bleed again. She was praying. She wondered aloud why God had shown her Satan, to which Asmodei responded, "You've not seen anything yet, *ma chère*." And with one quick tug he stripped the nun of her shift, tore it from her. And then he tore from her the hairshirt, the rough-dried animal hide she wore beneath her shift. I saw more scars, those horrible markings of her false faith, the black and infected Xs that ringed her hips; the rose thorns she'd sewn into her shift to sanctify her sleep had scarred her deeply. "So," mused Asmodei, speaking to no one in particular while looking the nun up and down, "it seems the good sister has a fondness for pain. Interesting." He knelt, took up that same length of chain again, and leaning into the nun's face, said, "Well, this must be your lucky day, holy one." He fingered a dark scar at her side; this caused the nun to wince. I turned away, toward the window.

But he didn't beat her. All he did, chain in hand, was lift the naked nun and carry her to the table. He laid her down so that, head-to-head, Sister Claire and I covered the length of the table. I could no longer see her, but I could sense her—too near—and I could of course hear her cries until Madeleine, saying she'd heard enough, tore a strip of pink fabric from the dress and fashioned a gag, which she stuffed in the nun's mouth. And then I heard again the rattling of chains as Asmodei, presumably, secured Sister Claire to the table; perhaps he used those same shackles that had held me, perhaps it was some other lock.

Secured as she was, Sister Claire could do nothing but writhe and rock from side to side on the table. Her muffled screams and prayers, her curses and those rattling chains . . . she must have exhausted my saviors' patience, for I heard them confer—the men laughed, though it was Madeleine who first mentioned Maluenda—and next thing I knew they'd set the cat on Sister Claire, on her chest. As if to weight her, still her. Sebastiana cautioned the cat against the too liberal use of her claws. "Only if need be," said she. Sister Claire's cries stopped. Rather, the cries devolved to pleas and more prayer, whimpering, simpering prayer. I could tell she prayed, even though the words themselves tangled in the net of that gag. Yes, her voice was *fraught* with fear. But the cat remained, and the nun lay still beneath it. I wondered if she'd fainted away. I almost pitied her. Almost.

"Are you ready yet?" asked Asmodei.

"Nearly." Sebastiana, who'd been muttering her own imprecations over whatever it was she drew from the velvet case, came close to tell me, with apologies, that I had to be naked. Before I could wonder why, the priest appeared beside me to peel away the thin blue robe Sebastiana had wrapped around me earlier—a bolt of blue silk, really; unfitted, fine. He unwrapped me, slowly, as though I were a gift he'd been given. He *savored* me, looked me up and down. Admired me. "Amazing," said he, setting his icy hands on my small breasts, where the rush of blood took fast effect. He took each thickened nub between a forefinger and thumb and pinched, just so, lightly, as he said to Asmodei, "Come see." . . . Perhaps I was growing accustomed to the priest's . . . *attentions*, but as for this Asmodei . . .

The other man came to stand beside me, just behind Father Louis. "Look," said the priest, waving his hand over my body. "Have you ever seen the like?" But Asmodei did not answer. His eyes ranged up my body to stop at my eyes; his were the hard green of emeralds, emotionless. He neither ridiculed nor admired me. Mere appraisal, it was; and this I took as a kindness. Then I saw Sebastiana pass him the black velvet case. "It is time," said she. I saw again the flash of anger, the flush of blood to his cheeks as Asmodei looked behind me to where Sister Claire lay. Then he stepped back and I could no longer see him.

Hurry, urged the succubus. *The girls are gathered in the Great Hall, waiting only for Sister Claire to descend.* She said too that certain elders and villagers had just arrived.

"Well," said Asmodei, "I'm afraid they'll have to wait a long while, for their Head, as they call her, is . . . is distracted at present." He was teasing Sister Claire, teasing or torturing her; judging by Father Louis's laughter, it would seem both men were engaged in the playing of a game.

"Tell me now," said Sebastiana, busy beside me, working her hands over the contents of the case, "did everything go as planned in the nun's cell?" I'd assumed she addressed Asmodei, but it was Madeleine who responded:

Yes. Yes, said the succubus. *Perfectly as planned;* and then she went on to tell how she'd appeared to Sister Claire in her cell. How she'd taken the shape of *"the other one"* (only later would I learn that she meant Peronette) and had *"sexed the woman good."* Given her what she'd long desired and denied. Made a mockery of her desire and denial. And, laughing, Madeleine told how, in the throes of passion, she'd shape-changed and bled her own blood all over the impassioned nun. *Quite a show, it was,* said the succubus to me.

It seemed that Asmodei had appeared just as Sister Claire tasted the succubus's blood and started to scream; as planned, he silenced her, restrained her, and relieved Madeleine, who returned to Father Louis and me in the library. (Here again she referred to me as a witch—*"Louis and the witch,"* she said.) So she hadn't been in the shadows all night; she'd visited with Sister Claire as Louis had visited with me; but where Louis had sought to teach, to pave the way for belief, Madeleine had sought to terrify, to torture. . . . I could not, *cannot* imagine what she might have done to Sister Claire.

"And you, Asmo?" asked Sebastiana. "I was a bit worried. It's been a while since you—"

"Yes," admitted the man. "It's been a long while; and as you know," over this they shared a smile, "I have never been one for the subtleties of your craft."

"To say the least," concurred Sebastiana.

"And making a golem," said Asmodei, ". . . *c'est difficile.* The infernal words of that spell . . ."

"Infernal, indeed," said Father Louis.

Asmodei went on: "I stumbled a bit over it all, yes, but in the end it worked. It worked quite well, in fact."

"Excellent," said Sebastiana. It was then I saw she worked her fingers over a collection of silver needles, such as those Father Louis had suffered long ago in his attic cell. I said nothing. Sebastiana spoke:

"Creating the likeness from the soil and clotted blood, *that* is the easy part," said she. "It's animating the golem that is tricky."

"But a golem is not animate," said Asmodei. "That would be an effigy, no? That is what we must do here. Is that not the plan?"

"Yes, of course," said Sebastiana; "... minor distinctions...." She looked up from the needles, which she held fanned in her hand, and asked, almost dreamily, of Asmodei, "Do you remember back in Paris, on the eve of the Reveillon riots, when we—"

Please, moaned Madeleine. *We haven't an eternity!*

"No, dear," returned Sebastiana. "But *you* will, if I fail here due to your distraction. *Hush!*" Sebastiana, ignoring the specter's sulky response, said to Asmodei, in summation. "It went well then, upstairs?"

"As planned," said he. "A likeness now lies upstairs on the nun's pallet. Dead, or so it will seem to whoever finds it ... rather, finds *her* there." He spoke quickly of the fun he'd had stabbing a dagger down into the golem while Sister Claire watched. "Running it through, thinking all the while of *this* one!" He must have pained Sister Claire then, in some way, for a muffled cry escaped from her. Father Louis, too, took a turn: her cry built to a terrible moan, and under it he and Asmodei laughed lightly.

"Boys, no," said Sebastiana, unhappily distracted. "Wait."

Asmodei, as if to recap his achievement, told how, when Madeleine returned to check his progress, he'd had her splatter the nun's cell with her own blood. "No one," he concluded proudly, "no one will doubt that the newly named Mother Superior was murdered in her sleep." What's more, he'd had Madeleine leave a blood trail between the nun's cell and the lesser library, "to help the simpletons put all the pieces together."

"But the blood, it fades in a few hours," said Sebastiana.

And so they will have a slight miracle, too, answered Madeleine. *Now on with this, please! The girls are asking after Sister Claire, wondering why she has not yet descended. They speak of sending a party up to her cell.*

"All right, quickly then ..." This from Sebastiana, who placed the cool back of her hand against my cheek, caressed me, and said, "This will hurt, dear heart; but it *must* hurt if it is to work."

"And it won't hurt you nearly as much as it will hurt *her*," added Father Louis; I could see him nod toward where Sister Claire lay beneath Asmodei's ministrations. "Take solace from that," said he, "from your accuser's greater pain." Again, visions of Father Louis suffering the Question, the search for the Devil's Mark, the consuming flames.

"What ... what are you going to do to me now?" I asked.

"Do you trust me, totally?" asked Sebastiana in response.

I said I did. I heard again her words: *You are safe.*

"Good. Let us begin," and as she signaled Asmodei thusly, I saw the silver needles glinting in her grip. Each as long as my first finger. Each so sharp the tip was invisible. In her other hand was a small, crudely shaped wax figure. A doll. Fashioned, I saw, from the candle that had burned all through the night, until Father Louis had put it to illicit purpose.

"Close your eyes," said Sebastiana.

Yes, counseled the succubus. *Do.*

I prayed that whatever would come would come quickly; and I braced for the pain. "That's a good girl," said Sebastiana; and at this, Asmodei laughed till silenced by the succubus:

Three girls are on their way up to the nun's chamber, said Madeleine. *Please, hurry!*

Sebastiana bent over me now; she'd plucked hairs from above my right ear before I even heard her apologize for doing so. My eyes flew open as though those hairs had been strings tied to my very eyelids; and I watched through tears as Sebastiana wound the hairs around the head of the ill-formed doll. She said something. Part of a spell.

"Very . . . nearly . . . ready," said she. "And you?"

"Yes," said Asmodei. "Much easier on my end: no doll to worry about. I just stick the needles right into the flesh, correct?" Sister Claire screamed, screamed till she choked on the gag, beat her heels against the oak. Asmo, apparently, had needles of his own.

"Oui," affirmed Sebastiana. "As I stick the doll, and no sooner. Remember: timing . . . *c'est très important.*"

Father Louis stood over me, across the table from Sebastiana. He took my hand, and it was then I knew, truly *understood* that what they were going to do would hurt. And, though I am ashamed to say it, knowing that the rite— whatever it was—would hurt Sister Claire *worse* than it would hurt me did lessen my pain.

Madeleine reported that the girls were knocking now on Sister Claire's door. Indeed, I could hear them.

"Witch," said Asmodei with impatience, "what is taking so long?"

"Silence," commanded Sebastiana. "I haven't fashioned an effigy since, well . . . it's been some time."

"Perhaps you should have practiced."

"Perhaps I should have. On you. . . . *Now silence!*"

A muffled cry from Sister Claire. And light laughter from the incubus, who looked over my head at the nun. What was Asmodei doing to Sister Claire?

Whatever it was Sebastiana told him to stop, and he did, countering her command with, "Get on with it then, or I'll simply strangle this one and we'll leave the other!" He meant me, of course.

No! begged Madeleine.

"Brilliant," said Sebastiana. "Litter the convent with corpses and arouse all suspicion. Start an inquiry that will—"

"Surely you're not afraid of these fools?" asked Asmodei.

"Of course not. But neither can I be *bothered* with them."

Please, do not abandon the witch.

I heard Father Louis whisper to Madeleine, "Do not worry. They want her as badly as we need her. She," and he meant Sebastiana, "*has* to save her. It's part of their creed or . . . or some such thing, is it not?" Sebastiana said nothing.

We all of us heard then the cries from the girls at Sister Claire's door—cries that summoned townsmen upstairs. This was followed by the slow beating down of Sister Claire's door. Madeleine had bolted the door from the inside after Asmodei had taken Sister Claire away. *Hurry,* said Madeleine now. *They are almost in the nun's cell.*

"Genius, to have slipped the bolt that way," said Sebastiana. "We'll need the few moments that bolt will earn us." She wrapped pieces of the pink dress around the doll. "Genius," said she again.

"Thank you," said Asmodei. He was teasing Madeleine, whose response was: *It was* my *idea. I ought to be commended.*

"What I *ought* to do," said Sebastiana, "is leave you to bleed through another century or two. . . . Silence, both of you!"

How did Madeleine and her bleeding factor into all this? Why did she seem so intent on effecting my escape? What was this "plan" of theirs? I knew not to ask such questions. Still, Father Louis, mercifully, offered an explanation of sorts.

While Sebastiana worked, while Asmodei waited to play his part on the body of the nun and while Madeleine stole through the halls of C——unseen, Father Louis explained. "It's simple, really," said he. He bent over and whispered in my ear so as not to disturb Sebastiana, who worked the wax doll and seemed to struggle a bit with the requisite spell. (I know now that he sought to distract me from the coming pain, too.) "Madeleine left the library earlier, during our . . . tête-à-tête"—here he smiled and tightened his cold grip on my hand—"and met up with Asmodei in the nun's cell. She slipped into the cell, visited the nun in the shape of your lost one, Peronette—that was her

name, was it not?" I nodded. "Madeleine worked upon the nun, who took it all
to be delirium, some sublime dream. A dream she'd had a hundred times
before. But then Madeleine...my sometimes mean and mischievous
Madeleine, changed shape. I don't know what shapes she took. Perhaps just her
own—that can be frightening enough to a mere mortal." Here he laughed.
"Then again, in the past, she has been wont to adopt the shapes of the most
ghastly hags."

Sebastiana worked on the wax, the words of her spell having fallen to a
whisper. Asmodei stood silently by. Sister Claire was still. And Madeleine, I
assumed, checked the progress of my accusers.

"Meanwhile," continued Father Louis, "Asmodei worked up a golem from
soil and blood. A simple spell and such golems take the shape of the
intended." I wondered, Is this Asmodei a witch, or a warlock, or a wizard or
whatever one calls such a...? "No," said Father Louis, reading my thoughts.
"But he has...access, if you will—access to...let us just say he has access to
aspects of the craft." The incubus said that Asmodei had left the likeness in
the nun's stead and carried the true and struggling Sister Claire down to the
library.

So far I understood; and I nodded when he asked as much.

"Now Sebastiana is making an effigy. A likeness of *you*; but unlike the golem,
this one will be alive....A much more difficult task." It seemed he couldn't help
but laugh. "Oh, I know," said he, "believe me, I know how hard it is to understand all this. Indeed, it's only slightly easier to explain. But you'll see for yourself soon enough."

Finally, he spoke of the plan's end, said we'd leave Sister Claire—who'd
appear to be me—in my place and make our escape. *Escape.* I clung to the word.
That I could understand.

"As I say, you'll see for yourself." The incubus stood and shrugged his
shoulders at Sebastiana, as if to say, That is the best I can do.

Madeleine reported that the door to the cell was indeed down. She said too
that they'd discovered the *"dead"* Sister Claire de Sazilly. *And the blood trail as well.
They're taking fast to it now,* said she.

"I am ready," said Sebastiana; and then two things happened simultaneously: Sister Claire let go a pained noise and I felt a quick, sharp stab in my
chest.

"Hold her," said Sebastiana to Father Louis, adding, to me, apologetically,
"The first one hurts the worst. Just twelve more now..."

She was piercing the wax doll with thirteen silver needles. And as she was sliding the thin needles into the doll and causing *my* pains, Asmodei was driving his set of needles into Sister Claire's very flesh.

"Count with her, Louis. Twelve more."

The next pain came to my right hand. Then the left. Tolerable. Though not so for Sister Claire: she rocked the table and screamed despite the gag that choked her. Her screams were more than matched by Asmodei's laughter, which rang like a cracked bell and resounded through the lesser library.

"Nine more," whispered Father Louis. "Nothing to it." A cold kiss at my temple.

Each foot. My forehead. "Eight, seven, six," said the priest.

They're coming. Hurry! said Madeleine. Sebastiana tensed. The distant screams no longer seemed so distant. Asmodei no longer laughed. They were coming, indeed.

The final five needles were the worst. My breasts. My navel and my anus. The very last one was in my mouth, at the center of my tongue. "That's so she'll sound like you when she speaks," said Father Louis. "Or rather, screams."

"Done." Sebastiana held up the doll—a *thing* of white wax, pink tulle, and hair, run through with thirteen silver needles—and asked Asmodei, "Success?"

"Indeed. Nicely done."

Father Louis, too, commended Sebastiana.

Please, shouted Madeleine. *They are on their way!*

What happened from that point forward remains a blur of magic and motion. I rose naked from the table, aided by the priest, and stepped into the blue wrap proffered by Sebastiana. I then turned to see . . . I saw standing . . . right before me. . . . My twin! Sister Claire de Sazilly. As *me!* Dressed in that foolish frilled pink dress—resewn through some aspect of the Dark Art—she stood barefoot before me, and I stood staring . . . at myself! Perhaps I spoke. More likely, no.

Sister Claire did not speak. She was still gagged.

Asmodei hauled the effigy to the chair and chained her there. She did not struggle. Was she resigned, spell-bound . . . had Sebastiana, in changing her outward appearance, also rendered her docile, dumb? Or was it simply a trance?

The cuffs were clamped around her ankles, just as they'd been around mine. Sister Claire choked on the gag, seeping now like a second tongue from her mouth. Asmodei laughed, laughed till Sebastiana scolded him, told him to step back from the effigy.

... The shuffling of slippers and boots along the stony corridors, on the central stairway. The scratch of metal on stone: *They have weapons,* said the succubus. *They will strike.*

"They are too late," said Sebastiana. "We have already struck."

Father Louis shoveled the books from the sill into a large leather sack that he drew from I don't know where. Madeleine returned the library to how it had appeared when first my jailers had locked the door against me, not twelve hours earlier. The earthenware pitcher, the candle, the chipped crystal goblet, everything was put in its place. (The blood she spilled in the process only furthered their end. "That is good, yes," said Father Louis of the blood. "The Devil's Trace," he called it.) Sebastiana tied the needles into the black velvet case.

I stood watching. It was then I realized something: none of these four—two spirits, incubus and succubus; a witch; and a demon or sorcerer or devilman—none of these four feared for themselves, for *their* safety. . . . It was then I knew I would leave C——— alive.

Asmodei tore the wet pink gag from the mouth of the effigy. Sebastiana cast words in an ancient tongue. And Sister Claire . . . rather, *me* . . . the effigy . . . I started to scream. It was *my* voice I heard. Screaming.

"It worked," said Sebastiana. "Are you all right, dear? Not bad, I should think, considering." And then, to Asmodei, "Are we ready?"

He said indeed we were, and we—excluding Asmodei—gathered at the lesser library's back door. Sebastiana and I, hand in hand; Father Louis, holding the bag of books; and Madeleine. Sister Claire sat staring at us, at me in particular; and from her issued screams and screams and screams; and then somehow she stilled herself enough to speak. I stood listening to . . . myself, or my voice as it railed against devils and demons and all the misdeeds she'd seen; as it began to spin the tale she'd deliver to the disbelieving assembly, then being led by Madeleine's blood to the library's primary door. Dumbstruck, I would have waited to hear the whole tale told, but Sebastiana called me back with a tug of my hand. "Let us quit this place," said she, "as soon as . . ."

. . . It was Maluenda. I watched as Asmodei lifted the cat from the effigy's lap. It would not go without a final scratch, fast across the face. *My* face. I flinched when I saw it, fairly *felt* it!

"Shhh!" said Asmodei to the crying cat, holding it near enough to the effigy for its every third or fourth swipe to catch the disguised Sister Claire. "Your cries are loud enough to . . . *to wake the dead!*"

"Come," said Sebastiana, stepping from the library, into the gallery. We could all of us hear the footfall of my accusers, coming along the corridor. It sounded as though some already stood on the far side of the library's main door.

Please! Do it now! moaned Madeleine. She spoke to Asmodei, still holding the cat.

"Oh, all right," said he to the succubus; and I watched as Asmodei took Maluenda to the window and, throwing it wide, with all his strength hurled the cat out over the sill. Yes, *hurled* it out! Out the window! I let go of Sebastiana's hand and rushed forward a step, two steps . . . but I stopped when I saw:

There, against the rising blue, the cat had burst into a flock of blackest birds. Rooks, or ravens. Birds that darted and wheeled through the dawning light.

I stopped. Was still.

It's part of the plan, said Madeleine.

Sebastiana, coming to stand behind me, said I ought not worry, that I would see the familiar again, and very soon. She said too that she liked the name I'd given her precious pet (and I knew then: it was hers, not mine), liked it far better than the name she'd called it all these years; with my permission, she thought she'd keep it. "Maluenda," said she. *"Oui, c'est parfait!"* As for me . . . all I could do was stare out at the brightening sky beyond Asmodei, where the black birds soared and spun, looped and dropped away one by one. I stared till the last of the birds flew from sight. And I would have stood there forever, slack-jawed and staring, but for Sebastiana.

"Now!" she urged. There came the first, still-tentative rapping at the library's main door. "Follow me!"

"Wait," called Asmodei. "What about these chains?"

"Hang them from the door's latch," directed Sebastiana. "Let them think, let them *know* this witch's devils have snapped them."

"Of course," said Asmodei. ". . . Yes, yes, I like that."

Understand: to my accusers it would appear as though someone or something—Satan, or whatever lesser demons they cared to conjure—had broken into the library. And, at my bidding, surely, these Dark Beings had stolen up to Sister Claire's chamber and killed her. Now, having already found the nun lying lifeless on her pallet, my accusers were hurrying to the library as we stole from it. There they'd find "me" just as they'd left me at dusk of the previous day. And in the lesser library they would be met with a screamed story of witches, of spells and succubi, et cetera. "I" would insist that I was Sister Claire de Sazilly, Mother Superior of the House at C——. "I" would say that I'd seen

Peronette Gaudillon in the night, that she'd taken some horrible shape before me. "I" would swear that I'd met a cast of devils who'd done me indescribable harm. And every word would be heard as a lie. Or even more damning, as the truth. "I" would be condemned without further process. "I" would be deemed too dangerous to bring to formal trial. "I" was bedeviled. They'd do to me what they would.

Finally, with Asmodei, we all of us stood in the shadowed gallery, at the top of the covered stairwell. Madeleine reported that the first of the accusers now stood at the library's other door, but no one dared enter without the Mayor present. They stood listening to the screamed story through the closed oak door, screaming in their turn.

I pitied Sister Claire then, if slightly. Something in my look must have betrayed the sentiment, or perhaps Sebastiana could access my thoughts as Father Louis could, for she said, "Forget her," and added, "Her final prayer before sleep last night was that she'd wake to watch you die."

And I did forget Sister Claire, for just then the screaming redoubled. The screams of the girls and nuns of C——, for, damning the absent men, they did finally open the library door to see the *thing* there. It was this discovery, and the attendant disorder, that we'd been waiting for. Now, under its cover—the slamming doors and all manner of hysteria—we took to the stairs.

It was all I could do to keep up with Sebastiana and the others. All I could do to not be trampled by the blond monster coming down the stairwell behind me. Soon we stood in the shadow of the convent wall. To our right sat the path leading to the stables.

I was blinded stepping out into the early sunlight behind Father Louis. I closed my eyes against the sun—they were closed but an instant!—and when I opened them I saw no sign of Father Louis. Nor Madeleine. They had disappeared. I was left standing between Sebastiana and Asmodei, our backs flush against the cold stones of the wall, lest we be spied.

Asmodei made a noise, though I should say that had I not been looking up at his face I would not have heard it. It was a whistle, seemingly too high and thin a noise for a man to make, or hear. It was a summoning. And sure enough, I followed his green-eyed gaze to where a huge white horse came rounding out from behind the stables. A horse I'd never seen before. Not a horse of C——. It stood too many hands high for me to quickly count. From Asmodei, then, I learned the beast's name. Cauchemar, he called it. The ground shook at its approach. Its coat shone as bright as the risen sun. Its mane had been braided. A puzzle of muscle and bone worked beneath its flesh. It was unsaddled.

Seeing Asmodei astride it—up, up with an effortless leap—he appeared as blond and bright and strong as the steed.

Then: "Call her." Sebastiana spoke to me. I did not understand. Not at first. But then I smiled at her, turned toward the stables, and more exhalation than speech, let go the words, "Maluenda. Maluenda, *come!*"

And she came. Came to the fading accompaniment of the ravens, which were nowhere to be seen. . . . A horse black as pitch to carry us away. Rounding out as Cauchemar had in a flash of sleekness and strength from behind the stables. . . . My Maluenda.

She stood as tall as Cauchemar, was as black as that horse was white. She came up beside the other, stomping and steaming, eager. Asmodei reached over her and helped us both up, Sebastiana and I. I settled behind Sebastiana on the horse's unsaddled back. Sebastiana's legs hung to the side; I straddled the horse. Sebastiana held tight to Maluenda's black and unbraided mane—her ears were torn, forever ragged despite the shape she took—and I held tight to Sebastiana, my cheek flush against her blue silk, her warm back. I listened to the beat of her heart. I felt the warm horseflesh beneath me. Finally, Sebastiana kicked into the horse's flank with her slippered feet.

We rode up the drive, passing the bushes in which I'd hidden, despairing, fearing for my life. Too late, I remembered the cypress cross. The one I'd left in the cellar. I started to ask Sebastiana to stop, to . . .

But that cross had been a mere weapon. A weapon I neither wanted nor needed now. So I let it lie.

And clinging to Sebastiana, eyes closed, I listened with intent to the fast-receding screams spiraling flame-like from the stony casements of C——.

Book Two

Ravndal

She was aferde of hym for cause
he was a devyls son.
—*Mallory*, Morte d'Arthur

15

Meeting in the Roseraie

I WOKE SLOWLY, into perfect darkness.

When I calmed myself enough to lift my hand and reach out I . . . I touched wood. Carved wood. I was surrounded on every side by walls. Walled in. I began to breathe with difficulty. I came to the heart-stopping conclusion that I'd been interred. Buried alive!

. . . *Mais non, ce n'est pas possible:* so large a coffin, one with walls so intricately, so carefully carved? With effort I slowed my breath. Steady, steady . . .

I reached out with first one hand, then the other. I lifted my hands up, up and out, reached forward till both hands were flat on one of the carved walls. Still I could see nothing. I felt all around. A handle! And its twin. I slid two panels back and . . . *light!* Blinding light!

I squinted against the sudden strong light. I waited for the return of sight. Breathe, I reminded myself; breathe . . .

Ah, yes, of course: the carved mahogany walls of the large box into which I'd been laid—by whom, I'd no idea—formed what is called a *lit clos:* a traditional Breton bed; a tiny room, really, often tucked into the corners of bed-chambers to assure privacy. I had never slept in one, but I knew them well enough by sight. I ran my fingers over the skillful carving, its smooth ridges, its flatter forms. I was reminded of a fire screen belonging to Mother Marie-des-Anges, a gift, she'd said, from some prince of the Levant. That quick recollection, that sudden and unsolicited memory, was enough to flood my mind with questions, just as the *lit clos,* once opened, had flooded with light.

Where was I? How had I arrived here? So many questions. I knew the answers to some of them, of course; but part of me resisted the truths I knew. After all, I'd seen such strange and inexplicable things.

I *insisted* on the few simple facts I knew. I *refused* fear, refused confusion.

The truth as I knew it was this: I was at this place—she called it Ravn-dal—rather, her distant, discreet, and, simply, *scared* neighbors in the low-lying fields around it had renamed the place thusly, owing to the birds so often seen circling its turrets and towers and tumbling chimneys. She, Sebastiana, adopted the name long ago, preferring it to one the pile bore when first it came into her possession—I say again, all I knew was that I'd been brought to this manor by its chatelaine, Sebastiana d'Azur.

But as I sat thinking those first few moments, my eyes still adjusting to the sudden light, I came to *understand* a thing at once quite simple and quite complicated: I was alive, and unaccountably altered. Alive! *I am alive!* I think I may have said it aloud. What I meant of course was this: I had very nearly died. For I knew then, and believe still, that my accusers at C—— would have killed me; killed me or in some subtler way allowed me to die. And I, having seen what I'd seen that final night at C——, well . . . I could only wonder what *my* new life would be like.

So I was awake—*alive*—sitting on the edge of that boxed bed staring out through the carved panels at the most amazingly appointed room I had ever seen. It came into view slowly, as my eyes mastered the light.

I rose, stepped through the window of wood. I turned around, full circle, to take in the room. Awed, I verily fell into a fauteuil covered in worn green velvet, beside which stood a three-legged filigreed table of mahogany and inlaid marble, with a smooth and golden-red veneer of tortoiseshell and brass. On its top was a note, "Join me, S.," and a plate piled high with Chinese ginger, tangerines, and crystallized fruit. There was a tiny teapot of the palest faience, full of a steeping tea; betony leaves, I'd learn. I sat. I ate and I drank. Looking around the room, I forgot the note for a long moment.

There, nestled in the corner, was the *lit clos*. Sunlight shafting down into the room through tall windows lit the uncarved wood of the bed's outer walls, showed its grain and its age—oak, it seemed, inlaid with ebony; and veneered with tulipwood, perhaps kingwood. Soon I was wondering how long I'd been asleep. It might have been hours; it might have been days.

Seated, quite comfortably, I realized, with some embarrassment, two things: I wore a long white nightshirt (and so I had been *undressed* by someone) and I was sore. In places I had never been sore before.... Thoughts then of Father Louis and Madeleine. Where were they? Would I see them again? And who . . . *Alors*, countless questions.

I set myself the simple task of taking in the room, one object at a time.

Two of the walls were muraled, amazingly detailed. I could not be sure, having not traveled at all, but weren't these scenes of the great cities? Yes. For there was Venice, with all its decrepit beauty; and that scene's title confirmed it: "The Doge Marries the Sea and Saves the City." There was Naples (I knew Vesuvius). Rome (the Coliseum). Russia (the gilded onion-domes, the deep drifts of snow). And scattered among these murals were portraits, in varying degrees of completion. Interesting: I noticed that all, or almost all the Parisian scenes were unfinished, the horses and men of the street scenes outlined in lead or pastel, then abandoned, midstroke.

A carpet from the Far East covered the whole floor; over it were strewn smaller carpets from *la Savonnerie* or some such place.

The furniture was impossibly grand, almost gaudy. In a corner I saw a full set in miniature—chairs, tables . . . These were the child-sized models that were sent to the wealthy, from which they made their choices, ordering full-sized replicas. (Clearly there was, or at least had been, great wealth at this place, Ravndal.) Though I've never much cared for dolls or their trappings, I found these pieces irresistible. Approaching, I picked up the sofa with one hand. It bore the imprint of a Parisian upholsterer, Daguere. The name meant nothing to me, though no doubt his had been the atelier of choice in the Paris of the past. Looking up from these toys, I realized with a smile that the full-sized set of furniture was arranged before me. These larger pieces were uphol-stered in green damask, wonderfully worn, smooth as skin, while the tiny set showed a dainty printed silk. I sat on a wide chaise and resumed my inventory.

Armoires, full of who knew what. I didn't dare look. Not just yet. Neither did I approach the tall mirror that stood between two lace-draped windows.

In another corner were piled some bricks—rather incongruously, I thought; they seemed mere rubble. Intrigued, I crossed the room to take up a brick; doing so, I saw that it bore the seal of the Bastille: souvenirs.

There was a small escritoire, and on it a stack of stationery, each sheet weighty and crisp. There was a jewel-set inkwell—in the shape of a cock, whose head tilted back by the comb—and an assortment of freshly cut pens. The desk itself, I knew, was deceptively simple; surely it contained some secret compartments. Here again I was informed by the many novels I'd read; . . . nevertheless, I promised myself I'd look the desk over later.

As for the rest of the room, which I surveyed as I stood at its center, it was rather cluttered: stacks of yellowed, once-fine linen; books piled flat on footstools and shelves; a chess set carved of wood, each piece representing some Revolutionary personage. The commode, I saw, was from Sèvres; in it had been painted a careful likeness of Benjamin Franklin, who, throughout the pre-Revolutionary mania for things American, had been revered in Paris; but this vogue passed, of course, and nowhere was this more evident than in the porcelain bowl before me.

I noticed frames (so obvious I'd overlooked them), scattered all about the room. Some stood nearly twice my height; some hung crookedly on one nail, while others were propped up against the walls. Each frame was empty. Nothing but cobwebs in their gilded and carved corners. Smaller ones, I saw, had been broken; stacks of golden kindling flanked the fireplace.

Near a set of open doors, over which hung bolts of Alençon lace, billowing sail-like on the breeze, there sat an artist's easel. In its gentle vise sat a yellowed canvas, gone slack over its frame; beside the easel stood a tall table littered with pigments, tiny spatulas, palettes, and other tools. Brittle brushes stuck up from a cut-glass vase like so many dead flowers. So this was, or had been a studio of sorts. But whose?

I sat again in that green fauteuil, nibbled at a piece of ginger, and rediscovered that note. "Join me. S." Sebastiana, of course.

But where would I find her? Looking around for other doors leading from the room, I startled myself: there I was, far across the room, reflected in a freestanding, gilt-edged oval. Entranced, I walked toward the mirror. Toward myself.

How many times had I shunned such mirrors? For how long had I hidden from myself? . . . But now I looked, long and hard, and happily.

My hair hung loose, tussled from my long sleep. I ran my fingers through it, a rough comb, and admired (yes, *admired!*) the golden play of light as it set-tled down over my shoulders. Back-lit, dressed in that simple white shift, I appeared—dare I say it?—*seraphic.* At this I had to smile. I moved closer to the mirror. Closer still, till I stood mere steps from my reflected self, which I was seeing for the first time as . . . as beautiful.

You are a woman. You are a man.

I took the loose shift by the hem and slowly, slowly, began to pull it up. Higher. Higher. Over those long, long legs, so lean and muscled. I wanted to see. To look. At my body, at *myself.* As one looks at a lover. I wanted to *savor* the first-time sight of . . .

Just then I heard singing, and I let the shift fall—embarrassed: the *shame* should I be discovered in such a pose!—and I turned from my mirrored self toward the sound. It wafted into the room like the very *sound* of sunlight. It came from beyond the door, beyond the billowing lace. A woman's voice: soprano. An Italian aria, sung at half-voice, for the sole pleasure of the singer.

The studio had been sunlit, but I'd no idea if it was nearer dusk or dawn until I stepped outside in pursuit of that song.

Again, a blinding light. The light of a low-angled sun; and so I knew that I'd woken into late afternoon. As for the day or date, I'd no idea. The sunlight felt so fine on my face. My bare feet were warmed by the square of slate on which I stood. At noon (perhaps four, five, six hours ago?), the slate would have been too hot to stand on. But it was cooling now, and so too was the air. The sky was cloudless and deeply blue.

I stood on that slate, my senses wonderfully keen. Soon I was able to open my eyes fully and take in all that was so perfectly sunlit. Yes: it was definitely late-day light. I heard sounds: that lilting soprano, but also the chorus of birds that backed it, and the lazy fall of water from a fountain, and beyond, the arrhythmic churning of the sea. Ah, I thought, this Ravndal is on the shore. I wondered then, fleetingly, how far the manor sat from C——. I remembered nothing of the ride—only our charging away, and my holding fast to Sebas-tiana.

Sight. Sound. . . . Smell. The sea, of course; so familiar, that salted air. Stronger even than the salt air was the scent of . . . What *was* it? So familiar, yet . . . I remembered then the moment when Sebastiana had first held me close, comforted me in the library at C——. There'd been a single rose in her hair, woven into her braid. Of course, it was roses I smelled. But so strong a scent, as though from a million blooms. How could that be? This seemed the very *essence* of rose. Looking to either side of the shell path that sloped away from the studio door, I had my answer when I saw the first of those million blooms. Here was a garden in the grandest sense. There were buds tiny and tight, roses frilly and full. Petals the color of cream, of butter, of fruit, of meat from the knife. . . . Crimson. Blood-soaked scarlet.

Only then, wide awake, every sense so keen, was I able to take in the entirety of what I discovered beyond the billowing white lace. A garden, indeed, with beds laid out in geometries of green, their angles formed of box-wood. The shell path, wide enough for two strolling side by side, glistened under the late sun; its oyster shells were ground and broken, and looked like teeth fallen from a beast. Many of the rosebushes and all the bordering hedges stood quite tall; still, as the garden sloped down and away from the manor, I could see beyond it to the strand and the blue-black sea.

The singing had stopped. I realized this only when it began again. I could not see the singer. Neither could I see the fountain, which, judging from the loud play of water—so different from the sound of the sea—was large and near. I'd find both singer and fountain behind one of those tall hedges, no doubt. I moved toward the song, toward the trill of the falling water.

The song—more exercise than aria—was, I knew, Italian. Ornate and rich as any rose in the garden. Scarlatti, I thought. (There'd been stacks of scores in Mother Marie-des-Anges's chambers—she'd once studied that same violin I'd sawed upon—and I'd taught myself to read them passably well, imagining the sounds of unknown instruments and the preternatural voices of the castrati for whom the fanciest, most florid songs had been composed.)

Moving toward the song, I stopped beside a rosebush identified, as were they all, by a thin band of ivory bearing both its French and botanical names, calligraphed with a penknife; these ivory tags were tied to a branch or stem by a blue ribbon. This particular bush, I recall, of pinkish double blooms, was called Borboniana, after our family of kings.

I stopped at this Borboniana to savor its scent and, with a half-turn more, I discovered the fountain. Much larger than I'd guessed. Its waters rose over-head, arcs of silver glistening in the sun. It was old. Very old. The wide bowl of its base was lichen-covered, and the sculpted figures bore a deep patina. This was a narrative in stone and bronze, but its story was lost on me. All I saw were tens of toads, hideous things depicted at various hopped heights, some open-mouthed, others pop-eyed and grossly fat. It was *horrific!* I must have stepped back from it, repulsed, for just then I heard:

"Now, now . . . It's not *that* bad."

The voice startled me. Two paces to my right sat Sebastiana, on the rim of the fountain's large pool. She was as I remembered her: beautiful, so pale, her features framed by her jet black hair, its braid falling down over her shoulder, her eyes a wondrous blue—they would amaze me each time I saw them; bluer still were the diaphanous robes she wore.

She sat sketching in a large leather-bound book. She closed it at my approach.

"Come," she said. I took one step nearer and stopped. What if . . .

Sebastiana addressed my ill-formed concerns: "Heart, tell me: Would I have saved you then only to hurt you now?"

I took a seat on the edge of the fountain, too far from Sebastiana, apparently; she extended an open hand, saying, more to herself than me, "Ah, but I forget. . . . I was afraid once too."

"This fountain, you know," said she with a languorous wave of her hand, meant to take in the entire mechanism, "is an exact replica of one at Versailles. Hideous as it is, I had it built years ago as a reminder of . . ." She stopped with a sigh. Turning to me, she asked, "Surely you know the story it tells?"

I said I did not. Rather, I shook my head. Speech seemed beyond me still.

"Well then," said she. "Welcome to the Fountain of Latona."

I stared down into the pool as though I'd find there—in the murky, thick, stagnant water—some clarification of her words. I saw only fish, large fish, sun-colored: shades of orange, red, white, and yellow. Several broke the scummed surface with the tense, greedy white Os of their mouths. Carp, they were, ranging like pulsing hearts through the body of the pool.

Sebastiana went on:

"There, at the center of the pool, stands Latona. In her arms is the infant Apollo." She told the rest of the tale. How Latona had tried to flee from the wrath of Juno, whose husband, Jupiter, had openly desired Latona. Midflight, stopping to drink from a creek, Latona and her son were set upon by a horde of peasants doing the bidding of Juno. Just then Jupiter intervened and turned the peasants into toads, and that was the moment frozen in the fountain: toads, some of which retained the odd human feature—a hand or face—were crouched, poised to attack mother and child.

"Of course, there were far prettier fountains at Versailles, but I always favored this one. I sat beside it often."

Sebastiana trailed her hand through the water, cutting its viscid skin; there rose up those wide-open white mouths. "They kiss me," said she, smiling. "And they beg." Reaching behind her head, she plucked a petal from the rose in her hair. She let it drop onto the water and then, striking fast, she scooped up the first carp that came. Thick as her wrist, rubicund and muscled, she held it up to the sun. Its gills pulsed. Its eyes were lightless and empty. She held it so tight! Would she let it die in her grasp?

No. She returned it to the pool, held it underwater—I heard those horrible kisses breaking against the back of her hand, her forearm—and finally she released the fish. Only when she told me to sit did I realize I had stood and stepped back from the fountain, from *her*. I did sit. And again I moved nearer Sebastiana when she told me to.

"You've looked into my eyes," said she, flatly. I nodded that yes, I had. She referred, of course, to the strangeness I'd seen in them, those same twisting shapes I'd seen in the eyes of Maluenda. Thoughts then of the feline familiar. Where was she now? Would I see her again? *What* was she? Animal essence, as Father Louis and Madeleine were somehow *human* essence?

Sebastiana spoke of her own eyes. I listened for the one word: witch. I wanted to hear it, wanted Sebastiana to tell me that she and I were one. Witches both. I wanted her to say it until I believed it. Say it till it seemed no more fantastical than those acts attributed to the Catholic saints I'd long worshiped. . . . But she did not say it, not directly. Instead, she told a quick story:

"In the city of Ferrara," said she, "in the sixteenth century, two orphaned sisters were tried for sorcery.

"The older sister—eleven to her sister's nine—told the Inquisitor that she would, if freed, tell him how to find all the witches he wanted. 'How?' he asked, all the while intending to burn both girls, as indeed he did. It was then the older sister told the Inquisitor about *l'oeil de crapaud*. The eye of the toad.

"The sisters, you see, were indeed witches. They knew of the true witches' mark."

Was Sebastiana saying that witches *were* marked, as so many witch hunters had supposed? Was *I* marked?

"All those trials," she went on, "all that torture and death . . . the searching in vain for, and the false finding of the witches' mark. . . . All a horrible waste. For the few true witches ever tried bore the mark within, at the center of the eye, and could hide or show it at will." She looked at me squarely, and added, "It is, of course, the same for their familiars."

So it was the shape of a writhing, twisting toad I'd seen in Maluenda's eyes as she'd sat in my lap that afternoon, bleeding from her wounds. This led to more questions, and still more till it seemed I might lose my mind . . .

My voice rose up within me, came out like those streams of water croaked by the toads, and I heard myself ask, "Am I, then, a witch?"

Sebastiana took up a long-handled mirror in response to my question. I hadn't seen it at her side. It was wrought-silver, its shape that of a naked woman whose outstretched arms held the glass. "Look," said she, holding the mirror up before me. "And ask yourself that question."

I did not look into the small mirror. I looked over it into Sebastiana's eyes, so blindingly blue. "Not my eyes," she said. "Yours."

Suddenly, there was my face in the silver mirror.

"You are beautiful, you realize," said Sebastiana. I did not demur. "Beautiful and handsome too."

My eyes, in the mirror, were changing. I was not conscious of causing this. All I did was stare, and the longer I stared the less certain the shape of the pupil. I closed my eyes. I looked away. But I would *have* to look again, and there it would be: the perfect round edges of the pupil pushing out, here and there, into the striate green of the iris. Like the bulbous toes of a toad. The whites of my eyes were unchanged. Neither did my vision blur or change in any way. I asked myself, tacitly, What am I? Am I a witch? And I repeated the word— witch, witch, witch—till the deed was done and there, in the mirror, were reflected my own witch's eyes.

I had my answer.

I would have looked into that mirror till nightfall had Sebastiana not lowered it to show her own shape-changed eyes. "We are witches both," said she, holding tightly to my hand.

"You have questions," she said.

Finally! Which would I ask first and how would I—

"Ask none of them now," she said, standing. She let go my hand. Was I being dismissed? No; she was leaving me.

And with that she walked away. Took two or three steps from me. Turning, as though she'd forgotten something, she said, her arms opening wide as her smile, as if to encompass all of Ravndal, "Welcome." Her long blue sleeves caught the sea-scented breeze, moved as gracefully as she. "Enjoy the roseraie. Walk the lawns." A few more steps away. "And oh yes, dear heart," said she, turning fast, "do *not* go into the woods." She bent at the knee—at first I thought she was bowing, but no—and took in the scent of a small purplish rose (*"Belle sans flatterie,"* it was labeled). With thumb and forefinger, Sebastiana snipped the bloom off a double rose, pink and smooth as a shell's inner curve

("Abaillard") and tossed off, not deigning to turn toward me, "The dinner bell sounds at nine. Tonight we dine in your honor." She did turn to add, with what seemed a wicked little smile, "And, of course, we dress for dinner." She raised the pink bloom to her nose, breathed it deeply in, and with a wave of her hand she was gone behind a hedge, singing again what was or was not Scarlatti.

16

I Bathe

I SAT FOR some time in the roseraie. The roses were lit by the low-angled sun; their tiny angular leaves shone green above and gold below; and the petals showed infinite pastels. And the air was thick with rose perfume and the scent of the chocolate mulch mounded loosely around the bases of the bushes.

Occasionally I would raise my eyes to the horizon, to the sea. The shore was near, but the sea was distant: the tide was out. From where I sat on the fountain's edge, I could not see much of the manor; and so I soon lost myself in the play of the carp, shooting like flaming arrows through the shadows I cast on the water.

I might have sat forever on the edge of that fountain, awaiting the wonders to come. But no; I could not. I rose to return to the studio.

Turning left at a shorter hedge, I saw over it to the

horizon, and to the receded sea. Ravndal sat high on a hill above a large cove. The descent to the strand was all rock and friable dune. From the boundary shrubs of the roseraie, the land fell fast away to marry the vast expanse of beach, or exposed sea bed; the sea was but an undulating line, far away.

This was beautiful, starkly beautiful. The sun was setting; it bore the softest of palettes, as though the roseraie itself were reflected on the undersides of the fast clouds. Purple shading to red, red to orange, to pink, to cream. But too soon the colors of the sky all died to blue. A singular, simple blue. A sliver of moon rose like a scythe in the sky, its edge sharp, its light hard. . . . Soon I was chilled through, and lost.

How I longed then to return to the room in which I'd woken!

Having determined to retrace my steps, move as quickly as I could through the roseraie, back to the studio, I stopped, could not continue.

For it was then that I saw, truly *saw* Ravndal for the first time, set like a jewel in the sky, faceted and darkly sparkling. I stood awed before it. A long stony wing spread back behind the studio. I saw scattered windows candlelit, and dark stone walls rising up, up. It seemed immense, as indeed it was, *is*.

Given the size, the scale of the studio in which I'd awakened, why was I shocked to see Ravndal looming so large before me? . . . Yet I was. And so I wandered the rose-heavy hedgerows, looking up at the manor from every angle. The shards of oyster shell shone an ivoried blue, crunched beneath my slippered step.

Coming rather serendipitously upon the studio door, my only thought was of the hour. Had I missed the dinner bell? I *bounded* into the room. There, on the mantel, the clock beneath the bell jar—I hadn't much time.

Tall white candles, textured and thick, had been set about the room in wrought-iron stands of various heights; they lit surfaces I had not noticed earlier—burnished floors, gilded moldings, mirrors showing their metallic backing as ill-kempt women let show their slips. . . . The muraled scenes seemed suddenly animate in the shadows cast by the tall candles.

A fire blazed now beneath the marble mantel. I took a seat very near the fire, shielded by a beeswax screen; then I saw with excitement that two of the studio's *necessaires,* or armoires, had been thrown open. Clothes of every shade, shape, and style threatened to spill out onto the rugs! I progressed to a closer inspection of each garment and realized, with a sickening chill—as though I were being laughed at—that the armoires were stocked with men's and women's clothes.

I stripped myself of the shift. I rushed over to that tall mirror, tilted its oval till I stood staring at . . . I hesitate to describe just what I did next . . .

Mais non, I've come this far, and certainly there is farther to go, and so . . .

I wheeled the mirror nearer a short divan (covered, yes, in emerald damask, and with gold chenille piping!) and positioned it just so—yes! *there*, and now *here* . . . And I lay down to take a long and intimate look at my body. An assessment, if you will.

Was this the self-abuse I'd so often been vaguely warned against? Could it be? No, not possible—for this was pleasurable beyond words, not abusive at all. Quickly my thoughts . . . well, what followed were not *thoughts* at all. Instinct, was it? Something *sensory* overtook me, and I did what I did as though my hands were not my own. I slid my opened palms over the plain of my stomach and felt fine hairs all over my body rise; up, up went my hands to the undercurves of my breasts and . . . and when first I touched, with a fingertip, the rough, reddened centers of my breasts, I felt my eyelids flutter, I felt my eyes themselves roll back . . . it was a sudden, surprising and most welcome sightlessness that I settled into then.

. . . My hands! What new instruments they were! So . . . *utile*. With them I took in textures I had never known, not in this way—my lower lip, the tip of my tongue, the lobe of my ear; and with them I dared . . . I dared to be curious; and I let myself be satisfied. Or nearly so.

I was brought back with a start from that quite wondrous, uncharted place by the first distant ringing of the dinner bell. My eyes burst open. There I lay, splayed, perspiring, and smiling. The clock showed eight. That bell had been rung to warn me that I had one hour to bathe and dress for dinner.

Clothes I had in abundance, but where was the bath? Surely there was a bath. And indeed I found one. But on the escritoire, folded and laid atop that stack of stationery, I discovered another note from Sebastiana:

"Dear heart," it read, "do you adore my roseraie? Are you well rested? I trust you are. We let you sleep some time—so that sweet dreams in the night might temper recent events, so regrettably sour. Enjoy the wardrobes. Choose well. And should you wish to bathe, you may do so in the Grand Canal!"

Whatever did that mean? I read on:

"Do this—take a pen, and on five sheets, which you will fold into quarters, write the five questions to which you most desire answers. This is a courtesy I extend to you. It is a duty, too. Think well, and carry these questions to supper on your new and well-dressed person. *À bientôt.*" The note was signed, in full,

Sebastiana d'Azur, and bore a quick and familiar sketch: a toad seated in the lower curve of the S.

This note—the handwriting, the signature, the sketch—was the work of an artist. It came to me plainly then: the frames, the rolled canvases, the muraled walls, the fox hair brushes, in short everything in the studio was Sebastiana's.

Five questions? I might have asked five *hundred* questions.

Sebastiana had been right to assume I'd want to bathe. Desperately. And the Venetian riddle was easily solved: one push on the large painted panel depicting the marriage of the Doge and sea and it swung open, revealing the most exquisite bath, a model of Oriental luxury and comfort. (Sebastiana— who was, I would learn, not *merely* an artist but the premier portraitist of her day—Sebastiana had done the Venetian mural; too, she'd designed the bath and adorned its walls with scenes of the East.)

The low-ceilinged room was dimly lit by sconces fastened to walls the color of baked clay. Through the steam that rose from the just-poured bath- water, I could see that the room was quite large, perhaps half the size of the studio. The sunken tub could accommodate a small crowd. A broad banquette, covered in smooth black cloth, ran along three walls. On the fourth, beside the door, there hung the linen one used to dry oneself. Pendant from golden rods, adjustable to the bather's height, it was a fine Indian mull, embroidered at the bottom with flowers, the added weight of which caused the cloth to cling to the skin. . . . It was opulent. It was . . . orgiastic.

I circled the large marble tub. Shining in a corner were the copper kettles in which the warmed water had been carried into the room. (When? By whom?) I nearly tripped over a delicate silver set, from which I would pour a cup of piping hot chocolate once I'd stripped, stepped down into the water, and set- tled in up to my shoulders.

Heaven, this was! The water's temperature was perfect. (At C——, desper- ate to avoid the other girls, I'd only ever bathed in tubs too hot or too cold.) . . . I closed my eyes. I could not *help* but close my eyes. I lay back, my head at rest on a contoured pillow. In that water—which I was embarrassed to find strewn with rose petals—all my cares dissolved.

I bathed. I sipped the chocolate. Then suddenly, inexplicably, the water cooled; indeed, the entire room seemed to chill, uncomfortably. I'd have to stand and quit the bath. I was wondering what the hour was. Just then I heard . . . *something*. No; I *sensed* something. Movement. Shadow movement, as I'd seen in the lesser library. Then, an actual sound. It may have been present for some time, that sound; I may not have heard it, lost as I was in the sway of the bathwater as it lapped at the smooth, high sides of the tub. But now I heard it clearly. There it was again: the slow, steady, unmistakable sound of . . . of dripping water? . . . No. It wasn't water. Denser than that, heavier. More like pebbles in a pond.

There were no spigots, no well-spouts ringing the tub. I looked all about the bath. Nothing. I scanned the ceiling, where bolts of oxblood fabric billowed, drawn as in some pasha's tent to the center of the ceiling. Grand as this room was, it was unavoidably humid too: I searched the ceiling for condensation, down-dripping water. Nothing. But there it was again . . . That hollow *plock! plock! plock!* I lay perfectly still, staring straight up, thinking that if I did not disturb the water it would . . . No. There! It fell now at my shoulder, near my ear! It—the source—was above and behind me, and when I turned fast I saw with a start Madeleine standing there. . . . Blood. Blood it was, dripping down into the bath from her split-open throat.

What happened then, well, it is a bit of a blur. I cannot recall if . . . Ah, *nonsense!* False decorum, this. I know *exactly* what happened next, and I'll say it plainly: I scurried like a soaked rat to the far side of the tub, scrambled up its side till I sat shivering on the tub's edge. The water in which I'd bathed was dark with the succubus's blood. In the uneven light I saw that the surface of the bathwater was slick, as with oil or bile or excrement; islands of . . . of life-matter floated among the rose petals.

There I sat, naked, knees drawn to my chest. I shivered. I said nothing. Madeleine stood across the pool, staring down into its soiled water. When finally she spoke, it was in that horrible voice that was not a voice, that garbled rasp, thick with blood, which I—thanks to what strange talent?—could understand:

I've only come to help you dress, she said. Blood bubbled at her throat, fell down with that sickening sound into the water.

Standing there, naked in the near-dark, wraith-like, Madeleine wondered aloud, *What will you ask of her? Of them? Tell me.*

In the lesser library, that last night at C——, I'd heard anger in Madeleine's voice, *seen* anger in her actions. There was none of that now. It was sadness I discerned in that voice of hers, and I was no longer scared. When our eyes met, I returned her steady gaze without difficulty. Her face . . . so beautiful above the bloodied gash . . . The expressive eyes . . . that immobile mouth . . . In fact, I could not look away from her face. And I stared as her "speech"—again, I know no better word—as her words spurted forth, as that watery viscus broke from her open throat, the black-red edges of which moved as though to mimic true speech; yes, it was as though the cut itself spoke. *What will you ask?*

"I have my questions," I lied.

Good, she said. *Then you've only to dress. The second bell will sound shortly, and there will not be a third.* Moving through the room, with its half-light cast by those bitter-burning sconces set with vials of whale oil, Madeleine seemed *composed* of shadow. More so than she had in the library. Her body . . . well, it was as though she absorbed the light. She seemed to reflect it, too; and a nimbus, a halo of sorts surrounded her. She moved with such fluidity, such grace and ease. She stopped before one of the sconces, and by its pale light I saw her from behind . . . the sweet and perfect curves of the girl she'd been, the long plait of black hair bisecting her narrow back, her high buttocks and long legs . . . In an instant she turned again to face me and that same sublime body seemed a *grotesquerie!* The slim hourglass of her torso, the small tight upturned breasts visible beneath the rags she wore . . . *enfin,* all her beauty bore the blood, its spoil, flowing from her throat down between her breasts, over her stomach toward the fork of her legs. What light there was caused that bloody course to glisten, and in it I could see those bits of viscus that slowed its flow. Was Madeleine *rotting* from within? The accompanying stench—a description of which I will spare myself—seemed to indicate that yes, she was. Or perhaps she'd achieved over the centuries some terrible stasis, and her dissolution would never end—she'd rot but never rot *away.* . . . Such were my thoughts when again I heard her voice:

May I speak?

"You may, of course."

Madeleine cast her eyes down, shamefully. She played with her braid. And it struck me: She is a girl. I nearly said it aloud. Madeleine, when she died, was but three or four years younger than I am now. Yes, we were near in age, discounting the nearly two hundred years separating our birth dates. Madeleine, centuries dead, come from Beyond—she seemed to me, simply, a girl. A sad girl. I pitied her. "Please, say what you will." I rose and wrapped myself in the linen.

Madeleine approached. *Do you forgive us for . . . for what was done to you at that place?* She was a horrifying sight, yes, at once beautifully pure and putrid. And I'd no reason to believe her to be benevolent. Hadn't she shape-changed to torment Sister Claire as Peronette, and then as her bleeding, licentious self? But now I knew that those tricks had been played in the service of a larger plan. And I knew too—I cannot say *how* I knew it—that Madeleine, though far from harmless, would not harm me.

"I do, yes," I said. There was *sympathy* between us, unspoken. "You saved me, all of you."

Madeleine stood before me now, looking down at my body. *I am sorry*, said she. I'd grown even colder with her approach. The wet fabric shaped itself to my body. I flushed, moved to cover myself with a second embroidered bolt of cloth.

"You refer to my—" How dare she pity me *my* strangeness?

No, she said; *I . . . I should have thought . . .* She took up a small cloth and dipped it into a bucket of clean, cold water. *I ruined the water*, she said. *I didn't mean to. I am sorry.*

Madeleine then began to lave my neck and shoulders, for I was covered with flecks of her . . . her *being*. I held out my arm to her—so *cold*, so light her touch—and saw that it was red-tinged. Taking care not to bleed on me again—I watched the blood slip down her legs, pool at her bare feet before running into the tub—she washed me clean.

We stood face to face. I looked into her eyes, looked away from the wide-open wound. I could not escape its smell: a malodorous mélange of . . . of soil, rusted iron, and butchered meat. (Ah, there it is! I *knew* I'd have to describe it.) I'd seen such anguish in those eyes, but now they were soft with concern, with sorrow and longing.

You must go, said Madeleine. *Your mortal clock ticks.*

I loosed another length of linen from the golden rod, wrapped it around me. I sat on the banquette and looked at the succubus, fast fading away. She moved to trail one foot through the tub. When she bent to take up some water, I saw that she was unable to hold it: it passed through her cupped palms as though they were porous cloth. *I have laid out clothes for you*, she said. *The choice, of course, is yours.*

"Thank you." I rose, ready to return to the studio. "Will you be at supper?" I asked.

Perhaps. Though Sebastiana may not allow it. Looking at the blood sluicing from the corner into the tub, seeing the slick tiles and the stained cloth with which she'd washed me, I did not need to ask why. *It fades in seven hours, the blood, leaving no trace, but it is so . . . unsightly in the meantime. I cannot blame her.*

"Why seven hours?" I asked.

Will that be one of your questions? I'd be grateful, as not even I know the answer to that one. . . . Neither does Sebastiana, though. I discerned for the first time, in the sound that was her speech, a lightness not far from laughter. But then she added: *Guard your trust. There are things your Sebastiana does not know.*

"Such as?" I asked.

Such as how to loose my bound soul into the void. Such as how to let me die, and pass from this world.

"She has tried to do this for you? She has tried to . . . to help you?"

Madeleine sighed—it was at once sad and dismissive of my question. *She tried, yes; or so she says. But that was years ago, and she refuses to try again.*

"Why?"

She is, she says, an old witch; and what is needed is the strength of a new witch. . . . A witch like you. But the truth is this: still she is afraid of her own self, her witchly self. She rose so fast from the tub I did not see her in motion—a watery wave through the air and a sudden chill were all I discerned; but there she stood now, across the shadowed room. *Go now,* said she. *Go and dress.*

As I moved toward the unmarked panel through which I'd entered the bath, I heard the expiring sizzle of the sconces, and what little light there'd been seeped from the room. Thankfully, just then, the door swung open into the studio.

I turned back to the bath. Into the darkness I called, "Madeleine? . . . Madeleine?" What did I intend to say? I don't know. I only know I said nothing, for the succubus was gone. Still, I called her name once more before closing the decorated door.

Where had she gone? Had she slipped past me, out of the bath, into the studio, away? Perhaps there was a second door? No, impossible.

I hadn't much time. I found the studio warm and bright: the fire blazed, more candles had been set about. (When? By whom? Questions. A surfeit of questions.)

. . . I somehow composed myself and dressed for dinner.

17

I Dress for Dinner

THE TALL white tapers that had been set about the studio showed no red signs of Madeleine. Neither did the lantern on the escritoire, lit now to illumine the stationery on which my questions were not yet written. I despaired: how would I ever distill so much mystery into five simple questions?

I saw that there remained little more than a quarter hour till dinner. I had to dress. Determined to do so, and moving toward the armoires, I saw that Madeleine had indeed been in the studio. The escritoire, that tiny desk balanced on bowed and gilded legs . . . something about it was not right, was not as it had been. And then I remembered that the Savonnerie carpet beneath the desk had been a pale green, with a rose-and-vine motif. Had someone switched rugs for some reason, or had . . . No, it was the same rug all right, but blood-soaked now, its green appeared much darker.

Madeleine. She'd sat there. The chair's cushion showed it, as did the corner of the escritoire itself. Some of the stationery too was stained, by fingertips, by down-splashing droplets of blood. One sheet of stationery, folded in half, had begun to crinkle and swell, absorbing the spilled blood.

I saw that the folded sheet was addressed to me. Across it, in a large, loopy blood-script was scrawled the single letter *H*. I too easily imagined a seated Madeleine, dipping her quill in the blood-fount of her throat, setting words to paper. So repulsed was I that I could not pick up the paper. I stood staring down at it for I don't know how long. But the bell would soon sound. And I dared not set the letter aside, for hadn't Madeleine said that the blood faded in seven hours?

So I took it up. I read it then and there, undressed, seated at the escritoire.

And this was wise, for the blood *did* fade. I'd return to the studio hours later to find that very page blank, nothing but the subtlest change of texture betraying the words I'd read, which were these: Help me, please. . . . I made no sense of the words, not for a long while.

Poor Madeleine. She'd have little luck hiding anywhere, that much was clear. She'd bled a red trail from armoire to armoire. (She had indeed chosen two ensembles for me; they lay, mysteriously unstained, on the divan.) The Venetian panel, too, bore the dark print of her hand. It was a cold comfort to see that she had entered and quit the bath by common means. But how *had* she left without my noticing?

The clock on the mantel ticked ever-nearer nine. The supper bell would sound, and still I stood naked in the studio. As for the five questions, I scratched out the first, and second, but soon my predicament was plain: dress now or dine naked.

The first outfit laid across the divan was a lady's riding habit. The label sewn into the sleeve said it was of Venetian origin. It was not new; which is not to say it was unstylish. Quite the contrary. I mean only that it was not newly sewn: it was well-worn, with a slight tear at the elbow. Otherwise, it was exquisite. Sewn of yellow-green and cerise watered silk, it bore basket buttons and braided trim. The skirt opened at the front and back, and there were drawstrings in the side seams, allowing the rider to hike her skirt higher than the mud. There was a waistcoat, of course, and an overcoat with exaggerated cuffs and lapels, both lined with pale blue linen. The shoes, I saw at a glance, would never fit, and so onto the second outfit.

A man's livery suit. Interesting. And my naked feet took easily to the slippers.

What a piece of work this was! I'd long known that gentlemen, nobles and such, had dressed like this, but what *wealth* to dress one's servants so!

The coat, three-quarter length, was of forest green wool broadcloth which I deemed too heavy to wear to supper, and so left it behind in the studio; also, the waistcoat it would have obscured was magnificent. Sewn of bright yellow silk, and featuring a high-standing collar, this waistcoat was embroidered with forget-me-nots, Queen Anne's lace, and fern fronds. Even the button covers were embroidered, with an unknown crest. The breeches were of a paler yellow broadcloth; they buttoned at the knee. Madeleine had set out a pair of downy calves: pads for slipping into the stockings to accentuate the leg. I smiled as I donned these and slipped my stockinged foot back into those slippers.

I took a turn before the mirror. Such vanity! I thought to scold myself, but I was having too good a time. Imagine it: me, sporting something as vainglorious as a pair of downy calves and, moreover, reveling in my costumed reflection!

And so it was the livery suit I wore to supper that first night at Ravndal. I added to it a simple blouse of white linen, with irresistibly lacy cuffs; it was to be worn with the riding outfit, but I didn't care. Along with the overcoat, I left behind a tricornered hat. I twisted my hair into a loose braid, one that hung down over my shoulder; the blondeness shone against the yellow silk of the vest.

My turn before the mirror—first this angle, now that—was interrupted by the second ringing of the dinner bell. *"Parbleu!"* I cried, sounding like a confounded character out of Molière; but it, such grandiosity, seemed to suit . . . well, seemed to suit my new suit. Rather more myself, I added, *"Merde!"* For still I had three questions to write. What's more, I'd no idea where the dining room was; and, if Ravndal were half as vast as it had appeared from the roseraie, the search would be lengthy.

I had just finished folding the fifth sheet and was about to slip it, along with the others, into my vest when the dinner bell sounded a third time. Madeleine had said there'd not be a third ringing of the bell. But there it was, rather insistent. I hoped the bell would sound a fourth, a fifth time so that I might follow its resonance to the dining room.

As it happened, finding my way to the dining room was simple; finding my way out of the studio, however, was not. The only doors I saw were those that gave out onto the garden. . . . I deduced the following: if the Turkish bath lay behind the Venetian mural, surely another panel secreted a door from the studio. Vainly, I pushed on every painted scene, waiting for a wall, praying for a panel to spring back or slide away.

Then I saw a tapestry. A classical scene I did not recognize hung in three thin panels, the outer two of which were cut to accommodate wall sconces. The middle panel moved suspiciously. A draft? Indeed. Behind it I discovered an open door. Thankfully, signifying torches had been lit and set high in their wrought-iron holders; otherwise, I might have wandered those dark halls of Ravndal till dawn. Those sticks, wrapped at their tips with sulfur-soaked rags, had only recently begun to burn: their acrid smoke still hung in the air. They rose at angles from the stony wall to my left. A chilling draft toyed with the torches' light, and the flames flickered. To the right, the hallway disappeared into darkness. Yes, I remember well that first darkness and bone-deep cold. I wanted to retreat to the warmth and candlelight of the studio, not make my way along those corridors seemingly carved from earth and ice.

I walked on, spurred by the promise of answers. The only sound was that of my slippers on the smooth stone floor. The light of the lantern was feeble, and the torches threw shadows all about me; several times I stopped, wheeled around, certain I was not alone, but all the beings I "saw" were but creatures of darkness and light, easily vanquished. Still, at every step I expected some specter, some *undead* thing to rush me. Ravndal might well be crowded with . . . with *what?* With things *inexplicable*.

Just then there came a high-pitched, hollow cry to still my steps. An owl, so near it must be within the house. Again. This was not the plaintive interrogative of a child's imitation; no, this was a throaty and murderous screech, scratching and clawing its way through the manor. The owl's cry was soon answered by a frightful chorus of raven-cry, a sound which, once heard, is never forgotten. These black birds with their blacker cries were nearer even than the owl. Surely they were within the so aptly named Ravndal! Of that I was certain; and so I walked on, bent low, watching and waiting for those shadows, which surely would come alive, to swoop down and strike me.

I passed several arched windows cut into the stone; there were no panes of glass to impede any bird's progress. Anything's progress, for that matter; for who knew what passed in and out of Ravndal, and by what means? The views from these arched windows were of open fields. Above, there hung the bladed moon, which gave its light charily, and so I could not see if these fields were cultivated, fenced for grazing, or put to any purpose at all.

Of course, I'd assumed it had been Madeleine who'd lit my way along those serpentine halls. I *knew* it had been she only when my slipper slid in a slickness spread upon the floor. A blood puddle. . . . Yes, the fire-lit path had been another favor from Madeleine. Strange, that she who'd at first seemed uncaring, even cruel, offering up her curt commentary and bedeviling Sister Claire . . . strange that she was now a protector of sorts. I wondered, had she watched jealously from the shadowed depths as Father Louis had lavished his attentions on me? Certainly she'd loved the priest in life; why should death— if death was indeed the state in which those two *lived*—why should death upset the balance of love?

Huge doors of slab oak with hammered iron hinges broke the walls at irregular intervals. I dared not try one. Somehow I'd know the dining hall when I arrived at it. Between these doors were hung tapestries and paintings. Typically, I'd have held the lantern high to inspect some of the art, but not that night. No. Doubtless I feared another strange discovery. Another threadbare saint bleeding upon a sewn landscape, or a portrait whose subject would speak or whose eyes would shift. No. I would wait for the safer-seeming light of day to see any more of the manor. Quite enough now to simply find the dining room.

First came the aroma: roasted meats, spiced sauces. Then the clear tinkling of silver and crystal. . . . There. Before me. The double doors behind which sat—I was *sure* of it—the dining room. Seeing no lit flambeaux extending in either direction, I grew more certain. Still, I stood listening at the thick oak. I had barely taken hold of the icy iron latch when the doors suddenly, smoothly, soundlessly opened inward, pulling me into the room, sweeping me in to see—

To see nothing. Only light. Blinding, disorienting light. And there I stood. Dressed in the suit of a manservant, sightless, on the threshold of the dining room. I could not see, but I sensed, *knew* that I was seen. Was being stared at.

No wonder I'd been blinded: hanging above the dining table was a vast, multibranched chandelier of Bohemian crystal set with white candles. It was an intricate, elaborate piece, with pendants and rods and a complicated system of stems; white wax spread over its faceted angles. As for the table, a solid slab of red-veined marble, it spread in either direction—it'd take a tall man twenty, twenty-five paces to walk its length—and I saw Sebastiana away to my right, Asmodei to my left. It was they who stared.

"Welcome," said Sebastiana, rising, gesturing to a third, empty seat, at the center of the table on its far side, just under that crystalline sun. I took two steps in Asmodei's direction and stopped, turning to round the table at Sebastiana's end. It was a long walk, and all the while nothing was said.

When finally I arrived at my seat, I said "Thank you." I had no idea just *who* I was thanking, or what I might be thanking them for. But what else was I to say? Life among the nuns had rendered me polite, at least. In truth, I was relieved to hear myself speak, for speech seemed an impossibility just then. The chair was throne-like, high-backed and heavy, each thick wooden arm carved down to a bird's beak at its end; covered in worn velvet—crimson—it was comfortable. Sitting, I said again, "Thank you." This drew Asmodei's rattling laughter. I sat straight-backed, and looked to Sebastiana, who said:

"You are an honored guest, and most welcome."

I remember raising my unsteady hand to the five questions, tucked into the inner pocket of my waistcoat. I patted them as a lover pats a fluttering heart. Indeed, through that thick embroidered silk, through those five folded sheets of paper, it seemed I could feel the quickened beat of my heart.

I sought something to say. My hosts sat silently at my left and right, far enough away that I'd have to practically shout. I did not want to hear Asmodei's grating laughter again; I would do nothing, say nothing to elicit *that*, for its effect on me was visceral, like a bee-sting or a slap, or the rush of desire.

So what did I do? One small thing, the telling of which embarrasses me now. I took up a fork, heavy as a hammer, and sat staring at it. It shook in my hand. The chandelier's light tangled in its three silver tines.

"Are you hungry, dear heart?" Sebastiana was smiling.

"Or have you never seen a fork before?" With that, Asmodei leaned forward so that his white-blond hair framed his face, his eyes sharp and cold. He went on: "If it's me you fear, *arrête*. I've been told I cannot have you. Of course, that does not mean I will not *take* you." His icy eyes held me fast; when he finally sat back, satisfied, I fought the urge to flee, to run from the room and never—

"Asmo, *really!* You are an absolute boor! Insufferable!" And turning to me, Sebastiana apologized: "You'll forgive him, heart. I'm afraid he's quite out of the habit of company."

I smiled, politely; still, I was disturbed. I would settle myself by focusing on what was before me. I set the fork down beside its three companions at my left (twelve pieces of silver in all, among them a tiny pair of scissors; this last utensil puzzled me). I looked down into the white china bowl set atop a plate. I tried to lose myself in its pattern—a tangle of thorny black vines winding up and over and along the lip of the bowl, then back to its center, where there bloomed, in exquisite hand-painted detail, a red rose.

One of the smaller crystal goblets was full of something. Something deeply dark, purplish. Wine, presumably. I willed my hand to still itself. I wanted that wine badly, and hoped it was more of the magical vinum sabbati. I wanted to drink and drink and drink, drain that tiny vessel then and there. When I knew that I could hold the glass without spilling its contents, I drank the whole of it down, inelegantly, sloppily. And I was quite conspicuously casting an eye about for a decanter, a bottle, when I heard Sebastiana speaking; she was mid sentence, saying something about my suit.

"...but I wonder: whatever made you choose it? Of course, it looks *wonderful* on you. It's quite complimentary, but still..."

I waited for some witty, inspired remark and, for once, one arrived on cue. "I thought it appropriate to come among you in servants' dress. I owe you all," and here I dared to look down at Asmodei; I even made a quick and vague gesture meant to encompass our *undead* friends, wherever they were. "I owe you all a debt of gratitude, one I pray I will somehow be able to repay."

"Well, bravo!" Asmodei raised an empty glass in mock salute. "Or should I say, brava!... Fear not, witch, you *will* repay the favor."

Exactly what Asmodei meant, I'd no idea. But it was clear he'd betrayed a confidence, or at least spoken out of turn, for Sebastiana interrupted him by slapping her hand on the table. Too, she shot a look like a poisoned dart down the length of the table. Asmodei said nothing further.

The dining room was perhaps twice the size of the studio. And the furnishings! At subsequent meals I would count twenty-eight chairs (and ten fauteuils for after-dinner lounging) lined up against the walls. The walls were so densely adorned with art that I'd only later realize they were painted a deep, deep red.

Sebastiana, seeing me staring openmouthed at the art, asked, "Are you an admirer or an adept?"

I stared at her stupidly.

"Of art, dear," she added. "Are you an admirer or an adept?"

"Oh," said I. "An admirer only." I'd essayed a few sketches in the past, the best of which evinced not the least bit of talent; I did not hesitate to say as much. "Pardon me," I added, encouraged, "but these... surely these aren't..."

"Real? Oh yes. Most of them. Some are copies, of course, or the works of some lesser member of a school. Still others are—"

"Still others are stolen," said Asmodei.

Sebastiana, as if the man hadn't spoken at all, finished her sentence. "Still others were traded for, or accepted as payment for... services rendered."

" 'Services rendered,' " echoed Asmodei. "Indeed."

"The Watteau?" I asked, pointing up at it.

"Real," said Sebastiana. "Signed and dated—1718, I think. The sketches too are Watteau, though they are unsigned."

"And that?" I pointed to a small and wonderfully grotesque work. It was a dark-hued vase of dead flowers, which I did not yet know was in the style of the Dutchwoman, Rachel Ruysch.

"Ah, a copy that one. Down to the worms on the buds. Exquisite though, don't you think? I may sneak that off someday to be sold, just to see what happens."

"Just to fuel the fire of your ever-waning self-regard," countered Asmodei. Had Sebastiana painted it herself? I assumed so.

Summarily, pointing to the wall behind Asmodei, and ignoring him with practiced ease, Sebastiana said, "As for all those Italians down there, they are all real, all Neapolitan, a few from the holdings of the d'Este in Ferrara." Asmodei said something which I did not catch; from his tone I knew it to be rude. His words drew from Sebastiana a withering look; still she did not succeed in wiping from his face a sly and somewhat menacing smile. The silence that ensued was thick with enmity, and I sat waiting for whatever would result from Sebastiana's having just rung the small brass bell that sat on the table at her right. As my hosts were distracted, glowering at each other, I was able to take them each in. Indeed, they too had dressed for dinner.

Asmodei sported a wrap-rascal, a greatcoat cut from black Genoa velvet. Beneath it he did not wear a waistcoat, but rather a simple mantle of white linen, high-collared and edged with lace. As he sat with his long legs extended out to his side, and crossed at the ankle, I can report that he was unstockinged; too, his black breeches were unbuttoned at the knee. His legs, bare between ankle and knee, were hugely muscled. No downy calves for him! On his feet were simple wooden clogs—sabots, as the Bretons call them—which he would later kick off. His yellow-white hair was loose, with just a dab of orange-butter applied to slick the sides. He wore three large rings on his left hand, two seeming to bear inscriptions; the third was a square-cut sapphire. He wore no rings on his right hand. At his side, propped against his chair, was a cane woven from the fronds of the dragon palm. Asmodei had no difficulty walking, at least none that I'd noticed; the cane was an affectation, or a weapon.

As for Sebastiana, she wore a sort of *undress*, a simple shift of her favored bright blue. It was the addition of a fichu of Antwerp lace (its vase motif identified it as the lace of Antwerp), which barely concealed her ample bosom, and a long silk scarf of that same startling blue silk that bespoke her delight in fancy dress and fine things. Her dark hair was down, unbraided and held back from her face by her combs of red coral. Red too were her jewels: rings and bracelets, earrings and necklaces set with jasper, carnelian, agate, heliotrope— "enablers" all, stones said to assist in bringing about the wishes of the wearer.

In response to a second ringing of that brass bell, a paneled corner of the wall fell away. It was a concealed door, of course; its sudden swinging open startled me. There appeared in the dining room a boy of roughly my own age, bearing a huge silver tureen and a crystal decanter. A boy of striking beauty, whose perfect pale skin showed a flush of anger as he said, in an admixture of Breton and French, "Madame need never ring twice, *eh*?" He set down the wine and proceeded to serve the soup—turtle soup it was, heavy with sherry, as spiced and steamy as his admonition. It was the server, not the soup, I'd drink deeply down.

A few inches taller than myself. Fine-featured, with pale blue eyes. Wavy black hair hanging down to his broad shoulders. He wore a simple work shirt, kitchen-stained, of white linen, and loosely belted blue half-trousers. He'd been perspiring in the kitchen (could it be *he* was the cook?) and that thin shirt clung to his skin, so wonderfully hale and tanned. Having ladled out the soup, the server disappeared into that same corner door from which he'd come. With each slap of his sabots I'd *fought* not to call him back. What would I have said, had I dared to speak?

I didn't dare. Instead, I ate and drank. And longed for more—more food, more drink, and more of the boy who brought both.

18

Origins,
Part I

I<small>T WAS AFTER</small> the Blinis Demidoff, just as this
Roméo came from the kitchen with the *cailles en sar-
cophage*, that Sebastiana said, summarily, "So then, your
questions."

At Sebastiana's direction, Roméo approached me
holding out a small silver salver on which I was to
place my questions. I marveled at the simple strength
of the boy's hands, so much broader than mine,
shorter too. Sparse dark hairs curled on his knuckles,
and his palms (too quick a glance!) were scarred,
showed callus upon callus. Yes, he was a servant at
Ravndal: with those hands he'd never be able to hide
the fact. Most probably he tended the animals—surely
there were animals, in addition to Maluenda?—and the
gardens, which I already knew to be complicated and
vast. . . . Roméo placed the tray beside Sebastiana,

and there the questions lay, undisturbed, for the duration of the meal. (The questions: I burned to change them! To ask five others, mais non. . . . It was too late.)

Finally, that delicious quail eaten—Sebastiana had explained the tiny silver scissors, plate-side: the baked birds' wings and tiny talons were to be shorn, the head snipped off—Roméo came to clear away our plates. He soon returned from the kitchen with four small baskets and an undusted bottle of Amontillado. Surprising me, quite happily, he took a seat across the table from me; he had his own basket, identical to mine, piled high with plums, apples, a wedge of white cheese, grapes in several shades. . . . Odd that the servant would join us at table; but there sat Roméo, slick with perspiration, fairly glistening under that brilliant chandelier.

Asmodei ate from his dessert basket, littering his end of the table with apple cores, the pits of olives—which he spat into his fist before scattering them like dice over the tabletop—and the remains of other fruits I'd never seen before. These same fruits I discovered in my basket too, of course, but I stupidly didn't dare to taste them. The cheeses I ate, washing them down with the wine.

Sebastiana seemed to prefer the Spanish sherry; she sipped her Amontillado from a tiny flute of etched crystal. Occasionally, she'd place a grape into her mouth, quite delicately.

Roméo, who spoke hardly at all, who seemed at times disinterested in what was said, would slip from his seat to refill our glasses, see to the candles, or clear away the detritus of dessert. As Roméo moved, I—despite whatever was being said, words on which my fate depended—I would stare at the boy, dazed, dumb, and delighted as a puppy. I couldn't help myself. The low collar of his shift, its top buttons undone, revealed his thick neck, hinted at the muscled plane of his chest. His collarbone fanned out so gracefully; rather like the base of angels' wings, or so I fancied. His black hair caught the candlelight and gleamed; it seemed threaded through with silver, silver that perfected the blackness, rendered it that absolute black that is nearly blue. And to see those rough, tanned hands handle that silver and china and crystal with such care. I watched his now-bare feet, dark with dirt, crude from use, so practical, so perfect, as he walked the length of the table toward me, passing from Asmodei to Sebastiana, stopping to fill my glass and—yes! yes!—press his hip against me, against my upper arm. Innocently? I cannot say.

Dinner and dessert done, our baskets overflowing with rinds and pits and skins, our glasses full . . . finally, the answering began.

That tray of questions lay beside Sebastiana, the five folded sheets at her fingertips. I thought then of all the hopeful pilgrims down the ages who'd prayed at the mouths of caves, or at the base of large and strangely shaped stones, attendant upon the oracle who would or would not speak, sealing their fate either way. There sat my oracle at table's end, dressed in bright blue robes, adorned with red jewels, sipping the sherry and smiling my way, about to speak:

"Sadly," sighed Sebastiana, "I must preface this game of ours by saying that none of us knows anything, not really." Her thin shoulders rose up and fell. As did my heart; yes, at her words—this *game?*—my heart fell like a rock from a height, dropped soundlessly down, down, down. A *game?* I'm embarrassed to say my eyes teared and I started to perspire. Just then Asmodei spoke:

"Sebastiana exaggerates," he said. And to the chatelaine herself, in a voice measured and low, he added, "This witch knows nothing. Our knowledge— nothing to us perhaps—will be welcome. Is in fact *needed*, no?" His words were weighty with implication.

"Yes. Yes, of course. You're right," answered Sebastiana. "I meant only to warn her that there are no answers. No absolutes. Merely ideas, beliefs, suppositions, and—"

"And it's just these things that mold every age, every sad and stupid age." It was a quite different Asmodei from the one I'd seen who went on: "I say, first, that you underestimate this new witch. Second, that the world we have to offer stands—none too steadily, it's true—on such ideas, such beliefs and suppositions." He sat back in his chair, heavily; he seemed disgusted at having to speak at all. Impatiently, he added, "Move on. Without further qualification."

"Yes," agreed Sebastiana. "It's just that the young"—and here she looked sadly, sweetly, at first Roméo and then me—"the young are always so hopeful."

Asmodei bit heavily into a green apple—bit it in two, in fact; I'd only ever seen horses do that—and sat back resignedly. "Sorceress," he warned, "the night wears on."

"We will tell you what we know," resumed Sebastiana, "but it will not be enough. It will never be enough." She was apologizing for all she'd not yet said.

With a nod I accepted her apology. "Please," I said, "go on."

In response, Sebastiana rang the brass bell again. Rang it long and loud, insistently. I watched that corner panel, waiting for it to fall away and show a second servant. None arrived. She rang that bell for well-nigh a minute, without cease, without explanation. When finally she stopped, satisfied, it was to say, "Yes, we may begin now"; and we did.

In the blessed, welcome silence that followed the ringing of the brass bell, I'd heard something: a fire crackling, spitting to life in the large fireplace behind me. I'd felt its heat, too, and I all but turned to see its flames. I knew that there'd not been a fire when first I'd entered the dining room. I would have noticed it.

I watched as Sebastiana read each of my questions to herself. She said not a word. Her face was free of expression. She'd read each sheet, refold it, and set it back on the tray, arranging them in an order known only to her. The crisp white sheets lay on the silver salver like gulls on the wing.

When it seemed I could not suffer her silence any longer, Sebastiana spoke: "The first question is this," said she, not looking up, her eyes on the three simple words I'd written, which were these: Will I die?

Her eyes rose up slowly. Training their marvelous blue on me, she said, "Yes, of course you will."

"Fool," spat Asmodei. "Did you think you'd live forever?" He motioned roughly to Roméo and the boy stood, walked the length of the table to refill Asmodei's glass from a decanter that sat well within the older man's reach.

I flushed at Asmodei's words. I was embarrassed, and angry. Why had I wasted one of my questions so? *Immortal*, indeed! But there'd been that fleeting thought, the hope that . . . well, simply, I had wondered if witches lived forever. Now I knew. They didn't: they died.

"I know of few immortal beings," said Sebastiana. She would answer the question, though it seemed to me she thought it a silly one, too. "There do exist some, yes; but we witches are not among them. More's the pity," she concluded with a simple shrug.

"Yes, dear, you will die. As will I. No method of divination with which I am familiar can tell us *when* we are to die. Indeed, I tried once, long ago, to divine the date of my death, and I came up with nothing. I read the flight of birds, as our Roman sisters did. I pondered the illegible dregs of countless teacups. I scribbled all sorts of nonsense on mirrors. I even"—at this Asmodei laughed—"yes, I even split the belly of a pig to seek some sign in its entrails. All for naught. Of course, I could teach you how to do this, if you insisted; but I'd be teaching you little more than ancient history. And besides, divination has always seemed to me a *secondary* talent."

"*Alors, vite, vite, vite!* Aren't there four questions more?" asked Asmodei.

Sebastiana hushed him and said, "Now, though I cannot tell you *when* you will die, I can tell you how." The meaning of her words was slow to reach me, overwhelmed as I was by the image of her sifting through a sow's spilled, still-steaming guts.

What I finally managed was this: "Please do." My reaction to this talk of divination must have been plain, for Asmodei then let go that laugh of his and Sebastiana said:

"I know, I know, dear. This *is* difficult. But I know no other way to prepare you, to preface these things." She gestured that I should take a bit more wine, and my hand went toward the decanter as though shot from a bow. As I was about to ascertain the details of my own death, I allowed myself a nice long draft of wine.

"Your mother . . ." began Sebastiana.

"She died," I said. "Some time ago."

"Yes. Of course," said Sebastiana.

"You knew that?" I asked.

"What I know is that every witch is born of a witch. And every witch dies a witch's death."

"No," I said. I simply said, "No."

"I am sorry, heart," said Sebastiana. Roméo played at corking and uncorking the Amontillado, the squat bottle coated with cellar dust and grime. Even Asmodei offered what seemed a respectful silence.

"Do you mean . . ." I began. I raised and drained my glass, and did not need to go on, for Sebastiana said again:

"Every witch is born of a witch."

And every witch dies a witch's death.

Was it a vision or mere memory I suffered then? Regardless, I shut my eyes and saw again my mother's blood seeping from her eyes, her nose, her ears, her mouth. . . . The choke of blood bubbling from her mouth, trickling from her ears and nose to slide down her long slender neck. However did she manage to speak, to point, and send me "to the Stone," doubtless the only *kindly* refuge (or so she'd have thought) within walking distance of our home? Afraid to leave her, afraid too to stay, I ran away. Left her. Never to see her again. Never hear of her again. Oh, I'd asked the nuns—asked till they forbade it—but all I'd ever been told was that no body lay beside the brook. All there'd been was a note, pinned inside my dress, that said, "Keep and save this child of God."

What stunned me then, I wonder? Was it learning that my mother had been a witch, or learning that I would die as she had, suffocating, suffering the throes of that same red death? What stunned me and precluded my asking anything more than this: "Did she know?"

"That she was a witch? Probably not. That she was about to die? Probably so. On neither point am I certain. I did not know your mother. But few witches ever learn of their true natures. If they are not *told*, as you were . . . well, often they do not discover the truth on their own."

"Why." I repeated that single word. It was not quite a question; an utterance. Finally: "*Why* do we die like that?"

"The Blood has always been the Craft's great mystery." Of course, Sebastiana spoke of her own death as well; she'd die by the Blood as I would, as had our mothers and theirs before them. Perhaps that explains the somewhat distant tone she then adopted to say, "It has long been held that a witch's power resides in the blood. So it was that they first began to burn us—rather, burn the *accused*, few of whom were witches; for it was believed that the boiling of a heretic's blood was the only way to save her soul. This according to Augustine, who—"

Sebastiana's exposition was interrupted by the awful coming-down of Asmodei's fist on the marble table, sending each piece of flatware skittering from its place. "Ah! Augustine, *le bâtard*! He had entirely too much to say on matters quite beyond his ken. Would that the sainted one were here to hear it from me! Would that all those death-dealing deities—Aristotle, Augustine, and Aquinas . . . Let *A* stand for ass, I say!"

"This from Asmodei," said Sebastiana to me, "whose A stands for arrogance."

Roméo stifled a laugh, as did I. Asmodei cursed us both with words I'd never heard—the meanings of which were nonetheless clear. Only slightly calmer, he explained:

Aquinas, said he, had seen fit to side with Augustine, championing flame as the only way to win the heretical soul to heaven. Worse, he—Aquinas—had refuted the *Canon Episcopi*, which held that witchcraft was illusory and recommended that its practitioners be ignored, by stating his absolute belief in witchcraft, transvection, shape-shifting, storm-raising, and miscellaneous maleficia, and concluding that witches had pacts with the Devil that fire alone could annul.

Asmodei then turned his rage toward Aristotle: whereas Plato had held that natural magic was morally neutral, Aristotle said there was no such thing as *natural* magic. All magic—including witchcraft, white or black, natural or not—was demonic *or* divine; and its classification was to be made by the Church alone.

Asmodei's tirade went on for some time, his voice rising to a roar, his history peppered with expletives, punctuated at one point by shattering crystal. When finally he paused, more for want of breath than words, his face was flushed. It was Sebastiana who spoke next:

"And join us tomorrow evening," said she, theatrically, "when Asmodei will favor us with his thoughts on Balthus, Boethius, and Boudin.... Thusly, within a month of suppers, we will make our way letter by letter through his entire Encyclopedia of Hate!"

Next thing I knew we were all of us laughing. Roméo stood to applaud. Sebastiana struck a crystal goblet with her knife and smiled wide.

Even Asmodei smiled, cursing us all the while. Finally, gesturing to the four folded slips of paper beside Sebastiana, he said, "Choose another. This *lesson* of yours ought to have at least the semblance of structure, or it will go on all night. And I, for one, am eager to retire to *other* pursuits."

"This one seems to follow nicely," said Sebastiana, a second unfolded sheet in hand. The second question of the evening was the first I'd written: "What am I?"

Sebastiana sat considering her response. Asmodei yawned, loudly; his mouth opened wide, he stretched his muscled arms overhead, and ran a hand through his blond mane. Leonine, he seemed always suspended between indolence and violence. "I thought you all made that clear already," said he. I looked back to Sebastiana, but the next words I heard came, regrettably, from Asmodei:

"I'll tell you what you are. You are a herm—"

"No!" shouted Sebastiana. *"Arrête!"* Sebastiana rose from her seat, as though to somehow *physically* stop Asmodei's words. She smacked that brass bell on the table's edge and it resounded through the dining room. Roméo sat perfectly still, as did I. Asmodei, tilted back in his chair, sucked at a sliver of green fruit.

"Stop it! It will *not* be like that. I will not have—"

"Ach!" said Asmo, dismissively, "I simply thought we ought to—"

"Silence!" commanded Sebastiana. And, surprisingly, Asmodei obeyed.

As Sebastiana retook her seat, Asmodei, fast as light, *flung* that sliver of fruit at me. (I can laugh at this now; then, my heart thumped to a stop.) . . . He missed. The fruit flew past me where I sat, stock-still.

Sebastiana, who may not have seen Asmodei throw the fruit, said to me, "There are words, *base* words from the Latin and Greek, that may, that *do* describe your state. We shan't use them. Ever." She would not label me like one of her roses. And in choosing to *not* reduce me to some four-syllabled, freakish thing, she allowed me to become something other, something more. For that I will long remain grateful.

"Too many sisters were staked on a single word: *witch*. No one, man or woman . . . no one, I say, is reducible to one word."

"That's well and good," allowed Asmo, "but surely you will tell he, she, or it what it is we know of—"

"I will tell her that she is graced. That she is unique. That she is one of us. Family."

Asmodei mumbled something. A sentence featuring words, common, coarse words corresponding to parts of the male and female anatomies.

"I will tell her," said Sebastiana, "that Hermaphroditos was the offspring of the gods Hermes and Aphrodite, the literal union of the male and female aspects of God."

"Whose brother," added a sneering Asmodei, "was Priapus, a troll known only for the enormity of his—"

"I will tell her," interrupted our hostess, "that Plato held we were all descended from a great and powerful race of dually sexed beings—"

"Who," took up Asmo, "rebelled against the gods and were split in two."

Silence then, before Sebastiana—having stilled Asmodei with a burning look—spoke on: "None of us knows where we come from. We are all orphans of a sort. As you remember so little of your mother, so too have we forgotten those who brought us into this world. I cannot be certain, but it—this orphan state—seems requisite: I have never known a sister who was not abandoned.

"And so we forge families—such as they are," and here she looked down the length of the table to Asmo, just then turning his dessert basket upside down, shaking its contents out over the table, "from those we find, from those who—for whatever reason—find us. And, I assure you"—here she pointed a jeweled finger at Asmo—"those reasons are not always clear."

"But why me?" I asked. "Why did you choose me for your family?" I tried, innocently, vainly, to sneak in a sixth question.

"Ah," smiled Sebastiana, "I return to your second question. Our bullying friend is right to say that this night must have some structure."

Roméo stood behind me now, tending the fire. I reacted *physically* to losing sight of him. I dared not turn to look behind me, but how I wished he'd return to his seat or walk toward the kitchen or . . .

"It is true, dear heart," said Sebastiana, "that you are, physiologically speaking, different." She spoke slowly. She chose her words well.

"Indeed!" was Asmodei's sharp, far less considerate aside.

"But we will not speak of *that* just now." Roméo returned to sink into his chair; so too did a smile sink from his pink lips. He seemed bored; better that, I thought, than disgusted by talk of my . . . my *uniqueness*.

"You learned a great deal that night at C——," said Sebastiana. "I trust you remember it well."

I could only nod in the affirmative. When I thought to ask if . . .

"Ah," said Sebastiana, "the *history* of it all. Is it all true? Allow me to answer your unasked question with this, a far less *personal* lesson than that of your final night at C——."

Asmodei said something; I did not even deign to turn his way, intent as I was on Sebastiana, who commenced then a quick history of the Craft. Some of what she'd say was familiar to me: I'd culled as much from books, from histories and religious tracts. Hearing Sebastiana say it was quite different, though: her words were *fire* compared to the ash heap of history I'd read.

"In medieval days," said she, "sorcery and witchcraft were synonymous; and as neither was yet associated with heresy, so-called sorcerers and witches were not persecuted. It was the eventual association with heresy that ushered in the Burning Days, during which tens of thousands of people—women mostly—were massacred, murdered by the Church; of course, heresy had long been punishable by death, since, I think . . . Asmo, the date please?"

"A.D. 430 " Having spoken, Asmodei returned to his wine and the close inspection of a thumbnail.

"Since A.D. 430," resumed Sebastiana, adding, "Forgive me. I haven't a mind for dates. Luckily, *he* has." She gestured to Asmo and went on:

"Over time, canon law stopped distinguishing between sorcerers, witches, and heretics, and began to identify them *all* as heretics and mete out punishment accordingly. This began sometime in the eighth century. . . . Am I right?"

"You are." Asmo shifted in his seat. So too did Roméo. They each of them drank. Sebastiana spoke on:

"By the eleventh century heretics were being consigned to the flames, due largely to the followers of our friend Augustine, who held that only fire could purify, could save the heretical soul. And so it was the Church began to burn, and burn, and burn. First it was the Albigenses of countries to the east and in our own southern lands; then it was the Cathars, and the Waldenses. All because the Church feared the beliefs of these people."

"Dismiss them all as heretics and fan the flames!" This from Asmodei, with forced calm. He held his wineglass up to the light, twirled the liquid around the rim. It did not spill.

"It was Lucius III in, I think, 1184 or thereabouts"—Asmo assented and

Sebastiana continued—"who directed his bishops to investigate all deviations from Church teaching. And, not long after, when Gregory IX issued a bull establishing Dominican investigators, answerable only to the Pope, the Papal Inquisition was *officially* born." It was, said she, "the proverbial beginning of the end."

At the time of those first papal bulls, ecclesiastical belief in witchcraft was relatively uncommon. The *Canon Episcopi*—holding witchcraft to be merely illusory—was still in favor. But there followed more bulls against sorcery and its associated practices, more writings by demonologists and theologians, all of which led to a burgeoning interest in things demonic and divine.

Laws were widely enacted distinguishing between black and white witch-craft and setting forth punishments for both: white witches were to be branded or exiled, while black witches, those convicted of injurious witchcraft, were to be burned along with those convicted of bestiality and "unnatural familiarity" with members of the same sex.

In 1522, Martin Luther, discarding distinctions between white and black witches—"the Devil's whores," and heretics all—railed against existing laws, which required, said he, "an excess of proof" for condemnation and proper punishment. Not long after there came the *Malleus Maleficarum*, which taught all interested parties how to track and torture a witch.

Soon every condemned witch was sentenced to death. In France and Switzerland and Germany, burnings beyond number. Scandinavia burned later, in the seventeenth century, as did England, and its rebel colony across the sea.

"And so," concluded Sebastiana, "thus began the Burning Days. And as you know too well, my dear, those days have yet to end."

It struck me, then: I'd come so very close to joining "the burned." My grat-itude was profound. I drank, and drank some more in silent salute. And then I asked, again:

"So then, I really *am* a witch?"

"And much else," mumbled Asmodei.

"Suffice to say," said Sebastiana, "that you are on your way." Her words were punctuated by the hollow, low call of an owl. I waited for the ravens' response, which did not come. That plaintive *who*. I remember it well, for it came to mock Sebastiana as she read the third question:

" 'Who are you?' She looked to me for clarification. "Presumably you mean: who are *we*? Asmodei, Father Louis, Madeleine, and me. Do I under-stand the question?"

I nodded. And I cast a glance toward Roméo, lest he be excluded.

"Of course: Roméo too. Very well. Let us start then with the boy, our dear Roméo."

How I thrilled then! My skin rose in gooseflesh. Was it the imminence of learning about my Roméo? More likely it had to do with that owl's cry; and Sebastiana's ringing, again, that brass bell, which seemed to occasion a chill of air to blow through the dining room, setting the crystals of the chandelier to tinkling. I shivered where I sat; Sebastiana smiled and shrugged her shoulders and said:

"Sorry, dear, but the boy is a *mere* mortal. Hopelessly, beautifully mortal. And though he is clearly gifted—one need only *look* at him to know it!—it is not preternaturally so. *Homo sapiens,* heart; nothing more."

I was disappointed. "Mortal?" I asked. It's an imprecise word: this I've learned.

"He is neither a sorcerer nor a spirit," Sebastiana explained. "He is no lesser demon, nor elemental. He is a mortal man of some sixteen or so years who will age and die in time, as will you and I. He has talents, yes, but no powers. You, dear, have both.

"Patience," counseled Sebastiana. She knew what I wanted to ask. (Talents for what? . . . What *kinds* of powers?) "All in time."

She spoke on: "This manor has been in my possession for many years, decades. Since before the Revolution. And in all those years, no one, no *mortal* has ever crossed its boundaries uninvited."

"Be accurate," chided Asmodei, "no mortal has *survived* the attempt to cross its boundaries uninvited."

Sebastiana did not take up the challenge, saying again, "No one has ever come uninvited, save Roméo." Suddenly she seemed at a distance, lost in reflection. ". . . A perfect little boy with hair dark as pitch and ice-blue eyes came wandering out of the woods. There he suddenly was, one summer afternoon, some years ago, standing in the meadow staring up at the manor, little taller than the wildflowers surrounding him. I looked down from a high window to see him standing in that sea of color, crying. Indeed, in the stillness of the late afternoon, I could *hear* him crying."

It seemed as though Roméo might cry now, sitting across from me. Candlelight caught the tears that welled in his eyes.

"Enfin," said Sebastiana, "this is what had happened:

"Roméo had been working a neighboring field with his father, turning a small square of soil, readying it for fall planting. It was his job to follow the horse and blade and gather up those stones too large to leave behind.

"Monsieur Rampal would sow whatever crop he could, but I'm afraid he was an unlucky farmer. That summer's crop had barely brought enough to feed the father and son and, as there'd been no surplus to sell, it seemed they'd have to 'do without' for a while longer." Here Sebastiana looked to Roméo, whose head was down. "I think that is why our Roméo has become the finest cook in France." Roméo did not respond. Sebastiana resumed:

"Madame Rampal had died bearing Roméo's younger sister, Mireille, who in her turn fell victim to a fever in her fourth winter. It was not long after the girl's death that Monsieur Rampal, embittered by his losses, died in the field. A horrible death.

"You see, the man had driven his half-blind mule over a nest of bees—or wasps, or some such stinging things—and the blade had split the hive in half. Roméo, turning back from his rockpile at the edge of the field, saw his father running around, draped in something strange and dark, something *alive*, flapping his arms as if attempting to fly. This made the boy laugh, of course."

Suddenly Roméo lifted his head and spoke. "I thought he was playing. Making like the scarecrow, which he had not done for so long. I thought he was playing again, and I was happy. But I should have known. He had not even smiled since *Maman's* passing."

"You'd no way of knowing," consoled Sebastiana. "From such a distance how could you have known that your father was fighting off those stinging things? Impossible. And had you known, what could you have done? There was nothing you could have done, Roméo."

"I just stood near the rockpile, watching him flop like a fish washed ashore. Watching him roll in the turned dirt. He was screaming. And I just stood there, even when I heard my name in his scream. I did nothing. Even when I knew this was not play."

"I tell you again, Roméo, there was nothing you—" But Sebastiana was silenced, for Roméo went on:

"I just stood there. Afraid and stupid. When finally I went to him, it was too late. He lay staring up at the sun, his eyes wide and dry, empty. The last of the pests crawled on his face, on the curve of his nostrils, in and out of his nose, in and out of his mouth until, before my eyes, his tongue swelled and shut that passage off. I *watched* his tongue swell beyond his lips, saw it grow first blue then purple then black till finally it split at the tip and it seemed two tongues pushed from his mouth.

"*This* was not my father, no. His eyes swelled shut; the thin purple lids stretched to contain them, and from under the lids there slid some horrible substance, like turned cream.

"I sat down beside him, not knowing what to do. No one was around. We knew no one; we'd not seen anyone but our creditors for months. What could I do but watch him swell and swell? First his face, till he was unrecognizable; and then his neck went impossibly thick. And his fingers. The blackening nails came off when I took his hard hand in mine and begged him, 'What should I do? Papa, tell me!'

"But he was already dead.

"I must have wandered then from the field, into the woods and to this place. Somehow I made it past—"

"No! *Attends!*" This from Sebastiana. "Speak not of the woods, not now."

Roméo shrugged. "I came from the woods. Sebastiana found me standing in the meadow." He turned from me to Sebastiana and added, "I have not left this place since. I never will." At this Sebastiana smiled. "They have helped me here. Fed me. Clothed me. Taught me much. They have gained my loyalty and love."

"It's enough already, boy!" said Asmodei, not unkindly. "Bring me wine to wash down this excess of sentiment!" As Roméo poured the wine, Asmodei placed his hand on the boy's knee; and farther up, to squeeze the muscled thigh. Roméo, before returning to his seat, crooked one finger and seemed to toy with a golden curl that clung to the man's neck. A filial gesture? Something more, something amorous? I cannot say.

Asmodei, raising high his reddened goblet, said, "To your boy!" Sebastiana accepted the toast and drank. "Now," said Asmo, "tell our omni-sexed guest what *you* are, dearest one."

Sebastiana was not so easily goaded. With a tiny knife, its handle mother-of-pearl, she peeled a large green apple; the skin curled around her wrist in one piece. We all of us watched Sebastiana, waiting. I drank. Finally, the white flesh of the apple weighty in her palm, she said, "I am the witch Sebastiana d'Azur. And you know well, Asmodei, just how this one will come to know me." She bit the apple. She looked to me, to Asmodei, and said, "I think it is time to speak of the great demon Asmodei."

In a single swift motion, which startled us all, Asmodei pushed back his huge chair—a horrible scraping on the stone floor!—and with a giant's stride moved to the fireplace behind me. I thought I heard him speak, mutter some-thing—to himself, presumably. As my chair weighed more than I did and extended a body-width beyond me on either side, it was not easily moved; I did not turn to see Asmodei behind me. I sat still. I *sensed* him there. I heard him stoke the fire. And then I asked Sebastiana, in a half-whisper, "Is he *really* a——?"

Asmodei came up quickly behind me. I looked to my left, to Sebastiana; Asmodei stood to my right. Quite close. I dared not turn. I did nothing. I did not move. Did not speak. He bent down to me; his face was so near mine I could smell the orange pomade in his hair, could smell the wine and the fruit on his hot breath. I reacted *bodily* to his nearness. Finally, following Sebastiana's gaze, I turned—so, so slowly—and saw that Asmodei, with a stick aflame at one end, was relighting several candles in the chandelier. Such *relief*... ah, but it was short-lived, for just then I remembered the silly, showy, lacy cuffs of the blouse I wore. I remembered them only when I realized that they were on fire, had been *set* afire.

I sprang from my seat, waving my arms in macabre mockery of poor Monsieur Rampal. Asmodei reeled back, laughing. Sebastiana stood to chide the man. As for Roméo, I don't know what he did, for two things happened then in quick succession:

First, I tore the flaming cuffs from my blouse and smothered them underfoot in a quite indelicate dance.

Second, I turned to see Father Louis and Madeleine standing before the fireplace, the tall flames burning *through* them as though they were made of mist.

... Oh yes, a third thing happened then: I fainted. Fell dead away.

19

Origins,
Part II

WHEN I CAME to I was lying on one of those fauteuils that bordered the dining room. Overstuffed with down, it was a sort of truncated sofa. I'd been propped up on several lozenge-like pillows, varying in shade from coral-pink to crimson. I detail here the comfort into which I woke for its effect was to heighten my already profound embarrassment.

I'd fainted. This, I tell you, was mortifying.

Roméo sat beside me, urging me to sip from a small golden bowl. Its contents were warm: a curl of steam rose up like a beckoning finger. He'd dribbled a bit of the liquid into my mouth; perhaps that had helped rouse me. Awake now, able to resist, I declined to sip. Roméo insisted. Again, I declined. He persevered, and I gave in. . . . A long draft. It was dark and viscid, medicinal. (This was, of course, Sebastiana's

concoction. A true witch's brew. Had I known its ingredients I might well have
fainted a second time; for I would learn that Sebastiana had heated in the bowl
the oils of rosemary and van-van, stirring in some walnut liqueur and a touch
of hog's lard.) . . . Disgusting, the taste; but so sweet the way Roméo held my
hands in his as we cupped the bowl and I sipped, staring over its rim at his face.
That extraordinary face. What *wouldn't* I have sipped then?

The brew had its effect. The fog within me lifted, and I was able to sit up,
clearheaded, ready to resume. After all, there remained the questions . . .

Eventually, we returned to the table—me with my tattered and charred
sleeves. Sebastiana, apparently, had exerted herself in rousing me, for she'd
removed that fichu of Antwerp lace and now only her blue silk scarf, ever-
shifting, concealed her high, pale bosom. (I remember reveling in the brazen
ease, the openness with which she sat there, so very nearly naked.) Before taking
his own seat, Roméo helped me settle into mine. I sat beside him now, for
Father Louis and Madeleine sat where I'd sat earlier, across the table from
Roméo and me, in front of the fire. They sat shoulder to shoulder on a small,
unsteady bench that looked as though it had been brought in from the kitchen.
Regarding the sudden appearance of Father Louis and Madeleine . . . well, I
was glad to see them. Of course, would that they had *not* appeared so suddenly,
back-lit so eerily by the flames . . . How long had they been present? I think it
safe to trace their advent back to Sebastiana's ringing of the brass bell—the
time-honored means of summoning souls—and the resultant chill I'd felt.

As the answering resumed, with Father Louis attempting to tell what little
was known of Asmodei—and clearly he'd been chided, but not so well as to
take the smirk from his face—I remarked that Roméo, while listening intently,
did not look at Father Louis directly. Rather, he looked but seemed not to *see*
the priest. It was evident he could see Madeleine's blood, see it as a trickling
red fount in the air, falling slowly to puddle and spread over the stone floor.
But as for the *corporal* beings (such as they were) of Father Louis and
Madeleine, Roméo, the *merest* mortal among us, lacking our powers, could not
clearly see them. Only when they were backed by fire, as now, could he discern
their shadowy outlines. It was as though the fire seared their shapes onto the
very air, just as the outline of a burning witch was sometimes seared into the
stake at which she'd burned.

Sebastiana had asked Father Louis to speak of Asmodei. The demon (I use
the word for want of a better, more accurate one) . . . Asmo, I say, appeared
resigned to hearing his tale told. Of course, this seeming disinterest was all
show; and he bore this out when, in the course of what followed, he spat all

manner of remonstrance and reproof at the priest. (Father Louis actually began with, "Once upon a time . . ." before Asmodei arrested him with, "Surely you know this is no fairy tale, *mon prêtre!*")

The priest, unruffled, resumed in a rather grandiloquent tone, as if speaking to his parishioners, or the parliamentarians . . .

"Once, decades back," began the priest, "there was discovered floating in the Loire, near the foot of the centuries-old château of Angers, a hollowed-out tortoise shell. In it, swaddled in rags, there lay an infant. A boy, beautiful but for this: into his still-tender scalp a tattoo had been burnt. Behind the right ear, just above the base of the skull."

I stole a glance at Asmodei and, as I knew he must, he touched himself, *there*, where this tattoo lay hidden beneath his long blond curls. "Is *that* tale still being bandied about? . . . Father, I suppose you believe in the boy from the bulrushes, too?"

Father Louis resumed: "This child's tattoo was identified as the seal of Asmodeus. No priest of Angers would baptize the child. No church would claim him. Neither any family. And so the child was consigned to the care of the crazed women of La Défense."

"Fabrications! Every word fabricated, you fool!" Asmodei would have further berated the priest had Sebastiana not then cued the cleric: "La Défense," said she, "speak of La Défense."

Father Louis nodded. "For centuries," said he, "the crazed and criminal women of Angers and its environs had been hidden away at La Défense. It was there, in the dark, airless catacombs of that secret asylum, that the city elders placed 'the demon child.' "

"They shared me, those women," said Asmodei, quite calmly, too calmly. He sat staring at his left hand, twirling its jeweled rings with the fingers of his right. "I grew, and they trained me to please them. And please them I did." He looked at me, long and deep. "Only among the prettiest and most crazed did I sow my seed. There, in the depths of La Défense, I begat a race of devil bastards! . . . Or so it is said." His laughter rang through the room.

"Finally I escaped, and made my way to Paris. The rest, as they say, is history." Asmodei sat back in his seat, sated and gross, and belched. "More wine," said he to Roméo.

"Let the priest tell it," said Sebastiana. She motioned to Father Louis to continue, and he did, telling how Asmodei was reputed to have killed the Taker of the Dead, the man who descended monthly into the depths of the asylum to gather up the deceased women in their varying states of decay. More was said, but so thoroughly disgusted was I with it all that I recall none of it, remember only that Sebastiana pointed at Asmodei and said, to me, "He is, we think, somehow descended from the demon Asmodeus."

Father Louis explained: "In old Persia," said he, "Asmodeus was associated with Aeshma, one of the seven archangels."

Hah! said Madeleine; the sound burst in a blood bubble from her throat. *An archangel as forebear? Him?*

"Oh, the pleasure I'd take in making you bleed, if only you weren't already awash in—"

Father Louis interrupted Asmodei: "Among the Hebrews Asmodeus attained an even higher place as part of the Seraphim, the very son of Naamah and Shamdon. Still other Hebrew legends hold that he is the son of Adam and Lilith—Lilith being Adam's first wife, the Demon Queen of Lust. She, made from filth before the birth of Eve, objected to Adam's lying atop her and sought to procreate side by side. Denied, she mated with the Luciferians, the fallen angels, and spawned a race of sex-crazed spirits."

"Rather more to the point," added Sebastiana, "among Christians, Asmodeus was said to be the Devil's agent of provocation—the demon of lechery, anger, and revenge, charged with preventing coition between man and wife, wrecking new marriages, and winning men to the ways of adultery."

Sebastiana was describing his avatar as the chief demon of possession when Asmodei interrupted to say, disdainfully, "Yes, yes, yes! And be sure to tell this he/she witch that the great Asmodeus was said to have three heads—those of an ogre, a ram and a bull—and also the claws of a cock, and wings as well! Give it the *grand* details! Tell it of our great good friends Astaroth, Baal, Beelzebub, Belial . . . Or shall I simply recite from the fool Barrett, and tell our double-sexed fledgling of Oriax, 'who, with his lion's mane and serpent's tail, rides upon a horse mighty and strong, serpents in both hands.' Or Agares, 'who saddles crocodiles and carries a goshawk on his fist.' Or maybe it will fancy Apollyon, 'overlord of demons and all discord, who looks for all the world like the simplest of merchants till he spreads his great black wings and . . .' " He glared at Madeleine, for no reason I could discern. "Correct me if I am wrong, sweet spectral bitch, but has not Apollyon ridden dragons down through time, breathing fire all the while? You ought to know, old as you are."

Madeleine, seemingly unmoved, looked to Sebastiana, who said:

"We agreed to all this before rescuing the witch." She spoke in an imperious tone, cold as the roseate marble on which her hands rested. Suddenly it was as though I were not in the room. "You will abide by these rules or you will leave this table."

"This table . . ." spat Asmodei, standing.

"And this house. *My* house." Her measured, steady words had immediate effect: Asmodei sat, adding only, in a controlled tone, "You'll tell the witch about the idiot Weyer, won't you? Now *that's* rich!"

It was in concession that Sebastiana added, "Christian demonologists, through centuries past, have cataloged demons into hierarchies of hell, ascribing to them attributes and duties, even ambassadorships to various nations. Johan Weyer was such a one. He claimed—"

"He *claimed*," took up Asmodei, "that hell held no more and no less than 7,405,926 demons, all in the service of seventy-two princes! The math alone must have been a life's work! Such *fantastic* idiocy!" And Asmodei, in imitation of the demon Apollyon, set then to flapping his arms as though they were the very wings of the merchant/demon. Sebastiana could not help but laugh; I remarked a fondness in Sebastiana's eyes as she looked down the length of the table at Asmodei. Vainly, she tried to hide a smile behind her hand. "Asmodei, dear," she asked, "what supper would be complete without your particular style of . . . of *discourse?*" There was laughter, I recall—it was not mine; but this levity was short-lived, lasting only until our talk turned to incubi and succubi.

"The objective here, as I see it," said Asmodei, coolly, "is to teach this young witch about this *family* into which he, she, or it has been flung. Correct? *D'accord*. And so let us speak now about our incorporeal fiends, or rather *friends*. Succubus and incubus, paramour and priest. Where, oh where, to begin?

"Of course, they'd like us to pity them as they swirl unseen through their spheres of illimitable sex? I think not. Pity the desirous living, not these over-sexed souls!" He was taunting them. Taunting us all.

Asmodei sat back in that throne of a chair. His legs lay over a corner of the table, crossed at the ankle. They seemed impossibly long, his legs, entwined, tapering to his bare feet. Tightly curled hairs, like shavings of gold, gleamed on his muscled calves. His large feet were all bone and sinew, callused and crooked. Oh, how he reveled in the attention (such vanity I'd never seen!). Finally, he tipped the heavy chair back, rocked it on two legs, and slowly, slowly brought his index finger to his lip, furrowed his brow, and said, absently, "Yes, yes, yes. Where to begin?" We all of us waited out his charade. Finally, he began, addressing me:

"They shape-change, as you know." Leaning toward me, his arm stretching toward me till it seemed he might touch me, touch me though he sat impossibly far away, he added, "You'd best beware. All they'd need is a strand of my hair," and slowly he ran his hand through his hair, finally, suddenly pulling free several strands, causing himself pain and obvious pleasure—"that's all they'd need to take my shape upon you. To touch you. Kiss you as I would. On your open mouth, on your *strangeness*. To tug at, suck on your—"

"Asmodei! *Ça suffit!*" This was Sebastiana.

"Ah, but no. It's not nearly enough. Is it not my turn to talk, to teach the witch?"

"Teach then, do not terrify."

"Oh, but it's not scared. Is it?" He looked into my eyes. How I hated him then. Hated that simple word, *It.* "In fact, I think it fancies the idea of a night visit from me. Do you? Do you want me to come to you, to work *my* ways upon you? *Answer!*"

I sat back, startled. He'd lulled me; and now his shouting stirred me terribly, so terribly I thought I might cry.

It matters not, said Madeleine, *for we will not oblige you. Neither of us will take your shape upon the witch. Never!* Madeleine turned to me. *We vow it.*

"Ah," resumed Asmodei, "the blood-dripping bitch speaks! Tell us, succubus, righteous one, why it is you disdain *my* shape?"

Madeleine could not continue. She was overexcited; she'd spoken too quickly; she began to choke on the blood. I watched helplessly as the blood was blown out and sucked back into the mouth-like gash that ran the length of her throat. Long moments passed. . . . Staring, aghast, I had this horrid thought: that, I said to myself, *that* is what it must mean to die of the Blood. To die as a witch dies, drowning in her own blood.

Father Louis succeeded in calming Madeleine, and she continued:

Louis said we had a lesson to teach you. I had only to take form, and come to you; then you would believe.

Sebastiana spoke. "We are ahead of ourselves here, Mademoiselle, don't you think?" The succubus made to answer, but Sebastiana overspoke her again: "Asmodei," said she, "I wonder: can you be trusted to speak—*sans* theatrics—of the succubi and incubi."

"I don't know that I'd describe my speech as *theatrical*, dearest; unless of course you refer to the theater of war." Apparently, the answer to Sebastiana's question was no. Nevertheless, Asmodei was allowed to resume.

First, surprisingly, he motioned for me—not Roméo—to refill his crystal, to pour him more of the vinum sabbati. This I did (albeit with an unsteady hand). He then proceeded to ridicule me when—foolishly, perhaps—I offered drink to Father Louis and Madeleine.

"Oh, how kind of you," said he. "But they've not touched a drop in over two hundred years..." Again that rattling metallic laugh. "You *do* abstain, don't you, dear?"

I stood beside Madeleine; I felt her chill, but still the flames within the fireplace heated my body, mocking the inner flame of my embarrassment. That crystal decanter might have been made of stone, so heavy was it in my hand.

"As you see us now," explained Father Louis, "we are not real. Not corporeal. We will at times hold to our mortal shapes, the shapes we held in life, and appear... *bodily;* but even then, when we might well pass for living beings, we've no need of sustenance, of food or drink."

"Ah," said I, "I see." I sat back down. Even Roméo was smiling.

"You were kind to offer," said Sebastiana.

"Foolish," added Asmo, "foolish and kind."

These, what you see before you, are but approximations of our earthly bodies. These are, more precisely, and here Madeleine hesitated, looking to Father Louis, *these are the bodies we had at the moment of our deaths.*

"When the good father went up in flames and the suicide tore open her own throat, pried out the tongue that had—"

"Asmodei, please," said Sebastiana, rapping her bloodstone ring on the tabletop. "Stop yourself, won't you, when you feel such speech welling up like vomit?"

Madeleine looked longingly, desperately, at me. It was unnerving, and I wonder that I did not look away. *What he says is true,* said she. *I took my life. And now I cannot escape this living death, unless you—*

"Wait! Please," said Sebastiana. Again the rapping of the ring. "All in due time."

Madeleine sat back. She seemed so eager, so sad and impatient.

Unable to stop myself, I asked if Madeleine could not take a more... a *different* shape? I meant, of course, a more *appealing* shape? Why suffer the blood flow for all time if—?

I haven't the strength to sustain another shape. Not for any length of time.

"It, like much else, is a question of the will," added Sebastiana. "Strength of will."

Father Louis explained that he and Madeleine could, on occasion, summon strength enough to take other shapes, as Madeleine had done with Sister Claire. Excepting such "trysts"—that was Asmodei's word—they were bound to their death-shapes. Further, they were bound to water, for it was from water that they drew strength enough to appear as anything at all. It was this watery state of theirs that caused rooms to chill when they came. "We are elementals," said the priest. "As we appear to you now, we are made of water and air."

Like ice. Like snow, added Madeleine.

I wondered why, if Madeleine appeared in her death state, her throat ripped wide, why then didn't Father Louis appear, well ... charred, burned? I asked this of Madeleine. As Father Louis, said she, had burned down to bone and ash, he could not hold the shape of his death. Rather he had to resort to a shape approximating his living self, and to do so was difficult. *His is by far the greater effort of will*, she added. She was the lucky one; for her there was hope.

I remember asking another question that night. "The blood flow," I said. "Will it ever cease?" That incessant bleeding, how to account for it? How was it that an elemental could bleed? Or was blood an element too, like water, air, fire, and earth?

"I must insist, again, on order," preempted Sebastiana. "These five questions only," said she, taking up the salver, "and no more. You see, don't you, dear" she added, apologetically, "that without structure we might sit here forever, tossing innumerable questions back and forth and—"

Interrupting Sebastiana, Madeleine answered: *The blood flow has never stopped, not once since I passed from the living. Will it ever stop? I do not know. But I have hope, great hope. And we have a plan. And you will . . .*

Sebastiana was unhappy, impatient; she interrupted the excited succubus in her turn, saying to me, "I see that if you are to know of these *beings*, it's I who must speak of—"

"Yes, please," urged Asmodei. "*You* do it. So boring, all this claptrap, all this arcana and apocrypha. . . . I'd much rather take my turn upon our witch. I'm quite curious, you know. Tell me," said he, leaning nearer the priest, "what was it like when you slipped your—" Sebastiana stopped the fiend with the clatter of silver on crystal. "Bah!" said he, "so *chaste* you appear, S. But I am not fooled."

"No," retorted the chatelaine. "Impossible to fool a fool."

Asmodei said nothing. He sat rolling grapes between his forefinger and thumb, popping them, sucking them, spitting the seeds this way and that. All the while he stared at me. Finally, he took to spitting the seeds at me. Several landed too near my place; they glistened darkly on the marble.

Ignoring him, Sebastiana spoke of the elementals. "It seems their origins are similar to ours," said she, "that of witches and demons. Tales of succubi and incubi go back to the Hebrews, Egyptians, Greeks, Romans, Assyrians, Persians . . . nearly every faded culture has left some record of such beings. Beings born of 'polluted semen.' "

"Whatever the hell *that* is," added Asmodei. "*My* seed is pure as honey from the comb." He trailed his ringless right hand down his chest to his lap, where he worked it fast and loose; he let his face fall into a mask of pleasure, and I had to turn from him.

"Some say they are beings borne of the semen of self-abusers. Or borne of 'impure' thought—the mind's ejaculate, if you will."

"Sebastiana," sang out Asmodei, "I've a *splendid* idea: why don't we just let these two give us a show. Or better yet, let's set them to work again on the witchlet!"

Sebastiana went on as though Asmo had not spoken. "Some say that they are borne of women. That the succubus takes the semen and passes it to the incubus, who then plants the demon seed in the womb of a mortal woman. Others hold that the succubus draws the semen from the recently hanged, storing it in her womb until—"

"And doesn't *that* make for a pretty picture?" asked a sardonic Asmodei. "Tell us, Madeleine, have you ever wandered the gallows in search of such sex? Is it true that hanged men go hard, that they stiffen and stay that way till all their seed is spent? Do tell us!"

Sebastiana went on without comment. "Christians called them the Lilim, the Children of Lilith."

"Do you mean," I began, "that you don't really know—"

"We know no absolutes," said Sebastiana—and without much effect, she went on to offer this: "But it is our belief in nothing that frees us to believe in everything, in anything."

My mind slowed, stilled itself in the brief silence that ensued and was broken, of course, by Asmodei: "Of course, none of *that* precludes our telling sweet and atrocious tales of incubi with cocks carved of horn and covered with icy scales; or of succubi with cold lacunae, devouring mouths dripping—"

The rapping of Sebastiana's ring. "Be silent, beast!"

"Ah, but none of this is of my own devisal," countered Asmodei.

And remember too that I am *just such 'an atrocity.' I am kin to the legend and lore.* Madeleine was indignant, mad.

"That, my dear, is your problem," said Asmodei, dismissing the succubus with a wave of his hand; this might well have been the start of a fantastic row, but Father Louis precluded such with these words:

"Stop it now! I insist!" Father Louis spoke not to Asmodei, but Madeleine. "Why," he asked, "*why* must you take up this anguish, this suffering for all time?" More was said, whispered from Father Louis to Madeleine. I cannot record it here, for I could not hear it clearly; but I can say of his tone that it was consoling. Madeleine's anger or anguish abated; and she, with a nod to me, *disappeared*. Vanished. As I know of no corollary in the movement of fog or steam or rain or snow, I say simply that one moment she sat across the table from me and the next she was gone.

I rose where I sat, stood staring at the leaping flames. I remained like this for some time, till the flames stilled and Roméo, his hand on mine, gestured that I should sit. Clearly, even with his mortal's sight, he'd witnessed such trickery before; he was undisturbed. Indeed, he was already busying himself with tablework: scraping plates, gathering goblets onto a tray.

"The small hours are upon us," said Sebastiana, "and a witch needs her sleep, as do demi-demons and Breton boys." As she'd made no reference to the elementals, I looked to where Father Louis sat . . . or *had* sat, for he too was gone. The active flames confirmed it.

Sebastiana bade good night to Father Louis and Madeleine, in absentia, and rang again her tiny brass bell. This, accompanied by a fast incantation, comprised a ritual of some kind. This further unsettled me, but Sebastiana drew my attention when next she spoke: "Two questions remain. Allow me." She took up the first of the folded sheets and read it aloud:

" 'Why did you save me?' " Her reply came fast. "Two reasons, heart. One: you are a witch—a most unusual and, I think, talented witch—and so worthy of protection. Two: had we not rescued you, you would have been . . . you would have met an unjust end at the convent." I thought then of Sister Claire, and my heart constricted like a fist. "And there's a third reason, too: we wish something to be done—certain of us, in particular—and only you can succeed at it." She did not explain further, not then. She stood, peeling the blue silk from her neck; it slithered away to show one ample breast, heavy and high; she made no effort to conceal herself.

"Last question." I alone sat enraptured. Roméo shuffled between the table and the kitchen, clearing away the china and crystal and silver. Asmodei, with bare hands, shoveled ash onto the flaming logs of the fire, smothering it. " 'How do I live?' Hmm, rather broad that one. But as it happens I have an answer.

"In the studio, upon your return, you will find two books and an assortment of papers. The black book belongs to me. Rather, I wrote it. It is my *Book of Shadows.* Plainly, simply, it is the record of my life's lessons. It is the story of my apprenticeship, my novitiate if you will. The other book, the red one, is yours. It is blank, yours to fill. It is your *Book of Shadows,* for every witch must have one—several, actually, written over a lifetime. Read mine. Copy from it all that seems of use. Take care to use it well, to *learn* from it. Trust and learn. In it is all I know.

"And now, good night all," and she quickly, blithely, slipped from the room, having summoned Asmodei to her side with something of a low whistle, or whisper. He, as though he could not resist, came up fast behind me before answering Sebastiana's call and with his large hand he reached down and raked his steely fingers over my chest, pinching and laughing till Sebastiana stopped him with a hiss, a frightful protracted hiss. The rigidity I felt poking into my back, well, I did not know it for what it was till I wheeled around and saw the . . . the *flare* where Asmodei's loose linen blouse overhung, just barely, his black breeches. Long after they'd gone I sat staring at the door through which they'd parted, stunned and silent.

"Don't pay him too much mind," said Roméo, continuing to carry things off to the kitchen. "With Sebastiana around, he is rarely much more than very, *very* rude." I offered to help, but Roméo refused me, thankfully; my offer was somewhat disingenuous: I knew myself to be incapable of the simplest act. I was stricken. Overawed. So, I sat.

Will I die?

What am I?

Who or what were my saviors?

Why had they rescued me?

And, How will I live?

The five questions had been asked and answered; and so how was it that I *knew* nothing? The answers were already lost in the questions to which they, in their turn, had given rise.

Finally, I rose to stand before the dying fire. Staring into the smoldering ash, wondering could *I* summon the elementals, Roméo reappeared. " 'Witches and Breton boys need their sleep,' " he quoted, smiling wisely. "I'm sure they've lit the torches, but here, just in case . . ." and he handed me the lantern I'd carried to the dining room a lifetime earlier.

That night, returning to the studio, I did indeed find the two books Sebastiana had described. And though she'd said the books were black and red—the former hers, the latter mine—*that* is not a satisfactory description.

These books were huge, quarto-sized. The paper was thick and slightly waxy, vellum of a sort; despite their slickness, the pages took ink well. The early pages of Sebastiana's book, looked at cursorily, seemed to have been written some time back yet they were still in fine shape. Perhaps the wax had been added later, as a preservative? No—I discovered that the blank pages of *my* much newer book had a similar quality. Both books were thick as Bibles; indeed, they very much resembled overlarge Bibles, their pages gilt-edged, their spines embossed.

I took up my book from where it lay on the escritoire. It was heavy; I held it in both hands. Its cover was oxblood satin, vibrant, vital, a thing *alive*. And into the satin of the cover had been sewn a large, ornate H, a sister ornament to the S on Sebastiana's book; my initial was sewn in black and gold and red thread—ten shades of red, it seemed. Yes, it was needlework, fine needlework, yet it reminded me of those medieval manuscripts whose margins had been adorned, illuminated by monks painting with single-bristle brushes till the onset of blindness.

I opened my book for the first time that evening, as though to confirm what I already knew to be true. It was indeed empty. Nothing but an inscription in the upper inside corner of the front cover. That handwriting—tight, angled, and neat—had already become so familiar. It was Sebastiana, of course, who'd written:

"And if it hurt none, then let it be." She'd signed it, simply, S.

I opened the black book, Sebastiana's. Its cover was faded to gray in places, and small silver triangles both reinforced and adorned its corners. A silver rod had been sewn onto its spine for strength. The pages showed their age: some were torn, others stained. They lacked the suppleness of my untried pages. But this was a book for the ages, of that there could be no doubt, hand-sewn in the old style, covered with care. And page after page was filled—left to right, top to bottom—with Sebastiana's orderly, exact script. Its inside cover bore that familiar S, complete with the toad sitting in the lower curve; it was colored with care. There too I found an inscription:

"*Tutto a te mi guida. Ciao, Soror Mystica . . .*" *Everything guides me to thee. Farewell, Mystic Sister*. It was signed, *Téotocchi*, and in the same hand dated, Venice, 19 May, 178—.

I opened by chance to an entry dated 6 August 181—, and I began to read.

20

From the Book of Sebastiana d'Azur—

"Beginnings—I Yearn for Old Paris—Russian Friends"

IN THE PARIS of my day, there were suppers everywhere; nothing was embarrassing but your choice. These long years later, I struggle to convey a sense of the urbanity, the grace of ease, the affability of manner that made Paris such a charmed place. Women reigned then; it was the Revolution that dethroned them.

We would meet at nine, dine at half-past ten. The company was numerous and varied; no one thought of anything but amusement. Talk of politics was discouraged. We would chat easefully of music, art, literature. We would share anecdotes of the hour. And when the wine flowed we'd act charades—and, as many of our fellows came off the Paris stage, this was an absolute delight.

Need I report that certain rivalries were intense? There were arguments between the Gluckistes and Piccinnistes, which, like as not, would end in furious but funny bouts of wig-snatching! Another time some supposed friends of the writer Poinsinet, having gotten him quite drunk, convinced him that there was an opening at Court for an office called the King's Screen; as audition, they persuaded the poor man to stand before my fireplace till his calves were fairly roasted.

As for the suppers themselves, they were simple—some fowl, some fish, a dish of vegetables, and a salad. The first courses were but necessities, for without them dessert could not be served; and it was over dessert that the singing would begin. Nine was slow in coming; but then the hours passed fast as minutes, and midnight would arrive as a surprise.

I preferred to have a dozen at table, though there were many suppers that saw twice, sometimes thrice that number; often marshals of France sat on the floor for want of chairs. My only rule was to never dine at tables set for two or thirteen; the former was apt to be boring, and the latter begged bad luck.

My guests? There might be the Comte de P———, who lived near me in the rue Cl——— and whose company I enjoyed. Or Madame M———, born of a famous father but charming in her own right. Most esteemed, most fun of all was the Comte de Vaudreuil (governor of the Citadel of Lille, Grand Falconer of France, et cetera), whose mistress was the Duchesse de Polignac, confidante to the Queen. Vaudreuil was equally esteemed as epicure and statesman, and he was rich beyond measure, owing to his family's acres of sugarcane on St. Domingue. . . . Such names! How they ring still in my ears! . . . Let me add: no name rang louder than my own; but it was a name I disdained.

Alors, my name is . . . rather, my name is *not* Sebastiana d'Azur. That is the name I have taken. My birth name is a secret I will keep, and my married name I rejected long ago. In truth, *that* name would be easily discovered by one who wished to learn it, for I was famous in my field of portraiture. Of course, the name by which I was then known was my husband's name—a woman had little choice; a woman artist had no choice at all. A woman wishing to paint *had* to be allied to a man, preferably a dealer in pictures or a painter himself; and so it was I would attach fame to my husband's name. In time, of course, I'd drop the name, the man, *and* the fame.

I was orphaned at an early age. My father found his death at sword's end in some faraway place when I was four. My mother died before my eyes when I was eight. She was a witch, of course. Did she know it, did she practice the

Craft? I don't know. And, as you know how witches die, or will learn soon enough, I spare myself the telling of *that* tale.

A neighbor raised me along with her own five boys. She was a good woman, though husbandless and poor. I left her house when her middle son tried to misuse me and, I am proud to tell it, lost an eye in the attempt. Not yet fourteen, I took to the streets of Paris.

Though I hardly thrived, I survived; and never once did I sell my womanhood, due not to some scruple, but rather because it was expected of me, and so repugnant to me.

It was during those early years, spent begging, stealing, going where the day took me, that I somehow discovered my talent: I could draw. I could draw *well*; and I did so, decorating the banquettes of Paris with chalk and chunks of coal. I determined to become rich and famous when I grew up; and I succeeded, beyond the scale of my most fanciful dreams.

Which brings me again to that man who will remain nameless. My husband.

He was much older than I. A minor portraitist whose canvases possessed *nothing* of their subjects. He and his first wife, *une chocolatière,* had moved to Paris from Brest. She died of consumption. It was shortly after her death that I met the man; soon—aided by an acquaintance who knew of our mutual needs—we'd struck a deal. I would be, in appearance, his youthful bride; as for "conjugal favors," he would seek them elsewhere. In exchange for my public if not private company, and my limited housekeeping skills, I would gain access to the tools of his trade, to his studio, to private collections, to other artists' studios, and to the Salon exhibitions.

It was an arrangement that might have worked well. He, however, soon sought more than I'd agreed to give. Worse, he fell in love. I put him off, retiring to the studio he rarely used and painting all through the night while my husband slept; when he woke at dawn, I would head off to bed. Eventually, quietly, I began to paint portraits professionally, keeping my fees. This was illegal, of course. I was reported—need I tell you by whom?—and officers of the Chatelet seized the studio in which I'd been practicing unlicensed. It was then I left my husband. Within the year, not yet nineteen but at long last having achieved my license from the Academie of St. Luc, I left Paris, too, taking my husband's name but none of his money.

I traveled for some years and only returned to Paris in 178—. Summoned by the Queen of the French, I had no choice but to put my studio under seal and quit Russia. Hastening a life-sized portrait of Prince Galitzen and leaving undone several half-length studies, I set off for Paris. (I was famous by then, though not as famous as I'd be by that decade's end, in the years nearer the Revolution.) This royal commission—among the most coveted in all of Europe—I owed to the Countess Skavronsky, Potemkin's niece, who *suffered* her wealth as no one else I've known. . . . Ah, Skavronsky . . .

Catherine Vassilievna Engelhardt, the Countess Skavronsky, was famously indolent, passing her days recumbent on a chaise longue, wrapped in a black cloak and wearing no stays. With neither education nor talent, her conversation could bore a nun. Yet she had a ravishing face and a sweet if simple disposition, and these things in combination with less readily defined characteristics constituted her charm. I liked her. And she me.

Typically, I would arrive for a sitting to find the Countess prostrated on one divan or another, black-clad and barefoot. On the carpet beneath her lay one of a corps of serfs charged with the recitation of the Countess's favorite stories, to which she'd doze each day between the hours of two and six. During our sittings—which were uncommonly easy, as the Countess could sit still for hours, like no other model I've known—box upon box would arrive from the capitals of fashion. The Countess would offer these boxes to me, unopened. She was disinterested, in fashion as in all else. Having hired a seamstress both talented and discreet, I eventually appeared in society very much à la mode; and jeweled at the ears, throat, wrists, and fingers. Doubtless it was Potemkin who caused to flow this steady stream *de luxe*.

Prince Grigori Alexandrovitch Potemkin was said to be the richest man in all the Empire. He was uncle to Catherine as well as her four sisters, two of whom, Alexandrina and Barbara, had preceded her as his mistress. For reasons I neither know nor care to contemplate, the Prince preferred his third niece to her sisters. The Prince showered her daily with silks and satins, and jewels. She had a jewelry box the size of a child's coffin!

I am reminded of a particular day that I must and will recount, shame-faced as I am.

This day, which, for reasons that will soon become clear, I will never forget . . . this day I arrived early for our sitting (for I was always rushing to paint by the earliest light, though the Countess would not be woken before noon) and I witnessed, in a far corner of the salon, the scene of the serf's preparation. *Mon Dieu*, what a tableau it was! Behind a half-screen of taut muslin, which was of no effect against the noonday light, a young serf—raven-haired, pale, and lithe, no older than eighteen, perhaps twenty—stood shin-deep in a copper tub while two other lecteurs washed him. These three possessed a fraternal familiarity with one another's bodies. Clearly, the ritual was familiar to them all. Clearly, too, it was conducted at the Countess's insistence: wafting up from beneath her divan would come not only her favored tales but the scent of rosewater and lime powder. Finally, the serf stood robed, awaiting the Countess's sign; with a wave of her fleshy hand, he came and took his position beneath her; a second wave of her hand and his recitation would begin. But on the day in question the Countess sought no story; instead, uncharacteristically, she spoke.

Trailing her hand through that jewelry box—always within reach—she said, rather absently, "It is a shame, really, that I dislike such things. So hard, so bright." She moved her hand through the jewels as one would through water. She held a diamond up to the light. She could not close her fist around this rock, which shot light to the four corners of the room! She added, addressing me, "... but I was heartened to hear you say the other day that *you* dislike them as well—and you so *fine* an artist."

"I beg your indulgence, Countess, but I meant only to say that diamonds are rather difficult to paint." (This is true; one tries to render their brilliance without success, achieving but a mass of white pigment.) "In fact," I ventured on, "I am quite *fond* of diamonds."

"Are you?" she asked, her voice uncommonly light.

"I am indeed."

"Well, then . . ." and she handed the diamond down to the serf, gesturing over to the large canvas bag at my side in which I carried my brushes, half-opened tubes of pigment, spatulas, blades, and . . . The serf dropped the diamond into the bag: it was mine. The Countess proceeded to arrange herself just as she had for our previous sittings.

The serf, returned to his place, showed his amusement at my shock and surprise; and he showed much else. In crawling toward my bag, his robe had opened, and now he let it fall open farther. And there the two of them lay: the Countess teetering on the brink of sleep, the serf penetrating me with a stare so deep, so . . . Dare I tell all?

Within the quarter-hour it was the sighing of the serf I heard, broken only by the dissonance of Skavronsky's rattling snore. My subject asleep (as often she was), I finally felt my brush fall still; and I returned the boy's dark, unsettling, and oddly satisfying stare. Did I raise my skirt well above my ankle, did I unfasten the brooch that held tight a lace fichu over my bosom? Perhaps I did. . . . Time passed. We did not touch, of course; but with our eyes in a heated lock, that boy—and what life was that, for a boy of such beauty and grace?—from that boy's flattering tumescence there issued a stream of . . . of pearlescent compliment. Or at least I took it as such. No words were said, but there came then two complicit smiles, sighs, and finally laughter loud enough to rouse the Countess.

"I am ready," announced she, her piled hair askew; she wiped backhandedly at a string of spittle that slid from her thickly painted lower lip.

"Ah," said I, "but the day's work is done." My brush was *atremble* in my hands. I stood no hope of harnessing discipline that day; indeed, what little I'd managed to add to the countess's portrait had to be scraped away that evening.

"So it is," sighed the Countess, "so it is." She excused the serf. (I asked his name, but she did not know it; indeed, stunned was she to consider that he might even *have* a name.) Soon, she descended again into sleep. And I took my leave, amused and newly rich.

(Eventually, upon my return to Paris, I took the diamond to three jewelers. Finally, a fourth dealt honestly with me and said these things: that the diamond belonged in a museum, not a jeweler's shop; that I was doubtless being trailed though the streets by agents of the first three jewelers; and lastly, should I ever find someone with resources enough to purchase the diamond, I might live out my days in an excess of luxury. As I was making money enough, and as no purchasers, presented themselves, I kept the Countess's diamond. I have it still.)

. . . Ah, yes, such luck and fun I found in Russia! . . . And first love, too; or so it seems now.

When I met the Prince of Nassau (at a supper held at the home of the Countess Stroganoff) he was in full bloom. As a younger man, he'd proven himself in the Seven Years' War, and spent three years with Bougainville circumnavigating the globe. Wherever he went, detractors and admirers alike spoke of his storied encounter with the Tahitian Queen. It was reputed that she'd offered him a crown. (She had, and he'd declined.) . . . Tall and broad, he was, with black hair and the bluest of eyes. And what a repertoire of love he'd amassed the world over!

Knowing each other but a few weeks, the Prince and I set out one winter morning in a carriage-and-four, eventually debarking along the banks of the Neva, where, to my astonishment, there were gathered hundreds, nay *thousands* of pilgrims, come for the blessing of the river.

When the ice of the Neva is about to break, the archimandrite comes to its banks in the company of the Imperials to bestow a benediction. Holes are cut in the ice and the faithful draw up a share of what is now holy water. In a cruel custom, women dip their newborn children in the water; not infrequently one slips away beneath the ice, leaving the mother not to grieve but to give thanks for the angel that has ascended.

The horror of having this told to me by the Prince—while we sat riverside in the fur-lined comfort of his carriage—was underscored by the groaning of the ice. I watched horrified as the pilgrims leapt from floe to floe, each making the sign of the cross, each convinced that should they fall in the river and freeze it would be . . . providential. The first to succeed in crossing the Neva presented a silver cup of river water to the Imperials; they, in turn, filled the cup with gold and passed it back.

The Prince enjoyed this day-long spectacle. I found it enervating—two men and a child drowned that day—and so perhaps I did not respond appropriately when, timed to coincide with the presentation of gold to the pilgrim, the Prince slipped a large bracelet onto my arm. Made of hammered gold, and inlaid with sapphire and pearl, it bore this inscription: "*Ornez celle qui orne son siècle.*" *Adorn she who adorns her century.*

It was days later that I was summoned home by my Queen, never to see the Prince of Nassau again.

. . . Jewels, jewels, jewels. Just so many rocks and stones, really, however exquisite. But that bracelet—touched as it was by first love and bearing that inscription—means a great deal to me. I do not wear it. I never have. (What painter wears bracelets?) But I have it here now, heavy in my free hand, as I write to you, *for* you, whoever you are.

Adorn your century, witch, in whatever way you can, for it is the application of our talents, with beauty our intent, that empowers us—and power, thus achieved, that renders us whole.

21

From the Book of
Sebastiana d'Azur—

"To the French Court

I Meet My Queen—Preparations

for a Southerly Escape"

W HEN WORD of my return to Paris—and my riches—reached my husband, he sent his man around with his card, seeking my assent to a visit. I struck a line through his name and sent the card back; this quite piqued him; and when next his man came around it was to deliver a letter bearing a thinly veiled threat. (My husband alone knew of my provenance; and it is far easier to fake the provenance behind a portrait than behind a person, this I know.)

We met at a café, and spoke at length of nothing. Eventually it became clear: I sought his silence and he sought a quantity of my cash; a deal might have been struck if only I hadn't ... *Alors,* it was when the man *dared* speak of that sum of money that would secure but one year's silence—he'd keep me on a tether, would he?—that I began to . . . to *trouble* him. Pain him. (It was my witch's will at work, perhaps for the very first time; of course, I did not know that then.)

And so, as he drew from his breast pocket a contract of sorts, I, indignant, angry, envisioned his heart to be a seizing machine; and watched with satisfaction as his hands returned to pat that same pocket, this time to press away the sudden sharp pains beneath it. Had *I* effected this? I wondered. *Impossible!* A moment later, when, recovered, Monsieur oh so politely suggested we might *negotiate* the sum, my world went red again, and this time it was his tongue I imagined as I knotted a cherry stem with my ungloved fingers. And, yes . . . he set to choking. Perhaps I *was* somehow effecting this. Intrigued, I was; and pleased. I watched as his hands ringed his thick neck and the flesh of his face progressed from pink to purple to white. If it *was* my will at work, what a wondrous discovery! (Of course, never for a moment did witchery figure into this; only in hindsight would I understand what I'd done that day.) . . . For certainty, for vengeance, and yes, for fun, I played upon my husband's lungs, saw them as the closing locks of a canal; and when he tipped backward in his cane-backed chair, I rushed around the tiny table to his side—ever the faithful wife—and, kneeling, lowering my lips to his ear, whispered, "You'll go away, won't you? And never utter my name in less than admiring tones?" Only when he nodded and snorted out his assent did I stand; closing my eyes, I let the locks of his lungs open and air flood in. Leaving him to the ministrations of strangers, I slipped from the café unseen, and greatly satisfied; but still I attributed the "success" of the mission to luck and the dissolute ways to which my husband had long ago taken, the toll of which showed: his burgeoning belly, his cherry nose, his shallow breathing.

As for my old friends, the people of the streets of Paris, they'd helped me so often, had taught me so much; but hadn't I crossed the continent in search of a new life? I had, and so I saw none of them. I even denied a few of them. I am not proud of this—no, not proud at all—but neither do I have any regrets. When I saw someone I knew from days past I ignored him or her. Those people did not recognize me, for I bore no resemblance to the girl I'd been. Once, in fact, an old woman with whom I'd huddled one winter night begged of me, of *me*. I gave her all I had, of course—money enough for several weeks' worth of food, or drink. But I found I could not bear the sight of my new and finer self as reflected in her jaundiced eye.

Some days after my arrival, I sent word to the Court that I was prepared to paint the Queen. I received this response: I was to copy four existing portraits of the Queen, hanging about the capital, in both public and private places, and only upon approval of these would I be invited to paint a portrait from life.

I was *enraged;* naively, briefly enraged. But what choice did I have? And so I dashed off the four copies and had them delivered to the Court. By what criteria they were judged, I've no idea. In due time, three liveried men arrived at my door bearing my invitation to Court—I noted pridefully that it bore both the royal seal *and* signature.

And so I went to Versailles, the splendors of which I will not describe, as such accounts are easily come by.

That first day I sat waiting for hours on a stiff-backed chair in a hall whose every surface seemed mirrored. The walls—mirrored, yes—were hung with mostly inferior portraits. Thankfully, there was a lone Van Dyke, as well as some heads by Rubens and Greuze to hold my interest.

Long hours passed. Finally, another coterie of liveried men arrived and issued me into an antechamber. (At Court, wherever one looked, there were servants or nobles in attendance; the French Court suffered a surfeit of servitude, the like of which I have never seen elsewhere.) More waiting. Finally, I was joined by Madame de Guéménée, a favorite of the Queen; she was also governess to the King's sisters, Clotilde and Elisabeth. This woman—and here I will suppress my *initial* opinion of her, owing to later kindnesses received from her—this woman, decorated to excess, entered the antechamber trailed by no fewer than a half-dozen pugs.

Soon more attendants arrived to lay a small table with the midday dinner. (I'd arrived at the palace just after break of day—as always, seeking to paint by early light—and now here it was suppertime!) Madame and I—and the dogs, porcine pests, no higher than my shin—proceeded to dine. The dogs had bowls with a china pattern all their own. An attendant fastened bibs around their thickly fleshed necks.

Some of the dogs, said Madame de G., were the Queen's. Indeed, they bounded about that antechamber barking and nipping and . . . and *relieving* themselves as though the throne were theirs. Amazingly, not one of the many servants present—there was one in each corner of the room, and two beside each door—seemed to have full charge of the mean-spirited, muscular mutts. I watched in horror as these dogs chewed the edges of age-old tapestries, shat on the Savonnerie carpets, and scratched at the parquet floors with their tiny clicking black-lacquered nails. They scrambled up onto damask-covered couches. They chewed the gold leaf from chair legs. (Perhaps that is the true and lasting measure of Versailles: that the dogs there passed precious metals!)

Only after supper was I informed that the Queen was unable to see me that day. "You are to return on the morrow," announced de Guéménée, reading from the note that had been carried into the room by not one but *two* men— the one to carry it and the other, presumably, to catch it should it fall.

I was angry. Again, what could I do? I could refuse to return. I thought of those artists, my lesser peers, who sought *constantly* the Queen's attention. Tischbein, Grassi, Lampi, Vestier, Mosnier; and the women, Marguerite Gérard, Marie-Victoire Lemoine, Rose Ducreux—and *despicable* Adélaïde Labille-Guiard, whose work was indistinguishable from her master's and who . . . ah, but it is of no import now. . . . Yes, I thought then of those painters, rivals all, any one of whom would have *crawled* to Versailles to paint that corps of the Queen's pugs, and I said yes, fine, I would return on the mor- row. I departed then, but not before I succeeded in showing the snapping, cerise-collared pug—it was worrying my hem—the pointed part of my shoe!

Neither did I meet the Queen my second day at Court.

The third morning at Court, I left my assigned chair in yet another vast and drafty hall, this one crammed with history paintings hung floor to ceiling, four-high, and went for a walk. I was growing increasingly indignant with each passing hour. I determined that I would never again be used in such a way, nei- ther by queen nor pauper.

I was walking along a thin avenue bordered by high shrubs, fragrant with jasmine and honeysuckle, considering my proper vengeance—perhaps I'd por- tray the Queen with pendulous earlobes, or a too-thin upper lip, or large hands. Just then, hearing a commotion, I rounded a hedge and came full upon the Queen and her party. There she stood. Only at some pointed sign from an attendant did I remember to curtsy; unpracticed at that art, I nearly overbal- anced.

It was Madame de G. herself who stepped forward and presented me to the Princesse de Lamballe and Yolande de Polignac, and then, finally, the Queen herself.

I said nothing. The Queen said nothing. Only the birds in the trees dared speak. And then, in a move which sent her party into paroxysms, the Queen slowly, slowly, took a half-step backward, snapped shut her fan, and with a grand gesture bade me continue my walk in whatever direction I chose. The sudden intake of breath among the Queen's courtiers sounded like the whistling mistral! This was, of course, an *uncommon* courtesy. Quite uncommon.

Arriving at Court for the fourth consecutive day, I was told that the Queen would see me directly, and so she did.

I confess: I became an admirer the moment I met her. Then—this was the middle eighties—the Queen was still quite beautiful, or so she seemed to me. She was tall and well-built; if one liked her, she was "large-boned," "stout" at worst; if one disliked her, well, there were adjectives in abundance. Her features were not quite regular: she had inherited the long and narrow, oval-shaped face of her Germanic ancestors. Her eyes were a beautiful blue, but not large. They seemed to me *kind* eyes. Her nose was slender and fine. I will say that I found her mouth too small to be beautiful, and yes, her lips *were* a bit thick—but these faults will not be seen in any portrait *I* painted of her! No indeed.

Her walk was . . . stately. She carried her head—*mon Dieu!* the irony there— she carried her head, I say, with a dignity that stamped her "Queen" in the midst of all the Court.

What I most clearly recall these long years later is the splendor of her complexion. Her skin was nearly transparent. I had some difficulty rendering its true effect, for it bore no umber in the painting. I chose a fresh, delicate palette, and after only three sittings showed the Queen a bust that pleased her greatly. It was then she extended that invitation *most* sought after by all the portraitists in France—*no*, in all of Europe! She invited me to paint the royal children.

Soon all the Royals, or nearly all, had sat for me. The King's brothers, the Comtes d'Artois and de Provence, and their wives; plus other Princes of the Blood—the Ducs de Bourbon, Condé, Penthièvre, Conti, and Orléans. And Madame Royale. And Madame Elisabeth. And a *host* of lesser nobles. Those who had *everything* had nothing till they posed for me! Of course, I charged what I pleased, and it was quickly paid. In one six-month span, I declined *five times* the number of commissions I accepted. Of greater concern to me then was the hiring of bankers: I painted only between appointments with same.

The wealth suited me, but the renown did not. It was when a portrait bust of *myself*, sculpted in terra-cotta by Pajou appeared in that year's Salon that I *knew* it was time to travel. I'd evolved from an artist into a work of art! Unwittingly, I'd traded away my anonymity. Yes, it was time to leave Paris. Again.

Preparing for my departure, I discovered a slight problem: my fame had outstripped my credentials. And one *needed* certain affiliations, certain credentials. Licenses. Memberships, et cetera. A bother, really, but still a necessity. And so, I determined to gain admittance to the Royal Academy of Painting and Sculpture.

I set to work. I retired to my studio. I saw no one. I spurned suitors, rejected the few friends I'd made. I completed my outstanding commissions and took no more.

What followed was a difficult period, artistically. It was a time in which I learned the value of discipline. Let me explain: history was the most respected genre, not portraiture. I had never done a history painting. What's more, I never *would* have done a history painting if the Academy had not. . . . Suffice to say that inside of three months I had produced five histories—"Innocence and Justice," "Peace Bringing Back Abundance," "Venus Binding the Wings of Cupid," "Love Testing an Arrow in the Presence of Venus," and "Juno Borrowing the Girdle of Venus." (This output would have taken another painter two, perhaps three years; indeed, I had to "play" with the dates of composition.) These paintings were all mediocre, by my standards, but they were more than good enough to gain me admission to the Academy. In truth, I might have painted anything, for the Queen was rather vocal in support of my application. Indeed, one day, in the course of a final sitting, I confided to her that these works shamed me, that having to do the histories angered me, and she paid me thirty-five thousand francs for all five paintings and promised to store them and never show them.

That same day the Queen gave me a letter of introduction to her sister, Queen Maria Carolina of Naples. And so it was I decided on a southerly route from France, from unwanted fame, and from a name not my own.

22

From the Book of Sebastiana d'Azur—

"Séjour en Italie:

Away from Rome—Sublime Naples!—

La Serenissima—I Meet My Soror Mystica"

I WENT STRAIGHT to Rome, but as I found that ancient place overactive—owing to some high ceremony involving Pius VI—I stayed but three days before hastening to Naples. I went via the inland valleys, the mountains rising all around and showing their high-lying cities and castles and churches and convents as some women show their jewels, high on an ample bosom.

Naples . . . Sublime! It was summertime, and the blazing golden light—the color of the palest topaz—was spectacular. That Neapolitan light—and the true artist will always ask of a place she has not seen, What *is* the light like?—the Neapolitan light *enchants* as it filters down through vine-covered trellises, flows over marble and stone. Yes, nowhere is shadow so charming, nowhere is color so charged. Nowhere has accident such grace. Coming as I had from the clutter and clamor of Rome, I savored the higher pitch of light and color, as well as the lower pitch of everything else.

I settled at the Hôtel du Maroc at Chiaja, south of the city. The view from my room was splendid: the sea and the Isle of Capri in front of me; to the left stood Vesuvius, belching up smoke and steam; and to the right spread the hills of Posilipo, dotted with white villas, diamantine under that strong sun.

I was so taken with the city itself, I did not hurry to Court.

In the evenings, as the purple wine flowed and the golden light faded, I dined among the natives. I forged good relations, as every traveler should. Once or twice too often, perhaps, I danced the tarantella with men whose names I did not care to learn.

Those first days were passed near the Porta Capuana and the Piazza del Mercato, its trundle carts and stalls fragrant from their wares. I ate from those traveling restaurants, which come along on wheels, announcing themselves by the rattle of their hanging pots and pans, wherein bits of cuttlefish are always on the boil in a spicy sauce, to be served with spaghetti and with fruit to follow, the whole of it washed down with cooled lemon water. *Exquisite!* Finally, after faring out to Pompeii one Sunday afternoon—and there I enjoyed the late-day hours of lengthening shadows—I resolved to go to Court the next day. It was time. I was due, if not expected.

I'd heard that the Royals were about to venture abroad. The King, Ferdinand IV, and his consort, the Queen Maria Carolina, sister to the French Queen, were going to Vienna, the first stop on a tour intended to secure dynastic marriages for their children. Through a quick correspondence, it was determined that I would paint the Prince and Princesses in their parents' absence.

Eventually, the King and Queen sent word of their successes. Their daughters, the three Marias—Theresa, Luisa, and Cristina—would settle upon lesser thrones in Austria, Tuscany, and Sardinia. Happily, I had painted the last of the Marias by the time the first of these announcements arrived in Naples, and so I was able to avoid the ensuing pomp. I focused instead on the full-length portrait of their brother, Prince Francesco di Borbone, who was seventeen and nicely handsome, not marked—as were his sisters, mother, and aunt—by his Austrian forebears.

The Prince . . . I decided to paint him in a rather traditional pose—just a hint of a palatial setting, with swags of heavy emerald drapery behind him, two columns framing an easy scene of the distant Bay of Naples. I would add several stock accessories, such as the corner of an ornate desk upon which I would place a globe and several laid-open books, all intended to portray the Prince with a worldly, educated air that he did not, in fact, possess.

I painted the Prince in profile. Despite this pose, he would not stop turning toward me to stare, smitten, wide-eyed and smiling. I would announce playfully, "I am doing the eyes now," and urge him to resume his pose. Invariably, he would turn slowly back toward me, as a flower finds the sun. So tempting. Indeed, I received many commissions to paint the forms of those who admired my own. But in the Prince's case, I was disinterested, merely flattered; and this was no impediment to the work: I could have completed the portrait of the Prince in his absence: sittings are more often than not a rite, a ritual conducted for the subject's benefit.

As Court Portraitist, I sat beside the Prince at the Te Deum—for four voices and orchestra—written and sung in honor of the newly affianced Princesses. This gave rise to rumors; two ministers suggested, strongly, that I absent myself from Court before the Queen's return.

As I'd come to Naples by the mountains, I returned to Rome in sight of the sea. I preferred to travel at night, saving the days for the happy hazard of things. I was on the road a long while, stopping whenever I wanted, enjoying the hospitality of the natives. Every Italian, just met, seemed a friend.

Sadly, Rome—save for its many Raphaels—remained unimpressive. I cannot say why. I played the tourist, took some quick commissions—nothing more involved than some pen-and-ink busts. Within a week of my arrival, I'd made plans to decamp to Venice.

Upon my arrival there I sought out one Dominic Vivant D———: I had a letter of introduction from a Neapolitan nobleman. . . . Or was it a *Parisian* nobleman? I forget Signore D———'s profession; it is probable he had none, and was merely, idly rich. All I remember of the man is that he possessed neither talent nor charm, and I would not have passed a second evening in his company had it not been for his mistress, Isabella Téotocchi.

Téotocchi was a popular hostess, reputedly quite "liberal" in her ways. Well known by one name, regardless of her marital state—which varied suddenly and often—Téotocchi had taken on D——— as a lover for reasons all her own. Indeed, while I was still in Venice she would drop D——— and marry the State Inquisitor, Count A———, whom she did not love. This alliance was purposeful, and it was as the Countess A——— that Téotocchi oversaw a salon frequented by the likes of Casanova, Chateaubriand, and Madame de Staël; too, her influence over Venetian legal affairs ought not to be diminished.

Téotocchi! She had a talent for life, and her death, some years back, shook me badly. The Blood came to her in public; she had not felt its advent. One moment she sat along the Riva degli Schiavoni, taking tea among the tourists, a white silk parasol aslant on her shoulder against the sun, and the next moment she lay fallen from her chair, choking, the Blood bubbling from every orifice, seeping from every pore . . . Ah, but perhaps I should temper this? Perhaps this is more than you care to know about the Blood? I will say only this, then: you *must*, sister, avoid such a fate! Listen to the Blood. They say it warns of its coming.

When first I met her, Téotocchi—my Soror Mystica, the one who taught me so much—was, though in her middle years, possessor of a *full* beauty. Standing quite tall, she'd go about black-clad through the hottest Italian summers; she preferred, as I do, draped fabrics as opposed to those of the tailored type. She favored the cape-like, concealing domino and wore it whenever she pleased, not just at Carnevale. Black hair, fair skin tinted by the Italian sun . . . and those eyes! Their green-blue sparkle *shamed* the Venetian lagoons. They were the first eyes to show me *l'oeil de crapaud*.

And so it was in Venice, in the years before Revolution came to Paris, shaking society off its axis, that I began to learn. To trust and learn. Of course, the first thing I learned was my true nature: that I was a witch. Then, there came the Knowledge, which, I assume, someone or something has shown you, or is showing you now. I wonder, is it me? Am I, Sebastiana d'Azur, *your* Soror Mystica? Have you come to read, to transcribe from *this*, my *Book of Shadows*? Am I with you? Am I alive or have I suffered the Blood?

. . . I spent several months secreted away with Téotocchi. I faked my taking leave of Venice—I was rumored to have accepted a lucrative offer to paint the daughter of a Portuguese merchant; which rumor I started—so that, should I be spied, the spy might doubt his or her own eyes.

Our days were spent in the upstairs rooms of Téotocchi's well-appointed palazzo; a catalog of its contents would include the finest furniture, Chinese prints, Egyptian papyri, and countless books and manuscripts. Each morning, boats would arrive laden with fruits, flowers, and vegetables, and we had only to drop our baskets down by their strings to secure such things as oranges from Palermo and fish drawn from the sea not an hour earlier. We ventured out onto the canals and into the piazzas only at night; even then we went disguised. In Venice, a city accustomed to costumery, this was easily done.

Yes, we "studied" by day, and at nightfall we descended, disguised, to dine. We favored the restaurant of Santa Margherita, which had paper lanterns of every hue hung about its arbor. Each night we ordered the same dish—filet of sole cooked with raisins, pine kernels, and candied lemon peel—and never tired of it. Over Braganza wine and clove macaroons, we'd talk away the small hours of the morning, me struggling with the Italian I'd not yet mastered. Other nights, nights when it was too hot to sleep, so hot it seemed even the nightingales and gondoliers had lost their voices, we'd descend to sit in silence beside the canal, where innumerable shellfish glittered at the foot of the sea-wall, where seaweed shone black on the moon-silvered water.

I remained in Venice through a season of festivals, and I might have stayed forever if not for . . . Well, Téotocchi had always said, without explanation, that I'd have to leave Venice. I had turned a deaf ear, but finally the dreaded day came, and Téotocchi would brook no debate. We were to witness the marriage of the Doge and the sea; then, said she, I was to leave the city.

On the appointed day, we boarded one of the thousand crafts that clogged the canals and we sailed out into the harbor. At the head of our tiny barque stood Téotocchi's beloved servant boy, Nicolo, so richly, so darkly beautiful. (Indeed, Téotocchi had a household rule: when she was at home, which was often, Nicolo was to be unclothed, regardless of his pursuit, chore, or leisure. It was an arrangement that seemed to *suit* them both, and though I soon grew accustomed to his nakedness, never did my admiration wane. Far from it: indeed, much later, when Nico was made to perform at my esbat in Paris, I . . . Ah, all in time.

(For now, I'll say this: in Venice, Nicolo was directed to love me, or rather to make love to me. And this he did with all the ardor of an aficionado. Téo-tocchi had a jeweled hourglass with two handles of jade; and so it was that the slow, slow passage of sand governed Nico's use of his lips, his tongue, his fingers, and his quite dexterous and durable member. Lessons, they were. And Téotocchi witnessed each one, including my . . . deflowering. On that occasion, she gathered up the bloodied silks on which we'd all lain, boiled the blood from them, and gave the extraction to Nicolo—a love philter that heightened his attraction, strengthened his attentions, tiringly so. Finally, with-drawing from Téotocchi's *laboratoire d'amour,* I left her to suffer Nico's boyish aggression alone, and I resumed a less strenuous course of study. . . . Of course, you know, witch, it is common among the sisterhood, the keeping of boys.)

The city was deep in celebration, the canals chock-a-block with boats.

Finally, too sad to speak, I saw come the great, gilded vessel, the *Bucintoro*. The Doge sat high upon it, senators at his slippered feet. In its wake came boatfuls of musicians, all brightly clad. The smooth dark wood of their instruments shone under the sun. The sea sparkled, the city itself seemed cast in gold.

As the *Bucintoro* neared—Téotocchi had known just where to anchor, and Nicolo had guided us expertly into place—I could see clearly the old Doge and the older senators, skeletal in their black gowns, clownish in their three-bowed wigs.

Then, the ceremony itself: the Doge stood—cheers from the flotilla, washing back like a great wave over the city—and quite showily slipped a ring from his finger. He held it high, as high as he could, as though seeking to set it on the sun. It seemed he stood like this for an eternity, until the cheering stopped and silence spread from the sea to the shore. Perfect silence. No sound but the sea's music, the hollow batting of boats one against another. And then, finally, the Doge sent that glistening gold ring arcing through the air to fall slowly, slowly—and, I swear it, *audibly!*—into the sea.

A thousand canons announced to the citizenry the consummation of this marriage, said to ensure the safety and prosperity of the city long known as La Serenissima. Bells rang above the canons, summoning all Venetians to masses of celebration.

We three remained at sea. Finally, Téotocchi took from a pocket deep in her own black robe a simple gold band and, with far less ceremony but with equal solemnity, she slipped it onto my finger, ensuring *my* safety, *my* prosperity.

That evening—it was a starlit summer evening some seven months after I'd arrived—I left Venice.

23

From the Book of Sebastiana d'Azur—

"I Return to a Troubled Paris"

I TRAVELED, alone, and all in the service of my art. . . . In those days, I would travel any distance to see a certain painting. I had boundless energy for such trips. In some places I passed months; in others, weeks or days, hours even. Finding a place anything less than exquisite, I would simply summon my coach. All the while, of course, I missed Téotocchi.

It was always the same, my modus operandi. I would arrive in a city noisily, splashily, attending one or two soirées—and then I would disappear. I made sure my name was known, that word of my presence was whispered in all the finer salons. In each city, I would contract a young man to do my bidding— shopping, for foodstuffs as well as pigments, canvases and other painterly supplies. Usually it was a university student. Eventually, these boys—they were not quite men, at least not when I met them—these boys would deliver the lesser portraits, collect the smaller fees. Payment far in excess of services rendered guaranteed their silence, their loyalty. (I admit to other means of inducing loyalty, means which were mutually satisfying.) So, I would not be seen in society, sometimes for weeks on end. I would tell everyone that I was simply too busy to accept invitations. I was the author of countless regrets.

Occasionally, the privileged would come to my door. Oh, the deep delight of looking a prince in the eye and telling him, squarely, no. "*No!*" And then, as his fleshy cheeks flush with anger, as tears of frustration well in his rheumy eyes, at the very *instant* when it seems you might fall out of favor, you recant. "Oh yes, yes, yes," I would say, flustered, "I *will* do it. For you, sir, I *must* do it!" And then I would shoo him away, always, *always* having upped my original price, and I would turn out the portrait in a half-day. (Indeed, the portraits were often completed before negotiations were!) "No, no, no," I would say, "one sitting will do. The Prince is *far* too busy to sit twice!" In truth, I could not bear sitting idly through more modeling than was needed, for in the presence of my subjects I had to slow the speed at which I painted.

Then, with the agreed-upon date of delivery at least three days past, I would touch-up the portrait—so that it was wet when delivered—and bring it myself to the subject's city mansion or his summer estate, careful to appear a bit disheveled, dressed in a paint-smeared smock, a touch of kohl under my eyes. Breathlessly, I would apologize for the delay; and then, payment in hand, I would humbly take my leave, denying all manner of invitation to sup, to dance, to pass the weekend, *"Mais non,"* I'd mutter, "So-and-so sits, this very minute, in my studio!"

It was a grand scheme! Skillfully, playing prince against prince, court against court, I managed to send my fees skyward! Previously, my peers had charged two or three prices for their portraits. Eventually they would all adopt my pricing policies—that is, one price for a bust with one hand, half again as much for both hands. To the knees? The feet? That would cost more. Posed thematically, and accessorized? For a full-length portrait with a minimum of attributes I might receive six or eight, maybe even ten thousand livres.

When I'd left France at the age of nineteen, I had twenty francs tucked in my shoe. In the course of my travels abroad, I earned in excess of one million francs! No painter in the whole of Europe earned more than I. For this, of course, I was reviled by my fellows.

As they will, rumors arose. It was said that I'd been spied in the streets of this or that capital, wrapped in sable and dripping sapphires. My favorite story had me receiving—from the very Minister of Finance, no less!—a quantity of sweetmeats wrapped in banknotes, payment for a portrait of his mistress done *sans robe*. As reputed, it was a sum large enough to topple the treasury of the tiny country in question. Nonsense! The Minister sent me a mere four thousand francs in a box worth twenty louis. What's more, his mistress, the charming Mademoiselle B——, was not, in fact, naked, but rather ... *erotically* accessorized. Dressed as a shepherdess, she was, posing recumbent on a length of sod brought into my studio at the Minister's expense. I had to cut those sittings short, in fact, for the Minister insisted on being present and he ... well, he became *overly enthused* at seeing his mistress thus arranged. Finally, I could no longer suffer his bleating! I turned them both out and completed the portrait in private.

Those were great days, yes; but at long last I returned to Paris.

I drove through the streets of my city, just as I had when first I'd returned from Russia, summoned by the Queen. I was eager to see what had changed and what—blessedly!—had not. I'd been gone now several years; but always, *always* the larger part of my heart held to Paris as my home. I have always believed one can love a place as one loves a man or woman: passionately—any true traveler will tell you as much. So it is with a heavy heart that I speak of the Paris to which I returned, for it was not the Paris I'd left, and loved.

Paris still had that certain sheen, that appeal that is, or *was* hers alone. But, trite though it may be, I find I must liken her to a courtesan whose day has passed, whose gross *maquillage* obscures what might remain of her true beauty, who clings tenaciously to her ceremonial ways. I saw this whore close up now, harshly lit by my long years' absence. I saw how her rouge was applied in circles too perfect, how her goat's-hair wig had shifted, how it sat crookedly on her head and stank of rancid butter, I saw how her one real gem sat loose in her ring and rattled as she beckoned with her puffy, brown-spotted hand. But then my coach would turn a corner and there she'd be, the sweet brazen bitch of old, snapping her fan, batting her long lashes, thrusting out her high bosom, and having her way ... and all was suddenly set right.

I speak, of course, of the final days of Paris—though none of us knew it was the end. It would be a few years more before Dr. Guillotine's girl would clog the gutters with gore, but looking back there is no doubting it: *those* were the last days of Paris, the Paris I knew, the Paris I loved. *My* Paris.

Those were the days when Madame de Genlis and her sisters-in-law would dress as peasant girls, have their women gather all the day's milk off their estates, and transport it, by donkey, to Madame's manor house. There, Madame and her "girls" would dump it into a bath built for four, strip and wallow in the milk for hours, its surface strewn with rose petals.

Those were the days when nobles had gemstones sewn onto their shoes, silver buttons sewn onto their cuffs.

Those were the days when women paid huge sums of money for bonnets honoring Turkish sultans and Carmelite nuns, as Fashion saw fit. These same women would sit for hours as their hair was wrapped in curling papers and frizzed with hot irons, combed out with nettle juice, and powdered with rose root, ground aloe wood, red coral, amber, bean flour, and musk, the mass of it then wound around a horsehair cushion and festooned with flowers, fruit, feathers, and figurines. The resultant works rose so high that the finest ladies had to kneel in their coaches, as it was impossible to sit.

Those were the days when courtiers vied for innumerable positions, and wit could be traded for wealth. Indeed, anyone applying himself at Court seemed capable of drawing a salary, for there were positions aplenty and money enough. The King's kitchen supported some twenty-odd cup bearers (answerable to the four carriers of the royal wine), as well as sixteen hasteners of the royal roasts, seven candle snuffers, ten passers of salt, et cetera, all of them handsomely paid. As for the Queen, half of what she billed the treasury for perfumes would have fed the starving families of Paris.

For those were also the days when countless children of the city subsisted on chestnut gruel, boiled down from bark, sometimes but not always salted— how many parents rotted in jail for having stolen salt? Men mutilated themselves to fare better as beggars. Each day at sunrise, on the steps of the Foundling Hospital, the sisters would find shivering infants, notes pinned to the bawling bundles begging baptism, and forgiveness. In the provinces, too, peasants starved as feudalists fed what little grain there was to their game, resulting in the vengeful slaughter of animals of the hunt by the starving peasantry, and, in turn, the retributive, legal slaughter of the peasants.

When before had so few had so much, so many so little?

Meanwhile, at Court, the King might be found hunting or forging ever more intricate locks in the company of his smith. The Queen busied herself showering all manner of excess on her friends and her Swedish lover, Fersen.

The press was beginning to flex its newly discovered muscle. And the politicized organized themselves into clubs—Jacobins, Cordeliers, the Minimes, the Society of Indigents, the Fraternal Society for Patriots of Both Sexes. Bad men were revered; good men met with unjust ends.

The city, the old whore hiking up her skirts, offering herself to whoever would have her, was rank with the stench of coming catastrophe.

And here I was, returned to *this* Paris, rich from *un métier de luxe:* the Continent's Portraitist. To whom did I belong? No one. The poor resented me, and the privileged would soon sicken me. Where did I belong? Nowhere. Had I been wise, had I *known*, perhaps I would have stayed away, holding tightly to the *dream* of home, as the exile does, and never sought its fulfillment.

But was I really so melancholy, so maudlin when first I returned? No, I was not. Time distorts things; time bends and shifts. In those few years leading up to the Revolution, I am ashamed to say I clung to *old* Paris, to the *douceur de vie* I'd known.

I was beautiful, rich, talented, famous, and free. Had I left Paris a *nobody* to make my name abroad to return to this ugliness? *No!* I would have my fun. I would *insist* on old Paris, *refuse* this doomed and dying Paris. I too could step over the poor on my way into the city's finest salons. I was, after all, a *witch!*

Immediately upon my return to Paris, I made my presence known. Happily, I discovered my husband had been fast forgotten. I sent word to the various academies to which I belonged. I wrote to the Queen with news of our mutual friends. In reply I received a commission to paint—yet again—the royal children.

I purchased two homes—properties that backed up to each other, the one in the rue Gros Ch———, the other the rue Cl———. A huge garden spread between them. The homes were well appointed, decorated under the direction of the Queen's dressmaker, Rose Bertin.

I took up residence in the rue Cl———, the house resplendent in satins, silks, and damask, with the wallpaper and furniture all commissioned from the finest ateliers. The house opposite I had fitted out as a conservatory and studio; my guests would stay in its upper stories. There too I kept the vast store of wine I decided to amass, quite cheaply, for many of the finest cellars of Paris were being auctioned off in lots, a sign of the coming bourgeois panic.

As for the garden between my two homes, well, it was there that I quite literally cultivated my love of roses.

Finally, settled, I took the advice of a lady friend and, as my reentry into society, I agreed to host a concert for a violinist of (as it turns out) no consequence whatsoever. I entered the crowded conservatory last, of course. All turned to greet me. There was an exquisite silence—like that which follows the final note of an aria, before the eruption of applause—and then all present stood, and bowed. I was back.

The ovation that followed, as I made my way to my front-row seat, lasted several minutes. The musician rapped on his violin with his bow, the ladies slapped their fans in their gloved hands, the gentlemen tapped the parquet with their canes. Needless to say, I did not hurry to my seat. Here I was, having risen from the street. I'd traveled and returned to the acclaim, the adoration of *le tout Paris*. Ah, yes, I was happy as any fool. Then, that day's reception seemed to mark my ascension. I feel differently now.

In the fit of excess that followed my return to Paris, I also bought a cottage in Chaillot, to which I would repair on Saturdays, returning to Paris on Monday afternoons. Yes, Paris. It was there, not long after my "debut," that I hosted—to my great and long-lasting regret—my Greek Supper.

24

The Greek Supper,
Part I

I HAD JUST come home from a stay of some length at le Raincy, where I had painted a royal niece, some lesser princess, at full-length and to great profit. Awaiting me was a letter from Téotocchi.

Much time had passed since Venice, but still I thought longingly and often of my days there. Knowing my nature had changed my life little. I was as I'd always been, more or less, except now there was a word—*witch*—to explain the distance between myself and others. I found myself, for better or worse, defined. Still, I was not to be seen late at night in my studio toiling over a brass cauldron, slicing the hearts of hummingbirds or plucking the eyes from newts. I cast few spells. It's true: there'd been bouts of unbidden clairvoyance now and again, but nothing to speak of. As for my "talents," I had come to appreciate only those that applied to my art, and since returning to Paris, my output had been prodigious—this despite a quite active social calendar.

How thrilling—Téotocchi was coming to Paris. Her three-line letter said little else.

Within the week I received two more packages from Téotocchi. The first—too wicked—was a long letter all in cipher. The second package contained a popular novel of the seventies, *Paul et Virginie*, and the cipher's code. The letter was little more than a listing of numbers corresponding first to pages in the novel, then lines, and finally words. Distilling sense from Téotocchi's letter took me whole days. Word by word, filling with guesswork what gaps existed. Only when I read the letter entire did I stop cursing my sister, for I understood why she'd gone to such lengths to conceal its contents.

The letter contained the names and addresses of eleven witches. I was to write to them all, using the same cipher, summoning them to my home.

According to Téotocchi's letter, a new witch must, within the first few years of discovering her nature, host her Soror Mystica, her first sister and discoverer, as well as eleven other witches loosely affiliated by geography, interest, or affection. The new witch summons these sisters, hosting them for a period not to exceed one and one-half days.

Téotocchi wrote that the eleven sisters—with addresses ranging from Paris to Angers to Brest, from the Auvergne to the Cambrésis, Corsica, Naples—would all have a copy of *Paul et Virginie*. I need only write a brief letter of introduction; in it I should state that Téotocchi was my Soror Mystica. I was then to copy the letter into cipher eleven times. Finally, my original, unciphered letter burned, I was to post my invitations and plan my party. No, no, no—let me say here that Téotocchi never referred to this esbat as a "party"; all she said in her letter was that its purpose was threefold: to thank my Soror Mystica, to meet the witches of my coven, and most important, to learn. It was I who thought it would be a party. . . . It was not.

Téotocchi had set the date for the esbat in her letter. Samhain, or All Hallow's Eve. The 31st of October. The year: 1788.

When finally I'd deciphered Téotocchi's letter, and composed, copied, and posted eleven of my own, it was already mid-September. I'd little more than a month! And I was determined that this would be the esbat to end all esbats! (I was a *fool* indeed.). I wanted my *party* to be as grand as any Parisian soirée, as any storied sabbat of the Burning Days.

Plans had to be made, immediately. Of course, I could not confide in my corps of servants. So what to do? I had hosted heads of state, kings and queens, artists of the first order, but surely *other* rules applied when one opened one's doors to a coven. A coven. I'd only ever met Téotocchi; and here I was, set to meet eleven other witches.

Weeks passed; still I had no plan. Finally, I woke one night in early October to find my blue silk sheets slick with perspiration. I sent for Narcise, a friend, a fixture at the finest suppers, something of a mascot to the Elite.

Narcise, of course, came without question. Darling, dark, diminutive Narcise . . .

Long ago, a traveler returning from Africa, desperately currying favor with the Dutch Queen, presented that lady with a black child, snatched off a Senegalese beach as though he were a shell. This child was Narcise's grandfather. As a child, and later as a man, he moved from court to court with the Queen, unequal to the royals but superior in station to everyone else. His only duty was to delight the Queen. He was taught to read, and he read well; he became the Royal *Lecteur*, renowned for his strangeness and grace as well as the deep, deep voice that belied his stature. (The Queen, it was said, had her stunted man stand beside her at state ceremonies so that she might rest a jeweled hand on his turbaned head.) Narcise's grandfather lived and died at the Dutch Court, conferring upon his heirs a strange cachet, one that faded within years of that man's death. If there were bequeathed a title or a royal pension, Narcise—who'd long ago left the Dutch—knew nothing of it.

Narcise was a poet by vocation, or so he would say. In truth, he read much and wrote little. He scratched out short, insipid sketches of his lovers. Dependent on the kindness of a bevy of mistresses, he was a flatterer *par excellence;* with no money of his own, he managed to live quite well. Quite well, indeed. His carriage was noble, his name was known, and his favors—favors of *all* sorts—were widely sought.

"Surely, *mon vieux*," said I when he arrived in a bit of a huff, "this is not the first time you've been summoned to someone's parlor in the middle of the night?"

"Indeed not; but it has always been for a far better reason than hostess anxiety." Narcise then produced two bottles of esteemed red wine, gotten, he said, from the cellars of Madame de X——; and he took from the pocket of his waistcoat his own corkscrew. "My dear," said he, "there are tools a society man must carry in addition to his own," and with that he pulled both corks. "But now tell me, *what* in the name of Christ on Calvary has you so troubled?"

That night, as I told Narcise all I could of my predicament, he stood to pace the floor. He hummed, scratched at his stubbled chin, mopped his furrowed brow with a pink silk kerchief. He *exerted* himself, all for my benefit. Finally, removing his waistcoat and tossing it across the foot of my bed, where the green and gold brocade shone in the firelight like the scaled skin of a fish, he asked why this particular soirée had me so upset; I'd hosted scores of such suppers. I lied, saying that I worried like this before each supper, that *each* of my suppers had to be perfect (as indeed they were) and he let the topic fall, taking a seat and turning instead to the guest list. I batted the topic away with a wave. "Every hostess," said I, "knows the list to be secondary to the theme, *mon petit homme.*"

That long night my friend and I considered and dismissed one idea after another. Finally, I despaired.

It was well past midnight—yes, the hour was small, perhaps two or three—when Narcise and I decamped to the plush plane of a golden-blond divan, for my bed was ridden with the debris of our late-night snack—apple cores, rinds of cheese, a small Chinese bowl half-full of pits sucked from grapes and black olives. And, of course, the two empty bottles of wine.

A perfectly pale and opalescent moon slid from behind a bank of clouds, its light overtaking that of my candelabrum and my fireplace. "Sleep," I said. "I need sleep." I reclined, sank into a bank of pillows. "Recite something, anything. Lull me with one of your poems." For that I received a pinch.

Narcise took from his pocket a copy of "Anacharsis," and, though I was half-asleep already, when my friend got to the part in the poem wherein a Greek supper is described—specifically, that part which touches upon the preparation of sauces—I bolted up to exclaim, *"Voilà! C'est ça!"*

"Woman," asked a startled Narcise, "what's gotten into you?"

"Go on!" I commanded. "Read!"

And read he did, not knowing what possessed me. I took up paper, pen, and ink from my nightstand and scribbled away. "Again," I would say, when he'd read all the way through a certain passage. "Repeat it, please!" And he would. A perfect angel, so compliant! I am sure he thought I'd lost my mind, for it was some time before I calmed enough to explain my plan, which was, of course, to host the esbat as a Greek supper.

Inside of an hour the details were done.

I wondered, would my sisters take to the idea of an Athenian evening, a Hellenistic honoring of our sororal alliance? Suddenly nothing less grand would do. What a *show* I'd make of it!

In the days following this inspiration, I combed countless markets and finally found thirteen suitably simple chairs, which I arranged seven versus six at the table. Behind the chairs I set up tall screens, and looped white cloth at intervals (you've seen the same in Poussin's pictures). I fashioned thirteen wreaths of laurel. A neighbor, the Comte de P——, had a superb collection of Etruscan pottery; I persuaded him to loan me drinking cups and vases, which I arranged on my long mahogany table. A hanging lamp lit the scene.

I cleared my kitchen to practice my sauces in private. And perfection they were—one for fowl, one for fish, and the most exquisite for the eels my fish-monger swore he could secure.

For music, I converted an old guitar into a gilded lyre. It was Narcise who suggested Gluck's "The God of Pathos." (But who would play it? On any other evening, I'd have had a stable of fine musicians to choose from.) Narcise was my partner in planning the party, and this of course posed a problem: I knew all the while that he could not attend.

On 29 October, I summoned my friend. "Darling," I lied, clasping him to my bosom, "something has come up, something I should have anticipated but did not. You must help me! You *must!*" I told him that some months back I'd executed a commission from a Mrs. Jameson W—— of London. I had com-pleted the portrait and then I'd simply forgotten to arrange for its delivery. "Now it seems her newly refurbished London home is ready for guests, and a party had been planned to unveil the portrait! The lady"—allied by secret affections, said I, to the Prince of Wales—"has been most patient, but if the portrait is not hanging in her home by the first of November I will be ruined! Finished forever among the English elite!" I then produced a tightly rolled, sealed canvas (it was, in fact, a throw-away study of Skavronsky) and begged, *begged,* Narcise to deliver it for me.

Narcise left the next day for London. I gave him money enough to keep him across the Channel a month or more. I'd already written an agent in Lon-don, one whom I'd used in the past, telling him that my man would be arriving from Paris on the thirtieth with a portrait which, for reasons I could not detail, *had* to be secreted out of France. I asked would he hold it for me; as far as I know he's holding it still, these long years later. All in all, it was a costly and distracting scheme.

Finally, the last day of October arrived. All was in readiness. I finished the cooking and laid the table myself. I'd dismissed my staff with a week's wages, telling them that I was readying to paint a large group portrait ("The First Supper," I called it) and had no need of their help.

As the hour approached, I decanted the bottles of Cypress wine I'd bought at considerable expense. I baked honey-flavored cakes crowded with

Corinthian raisins. I saw to the details of the table, set with my finest china and crystal. I lit the beeswax tapers. I dressed. And I was nearly sick to my stomach. To see my beloved Téotocchi again! To meet the other sisters, from whom I would learn—*finally!*—so much. . . . Yes, after this night my life would never be the same.

As my mantel clock struck the appointed hour, there came a knock at the door. I answered in my mock-Athenian garb, laurel wreath in place atop my piled hair, and immediately I felt the fool. Téotocchi looked me over, head to toe: one eyebrow arched, a slow smile slid onto her lips. Finally, flatly, she said, "Oh my . . ." and simply slipped past me into my home.

I was stunned to see Nicolo at her side: I'd thought these esbats were the strict province of women, and to Téotocchi I managed to say as much.

"Ah, him," said she, shoving my beautiful friend forward, "he is here to . . . to fill a void." Nicolo—and he was somehow different from the boy I'd known in Venice—hid behind his mistress, showed little more than one black-suited leg and a tall riding boot, mud-splattered. He would not meet my gaze; he turned from me, shyly, as I moved to embrace him. I stopped.

"Surely," said I, "having shared what we shared, shyness seems hardly appropriate to—"

Only then did he raise his face to mine, and I saw that it was not shyness but shame that worked within him. At first, I did not notice, for I did not look *at* his eyes but into them, searching for the smile I'd always found there. But when Téotocchi stepped aside, and the light in the foyer shifted just so, I saw that Nicolo's eyes had turned the color of perfect, palest topaz. These were irises unknown to the human spectrum.

"Mais non!" I rather indelicately exclaimed—I was shocked, not repulsed; the color seemed only to set his darkly beautiful features in greater relief. Finally I managed to ask, "Whatever has happened to your—"

"Go outside," commanded Téotocchi to the boy, who proceeded to do just that; here was mindless obeisance the likes of which I'd not seen from him in Venice. "Prepare yourself for the Maiden," said Téotocchi, further. Nicolo nodded: even he, it seemed, knew more about what would transpire that night than I.

With the boy outside—we watched as he removed his short-waisted jacket, rolled his blousy cuffs, and launched into calisthenics with Spartan ardor—I asked of my Mystic Sister, "What have you done to him?" Was I angered? Protective, perhaps, for I continued to consider Nico a boy, though he was but a few years younger than I.

"Oh, that," said a smiling Téotocchi. "He doesn't know it—simply because I continue to lie to him—but it is reversible. Flattering, don't you find it, that harvest-like hue?"

"But . . . but why?"

"He had an idea about independence not long ago; and I cannot, simply *cannot* brook the thought!" I waited patiently for what would follow. "Sometimes, dear, it behooves us to remind our men that we've rendered them . . . *unfit* for the larger, lesser world. He sees those eyes in the mirror and he understands that he is mine." She did not say what I knew to be true: she loved him.

"But how did you do it?"

"Never you mind," said T. "A bit advanced, that lesson, and you'll learn enough tonight to keep you busy for a long, long while. But fear not: you'll have occasion to admire our Nico. For now," said she, looking this way and that, smiling wryly at my home's finery, the surfeit of gold-leaf, carved wood, and marble, "for now, can you guarantee that we are alone, that we will not be disturbed or espied in this palace of yours?" Before I could answer, Téotocchi turned, threw open my front door, sent up a signal—perhaps it was a whistle, perhaps a wave—and . . .

And there came tramping past me in single file the strangest assortment of women conceivable. Some were richly adorned; others were clad in rags, and stank. One I thought I recognized. I heard several languages being spoken. Not a one, not a *single* one offered a word of salutation to me. A few remarked with smirks and arched brows my outfit. Once inside, they passed through the foyer, through the dining room—not a one seemed to notice my well-laid table—into the grand salon, and, finally, through double doors out into the gardens.

Still standing, stricken, in the foyer, I heard the glass doors slam. Silence, a sudden and absolute silence struck me then, sure as a blow. I made my way to the grand salon. I could see the group gathered in the gardens. They'd formed a loose circle, with Téotocchi at its center. They held hands. Téotocchi spoke; I could not hear her, but I saw it was she who spoke. I watched through the thick glass as the circle suddenly broke and the witches sprayed like shot through my moonlit gardens.

Never had I felt so alone, for never had I so anticipated the end of loneliness.

I remember being thankful that the ragged assembly had come into my home under cover of darkness, unseen from the streets, or so I hoped; for, if I was not to have a life among them—already I knew this to be the case—then at least I might return unsullied to society proper.

I admit it: I considered walking from my own home. But instead I walked past my beautifully laid table—seeing the laurel wreaths tied with white ribbon to the back of each chair *pained* me—and I made my way out to the gardens.

The gardens, of course, were extensive, of a scale complementing the two homes between which they spread. There were innumerable plants and flowering shrubs and trees, all contained by borders of boxwood. I concerned myself with the roses only, deferring to my gardeners on all other matters.

Stepping out onto the flagstone path, I saw no one but Téotocchi. She sat on a stone bench, straight ahead. Where were the others?

"Oh," said Téotocchi, apology in her tone, "they're here. Having a look around." She shifted to one side of the bench. Moving toward her, I saw movement in the shadows. I was about to protest. Eleven women, witches or not, traipsing through my well-tended gardens? I did not like the idea, not at all.

"There are things you will need," said Téotocchi as I sat down beside her. "Things you will need to practice the Craft. They are simply seeing what it is you already have, what it is you need." One of the witches had presumed to light the votives that sat waist-high on wrought-iron stands, beneath glass bells; with the flagstone paths lit, I saw several more of my "guests" skulking and slinking about, some on all-fours. I rose, angry. This was too much! "Now, now," said Téotocchi, patting the cold stone beside her. "Sit."

I sank onto the bench, heavily, as though there were no breath in my lungs to buoy me. Tight, too, all through the neck and shoulders. I could not sit up straight. My hands lay palm-up in my lap. I felt like a tree that has survived a fire, lifeless and dry. I'd crumble if touched. Crumble or cry.

"Perhaps I misled you as to the purpose of the evening?"

I looked at Téotocchi, and suddenly there came this rush of words: "But there is no account of an esbat in your Book. I did not know what to do. What to expect. I thought—"

"I know, I know, dear," and she guided my head onto her shoulder. "The Books cannot contain all," she explained.

She stood. Her black robes were one with the shadows; the moonlight fell on her face and neck and hands, showed them whiter than white. Beautiful as ever, she seemed afloat in a pool of deepest night. "This is my fault," she said. "I should have—"

"No," I interrupted. "It is done. Leave it be."

"But you've gone to such trouble." She nodded toward the house. "Knowing your penchant for *excess*, I should have—"

"*Arrête*," said I. We laughed, and I rose to stand beside her. All around us, the sisters scavenged. "No more blame," said I.

Just then we were interrupted by a terrifically tall sister sticking her head up from behind a bush to observe, breathlessly, incredulously, "But there is not a sprig of rowan to be found anywhere! Not a *single* sprig!" This said, she sank back behind the bush.

I laughed. Téotocchi scolded me, but I could not help it. "Laugh or cry," said I, adding, "Tell me: the one in black, who came with you and Nico, it seems I know her from somewhere. Perhaps the—"

I stopped, distracted by that same tall witch, for here she came at us, swiftly, down the flagstone path. Standing a full two heads taller than I, dressed in pale yellow robes, with her long hair flying out behind her as she moved, she looked for all the world like a giraffe loping across the African veldt. Her gaze, I saw, was fixed on me. When it seemed she might step right *over* me, she stopped, suddenly, and lowering her face to mine, she asked, "Surely, dear, you've a rowan tree or two?"

I said I did not. I said I could plant one or two if need be.

"Need be, dear. *Need be!*" This witch looked down at me, her eyes separated by a nose so long and crooked it seemed she could only see me with one eye at a time; indeed, she did tilt her head this way and that as she took me in. Finally, stepping back to take in my attire, she turned to Téotocchi and asked, "*Whyever* is she dressed like this? . . . Esbat as . . . *un bal masqué*, perhaps?"

Téotocchi did not respond; instead, by way of introduction, she said, "Sebastiana, this is Cléofide; she comes from the Cambrésis." Neither I nor the tall witch said a word. We stood staring at each other, tense as cats in the street. When finally she extended her hand—the unadorned fingers were whip-like, the nails red-lacquered and sharpened to points—it seemed impossibly long. Her hand was without warmth; shaking it was like shaking a bone. When finally she relaxed her mouth, which had been drawn tight as a miser's purse as she'd appraised me, it was to say, without inflection, "Charmed," adding, "But I know of *no* witch without a rowan tree or two."

Téotocchi teased this Cléofide, wondered aloud if perhaps she wasn't *overly* fond of rowan, *too* trusting of its powers. She reached out and fingered the long, looped necklace of wine-dark rowan berries that Cléofide wore.

"Not at all," sniffed Cléofide, worrying her berries as one does rosary beads. "Rowan has served me well," said she. She then turned full-bore on my Soror Mystica and asked, her free hand at rest on the bony shelf of her hip, "Do you mean to imply that this witch has no need of a rowan tree?"

"I mean to imply no such thing, dear Cléofide," replied Téotocchi.

"I am relieved." Silence. I expected the witch to turn and leave, amble off into the gardens. Instead, and to my great surprise, she unwound one strand of the berries from around her neck and raised it up. Instinctively, I bent ever so slightly forward; Cléofide approached, and I felt the strand fall down over my shoulders. Still, I did not like this witch; and the sermonic way in which she said what followed won her no farther toward my favor.

For centuries, said she, throughout Europe, believers have fashioned crosses of rowan twigs and placed them over the doors of cottages, stables, cowsheds, and pigsties to ward off witches. "To little effect," said Cléofide. "It's true: I have seen a few efficacious crosses, but those were formed of twigs cropped from a tree the harvester had never seen! Such a cross is but one in a thousand."

I wondered what she meant by "efficacious"? Did the transgressing sister die, cramp horribly as she stepped over a threshold thus adorned? I did not ask: I was battling multiple distractions, for I could see other sisters in the gardens, some of whom carried things they'd torn—roots and all—from the ground. Elsewhere I heard branches being broken. I even heard the *snip, snip* of shears. And I was cold: the night was starry, clear, and crisp, and I wore only my Athenian costume (I'd stuffed the laurel wreath deep into a bush when it seemed no one was looking).

"You'll excuse me," said I, interrupting Cléofide, "I must go inside to see to—" But I hadn't taken one step toward the house when Cléofide sprang at me, grabbed my upper arm and held it tightly, *too* tightly, and said, with a hiss, "Go if you wish, Sister. But hear this: plant the rowan for one reason and one alone: to keep the unquiet dead at a distance." She took her hand off me, roughly. It seemed she might strike me. Pathetically, I pointed back to the house, ". . . my sauces . . . they'll burn . . . and I—" but I fell silent when Cléofide spoke again:

"And when you search out a rowan to uproot and plant, look in a churchyard. There is always a rowan in a churchyard." She came close to me now, closer, till I felt the heat of her breath, and added, in a whisper, "It stands besides the yew, for the wise know to plant them side by side." That said, she stood straight up and smiled widely. Her demeanor suddenly, inexplicably changed. Fingering the strand that now hung around my neck, she added, "What's more, the berries are beautiful!" With that she turned in a swirl of yellow silk, let go a rolling laugh, and galloped off.

If I'd been chilly before, I was stone-cold now. I stood shivering—Cléofide had scared me—wondering how best to slip from the gardens before another sister could "greet" me. . . . I did not make it.

This one was called Zelie. She was short and fat and wore black, and as she came at me fast down a flagstone path she had the aspect of a boulder breaking through my gardens. When this Zelie spoke her words were underscored by a whistle, for she hadn't many teeth and the few she had were . . . let me say they were *unluckily located*—two on the top formed a groove through which her tongue slipped as she spoke. And she spoke quickly. It was hard to tell—what with all that whistling—but it seemed she had a southern accent. French, of course, and easily understood; but decidedly, liltingly, bouncingly southern. I do not mean to slight this witch. She was, in fact, the first sister to show some civility. In fact, she'd brought a gift, which she presented with words similar to these:

"You have a hazel tree, I am happy to see." This she found amusing. "That sounded like a spell, didn't it? *'You have a hazel tree, I am happy to see.'* " She fell into a fit of laughter, wheezing and whistling, her black-clad bosom heaving.

Why yes, I said, I believed there were several hazel trees in the gardens.

"Hazel is good," said she.

I averred that yes, it seemed so to me.

And then, from the folds of her robe, this Zelie drew forth a hazel rod, delicate, expertly carved. Her face settled into seriousness—a moment earlier, those same features had been aswim in a sea of fat. "This," she said, presenting the rod, "is a caduceus, like that given Mercury by Apollo. It is the symbol of an enlightened spirit." Enlightened? Surely the one thing I was *not* was enlightened. Nonetheless, I took the wand from her. It was unaccountably light. Carved to resemble two entwined sticks, and with a snake winding up its length, it seemed . . . how else to say it: it seemed . . . *alive*, and I very nearly let it fall. But I held to it as Zelie informed me that Pliny had used a hazel rod for divination. Moses, too, possessed a hazel rod, harvested by Adam from the Garden of Eden; it was with this rod that he and Aaron had issued plagues into Egypt. "So you see," said Zelie, "it is rather a powerful thing, in the right hands."

"Surely mine are not the right hands," I asked.

"Not yet, sweetie," she whistled, "not yet"; and with a giggle she was gone.

This went on for some time. The sisters stepped from the shadows to show me what they'd discovered in my gardens, or to tell me what it was I lacked.

I had hazel. But in addition to rowan, it seemed I'd have to plant ash, aspen, elder, birch, holly, oak, hawthorn, and bay. Hawthorn to protect my homes from lightning. Holly for use in spell-casting. Elder to fashion into amulets, and to make wine of its berries. Aspen to lay atop "unsettled" graves. Et cetera.

I confess: I heard little of what was said to me as I stood at the head of that strangest of receiving lines. Finally, chilled through, unable to stay a moment longer, I said, to whoever was speaking *at* me, "All this talk of trees and bushes and berries is well and good, but it must be continued inside. Beside the fire." And then I left the gardens. A bit brazen, perhaps, to leave my Soror Mystica and all the other sisters standing in the shadows. But not a one had introduced herself properly, most had come without gifts, and the trouble I'd taken had gone unremarked by all but Téotocchi... *Damn* them, I thought. Let them slink about the gardens till sunrise! Oh, I damned them indeed, the whole pack of hell-born bitches!

My sauces had long ago curdled or burned; and so I sat beside the hearth and stoked the dying fire back to life.

One by one the witches came into the house, Téotocchi first.

She came to me fireside. "Strength," she whispered. "Strength, dearest. The sisters come at significant peril, you know; and for your benefit.... It is dangerous to gather." I put my hand atop hers, where it lay on my shoulder. I wanted to say so much: that I had thought by night's end the course of my life would be determined, my way in the world set. That I would know what it meant to *be* what I was, who I was.... Instead, ridiculously, I stood to ask of all present, "Shall we eat?" But Téotocchi bade me sit. "It's being taken care of," said she.

With a churning stomach I turned to see several sisters in the dining room, dismantling the scene I'd so carefully set. Folding up the screens. Tasting the cakes, tossing them back half-eaten. Gulping the wine as though it were water. Twin Ming vases smashed into octuplets when a broad-ended witch backed into the pedestal atop which they'd sat; she made no apology, simply nudged the sea-green shards aside with her sandaled foot. "Pearls before swine," whispered a smiling Téotocchi. Others rolled up my rugs, shoved the salon's furniture against the walls. They rearranged the thirteen chairs in a circle before the fire. One sister set about pitching the wreaths of laurel into the fire, "to scent the room"; too, she stuffed into her smock the white grosgrain ribbon I'd used to secure the wreaths to the chairs.

So be it, I thought. At least the night was taking shape, and the esbat was coming to order; for the sooner it started, the sooner it would end.

We took our seats. A convocation was read by Téotocchi. My duties as Summoner were set forth—I was to listen and learn. And somehow record it all.

25

The Greek Supper,
Part II

Excerpted from "The Record of the Esbat

of 1788; or The Witches' Pharmacopoeia, with

Advice on the Proper and Right Casting

of Spells"

HE SISTERS have formed a circle. I sit savoring
the fire's warmth and writing by its light, for they have
darkened the salon. I will do as I've been told, and I've
been told to sit here in silence, this Book in hand, listening, recording, and, as Téotocchi has rather cryptically said, "learning so that I may live."

A very tall witch has gone center-circle to speak. (Not
Cléofide, met in the gardens earlier—not as tall,
but thinner.) She has closely cropped hair, gone gray.
Her eyes are the palest blue. There is a most welcome warmth to the smile she offers me, a smile

that shows charmingly crooked front teeth. She is beautiful, I think; plain, but beautiful. Her slate-gray robe is tailored to her frame; the man's culottes she wears beneath are black. She is barefoot; her sandals—the kind that wind up the leg, Roman-style—sit coiled snake-like beneath her chair. "My name," she says, "is Hermance." (Perfect Parisian French.) She says she has chosen to speak of the Witches' Calendar, its six great festivals. "One of which," she says, "is this very night. Hallowe'en, the eve of hallowed souls."

The dates she gives are these: Candlemas, the 2nd of February; May Eve, the 30th of April; St. John's Eve, on 23 June; Lammastide, the 1st of August; Hallowe'en; and on the 21st of December, St. Thomas's Day. She says a bit about each, but she speaks too quickly for me. . . . I am lost, as this Record, as Hermance's *unrecorded* words, attests.

. . . *Attends*. . . . Yes, she speaks now of Candlemas: ". . . the feast of Purification of the Blessed Virgin Mary, the day on which She underwent ritual purification in the Temple of Jerusalem and lit a candle to signify that her Son would be 'the light of the world' " . . .

. . . Talk. There is chastening talk. It seems that at Hermance's words another witch—Sofia, they call her—has spit on the floor. (The parquet floor of *my* salon!) In disdain, this Sofia says, "*Ach!* All this talk of the Virgin and her Brood!" (Brood? Presumably she refers not only to Christ but to *all* Christians?) She stands now, Sofia does. (Hermance remains center-circle.) Her dress . . . rags! Waxen black sheets, wrapped around her person. Stained, ripped. Is she mad? It seems so to me. I am surprised the sisters let her speak now, out of turn.

"Tell her," says Sofia, pointing to me but speaking to Hermance, "tell her of the days *before* your Virgin. Tell her of the *true* Candlemas, as you call it." Virgin, Candlemas—Sofia lets fly these words like venom. (Her accent . . . I cannot place it.) "Long before Christ," she says, "and long before talk of his pure, *pure* mother overtook Europe, *true* witches marked the coming of February with the great Festival of Fire, inducing the Goddess of Spring to drive away the darkness and warm the soil. *That* is the true rite of winter!"

Téotocchi reminds the witches of their mission, says they have not come to indoctrinate me, to win me to one set of beliefs or another. Their mission, as best I can understand it, is to give me information that I may use, that I will need to survive as a witch in the larger world. She is interrupted now as ——— stands and tells how best to break a curse: a cloth doll stuffed with nettles and inscribed with the name of the cursing witch will work, as will nettles sprinkled about the room where the cursed person sleeps. . . . Now Téotocchi insists on order. She deems it best to proceed around the circle. Each sister will rise in ritualized turn, sharing what she pleases. She hopes in this way to avoid debate and spare time. "It is, after all," she says, "Hallowe'en." (What does she mean? Best not to think on *that*.)

So, seated to Téotocchi's right, for we will proceed widdershins around the circle—that is, against the clock, for "It is the witches' way," they say—an unnamed sister stands and recites the following, which she knows from a text of old Egypt. "To secure the sexual services of a woman, make a wax image of her, pierce it with thirteen needles, as though making an effigy, then place the doll at sunset on the grave of someone, male or female, known or not, who died young or by violence." This has never failed her. The secret, says she, lies in the state of the deceased's soul: best to seek out the grave of one who died young *and* by violence. "The more violent the death, the better," she says, adding, "A suicide is best."

I wonder, is it shame I feel as I watch this witch, this street-hag rise again to speak? Sofia, it is. Truly, I am repulsed. Yet I know I ought to accord her the same respect as the others, those who are set with jewels and dressed in silks. (And who *is* the younger witch, so familiar?) . . . I have much to learn from all of them; this I know. . . . But I cannot help it, I *am* shamed and repulsed by my association with this sister as she drags her chair center-circle and draws from her burlap bag a . . . a Hand of Glory, she calls it. . . . *Hideous* thing, this relic! Dark dirty shriveled thing. Can it be? . . . *Mon Dieu*, it *is* a human hand, petrified and—

It is indeed the severed hand of a murderer she holds, sawed free while the corpse still swung. "Of course," she adds, apologetically, "the most effective Hands are harvested during the moon's eclipse. This Hand is not such a one."

(Am I to be sick to my stomach? How do the others even look upon the Hand? . . . I will continue. I must continue.)

The hag comes closer to me now. (The breath that seeps from her tooth-less smile bespeaks a diet of vermin and dirt! Foul, *foul* thing she is!) Lowering the Hand to my face, she says, "You must take the Hand and tie it in a shroud." A pause; she waits, asks am I getting every word into the Record. "Then you must wring the blood from the fingers; saving it for love philters, of course." Some others laugh now at this witch's economy. She curses them and continues on: "Pickle the Hand in an earthenware jar, with salt, long peppers, and saltpeter; let it sit two weeks. . . . Write it!" she adjures me. I show her that I have written it. "*Bien*. Then dry the Hand in an oven with vervain; or better, set it out beneath the summer sun."

(She unnerves me; the proof is here, in my unsteady hand. . . . Step away, witch. *Step away.*)

She returns center-circle. She tells how, once preserved, she fits her Hand with candles, fixing them between the splayed fingers. The candles should be made from . . . from the hanged man's fat, from a slab of it sliced from his buttock or thigh and boiled down. (Can I go on? I am sick. I am disgusted and sick. I am disgusted and sick and so very disappointed.) "And take care to save the skin," she adds. "And a few hairs from his head, for they'll serve nicely as wicks."

Go on. Write.

"Forty-four years I've passed uncaught through the finest flats of Paris," brags the hag, "and all thanks are due to my Hands of Glory." Apparently, she uses the things thusly: she takes a Hand to the targeted place, presumably a home she hopes to burgle. She waits there, watching. Then, in a place where it will burn undisturbed ("beware of cats," she warns), she lights the thumb and first finger—the thumb for protection, the first finger to still the wind—and then she enters the place through a window, in case the homeowner has placed some repelling iron on the threshold—split scissors are favored—to ward off a witch. As long as the Hand burns it is safe to walk about within the house "for whatever purpose"; it is clear, from the snickering of her sisters, that this witch's "purpose" has always been burglary. The sharer drags her chair to the circle's edge, sits, satisfied. . . . She is suddenly up again, and nearing . . .

"I almost forgot to tell you!" cries the foul one, rushing back at me, "there is but one thing that can extinguish a Hand once lit, and that," she comes nearer, nearer still, ". . . and that is Mother's milk"; and with a horrid crack of laughter she—the *beslimed* bitch!—she takes my left breast in her knotted hand and squeezes!

. . . Tears. The hag laughs. Téotocchi reprimands her and she sits, laughing still.

I ask for some moments alone, and it is granted.

They have called me back to the salon from the kitchen, where, crying, I surveyed the damage done. The dining room too: a shambles. . . . My recess has ended.

———— speaks now, re: the efficacy of blood:

The blood of executed criminals is of use in the distillation of philters. Some hold that the blood of a redheaded murderer is most potent; others say it is the semen of such a one. The point is argued for some time. I sit, my pen still.

The blood of menses, it is said—though *never* that of a witch's flow—is potent indeed. A few drops mixed into a man's meal will secure his love. "Carry seeds to planting in a cloth thus stained or soaked," says ————, "and crops will ripen regardless of the season." None present can attest to the truth of a belief popular in old Rome: that a woman's blood could blunt knives, blast fruit, sour wine, rust iron, and cloud mirrors. "The Romans were right about much," says ————, "but they knew neither their women nor their witches."

There is laughter; and this same witch leads a song—spell? incantation? prayer?

"Rue, vervain, and dill,
Hinder witches from their will . . ."

she sings.

More laughter. Is it because the song is wrong? ———— rises to speak of vervain, "the Herb of the Cross," said to have stanched the flow from Christ's wounds. The undiluted juice of vervain, says she, will bring to pass the simplest of wishes, may bestow immunity to disease, can enhance clairvoyance.

Another song, this one from ————; more recipe than song, it seems to me:

"Hemlock, juice of aconite,
Poplar leaves with roots bound tight,
Watercress; now add oil,
Rat's fat, and let it boil;
Bat's blood, and belladonna too—
Now kill off those that bother you."

At this last line the sisters fall into hysterics. I transcribe. I am the Summoner of the coven, the one directed to call these sisters together; I am hostess of this esbat and keeper of this Record; and these women, witches all, have come together for my benefit, but how am I to learn when they—

Téotocchi. She stands and quiets the sisters, insists again on order; and so the din evolves from songs and spells and talk of Christ's blood to organized Sharing. (T. calls it that.) The circle is rejoined as several sisters return from the far corners of my house, to which they have wandered for purposes all their own. (Before she leaves, I must check the bag of the one who hoards my white ribbon.) I sit fireside. Téotocchi counts twelve heads, excepting her own—

always thirteen at an esbat—and the Sharing resumes. I cannot identify the speakers: I know few of their names, and often they speak, several at once, in a sort of contradictory concert. I shall scribble all I can discern from this cacophony of curses, spells, and stories.

The subject now, it seems, will be the use of herbs. (This will not be as orderly as T. would wish; I can see it.)

"Beware the nightshade—belladonna, mandrake, henbane," says ————. "I have seen the like of these send a man elsewhere, never to return." (Q: "Elsewhere," she says. Does she refer to a prolonged dream state? Or does she mean death? I cannot ask this aloud; that much has been made clear.)

"Do not listen to her," counsels another witch. (I have met this one in the kitchen. Her name is Yzabeau.) "To deny the mandrake is foolish. Perhaps our Sister has simply misused it." The first witch takes umbrage, rises to counter the claim that she—But Téotocchi calms her. It is Yzabeau who continues to speak of mandrake, of its history and "proper" usage:

"The Greeks and Romans used it as an anesthetic before surgery," she says. "It was said that Circe used mandrake juice to transform Odysseus's men into swine."

"Which trick," interjects ————, "they so often effect themselves." (This witch speaks slowly, deliberately. A southern accent, is it?)

Yzabeau tells how her Soror Mystica—whose name, I see, is known by some here, and revered—harvested mandrake at night, from beneath a gallows tree sprung up from "bodily drippings." "Wash the harvested root in wine," she says, "and wrap it in silk; or better, velvet."

"No, no; too dangerous, that," says another witch, speaking now for the first time. "If the torn-away root resounds like a struck fork or seeps a bit of blood, the harvester will die." She has seen this happen. "Far better to harvest it thusly," says she. "Dig around all but a small portion of the root with a silver spade. Tie one end of a string to the exposed root and tie the other end to a bitch. Turn away at once—*at once!*—and let the bitch pull the root from the ground. The dog will die, but you will be safe."

Three others testify to the efficacy of this method. One adds, "Never but *never* use a male root; neither a female if the berries of its bush glow at dawn."

I am exhausted. I ask for a respite, a second recess. T. grants me a quarter hour, and I think her ungenerous until she draws from her robe a vial of the most fragrant oil and asks for my writing hand. Ah, yes, yes . . . Happily, I set down this pen.

_____

We resume.

——— explains the proper use of those herbs that, in combination with certain spells, she promises, will induce "dreams of divination." She lists the herbs: "Sinum, sweet flag, cinquefoil, oil, and solanum somniferum; add to these a bit of bat's blood. Rub all this into a ball—fist-sized—formed of an animal's fat." These words, this hideous recipe, sounds so strange, coming as it does from this exquisite Italian witch standing before me in bright silks. Though in fact her gold-bladed athame, pendant from her necklace, its blade glistening, does look more like an instrument of murder than a tool of white magic. She has paused now to take some wine. Mine? Or has she brought her own? She resumes, speaking in a richly accented French. In summation, this: "the ointment, thus rendered, is best absorbed through the moist tissues of the vagina, upon which it is to be liberally applied." With a nod to me she sits, rejoins the circle.

Some commentary now, none of which I can distinguish. And so:

It is ———'s turn to speak. She is old and worn. She sports a Breton scarf of finely worked lace. The sisters listen respectfully. "What has worked best for me, in late years," says she, regarding divination, "is this: aconite, two drops of poppu juice—no more than two drops!—foxglove, poplar leaves, and cinquefoil, all married in a base of beeswax, and almond oil." Talk now, the topic of which is this: how best to procure two drops of poppu juice! (Q: What _is_ poppu juice?)

Lest she be doubted, the Breton witch reminds all present that it was she who "saw" the death by drowning of _la famille Gremillion_ some days before it occurred; what's more, it was she who "witnessed" recent and weird events in Quimper involving two cows and a daft dairy farmer. She sits, triumphant.

——— counters with _her_ ointment: "Deadly nightshade, henbane, wild celery, parsley, and a fistful of thornapple ground with an alabaster pestle; all in a base of hog's lard." Discussion now, which I cannot record. Instead, I am imagining ———'s cuffs of Brussels lace trailing through a bowl of boiling hog's lard! There is something about this witch I do not like. (Is she from the Lowlands? I wonder. It is possible, for I have overheard her say that last night's coach ride took some seven hours.) I am glad now that she sits.

Oh, but _who_ is this? A grimy, malodorous creature comes center-circle. (It is whispered that this one lives in the hollow of a tree, deep in the Bois de Boulogne. Is that possible?) She offers this, re: divination:

Recipe the first: hemlock, aconite, poplar leaves, and soot, stirred into the boiled fat of . . . of a dead baby.

Wild censure from the circle.

The witch demurs that never has she *killed* a baby for this purpose; no, she harvests the tiny corpses from the cemetery of the Infant Asylum of St. Adolphus, where the sexton, for three sous, turns a blind eye to her and her shovel. Again she is abused. ———— raises an amulet against this witch, who spits, who damns her supposed sisters. Some laugh, others curse her in turn. She calls her sisters hypocrites, says they've all trafficked in corpses. (Could this be true?) She returns to her seat; now, maligned, she says she will not share her most effective recipe, learned from none other than La Voisin.

Silence now. That name has stilled the witches. (Q: Who is La Voisin?)

Téotocchi assuages this witch of the woods. She *must* tell. For my benefit. "It is why we have come," says she, "why we risk gathering." As Summoner, I must hear it for the Record. The foul one resists. She sits with her withered arms crossed over the concavity of her chest. Her drawn and too pale face resembles nothing if not the skull and crossbones of a pirate's standard! (How I want these hags out of my house! How I want this night to end!) . . . Finally, the Witch of the Bois stands. It seems no witch here will disobey Téotocchi.

"This," she says, "*this* no one knows." The sisters scorn her; still, they listen raptly. She repeats herself, teasingly, and adds, quickly, dismissively, "No, no, no. I cannot tell it. It is too strong . . . it is untried; not ready for the Record." Again she sits.

The sisters are piqued. . . . Pleas and insults. Entreaties, threats. Rules of the esbat are cited. Still the witch sits, silent. She will not, she *cannot* share something so strong, so dangerous, so . . .

But of course she does.

"This," says she, finally, retaking the circle, "was taught to *my* Soror Mystica by hers, who'd heard it from a disciple of La Voisin." Again, that name stirs the sorority. La Voisin . . . haven't I heard the name before? I have, I'm sure of it, but just who is. . . . ? I look to Téotocchi, and it's she who explains:

"La Voisin," she says, "was the witch of the Marquise de Montespan, mistress of Louis XIV. For the Marquise she said many Black Masses, read many rites." Reluctantly, T. adds that La Voisin favored the blood of children in her recipes; indeed, she is said to have mixed it with her wine, even bathed in it. At her trial, it was reputed she'd sacrificed more than two thousand children. In

1680, with all her noble patrons exiled or jailed, La Voisin was burned along with thirty-six of her disciples.

The sister resumes: "La Voisin had a papyrus, Egyptian, from the third century, seen by very few—and this papyrus bore this recipe, these instructions: make a salve of water and the ground flowers of the Greek bean, which," she says, her voice a hush, "can be bought from a garland seller. Add to it what you will. Seal this flower paste in a container for twenty days exactly, leaving it undisturbed, untouched, in a dark place, at the end of which time, the opened container will reveal"—this I *cannot* believe!—"a phallus and testicles." Smirking, and derisive speech from the circled sisters. Téotocchi quiets them. "Reseal the container and set it aside for twice as long—forty days; no less, no more—and open it to find the same contents blood-covered. This blood is strong beyond measure, and is to be kept on glass in a black, covered pot." She pauses. "When daubed above and below the eyes, this blood will give dreams to answer any question."

———— sits. She bows her head, closes her eyes. The skin of her hands, which lie in the folds of her filthy apron, is cracked and dirty, dark as bark.

The sisters start to comment. Téotocchi quiets them, asking of the Sharer has she ever tried this recipe. "I have not," says she, "but I knew well a Sister who did. Twice she tried it, with success. But the third time she was struck blind; and she was dead of the Blood before two nights had passed." Now she lets it be known that she has said all she will say.

I beg another recess. During it I will ask T. to name the witches.

Marithé speaks now. She is clad in saffron and black, a black woolen scarf wound around her long, slender neck. She resembles Hermance, beside whom she sits; she too speaks the French of Paris. She talks of candles; and as she pulls a store from her bag she lists their attributes.

Marithé says one should burn a blessed white candle for spiritual strength, or to break a curse. (Q: Is a blessed candle merely one stolen from a church precinct?) Yellow candles endow the burner with charm and powers of persuasion. Green candles heal, further good luck and fertility. Pink candles allow the witch to alter the course of love and friendship. Sex and health are enhanced by the burning of red candles. Courage comes from the burning of orange ones. Purple reverses a curse. Gold: to intuit. Black: to sow discord and sadness. Blue: to heighten awareness, achieve peace, protect one's sleep, and induce prophetic dreams.

No witch dissents. Marithé (I like her) has taken up the candles and brought them to me, a gift. Wrapped in white cloth and tied with silver ribbon, they sit beneath my chair.

"Next," calls Téotocchi. (N.B.: There is little joy in this for these witches. Above my head the mantel clock ticks, ticks, ticks . . .)

Luchina, my Maiden—the least senior sister, who is to keep the Record if for some reason I cannot—will speak of amulets. She is Italian, and has traveled north with Téotocchi and Nicolo. Luchina's French is good. Her voice is wonderfully mellifluous, and her words elide with grace, as those of the Parisian sisters do not. (That voice . . . There is something so familiar . . . Yes! It is she! The star soprano. I *knew* it!)

Luchina wears an amulet herself, on a fine, frilled blouse of black silk. It is a large, bejeweled udjat, or Egyptian eye. She says it brings good health, comfort, and protection to the wearer. I had not noticed the amulet earlier, when first I saw Luchina; I'd been drawn instead to her deep green eyes (she alone of all the sisters has shown me *l'oeil de crapaud*). I noticed too her long braid, black as her silks; and her skin, so perfectly pale. She is beautiful, this Luchina. (Luchina is not the name she uses on stage, of course; and I will not, *cannot* compromise her by stating her true name here. "It is prohibited, such disclosure," warns T. in a whisper, seeing that I recognize my Maiden.)

"The word 'amulet,'" says Téotocchi, speaking to the assembly, though for my benefit alone—the others are bored; some sit awkwardly in their chairs, turning this way and that to take in the salon's art, sculpture, et cetera; some pick at the last of the food—"comes from the Latin *amoletum,* a 'means of defense.' The Egyptians were fond of amulets, crafting frogs to enhance fertility, and scarab beetles to ensure resurrection and passage to the Afterlife." It is Luchina who adds, "And of course there is the Egyptian ankh, representing the union of the male staff and the female loop; this was said to bestow everlasting life and . . ."

. . . Luchina comes to me now and . . .

. . . She has given me an ankh! An amulet all my own! She drew it from her horsehide bag. It is quite heavy. Could it be *true* gold? Its loop is as wide as my palm, and the staff is set with—*impossible!*—sapphires! If not sapphires then another stone equally shiny and blue. (Luchina's smile says it is gold, these *are* sapphires!) The ankh hangs on a golden chain. She sets the hasp behind my neck. She seals the gift with a kiss on each cheek.

What to say? I smile and say nothing. I do not *know* what to say. Already

Luchina has returned to her seat and Zelie stands center-circle, ready to share; she will speak of Black Masses—specifically, the Mass of St. Secaire, read to curse one's enemy to death by slow, wasting illness.

This amulet is so *heavy* on my chest. It has settled just over my heart, which leapt at Luchina's kiss. . . . I *feel* this golden thing. I swear I feel it! Like Zelie's caduceus, given to me in the garden, this too seems somehow *alive*.

A recess is announced, blessedly. I must search out the soprano, and thank her.

26

The Greek Supper, Part III

It was indeed she: the soprano I'd seen—in Naples? was it the Teatro di San Carlo?—in Paisiello's *La Molinara*. It was over the last of the eel that I got my Maiden to admit as much; she'd hoped to hold to her alternate identity (far safer, even among the sisters).

"And you," I ventured, "... your esbat?"

"It did not go so well," said Luchina. "Téo introduced me into a coven of all Spanish witches, and they can be rather . . . how shall I say it?"

"You needn't." So Téo, as she called her, was Luchina's Soror Mystica as well? Interesting. (Would I have been more or less jealous if this Neapolitan had not been so beautiful, so talented?) "It did not go well?" I parroted.

"It did not. That is why Téo has introduced you into a more varied sorority."

"*Varied* is the word, indeed," said I, and we laughed. Luchina complimented my home, my efforts as hostess—"Mortifying," I demurred. "If only I'd *known*."—and we shared fast accounts of our travels. Luchina had not yet gone to Russia, but had plans to do so within the year. I offered letters of introduction; she—and I was not offended—declined: she already had one from Paisiello, who had composed *La serva padrona and La finta amante* under the Czarina's patronage. I gave my impression of the French and Neapolitan Queens. Luchina told of her recent successes in Lisbon and Venice. When asked about my beginnings, I turned the question back on the questioner—the first law of social inter-course—and learned that young Luchina, motherless, of course, had been sent by her father, a dealer in precious gems and a primo basso himself, to study with the great Marchese in Florence; it was he who arranged her debut at sixteen, after which she soon progressed to prima donna roles in operas by Cimarosa, Pic-cinni, and her beloved Paisiello. "So distinguished a career," said I, rather grandly, "and you not yet into your vocal prime!" "No, no," said Luchina, "it is *you* whose accomplishments humble every artist." "*Mais non!* You flatter, and I must return the compliment and say—" Our mutual adoration was interrupted by Téotocchi, who came to announce the end of recess and ask, mysteriously, of Luchina, "Are you ready, my dear?" My eyes went wide as T. proceeded to cup Luchina's heavy breasts, and lean in to kiss her crimson lips.

We retook the circle, my Maiden and I, but not before I gifted her with the tiny Canaletto she had admired in the foyer. I liked Luchina immensely, but events would preclude our . . . *Eh bien,* on with it. There commenced then a rit-ual that was as unexpected as it was, in the end, satisfying.

"Nico!" shouted T., thus summoning her boy in from the cold yard, where he'd been standing at the glass doors, arms wrapped tightly around himself, stamping his booted feet against the bone-deep chill. So distracted was I by all that had happened, I'd not thought to offer my friend a blanket or shawl; indeed, I'd forgotten he'd even come.

Nicolo entered the salon now to a shrill and inelegant chorus of catcalls and whistles. Several sisters took liberties with him as he passed—it was old Sofia, I think, whose knobby hand appraised the muscled weight of his but-tocks. "Off with it all, son!" said she. "He'll make the Maiden dance, indeed," said another. "It is the Beast with Two Backs we'll see dance!" added a third, and so on until finally I understood:

Nicolo had been brought to take the Maiden, Luchina. I'd read of such ritu-als; and now, I, stunned, watched, as a quite calm Luchina was prepared for what would ensue.

Cream- and pearl-colored pillows with black piping were pulled from my settee and chairs, piled center-circle. Luchina stripped down to naught but her scarlet stockings, fastened by black leather garters; in her hand was a bean-filled phallus crafted of the same leather, so large I'd not known it for what it was when first I saw it. Weaponry, it seemed to me. "You are ready, *ma petite?*" asked T., kneeling at the Maiden's head, bending to once again grace with a kiss her flushed cheek.

"I am," whispered the Soprano. T. said something to her I did not hear, and Luchina said again, rather more emphatically, "*I am!*" and then let fly a note that caused a crystal in the distant chandelier to burst like a dying star. This the sorority loved! Through what followed, they would show their appreciation of the Maiden and boy with rhythmic applause and occasional cries. "A lucky Maiden she is," said one, "to get that fire-eyed boy!"

What had come over Luchina, that sweet, demure woman with whom I'd conversed not a quarter-hour earlier? The pride of every opera house on the Continent. Here she was now, writhing on my salon floor in anticipation of— And what had happened to me? For here *I* was, kneeling at T.'s direction to . . .

I separated Luchina's stockinged knees with the lightest of touches, and took from T. the heavy phallus: I was to ready the Maiden. And this I did, slowly at first, wondering was I hurting her; but by the slight bucking of her hips, I knew I was not; and so I sped my hand, and Luchina's breathing grew ever more shallow. I would have worked on but for Téotocchi, who stopped me. "*Ça suffit,*" said she, laughingly. I leaned down to kiss Luchina, deeply; and whisper to her, as I looked over my shoulder at Nicolo, "Pay heed to the taut fullness of his lower lip, Sister, for it's fine as the finest steak." (I hear those words now in a voice not my own.) With that said, I rose and stepped aside. Nicolo, naked and roused to purpose, was led forward by T. He looked at me. How *well* I knew my friend! I saw through the sad, sad mask he affected, saw through it to the insatiable Venetian I'd known, who'd been my first and best, my beloved.

I, as Summoner, sat on the floor beside the Maiden and boy; and watched.

For how long, I cannot say. I was . . . was overcome. By the flowing wine? By the strange occasion? By such a shameless sorority? By simple, strong lust? Had someone cast a spell? . . . Or was it relief, now that the long-anticipated hour had come, and soon would pass?

I was called back, literally—from watching that puzzle of love being put together in seemingly infinite variations—by my own name. "Sebastiana," it came. "*Sebastiana!*"

"What is it?" I asked impatiently, pulled up so suddenly from the sweetest depths. It was then I grew conscious of the blood that had risen to flush my neck and face, my body entire, and render so very pleasant the feel of my trailing fingers, the teasing touch of my own hand.

It was Téotocchi who'd spoken; and so she did again: "I must apologize," said she, settling on the floor beside me. Cheek-to-cheek we watched the copulating couple.

"Whatever for?" I could not be distracted; it was as though I alone watched Luchina and Nicolo; it was as though the sorority, to a one, had dissolved, disappeared, but then I would *sense* my sisters, see them, and the hot chill I savored would redouble, and please me anew.

"The senior among us know this to be a breach of protocol," said T.

"Doubtless it is," said I.

"I am serious," T. went on. "It is first blood that is to be drawn at an esbat, but as we have all been . . . *spoiled*"—here she laughed—"I determined the Maiden would do."

"And she does nicely, indeed," said Marithé, who, having slid her blouse from her shoulders, had settled near us, unremarked by me. Hermance, beside her, teased Marithé's nipple between forefinger and thumb: it was the infamous tableau of the famed Fontainebleau portrait—*Gabrielle d'Estrées and One of Her Sisters*—with both subjects staring daringly, impassively, out at the onlooker—*moi, bien sûr*—while a nameless maid works busily in the background.

The circled witches had quickly donned masks of pure pleasure. Never had I been party to anything so private—so unself-conscious, they were. Among the older, heavy and ungirdled flesh was exposed; it bore the color of butter gone bad, was the texture of unset pudding. Some of the younger stripped entirely. It seemed the sisters were familiar with one another's paths of pleasure—from practice or instinct?—and I spied jeweled fingers prowling shaven clefts and bared breasts. Directions were spoken without shame; and shamelessly, openly, were the directions followed. "Here, Sister," breathed one. "Yes, yes, yes! And kiss me now, there. But will the same work for you, my sweet? Let us see." Some had brought favored props, which were passed hand to hand—agate balls, tiny clamps with tight springs, prods and oils; and a sort of necklace, strung beads of increasing size, "Used well," said a smiling Yzabeau, "by a Chinaman of my acquaintance." . . . All the while, the scene went on centercircle.

As cued by T., Nicolo and Luchina rose to mutual release. The sounds from the sorority were deafening, and thrilling. I turned—first with laughter, then, as my *self* returned, shame—from several of the self-abusing sisters, quivering like shot arrows. . . . Hisses and cheers, laughter. And it was over.

. . . Again, I can render no account of the clock. Time passed.

And then I was directed to draw baths for my spent friends. I'd been told by T. to do so quickly, for the sharing was soon to resume: all were attendant upon me. But I dared to speak to Nicolo in my bath, dared to tell him those gemstone eyes would not be his for all time, that T. could be persuaded to . . .

"Yes, I know," said he, stopping me, "and won't the persuading be fun?" He smiled. Here was the boy I'd known, and so it was a great temptation to hear him ask, in hushed and hurried tones, "Won't you come back with us to Venice, to our mutual amusements?"

Flattered, I made no response: I hadn't the time. Téotocchi called from the salon. Luchina and I hurried back, leaving a weary Nicolo to soak in a candlelit bath. We entered the salon to the applause of the assembled: it was not for me, of course, but for the sated Maiden at my side, who bowed as though she stood in the footlights of La Scala. *"Brava!"* came the cries.

The esbat resumed, though the Record becomes rather scant and a bit sloppy at this point. (Need I say I was no longer the quick-scribbling Summoner I'd been earlier?)

It was midway through the evening before I learned all the witches' names; and, as I was suffering a rush of emotions and they spoke so fast, interrupting one another, casting off asides . . . What I mean to say is this: it doesn't much matter if the Record errs, attributes to one witch the words of another, for, though the night would be of consequence—owing to that one careless, *careless* act!—none of the witches would be. Not to me. I would never see any of them again. Téotocchi would soon be surprised by the Blood as she sat taking tea in the Riva degli Schiavoni. As for Luchina, I'd know of her only through gossip and untruths told in the journals. . . . No, the coven of the esbat of 1788 would never reconvene, and for good reason: we'd done damage enough.

That said, the excerpt from the Record has introduced, by name, seven of the witches present that evening. In addition to Téotocchi, we know of yellow-clad Cléofide, she of the rowan berry necklace; the squat sister from the South, Zelie; the elegant pair from Paris, Hermance and Marithé, the former speaking of the Witches' Calendar, the latter of colored candles; that dreadful Sofia, she of the Hand of Glory, who I would learn was Basque; and Luchina.

The crone who lived hidden deep in the Bois de Boulogne was named Inez. Others in attendance were Giuliana and Renata, who'd come from somewhere in northern Italy; Mariette of Paris, a nun who scared me, scared me *terribly*;

and, finally, Léocadie, come from some faraway part of France. (Léocadie, for reasons all her own, had earlier given her name as Yzabeau; indeed, that night she'd use *three* names, but here I will fix her as Léocadie.... Indeed, as I did not like her—she too readily took every opportunity to laugh at my *gross* misunderstanding of the esbat's nature—I will further fix her as the widow of one J.-F. de Bonnegens, Presiding Judge of the Civil Court of X—— de M——, dead of an excess of cantharides, used "to secure his love.")

That makes eleven. Thirteen, counting Téotocchi and myself; and only with Luchina did I sense any affinity. The Parisians, Hermance and Marithé— the latter having access to the Queen through medical channels; indeed, she offered for sale vials of the Queen's "blue" blood; and the former reputed to be the mother of six—were refined, friendly, but no.... True to say I liked few of these women.

I should say that none of the sisters seemed enamored of me, either. The intimacy borne of our sex charade proved false, and short-lived. A few of the witches were openly contemptuous, and comments were made regarding my high style of living. Others thought I courted fame, that I risked discovery, thus endangering them all. What did I care? A few hours more, I told myself, and I will close my door on these women forever. The night would distill itself down to little more than a cautionary tale in my *Book of Shadows*. What came to matter was not that this was *my* esbat, *my* chance to meet my sisters and learn and...No. What came to matter was the clock on the mantel. I *willed* the hours on. I wanted the night to simply end.

Would that the night had ended simply, that the sisters had slipped from my house out into that Hallowed Night unseen, fast to be forgotten. Instead, what happened later that evening would change...everything. *Everything!* No amount of prevision, practiced by the most senior, the most adept among us, could have told us what waited in store. And even if we had seen it, we would not have believed it, *could* not have believed the magnitude of...of all that would happen in the days, the weeks, the months to come.... I wonder, if one among us had seen just what that simple dance was to draw down on our city, on all France, would we have done it? Certainly, if I'd seen as much, I would have stopped the esbat then and there, thrown the witches from my home no matter the repercussions.... *Hélas*, none of us had such a vision that night, and so...

How, *how* could this ragtag assemblage of sisters, no two of them very *sisterly*...how could this coven effect such long-ranging change? The answer, in a word, is this: accidentally.

... I will explain, yes.

According to the Record—I have it here before me—Zelie finished speaking of the Mass of St. Secaire and the twin Italians, Giuliana and Renata, presented me with rings. Giuliana's was of jasper, that greenish-black stone that warriors and witches have long worn to stanch their blood flow. It was set in gold, with chips of diamond around its rim. Renata's gift was a much larger ring of quirin, a stone harvested from the nests of lapwings; this ring, if placed beneath the pillow of a sleeper, will cause him or her to speak the truth, steadily, intelligibly, when a question is put to them. I have these rings still. The quirin, I must say, has done its duty well on occasion. The jasper, happily, has never been tested.

... Looking over the Record now, I am reminded of Mariette, the nun, who spoke of demons. She was wide-eyed, with thin and colorless pursed lips; her hands were frozen into fists, like those of a paralytic. She sat stoop-shouldered, her chin drawn to her chest, as the others spoke. Time and again she'd raise her head and her dark eyes would dart about the room like bats, as if an unseen Tormentor had returned.

No one spoke when Mariette did; all the sisters seemed fearful, as though the horrors the nun knew were somehow communicable. To *hear* this witch required a great effort, for her whispered words fell down into her lap, like drool from the lips of a fool. When finally she spoke it was of devilish pacts, and the summoning of demons. (Her words are in the Record, but I will not copy them here: having met this Mariette, I will *not* encourage you to attempt her Craft.)

As Mariette spoke, I wondered if she weren't summoning a demon to my salon just then, for her head set to swaying, rolling atop her bone-thin neck. She snapped her head forward and back, faster, and faster still. A child's barrette flew from her hair. Tears slid from her wide-open eyes. She raised her hands to her head. She pulled at her hair. She tried to *stop* her head—vainly; still it snapped forward and back, forward and back, till it seemed her neck might break! And then, as if the *sight* of Mariette in this state weren't enough to chill the blood, she let go a howl the likes of which ... It was ... diabolical! And when next she spoke—my handwriting in the Record is rather shaky at this point—it was to tell how best to protect oneself from "the demons who come unbidden." Calmly, she took up the barrette and fixed it back in her lank hair. She smoothed her forest green skirt and, never raising her head, went on:

"The *agnus dei*," said she in a whisper, flecks of spittle on her pale lips. "It's the *agnus dei* will best protect you against such demons." According to Mariette, this small cake made from the wax of paschal candles and shaped to resemble a lamb would protect one from demonic possession, but only if it were blessed by the Pope. (She said this as though to secure the Pope's blessing were no achievement at all.) Then, Mariette—the weirdest of *all* the witches—drew from a deep pocket of her skirt an *agnus dei*. I thought she would simply show it to the circle, perhaps pass it around; but she stood, came over to me, and presented it, wordlessly. I took it with a trembling hand. I thanked her. (Weeks after the esbat I discovered this *agnus dei* on a windowsill, where I had left it, consciously or not, to melt into a sorry, misshapen thing.)

Mariette (the nun, now, not the witch) concluded by coming center-circle to stutter, say that should the *agnus dei* fail, one could of course resort to the Church's sanctioned nine-day regimen of holy water and wafers, "accompanied, *bien sûr,* by the hourly recitation of three Paternosters and three Aves in honor of the Trinity and St. Herbert." This said, Mariette made the Stations of the Cross and—having taken care to add that the Church's regimen also protected one from rabid dogs and rashes—she started again to snap her head to and fro. She fell into her seat, and sank into a trance from which no one could rouse her. . . . In truth, no one tried.

Mariette done, we had gone round the circle twice. Another recess was granted; and it was at the resumption of the sharing that the end began.

During that final, brief recess I saw Zelie come from my cellar with five bottles of red wine, all of which were decanted without my being consulted. At first I was resentful of this, not wanting to waste good wine on these witches; but as it became clear Zelie would somehow render the vinum sabbati . . . well, perhaps the bewitched wine, if heavily poured, would hasten the night's end. And indeed it did. It also rendered us sloppy, careless, and overconfident, which in turn contributed to the trouble of which I'll speak.

. . . Yes, the trouble. On to that now, with this as necessary preface:

Cléofide rose to speak of spiders and ants; and it was the mentioning of ants' eggs that prompted old Inez to stand and, swaying from drink, stumble through a horrific, ant-related story of her own. And *that* in turn led to foul Sofia's leading us all outside to dance and . . .

Wait. I must return to Inez, and the tale she discovered in the first *Book of Shadows* she'd ever read, a Book written by a witch named Grethe, a coven-sister to Inez's own Soror Mystica.

This Grethe, according to Inez (who added that it had been years since she'd read the story; she'd tell it as best she could) . . . this Grethe lived a long and quiet life in the Massif Central, subsisting on coins given her in exchange for medicines, powders, and potions. As her witchcraft was more white than black, she was known among her neighbors as a healer; indeed, she'd delivered several generations of villagers. It was said she'd cursed a few as well, and blasted the crop of a man who'd abused her; but Grethe, said Inez, had struck the perfect balance: feared, suspected, and sometimes needed, she was let to live peaceably among the villagers.

Then one day late in her life a spell went horribly wrong. Just what Grethe had been trying to achieve, none can say. Her Book made no mention of her motive, showed no record of a fee received or a favor granted.... What she did was this:

She somehow cast a spell over the whole of the Sologne, that part of France covered, then as now, with unarable land—boggy, badly drained, and horribly humid in summer, iced-over in winter. If famine threatened any part of France, it was said, surely the peasants of the Sologne had already starved. It was there that Grethe went—for reasons white or black—riding along the region's borders, imprecating all the way.

These spells, said Inez, were written in Grethe's Book. They were simple, the rites accompanying them simpler still—all one needed were hayseed and powdered bone. Inez refused to recite them for the Record. They were, she said, too strong. They had, she said, brought down death. For within two months of Grethe's spell the Sologne had lost all its crops, sparse to start with, and its rye harvest had been horribly blighted. Still, the hungry peasants had to reap and eat what they could, even the diseased rye, spotted with fungus and crawling with vermin. Apparently, it was the fungus borne on the rye that brought on the dreams. The terrible, *terrible* dreams.

All the Sologne was dreaming, and yet no one slept. Doctors and other experts in fields ranging from agriculture to mesmerism traveled to the Sologne from all over France. Each quickly left. The Paris newspapers reported that peasants, seemingly sane, swore they were covered with ants, ants that were eating them alive. Red ants, large as a man's hand. None of the afflicted peasants could see anyone's ants but their own; but not only did they see their own ants, they *felt* them tearing into their flesh, thousands of them, devouring first digits then limbs then ... (Drunken Inez mimicked the ants; with cracked and blackened teeth she "gnawed" the flesh of her upper arms.)

The situation in the Sologne went from bad to worse. Neighbors turned on neighbors. Fights within families ended in murder. Not only the imagined ants ate flesh: there were acts of cannibalistic excess. The peasantry was both famished and, at least temporarily, insane; packs of children gone savage chased down livestock—ten of them, aged two to six, were said to have brought down a bull; women ate the newly born.

In the Sologne that terrible season it was a *human* crop that was harvested. Corpses of the mad dead were pitched into pits and quickly covered with lime, lest the equally mad and ravenous mourners leap down among them to feast. Families wandered the roadside in search of carrion; they might set upon a traveler, a pet, or a person they'd known all their lives; they might set upon one another, all the while scratching at their ants till their skin was raw, till they bled and their suppurating wounds went dark with infection.

Hundreds died horribly. The fortunate never regained their sanity, for who among the formerly afflicted could live with an understanding of what they'd done? . . . Yes, it was a curse upon the land, a plague of the mind. And it was all the dark work of one witch.

Inez did not know what had become of Grethe. Her *Book of Shadows*, as Inez recalled, ended with the account of events in the Sologne—rather more horribly detailed, Inez assured us, than her retelling, which in turn has been tempered by me.

That night we all listened raptly to Inez. I wrote furiously. . . . But not a one of us *heard* the tale. We listened, but we did not learn. For, by night's end, with much of the vinum sabbati drunk, at the urging of Sofia, all thirteen of us—coven-sisters, Soror Mystica, Maiden, and Summoner—took to my gardens and danced and . . .

The night was fair and bright. The autumn air bore a wintry chill, and a crescent moon hung overhead like a blade. (How much *worse* might things have been had the moon been full?)

There was no music—forgotten was my gilded lyre!—but the sisters sang. And Inez, Sofia, and Hermance all went suddenly "sky-clad," letting their dresses fall to the ground—"far better," said they, "to meet the moon this way." Several others dropped their dresses down to bare their breasts. (I opted to not.) Fortunately, the tall walls bordering my property precluded our being spied by my neighbors, but still I feared our singing would rouse them: I had Téotocchi reduce the singing sisters to a whisper. In time, I'd care not a whit who heard. Need I tell you that Inez, drunk as *she* was, could not keep the words of Grethe's spell to herself? Once outside, having slipped quite naturally into a circle, we listened as Inez—having been asked but twice—shared the spell as well as the accompanying rites. Renata had on her a bit of hayseed, but none of the sisters had powdered bone. Each contributed something—a pinch of this or that drawn from a pocket or purse and tossed center-circle—

as well as a lock of hair. My contribution was involuntary: it was Zelie who slipped up behind me with long-handled shears; she dropped a lock of my hair into the first of two holes dug in the garden, and each sister followed suit.

What I did not know at the time was that Sofia had taken the occasion of our final recess to slip outside and . . . and urinate in the holes; and now she, setting a large rock between them, produced a dark rag, which she stuffed down into the "lock-blessed" hole and withdrew to smack on the stone, imprecating thusly:

> *"I knock this rag upon this rock*
> *to tease the seasons from their clock;*
> *We raise a wind in this new witch's name;*
> *Let it not settle till she calls for same."*

Soon we'd crafted Grethe's spell into a song, and we sang it as we danced Sofia's dance. It was a simple dance, which many sisters did while untying three knots from leather cords of varying length, thereby freeing "the wildest of winds." All the while Sofia *swore* that she'd never effected more than a storm cloud or two, perhaps a few drops of rain. . . . (The Record reads simply: "We dance and dance and dance. We dance and sing." I wonder, was I simply drunk or otherwise enchanted? As Summoner, at this point, I failed miserably; but who could be expected to dance and sing and keep the Record all at once? And I assure you, I *did* dance and sing.)

My esbat ended as Hallowe'en ceded to the Day of All Souls. The sun was rising as the witches slipped from my house as stealthily as they'd come. None save Luchina and Téotocchi, who were the last to leave, in Nicolo's dazed company, offered a proper good-bye.

T. stood silently by as Luchina blessed me, all the while detailing said blessing—clearly she'd only recently learned it from T. "Pluck a lemon at midnight," said the Soprano, drawing a plump piece of citrus from the deep pockets of her dress, "and stick it with colored pins." This she'd already done. " 'Arise ye to action, forces of the Moon Divine!' " T. shushed her. We stood now at my open door. Luchina repeated the spell thrice more: in Latin, in her own Italian, and finally, my French. Thusly were we, supposedly, mutually blessed and somehow wed.

"*Très bien*," said Téotocchi, who bowed to me, snapped her fingers—driving Nico, who now sported blue-lensed, concealing spectacles, to some unseen action—and draped her arm over the Soprano's shoulder; it was then they all three walked from my door.

Finally, I was alone. I drew on a shawl and went back out into the gardens. I sat down on that stone bench, drained the magical dregs from two bottles of wine that I found, and I cried. Cried until I could cry no more, until the muscles of my face and heaving shoulders ached. Even now, these many years later, I'd be hard-pressed to say just *why* I cried.

Then, among my roses dew-wet and bright, with the gray moon dissolving and the rising sun casting the walls of my home in palest gold, I rose from that stone bench and I danced, danced like a dervish! (That *damnable* wine!) I declared aloud that I would not be defeated, reduced to tears by disappointment! Yes, I sang and danced as I had with my sisters; but I sang louder now, and I danced at double-speed, spinning with my eyes shut and my arms open wide, casting off that simple shawl as well as the smothering mantle of sadness that had settled over me. . . . *Mon Dieu*, what a show I must have made, lost as I'd been when I'd watched the Maiden and Nicolo! What a witch I was! Singing the spell and dancing the dance that would bring down death, yet again.

I woke later that day—All Saints' Day, 1 November 1788—and wondered what I'd done. In time I'd know; but it would be too late.

Within days of the esbat and that dance we did, the weather turned. Paris, in the months to come, would suffer her worst winter in three generations.

The bridges spanning the Seine were oddly beautiful; coruscant, coated with snow and bearing icicles that hung to the still surface, they looked like diamond necklaces. But beauty, then, was illusory. Wrapped in layers of wool and fur, I sometimes walked the city. The gutters were piled high with filth, for the carters could not navigate the snow-clogged, icy streets. Rats scampered about at eye level as one walked, for the mounded offal was that high. Excrement froze wherever it was flung. Bodies curled fetus-like in the crevices of buildings, lay deathly still in doorways. Everywhere one turned the blind, the lame, the poor held out battered copper bowls, begging. The only sound in the streets was that of this ragged corps tapping their walking sticks over ice-slick cobblestones or against the sides of shuttered buildings; this sound seemed to mock the grinding ice of the river. Occasionally, the last of the street peddlers could be heard, hawking old boots or ribbon or "New Songs for One Sou," but there was no one about to buy. No one but me; and I, wracked with guilt, bought all I could carry. I'd buy boots on one corner and give them away on the next. What more could I do?

With the Seine frozen solid, barge traffic stopped, and so no wood arrived to heat the houses; soon the laundry boats stopped working as well. The grain markets closed: what little wheat was stored could not be ground, as the mills ran on water and every source of water was still. With the capital too cold to be about in, businesses started to shutter-up: first the inns and eating houses, then the taverns. Finally, even the brothels closed.

It seemed that those traveling through Paris could speak only of the weather they'd witnessed in other parts of the country. Wolves were spotted in the cities, come down from the frozen forests to feed. Hailstorms occurred all through France, falling unannounced and with hellish fury. Hailstones large as a man's fist fell fast to the ground, killing what small game survived, cracking their tiny skulls as they scurried about barren fields in search of shelter. No crops could survive such storms. Lost were budding vines in Alsace, Burgundy, and the Loire Valley. The late-ripening wheat in the Orléanais was crushed, as were the apples in Calvados, and the oranges and olives of the Midi.

Red weather sprang up suddenly at sea. Boats sank all along the coast— some even in port—as wind and wave conspired to dash them against rocks or their own moorings. Few fishermen dared venture out. First no crops, then no fish. Talk turned fast to famine.

The frozen Seine, the crop-crushing hail, the stilled mills . . . all this resulted in the rising cost of bread. The price of a loaf—which stood at ten sous the night of the esbat: I know because I shopped myself that evening, something I rarely did—rose to twelve sous, then fourteen, and fifteen by February. As a family of four could easily consume two loaves of bread in a day, and as the father of that same family might earn twenty or thirty sous for one day's work, well . . . The math is simple, and it equates to starvation.

As for my emotional state then . . . I was sick. I could not sleep. I felt so responsible. . . . Never, not once did I doubt that we witches had brought all this on with our dance. Many attributed the weather to the supernatural; only I knew how right they were.

After days, then weeks of ever-deepening depression, I roused myself. I did what I could. I wrote to my coven-sisters, telling them what had happened— how could they not *know*?—and asking after any spells I might cast, any Craft I might practice to undo the effects of the dance? Few responded—Zelie, Luchina; surprisingly, Mariette—but they had little to offer: a few imprecations, not quite spells, which of course I tried to no avail. It was Mariette who recommended I invoke the Holy Trinity, the Lord's Prayer, and the Angelic

Salutation (each repeated thrice) and then read aloud the whole of the Gospel According to St. John; of course, all this was to accompany the casting of thirty-three hailstones into a fire.... Téotocchi responded, too—again, in cipher; but this time her letter was short, and quickly *deciphered*. There was nothing she or I could do, *"rien du tout."* She wrote that she—as Soror Mystica—and her fellow *"tempestarii"* should have known better, should have shown more "discretion." My Book should reflect that the fault was hers, not mine. She closed with further apology, and wished me well. (That was the last I'd ever hear from Téotocchi. The last she'd hear from me ... well, reading her words, so terribly *insufficient*, I was incensed. I scrawled across her ciphered note, "Hope all is well in Venice. Paris starves. *Adieu*," and I posted it back to her.)

That winter, I opened my home in the rue Cl—— to those who might otherwise starve or freeze in the streets. I fed them as best I could. I opened my cellars, and tried without success to convince all comers that they'd do better to *sell* rather than drink my wines. Indeed, I told those who came to take away whatever they thought they could sell.

From the house across the gardens, in the rue Gros Ch——, I sold off all my furniture, my silver, my crystal, and my art. I converted all I could to money. I raised eight million francs, and gave it all away. There were those who sought to dissuade me, of course; I ignored them all.

Once my charity was discovered, crowds came daily to my home. I could no longer live there. With only my paints and brushes and a few simple things, I decamped to a studio deep in the city. Of course, I could not paint, doubted I'd ever paint again. I barely had strength enough to survive. I was disconsolate. And hungry, too: no amount of money could procure what simply did not exist. I thought ... I thought often of death. I knew I did not want to live. But never, *never* did I consider self-murder. It seemed to me cowardly. And I was ... curious. Where would it all end? Would the sun ever shine again? Would spring come? Would the ice that rendered Paris as fragile-seeming as glass ever melt, would the drifts of snow sink, the river flow? Or would the world end in a choke of blue ice, all activity slowed to a deathly stop? Yes, wanting the answers to such questions is what kept me alive.

Let me say that never once did I think it would end as it did. *Never!*

But what choice did the ignored poor, the starving people of Paris have? None. The King and Queen, the nobility, the rich, the privileged—I and my circle—these parties seemed prepared to let the Parisians starve to death. Soon the starving started to steal, and then they started to kill. A simple devolution, really, but one that so few of us saw coming. And when finally we did see it, it was far, far too late. For the fortunate there was time enough to run, into exile; for the less fortunate . . .

Soon murder was little more than a means of expression. Severed heads were seen in the streets. I was present when a mob formed outside the shop of a guiltless baker, a merchant refusing to simply *give* his goods away. This man was condemned, and saw his shop, his life's work, destroyed. Daring to resist, the baker was then carried off to the Place de Grève, where he was hanged and decapitated ("in that order, of course," reported Marat, wryly, in his paper, *L'Ami du Peuple*). The baker's head, stuck on the end of a pike, was then paraded outside his shop before his friends and family. On another occasion, the mob killed two guardsmen, took the severed heads to a wigmaker, and forced the man to groom and powder the hair. Those heads, affixed by their hollowed spines to poplar branches torn from trees in the park of Versailles, were paraded before the palace windows.

Yes, the people were beginning to close in on the King and Queen. Their actions were not planned, but rather . . . *instinctive*. They were like those wolves wandering down to the cities from the woods, sniffing the air, scratching at this or that, sinking their teeth down, *striking* when somehow the time seemed right. And in time, of course, the people would have the heads of their Sovereigns.

All I could do was watch, watch all this unfold. What I could offer—opening my home, raising what cash I could—it all amounted to nothing. It was a long time before I realized, or rather resigned myself to the fact that there was no way, *no* way to undo the damage I'd done. The damage *we'd* done with that diabolical dance, that spell so blithely cast. I'd blighted Paris, *my* Paris. (Beware, witch! Beware your strength! And know that though we may be peripheral, we are *not* insignificant. . . . No, we are not.)

Is there some other explanation for that sudden, strange change of weather? If there is, I never learned of it; and I searched, searched long and hard. Yes, yes, yes, there were a host of other, *lesser* factors contributing to the fall of Paris; I could list twenty, fifty, a hundred if I cared to. . . . But no, we did it. We witches did it with our dance. *We* drew that weather down. *We* caused that climatic change; and all that happened rolled on from there—just as snowflakes fall a second time in avalanche.

27

Roméo Rampal

I READ THAT first excerpt from Sebastiana's *Book of Shadows* deep into the night. Curled up in a corner of the *lit clos*, having secured two candles, three bottles of ink, and several freshly cut goose quills, I copied the story of "The Greek Supper" into *my* Book, *this* Book. That done, I sank into a dreamless sleep.

Some hours later, I slid back the panels of the box-bed. It was early afternoon: I knew the light, mellow, deeper than the bright light of dawn. By that light the burnished frames and the brushes sitting up-ended in various cylinders and the rolled canvases leaning in the corners... all of it shone doubly bright now that I knew its story. Unfurling a tall canvas or two, would I find there the indolent Countess Skavronsky, perhaps the Neapolitan Prince or the children of the French throne, toppled some thirty-odd years ago? No; I dared not do it. Sebastiana would not approve of my snooping around the studio. Or would she? Surely there were many other rooms in which she might have had me sleep—why here, in her studio?

The studio. . . . It seemed settled into a state of disuse. The bristles of the brushes were stiff. Small glass jars of paint, scattered beneath a rickety easel, like a child's marbles, were sealed shut; those few I could open showed paint that had thickened or separated, gone bad over time. Did Sebastiana no longer paint? And what about witchcraft? Had she forsaken *all* her talents years ago, when she knew such regret, such remorse for having so innocently sung a song, danced a dance?

I found a warm bowl of coffee on the desk. I cupped that blue and white Breton bowl and sipped. Who'd known when I would wake? I shot a quick glance to each corner of the room. No one. But this did not discomfit me, not at all. Company of any sort—seen or unseen, mortal or not—was welcome. I retrieved both Books from the bed—Sebastiana's, so full of wonder, and mine, empty but for the story of the esbat. I would settle at the escritoire, resume my reading, my copying from Sebastiana's Book to mine.

But instead, I found myself walking, bowl in hand, toward the studio door, the one that gave out onto the roseraie. Stepping out into that late-day light, so wonderfully warm, I tilted my face to the sun and smiled. Then I sat, right there beside the door, sat cross-legged, my back against the centuries-old stone wall, the bowl of coffee balanced on my lap. How *full* I was then, how happy! I believed I'd finally found a refuge, a place where I might hide away a happiness all my own. I wanted nothing less than to live and die at Ravndal. As for Sebastiana's Book, I was quite eager to read it, but I thought I'd have days and weeks and months to devote to both our Books. Why devour what I might savor?

It was perhaps a minute, perhaps an hour later that I resolved to find Sebastiana. I cannot say why, exactly. Doubtless I was eager to ask the innumerable questions, large and small, that our supper had left unanswered. (I thought then that Sebastiana's answers would set my life aright. Too, I wanted to be near her.)

Wearing only a simple white nightdress and the slippers I'd worn to dinner the night before, and with my hair loose and falling full over my shoulders, I went off in search of my Soror Mystica.

I walked into the roseraie, to where I'd first found Sebastiana beside the fountain. But she was not at the fountain. She was nowhere in the roseraie. It never occurred to me that I might call out her name; Ravndal, even its grounds, had about it the feel of a church, a great cathedral where silence was preordained. I turned to head back to the studio, still determined to find Sebastiana, or another of my saviors.

Smarter this time, I'd left a trail of rose petals behind me as I'd made my way deeper into the roseraie, winding this way and that among the tall hedgerows. I retraced my steps now, following crimson and pink and purple and yellow and cream petals. I congratulated myself: quite clever, I thought, to thus mark my way through the labyrinth. (Of course, I'd later discover a note in the studio, the handwriting already quite familiar. "Dearest," it read, "should you put my roses to such purpose again, I will curse you till your teeth fall from your head as those petals of mine fell from the vine. Yours, S.")

Returning to the studio, I felt a chill; the sort of chill that is ever present in places made primarily of stone. From a tall armoire, I drew on a dark green gown of silk, its hem heavy with embroidered leaves; I wore it over that white shift. I then set out through the tapestried door of the studio, stepped from the sunlit studio into the dark halls of the house.

In construction, if not in aspect, Ravndal was very much like the hated C——. Such stony structures not only exude a steady chill, they suffer no light. Their interior rooms are invariably lightless. So too are the corridors lightless, and chilled. Such places seem not so much constructed as *born* of stone, as statuary is.

Stone. Stone everywhere. . . . I thought then of my mother. How horrible it must have been for her when the Blood came! A witch who knows her nature *knows* to expect it, knows every sister will die that way. For my mother it must have been dreadful. She knew enough to pack my few belongings and take me to C——, where, in sight of that stony edifice, the Blood overtook her. There, on the packed-dirt road, beside that brook that her blood would cause to run red. She'd known enough to tell me to "Go to the stone." . . . Yes, as I wandered the corridors of the manor that afternoon, I thought of my mother. I imagined her smiling to see me there.

I walked and walked through Ravndal, lantern in hand, my progress marked only by the sounds of the slippers I wore, their waxed bottoms whispering, their low heels tapping like tiny hammers along those long avenues of stone.

I stood with my ear pressed against locked doors. I peered through keyholes. Nothing. I searched out signs of Madeleine's presence: blood pooled here or there, red prints on doors or walls or banisters. In the darkness, it was hard to discern substance from shadow. Spying a suspicious spot—blood, surely—I'd reach out a finger and . . . no. Nothing.

The first-floor rooms were large common areas. In addition to the studio, *my* room, there were twin parlors, sparsely furnished. There was a second dining room—empty but for another huge table, this one of carved wood, much simpler than the red marble one at which we'd dined. There was another room, adjoining this secondary dining room, spacious as a ballroom; its herringbone parquet tiles were loose, and walking, let alone *dancing*, over this floor would be a slippery affair. I came across a smallish room with a vaulted ceiling painted sky blue; its dark wood shelves rose from ceiling to floor, lined every wall, including the back of the door; but the shelves of this library were bare, supported not a single volume. Surely there was another library somewhere, stocked with all those S-marked volumes I'd read that final night at C———.

What few pieces of furniture I found in these first-story rooms were exquisite but in disrepair. A table of inlaid marble, lame, missing one of its thin and bowed legs, stood propped against a windowsill. A chaise longue, its yellow silk torn, let go its downy stuffing. Chandeliers sat on the floors in corners, like drifts of icy snow. Wallpaper hung from the walls like the skin of half-flayed livestock. Wooden baseboards had fallen away, disclosing avenues for the many mice that must be resident. The furnishings, fit for Versailles, were scattered about, broken and forgotten, relics. Yes, the house was little more than a reliquary. A fantastic tomb. If it had once been a home, it was now but a refuge. A place set apart from the world. Yes, here was a *strange* haven indeed— and how I loved it! Granted, it was not what I'd expected; the studio, by far the most well-appointed and comfortable room, had set a standard that the rest of the manor—what I saw of it anyway—did not meet. Still, it seemed as if I'd come home.

On the second floor I came across a large room full of chairs, all turned to face the same, stageless wall. These were complete sets of chairs; I counted thirty of one style, each bearing the signature of that Parisian upholsterer, Daguere. In the hallway outside this room, a deep armoire was crammed with Sèvres settings, hundred of pieces of hand-painted porcelain, some sets complete, others chipped and in pieces. As I opened the armoire door, a tiny teacup, delicate as an egg, fell and cracked beside my foot.

A chapel occupied more than half of the third floor. Whole panes of stained glass had fallen from their moorings and lay shattered on the floor. A huge wooden cross standing in a corner showed an active nest upon the nape of Christ's neck. There were wine bottles on the altar, bound there by silvery cobwebs. Candles had burned to nubs, and had not been replaced. The fount at the door was crammed with foul-smelling rags. Dried flowers flowed from tipped vases; a white chrysanthemum, perfectly preserved, crumpled at my touch. The wood of the many icons scattered about was slick with mildew, pocked and splotchy as though with disease—the stained-glass windows, fallen inward, had left the chapel open to the sea air, the rain, the seasons, and time.

Finally, I found myself on the fourth-floor landing, despairing that I'd found no signs of anyone. This was the top and brightest floor. It was the brightest for one simple reason: parts of the roof had worn away, and the sun shone directly down into those tiny, low-ceilinged rooms tucked up under the eaves. Perhaps they'd once been servants' quarters, or spare bedrooms for children—hard to imagine children ever having lived at such a place—regardless, they'd long been used as attic space. Some were crowded; others sat empty. Yes, these rooms had seen the rain and snow, and long hours of summer sun: I watched as mice wove among the warped floorboards. There were nests scattered everywhere. Surely some of the bird-cry I'd heard the night before had come from these fourth-floor rooms. It seemed at least one horned owl was resident at Ravndal, for, as I explored, I came across more of its handiwork: the headless skeletons of rodents, some quite large, littered the floor as they did the surrounding fields.

Nearly tripping over such a skeleton—and sending it skittering across the floor in the process—I determined to descend, return to the relative luxury of the studio. But as I made my way back to the landing, I came across a half-open door and as I pushed it open the door fell flat at my touch, slammed down, resoundingly, on the wooden floor! Stooping—as I am accustomed to doing—I walked into the room.

This particular room was empty but for a few scattered trunks and crates and piled wares. Wallpaper had been torn from the walls; whatever its original design, it now showed wide stripes the colors of rotted citrus. The ceiling was sound, or appeared so, but the floor gave a bit too much as I entered the room; the groaning of one plank in particular gave me pause. Not wanting to return to the first floor by any means other than the stairs, I stood as still as I could on that creaky, springy floor; and it was from the room's threshold that I took a quick inventory. In the corner farthest from where I stood were piled wood-slatted crates that had sunk under their own weight; their slats were host to a white-green slime, mold grown so thick it was moss-like, furry. Only the top crate was intact. Something in it caught my eye.

I made my way into that corner, carefully. From the top crate I took up an old ledger. (I'd hoped, *fancied* it was another *Book of Shadows*, but no.) The book, wider than it was tall, was covered in faded blue cloth. Its spine popped and pieces of rotted paper rained down on my slippers when I opened it. It bore the musk of age. Its pages showed a neat, careful accounting of household expenses from when Ravndal—known then by another name, of course—had been an active farm, the fields worked by tenants or those otherwise bound to the nobles whose home it had been. This accounting predated Sebastiana's tenancy by many, many years. Most likely, whoever'd written these figures, in so tight a script, had not even known the dissolute noble who'd one day trade away the house and land for a portrait of the bastard branch of his family. (Yes, that *is* how Sebastiana came to call the place her own.) Perhaps this was the hand of that nobleman's grandmother, or great-grandmother; I'd no doubt so careful a record was the work of a woman. It made me melancholy to think that her home, the land she'd clearly cared so much about, had been traded away. If she'd known of such plans, she'd have had no say. Men, even boys, could do such things then, and their women could only stand by and watch. The rules of primogeniture would change with the Revolution, of course, and then women—sisters, wives, and younger brothers too, who'd long seen everything pass to their older brothers . . . those individuals finally gained a say regarding inheritances. I was quite caught up in my imagining of an entire family of the *ancien régime,* had even grown indignant at all I attributed to some callous, imagined man, when . . .

I heard a noise.

I replaced the old ledger.

This was the first noise I'd heard all day, or so it seemed. Fearing the floorboards—were they giving way?—I stood still, listening. But no, this was not the sound of wood, of floorboards settling or shifting. This was the sound of something . . . something *forged,* a thing of iron striking down, down into something soft. A shovel. Yes, a shovel . . .

Slowly, I made my way to the window. I undid the old iron hasp that held two wood-slat shutters together and carefully, *carefully* pushed them open. I half-expected the shutters to fall from their hinges, as the door had; or perhaps the hinges themselves would slip from the stone walls and the whole works, shutters and all, would sail four stories down to the ground. This didn't happen. There was, though, a sudden fluttering of wings on the roof just above the window: it seemed I'd disturbed some section of a great rookery. I leapt back from the sill with a start as scores of the blackest birds rose to shoot like dark stars across the sunlit sky. . . . It seemed an eternity of seconds before this lightless constellation calmed itself . . . and again, silence.

This window did not give out on to the sea, as I'd expected; rather, this was the other side of the manor and the view was of the fields that sloped down to the bordering woodland of which I'd been warned. Those distant, densely packed trees shone black; the forest, I could see, was a lightless place. As for the fields, they'd not been farmed in some time, that was evident. They were, however, fenced, indeed, this was pastureland *still*, for I discerned a few graceless, angular shapes at a distance: cows. Of course, it made sense that a few cows would be kept at this isolated place; surely there were hens somewhere, pigs, perhaps goats as well. What other land I could see had reverted to its natural state: grasses grew tall, had been burned to a brownish-gold by the summer sun; wildflowers sprouted here and there in variegated patches; a stand of sunflowers, much nearer the house, bowed under the weight of their bright heads. Most striking were the bright red poppies that spread over the sloping land like rubies cast by a great hand.

. . . That noise again.

Down; and to the left. I leaned out over the casement so I could see nearer the house and yes, *there*. . . . A garden. Alternate bands of turned and unturned earth unfurling from the foot of the house. In the dead center of that garden stood Roméo; rather, *stooped* Roméo, turning the soil with a hoe.

I quite forgot about those creaking floorboards. Slippers in hand now—with those slippery bottoms I could only go so fast!—I quit the attic and descended those three flights of stairs. Taking a quick turn on the second-story landing, I ended up on a staircase much narrower than the one I'd climbed earlier; a servants' stairway. At the bottom of that dark, serpentine stairwell, I saw a doorless opening that gave out on to the grounds.

At long last I stood in the yard.

Not far from the doorway sat the strangest contraption—it seemed a scarecrow made of glass. Closer inspection showed it to be a multilimbed wooden *thing*, standing as tall as I did, built, apparently, for the purpose it now served: on it, hung by their mouths like hooked fish, were large glass jars. Hung there to dry after being washed? Or were they being seasoned, somehow, by the sun? Surely not the greatest mystery I'd encountered, but a mystery nonetheless. (Roméo would later tell me he'd emptied the jars of old preserves, washed them, and hung them on his "tree" to dry, in preparation for the fall's putting by of fresh preserves. He did this all by himself; I liked that, tremendously—I thought it romantic.)

Keeping to the cool band of shadow near the manor's wall, I moved toward the sound of Roméo turning the earth in the garden. Just around that corner. Slowly, stealthily. . . . *There!* . . . A beautiful tableau it was, worthy of Sebastiana's beloved Raphael: Roméo in the garden, lit by a low, strong sun.

The garden was bordered on three sides by a tall hedgerow; the wall of the house completed the loose rectangle. Though the hedge obscured him from the shoulders down, I could see Roméo at work. Indeed, it was those strong shoulders that determined me to move closer. I had to see more. Of him.

But how to get closer, close enough to see all I could, *all* I could, and still remain unseen? I was conscious of my quickening heartbeat. This boy, his simple proximity, caused me to feel things I'd never, *never* felt before.

In its way, the garden was as beautiful as the boy who tended it. It was resplendent. And through the combination of Roméo's tending it, and Sebastiana's offerings of potent powders turned into the soil (not to mention a certain rite read each February), the garden bore outsized produce: tomatoes one had to hold in both hands, pumpkins that had to be carted from the garden in a wheelbarrow. What's more, things grew in that garden without regard to their proper season, and so Roméo might serve a corn chowder in May, fresh ratatouille well into winter.

Turning the corner, stepping from shadow into light, I saw several espaliered apricot trees, expertly tied and trained, standing flush against the wall. I crept ever closer to the garden, imagining myself hidden among the perfectly flat fruit trees. Finally: a full view of garden and gardener.

What I saw then, as I stood so perfectly still, as disciplined as one of those trees . . . what I saw then, what I drank so deeply in, was a sight I'd never seen: a beautiful and very nearly naked man. (No: the incubus does not count; his beauty was of a *quite* different sort.)

Roméo, as he worked under that hot sun, wore nothing but his old wooden clogs and a pair of indigo-dyed pants, cut off well above the knee and tied at the waist with a white cord.

His black hair, shoulder-length and loosely curled, draped his face as he bent over, working the iron blade through the dark soil. Though I could not see his face, I already knew its beauty well: the high forehead, the wide-set blue eyes with their long lashes, the almost-broad nose, the lips red and thick, and . . . *Mon Dieu!* My blood races now at the recollection!

As I could not see Roméo's face, I assumed that he could not see me where I stood, against that wall, between two of those flattened trees. (I was like a child who, wanting to hide, covers his own eyes with his hands.) I've no doubt I stared at him, took him in brazenly, boldly. Took in those broad shoulders, *so* very broad, and the muscles moving beneath his tanned and sun-freckled skin, moving just so, with every toss and pull of the hoe . . . Took in the rippling plane of his torso . . . Took in the taut fan of his back, tapering down to his tight waist . . . Took in the thickly muscled thighs and the rough fabric of those half-trousers . . . Took in the high muscles of his calves, and their descent to the ankle, to the soft and thickly veined instep that showed just above the worn leather of those clogs. . . . I took it *all* in.

And yes, standing there in the full-on sun, Roméo not fifteen paces from me, my blood coursing from my brain to places unknown . . . yes, I am willing to concede that, once or twice, I turned to that stone wall for support, perhaps even held to the stunted branches of the apricot trees. But at least I did not faint, as I had when set aflame by Asmodei at dinner.

Eventually, Roméo stood up straight. Cupping both hands over the top of the hoe, he leaned on it and squinted into the lowering sun. He shook his head and sweat flew from his brow; I saw these as shavings of silver, chips of diamonds, and—shamefully—I *yearned* for their salt taste. The hoe at rest against his chest, its handle against his heart, Roméo ran both dirty hands through his thick black hair. He then trailed one hand, lazily, over his chest, and I heard, *felt* my breath seep from me as a sigh.

Throughout, Roméo was attended by an extended family of roosters, hens, and chicks. The hens worked the earth with their talons, undoing Roméo's work, raking it into random piles, places to roost, places for the still-downy chicks to play. The chicks wandered underfoot, and Roméo nudged them away. The vicious-seeming hens chased each other in crazed paths, clucking, bounding waist-high off the ground. The roosters, so regal, stood to Roméo's knee, their feathers shining black and gold and red and green in the sun, the points of their combs burning back off their narrow heads like flames. Their cries, so easily imitated, broke forth, unprovoked, to crack the sun-white silence of the day.

Letting the hoe fall, Roméo moved to stand on the archipelago of blue, green, and gray slate that led from the garden. Stepping from his clogs, he started to walk, flag by flag, toward where I stood. I flattened my back against the wall. . . . Still, he came on.

I *willed* myself to disappear. Failing that, what could I do? Step forward as though I'd just arrived? Stand as though I were admiring the expertly tended trees? Or should I run, run to the far side of the property and fling myself into the sea?

I'd all but decided on this last plan of action when Roméo, without a word, without a glance, passed within five paces of me. Turning to his left (a right turn would have brought us face to face!), he made his way toward a pump, a curl of black iron that rose up from the earth like a question mark.

I watched from my station as Roméo bent to pick up an old wooden brass-studded bucket. Placing the bucket under the mouth of the pump, he started to work the handle. He stood with his back to me. Drawing on what reserve of nerve, what lack of caution or discretion I've no idea, I took first one, then two, three, four steps toward him, till I stood flat against that wall, beside the very last tree in the row.

Did I have a plan, an excuse at hand? What would I do or say when Roméo turned to see me standing there, staring, as he invariably would? If I did know what I would do, I've no such memory now, thankfully: if I could recall what it was I was thinking I'd feel duty-bound to record those thoughts here, increasing by a factor of ten my already considerable embarrassment.

Roméo filled the bucket. He stood. He untied the knotted cord at his waist: his blue trousers fell fast to his ankles, and he kicked them away. *Naked*, he was! The blue of the fabric was replaced by the alabaster of his untanned flesh, his firm and rounded buttocks. His back still turned to me, he bent to lift that bucket up. He raised it high, high over his head, holding it with both hands. Then, with a shiver—mine, not his—he tipped the bucket and poured the well water down over his head, over his back, over his whole body.

Done, he stood still, holding the bucket overhead. The last of the water coursed down over his skin. He glistened, *glittered* under the sun. Finally, wildly, he shook out his hair, as a dog does when it's come from a puddle or pond.

Watching, *staring*, I saw that he was shaking. Could the water, drawn up from deep in the earth, have been as cold as that? Or was *my* Roméo (I'd thought of him as *my* Roméo from the first time I saw him, coming from the kitchen, soup tureen in hand) . . . was my Roméo crying?

No, he was not. As he turned, suddenly, startling me, I saw that he was *laughing!* Yes, he stood returning my stare, smiling a smile broad and bright. *"Bâtard!"* I said, but embarrassed as I was, I couldn't look away from his . . . from *him*.

Only when he lowered that bucket, tucking it up under his arm like a game ball, only then did I look away. Indeed, I stood staring into the dirt as he said lightly, in an admixture of Breton and French, "We don't all have Turkish baths tucked behind our rooms, you know." He said something else—something about "the open air"—but by then I was quite beyond comprehension.

Again, I did not faint, thankfully. But neither did I die, as I wished I would, right then, right there. No, instead I stood dumbstruck. Couldn't hear, couldn't speak, couldn't walk or turn away. Dumb as those turkeys that drown staring up at the falling rain. Yes, there we were: me, slack-jawed, stupid, staring, and Roméo, smiling and quite comfortably naked.

He came to stand beside me; but not before he drew on those blue pants and recovered his sabots from the garden path, which acts I witnessed as though they were the very Creation.

Standing beside me, Roméo said, simply, "Come," and, appraising the sun's height in the sky, he added, "We have some time yet." He placed his hands on my shoulders. We stood face to face and one step apart. It seemed he might kiss me—I'm embarrassed to say I readied for it—but instead he turned me around and I felt the green robe slide from my shoulders.

"May I wear this?" he asked. "Will you be warm enough without it?" I somehow managed to smile my assent, standing there in only that thin white shift. The robe looked improbably beautiful on Roméo, tight though it was across his chest and shoulders. His tanned skin seemed to *burn* through the silk, deepening its emerald color. He tied it off at the waist, loosely. Following Roméo's gaze downward, I saw that the tips of my breasts bespoke my excitement. Roméo's smile spread wider. He grabbed me by the wrists as I raised my arms, readied to cross them over my chest. "Why?" he asked. Having no answer, I let my arms fall.

I was conscious then of feeling many things for the first time.

"Let's go!" said Roméo, and I followed him. His sabots drummed over the packed dirt of the path that led from the garden. Quicker and quicker till finally he broke into a run, the green silk spread out behind him like wings. We ran along a length of sun-lit wall. Down past the studio windows and the roseraie. Roméo ran faster and faster and I followed, not knowing where we were going. He turned back toward me—he was smiling still—and he slowed, offering his hand; but when I reached for it . . . *alors*, I was too far behind him to take it, and he may have been teasing anyway. I drew up beside him as he slowed, stepped out of his sabots, and slung them against the wall, gracefully, barely breaking his stride. Happy to lose my silly slippers, I followed suit.

Beyond the roseraie, as we neared the bordering dunes, Roméo reached behind him again, and this time I took his hand. We ran on side by side, both of us barefoot, both laughing. I felt the silk of the robe he wore wash over my legs like waves. . . . Waves, yes. It was to the sea that we were hurrying. . . . I stopped. My *body* stopped—and only then did I understand, for fear quickly overtook my *whole* person. It was a memory of Peronette. Recollected too were the many real and metaphorical tides that had so recently turned, bringing me to danger, and very near to death. Ah, but hadn't those same tides carried me here, to this sweet refuge, and set me down beside this beautiful boy?

"What is it?" Roméo asked, turning back to me. "It's nothing," I said, and on we ran.

That afternoon Roméo and I descended from Ravndal, down its dunes to the sea. We followed a path, but still the tall grasses cut, snagged at our silk and our skin.

Through the late hours of the day, before sunset, before the tide's return, we walked in the ash-gray loam near the shore. Roméo let go my hand only when necessary, and he was fast to reclaim it. We coaxed razor-shaped clams up from their narrow dens with fistfuls of salt, salt from a small bucket Roméo kept in the crook of a tree atop the dune. We gathered mussels from the sharp rocks into a pouch Roméo made of the robe, holding the fabric away from his body with one hand.

It was late. Soon the sun would set. And soon too we'd hear that distant rumble that heralded the return of the tide; and it would come fast to imprison constellations of starfish and jellyfish and hermit crabs, to stir the mussels and redefine the harbor entire. By then I'd be safely ashore, not wanting a tidal reminder of dangerous days with Peronette.

Wordlessly, we retook the dune by a less worn path. This time the grasses—some colorless, some brittle as rusted blades—cut our skin; half-buried shells and stones further slowed our progress. Roméo, ahead of me, would turn and offer his free hand; with the other he held to that silken pouch of mussels, and I could hear the slick shells clicking, chattering like a mouthful of black teeth as he climbed.

Later that evening, Roméo and I would sit in the dining room, just the two of us. I was disappointed to learn that we would not *all* dine together each night. But my disappointment was short-lived, for I entered the dining room to find the great table set for two, simply: two brass bowls, two mugs, and two tiny forks. There was a loaf of thick-crusted bread, a block of butter, and two bottles of wine, *ordinary* wine. Roméo, of course, was there. When I'd returned to the studio to change he'd gone I don't know where—I would never see his rooms. He'd changed as well. Now he wore loose-fitting brown pants that ended just below the knee and a billowing white shirt, something akin to those famed pirates' blouses. He wore a newer, cleaner pair of sabots. I wore the first thing that had come to hand when I reached into the armoire: two pieces of

loosely tailored red silk, pants and a button-down blouse, gold-embroidered—
pajamas in the Eastern style. I'd come barefoot over the cold stone of the corridor to arrive at the dining room, and so, entering that room, I proceeded to
the warm stone near the hearth. There I stood, watching Roméo tend a boiling
black pot.

"I've boiled our take in seawater," said he. Now he was stewing the mussels
in the sauce he'd made—a white wine base, with garlic and *fines herbes*. "Are you
ready for *une fête aux moules*?" he asked.

Indeed I was. I ate my fill, and then ate some more. We talked and laughed
lightly. I recollect precious little of what was said, but it was so wonderfully
easy being in Roméo's company. And all the while we drew mussels from a
common pot, discarding the spent shells into a second. I scraped the sweet
orange meat from the shells with my fork, with my fingers. The broth, the
bread, the wine. . . . It was delicious.

Within hours, I would be the sickest I'd ever been in all my life.

A single mussel—"bad" by some definition I don't care to contemplate—
induced in me fits of nausea and diarrhea, cramps and spasms that I won't
describe further.

Eventually, I managed to install myself on the divan in the studio. I sweated
beneath the flimsiest sheets, then shivered under mounded cotton and wool. I
could not ingest even the weak black tea that a distraught Roméo brewed for
me, and the sight of the crackers he carried into the studio caused me to retch.
The sheer violence that erupted within me was . . . Well, so sick was I, I did
not, *could* not care that Roméo, *my* Roméo witnessed the whole episode. Yes, he
was beside me the whole time, caring for me all that long, long night.

At one point, fairly desperate— this was after the failure of the black tea
and crackers—Roméo disappeared from the studio for a short while, returning with some concoction he'd gotten from Sebastiana. I drank it. She'd said
too that there wasn't much that could be done; such an illness—not at all
uncommon—would run its course within twenty-four hours, at which time I
would feel remarkably, wholly better. Still, by my quick calculation there
remained many long hours of abject misery. Unable to sleep, and desperate for
distraction, I would eventually ask Roméo to read to me from . . .

Roméo knew of the existence of Sebastiana's *Book of Shadows*, but he'd never
read from it. That night—against all custom, as I'd learn—I asked him to read
aloud to me from her Book. He did so, with a modicum of difficulty: I helped
him with words he did not know, with others he recognized but had never

pronounced. I remember the story well, for I listened intently to every word read in that deep, Breton-accented voice, the voice of the beautiful, beautiful boy I would have beside me but one day more.

Roméo read to me all through that night, till finally sleep came. He sat on the floor, his back against that divan covered in yellow watered silk; on it I lay in those red pajamas, the perfect picture of some eastern Empress, or Emperor. (Our pose was that of Skavronksy and her serf.) There were two golden bowls on the floor within my easy reach; their purpose ought to be plain. . . . *Enfin,* I took in *every* word Roméo read, watching him—*my* Roméo—all the while. Such sweet distraction he was from my body's betrayal.

28

Bufo Vulgaris

WHEN I WOKE, having slept for I don't know how long, it was to the sound of a slow-opening door.

The room was dark, impossibly dark. Every muscle in my body was sore. And my head felt like a saturated sponge, too heavy to lift off the pillow. With what little strength and coordination I could summon, I reached up and found a cool and dampened cloth, folded lengthwise and laid over my eyes and brow. I pulled it away and the sun rose that day a second time.

I'd lain on the divan all through the long, long night, chilled, variously uncovering and covering myself with the blankets Roméo brought me—and all that long night he, *my* Roméo, had stayed by my side. He felt guilty and apologized a thousand times for not warning me away from the shut mussels. All I cared about was his company. Sick as I was, I'd been so content to listen to him read. I'd thought of asking Roméo to read to me from the books I'd discovered in the studio: *Confidences of a Beautiful Woman, Memoirs of a Young Virgin, Anecdotes of Conjugal Love* . . . but of course I'd chosen instead Sebastiana's Book.

I felt a slight, slight return of my strength. It was as though I were slowly reoccupying my body, limb by limb. And as my eyes adjusted to the light, a certain shadow moving toward me took on a human aspect.

There stood Asmodei, dressed as he'd been two nights prior at dinner: white blouse open to the plane of his chest, long sleeves falling unfastened and soiled over his wrists, black culottes cropped at the knee, dirt-darkened sabots. He stood at the end of the divan on which we lay; in truth, Roméo, still asleep, lay alongside it on the carpet.

"Boy," said Asmodei. He towered over the divan. Early light entering the studio through the tall windows behind him gave to his blond mane a golden cast; so bright did he seem, I had to look away, turning back only when he said again, "*Boy!* Wake up!" I saw with relief that he spoke to Roméo, whom he nudged now with his foot.

"Talked the night away, did you, young lovers?" Asmo stood staring down at me, clad so splendidly, so incongruously in the red silk pajamas, which clung to my every contour. Damp too was the yellow silk of the divan, on which I'd sweated all through the long night. I drew myself up and curled into the divan, as far from Asmodei as possible—"cower" would be the word, had I not taken pains to sit straight-backed and hold, hold at all costs, that man's appraising gaze. There he stood, hands joined behind his back, rocking up and down, heel to toe, in a contemplative pose—but Asmo, I know, was not given to contemplation.

Roméo woke. He asked how I felt. "It has passed," said I. "Thank you." And turning to look up at Asmodei, Roméo added, smiling, "I dreamed of you." This struck me.

"A pleasant night's work, I trust? Speaking of work, you've a great deal of it. The cocks have been crowing for more than an hour; so leave *her* crowing cock alone and see to them."

"Do you need anything?" asked a still sleepy Roméo of me. "Can I get—"

"You can get yourself gone, boy!" Asmo kicked at Roméo's bare foot. "The witch and I have some *work* of our own to do."

Doubtless it was fear, perhaps even panic Roméo read on my face as he rose from the floor. *Don't go*, was my tacit plea; but he had no choice: in Sebastiana's absence he answered to Asmodei.

"See to the fire first," commanded Asmo. "There's a chill to be burned off; and it *stinks* in here. Take these away with you," and Asmo gestured down with a nod to the bowls I'd put to sickly purpose all through the night.

As Roméo passed him, Asmo let fly out an elbow, catching the younger man in the chest and causing a rush of air from his lungs. The boy cursed; the man smiled; and nothing more was said. Only when Roméo, having resuscitated the fire, eyed him from the door did Asmo feint a second strike. Oddly, Roméo's suspicions—I know now that he had suspicions—dwindled to a simple smile, and he left us.

It was in the course of that boyish jousting, as Asmodei turned, took two quick steps toward Roméo, that I saw he bore a gift, hidden behind his back: a square box wrapped in slick golden paper and festooned with a great green ribbon.

I asked, reflexively, rather boldly, "For me?"

"Drink your tea," said Asmodei, setting the box beside the silver tray he, presumably, had brought. I eyed the steaming green-black tea. I'd seen enough of this man to worry. "Oh, drink it down, for the love of Lucifer! Your Sebastiana sends it."

I sipped at the tea. I was feeling markedly better. The revolt of my innards was over; cramping was all that remained of the sea's assault on my person. The tea, if somewhat brackish, seemed to help; soon I was wide awake. "And the present," I ventured, "is that from Sebastiana as well?"

"No," said Asmo; he sat now on the far end of the divan. "Not directly." He looked down at his hands, shyly, as if he'd an admission to make. "We men on the periphery of the sisterhood have our role, too, you know. Traditions and such."

I was glad for that; and I found myself unafraid. Had I forgotten the flaming cuffs, the insulting play of pronouns he'd used since first we'd met, the thinly veiled threats? Ah, but who, I ask, is not won over, however fleetingly, when one finds oneself in receipt of a gift? "Shall I open it?" I asked.

"The tea. Finish the tea."

I did. It was pleasing—was that salt, that crystalline silt that swirled through the sea-green tea? It had just enough coffee-like bitterness to rouse me. We spoke as I drank, though I recall not a word of what was said, so distracted was I by the gift—I admit it, and add that I have received precious few gifts in my life—and by Asmodei's presence. . . . Yes, I drank, and having done so, it was to the above-mentioned—the gift, its giver—that I attributed the quickening of my heart.

"This tea, what is it?" I asked.

"Do you feel its effect?"

"I do." The dregs of the tea had already dried to a dark scab in the cup's bottom. Asmodei neared to spoon-feed me its silt—salt, yes, or perhaps sugar—which stung my tongue, just slightly.

"Good," smiled Asmo, "and now, my little gift." He carefully, *too* carefully, took from me the cup and saucer, replacing them with the beribboned box. As I set to work, smiling, on the emerald bow, the embossed paper, I felt the sudden heat of Asmodei's hands on my bare ankles. On raced my heart. I felt my face flush and to draw breath was suddenly difficult. Still I attributed it to the man, his mere proximity. "Yes," said he, "something of a tradition, that I gift you with this. Not many men are allied to the sisters, you know. . . . You, of course, will be. Or would have been." And at this riddle his hands rose from my ankles, up, up, under the wide-cut legs of the silken pants. His grip was tight and would have tightened had I tried to move. And so I hastened the strange ritual, and tore into the box; all the while the muscles of my throat contracted, as if in anguish. I was breathing now through my mouth, and my heart leapt about like—

Like the two blue toads that bounded onto my chest from the opened box.

Asmodei's metallic laughter, ringing, ringing. . . . I drew back but was held, fixed in place by his hands, so near my knees. He settled closer. The toads sat fatly on my chest, as if to mock the twin weights of my breasts. . . . Dreadful, they were, the size of a child's palm, blue- and black-speckled. . . . My pulse, racing. My heart about to burst.

"But don't you like toads," asked Asmo, much nearer now, too near. "Toads to mirror your witch's eyes?" His body, his weight pinioned me; and his face was less than an arm's length from mine. "Pets," said he, "that's all. Sebastiana said I was to—"

"Sebastiana," I echoed, but the name did not calm me as I would have wished.

"Yes, of course. She has sanctioned it all. . . . Take one up, witch. Do it. . . . *Do it!*"

Scared, I soon had a toad in each hand. Asmo sat back, satisfied. "There's a good girl, or boy, or whatever." He was settled in the fork of my splayed legs . . . surely it was that which caused my heart to lurch? . . . Yes, painful now, that crazed pulsing; and every breath, too shallow, rattled my chest. I tried to move but couldn't. I tried to speak but . . . my tongue seemed made of cloth;

my whole body felt hollowed and packed with cloth, like a mummy bound for the Afterlife. Still, reasoning that if I did as I was told the whole bizarre ceremony would end all the sooner, I settled the toads in one palm—I *hate* such things—and I petted them with trembling fingers. "That's it," said Asmodei, whose own hands ranged over me now with far too much freedom. With shame I'd gone stiff, stiff and slick at his nearness, and the play of his powerful hands rendered me short of breath.

"Please," I begged, when it seemed I could not hold to the scaly weight of the toads a moment more, "please take them." I held them out to him. "And please, take your hands from—"

"*I* don't want them," said Asmo, standing fast, raising his hands in mock surrender. "No, no, no." At least I was free of his crawling fingers. "Don't you favor your new friends?"

"I'm sorry," I said, "but I do not."

"No matter," said he. "You'll not have to suffer them much longer. Indeed," he added, looking to the clock on the mantel, "it has been some minutes since the tea. Your heart must feel like it's fit to *pop!*"

"It does," I said through welling tears. "It does.... What have you...?" I could not complete the sentence. I put the toads back in the box, settled the lid tightly over them. Something clung to my hands like sap from a tree, like ... like poison from a toad's skin.

"*Bufo vulgaris,* or some related species," said a gloating Asmo from over near the fire. "Terrific little creature, deadly to the touch." Lifting his shirt to show a pair of canvas gloves tucked into his belt, he added, "And requiring a quite dexterous handling.... Why, *hours* it took me to milk enough venom from the little beasts, to carefully, carefully raise the flames just so—no good cooking them, after all—and oh, what a game of patience, waiting, waiting for the slow dripping down of the toxin into that teacup.... I slept nary a wink!

"Oh yes ... you've been toaded, dear, from without and within." That laugh like the striking of cold irons. "Not much longer now, and your heart will screech to a sudden—"

"But ... Sebastiana?" I managed. My throat was swelling. Soon speech would go. Then breath. Then life.

"Your trusted sister sleeps, sleeps soundly in her rooms beside her den, from whence your sticky killers come.... But you've not seen her den, have you? Pity—now you never will. Fantastic, it is, with contents to rival the dens of the witches of Thessaly. Where she gets such things I'll never know...."

Chunks of salt-cured flesh. Beaks, sawed from birds of ill-omen. Briny bottles holding the noses of victims of crucifixion. 'Holding the noses,' get it?" He mimed the action, giddy as a boy until . . .

"And antidotes too, you fool!" Sebastiana, sleep-disheveled, wild-seeming, stepped into the studio from behind the tapestry that covered the corridor door. "That studio has the antidote for any aspect of the Craft *you* dare attempt." In her hands was a glass vial. She brought it to me, poured its thick black syrup into my cupped palms, instructed me to spread it on the thin skin of my wrists, behind my ears, and . . . and as far back on my tongue as I could manage without gagging.

"You," said Asmodei, flatly. "You." And I saw that the unfinished accusa-tion—of betrayal? of perfidy?—was directed at Roméo, standing half-hidden behind the tapestry. Sebastiana called Roméo forward and handed him a lid-ded porcelain bowl, which sat in his callused palm like a dove. "As I directed," said she to the boy. "And quickly!"

Roméo came up behind me and, with awkward apology, ripped open the red silk nightshirt. Dazed, I'd no strength to resist—from ever-increasing shame? from mere propriety?—as he opened the bowl, doused my chest, my neck, and my breasts with a powder that had the consistency of . . . of ground bone, and bore a quite indelicate smell.

My heart slowed. My throat opened. And I heard Sebastiana say, "*Devilish* man! . . . I knew before the boy came to me. I need no *mortal* warning of sisterly danger! . . . What," she went on, "*what* were you thinking? . . . I should have known you'd try to—"

"To what?" challenged Asmo. "To put down the witch like the monstrous anomaly she is? Yes, you *should* have known I'd not suffer such as that among us." He waved dismissively at me. "In truth, all I hoped for was a quick going-over of the still-warm witch. The incubus, after all, spoke so admiringly of its attributes. And if it died, it died." All the while Roméo worked upon me, and so perhaps Asmodei's words did not fall before me with the desired effect.

"*Brute!* I know you are capable of the most lowly mischief, but here, in my house, to *attack* one of our own?"

"You'd have me accept *that* as one of our own?"

"Oh, you *are* a brute, a beastly, jealous brute!" Sebastiana let fall her voice to a whisper, asking, "Do you forget what I have the power to do to you?"

"I do not," answered the man, coming nearer the divan. Sebastiana put her-self between us. Cower *is* the word for what I did then. "Do *you* forget," asked he, "the very *earthly* hold I have over you, my dear? You who have been dumb with love all these long years?"

"You flatter yourself," said Sebastiana. "You have become little more than a dog in my home, a once-favored pet that has no role now but to die. To obey until the day it slinks away to die!"

"A dog, is it? . . . If it's a dog I am, you are but my bitch."

"*Arrête!*" This from Roméo, who came nearer now. "Stop it, both of you. And you," said he to Asmo, "you go now. *Go!*"

"Go in shame," added Sebastiana, "and before the succubus sees what it is you've attempted—to take from her the only hope she has of . . ."

"I'll go," agreed Asmodei, "but I will return. And when I do, *this* had best be gone." And with that he moved fast; leaning over the divan, taking my chin in hand, so that I could not turn from him, he lowered his face to mine and . . . and he made the croaking call of a toad. Much amused—his laughter *exploded* within the studio—he left through the garden door, and was gone among the roses.

At the slamming of the door, at the rattling of the glass panes, I *leapt* into Sebastiana's arms. Roméo, at her direction, knelt to wrap my hands in bolts of black damask torn from beneath the divan. "In two hours' time," said Sebastiana, "the venom will be dry, of no danger at all."

Apologies and plans were made, but all I can recall is Sebastiana whispering, more to herself than to me, "I feared this might come to pass."

Soon it was agreed that sleep was the wisest course of action; and so I found myself settled into the *lit clos*. Sebastiana spoke somewhat cryptically of a "mission," and of "the long, long days to come." As if to assuage me, she added, "It was never meant to be *permanent*, my dear." Then—with a blessing or spell—she slid shut the doors. I tried to stifle my tears, for Roméo, I knew, stood sentinel in the studio.

My sleep, when finally it came, was deep, aided by a second tea I'd warily accepted from my Soror Mystica, this one thick and pulpy, pumpkin-colored.

Sometime later, I woke and stepped from the *lit clos* into the cold and dark studio.

It seemed whole days had passed, so deeply had I slept; but the clock, its golden works plain under a glass bell, showed an unlikely hour. It was dusk of the same day. I'd not even slept the night away.

I turned from the windows to see Madeleine standing across the studio. The *depth* of the chill told me Father Louis was near as well, though I could not see him. Asmodei was gone, I knew not where. Within minutes, Sebastiana would come. And Roméo too: he would have with him the makings of a meager, but satisfactory supper.

In contrast to when I'd last seen her, when she'd rushed gracelessly into the studio in Roméo's company, dressed in only a single blue robe, her black hair in a hastily pinned-up pile, Sebastiana came as impeccably dressed as when she'd come to save me from C——. She wore her standard robes of azure silk, carefully draped and pinned to conceal her naked self; indeed, her form did sometimes show clearly through those folds of silk. She'd brushed her hair out, and now sported one long braid; wisps of blackest hair were contained by her red coral combs. Her feet were bare. A thin silver chain adorned her right ankle; it was hung with two scarabs of lapis lazuli. She wore no necklaces, no rings or bracelets; but her exquisite eyes, and perfect pale face, were set off by earrings of hollowed pearl, pendant from delicate silver chains and full of a scented oil, which dripped, at long intervals, onto her bare shoulders.

Sebastiana suggested I bathe, but it was Madeleine who brought me a bathing shift of sheer muslin, who led me to the bath behind the muraled wall. There, in the quiet dark, Madeleine—so *kind* she was—sat plaiting my hair.

Then, in the bath, Madeleine let me cry, encouraged me to cry. I did not notice the blood she spilled on the dark tile, on my skin and hair as she comforted me. (Discovering it, on my person, I simply washed it away.)... And Madeleine did comfort me, truly; it was as though she were able to distill her own pain and make of it an elixir. I relish the memory of it. I relish too events that commenced when there came a light knock at the paneled door; and before either the succubus or I could respond, we were joined by Roméo, who asked, simply, "May I?" Before I could answer—did the succubus answer him, or somehow draw him there?—he stripped and slipped down into the tub. "I could use a washing too," said he. "It has been a . . . a *dirty* night and day."

Now my embarrassment was acute, relieved not at all by the ministrations of Madeleine, nor by Roméo's sweet and constant smile. I was embarrassed *bodily*, of course, but also at the recollection of the dirt to which Roméo referred. Yes, he'd cared for me so patiently all that long night, he'd tended so casually to the base aspects of my body—dumping out those enameled bowls of spittle and vomitus and excrement, wiping the sweat from my brow, swapping out the sweat-darkened blankets he'd laid over me, holding back my hair as I retched again and again, my head hung over the side of the sofa. . . .

This grim recollection was interrupted by the succubus, who leaned nearer to whisper, *Perhaps you owe the boy the washing he seeks?* And before I could demur, could act in any way, she repeated her words; and, strangely, this time Roméo seemed to understand her every word, for he rose and came nearer, stopping to stand in the very center of the tub, where the water rose to his full thighs and . . .

Roméo neared, and Madeleine shoved me forward: soon he and I stood face-to-face. Naked. "I never thought he'd be more than rude," whispered Roméo. "I never would have left you alone with him."

Ah, the differentness! The sameness! Never have we seen the like of this! Louis . . . if only Louis. . . . My sudden, paralytic shivering amused the succubus. (Roméo was far calmer, and already aroused.) *Yes, witch,* said she, *the sexual is the preferred means of communication among us, and the boy has been well-trained.* And it was then she fully ceded to her nature, and directed us in a dance, the likes of which . . .

You've no reason to be shy, dears, said she. *Your wishes, your desires are known to me.* And this she proceeded to prove. *Ah, but wait,* said she, and were it not for the fluctuating temperature in the steamy, dim room, I would not have known she'd left it; but leave it she did, returning in, quite literally, no time, with the standing mirror I'd put to purpose earlier. Too, she'd brought candles into the bath, and arranging these in their silver stands just so before the mirror, I saw what it was she sought to achieve—for now, by their doubled light—I cannot say how she caused the wicks to suddenly take flame—she would be visible to Roméo as well as me. He would see her in the mirror, a murky mass of steam, of condensation . . . of I know not what else.

Now, said the succubus, settling on the tub's ledge, before the mirror, *what he seeks is the knowledge of what so drives Asmodei to distraction. As for you, witch, well . . .*

"May I see?" asked Roméo. "May I see your . . . your . . ."

"But I cannot," said I, shrinking back in my clinging shift, nearer the succubus.

Madeleine's laugh came like running water. *You want to, witch; and so do it!* Again I felt her cold shove, sending me tripping into Roméo's opening arms. *Do it!* she commanded, adding, *If there is an occasion for shame, I've never known it. . . . Now show him your . . . your* self; *he asks out of a tender care and attraction. Why look at him! Here you stand before him, that muslin a second skin, and yet his eyes are trained on yours. He awaits permission. . . . And what you fear will not come to pass: he will not turn from you, from the* truth *of you.*

"Can I not tell him? Must I show him?"

No, no. Far more articulate, the showing. . . . But time . . . time is of concern to us this night; and so . . . Boy, raise your arms high above your head.

Roméo stood still, and I realized with a sinking heart that I would have to translate for him the succubus's every command; this, at her urging, I did.

Madeleine directed me to mirror Roméo's every move. *We shall compare,* said she, *for his benefit and yours—and,* she added with just a hint of apology, *for my amusement.* Again, the liquescent laughter.

And so Roméo flexed this muscle and that, raised his spread palms to meet mine. We tested the slopes of each other's shoulders, patted the flat plains of stomachs, smoothed the wet hair of heads and . . . *Touch it,* said the succubus to me. *You first, then the boy.*

As my trembling hand rose from my side, as the fingers splayed and curled, and as I readied to take his tumescence and . . . Just then the near giddy succubus spoke: *Ah, but wait,* mes enfants, said she, in mortal years younger than us both. *The pleasure is in the slow play, and I ought not to deprive you of it.* She bade me touch Roméo's brow, the curl of his ear; she bade me touch his lips, and tell him, repeat to him that he was to take my fingers, gently, slowly, with his tongue. It was then she directed my glistening fingers to his chest, so firm, so . . . so unlike mine. I told him: Touch me, as I touch you. (Was it the succubus's command, or orders of my own?)

It was then Madeleine sank her hands into the tub, and, with a smile, caused the water to heat; soon it churned as though rolling to a boil. "Does she mean to cook us?" asked Roméo, in half-jest.

I mean only to heat *you,* said the succubus. . . . *Now continue. Revel in the difference, seek out the sameness . . .*

Take to each other's most tender spots, with fingers first, then perhaps mouths, and . . . Her words, discernible now only to me, were lost in laughter. But I knew what it was she meant me to do: I took Roméo's hands in mine and placed them . . . placed them on my breasts. *The nipples, yes! Always best to begin there.* Madeleine verily howled this; and by instinct Roméo understood, and when he, with forefinger and thumb, took both my . . . It seemed I would faint, but falling this time into pleasure, not fear.

I did the same to Roméo, teased the ripening buds of his chest till his neck went slack, his head rolled just so, and his fruity breath—so intoxicating!—came in great waves from his mouth and. . . .

Still her with a kiss, said the succubus. "Kiss me," came the echoed command from me; but as I readied to receive same—eyes rolling back in my head, lips pursed, my own fingers still at play on Roméo's chest, as were his on mine—the succubus dug into her bag of tricks and . . .

"Damnation!" I dared say when the cold, cold splash came over us both. But we all three of us soon dissolved into laughter, Roméo and I clinging fast to each other for warmth. As for Madeleine, she'd amused herself well; she applauded now by cracking two silver candlesticks together.

Damned, indeed, said she, rising . . . *and so I am reminded. Quickly, into the studio with the two of you! Such games as these will have to wait.*

"But," I began, having hoped our game would resume. Roméo, I saw with relief, had hoped the same. "But . . ."

Tonight it is you mortals who have eternity on your side. As for me . . . Now come! And she dipped her hands deep into the bathwater, threatening another rain of wintry water.

We leapt from the tub, Roméo and I. We took to the hanging bolts of cloth and dried ourselves. And it was then, on our own terms, that we took each other in—with eyes only—and all of our questions were answered. When Roméo looked at me and, far from turning away disgustedly, smiled, I felt a flood of tears, for a dam of loneliness, long years in the making, had burst within me. Then came his final kiss, and hand in hand we left the bath, Roméo whispering, urgently, "You were never meant to stay." I did not hear his words, did not understand them, not then; for too quickly came the light of the innumerable candles that had been set about the studio.

29

Preparations; and Departure

RETURNING TO THE studio—and let me say deep, *deep* was the ache of delayed satisfaction—I saw a purpose in Sebastiana's eyes that I'd not seen since she'd entered the library at C——. I remember she'd fallen into conference with Father Louis then, and it was they who made plans now; rather, it was they who decided that the plan that had been in place, unbeknownst to me, had now to be put into action. "It's time, yes," I heard her say.

"Madeleine will be pleased," was Father Louis's response.

"That," sniffed Sebastiana, "is of secondary concern."

What are you speaking of? asked the succubus from across the studio, where she stood helping me to dress in a simple shift and slippers. As for Roméo, he'd gone naked to Sebastiana's side; and there he stood a long while before seeking out a robe.

Ignoring the succubus, Sebastiana said to me, "*Mon coeur,* you must leave. Your safety cannot be assured." And so, with no appeal, it had been decided: I would leave Ravndal, and soon, in the company of Father Louis and Madeleine.

The mission? What I learned that night was that Sebastiana had little invested in it; it was of little consequence to her. It was, however, of *primary* concern and consequence to Madeleine, and Father Louis, too; and it was they who now pressed for a hastened departure. "She's been most patient," said Father Louis, referring to the succubus, and speaking to Sebastiana. "And need I remind you, there were promises made and—"

"You need *not* remind me, Father," interrupted Sebastiana. "I well remember.... How could I forget, *haunted* as I've been all these years?" It seemed Sebastiana had made Madeleine a promise long, long ago; somehow, *I* was the fulfillment of that promise. I understood too that there'd been a plan in place; this mission, as it were, was nothing new. There was much talk that night: routes discussed, details seen to, and from it all I gleaned this: I was only ever going to stay at Ravndal a few days. Now those days had been shortened farther, and mere hours remained to me.... *It is time,* said Madeleine, again and again. *It is time.*

"Time for what? *Tell* me," I insisted.

"Time to make preparations," said Sebastiana. She beckoned me. The two of us stood in the dead-center of the studio. Madeleine, in full-form, was to my side on a spread of worn purple velvet, wet with her spill, near enough to hear every word Sebastiana spoke but far enough away so as ... so as not to *offend* the chatelaine. Roméo, sullen, silent, sat in a far corner. Father Louis was near but took no form.

When Sebastiana leaned nearer, it was to whisper, "As Téotocchi told me, long ago, to go north, I tell you to take to the sea. In a dream I had—a dream *of* you, a dream *for* you—I saw the sea."

What is it you whisper? asked an agitated Madeleine. *Have I not suffered enough from the secrets you keep, the secrets of your precious Craft, which might have spared me ... spared me this, if only you'd been brave enough to try, to try to—*

"Silence, sanguinary one," shot back a slyly smiling Sebastiana, who went on: "Once again it is *I* who am to blame for your state? But was it *I* who bedded my parish priest with so little discretion, *I* who—?"

Suddenly, the temperature in the salon plummeted; the fire sputtered and spat as Father Louis fast appeared. "Now, now," said he, coming to full-form beside Madeleine. "Ladies . . . we've agreements, have we not?" But it went on:

"I," said Sebastiana, "*I* should again risk calamity—like the winter I wrought—just to aid you in your crossing over, in dying the second death you seek?"

Yes!

"And why? Tell me why?"

I've told you over and over and over—

Father Louis interceded. "Madeleine, perhaps with this *new* witch . . ." but the succubus did not hear him, for already she'd begun to wail, wail in horrid tones her sole truth:

I cannot live this death any longer!

I fell back from this little circle, nearer Roméo, fearful. But then Sebastiana, with a nod toward the succubus, said, to me, "I tried to help this pitiable one once, but I could not." She smiled, rather wistfully. "I was . . . I was not *new*, then; and when I tried to . . . Ah, let me simply say this: you, as a new witch, are in some ways more powerful than I. And this one"—another nod in Madeleine's direction—"this one needs your power. . . . *Regarde!* She all but *begs* it of you. Rather pathetically, it seems to me."

"What can *I* do that you cannot?" I asked of Sebastiana.

"They'll tell you in time," said she, with a wave toward the elementals. "But now," she went on, a too mischievous smile on her red-painted lips, "now I need something from you, something *of* you. Turn around, won't you, dear?"

I did. My back was to Sebastiana; and it was in that tall, free-standing mirror that both Madeleine and I had used earlier—for purposes perhaps illicit, but true—that I saw my Mystic Sister bend and draw from beneath the paint-splattered easel a black sack. It was sewn of velvet; rather large, it seemed *heavy* with something. As she stood, she nudged the bag away with her foot, and this set to tinkling the two scarabs at her ankle. The bag's angles, the hard noises of its contents called to mind bones, or stones or shells, or worse. . . . Did I think the bag's contents were *alive*? That Sebastiana would loose some scuttling beetles or crabs or rodents into the studio? . . . When I took a step nearer the mirror, Sebastiana laughed. "Nothing to fear, my dear. Nothing at all." And I might have believed her, had she not already drawn from the bag a pair of large shears. Seeing the reflection of those glistening gold blades, I took another step, away; still I did not turn to face her. *"Eh bien, arrête!"* said she, barely stifling her laughter.

Sebastiana came up slowly behind me, the shears somewhere in her blue silks. She came so close I could feel her hot breath when next she spoke: "Such a sweet one you are," said she in a whisper. "I wish you could stay. I would *let* you stay, were it not for . . ."

For our mission! said a nearing succubus.

"Get back on your drape, ghoul! What I whisper to this witch is of no concern to you." Sebastiana then, rather roughly, lowered the robe on my shoulders. She took my long and still wet hair in her hands and I felt the cold blades come to rest against my neck. I could see them now. . . . Something—the hard cold shears, the words she would soon whisper—something caused my skin to contract. I was all gooseflesh, and I began to shiver.

"Do you trust me?" Sebastiana stood behind me, winding my hair tightly around her tiny fist. "Answer," said she—and I affirmed that yes, I trusted her, wondering all the while if she knew of my uncertainty. I couldn't help but recoil from the blades. My eyelids fluttered; I worried that I might faint. But I was roused just then by a tug at my scalp, and in the mirror I saw the first strands of hair fall at my feet.

I wheeled around and grabbed Sebastiana by the wrists. "What are you doing?"

Perhaps I held too tightly to Sebastiana's wrists. Perhaps I pained her. . . . Regardless, what I saw then stilled me, for . . . for, with our faces so close, Sebastiana showed me *l'oeil de crapaud*. It *burst* into her eyes, flared there like a flame. And I knew that yes, I did trust her. I let go her wrists and slowly, slowly turned back around. I saw then with surprise that my own eyes had turned as well. . . . And so I bowed my head, and bent at the knee so that my sister could more easily cut away the thick blond hair that I'd only recently begun to prize.

"It is for our protection," explained Sebastiana, "you'll see." She then directed Father Louis to go out to the roseraie, candle in hand, and half-fill the hammered-tin watering can beside the door with soil scooped from under the Ambrose Paré. "Read their labels," said she, but the priest did not understand. I directed him to that double-rose of medium size, purple-crimson in color; and this pleased Sebastiana—she told me so.

While the priest worked, with Madeleine standing near, Sebastiana incanted, "Hellish, Earthly and Heavenly Goddess of the Light, Queen of the Night, Companion to the Darkness, Wanderer, Traveler, you who crave the terror of mortals, Great Gorgo, Mormo, Keeper of the Moon in Its Thousand Shifting Forms . . ." She invoked the infamous gorgon Medusa. She continued on, stopping only to scoop my hair from the floor and place it carefully in the watering can, first separating it into long strands, which she tied at one end with bits of black string—"soaked," said she, with a wince, "in cat's urine."

I watched as she worked her Craft over the can, planting the hair and with-drawing her hands fast. "Snappish little devils," said she. A spitting hiss rose now from the hammered-tin can, which sat like a kettle at slow boil.

...Understand: the hair of a witch will—when cut, imprecated, and planted...the hair of a witch will, when next the moon wanes, evolve into ser-pents whose purpose it is to guard whatever perimeter they are planted along. (Ravndal, bounded by the sea on one side, was protected by these snakes on its remaining three sides.) They—and what I saw in the watering can that night were but their squirming larvae—they are white, nearly translucent by day, and black by night: they are rarely seen, even by their victims, for they reside in the deepest dirt and rise only to strike at those who come uninvited or unescorted by their Creator or that witch's surrogate. They spring from the soil, fast as a flash, to bury their single fangs deep in the intruder, extruding a necrotic venom that works on the soft tissues of the body, consuming the flesh from within. "Three of our snakes," said Sebastiana, "can take down a horse, devour it whole—bones too—in two days' time." She added that it'd been years since she'd "augmented the guard." At Ravndal, it was "time to sow snakes." (N.B.: Plant the snakes thirty-six to a row, with a six-pace break between rows.)... And snakes born of my hair, said Sebastiana, would produce a most potent venom, for I was a *new* witch.

...Too, I needed to get rid of all that hair, for, as Sebastiana opined, "I think, dear, that you would do best to travel southward as a man."

I was easily convinced: she showed me men's clothes. The fabrics were impossibly rich, the needlework exquisite! And though certainly not lacking in detail or decoration, they showed infinitely fewer buttons, clasps, and clips than women's clothes, and they were much more comfortable. Yes, I must have said it a hundred times: *Yes, I'd dress as a man! And why not?*

The hour had quickly grown small. Father Louis and rather sullen Roméo had long since disappeared, leaving Sebastiana, Madeleine, and me in the studio.

"*Ah oui,*" said Sebastiana ruefully, sticking her finger through a moth's work, done on a dress of white chenille. She cast the dress aside and dug again in the tall armoire, coming up with this, her clinching argument:

A suit—coat, waistcoat, and breeches—cut from light green silk. The coat, which fell just above my knee and not below, as designed, was embroi-dered with fleurs-de-lis and fern fronds sewn in threads of variant browns and gold; the buttons had embroidered covers as well; and the collar of the coat stood high. The sleeves, though, fell a bit short: we chose a blouse with extra-long and lacy cuffs to compensate. And that is how I was dressed some hours later, at dawn, as we drove from Ravndal with that bulging *necessaire* fastened to the back of the coach.

That *nécessaire*—a large trunk, or traveling armoire—was in fact a bit more complicated than that, with interior and exterior drawers, both plain and hidden. It was constructed of dark woods, with inlays of mother-of-pearl and ivory. Its lining and outer strapping were of heavyweight canvas. Its sturdy buckles and locks were brass, and brass too were the rods within, for the hanging of clothes. The *nécessaire* sat before the stationary armoire, the one I knew to be crammed with clothes, the one from which I'd already chosen a few outfits, including the robe of green silk that Roméo had worn and those regrettable red silk pajamas. The *nécessaire*, when first I saw it, was already half-packed: Sebastiana had begun packing it as I slept. Now she was *unpacking* the trunk: I simply *had* to see this *blouson*, these culottes, et cetera. . . . Yes, I daresay she was giddy. (She sought with her lighter mood to distract me from the events of the day and the coming dawn. She succeeded, briefly, and I remain grateful.)

"Mon Dieu!" said she, "I'd forgotten just how much I'd collected over the years. It's all sat packed away for so very long!" Only that very night, struck by the notion that I ought to dress as a man—"at least to leave here," said she, "and maybe longer. Who knows?"—only then had she thought again of those clothes.

"Ours was a world of masquerade," sighed Sebastiana, rifling through the armoire. "We were"—and here she looked up, rather dramatically, at me—she deigned to address Madeleine, too; Madeleine, who sat at a distance, her blood pooling on that purple velvet spread—"We were," said Sebastiana, *"les Incroyables.* Dress was an art like any other. We didn't give a *damn* for the accepted fashions. We defied them at every opportunity!" Here she paused. "That is, until a man's wearing the wrong color hat could lead to his death in the street!"

She raised a half-robe to the candlelight just then; its whiteness had gone gray. "These clothes, each piece," said she, with a sigh, *"each piece* is bloodstained. Do you understand?" I said I did.

"How is it you have all these clothes?" I asked.

"How is it," echoed Sebastiana, "that I've ended up with this ragged, tattered, and moth-eaten *musée des modes?* . . . You have read a bit in my Book, no?"

"I have," said I.

" '*Le souper grec*', and its preceding chapters?"

"Yes."

"Eh bien," said Sebastiana, "then you know of the royals and aristocrats, the privileged people I painted. And you know too that I had property safely

beyond the city." I nodded. Madeleine sat silently by. Sebastiana fingered a length of blue damask. "When these ... *acquaintances* of mine slipped into exile, I agreed to store their wares, 'hold them' till they came to reclaim them. Of course, the few who may have returned would have searched for me in vain, for I was secreted here by then."

It was rather dangerous, what you did, no? asked Madeleine.

"Sedition would have been the official charge," said Sebastiana. "Punishable, of course, by death." Then, with forced lightness, she cast aside the memory of that long-ago day just as she cast aside this moth-eaten dress or that unraveling blouse, and she drew from the armoire a suit of salmon damask.

"No, no," I demurred. I could not imagine wearing such a showy thing, and I said as much. "Ah, but this was the color of the *proper* Van Dyke costume," said she, passing her hand over the smooth fabric on the back of the jacket, which was broad, too broad for me. I wondered were these ... Asmodei's clothes?

"Some of them are, yes. Asmodei *was* known to dress in his day. 'The glass of fashion and the mold of form,' " she added, wistfully, quoting some unnamed source. "But *this* suit," she went on, "this is an archer's suit, one worn by a friend, a certain Marquis, whose days ended in Spain, I believe." The suit was topped with a short cloak. I tried the ensemble on, at Sebastiana's urging, and Madeleine's too. To my surprise, it fit passably well.

"Mais non!" I said. "I cannot! It's too. . . . *pink!* I look like . . . like an overlarge salmon! I'd feel obliged to walk *backward* down the street in such a suit!"

It was great fun. We whiled away the night like that, the three of us. Madeleine, sitting cross-legged on her spread, grew ever more at ease as the hour of our departure approached. Sebastiana, her arms turning like the wheel of a mill, pulled from the seemingly bottomless armoire suits of ditto and suits cut of Genoa velvet, and shirts edged in varieties of Flemish lace—the laces of Antwerp, Mechlin, Brussels, and Binche, all of which she could identify by their motif. There was damask, chenille, dimity, and brocade. There was the most exquisite passementerie. I modeled the clothes that Sebastiana *presented*, for yes, each outfit came with a story of its provenance. And then we'd all opine; *enfin*, we voted, the three of us, and the clothes were packed or discarded, depending on majority rule.

Many of the outfits did fit; there were droppable hems, and the trousers buttoned at the knee, or near enough. We'd a store of pins, too: Sebastiana made minor alterations. It was fun! Truly, it was. Sebastiana spun her tales faster and faster. We doubted fully *half* of what she said that night, so exaggerated did the tales become. Madeleine would laugh from time to time, the mechanics of which act were, of course, grotesque—Sebastiana, as kindly as she could, told the succubus to sit back, lest the spurting blood stain the clothes; still, it was nice to see the ancient girl smile and laugh.... Poor Madeleine, I miss her; I began missing her the moment Father Louis and I—

The mission! Alors, my mission, *our* mission, was simply this:

The elementals would accompany me southward, to the city of Madeleine's birth; at a crossroads beyond that no longer extant city, she, or her mortal remains, lay buried in unconsecrated earth. There, by means still quite mysterious to me, we—Father Louis, Madeleine, and I—would seek to undo whatever trick of the Church had consigned Madeleine to a centuries-long deathless death. She sought to live again, to live so that she might finally and truly die. Yes, Madeleine wanted desperately to die.

It seemed that in years past, when first they met, Sebastiana had tried to help Madeleine effect this, but for whatever reason she had failed, and refused to try again. Madeleine and Father Louis had then tried all manner, *all* manner of ways to win her release over the centuries, to no avail. My saviors had come to believe that to effect Madeleine's death it would take the strength of a new witch. They'd waited a long time for a new and untried witch, a *powerful* witch to make herself known—Sebastiana *had* agreed to assist in the finding of such a one. Such a one as I.

Our *"soirée"* ended at the first light of day. Again, as it had at C——, dawn came to redefine my life.

Sebastiana and I packed the *nécessaire*. Crammed as it was, we could barely close it. *"Ah, attendons!"* exclaimed Sebastiana, just as I'd secured the first of the brass buckles. "I nearly forgot." With that, she took from under the easel that bag of black velvet, to which she'd returned the golden shears hours earlier. "You won't be needing these, at least not for a while," said she, withdrawing the shears; she secured the mouth of the bag, tied around it the leather strap that had held my braid at its base. "But the rest of this, all this, is yours."

"What is it?" I asked, watching as Sebastiana shoved the bag deep into the *nécessaire*.

"Let us say that it contains a legacy of sorts, passed from me to you; the contents are yours to dispose of as you please."

I thought then that the bag contained certain *trinkets*, things Sebastiana knew I'd need, or thought I might want. I thought specifically of her red coral combs; though those remained in her hair, I took the bag to be full of similar items; and, once I tasked myself again with the brass buckles of the *nécessaire*, I gave the bag not another thought.

And then I saw the coach that would carry me from Ravndal. To say that I have not traveled widely is, of course, a gross understatement. Still, even *I* knew that one rarely if ever came across such a coach as *that* on the backroads of France. Indeed, it had been years since so showy a thing adorned the streets of Paris. I said as much—once I'd steadied myself—when Sebastiana led me outside at dawn and I saw . . .

"You cannot go fast," said she, "it's true; but you *can* go in style." Style, indeed! I stared as the thing came rolling to a stop before us, Roméo at the reins of its two horses. "It could take four horses," said Sebastiana, "but you'll have to make do with two." Roméo, lantern in hand, remained atop the box; his smile—so *pleased* I was to see him smile—outshone the low moon, the blue light of which caused the coach to glow. The elementals? They were near, doubtless hovering as little more than misted soul, clouds of life-matter drawn out along the shore. Asmo? Nowhere to be seen. Sebastiana stood beside me wrapped in an ermine stole, smiling and stifling her laughter.

"Isn't it grand, great heart?" she asked.

"Grand," I echoed. "Yes; *grand*, it is. Surely you don't mean for me to—"

"Roméo, my boy," directed Sebastiana, "the *nécessaire* sits ready, inside the studio. Would you please?"

Roméo came near us. He leaned nearer Sebastiana. I heard what it was he whispered; he wanted first to show me the coach. "Go right ahead, then," said she. "But it's properly called a berlin."

I was in possession—*incredible*, this!—of one of three carriages built by a Parisian saddler in 1770, all of them intended to lead young Antonia and her senior attendants into France. Problem was, the girl was sent from Austria in a hurry, and this last of the berlins was not yet completed.

The young Archduchess had been promised to the French for a full year before they were able, as Father Louis put it, "to take delivery." Heads of state had waited with lessening patience upon the girl's first blood. Maria-Theresa, most eager of all to ally Bourbon and Hapsburg, had ordered that her daughter's inexpressibles be checked thrice daily. The Empress's private correspondence with the French envoy, Dufort, made repeated reference to the *imminent* arrival of one "General Krotendorf." When finally the future Queen of the French spotted her silks, her mother was ecstatic! The "General" had arrived to save Austria! Long-standing plans were quickly set in motion.

One thing *not* set in motion was the third coach, still unfinished. Paid for in full and forgotten, the trap would come to sit for years in the saddler's garage.

At first, no one could afford it; later, no one wanted it. Twenty-odd years later, in the early days of the Revolution, when all workmen and merchants engaged in the opulent trades sought desperately to drop their wares, Sebastiana bought the berlin—"A bargain, *je t'assure!*" said she—and used it to decamp from the rue Cl—— to Chaillot, under cover of darkness; later, laden with all it could carry, Sebastiana had it driven to Ravndal, where it had sat unused in the stables ever since.

That morning, beneath a brightening sky, I took Roméo's hand and climbed into the coach for a closer inspection. The inner walls of the cab were lined in red satin and trimmed in cherry wood. The facing banquettes were upholstered in blue velvet; the cushioned seats themselves bore thread-paintings depicting the four seasons. I smacked a seat and a thick puff of dust rose up. *"Regarde!"* said Roméo, and with that he lifted the same cushion to disclose a commode! In addition, the carriage bore a larder for storing provisions, a simple stove, and a dining table that could be lifted up from beneath the deep blue carpet. I inspected a tall box beside the larder—a portable set of cutlery, complete with spice box and egg cups, the whole made of porcelain, gold, and hammered steel. Four hooks bearing unlit lamps were screwed into the dark wood; two lamps hung between each set of windows; over the windows were black shades of fine, doubled linen.

What a fool I'd feel like rattling south to the sea in so ostentatious a trap! "Isn't there a simple diligence I might board and . . ." But Sebastiana dismissed my concerns with a wave of her hand.

Climbing from the berlin, I saw that someone—Roméo, no doubt—had toned down the rich appearance of the outer carriage. Gilded wood had been painted over; still it shone through in spots like gold in a streambed. The door handles had small black sacks tied over them; along the road I'd steal a peek: solid gold. What band of brigands would *not* set upon such a contraption as we crawled along the backroads of the country?

"My dear," said Sebastiana, in response to the question I had not voiced. "You have read too many novels. And we don't call them *brigands* any longer; they are mere thieves."

"Call them what you will," I countered, "but as we near the southern port cities they'll pick us apart!"

Sebastiana assuaged my fears thusly: "Heart," said she, rather dryly, "you're a witch traveling in the company of two entities several centuries old. I think you'll be all right." It was then I would have sworn I heard Asmodei's quite distinctive, ferruginous laugh somewhere above us. It came like sounds from a forge, issuing perhaps from an upper-story casement, perhaps the roof; but, looking up, I saw no sign of him.

All that happened next happened quite fast. It's a blur to me now, though these events transpired but a fortnight ago.

Sebastiana had left me a bit of my beloved blond hair, tying it back with a green silk ribbon, and Roméo, seemingly amused by my new suit and hairstyle, single-handedly loaded the *nécessaire* onto the berlin before climbing back atop the box. "Is he . . . ?" I asked hopefully of Sebastiana.

"Yes, dear," said she, "but only as far as"—here she named a village a half-day's drive from Ravndal—"and then he returns to me, to us." Roméo would drive me to P—— and there he'd help me hire a driver and fresh horses. He'd return to Ravndal on one of the horses, the second of which he'd sell in P——.

Eager though she was to see me take to the road, Sebastiana let me return to the studio. I lingered there a short while, alone. I left the chatelaine standing beside her boy; they spoke admiringly of the berlin. I sought to *absorb* the studio, take in its every detail. But all I remember now is staring at the map that Father Louis had clipped to an unpainted, yellowed canvas set atop the easel; early the previous night, he'd detailed the route we would take south, to the crossroads, to the sea. Finally, I stepped out into the roseraie. The air was chilling and wet and sea-scented. Mist rose at the base of the bushes. I dared not snip a bloom, but I did sniff those few that had fast become my favorites. Would that I could retain their scents, take with me their sweet perfume. It was then a tide of anguish rose within me, but it was without depth, and I mastered it fast, fast as it rose. *I would not cry.* Quickly, I quit the garden. Passing through the studio, I took up the two *Books of Shadows*—Sebastiana's and mine—and made my way out to the coach.

Sebastiana stood in her ermine wrap. Roméo sat high on the driver's box, reins in hand. The elementals? They had neared; I knew it somehow. And I know now that when Sebastiana, rather mysteriously, addressed . . . addressed the very *air*, saying, *"Courage!"* and offering a quite literal *"Adieu"* . . . I know now that she spoke to an unseen Madeleine.

Sebastiana, taking my hands in hers, suggested I sleep at P——; she suggested too that I summon the elementals at dusk. For this purpose, said she, I'd find in the cab a brass bell, its tongue carved of mother-of-pearl. I'd find it, indeed, in its sheath of gold velvet, well worn and embroidered with three initials that remain unfamiliar to me. "Ring the bell as near to the shore, as near to a source of water as possible," directed Sebastiana. Hearing it, the elementals would come. "They most easily take and hold their true shapes in the cooler hours of evening," said she. And then, quickly, she explained to me something that had puzzled me regarding our route since first Father Louis had detailed it. Father Louis and Madeleine had much to tell me, said Sebastiana, and it was best they do so while fully-formed, that is *corporeal*, visible to me. To achieve this, the elementals required a store of water, salt or fresh— they are, after all, *elementals*. So, even though it would slow our progress considerably, we would keep as close to the "coast" as possible; that is, our route would be dictated by the meandering paths of rivers, lakes, and streams. The Coast Road. Madeleine was the first to call it that.

I said good-bye that early morning to Sebastiana. I saw her for the last time by the light of the lantern she held. First light was coming. Golden waves had begun to break over the dark fields.

I climbed into the berlin. Sebastiana handed me up her ermine wrap. She held my hand in hers. She kissed it, and whispered, "Go. I send you now across the sea." It would be some time before the enormity of her command struck me.

Settling into my seat, looking tearfully down at Sebastiana through the open door, I saw a shifting of the shadows in the tall elms that lined the drive, and then flocks of ravens flew up and away, with one, quite large, swooping down with a great cry, nearer, nearer, till it seemed it might fly into the berlin as it began to roll and . . . But no. The bird perched atop the cab: it—she, Maluenda—would accompany me.

I watched Ravndal recede through the small oval window cut into the back of the berlin; its glass was thick and ill-blown, and so the scene was blurred. Certainly my tears played their part, too. Regardless, all I could discern was a mass of stone and timber and glass, Ravndal, aglow in the rising light. I saw too a waving figure clad in blue.

Finally, I sat forward in the coach and drew down all the black shades. Then I closed my eyes to see the sun rising higher, higher in a new sky.

Book Three

The Coast Road

Nor is his mortal slumber less profound,
Though priest not bless'd nor marble
deck'd the mound.

—*Byron,* "Lara"

30

A Divining Dream

THERE WERE many things I might have considered as we drove from Ravndal that morning. I might have wallowed in my anger at Asmodei; regardless of what I'd learned of the standing plan, it was *he* who'd deprived me of what surely would have been a long and happy life at Ravndal. I might have considered all that was called into question by my adoption of a manly guise. By deciding to dress as a man, had I not altered, markedly, my role in the world . . . whatever *that* was? I might have considered, with measures of worry, just what I would do when the southern road spilled into the sea—in Marseilles, most likely—and I had to secure passage, cross the sea as Sebastiana had commanded, quitting motherland and mother tongue. I might have considered *la nature surnaturelle* of my companions, and our mysterious mission. I considered none of this. Not then.

Instead, I sought and found distraction in the landscape, in the history that would soon come alive all around me, in a world of which I'd only ever read. Now here it was. Too, the pure *strangeness* of events as they occurred would prove a sweet distraction from considered thought. And there was, of course, the Craft, and Sebastiana's Book.

In addition to those entries I have copied from Sebastiana's *Book of Shadows* into my own book, *this* Book, there were many other, far simpler entries, journal-like, relating to events of the day—chiefly, the years of Revolution and Terror. Many of those entries were political, and this surprised me. Sebastiana, it seemed, had long ago disavowed all things political. Surprising, then, to read of her early admiration of Robespierre; of course, in an entry dated not one month later, she dismisses "the Incorruptible" as a slight, sere, exceedingly proper man, heartless, his every move coldly calculated. She seems always to have been amused—yes, *amused* is the word—by the beast Danton, with his outsized nature and vulgar ways. Variously, she envied and pitied Madame Roland, whose ambitions had by necessity to be channeled through her husband, the on-again off-again Minister, and whose salon was the center of so much, including debates of which Madame, the sole woman, missed not a word, sitting as she did at a smaller table beside the larger, hurrying her pen along. Sadly, as though she lacked the strength to record the deed in words of her own, Sebastiana had slipped into her Book that edition of *Gravures Historiques*, which, through engravings and eight pages of inflated text, tells of Madame Roland's execution.

But what interested me most in Sebastiana's Book were not those entries regarding the Revolution, but rather the accounts of her earliest experimentation with the Craft. Those entries—little more than recipes, really, the results of which were not always recorded—served as my primary distraction at the beginning of our journey south.

And I had ample time to read, for as we rode out of Brittany, from Ravndal and the coast, toward Rennes, the elementals rarely showed themselves. Roméo, who'd helped me find and hire a driver before leaving P———, had returned home. Our farewell? It was chaste: shy, wordless, with simple kisses, the kisses of siblings. There was . . . there *is* much I wished I'd said; but I lacked the vocabulary for any good-bye but the most abrupt. (How I longed then to summon the succubus so that she might lead us through a dance like the Dance of the Bath!) . . . He, Roméo, with unexpected guile, had told the driver, Michel, that I was French by birth but Italian by residence; and that it was to Firenze I was returning to settle some family business. . . . Yes, save for

Michel—unquestioning, *petit* Michel, so wonderfully willing to drive through the night; and save for Maluenda, who dipped and dove and sang a discordant song overhead—I was alone for long stretches. And solitude, I found, made it more difficult to master my anger. Yes, I was angry. At Asmodei. Perhaps at Sebastiana, too, for why couldn't she *master* Asmodei, control him so that I might have remained in safety? Anger colored my reason, and my thought was this: if *he* had deprived me of what might have been, *she* had shown me a way to see what would be. I would work the Craft. I would divine my future, my *true* future.

So it was that, in the quiet of the rocking carriage, troubled by every pebble half-buried in the road, I read of the Craft. I grew eager, the more I read; eager to practice the Craft myself. I was ready, ripe; or so I thought. I would have been wise to remind myself just how quickly ripeness turns to rot; but my actions then were fired by anger and, yes, a measure of blinding fear.

I hadn't much at hand: no charms, no amulets, no tools; nothing but fragmentary recipes and disparate spells, and a trunk of dandified clothing that I'd soon discover I was far too shy to wear. And so, I'd soon scratched out a shopping list; and here and there, at Rennes, at Angers, and at places in between, I "went to market." I'd have Michel stop at farms, or alongside streams whose banks were dense with herbs that I tried to identify from sketches in Sebastiana's Book, all the while reminding myself that a mistaken herb could mean the difference between a successful spell and death.

. . . I'd been staring down at the road, which ended an arm's length from the carriage wheels, dropping precipitously down to a rock-strewn strand, when I felt that chill that heralds Father Louis's coming. Convinced that the slightest move on my part would set the whole box to tipping and tumbling to the beach below, I remained still. Was the succubus seated across the cab as well, beside the priest? I saw just a hint of their shapes, for the sun was high, the day hot. I drew the blinds; in the darkness they grew dense, and spoke:

"Have you any idea where we're headed?" smiled the priest.

"Vaguely," said I. "I heard our route discussed last night, but . . ."

You'll need to direct the driver, interrupted Madeleine.

"I can do that," said I, too assuredly; in fact, I didn't relish the thought. I would rather have stayed sealed like some delicate herb or fruit in the crate of the carriage, exiting only as necessary. "I can do that," I said again, speaking to myself this time.

"*Très bien,*" said the priest. "You'll begin now." And so it was he launched into the route I was to relay to the first of my hired drivers.

Of course, I had never traveled; the very notion was new to me. As were the cities, villages, and places—some seemingly too tiny to support a name— through which we'd pass. Along the way, I would acquire a store of guide- books, pamphlets, and maps, of course; for here finally was the world. I would *know* it!

Our route, then, would be as follows:

South off the Breton coast, past Rennes to Nantes and into Angers: our goal was to gain the mouth of the Loire as quickly as possible. Thereafter, we'd follow the flow of that and other rivers, making our way to the southern cross- roads.

From Angers we'd follow the Loire into Tours. Then into the Sologne, where it would seem we drove château to château through the valleys of vari- ous rivers till we took to the Cher. Bourges would be next. Then Nevers. Moulins, and Roanne. Thereabouts, we'd first learn of the flooding—some- what out of season—farther south. Indeed, as far north as Mâcon, the Saône was already expansive. At Lyon, it was said that the waters of the Saône and the Rhône—which would gain our allegiance after the Loire—were already risen to heights rarely achieved. (It was some time before I would let myself wonder *why* the flooding was the worst in generations, *why* the waters rose behind us as though we'd somehow harnessed the strength of the moon and caused the rivers' seasons to turn from their cycle. . . . Was this the work—conscious or otherwise—of my companions? The half-answer I arrived at would unsettle me, deeply.)

The Rhône would lead us down through Lyon, Vienne, Valence, and Mon- télimar. Orange, said Father Louis, would be our gateway to the South. Then it would be Avignon and Arles. And finally, at a place I will not name, a place no longer on any map, beyond Les Baux, north of Arles, we'd discover Madeleine's crossroads and our mission would end.

"Tell him," said the priest; he referred of course to the boy, Michel, who sat atop the box; and with that the elementals faded away—as morning mist, as steam or smoke will—and Father Louis was but a faint voice, repeating, "Tell him," and adding, "Instruct him to drive through the night, south past Rennes, on to Nantes and Angers. To the waters of the Loire." I screwed up my nerve, certain the boy—who was, perhaps, two years younger than I—would ques- tion directives given by a girl. Ah, but I was no longer a girl, or was I? Was it as simple as that, as simple as swapping hair ribbons for waistcoats, corsets for cravats? I rapped at the embossed leather lining the berlin's roof with the Jam- bee cane Sebastiana had foisted upon me; it was a rod of Sumatran bamboo, with a gold pommel, which until that very moment had seemed *utterly* purposeless in my possession. Immediately, the berlin slowed. "*Oui*, Monsieur?" asked Michel, opening the door to the cab; and "*Oui*, Monsieur," said he shortly thereafter, having received my directions with respect and intent.

I knew that we were too far from strong water now, for we'd driven sharply inland from C——; it was then I surmised, rightly, that I'd not see the elementals again until we gained the river Loire, near Nantes.

We reached Rennes by sunset; and in that charming light the city would not *scare* me as others soon would.

Outfitted as I was, Sebastiana had been unable to provide me with suitable footwear. I wore slippers. And so I waited in the berlin while Michel went in search of a tanner who'd open his atelier at that late hour. He found one; and among that man and his family—all of whom suffered stained hands, which I attributed not to working with skins but to some rare and pitiable disease—I chose a pair of boots. Or tried to. Whenever had I made such a choice? Never. And I found it bewildering. Michel spoke persuasively of a pair of plain brown boots, slightly worn at the heel, that rose to the knee. But I was not sure. Soon I sat staring at the boots strewn all around me, like severed limbs on a battlefield. I must have tried the traded-away shoes of ten or twenty men. Finally, the tanner's wife threw open the door of the family atelier and stood before it, hands on her broad hips, and Michel whispered that it was time to choose and leave. As unaccustomed to coin as to the act of choice, I left the tanner's with far fewer bills—I know now that I was overcharged when Michel took his leave to fetch the berlin. Retaking the road that night, having spilled the remaining contents of the purse in my lap, I wondered how much money I had; and I wondered what Sebastiana was thinking, sending me the length of France dressed as a boy-doll from the last century, and in a carriage that outshone every roadside cottage.

My escorts were unseen all that long night. I was on guard now as I read, and as I took in those sites lit first by the moon and then by the rising, brazen sun. I tried to sleep, but could not: I was anxious and eager, so very eager, to practice the Craft. Which, unfortunately, I did, that very night.

We were traveling slowly on a bad stretch of road. I'd directed Michel to drive until dawn; we'd speak again then. I'd rap at the roof of the cab with my cane if I needed him; otherwise, he was to drive on without disturbing me. It was time to practice my plan, and the execution of the Craft, its success or failure, was to be witnessed by no one.

Divination. In first reading Sebastiana's Book, I was intrigued by the notion of foretelling, the inducement of dreams of divination. It was an aspect of the Craft that seemed to me quite practicable. That is, I thought I could do it. At that first supper at Ravndal, Sebastiana had spoken of the ways in which sisters have long foreseen the future: by reading tea leaves, the spilled entrails of birds, and so on. But of greater interest was something I'd later read in her account of the Greek Supper; and it was to those pages I now returned.

I read again the recipe presented by that Parisian hag, that recipe allegedly passed down from the great Catherine Monvoisin, the ill-famed La Voisin, and involving burial and blood and mutilated male genitalia. Now, truth to tell, as grotesque as that spell was, *is*, I might have tried it had I the means and time; but, as the casting of that spell was to be effected over the course of many weeks or so, I simply hadn't the time. (Neither was I inclined to conjure some magical phallus!) So I resorted to a truncated version of that recipe, adding bits of another; and over it all I cast a quite simple spell. (*Whatever* was I thinking?)

I'd already set about stocking up on those ingredients mentioned time and again in the Book. At the market in Rennes, newly shod, I had procured a measure of what's known as the Greek bean. From its seller I received the strangest of looks, which made sense when he said, staring down at the payment I blindly proffered, "Monsieur, that is the coin of Portugal." "Ah," said I, in a lowered voice, "so it is. The coinage of my Italy is so much more manageable." That very evening in Rennes I had Michel detail for me the attributes of each species of coin and bill in my possession; not all of which *he* knew, for into the hurried mix Sebastiana had thrown the money of other nations— Portugal among them, yes—and other times . . . *Alors*, I invited the seller of the Greek bean to pick from my purse, and this he happily did.

I needed a few other things besides, all of them fairly easily come by. I harvested a certain berry roadside, Michel looking on, inquisitive but still. Finally, there remained but one problem: I hadn't a single blue candle.

Blue candles, I'd read, increase the efficacy of all divining spells; they clarify the vision, sharpen it. Then I remembered a lesson learned that last night at C——: blessed candles burn blue in the presence of spirits. Now spirits I had; as for blessed candles . . . Well, let me say they were easily had from a small church in a village whose name I never knew; and that church's priest or sexton, if he even noticed the theft, was surely distracted by the quantity of coin discovered in the collection box beside the door.

I wondered when I should summon the elementals, when I should burn the white candles in their presence. How would I answer the questions they'd ask? Or did they already know what it was I was up to? After all, weren't they *always* watching and . . . ah, then it dawned on me: it seemed they were never far away, and so perhaps they were sufficiently *present* to render the blessed candles blue. I was right: lighting the candles that very night, with everything else I'd need ranged about me in the berlin, I watched as first the flame and then the wax itself turned a powdery blue. Finally, I was ready.

Moonlight fell on the slow-going berlin. By my calculations, we were far from any place of distinction. I locked the doors of the cab. I drew the blinds lest the breeze disturb the burning candles, but they held to their ever-deepening blue. Indeed, they'd soon burned from sky- to sea-blue. I secured them, settled them into niches carved into the wall of the berlin.

I took up the simple potion I'd mixed earlier, which contained the Greek bean as well as other improvised ingredients that seemed, somehow, appropriate: chiefly, duck eggs, a peeled and seeded tomato (N.B.: this *will* sting when applied to the eyes, but it is necessary; "brook no substitute," wrote Sebastiana in one entry), and mandrake, which I'd carefully harvested from a dry streambed, according to the Book's careful directions. I worried that I hadn't mixed in enough of that two-legged root, or that I'd not powdered it properly, or had erred in the harvesting of it. As I knew that mandrake was possessed of considerable properties, it was with some trepidation that I spread the reddish paste over my eyelids.

I was uncertain, too, as to what spell to cast, what words to use. The Book, in various entries, is inconclusive as regards the efficacy of *spoken* spells—as opposed to those that the witch recites silently or sings. I'd determined to use the spell favored by the witches of Thessaly, the one which, according to Albertus Magnus, they read aloud while inscribing it on their magic mirrors. Why this spell? Perhaps it was because those witches had finished their mirrors by burying them at a crossroads, letting the trapped souls of suicides work upon them for three days. Perhaps because that was the first spell that came to mind? . . . For whatever reason I decided I'd recite a variation of the Thessalian spell: "S. Solam S. Tattler S. Echogordner Gematur," which means I know not what.

All was in readiness. The candles burned on. The paste sat waiting in my mortar and pestle (of white and unveined marble, as dictated by the pharmacopoeia). I'd decided on my spell. Coincidentally, it was the midnight hour.

The deed done, I sat back against the banquette. The berlin bumped on. I heard the clapping of the team's hooves on the hard-dirt road, and the occasional cry of the raven. In my mind's eye I watched the turning of the berlin's wheels; this steadied my nerves. My heart drummed: I *had* used too much mandrake, I was certain of it, and now . . . No. "Steady. Steady," I said aloud. The potion, thinned by my perspiration, seeped into the corners of my eyes and stung. I *willed* my eyes to show *l'oeil de crapaud*: immediately the stinging ceased. Perhaps that was the first time I truly understood the power of the will, so often alluded to by witch and elemental alike.

How long did I sit like this, perfectly *attendant*, my eyes caked with that red paste? (I imagine I looked like some third-rate actress of the Orient!) Not long, I think; no, it was not long before . . .

Suddenly, my eyes shut; from out of a murkiness that lightened first to fog, then mist, there *appeared* before me a familiar landscape. Its shapes, its colors, its features came into sharp relief. I'd never seen this particular landscape in life, yet it was familiar: it was a strip of coast like that bordering Ravndal. Sunlight lit the whole, and soon I could distinguish sedge and broom, and fishing boats left askew on sands laid bare by the departed tide.

Though I feared what might happen—would I lose the vision, somehow damage my eyesight?—I opened my eyes. Opened them wide. Then I raised the shade and looked out the window of the berlin. Night. Deepest night. We were riverside once again. I gazed out over the moonlit water. I could discern some stony ruin on the opposite shore. Noise too: the sounds of the unknown river, quite loud, for it had turned cataractal just there at some dropping down in its course. I heard too the hollow turning of the wooden wheels on the road, the creak and groan of the berlin, the thundering of those pairs of hooves, pulling, pulling . . . all of it so loud!

Ah, but then the sudden and abject silence as I closed my eyes again, as the sun rose up and there spread before me not a moonlit river but a sun-drenched strand. Time passed; it might have been seconds, or minutes; it might have been days, decades. . . . But I was conscious not of passing time but of *seeing*, of looking out over this landscape of my affected mind at the perfectly still grasses on the dunes, the cloudless sky, the abandoned sands drying under the strong sun. . . .

My eyes opened. Again, I saw the dark, rushing river. And the moon, which soothed me not at all. Still, my heart beat wildly. Surely I *had* mixed too much of the mandrake into the potion. I would achieve what Asmodei had failed at: *I would poison myself*. Surely my heart would rattle to a dead stop and . . . I dared not close my eyes again.

But I did just that.

I tried, by some exertion of the will, to see *myself* in the dream. But I could not. I raised up an arm, raised my hands up in front of my face. No doubt I would have appeared somnambulant to anyone seeing me then, in the cab, waving my hands, flailing my arms blindly about...But I had no hands, no arms...What I had in the dream were...were wings. The pinnate, ebon wings of the hovering familiar: the raven.

I opened my eyes. Again: the night, the moon on the river, the sounds of the berlin. . . .

I closed them. Again: the bright light of day, and a seascape I'd never seen but knew to be real, very real, above which I now rose, riding the currents of warm and salted air. Higher. Higher still, till, banking low and rising fast on a sudden rush of wind, I saw below me the dark mass of Ravndal. I sought to land. I could not. The choice was not mine. And, as if in defiance of my will, my host rose horribly fast and flew on. On and on, along the strand, and in no time—it was here I thought my human heart would slip from its casing, crack like crystal—we achieved C——, dreaded C——. I understood: at Ravndal I'd been very near C——; though the two places seemed worlds apart, they were not. *They were not.* This was a lesson I will remember.

. . . The down-falling, the deep flutter of wings, the reaching of talons to take this branch, no, *this* branch...and yes, a perch, high above the shrubs where I'd hidden days earlier. Why was I here? I'd not consciously asked to see, to be shown C——. *Au contraire,* it was my wish to never see the place again. Ah, but see it I did from my fixed vantage point: I saw it empty, the girls gone. I saw the black scratch left by flames on the sill of Mother Marie's rooms, where Peronette had danced. I saw the place in ruin. . . . It was then I felt the pull of the earth, felt the raven tip and slip from the branch, from the piney green of the tree, and take to the air. And it was then, spiraling higher—and I could *see* lesser birds scattering, could *smell* the fear of rodents far below—it was then I was graced with what I'd sought: a dream of my future.

But all I saw with the raven's eyes...I could not read it. Could discern no sense. Images, images only: water, rising water, dangerous water; and the shifting and various blues of shallow seas. I saw an old man covered in blood. I saw ships and a gabled white home with windows of beveled glass, and trees with narrow trunks the tops of which swayed like fishtails in a gentle sea of wind, and men, countless nameless men, and one woman's face, again and again. . . .

The great bird spun and dipped. My heart remained high, and still: a stone on a cliff that will fall, *did* fall. Down and down and down, toward the uprushing ground. A field. Grass sere from the summer sun. A leveling—the stillness of spread wings. And then...attack, and the knifing of fur from bone, the snapping of bone, the crack and spill of...

I broke from the dream. Such sweet release!

But there I was, sprawled on the floor of the cabin, face to its carpeted floor. On my raven's tongue I knew the taste of blood and brain.

Sightless, I scrambled up onto the banquette. I felt for the square of cloth that I'd set at my side. Wet with a mixture of egg yolk and rum (as written), I used it to wipe my eyes clean.

When finally I opened my eyes it was to see the moon cast a silvered net over the black and rushing river.

It was over. The cloth had come away clean, no trace of the paste. My shut eyes showed nothing now but darkness, utter and perfect darkness. Still, I had not returned, not truly; for I realized that, though I could see, could smell and hear and ... *Enfin*, though my senses had returned, certain functions of ... of the living had not resumed: I was not breathing, my heart did not beat. My body was but an empty barrel.

It was a deathly stillness. It was, perhaps, a deathly state.

And it ended only when my mouth opened suddenly and I gasped, *gasped* for air as one does when rising from a watery depth. Slowly, my breathing steadied; and I relaxed into that familiar rhythm, the rise and fall of my chest. As for my heart, I heard it: coming, coming like a stranger's footfall from out of the distant dark.

31

A Night in
Black Angers

As WE AMBLED along the quay into Nantes that
next morning, I was for the first time city-struck.
Never had I seen such hubbub! The river was busy
with commerce despite the very early hour, with tall
masts scratching at the sky and barges plodding along
among their sleeker sisters. The gray facades of the
quay-side buildings overshone it all. There rose up
banks and banks of colorless homes, their arched windows and iron-work balconies forming the eyes and
mouths of hard-set faces, overhung with heavy, slated
brows.

It was not long before all eyes fell upon the berlin;
the braver boys and men on the quay dared to jump
up onto the running board and peer inside. I was *terri-
fied!* Some asked for money; others offered services at a
price, love among them. There was a young boy, no

older than six or seven, who thrust his thumbless hands through the window, grimy palms open and empty. Running behind him was a man who said, simperingly, "My boy . . . how, Monsieur, will he fend for himself in such a state? *Please*, Monsieur?" And I gave in, generously, though I knew, *knew* the boy's "state" was not a natural one: with a hatchet his father had defined his son. I might well have struck at the man; for fresh in my mind was the willed effect Sebastiana had had, long ago, on her extorting husband. As it was, I knew to look away from him fast, for I felt a change . . . a *heated* change coming over me, and I dread to think what I might have done. I nearly retched as those tiny, filthy fingers folded around whatever bills I proffered; and then the boy fell back from the board and disappeared. With trembling hands I latched the doors and drew the shades. Fiercely, I rapped at the roof: Michel understood, and drove from that drear and dirty place as fast as the narrow streets allowed.

One look later at the guidebook I'd procured, penned by one Monsieur Joanne, and my impressions of the place were confirmed. For it was near Nantes, late in the Revolution, that the bestial Carrier and his *noyades*, his crews of "drowners," had set their enemies afloat on the Loire—coupled by iron cuffs, clinging to their weighted rafts—only to send them to its depths beneath a sky alight with fireworks. And it was that city's castle that had housed the Maréchal de Retz, executed in the fifteenth century for his complicity in the deaths of several hundred children by means of indescribable rites and rituals. Yes, the place bespoke just such a history. I wondered, would every city be the same? I would have Michel avoid such places, as possible, for surely they could only degenerate further as we made our way from river to sea.

Well beyond Nantes, the sounds of the city receded, I sat back in the berlin. I determined to sleep, without success—still my heart raced. For distraction, I turned again to Sebastiana's Book and by day's end I'd discover another aspect of the Craft I was *most* eager to practice, despite the fearfully divined dream of the night before.

And so, as finally we neared Angers late in the day, rolling west on a wide road that mimicked the wider river, I took up the brass bell that sat idly at my side, and, for the first time, I summoned the elementals.

I looked out over the Loire with tired eyes, saw it shimmering brown, almost gold beneath the low-angled sunshine. The bell's song sailed over the insistent rush of the river. There stood, beside the road, a bank of yellow-flowering trees; in the shade of these several old men angled away the twilit hours. I wondered, would I be able to see the elementals take shape, coalesce of air and water? Would the old fishermen see them too and, destined to be disbelieved all the remaining years of their lives, hurry home to tell of the fantastic fish they'd seen rise from the river?

I rang the bell again, holding it outside the berlin. I was tired, and perhaps I too rudely told my boy that it was *not* his attention I sought, and that he should simply continue on toward Angers without . . . It was then that I, as if involuntarily, drew my head back too fast—a bump above my right ear, large as an egg, attested to *that* graceless act for days—and . . . And as I dropped the brass bell onto the carpeted floor, I . . . I won't say I *screamed*. Let me say that I greeted the sudden appearance of the elementals, there, on the banquette, with . . . with an *audible* exhalation.

There they sat, shoulder to shoulder, full-form, staring at me.

"Witch," said the priest, "every time we appear you nearly leap from your skin. Even now that you've seen fit, for whatever reason, to *summon* us." Father Louis looked down at the brass bell as it rolled away beneath the banquette; though I wanted to attribute the bell's sudden motion to a bend in the road, I knew better.

What do you want? asked Madeleine. Her words were a challenge I would meet.

"How long have you bled, like that?" I asked. Madeleine stared at me and her form grew suddenly . . . *fuller,* dense as a cloud laden with rain.

Since the day I clawed my throat open. Two hundred years ago, by your calendar; an eternity by mine.

Father Louis turned toward the window and the river beyond. "Why ask such a question?" he muttered; clearly, he expected no satisfaction.

Yes, why? echoed the succubus.

"Because," I said, "I have an idea."

Neither spoke then. Rather, the elementals looked at Sebastiana's Book, which lay open in my lap; then, expressionless, they looked at each other.

"Come to me at midnight," I commanded; and I said again, "I have an idea."

We would pass the night in Angers; and there, I would put my idea into practice: I would work the Craft. All the long sleepless night before, having endured the dream, I thought, and concluded thusly: I had to practice the Craft again, and soon. If I did not . . . Well, it was a potent admixture of fear and intrigue, daring and denial, that drove me. Hadn't I brought myself near, *too* near death? Perhaps I had. And for what? To see through a bird's eyes unintelligible images of my future? . . . Ah, but it had all been achieved in the service of the Craft. The service of the Craft: it was *that* drew me on. But next time, *this* time I'd apply it more practically. And not to myself, but to another. Madeleine.

Having called for the elementals, having told them that I had an idea (which I did not then disclose), I said I wished to stop, indeed had already ordered the driver to stop. Father Louis concurred: he cared not what we did, as long as we arrived at the crossroads beneath the next new moon, rising five nights hence. *Yes,* stressed the succubus in parting, *we will need the new moon. Keep an eye on your calendar.*

So Michel turned from the banks of the Loire toward Angers, sitting inland on the Maine, an affluent of the greater river; and I took a room at an inn shadowed by that city's ancient fortress, a château built in the interests of safety, not splendor. Angers was charming, if somewhat *dark* in aspect. I wondered if I was already growing accustomed to massed humanity, cityscapes, and strangers.

Within the hour, I found myself being led up a dark and narrow staircase, its steps made of that slate, quarried locally, which earns for the city the appellation "Black Angers." Indeed, the steps seemed hewn from obsidian; they were dark and smooth as the river's night-waters. At each narrow step I expected to slip backward down the whole lightless flight of stairs, for I was off-balance: I had in my hands the makings of a simple meal, a torch, the brass bell, Sebastiana's purse, and our two Books.

When finally we'd climbed to a landing, the innkeeper handed me a heavy key and she, stout but unfazed by the steep climb, thanked me and asked did "Monsieur" have all he needed. "Indeed, he does," said I. "Rather, *I* do," I sloppily amended. She looked at me quizzically; then, accustomed to men far more foreign than I, she accepted my thanks and took her leave.

The room was tucked up under the eaves of one of those dark, cross-timbered homes, ages-old, which crowd the narrow streets of Angers, seeming to lean forward, shading the streets at midday with their heavy brows. There was a single window cut into the angled ceiling of the room; this gave on to the Maine, far below, whose waters had once filled the neighboring castle's deep moats. Leaning out that window and looking to my left, I could see one of the fortress's famed towers, a fearsome affair of dark stone and slate, unadorned but for a band of bright stone girdling its middle. "This will do," I said aloud. "This will do nicely."

It had come to me as I read Sebastiana's Book the previous night, once I'd recovered and my systems had settled; specifically, an entry dated not long after the Greek Supper, in which she writes of a sister she'd heard of who'd tried, in numberless ways, to avoid the witches' fate: the coming of the Blood. (She notes too that this sister fell to the Blood, appropriately enough, in a Finnish town; the year was 1802.) Sebastiana recorded but one attempt made by this unnamed sister. In the course of three quite sketchy sentences, Sebastiana writes that the witch failed, of course; but she did once succeed in stanching the flow of blood from a sheep's severed legs. The spell which worked on that unfortunate sheep—butchered while alive—involved the naming of "the four rivers that flow from Paradise," as listed in the Book of Moses, bracketed by what seemed to me a fairly standard spell.

Why not? I thought. Madeleine is no barnyard animal, but still . . .

That night, alone in that quiet and suitably clean little room, believing the elementals would not come till rung for some hours later, I lay down on what passed for a bed. I had requested a Bible from the innkeeper, and this she happily had delivered to me, posthaste. I had it and Sebastiana's Book beside me. Tired as I was, I doubted I could sleep: I was excited, eager to work the Craft, and my mind was busy as a mouse in a maze. I would read. . . . But as I lay on that thin palette, the rich river air filled the room, wafting in through the window I'd opened. I felt the temperature fall with the sun. I drew an old, tattered blanket up over my full belly—I'd already eaten the bit of black bread, cheese, and salt pork I'd brought—and I kicked off the new boots I'd gotten in Rennes. The welcome silence of her house stirred in me an unaccountable rush of affection for the innkeeper, who'd not distinguished herself in any other way, save for having called me "Monsieur." Yes, silence then; silence save for the river sounds. And this after hour upon hour of the berlin's wheels grinding over endless roadways. So there I lay, exhausted, excited, and sated, ready to read the Word of the Lord . . . but I'd not even lifted the book before sleep overtook me.

I woke with a start some time later, my left hand at rest on the Bible. My right hand shot like a dart to my side: yes, it was there: Sebastiana's Book.

A hand on each book, I surrendered again to sleep.

I woke later that night not knowing what time it was. More pointedly: how many hours remained till midnight?

I pulled on my boots and scrambled down the dark stairs, through the inn's common rooms, empty but thick with smoke and the scent of stewing meat, and out onto the narrow street. I'd gathered up both books off the bed, Sebastiana's and . . . well, God's. I stood in the dark street, a book tucked under each arm. A chill rose up off the cobblestones, and the air bore the scents of the river and the smoke rising from the city's innumerable chimneys. Looking up at the darkly timbered houses, which seemed to lean into the streets to stare down at me, I wondered which way to walk. I had maps and books that purported to inform, to guide, but I'd left them all in the berlin. I knew nothing of Angers. Finally, I walked off, down the sloping street, away from the inn and the fortified château that dominated all.

It was not long before I came upon a clock that said I'd two hours till midnight; a second clock—hung in the window of a charcuterie, amid pallid pig heads and crusted logs of pâté—confirmed the hour. Only then did I decide to seek out a café; and I must say I reveled, *reveled* in the freedom I now had to do so. (Had I *ever* gone here or there, this way or that, of my own volition, not driven by the clock of the convent, or even the wishes of my saviors?)

I found a café with the improbable name of La Grosse Poule down along the river. Of its few, well-salted patrons, certainly I was the only one settled in a dark corner with a beer and a Bible. I read by the light of a single white candle, which was greasy and burned too quickly down. I felt the heat not of that thin candle but of the Angevins' stares; thankfully, they soon resigned themselves to the stranger among them.

It was in the second chapter of the first Book of Moses that I read of the Rivers of Paradise: Pison, Gihon, Hiddekel, and Frath. I confess it: I consulted too a few more familiar passages, which had comforted me in times past. I'd not yet downed half my beer.

So, I had my spell with hours to spare. I might have sat quite contentedly in that café, had my mind not then taken a dark turn, directed by some Old Testament tale. I fell to the contemplation of yet *another* thing I'd not considered since leaving Ravndal: the Blood. At Ravndal I'd learned how I would die. I learned that the blood of every witch betrays, bubbles over like an untended kettle. And the accounts I'd read of the coming of the Blood in Sebastiana's Book were horrific: witches overtaken with little warning by the rush of red, pouring forth from every orifice. Most witches, it was written, see the Blood coming, literally. It's as though they are looking out a window up which a blood tide rises, and their worlds go red from bottom to top. Their very eyes turn crimson! First, blood seeps from the pores, a pinkish-red perspiration. Purer blood drips down from the nostrils and trails down the neck from each ear. Upwelling blood swells the soft flesh under the nails till finally they slip from the fingers and toes. Blood gushes from the nether mouths. And finally, violently, the Blood spews from the mouth. Every orifice then is an outlet for the Blood, and the witch dies her red death. For every witch the end is the same.

I ordered a second beer.

I tried to tell myself that I ought not to worry about the Blood when there is nothing I can do about it. All I can do is hope that it'll be many long years before I find out for myself exactly what the coming of the Blood is like. ("Such an end," writes Sebastiana, quoting Téotocchi, "though admittedly gruesome, is nothing compared to the life that might precede it, a long and magical life, an *uncommon* life.")

I opened Sebastiana's Book to the recorded efforts of that Scandinavian sister. I'd determined to proceed with greater care this time. I could not *kill* Madeleine, no; but neither did I care to achieve anything other than the desired end: the cessation of her blood flow. I sat practicing the spell I'd cast, whispering the words, committing them to memory. I envisioned myself, a witch at work. I also procured a third beer.

So distracted, so excited, so eager was I for the appointed hour to arrive that I was stunned when a man—a hugely muscled man, whose ropey forearms I'd been admiring as he read of recent events in *Le cornet d'Anjou*—stood and exclaimed. *Shouted.* For blood was flowing fast from his nostrils. Soon it slickened his shirtfront, and the tiny circular table over which spread the red-streaked newspaper. He raised his clenched hands to his face, but to no effect: blood burst from his fists.

I, several tables away, rose. I went to him. And I apologized, profusely, till finally the barman, who stood before us now as that great hulking château stands before the city, demanded, "What has this to do with you, my man?" Both men looked at me, one panicked and the other puzzled.

"I . . . I was just sitting over there, and I cast . . . I accidentally . . ."

"Get him flat on his back," called the barkeep's wife, reaching down rags from a distant cupboard.

"You think all problems are best solved by getting a man flat on his back," jested a bearded man seated where the bar curved around; men flanking him laughed, but only till the bleeding man turned toward them, fainted, and fell to the floor.

I drew a bill from my waistcoat pocket. I left it on my table, though Michel had told me that three such bills could buy a horse not too far past its prime. I left La Grosse Poule, unremarked, uttering the same spell in reverse, for I could think of nothing else to do. I headed out onto the dark, dark streets of the city. I found that I still had a beer in hand. I downed it fast, set the pewter tankard on a sill, and walked on, fast, scared, and none too steadily.

I returned to my room. The elementals were already there; to judge by the chill, they'd only recently come.

"But it isn't midnight," I said, too quickly—I know now that I expected punishment. I'd done wrong at the tavern, and now I'd hear about it.

"We are well aware of the hour," said the priest. "We are early, what of it?"

We are eager to hear of this idea of yours. I've known this blood for centuries; hopefully, with your help, I'll know it but a few days more. Still, said the succubus, *we are eager for you to prove yourself. Quite eager,* she added, turning to the priest.

"So eager," said he, "we nearly came to you in that squalid tavern, but you seemed to be so enjoying your Bible and your beer." The priest warned that, dressed as a man or no, I'd soon find trouble if I continued to carry and show as much money as I had that night. Did they not know of my little accident? Did they not care? I dared not ask. And I dared not deny them by excusing myself from any practice of the Craft. I'd a promise to keep. But how I regretted having convoked them that afternoon.

I sat on the edge of the bed. A small fireplace sat opposite; in it someone—the innkeeper, the near-idiot boy in her employ, the elementals?—had set a fire. Before the fire, on two cane-backed chairs, sat the elementals, the fire showing through them though they held strong shapes.

The elementals sat, staring. I said nothing. I listened to the crackling fire; and I heard too a boat passing on the river below: the rhythmic slap of oars. At the window, I saw a blunted triangle of boat trailing a silver line of moonlight. Two passengers sat lovingly entwined on its bow. As I was cold—autumn was already in the air—I took in hand the curves of the iron window-pulls; but then I heard the succubus say, in her garbled and grotesque way, *No. Leave the window open. . . . Far easier for us.*

Of course: the cold night air, the moisture it held. But why the fire then? Why the fire if the elementals were so dependent on water? I cannot say. Clearly, they had some need of fire too. I've yet to figure just how they made use of *all* the elements.

"Your idea, then?"

Yes, echoed Madeleine. *Your idea.*

"I think I can stop your bleeding," said I, flatly, boldly, though now, having stricken that innocent man, I was certain of no such thing. The elementals said nothing at first. Then:

Go ahead, said Madeleine. *Do it.* Was this a dare? *Do it,* said she, rather more emphatic the second time.

"I will," said I, like a child challenged.

I took up both books, the Bible and Sebastiana's. Madeleine watched my hands with eagerness. *And which of your books holds so great a secret?*

Did I toy with the succubus then? Perhaps. I passed my hands over this book, then that. I saw it was the Bible she hoped I would not open. When finally I set the Bible aside and opened Sebastiana's Book, Madeleine sat back in her chair and her shape, which had grown fuller, faded to what it had been; once again, she and the priest seemed a pair.

"Did Sebastiana warn you?" asked Father Louis. "Did she tell you that a new witch is quite strong, sometimes *too* strong; and that the Craft of such a one cannot always be controlled? . . . You've read of the calamitous cold of '88, I presume?"

"I've read of it, yes," I said.

"Do you *understand* the danger implicit in the Craft? . . . Do you understand what . . . what a *failure* to understand might result in?"

Madeleine asked, *Did Sebastiana warn you?*

I lied when I said she had. In truth, all Sebastiana had said was that I had powers in direct proportion to my witchly youth, and that the elementals had waited a long, long time for a new witch to appear, one who might lay Madeleine down, finally and for all time. Yes, I'd read the cautionary tale in her Book, but—I quite recall thinking this then, and convincing myself of it—it's a *mere* imprecation, a *simple* spell. What can go wrong? For the succubus was, I reasoned, already dead.

"You found this . . . this *trick* in Sebastiana's Book?" asked the priest.

I said I had. Giving voice to what it was we all thought, Madeleine asked: *Why then didn't she ever try it on me?* She turned to Father Louis. *Has she known all these years . . .*

"This witch cannot speak for the other," answered Father Louis. Already Madeleine's anger had begun to show: the blood at her neck began to pump, to quicken like water on the boil. "Besides, Madeleine—" began the priest.

Besides, took up Madeleine, *the other, as you call her, has hated me all these years, has never truly tried to free me from—*

Father Louis stopped her with a whispered word, one I could not hear; and just in time, for by a quick calculation I deduced that the blood she was spilling, spraying here and there in her agitation, her excitement, would not fade until morning, either delaying our departure or giving rise to all sorts of questions that I did not care to answer. How would I dismiss the red web Madeleine wove? The floor before the fireplace was already puddled, and the sill was slick with blood; and the chairs, would I need to burn the ruined chairs?

"What's done is done," said the priest to Madeleine. "Paris is passed," said he, referring to the unspoken something between Sebastiana and the succubus. "Now," he went on, to Madeleine, "listen to *this* witch; we've waited for her."

Witch, pled Madeleine, *if you are only experimenting, only teasing me with your—*

"Stop it now," said the priest, soothingly; he then turned to me to add: "Herculine—or is it Hercule, in this new casting?—if you've given us false hope and—"

"Pison," I began, "Pison, Gihon, Hiddekel, and Frath. Do you know what those are?"

"I do," said the priest. "The waters of the world. What of them?"

I read aloud the short entry from Sebastiana's Book, and together, the three of us, over the next quarter hour, worked out the spell I'd cast. And an odd litany it was: I had the elementals recite, repeatedly, the names of those waters while I said them widdershins—this I had *not* done in the tavern, thus causing that unfortunate man's blood to flow forth, not stop, as Madeleine's would; or so I hoped. And all the while I mixed in some simple witches' words, innocuous, as common to the blasting of crops as to the baking of cakes. I was confident I'd rectified the spell.

It's hard to say who among us was most relieved to see the succubus's blood flow cease; for yes, we succeeded. Rather, *I* succeeded. But not before there came a terrible, terrible mess; for the spell caused in Madeleine a great, spasmodic *voiding*. And so I sat, far across the room, with my new boots bloodied; and blood-flecked, too, were my face and hands, my clothes, ruined.

I had thought the blood flow would cease, or hoped it would; never did it dawn on me that it, as changeable as any liquid, could only disappear through a change of state. And thus it did: Madeleine's blood, freed of her body, would evaporate, rise as a fetid, ferric gas and disappear—from plaster as from cloth, from leather as from glass—in the seven hours to come. In the meanwhile, Father Louis and I scrambled about the room, plugging the warped floorboards with the bedclothes lest other tenants find them themselves redshowered, and wondering.

As the exsanguination wore on and on, I went to throw wider the window, thinking—I don't know why—that it might help; too, it might relieve the stench. But as I pushed the window open, it blew back at me and slammed against the casement so suddenly, so sharply, that I marveled that the panes did not shatter in their frames. This sudden wind, how strange. Strange too was the action of the river, which had been still not a half-hour earlier. Whitecaps wove along its middle now, and it splashed over its stony banks. That same boat I'd seen now lay at anchor, its two lovers in a clutch of a different sort.

"What is this?" I asked of the priest. "Is this—"

"It is to be expected," was all he said. "It will all settle in time."

Having controlled the red flow in the room as best we could—"Do not bother wiping the walls," said the priest; "time will work just as well."—we sat, Father Louis and I, staring at the succubus's slit throat. Madeleine sat immobile, her head back, her eyes closed, her delicate but dirt-caked hands hanging limp at her sides. As the last of the blood burst from her in time with my living pulse, I wondered, fearfully, if I'd accidentally— For the succubus seemed *gone*. If it was not her "death" I'd caused, certainly it was her . . . her dissolution.

Worried, I willed her to return to us, and she did. She came again to full-form and set immediately to crying; the last of her bitter blood flowed from her eyes as tears. When she spoke—her voice unchanged, regrettably—it was to curse Sebastiana. Sebastiana, who, all those years, had not bothered to try to stop the blood flow, even when begged, even when—

"Good work, witch!" exclaimed Father Louis, interrupting the succubus, who fell silent beside him. I watched as he pulled two fingers from Madeleine's open throat to show them bloodless and dry. "You did it!" . . . But as fast as he spoke, his smile fell away, and he sat staring at the succubus. I had succeeded, yes. Would I do the same at the crossroads? If so, the elementals, who'd come to believe they were bound each to the other for all time, would, presumably, part. This we all knew—though no one spoke it—and it greatly tempered what joy there was, or what joy there might have been.

The elementals took their leave. Vanished. Wordlessly. It seemed neither of them knew what to say; certainly, neither of them spoke. I knew too, before she quit that tiny room tucked beneath the eaves, that Madeleine felt no differently: she still wanted to go to the crossroads, still wanted to "die." So it was I wondered: what had I achieved besides a bit of the Craft? The only answer I could arrive at—"Nothing"—rendered me unaccountably sad.

The next morning, when the blood had nearly faded away, I sent word to Michel. I'd meet him at nine, not ten as we'd agreed. After a simple breakfast, I quit the inn to wander a long hour through the still-waking city.

32

Bell, Book, and Candle

UPON ARRIVING in Angers the day prior, I'd had
Michel hay the horses and hide the carriage on a back-
street; too, I'd asked rather guiltily if he'd mind spending the night in the berlin. Such had been his intention, said he, much to my relief. Still I gave him
some coin—it seemed to me a lot—and this, in what
seems a rather common act of transubstantiation, he
managed to turn to drink in the night. That next
morning, at our rendezvous, he was rank and apologetic. I was surprised—docile Michel, innocent
Michel—and sympathetic, for indeed I'd a certain *mal
à la tête* myself, owing to the several beers of the night
before. Regardless, when Michel asked me to stay on
in Angers another day, I denied him, and found I was
proud of having done so. What's more, I dispatched
him to La Grosse Poule—knowing full well he'd take

a hair from the dog that had bitten him—and directed him—in couched terms, obviously—to ask after the bloodied man I'd abandoned. He took with him coin enough to rouse the barkeep and his wife; but he returned with no news, reporting only that the place was "shut up tight as a frog's ass, sir, and that's water-tight."

It was late morning when finally we left Angers.

The elementals were elsewhere, as they typically were during daylight; and so I raised the shades of the berlin and the on-rolling cab flooded with light, just as the Touraine is often flooded by the waters of the Loire. Indeed, those very waters were already full, though not yet at flood height; the power of the river was evident as it ran steadily in long, slow curves.

Gazing out over the landscape, I never had to wait but a short while for a château to appear on the horizon; indeed, the orchards and vineyards, in which cultivation was evidently easy, were spotted with châteaux, some fantastic, others simpler though still grand in their way.

The Tourangeaux were everywhere at work. The white caps of the women spotted the fields like mushrooms. Time and again we'd pass a group of women walking roadside, or standing atop the dikes that defined one side of the road—always women; where were the men, I wondered?—and they would gape at the berlin. Their vacant faces, their wide-open eyes, gave them the appearance of dumbness, and this was in no way relieved by their simple dress and clumsy sabots; those shoes made it seem as though their feet—if not their bodies entire—had been cut from petrified wood. Feebly, I'd wave to these women; often—overawed, not *naturally* rude—they would not respond. My spirits would sink—for if I *knew* anyone in the world it was these working women—and I'd sit back newly resolved to rid myself of the berlin and hire a lighter, faster, and far less ostentatious trap.

Along this leg of the journey the road was well made and wide, and we were always in sight of the river, often running alongside it. The travel was easy and quick as we made our way through the Touraine.

Tours sits not far from Angers, and we gained it by midafternoon of that third day. We might have arrived earlier, but I'd had Michel stop here and there—to take in this vista, to marvel at the wares in that market; and he, unwell from the aftereffects of drink, had stopped once or twice for reasons of his own.

Rolling into the city, I was instantly charmed by the quay, which—blessedly, unlike vile Nantes—was devoid of any sign of commerce: no stacked barrels or bales, no dark masts rising to the powder-blue sky, no riverine types bounding up onto the berlin to beg; a few barges, yes, but these slow-moving ships seemed imbued with the indolence that characterizes all middays in late summer.

The place, on the whole, seemed to me a fair mix of man's work and nature's. There were gardens and vineyards, and villas here and there, their walls slick with moss, or the scarlet scrawl of woodbine, or five-leaved ivy. Among the simple homes of the Tourangeaux, there rose the gabled and turreted affairs of the affluent. And there was, of course, a cathedral.

As I strolled through the city that afternoon, not *quite* fearful of the place, and trying to make of myself a proper tourist, I saw the decorative towers of the cathedral rising up from the Place de l'Archevêché. Having taken a narrow lane embowered by flying buttresses and overhanging gargoyles, coolly shadowed by the church itself, I found myself standing before the middle of the cathedral's three tall, recessed doors, atop which softly-hued pigeons nestled and cooed. Old habits will have their way, and so it was that time alone in the church seemed to me just the thing; prescriptive, and familiar. Already I could smell the heavy and still air, dense with incense and flowers past their prime; feel the wooden pews smoothed by generations of the faithful; see the pied light from stained glass, thick with the dust of ages, the fiery glow of a bank of votives, and the cold but oddly commiserative faces of the statues.

A survey of the cathedral's exterior had shown it to be drab, dark with age, and weighted with ghoulish sculpture and ungainly buttresses, supremely Gothic if not downright grotesque: I *loved* it. I learned from an inlaid plaque that work on the cathedral was begun in 1170 and completed some four hundred years later, despite which dates there seemed to me a homely harmony in the architecture.

Inside, I found the place—dedicated, I remember, to one St. Gatianus, the first Christian missionary to Gaul—empty; there was not even an old sacristan, as one usually finds in such a place, offering for a coin a tour of every cobwebbed corner.

I sat. The silence and the solitude were luxuries; only then did I realize that what I'd sought was a place to hide. Hide from the elementals; their presence reminded me of all I'd left behind: the unfulfilled promise of a life at Ravndal. Hide too from the wide and prying eyes of the *paysans*. I didn't want to be seen by anyone, for I could not help but wonder what it was they saw when they saw me. *You are a woman. You are a man. You are a witch.*

Yes, that's all I wanted: to sit in silence, hide and not have to think. To still my mind, give over to the burnished wood and bright glass and smooth stone all those questions about who I was, what I was, how I'd live and die, and what it was I'd do across the sea. And I did succeed in stilling my mind, for a while; perhaps I did it with prayer, I cannot say. Old habits.

I settled into a pew not far from the altar, richly lit by the sun streaming through the stained glass. I moved, ever so slightly, with the sun, in an orbit all my own. I slid first into a shaft of red light, and then farther down the pew into a golden glow. In the coolness of the church that buttery light seemed wonderfully warm. I let it play on my face. I fairly bathed in it! I lifted my hands, turned them this way and that, played at catching first the gold, then the green, then finally the violet light.

Time passed; no more than an hour, I'd say.

I sat considering the tomb of the two children of Charles VIII and Anne of Brittany, nestled in a corner of the cathedral not far from where I sat. Its white marble was carved with dolphins, which are said to guide the dead, and the fox-like, emblematic ermine that everywhere marks the influence of Anne; too, it bore vines festooned with flowers, foliage, and fruit. The boy and girl— dead young, and of natural cause—lay side by side, pairs of angels at their heads and feet. I sat, engaged in the elegance of that tomb, wondering was my melancholy gone, or was it refining itself? Sharpening itself, grinding itself blade-like on the carved marble?

An answer to that question came in the shape of a woman.

I hadn't heard the great doors open behind me; neither had the darkness of the cathedral been diluted by any rush of daylight. Still, I heard something. Someone. Turning, I saw her coming down the center aisle. She wore a long black veil that, in company with the shadows, obscured her whole person. She walked at a bride's pace, and with a bride's stiffened gait. She did not slide into a pew of her own, as I expected she would. No; she continued on, toward me.

She stopped at the end of the pew, *my* pew. She turned and—without gen-uflection—entered the pew, slowly making her way toward me. Did she not see me? I cleared my throat. I slid a bit farther from her, but she came on, with an uncommon grace, as if afloat, not at all awkward in so narrow a space. She sat beside me.

She kept her long black veil lowered, but when she turned just so, and the colored light shifted across the black tulle of the veil, I could discern her pro-file. She was young, and beautiful, and a mass of unbound red hair fell over her shoulders. She wore a voluminous skirt of a powdery blue that fell neatly into its pleats and billowed out around her as she sat. I glimpsed her black boot, ankle-high, with three buttons of pearl up its outer side.

Clouds passed over the late-day sun, muting the cathedral's light. A moment later the sun burned its way through the clouds and the shafts of red, yellow, green, et cetera, were as bright as before. Blue light hung in the air like smoke. Shadows of birds passed over the stained glass; fixed there, trapped, were the pilgrims, the saints, and martyrs unaffected by the changeable light and the shadow-birds, unaffected too by the witch gazing up at their piebald shapes. I envied them their stillness, their perpetuity—the fixedness of their lives, long ended. It was then I discovered that my eyes were brimming with tears. It was then too that the woman beside me spoke:

"Don't cry," said she. Her voice was warm, mellifluous, and deep. But the wonder of her words soon ceded to this: How did she know I was crying? She'd not turned toward me. And I, from long years of practice, am expert at stifling my tears—no wracking sobs, no heaving shoulders.

"Don't cry," she repeated; and with that she knelt. At first it seemed she was falling, and I nearly reached to steady her. She moved as would a marionette with tangled strings, or an unsteady hand above her. But then I sat back and watched as she . . . as *it*, that body, was made to kneel. . . . Imagine a face rising up from underwater: I know of no better way to describe what it was like as that woman, as the arms of that borrowed body raised themselves jerkily up to lift that veil and show to me, *there*, like a mask, atop that deathly still and unfamiliar face, the quite familiar face of Madeleine de la Mettrie.

I'd seen what I'd seen, yes; but only when Madeleine caused the cold hand of the corpse to settle unsteadily over mine, only at that icy touch and the garbled, liquescent voice, *her* voice, to which she reverted, telling me again I ought not to cry—only then did I know it was Madeleine beside me, resident in a dead body.

"Mon Dieu!" I cried, standing up fast. "What are you—"

Sit, she commanded. Apologetically, she added: *It's so much easier, witch. Would you have me walk through the streets of Tours as I am?*

"Why walk at all?" I asked. "I thought you moved . . . willfully, without need of—"

Sometimes it's fun. Now sit!

I was to accept this and ask no further questions. So be it. I'd sit in church and converse with a cadaver.

"Who *is* that, anyway?" I had to ask it.

Newly dead, said the succubus, *but she's stiffening terribly* . . . She caused to flex the fingers of the left hand, then the right; she turned the head toward me. Dismissively, she added, *It's no concern of yours, witch, who she is.*

"Will she be missed?" Specifically, my thought was this: has she a daughter, or a son, who will be sent away?

She'll not be missed until she's found, answered the succubus, adding to that riddle, after a pause: *And I didn't kill her, if that's what you're wondering. I found her not far from here, dressed but fallen beside her bed. Her heart was young, yes, but faulty: it gave out not long after dawn. Let her loved ones find her here, nearer her God.*

That was exactly what I was wondering—if Madeleine had killed her witless host; and, though I thought to commend her on what seemed a kindness, I said nothing else. Nor did Madeleine speak, with either voice. There the two of us sat, shoulder to shoulder in the cathedral of St. Gatianus in Tours. To any worshiper who might come we'd appear to be two souls deep in prayer.

Finally, Madeleine spoke. She used the . . . the *other's* voice. "Kneel with me," she said. "I cannot see you. . . . This neck . . . it's already rigid and . . ."

I knelt beside her. "Please," said I, "don't use that voice. I'm finally used to yours, and I cannot bear to be reminded that I'm here with—"

All right then! . . . Now listen, witch. I've come . . . I've come to thank you.

Anyone near us would have heard Madeleine's voice as a rush of air, something like the beating wings of the lone pigeon I spied high up in the nave. Her voice was a bit different, *drier* perhaps. Still there was a watery quality to it, akin to an overrunning gutter; perhaps her voice *had* changed when I'd worked the Craft to stop her blood flow. . . . And it was that for which I thought she'd come to thank me.

"It worked then, the spell?" I knew it had. "The blood—"

Yes. Let us hope your Craft is as strong at the crossroads.

"You understand," I said, "I've no idea how. . . . I don't know if I—"

That's why I've come. That's why I followed you here, holding to this cold shape.

"Why?"

To thank you, and to tell you more about this mission of ours, as your Sebastiana calls it.

I said nothing. Could it be that someone was going to *offer* information, that finally I'd not have to pry, deduce, guess, worry, or wonder?

You know, of course, that for two centuries now I have been trying to die, trying to escape my fate. I have tried in so many ways. . . . Her voice trailed off. I watched as she awkwardly slapped the corpse's hands together and held vise-tight to that prayerful pose.

"I've heard you and Father Louis speak of that, yes; but I don't really know what you mean."

No, you don't, witch, said she. *You've no idea.*

"So tell me!" I said, surprising myself. "Tell me all you know of death."

That said, we sat staring forward a long while, both of us—*enfin,* all *three* of us—in the otherwise empty church.

Her words, when finally she spoke, were these:

In the years since my death I have traveled widely, and with one intent: to find an avenue back into life.

. . . What I sought, failing always, was some small portion of a life's span. I didn't care if the body I gained was that of a baby or a beggar woman, a fool or a nun; I wanted only to return to mortality, to live again so that I might finally, truly die. To quit this . . . this infinite suspension . . . or this suspension within the Infinite that some rite or ritual of the Church has condemned me to.

"You believe the Church has done this to you?" I asked.

I know she has. It was an act of the Church; not an act of any god. . . . But just how it was done, I've no idea. It was Madeleine's face I saw then beneath the veil, risen above the other, divorced from it and turned to me. *And if I've no idea how it was done, how then do I undo it? How might anyone, anything undo it?*

Of course, my thought was this: how am *I* to undo it? I didn't ask that question. Instead, I sat listening. And looking. In the cool dark, in the multi-hued shadows of the cathedral, I marveled at the hands of Madeleine's . . . host. Pretty, long and slender fingers tapering down to well-tended nails. Nothing like Madeleine's cracked and overgrown curling nails—filthy, always, hers were; like those of something . . . *feral.*

Madeleine resumed: *All I have learned these long years of searching is that I cannot suffer this fate for all time. I cannot! I need the whole of life, or the whole of death. I cannot suffer this . . . this stasis any longer!*

As she lapsed into silence, I looked from Madeleine to the bank of glowing red votives before which an old man had come to kneel; his grief—as evinced by his hands, clasped fast in prayer, and his heaving shoulders—was great.

I have sought a way in all the Church's rituals, without success. But I've a final hope:

We are traveling to disinter my body, to alter it at the suicides' unconsecrated crossroads to which it was condemned, banished from the Church's blessed earth. It's my hope that this—if done by the darkness of a new moon, and with certain rites read by both Louis and you, a new and strong witch . . . Well, perhaps I shall rest at last. Perhaps I shall finally die.

It seemed I'd little say in my own fate, yet here I was with the succubus dependent upon me to decide hers! All I could think to offer was a pathetic, "I'll try, Madeleine. I will."

Yes, you will, said the succubus.

"But what rites am I to read? You mentioned rites . . ."

Yes, yes, the rites. Bell, Book, and Candle, said she. Are you familiar, witch, with the rites of excommunication?

I said I was not, adding, "But those are for a priest to read, no?"

At this the succubus issued a derisive laugh. *No, thank you, said she. I've had my fill of priests. And Sebastiana says you have access to worlds priests and pagans can only pray to.*

"Why me?" I asked.

New witches are not so easily come by, said Madeleine. I've waited—

"No; I mean why me and not Sebastiana?"

Back in her day, you mean, when she was new? Well, by the time I met her, during the Terror, her strength had already ebbed, and she was still shy of her powers, having unwittingly rained down such storms as—

"Yes, yes, I know of the storms," I said.

And that witch, your Mystic Sister . . . well, she tried to help me but once, and only after much persuasion, by myself and Louis as well. The attempt was halfhearted and without effect; without effect on me, I should say.

I asked what she meant.

Madeleine hesitated. *Well, she began, Sebastiana worked the Craft that day with little confidence and an unsure hand, the result being . . . well, it was sometime later we learned of the unfortunate effects, the . . . the* hemorrhagic *effects her Craft had had on several dogs in the vicinity of Chaillot. Apparently, said the succubus with a mischievous shrug, it was not pleasant. "Explosive," was the word used by one tearful woman who, with the aid of the authorities, tried to puzzle out the loss of her poodles.*

Resuming her . . . her *graver* tone, Madeleine went on: *Ah, witch, said she, there are more important things to speak of now. As my priest says, 'Paris is passed.' . . . I ask again: what do you know of the rite of Bell, Book, and Candle?*

Before I could answer, she spoke on:

. . . It was the springtime of 1670 or '80; I forget the exact year, but I'd not yet been dead a half-century, that I know. From a traveler in the South, a dealer in champagne, I heard tell of a strangler in the Midi. This traveler had just received word from some man of his family that a suspect had been caught—a mute. I was suspicious; with good reason, as it turned out.

"But why would you be interested in—?"

—Because surely there'd be punishment meted out, and that most often meant the taking of life, the loosing of a soul into that same oblivion in which I dwell. And so, as I'd had my fun with that traveler—I was a bit more mischievous then—I set off.

"Mischievous?" I didn't ask for details; I didn't need to.

Louis was off in Bordeaux somewhere, keeping company with a family of daughters, so I traveled to the Midi alone. . . . To say I 'traveled' to the Midi is inaccurate; discarnate, I had only to will myself there. She asked did I understand; I lied that I did. In truth, that— the omnipotent will—seems destined to remain a mystery to me.

I don't recall the name of the village, but it doesn't matter. Neither does it matter that the priest involved in events there was one Monseigneur de Pericaud, the first priest I'd hear read the rite of excommunication.

The situation, I should say, was this: the mute stood accused of strangling, bare-handed, two women of that town. One victim was a widowed midwife, little better than a witch, it was said . . . dispensable, in other words. But the second victim was the pregnant wife of the mayor's son; and so a condemnable man was sought. It was easily decided that the mute who lived without family on the edge of the village, caring for hens and carrying their eggs to market weekly, would make a convenient suspect. The evidence was easily arranged. The trial was quick, the verdict unanimous. Interestingly, the mute was not to be strangled, as would have been customary: an eye for an eye, and so on. No, he was to be excommunicated, for he was of the Faith. And so, though his life would be spared, his soul would be cast off into damnation eternal. This, for the mute, was a fate worse than death. But it suited his accusers, for it spared their consciences—if not their souls.

On three consecutive Sundays the priest rang a large bell on the steps of the wooden church, distinguished only by the shortness of its spire, an embarrassment to the villagers, for it formed the town's sole renown. At the pealing of this bell, the villagers assembled. The monseigneur asked were there any present who might bear witness to the mute's innocence. No one spoke. Finally, on the fourth Sunday—and I assure you, by now I was ready for the rite to be read; I'd grown quite impatient, and I'd already ensured that the actual strangler would strangle no more—on that fourth Sunday, with no one speaking on behalf of the condemned, the verdict stood. The ritual commenced at noon.

A thick white taper, representing the soul of the condemned, was set on the church's top step.

"The rite is read outside?" I asked.

Not typically, said Madeleine, *but too many people had come to see the mute's soul cast out, and that ramshackle church, its timbers rotted, the whole resembling nothing if not a piece of carved coal, could not accommodate the crowd.*

"What happened then?" I asked. "Did the mute—"

Madeleine's slow turning . . . no, the *corpse's* slow turning toward me, accompanied by a terrible . . . *cracking,* told me wordlessly that I ought not to interrupt. Lest I misunderstand, the succubus added: *It's a short tale, witch; and I'll tell it fast.*

. . . The taper was lit, and a glass cylinder was placed over it, against the wind. More bells

were rung. As some of these were brass, I suffered a bit, had to surrender the shape I'd taken, that of an old hag, ignored at the edge of the crowd. No one noticed as the shawl I abandoned sank to the ground. I rose up unseen, hovered above the crowd and watched, disembodied.

"The bells . . . ?" I prompted. "Why brass?"

To ward off those demons who'd ascend to fight for the outcast soul.

"And were there demons?"

Again, that slow turning of the veiled face toward mine. *Just me,* said Madeleine; and the corners of the corpse's lips twitched, convulsed into a sickly smile.

"But you weren't there for the *soul* of the mute. It was the body you wanted, no?"

Yes, it was a body I sought, initially; but the strange verdict had fouled my plan. Still, I grew intrigued: if the soul and body were indeed to be separated, with some part of the soul of a still-living man cast off into the void . . . If this spell of the Church's worked, and body and soul were somehow severed . . . well then, I might be shown some avenue I'd not contemplated before.

Madeleine hesitated, lowered her voice till it was nearly inaudible. I wonder, did she worry what might happen when she recited those words, there in the cathedral? She did, after all, believe; she'd reason to. But then, in full voice, causing the grieving man before the votives to turn, Madeleine recited those words she'd first heard a century and a half earlier:

"We exclude him from the bosom of our Holy Mother the Church," said she, her voice so deep, her words so deliberate it seemed I was listening to the monseigneur himself; and I wondered did the elementals' talents for mimicry, effigy, and shape-shifting extend to the replication of voices lost to time? *". . . And we judge him condemned to Holy Fire with Satan and his Angels and all the Reprobate, so long as he will not burst the fetters of his demons, do penance, and satisfy the Church."*

Madeleine fell silent. The left leg of the redheaded woman twitched terribly, so terribly I thought Madeleine had meant to kick me. *It seems this body is dying still,* said she lightly, in fast apology; and then she spoke on:

With more of the rite read, the monseigneur closed his dark text and tucked it up under his arm. The wind twisted his black shift about his legs and he, along with all those assembled, stared not at the mute but at the dancing flame behind the glass, emblematic of the mute's soul. Carefully, the glass was lifted off the candle and the priest, quick as a cat, snatched up the taper and waved it in the air. The flame blew out, and just as quickly the mute's soul was cast from God's sight. The priest then, quite showily—this angered me, for it is not part of the prescribed rite— tossed the taper into the crowd, where, with shouts and cries and prayers, the assembled faithful shrank from it.

"And the mute?"

Yes, well, the mute . . . Nothing. He simply walked from the village under a shower of stones, all his worldly goods slung over his shoulder, tied into a square of soiled canvas.

"His soul . . . ?"

Unaffected.

"The rite, then, it didn't . . ."

"*Sound and fury, signifying nothing.*" *Such rites, you see, if they are to work at all, must be read by one who is "pure." The Roman Ritual, the rite of exorcism, states it plainly: the reading priest must be pure.*

"And the monseigneur?"

Impure, said Madeleine flatly. *As are so many, for it seems to me the Church holds to a standard quite apart from life. Mind you, I make no excuses for the impure, none at all.*

"The mute . . . ?"

Unchanged, as regarded the state of his soul. This I've told you—

"Yes, but did you tell *him* this? If he was a faithful man, then—"

No, I did not. I was, you understand, quite disappointed myself, for I'd learned nothing I did not know. And neither am I inclined to impart confidences to mortals; in this I do them a favor, for not everyone suffers as well as you the acquaintance of eudemons.

"Yes, but—"

Leave off, witch! It is over and done, and all those concerned have long since passed to their just reward. Would you have me somehow turn back time to talk to a mute?

Silence then.

But I believe still, said Madeleine, *that there is something to that rite. I've long wondered what it—or a rite derived from it—might effect if read by one who is pure. Pure as you are.*

Still we knelt shoulder to shoulder. The cathedral was empty and nearly dark now, the stained glass faintly aglow with the last light of day. I sat looking up at the windows when suddenly Madeleine abandoned her host and it—the redheaded corpse—toppled toward me like a felled tree! I scrambled out from under it to see Madeleine standing in the church's center aisle. She appeared as always, in her cerements, wild-looking. I saw clearly her ragged wound; free now of the obscuring blood, it was even more horrible. But then . . . above the throat, there floated her ethereal face, her beautiful face, frozen forever in her youth yet masking such a very old soul.

Madeleine held my gaze so long I nearly looked away. "What . . . what will become of *her?*" The corpse lay stiffening on the hard pew. There rose from it a smell I've not the stomach to describe, not now, not with these waves at work beneath me.

Madeleine made no answer, said only, *I'm leaving now, witch. I suggest you do the same. We've the calendar to consider.* Already she was one with the shadows, and gone.

"Pure as you are." Her words resounded in my head as I moved up the center aisle, out of the church. Indeed, I'd hear those words again and again, hear them as I stole back to the berlin from the cathedral, hear them as we retook the Coast Road to ride into the night.

33

I Wake
to a Surprise

WE'D BEEN traveling some days now. Lately, our course was that of the river Loire. It was not the most direct route—indeed, since Angers we'd traveled, as best I could tell, due east. In time, we'd transfer our allegiance to the Rhône, and in so doing take to a directly southern route. Of course, I had little say in mapping our way; Father Louis did that. And though I would sometimes insist on stopping here and there, and sometimes spending a night in an actual bed, it was the lunar calendar that set our pace, for we needed to arrive at the crossroads before the new moon rose; a new moon, I was told, would aid me in my work. And should we miss the coming new moon, we'd have to wait a lunar cycle for its return. This I did not wish to do: if I were going, and I was, *I would go.*

And so I would see that we arrived in advance of

the new moon in that part of Provence where the elementals had lived their actual, their *mortal* lives. And there, at the suicides' crossroads, beyond a ruined city I will not name, in the darkness cast by the blind side of a new moon, I would do what I could to free Madeleine; and then I would. . . . In truth, I did not know what I would do then.

. . . The dream I'd induced beyond Rennes had left me enervated. My breath was labored for a long while, my heart not quite right, and my limbs bore a lassitude that I could only attribute to the exertion of "seeing." The divining had a disorienting effect. So too did the work I'd done upon Madeleine in Angers, and all I'd learned in Tours. Which is to say, I was unspeakably tired.

I took up a map to try, without success, to situate myself, to find Bourges. I'd no idea what time it was, no idea at all. I saw that the moon was high, and the night deep. *Alors,* I sat so listlessly, contentedly staring out at the play of moonlight on the river, nodding off now and again.

The bright light of the moon lit the land blue, and so it was that I would see Blois—only later would I learn it was Blois; north, and off the expected route—on the bank of the Loire, in a pale and ghostly cast, the facades of its buildings aglow, banks of poplars swaying forward to admire themselves in the silvered river. Narrow streets rose steeply up from the river and wound their way out of sight. Overhanging the city was the great château, bright as a secondary moon. A timbered inn, riverside, tempted me; but no . . . We drove on.

Looking at my map, now, I see that we would have achieved Amboise before Blois; though the map is irrefutable, that's not how I remember it. . . . Ah, but the tired hours of that night are so confused in my memory . . . Confused too was our route, from which the elementals had us stray.

. . . I do, however, recall Amboise. Indeed, I can *see* the dark mass of its château above the river, its crenellations and platforms and balconies, its niched windows, its shadowed profile cut with *machicoulis* to which tiny cannons would have been wheeled in medieval defense. Seeing it through heavy-lidded eyes, I did not regret rolling on, owing perhaps to a historical tidbit that came back to me then: it was from the balconies of the château at Amboise that the heads of Huguenots had been displayed as the grimmest of ornamentation after the discovery of the long-ago conspiracy at La Renaudie. The silence that night in Amboise as we rode beside the river seemed the silence of those severed heads. Rolling on, I worried that they'd speak in my dreams.

. . . Eventually, Morpheus triumphed: I felt my neck go suddenly slack and roll heavily this way and that; my hand fell from my lap, heavy as a stone.... Soon I was fast asleep.

When I woke it was to the unmistakable sound of gravel being ground under the large wheels of the berlin. We were driving slowly, owing, I supposed, to a bad stretch of road. I remember hearing two other strange sounds immediately upon waking: a silence which said we were no longer beside the river, and the nearby cry of the raven. Had Sebastiana sent Maluenda, as raven, to watch over me ... or was *she*, Sebastiana, watching me through the raven's eyes? *Impossible!* But then again, I'd taken to the raven's eyes in my dream; and hadn't I already learned enough to banish that word—impossible—from my vocabulary?

(Here at sea, aboard this ship, I spy a certain fat black rat in my cabin on occasion. I'll look up from these pages, considering a certain sentence, or perhaps to dip my pen, and there it'll be, staring up at me from over beside the larder. Almost as large as a cat, I'm sure the rat fends nicely for itself on board, but I feed it nonetheless, leaving wedges of cheese and rinds of bacon scattered about. I verily *host* the thing. And sometimes—this is embarrassing—I smile at the rat and tell myself the smile is seen by Sebastiana.... And yes, sometimes I speak to it. I'm sounding like a fool here; and so I'll stop.)

... As I say, there was something about that combination of sounds to which I woke—the gravel; silence where there'd been the steady song of the river; the ravensong—that piqued my curiosity. The gravel was particularly curious—the roads we'd traveled over were, for the most part, smoothly packed dirt, pocked here and there, or else they were impossibly bad, slowing us to a crawl for long stretches. Gravel? No; there'd been no gravel. Only a private drive, one especially well tended, would be covered in a gravel deep and fine enough to grind like this beneath the wheels ...

And that's when I sat forward, looked out the window of the berlin, and saw there, *there*, looming ever nearer, a city wrought all in silver!

The sight took my breath away, literally: seeing that city spread before me, the breath rushed from my lungs audibly, as though I'd suffered a blow. And had I had a traveling companion, a *mortal* companion, he or she would have heard me utter an expletive or two, occasioned by awe, once I'd regained sufficient breath to do so.

The very instant I saw the city, my mind began to beat back my imagination, and I reasoned that this was no mythical place, no Camelot or Xanadu, no Atlantis rising from a sea of night, but rather that edifice known to every French schoolchild: the château de Chambord.

We had doubled back from Blois. But why?

I saw outlined against the dark sky the even darker roof: a compilation of cupolas, chimneys, pinnacles, spires, and towers. The walls, rising up out of the disfeatured park, the peasant's landscape, shone like sculpted ivory. The glass of a thousand windows glistened, gave back the moonlight as a prism would. It *all* glistened! It *all* glowed, all four-hundred-odd stone-carved rooms.

The château de Chambord. I will not offer here a detailed description of the place; I haven't the time. I'm told we sail ever-nearer port and I despair of finishing this record. For now, let me offer this, culled from a pamphlet I would purchase in Arles.

Begun under Francis I in 1519, the château bears his imprimatur all over: the flat and fairly plain F, and the royal (and *repulsive!*) salamander. Its luckless, loveless fate seems to have been ordained by Francis, who, it is said, chose the site in the soggy Sologne for no better reason than this: the Comtesse de Thoury, with whom the not-yet-ascendant Francis was smitten, had a manor in the vicinity. Francis's heirs took up the care and construction of the château upon his death; eventually, with Versailles, St. Cloud, Fontainebleau, and St. Germain all within easier reach of the capital, sovereigns were little inclined to decamp to Chambord, in perhaps the least appealing part of the kingdom. In succession, the royal barrack hosted Henri II and Gaston d'Orléans—brother to Louis XIII; and, most markedly, Louis XIV. The adornments and additions made by the latter, the most *decorative* of kings, are easily imagined. There later came the perennially exiled King of the Poles, Stanislas Leczinski, father-in-law to Louis XV, and his queen, Catherine Opalinska by name. The Maréchal de Saxe was given the château after his victory at Fontenoy, in 1745; and at present the sad vastness is unoccupied as the heirs of the Maréchal de Berthier wage a litigious war with the Duc de Bordeaux, whose mother, the Duchesse de Berry, is pressing her son's claim with great voice.

The berlin came to a standstill in the inner court of the château, passing through *La Porte royale*. Finally, I thought, a place whose scale suits this conveyance of ours! I climbed down quickly from the cab, wondering should I dress down Michel for stopping here of his own volition, for not conferring with me, his *master*. . . . But of course, it was not Michel atop the box.

There sat the smiling priest, holding fast to his own shape. "The driver?" I asked. "What have you done with the driver?"

"Dismissed," said the priest, "while you slept. Unharmed, newly rich, and . . . well, just a bit confused."

I could not help but smile—finally, Michel would get the rest he'd sought back in Angers; and I knew he'd do well, for his was a most adaptable nature. Just then I heard a horrible noise and turned to see an ancient set of iron-hinged doors—not often used, evidently—swing open across the inner court-yard. There stood Madeleine. With a sweep meant to take in the whole of the château, she said, smiling, and with the practiced grace of the greatest of chatelaines, *We thought we'd pass the night here, grandly.*

"Grandly, indeed," said I. Father Louis descended unseen from atop the berlin; and Madeleine came unnaturally fast from across the courtyard. Both their shapes were full, strong; still, the moon seemed to penetrate them and they gave back its light—that is, they glowed; as did the great château.

The château's towers—it is comprised of a larger structure enclosing a smaller, each sporting four towers— . . . its towers and their adjoining walls rose up all around us, and the sculpted stone, the gargoyles staring down from atop every capital . . . the many shadows gave to the whole a depth, a texture that made it seem a *living* thing. I stood in that inner courtyard for a long while, turning this way and that, trying to take in the whole magical *mass.*

Madeleine had disappeared, but there she was again, standing in the portal of the vestibule, which she'd somehow, soundlessly opened to us from inside the château. *Shall we?* She asked. So it was that I—like how many queens, how many kings before me?—entered the château de Chambord.

The huge door shut behind me; the clap of cold wood on colder stone resounded for a long while. The light of the moon was lost; an instant later, there flared up before me a flame contained in an oil lamp held by Madeleine. I did not see her strike a match, nor otherwise light the lamp; how she raised the flame I've no idea, but neither did it really surprise me, for it seemed that one comprised primarily of air and water could surely put a bit of fire to purpose.

Led by the light of her lamp, I followed Madeleine. Here and there the moon seeped through a narrow window to augment our light and I'd glimpse a tapestry, see a tall and unwound clock hulking in a shadowed corner. Father Louis was near, I knew, but if he held to his shape he did so beyond the light cast by our lamp. Shortly, Madeleine and I arrived at the foot of the château's famed double staircase, its entwined stairwells designed to allow two persons (mistresses? rivals?) to come and go without encountering each other. There stood Father Louis, three or four steps up the stairway, leaning against the thick handrail, his shape weak but easily discerned. All that night the elemen-tals would appear thin, almost translucent, struggling to draw what sustenance they could from the canal running near the château; they were too far from the Loire to draw on it for strength.

In deference to me, to my mortal limitations, the elementals rode that stairway in standard fashion: that is, step by step. They, in my company, would
always walk through doorways rather than walls, light lamps though the darkness was nothing to them, seat themselves on furniture when they might have
easily hovered, weightless but for the water they bore. No one spoke; and the
silence seemed only to increase the scale of all I saw. There was, in the construction of Chambord, no concession made to the commonness of man's lot.
No, the excess of adornment, the *scale* of all I saw bespoke the presence of
gods; was, in a word, Divine.

Up we went. Though I was tempted to break from my spirit guides at each
landing, to set out and explore on my own, I followed the elementals, wondering why we passed first this level, then that, why we kept to the stairs, climbing,
climbing? I had my answer when finally we achieved the openwork lantern that
tops the château. There I remarked a large fleur-de-lis of stone, which, in its
untouched perfection, called to mind all the scarred statuary I'd seen as we
headed south, all the limbless or headless statues on which the Revolutionaries
had made their mark. But here this stony flower, the Bourbon emblem, sat in
perfect bloom, and I understood that the château entire was but a monument
to a tradition, to a system that was once great and might, *might* have remained so.

From these thoughts, my mind and eyes were drawn to the jagged line of
the roof, which spread out all around us like a rough sea sculpted of stone and
slate and glass. Up a few steps more, a turn here, a turn there, and we achieved
the roof itself; nothing but night obscured my view. And the moon quite generously lit two landscapes: the expanse of park and woodland through which
we'd driven and the sculpted sea of the roof.

The night air was chilly; it bore the pungent perfume of burning wood. I
remarked the mold and lichen that had spread in corners, climbed walls and
the insides of arches, slid sideways over wide sills. I must have muttered something about the cold, for moments later I felt fall down over my shoulders the
ermine wrap that I'd left in the berlin. "Thank you," said I, casting the words
out into the night, for I did not know which of my friends had so quickly
descended to do me this favor.

We remained on that roof till finally it was time to settle—the elementals
intimated that they had something to tell me. It was decided—not by me—
that we would settle in the *Chambre de Parade*, in the *Appartement du Roi*. "That,"
said the priest, "should be suitable, no?" The succubus said nothing, but it was
she we followed.

Fabulous busts and tapestries and gilded mirrors, filigreed and finely carved furniture, some of it draped with white sheets. A bed where the Sun King and the King of the Poles had each lain with how many mistresses? But the three of us wordlessly chose a spot on the comfortably thick carpet, in front of the fire that one of the elementals caused to burn—instantly, a half-burned log showed flames end to end, flames that would burn all that night with little tending beneath a mantel of red marble. The mantel called to mind the dining table at Ravndal. Here, as there, I'd sit and listen. I'd trust and learn.

"Won't the smoke be visible?" I remember asking.

Perhaps, said Madeleine.

"I should hope so," added the priest, who hoped our fire might give rise to local legend: those living within sight of the château might come to speak of the night when smoke billowed up from its unused fireplaces, curling in purple plumes toward the moon.

I sat cross-legged on the carpet, wrapped in white ermine. What would the night hold? If the elementals had taken me to this spectacular place, and if they struggled to hold their shapes so far from strong waters, well . . .

And events as they unfolded did not disappoint me. Scare me, shame me, embarrass and edify me? Yes. Disappoint me? No.

34

Chambord, Part I

—L'Appartement du Roi

THAT NIGHT, with words akin to these, Madeleine introduced the tale she would tell:

It was in a southern city of no distinction, A———, in 1651, that I witnessed my first exorcism.

My objective was plain. I say again: I longed to live so that I might die.

I looked at Father Louis, beside Madeleine. We all three of us sat in the King's Apartment. I was facing the fire and the elementals, who sat with their backs to it; the arrangement suited us all: the elementals drew what they needed from the fire, and I could see them as they spoke, the flames burning behind them, *through* them.

"Yes," adjoined the priest, "I was there too."

Indeed you were, said Madeleine. *Indeed you were.*

"But I remind you, dearest," began the priest, "*that* was not your first exorcism." He paused. "There was, of course, Capeau."

Please, don't let's speak of that little screw-backed bitch!

"I should speak instead of Sister St. Colombe?"

You need not speak at all, mon prêtre, *for I will speak of Barbara Buvée.* Madeleine turned to me. *Barbara Buvée*, said she, *was Sister St. Colombe.*

"*La possédée*," qualified the priest. The possessed.

"Ah," I breathed. "Go on, please."

Madeleine began: *Sister St. Colombe was—*

"She was 'a woman of independent spirit,' " finished Father Louis.

Yes, agreed Madeleine. *And this nun, this Sister St. Colombe, had been a Mother Superior for some years, even though she was rather young. In that time she had managed to anger her superiors on occasion.*

"One such superior," added the priest, "was a Father Borthon, the convent's confessor; and he hated Sister St. Colombe."

Yes, he hated her as only a weak man can hate a strong woman.

"Strange to hear you speak of her as strong," said the priest. "She certainly wasn't strong enough to resist you, to fend off your invasion of her body."

"You *possessed* the Mother Superior?" I asked, quick and incredulous.

All in time, answered Madeleine. *All in time.*

It was Father Louis who then said, summarily, and to urge his companion on, "And so we have a man and a woman, priest and nun, each *possessed*, if you will, of certain powers, mortal powers; and they hate each other."

Of course, he is more powerful than she simply by virtue of his sex.

"Yes, that is true," agreed the priest. "Rather, that *was* true," and he proceeded to remind the succubus—and himself—that all parties concerned were dead these two hundred years. "Lest we forget," said he with a wry smile.

Madeleine, brooking no distraction, resumed her narrative, saying that she and Father Louis were late in arriving at A——; indeed, they only went to that city after learning of "the troubles" there.

The tension, long-extant, between the Father-Confessor and the Mother Superior had escalated over an issue that was, according to Madeleine, of no significance. Apparently the nun had openly and publicly defied an order of the priest's and received, as punishment, an equally open and public flogging; additionally, she'd been ordered to fast for six days.

One month to the day from the pronouncement of said punishment the priest was dead.

"First tell of the sisters," prompted Father Louis. "Tell of the priest's blood sisters."

Yes, of course, said Madeleine. Turning to me, she went on: *Father Borthon had three younger sisters in the Order, all of them under the auspices of Sister St. Colombe. They were, I believe, the Sisters Marie, Humberte, and Odile.*

"Precisely," said the priest. "And they were all three of them pious and ugly ... hideous things.... Without doubt, the three ugliest women I ever visited."

"You," I stammered, "... you, as incubus, moved among the nuns at A——?"

"I did indeed."

Emboldened, I went on: "Was it the Mother Superior who killed the Confessor?"

"Ah, but you jump ahead of our story.... No, she did not kill him." And with this the priest deferred to Madeleine, who hesitated before saying:

He died a suicide. A suicide like me.

"Oh," said I. "I see."

"He took himself for unknown reasons," said Father Louis. "Or rather, reasons unknown to us. That happened just before we arrived."

Yes, in the days before our arrival at A——, the priest disappeared. With two days passed, a search party was formed.

"One in which, of course, the Mother Superior *and* the priest's sisters took part." In groups of three, the nuns combed the village and the woods surrounding the convent. Sister St. Colombe searched in the company of a novitiate and the Confessor's youngest sister, Marie.

In the late afternoon of the second day of the search, as her party pushed its way through a dense patch of woodland, Sister St. Colombe—who, of course, prayed that the priest was gone for good, had run off for whatever reason—stooped to make her way through some brush. Brambles and thistles snagged the rough cloth of her shift, scratched at her hands and face. Father Louis imagined that she uttered words that were decidedly ... un-Christian.

The priest went on: "And when she made her way through that brush to a clearing in the woods, and stood up straight, she was struck in the back of the head by what she assumed was the blunt end of a dead branch. But it was, in fact, the blunt end of a dead man! The priest's foot!" Father Louis laughed, long and loud. "It was the self-murdered priest, swinging from an old oak!"

The Mother Superior screamed, said Madeleine.

"Indeed she did!" enthused the priest. "And the novitiate and little Sister Marie came quickly into the clearing behind the Mother Superior—who stood in hysteria beneath the rotting corpse that she'd set to swinging with her head—and those two joined in with screams that summoned the entire search party, all of whom soon stood crammed into that clearing, screaming, staring up at the puffy, purple, putrefying priest who—"

Louis, please, control yourself.

Ignoring the succubus beside him, Father Louis went on: "It's all rather easily imagined, is it not? The fervid prayer, the fainting onto the forest floor . . ."

Madeleine said they learned all this at the trial. "A trial?" I asked.

Indeed, said Madeleine. *And all we'll tell you will but confirm your low and accurate opinion of such proceedings. . . . But at A——,* she added, *things grew a bit more . . . complicated.*

"Yes, they did," said the priest. He showed his impish, sly smile; his words were light with laughter. "Once we arrived in A—— things took a quite *interesting* turn." Then, fast as light, lost to my eye, he moved to set a second log, already aflame, atop the first. He was back beside Madeleine before I understood what he'd done.

So, resumed the succubus, *having heard about the discovery of the priest's body, we went to A—— to see if—*

"Wait! Go back to the woods," said an excited Father Louis. "Tell what happened when first the body was found."

Well, when the corpse was seen swinging by the three women—that is, the Mother Superior, the novice, and Sister Marie—the latter, beset by the most extreme hysteria, was heard to scream at Sister St. Colombe, "Witch! You did this! You killed him!" The novice took up the cry too, and so it was that the search party, comprised of nuns and villagers, all loosely allied by faith or familiarity, arrived in the clearing to see Sister St. Colombe beneath the swinging priest, the two other nuns pointing at her, screaming, "Witch! Witch!" . . . What a sight it must have been!

I interrupted the laughing elementals to ask, "But those nuns had no reason to actually suspect the Mother Superior of being a witch, did they? Had there been other incidents where—"

"Now that is an odd question indeed," said the priest, "coming from you." When he went on to ask if I'd already forgotten recent events at C——, I realized, quite happily, that indeed the blessed forgetting had begun.

"Proof of witchery?" asked the priest. "None at all. Witch, this is but a tale of religious, embittered men and women set apart from the world, in equal parts privileged and deprived—and in such surrounds, as *you* well know, anything might happen. . . . Anything at all."

They were but children, continued Madeleine, *and they responded as children will: they spat the worst word they knew: Witch. And suddenly the Mother Superior stood accused.*

"Tell of the body, the priest's body," urged the incubus, who stood to circle the great room, graceful and alert and in full-form. I heard then a wild wind descend the chimney with a whistle; the flames leapt in time, as though to a tune.

No, Louis. There is no reason to speak of such things when all we want to convey to this witch is—

The priest, quickening his pace around the room—I thought then of the lions of Rome, starved in their dens, eager to rip at the Barbarians, the Infidels—accused the succubus of depriving him of his fun. She ignored him, speaking on:

Back in the woods, when first the corpse was discovered, and the cries of "Witch!" rang out, Sister Marie, brandishing the crucifix pendant from her beads, began to shout, "You've had your revenge, now God shall have His!" And with no other evidence against her but these words of the priest's sister, Sister St. Colombe was led back to the convent. From that moment on she'd not be free. . . . Soon talk turned to exorcism.

"Exorcism," I echoed. "But why? Who was it seemed possessed?"

"No one, at first," replied the priest. "But that's when I . . . that's when *we* set to work."

I looked to the succubus. *Yes,* said she, *I went along with him; but not, as he is wont to say, "for fun," but rather because I was angry.* She paused; what she said next bore the gravity of the confessional: *For a long time,* said she, *I was very, very angry.*

"You are angry still," said the priest. I expected Madeleine to turn on him, but instead she sat with her head bowed, her hands clasped prayerfully in her lap. She said nothing: the priest's charge was irrefutable. He spoke on. His words were truthful and not unkind: "She is angry now," he said, "but back then she was . . . she was *wrathful.* Her anger was unbounded. Each new disappointment fanned the steady flame of her anger to . . . to a conflagration and then, well, she could be positively Old Testament!"

"Disappointment?" I led. What did he mean?

Madeleine answered: *I went to A——— when I learned that there stood a nun accused of witchery. I knew there'd be an excess of priests, and of testifying nuns; rites would be read and most likely there'd be an exorcism.*

"We simply *ensured* there'd be an exorcism," added Father Louis.

You see, explained the succubus, *I'd already been disappointed by the rite of Bell, Book, and Candle—the rite of excommunication that had come to nothing at the hands of the impure priest who'd read it on the mute. And I thought perhaps an exorcism, if properly done, if done by a pure priest, might just . . . might show me a way. A literal way—an avenue unto death.*

"But it did not?" I hazarded. "And you were once again disappointed."

"Disappointed, indeed," answered the priest. "And angrier than ever. . . . And, witch, do not think I speak of simple pouting or petulance. No, when Madeleine is *agitated*, let alone angry, the four winds know it, the tides know it, the orbiting clouds—"

Enough, Louis.

"The exorcising priest?" I asked, leading the narrative. "He was—"

Impure, said the succubus. *Simply, he had an eye on the bishopric, and his vita lacked an exorcism.*

From the moment he—Father François, beautiful, arrogant, ambitious Father François— from the moment he arrived in A——— I knew that everything would devolve to a sham. Mere popery. Theatrics, nothing more. I knew that if the Church's rite had any innate power—and it does, I believe—it would not be displayed at A———. The exorcism would be as fraudulent as all that was done to—

"To Capeau," I finished.

Yes. Only then did I consent to his plans—she nodded to the incubus—*only then did I let him work his ways on those women. As for Father François, well . . . he'd be mine, all mine.*

Madeleine showed a smile that was jarring, for her mouth was . . . her smile spread over lips that did not otherwise move—she spoke not through her mouth but through her torn-open throat—and *those* lips, those of her wound, now dry of blood and all the more hideous, *those* lips vibrated ever so slightly, like the cords of a pianoforte, as her watery voice poured forth to say, *It was then Louis loosed himself upon those women.*

"It was shortly after her brother's death, if I recall," and clearly the incubus pleasured in the recollection, ". . . or was it when they discovered the body . . . ?"

Indeed it was that very night, said Madeleine. *You could not wait.*

"Yes, that very night," said Louis, "Sister Marie started to experience . . . let me think, how did she refer to such in the course of the trial? Oh yes—she started to experience 'temptations in the night.' "

"The priest, this Father François, had already come?" I asked. "You knew that all was already lost, that the exorcism would be mere show?"

I'd an interest in the rite itself, but yes, once the priest came nosing around—as the ambitious will—and insinuated himself into the search party. . . . Yes, it was the very day of his arrival in A——— that Louis and I decided—

"We decided to 'have at it,' " finished the priest. "To make a show of it before the priest could. And naturally, I started with the girls . . ."

"And Sister St. Colombe?" I asked.

She sat shackled, prayerful and doomed, awaiting a trial the outcome of which was already plain.

The Mother Superior was formally accused on 28 October, said Madeleine, *three days before Samhain, your great witches' festival. In early November, testimony was taken, and soon after the Parliament of Dijon heard the case, quickly convicting Sister St. Colombe of crimes against God and sentencing her, as Father François had arranged, to exorcism.*

"If I do say so myself," continued Father Louis, "I succeeded brilliantly. At trial, the nuns were unanimous in their accusations, and expressed themselves quite graphically."

Yes, averred Madeleine, looking not at the incubus but at me, *his talents, such as they are, were still new to him, and he honed them well on the nuns of A——.*

"Honed them, indeed!

"There was one—perhaps it was Sister Henriette; *she* was rather lively—who testified that, despite her incarceration, Sister St. Colombe came to her nightly 'to touch her bosom and kiss her all-about, and passionately.' She actually showed the officers of the court the bruises and bite marks on her breasts, and complained of the pain her swollen nipples caused her!" Louis stopped speaking then—he was laughing too hard to continue—thus affording me the opportunity to ask a question.

"But," I began, "how is it you went to her as a woman? I thought an incubus—"

I cooperated with him from time to time, demurred Madeleine; who quickly excused herself by adding, *He begged me to. We stole a few items from the rooms of the Mother Superior, and so I easily assumed her shape.*

My bewilderment at this was enough to elicit further explanation: it seems that we mortals sometimes invest our *things* with our *selves;* such entities as the elementals, taking possession of such *things,* can then possess *us.* . . . When, confused, I pressed the succubus, it was Father Louis who ended the matter by quoting the Bard—" 'it is all but a lust of the blood,' " said he, " 'a permission of the will' "—before going on to boast:

"And *I* managed to steal away with the dead priest's shoes before they buried him, so *his* shape was mine. . . . Brilliant, it was! *Brilliant!*"

And, rest assured, it was no burial at a crossroads for the priest, said Madeleine, her voice heating up somewhat. *So sure were her accusers of Sister St. Colombe's crimes— chief among them the bewitchment and murder of the priest—that no one spoke of suicide, and Father Borthon received a proper burial.*

"Anyway," sighed the incubus, which sigh was intended to forestall

Madeleine's increasing anger—an anger not unrelated to a roiling wind that rose then to wrap the château and rattle its windows. His sigh, coupled with a certain look, succeeded, and the succubus grew calm. "Anyway, I had the priest's shoes—dead Father Borthon's—and so I easily assumed his shape."

To torture the nuns, including his own sisters. . . . That was vile, Louis. Vile, indeed!

Father Louis nodded, accepting her words as one would a compliment, and continued: "I think it was Sister Humberte, another of the Borthon sisters, who told the court that she suffered visions—induced by the Mother Superior, of course—wherein her brother returned to her. What was it she said? . . . Oh yes, I remember: she said that he, doing the bad nun's bidding, placed a serpent upon her, *in* her, where it writhed about until she fairly froze."

"A serpent . . ." I repeated.

Father Louis laughed. "Yes, a *serpent!* She did not even know the thing for what it was! . . . And of course I took the occasion to grace the dead priest's form with a serpent more potent and better envenomed than his own, which was puny and weak from want of practice."

Oh, stop it, Louis. Tell the tale, would you please? I remind you: we'll need to regain the road at a suitable hour if we are to keep to the moon's calendar. With slight menace in her tone, she added, *I will not wait one day longer than I must. I will not!*

"Oh, all right," said the priest, "but you must let me speak a bit more of Sister Marie, for I did my best work upon that little nun." The priest turned from Madeleine to me, and I saw that, in his excitement, his shape had strengthened. He practically leapt about the room! He was as strong, as solid as I'd ever seen him, and the now-wild fire that shone through Madeleine's shape was testament to this. "Remember, witch, we'd been dead less than a half-century, I think, and so our sex-talents were still new to us, unrefined . . . But oh how the refining of them was fun!" He wrung his hands like a moneylender.

Louis, please. . . .

Father Louis went on: "Sister Marie testified that she'd sat on the Mother Superior's lap once and that she'd received that woman's fingers, like icicles, within her. (Which was true.) She said too that her own brother had worked a phallus fashioned of stiff linen upon her. (And he had.) And oh yes, she said," and here the priest cast an opprobrious glance at Madeleine, ". . . she said that the Mother Superior had railed at her about certain rites of the Church . . ."

I did get carried away a bit that one night, admitted Madeleine, which admission drew a wide smile from the priest.

"Now little Sister Marie—who was not, curiously, a virgin—began to take communion thrice daily. She washed with holy water, passed hours at a certain shrine of the Virgin, hung amulets from the four posts of her bed, swallowed a veritable herbarium ... but all in vain, for the more she sought to resist *me*, to 'save herself,' the more I visited her. As her brother, and as handsome Father François ... Yes, I stayed with her all through the gathering of testimony and into the trial. I enjoyed her resistance: most nuns simply surrender.

"By the time of the exorcism, Marie was quite addled, well on her way to insane."

"And that was all right with you?" I asked of the priest. "You rendered the girl insane with sex, and ..."

"Ah, but judge not the maned beast who brings down the weakest gazelle. Nor the bear who with bladed paw scoops salmon from the river. No. In my defense, I will say only this: I did what it is in my nature to do."

See, witch, said an amused but still impatient Madeleine, *see how he is prone to pontification? ... Louis, may we simply say that the trial progressed predictably, and that the verdict was never in question?*

"But it was an unusual verdict, no?" I asked. "I understand that this Father François arranged it, but wasn't exorcism more often used to elicit testimony, as with—" I stopped short of saying the name: Sabine Capeau.

Everything about such trials was unusual, said the succubus; *rather, everything about them is unusual, for these trials go on still, and will go on, I suspect, forever.*

"But you are correct," said the priest, to me. "It was unusual for the nun, Sister St. Colombe, to be sentenced to exorcism, but remember: a quite ambitious young priest was at work in A——, this Father François. And also, the Borthon family demanded to know why the priest was dead and why the nuns testified to having been so defiled, so degraded ..."

"And witchery," I finished, "was as good a reason as any."

"Precisely," said the priest.

"Save them with the rites of the Church," I went on. "In this case, the exorcism of their tormentor, Sister St. Colombe."

Idiots, spat the succubus, *to think they'd be saved by the work of one impure priest!*

"So this Father François—" I began, only to be interrupted by Madeleine, who stood to move about the room, as Father Louis did. In contrast to his density and the measured grace with which he moved, Madeleine held to so weak, so diaphanous a shape that it seemed she floated over the carpeted floor. ... I stared at them as they circled me where I sat.

Madeleine stopped to stand before the red marble hearth. *It's my turn*, said she. *I will tell of the exorcism.* On the mantel beside her there sat the bust of a man—the Maréchal de Saxe, in the interest of fact—and the dense white weight of the porcelain, the very *mass* of the thing seemed to mock Madeleine's incorporeal state. She was anxious. Angry. She seemed to slowly grow more . . . more *solid*. She said I would hear her speak of things of which she was not proud; regardless, she had done these things, and she would speak of them. She solicited the priest's assistance. Would he help her tell the tale her way?

The priest, bowing deeply, said, "At your service, sweet hellcat," and, smiling, he resumed his slow circling of the room.

35

Chambord, Part II

—The Continuing Charade

I<small>T WAS A</small> *day in late November,* said Madeleine, standing in front of the fireplace, some ten or fifteen paces before me. *Fresh snow had fallen in the night, its whiteness soon sullied by all those who came to witness the exorcism. By midmorning that white blanket was dark from the dirt dragged in on the heels of peasants and the mud sprayed from the wheeled conveyances of the rich. There were, perhaps, five hundred of the good men and women of God gathered in A———.*

The rite would not be read in the church. This was deemed too dangerous, for what might the exorcised demons do when loosed into the House of God? A stage was erected in the shade of an ancient oak and Father François refused no one as fine a vantage point as they could afford.

As the hour drew near, Father François, resplendent in surplice and violet stole, took the stage to rhythmic applause and murmured prayer.

Sister St. Colombe sat tied to a chair that was, in its turn, fastened to the oak where it abutted the stage.

"It appeared the setting for some druidic ritual," said Father Louis, "wherein the oak, the chair, and the witch would all rise up in one single, sacrificial flame."

Madeleine continued: *The Mother Superior was clad in a simple shift, too thin for the weather; but she was beyond discomfort, so hungry, so tired, so broken was she. The marks of the vermin with which she'd been confined showed red and purple and black upon her arms, her legs, her bare feet, and her face. Her head was shorn. To those who'd known her, she was unrecognizable.*

Finally, Father François opened his Ritual Romanum *and began. Louis and I were present, of course, but we held no shapes, though we might easily have done so, drawing from the depth of the drifted snows.*

Madeleine paused then. *Louis,* she said, not looking at the priest . . . *the words, Louis. Don't make me repeat those words.*

The priest understood. So too did I, for when next Father Louis spoke it was with a voice not his own. It was—I knew it instantly, though of course I'd never heard it—it was the voice of Father François.

I drew the ermine stole tighter around my shoulders. I heard the howling wind, felt it invade the château. I listened to the incanting incubus as he stalked around the carpet's edge, encircling Madeleine and me.

" 'I, Father François Sidonie, Minister of Christ and the Church, in the name of Jesus Christ, command you, unclean spirit, if you lie hid in the body of this woman created by God, or if you vex her in any way, that immediately you give me some manifest sign of the certainty of your presence . . . ' "

Madeleine resumed her narrative: *The first exorcism begun, Sister St. Colombe sat upon that stage seeming less alive than the great oak to which she was tied. All stared at her, awaiting some devilish sign. None came. And then, quite contrary to the prescribed rite, Father François turned to address the assembly. He declaimed that he would rid the Mother Superior of those demons who'd used her, who'd urged her to kill the good Father Borthon and torture the innocent nuns. He proceeded to address Sister St. Colombe, who wanted only to move on to her reward: death, however unjust. Father François commanded the demons within her to declare themselves, to state their names. He inquired as to their rank and their role in the Satanic order. He asked if they proposed staying a specified time, or would they use the woman for all eternity.*

"This," chuckled the priest, "drew *gasps* from the crowd."

He asked the hour and place at which the witch, or nun, had been entered. No response. Louder, ceding to some dramatic impulse, prancing about that makeshift stage as though he were host to demons, the priest demanded of the lead demon within the Mother Superior the reasons why it had come into her. Still no response.

"Madeleine," said Father Louis to me, "was biding her time."

I was, yes; with great effort. But then one of the assembled Faithful lobbed a snowball at the nun, who sat staring up at the priest, her face devoid of hope. Then suddenly there was an arsenal of snowballs in the air, fists of ice striking the Mother Superior. From these she could not shield herself, for her hands were bound behind her. Snowballs soon ceded to rocks, one of which split her lip. Another rent her cheek. . . . It was then I could not wait no longer, and I . . .

. . . Let me say that Father François, that all present were rather . . . rather surprised when the Mother Superior first responded to the rites read upon her.

I descended, discarnate still, said Madeleine, *and I hovered near that ancient oak, near the Mother Superior. Surprising myself—for it took no effort at all—I caused the chair on which she sat to rise up, slowly, as though on a current of air; it rose and rose till the ropes that bound it to the oak snapped like strings.*

"You lifted it up and—?" I was confused.

I caused it to rise, as I said. The act was unrelated to physical strength; it involved the strength of the will. I willed the chair to rise.

Madeleine went on: *It was then I entered Sister St. Colombe—true possession is but a simple, watery displacement—quite different from the shape-stealing effected with stolen shoes and skirts—and I caused her voice to rise up to a shout. My every word was heard.*

Into that wintry silence, I said this: "I was a servant of the right God and was unjustly condemned to a living death. From Purgatory I've come in search of a Christian burial." All the while I shared the body of the broken nun, who'd fainted away when I took her voice. . . . I willed the chair to hang high above the slatted floor of that makeshift stage. The nun was but a rag doll, and I willed her every move, caused her to jump and skip and flop about like a—

"The effect of which," interrupted Father Louis, "was extraordinary. Extraordinary!" He moved briskly about the room, excited by these recollections, and continued his testimony: "The mob fell back from the stage. Some screamed. Others ran home to hide in their houses."

"And what," I asked, "was the effect of all this on the Mother Superior?"

"She was a wondrous, a *frightful* sight!" exclaimed the priest. In imitation of her, a laughing Father Louis threw his arms out wide, let his head loll about his shoulders, rolled his eyeballs back in his head. "Indeed, she *was* like a rag doll . . . the only animate part of which was her mouth, from which issued such invective, such filth as to—"

As regards the nun, interrupted Madeleine, *she resisted me not at all; and she slipped the bonds of life as quick as she could.* I said nothing; but Madeleine responded to my unasked question. *You want to know if I killed her,* said she. This silenced the priest, who stopped in his dance to stare at the succubus. *That is what you want to know, is it not?*

"Yes," I said, "it is."

In response I say this: I broke that chair like a twig, dashing it and the nun's body against the oak. Freeing her of life's fetters, I had her charge that oak like a stuck and crazed bull. She stove in her own head. She beat her body against the oak till her skin was but a sack of shattered bone. . . . I caused all this, yes—taking care, of course, to spare the nun's jaw, for that I'd need if I was to continue speaking through her; but the nun was dead by then, dead and departed; her soul had slipped away. . . . So, no, I did not kill her; I merely occupied her, used her, and destroyed what remained of her.

"You were *in* her, no?" I reasoned. "You *possessed* her. So did you not feel that bodily pain, the breaking of every——?"

An approximation of the pain, yes. But it was nothing I could not suffer. It was like those phantom pains you felt that night at C——, reading of your tortured sisters. Madeleine hesitated, then added, raising her hands to her opened throat, *I've known pain far worse.*

I said nothing. Father Louis resumed his route around us.

I tell you, witch, the nun had already passed when I did what I did. She'd abandoned her body. She'd sat beneath that shower of stones, freezing, starving, clad in rags, knowing she would die. And so her will to live was soon gone, displaced by her desire to die.

"Still," I insisted, "you might have saved her somehow."

"No, no, no," explained Father Louis. "She was a mere mortal woman, unlike you. Would you have had us revive her, untie her, brush her off, and send her on her way? Introduce ourselves to her as the eudemons who'd saved her and share with her a teary farewell?" He paused before continuing, with—thankfully—dampened sarcasm: "You don't know, witch, how easily we can render insane those of a true faith, *any* faith. The streets, the asylums of every city are *littered* with those whose minds have been ruined by our kind, people who have seen things they ought never to have seen. No, to save Sister St. Colombe would have been unkind."

And I say again: she wanted to die.

"How do you know that?" I asked of the succubus.

I was in her! I assumed not only her form but her will, too.

"And through her will—whatever *that* is—she communicated to you her desire to die?"

Well, no; not exactly, said the succubus. *What I learned from her was that she wanted to kill, and only secondarily to die. . . . I did her bidding, that's all. I let her die and—*

"And whom did you kill for her?" I asked.

Madeleine, having made no response, spoke on:

With Buvée dead—with her soul departed—I remained in possession of her body. Now I was the sole target of the rite. I would judge its effect—if it had any: again, the priest was impure.

"You remained in literal possession of the dead Sister St. Colombe?" I asked.

"Possession," explained Father Louis, his patience thin, "implies that the possessed person lives; so to say Madeleine *possessed* the nun is inaccurate. If you must have a word for it, let us say that Madeleine revivified, or reanimated her."

As I did your red-haired visitor in the cathedral.

"I see," said I. "She was but a vehicle, a host. A vantage point from which you might view the Church's rite, sham that it would be."

Yes, said Madeleine. *I was busy with the broken body, with the rite and the priest, whom I addressed where he cowered, far across the stage. . . . Finally, I, within my host, approached him. . . . Louis, please. . . .*

Again, in that voice lost on the winds nearly two hundred years—the voice of Father François—the incubus intoned, " 'Who are you?' " The voice was tremulous, thin; and surely it was but an approximation of the exorcist's true fear. " 'Who are you?' "

With those words the elementals retook their parts. I sat cross-legged, still and silent, and I watched the charade played out to its end.

"You want to know who I am?" quoted Madeleine. *"Might I say that I am Mahonin, of the third hierarchy, and the second order of archangels, and that before I entered this woman I was resident in the seas? Might I say this?"*

Father Louis's line was this: " 'Mahonin! Oh, foulest Mahonin!' " The incubus circled the large room, circled me where I sat at its center. All the while he spoke, more and more animatedly, in that voice not his own. " 'I exorcise thee, foul Mahonin, most vile spirit, the very embodiment of man's enemy, the entire specter, the whole legion, in the name of Jesus Christ, to get out, to flee from this creature of God!' " The incubus then made the sign of the cross upon his chest, repeatedly, and did the same on the air before Madeleine, who rose up, actually rose up before that snarling, snapping fire till she hovered high above me. In the course of what followed she began to revolve, slowly at first, then faster, faster, her head thrown back and her arms extended. The wind rose to accompany her deathly dance; I would hear the distant shattering of panes blown from their frames, the hollow slam of doors, and that *tap, tap, tap* that I rightly took to be hail falling on stone.

" 'I adjure thee,' " continued Father Louis, " 'by the Judge of the Quick and the Dead, by thy Maker and the Maker of the world, by Him who has power to consign thee to Hell, I adjure thee to depart quickly from this servant of God!' "

Father Louis bounded about the room, turning circles and scurrying under the succubus's suspended form. Each time he passed before the fireplace, the flames rose up and spat like so many snakes, fairly *licked* the red marble of the mantel. " 'It is God who commands thee! The majesty of Christ commands thee! God the Father commands thee! God the Holy Ghost commands thee! The sacred cross commands thee! The blood of the martyrs commands thee! The constancy of the confessors commands thee! The devout intercession of all saints—' "

Spinning fast now, rising up nearer and nearer the ceiling, her head thrown back, her legs and arms splayed by the speed at which she spun, Madeleine sent forth a cry that was equal parts laughter, scream, and speech. Barely discernible within it were these words:

"Repeat that, if you dare, you faithless fiend! Do you dare to invoke the blood of the martyrs and the constancy of the confessors?"

" 'Thou art accused by Almighty God, whose statutes thou hast transgressed. Thou art accused by his Son, Jesus Christ, our Lord, whom thou didst dare to tempt and presume to crucify. Thou art accused by the human race, to whom—' "

"Oh, pitiable creature! Presume not to show me the face of my accusers, for I was accused by none but the likes of thee, and so it is to thee I have returned!"

" 'For what purpose hast thou returned?' " intoned the incubus.

"You denied me a Christian burial. It is that I seek. By your rites you condemned me to roam the earth in discarnate form."

Father Louis pranced on, beneath and around Madeleine. " 'I adjure thee, most vile spirit, the very embodiment of Satan, in the name of Jesus Christ of Nazareth, who, after his baptism in Jordan, was led into the wilderness and overcame thee in thine own habitations, that thou stop assaulting this creature whom He hath formed from the dust of the earth to the honor of His glory. . . .' "

They each of them rose to fever pitch. The windows blew open. The flames threatened to leap from the hearth. I worried that the fire, feeding on the swirling wind, might spill from its place, set first the rug and then the whole room aflame!

" ' . . . Therefore, yield to God, who by his servant Moses drowned thee and thy malice, who pitched Pharaoh and his army into the Abyss. Yield to God, who made thee flee when expelled from King Saul with spiritual songs sung through his most faithful servant, David. Yield to God, who condemned thee in Judas Iscariot, the traitor, who—' " and the exorcism went on.

Madeleine's spinning finally slowed, then stopped. Father Louis, not seeming to notice, capered on, reciting the rite from memory.

Madeleine descended to stand before the fire. Her descent seemed to tame the flames. She came at mortal speed to sit beside me, and by the din of the continuing exorcism, and the dying wind, she told me the end of the tale, fairly whispering it in my ear.

Spinning and spinning there, strong in the wet winter air, I . . . I did a dreadful thing.

I took . . . I took a short-handled scythe from someone in the crowd, snatched it up as they all scurried about like bugs, and I set to hacking at the stiffening corpse of the Mother Superior, at my bodily host. Madeleine mimed the actions she described. *I held the scythe in my left hand and with it severed the three lower fingers of the right hand. The fingers fell upon the screaming priest. I hacked at the chest, the neck—I would have severed the head but for the spinal cord, and the too dull blade. Spinning all the while, I loosed the nun's cold blood to spray the assembled, to spray the cowering priest. . . . Witch, I did dreadful damage to that body.*

"But why," I asked, "why would you do such a thing?"

Anger, perhaps; anger at my seemingly inescapable lot. Vengeance, vengeance for what had been done to the Mother Superior, and to countless others falsely accused. Perhaps I hoped to break the faith of those who were witness to the rite. . . . Perhaps it is the suicide's abiding impulse.

"What did they do, those who were witness to—?" I led.

It was a scene straight from the brush of Bosch, said the succubus. *Pan-demonium.*

"And Father François? What became of the impure priest?"

He was sanctioned, in absentia, by the Parliament of Dijon for having read the rite of exorcism without the bishop present. It was a sham verdict, for he'd had the bishop's permission, but the people of A—— demanded the verdict. Of course, by the time the Parliament concluded its inquiry, Father François was long gone, chased from A—— for having brought such devilry down upon the place.

"The priest . . . did you . . . ? You said earlier that you did Sister St. Colombe's bidding . . ."

Oh yes, I found and visited Father François some days later. And by the time I was done with him he'd determined to lay himself down in a deep mountain stream, his pockets full of rocks, his mouth open to the flow.

"The nuns?"

Dispersed. The convent was closed, and eventually razed. The townsmen fled, nearly to a one, and the town is not marked now on any map. Nothing remains but the shell of that church, the roof of which fell in long ago beneath the weight of a winter snow; the steeple sits now inside the church, as though retracted from God's sight.

"So, it ends there?" As I spoke those words, only then did I notice that Father Louis had slipped away, silently. He was gone.

Mais non, said Madeleine. *It begins there, with the rites of Bell, Book, and Candle, and exorcism. Just where it ends, well . . . we'll see shortly, won't we?*

Sleep now, said she; and, too fast to follow, she quit the room: so said the sputtering fire.

36

Avenues

I WOKE SHIVERING from a fitful sleep; dreams had plagued me, but upon waking I could not recall them. I'd no idea how long I'd slept. Neither did I know where I was.

I sat up and felt the ermine wrap slip from my shoulders. And the *Chambre de Parade* was cold, terribly cold; and colder still when I heard behind me, in a familiar whisper, *"Bonjour."* At that a fire, born of charred and cooled logs, rose sudden and strong; and I scuttled back from its flames into the arms of a kneeling . . .

"Mais ce n'est pas possible!" I breathed, my heart snared like a rabbit in a trap. I drew the snow-pure ermine up to my throat. To protect myself. Perhaps to stopper my throat, for already the word was rising up in it, the word I spoke though I knew it to be a lie. The word was a name and the name was Roméo.

I said it twice more as my waking eyes focused on that familiar figure, standing above me now. He did not speak. He simply smiled down. I cannot say what it was he wore, for suddenly he began to . . . to undress, and I took no note of the fabric as it fell. Only when I saw through tears his nakedness, only when I reached out to touch his cold bare calf, only as my hand neared the lifeless flesh . . . Only then did I know, and my hand, my arm, my heart, my . . . my very self and the whole of my soul drew back, disgusted.

"Bâtard!" said I, equally shamed and angry. "How *could* you?" . . . But the incubus was beyond insult.

"You are happy to see me, *non?*" he asked in the appropriated voice. To hear Roméo's voice pained me, even though it was not Roméo who spoke, not *my* Roméo; worse was the pain of *seeing* him, being subjected to the stygian illusion.

"You are happy," said the incubus again, coming closer, planting a bare foot on my trousered hip. Through the fabric I could feel that foot's weight! And the icy crawl of the toes as he worked them onto my inner thigh, and toward my. . . .

"No," said I, scurrying back. "I am *not* happy." I stared up at the creation: it was as though Michelangelo himself had set to work with pick and chisel on a block of ice. . . . Ah, but it *was* but a block of animate ice!

"But I've only come to thank you," said the priest in his own voice. "This is what you wanted, no?" With his hands he indicated the whole of the naked body, and with one particular gesture—so lewd, pure Father Louis—he indicated a certain *part* of that body, and asked again, *"This* is what you wanted, no?"

"You would *thank* me?" I asked, scampering crab-like toward the hearth, away from the cold temptation. "You would thank me with this . . . this *glamour?"*

"I would thank you, yes," he said—he seemed, unaccountably, sincere— and he went on, "for what you have done, for what you will do in the coming days—your Craft, your witch's work."

"But you . . . you are not him! And *that* . . ."—my turn now to envelop the exquisite body with a gesture—*"that* is not Roméo!"

"No," observed the priest, rather matter-of-factly, "it is not." Already the conjured Roméo was losing strength; what had seemed the densest of flesh began to dissolve in the light of the flames. "But, my dear, *this* is the closest you're likely to get." And lest I confuse his meaning, the incubus worked the body's member to rigidity, so grotesquely, so lasciviously . . .

I turned from him. "Go away," I said. (I would *not* cry.) "Please, go away."

The incubus did not, *would* not understand. He stepped around, into my sight, to proffer the icy member a second time. His appeals, though obscene, were . . . were pathetic as well, for yes, he was, in his way, sincere. I heard again his words of the night before: one cannot fault a being for doing what it is in his nature to do. My anger was lessening, for Father Louis retained in death the considerable charms he'd had in life. He'd heed no command or plea. Understand no reason. . . . I would need to manipulate the incubus more subtly than that. When he renewed his campaign a final time, I interrupted:

"Louis," said I, dryly, addressing him as Madeleine did, "go get the berlin ready. . . . Go now." And I waved a lazy hand in the direction of the door.

It worked, this superciliousness. It angered the incubus to distraction. Flames rose to scratch at the red marble of the mantel. Before the incubus could litter the air with invective, I spoke again: "If that . . . if *that* is your way of 'thanking' me, I say no thank you, and I tell you again: *Go!* Ready the berlin."

It was difficult to not look upon that beauty, illusory though it was. But I did not turn back to the incubus. I stared instead into the flames; and in their action I read it plainly: the incubus had surrendered, and gone.

I wanted only to quit that room, quit the château—how *silly* it seemed to me now, in its ostentation, its callous and arrogant scale—and retake the road. I took to the cold, dark halls, walked from the *Chambre de Parade* caring not a whit who'd slept there. I descended that famed staircase, and I heard with disdain the echo of all the jeweled heels, the swish of all the embroidered trains that had taken those steps over the centuries, and the conjured sounds left me unaccountably cold. . . . I hastened my own, less ghostly step; but I stopped when my thoughts turned to a practical matter: I had no driver. Father Louis had led us to the château, had dismissed Michel. What to do now? I'd never even guided a wheelbarrow, let alone a monstrously large coach led by a team!

I walked from the château, out into the courtyard. I stood surrounded by the smothering stone towers, aglint with dew. I judged the hour by the sun's height: perhaps six, seven o'clock. There sat the berlin. The horses were hitched and eager. I was not; for instantly, I understood: the rebuffed Father Louis would take a perverse joy in seeing *me* atop the box!

As I approached the berlin, which loomed larger, more *ludicrous* with every step, the gates through which we'd entered the courtyard opened, creakily, inexplicably. "No," said I. "There's simply no way . . ." and I stood with hands on my hips, shaking my head. "I will *not* mount the box."

The sole response came from the horses: they switched their tails, turned their heads this way and that, blew steaming breath from their flared nostrils . . . "*No!*" I insisted; it was the horses I addressed.

I heard then the priest's taunting voice on the air: "It's a thing a *man* would do," said he. I cursed him soundly, though he was nowhere in sight. And then I clambered up onto the box and took the reins. What else was I to do?

The horses tensed. There sat the gates: wide-open and straight ahead. "This will be easy." Whether I spoke to assuage myself or the horses I do not know. I made a vague motion with my wrists, wriggling the leather of the reins, and the horses lurched forward a step or two. With this, I was content: *slow* progress was still progress, no? But then my diabolical friend, unseen, somehow caused the reins to come alive in my hands! They were as snakes, snapping and biting at the horses! He issued a fast command in tones understood by equine ears, and that contraption, the candied coach atop which I sat flew forward, and we were off at a clip. I fell back against the short-backed drivers' bench. I looked down to the rushing ground—too high to jump, too far to fall; and so I held on as best I could, closing my eyes and bracing myself when it seemed certain we'd crash against the gates, shearing off the berlin's left side in the process.

Somehow we slipped through; and I felt almost triumphant. The priest's laughter grew faint as faraway birdsong. And then there came *true* birdsong as we roused the residents of the parkland. I listened to it, and to the gravel being ground by the carriage wheels. Perhaps the horses had a memory of the way we'd come, or perhaps the priest guided them. What I mean to say is this: though I held tightly to the reins, it was no achievement of mine that we eventually regained the Coast Road.

We returned to the river. Suffice to say that I never quite took to the role of driver; I did, however, do it, for, as the incubus had said, *It's a thing a man would do.*

As I drove that early morning from Chambord, listening to the murmuring river and the great grinding wheels of the coach, marveling at the muscular motion of the horses, I watched the sun rise higher and higher. Its light fired the undersides of the thin clouds, and nature's palette shone acutely. Violet and palest pink, recalling the smooth insides of seashells, ceded to nacre and bister and honey as the sun stood taller, stretched and surrendered its somnolent stoop. The dimmer twin of every shade swam atop the river. And light played in the trees too, tangled itself in branches still dressed with late-season leaves. I grew calm. I gave myself over to the light, and I recall it more vividly than many of the seemingly more extraordinary things I'd already witnessed, and would witness still.

When we reached our first village the hour was early still; and, as old men wake before younger men, it was to an assembly of such, fishing from two benches beside the river, just outside the village proper, that I made my appeal: did they know where I might hire a driver to go to Bourges and perhaps beyond?

None responded to my very direct question. Instead, abandoning their flimsy fishing canes to the bank, they came to circle the berlin, to marvel at and test its every surface. They stared as if it harbored the headless ghost of its intended inhabitant, dead now these thirty-odd years.

"Are the fish not about this morning?" I asked. The four men took up their poles again, my question still unanswered.

"They are not," I was told by the younger man. "Spooked by something, scared away." After a pause of some heft, he went on: "Seems the river over-rode its banks last night. Not here, but farther back. Nearer the château. Fickle as a woman, she is." He turned now to address his peers, saying, in a charged tone, "Témoigner told me it was wild in the night, that the fish rose up to beg for hooks!"

"Surprising, that," said the ill-married man. "It is early for the river to rise."

"It rose last night, perhaps," said he whose beret concealed a hairless pate that shone smooth and bright, and which he now bared; he ran a broad and roughened palm over it as he spoke on: "But see—is she not calm now? Higher than her summer low, oui; but we've some weeks before she truly rises, flexes like . . . like . . ." and he pushed high his sleeve to show his hale and withered left biceps, on which an anchor, festooned with chain, wavered. I'd see more tattooed men—in direct proportion to our proximity to the sea, it seemed—but then, I was struck by the bright patch of flesh and asked with outreaching finger if . . . I asked, regrettably, if I might touch it—at which the sleeve fell fast, as fast as those eight eyebrows arched.

"You might try the blacksmith's boy." This reprieve came fast from the tattooed man. Then, having stared at me a bit too long, he added as afterthought, "I hear he is itching to get away from his father's fires."

"He is gone already, cousin. Off to Nantes. Day before last."

"I need a driver." I said it plainly. (Still I was terribly embarrassed.) "I will pay fairly for a driver to take me to Bourges, perhaps beyond." I showed my purse, retrieved from the cab; indeed, I held it open in my palms like an overripened, split fruit. Money, I would learn, concentrates the attentions of men, and certain women, too. "My driver has deserted me and . . ."

And shortly, with money spent, I had what it was I needed: the name of one Étienne B———. I forget who it was gave the name, but all four men then set to scratching directions in the dirt with the blunt ends of their fishing canes, such that I marvel that I ever found my way.

But indeed, I'd soon contracted with my new driver, whom I'd found sitting before a squat and squalid home, his chair tipped back against a sill. He was whittling—to no end, no purpose I could figure—the handle of a broom. I made a quite generous offer. He asked for more money, and, flummoxed, knowing only that I did not wish to drive myself, I agreed. (I did not yet know that one is supposed to start low in negotiations of this kind.) This Étienne went into his hovel. Not long after, he came around the distant corner to which I'd directed him, rucksack over his shoulder, saw the berlin and stopped. I feared he'd turn and leave me. "It's nothing really," I urged, "just a trap, larger and fancier than some, I suppose." He smiled, threw his bag up onto the box, and climbed up after it.

Étienne—who would prove an able and devout driver, and would indeed drive me beyond Bourges, all the way to Avignon—was perhaps three times my age, unclean and ugly, broad-shouldered . . . but appealing. I knew him by his eyes, which were clear and bright. He had about him the air of one who will do anything for money, owing not to necessity but rather to the simple appeal of coin; and, as the chief characteristic of such a man is silence, the seeming absence of curiosity—Étienne would ask no questions; he made that plain—I was pleased with my new hire.

We drove toward Bourges, a stretch of some distance. I decided we'd drive directly; that is, we'd abandon the Loire. We'd not waste time seeking out rivers or streams or canals that would sustain the elementals. In truth, after recent events, I wanted time without them, time alone. What's more, we had but three days before the new moon rose, at which time we'd need to be significantly farther south. If the priest took exception to my decision, he did not come to say so.

The way was without event. I slept and read and wrote and took in what sights I could see from the on-rolling coach.

Later, as we gained certain cities—and, again, we'd head toward Bourges, then Moulins and Roanne, with Lyon the goal; later, it would be Vienne, Valence, Montélimar, and Orange, where finally we'd gain what seemed the true South, and then Avignon, and finally, just beyond Les Baux, the cross-roads—as we gained these places I would sometimes rap at the roof for

Étienne to stop. I might search out the resident bookseller; from their shops or stalls I would cull any and all books pertaining to . . . let us call them "the dark arts." (Near Vienne I gathered up a *trove* of works from an unpleasant man who knew not what he had!) I also, on occasion, divested myself of the *necessaire*'s contents: I'd never wear such clothes, and I needed the room in the trunk for my burgeoning library. I'd give the clothes to the needy; and so, if now an unknown hand, extended to beg for alms, shows a thin wrist framed in fine Alençon lace, it is my doing. By the time I set sail the trunk that had been packed with that wondrous wardrobe was laden with books and, yes, that black velvet bag, still tightly tied, the contents of which remained a mystery.

. . . The elementals eventually rejoined me—deep in the night, near Lyon—drawing on the strength of the Rhône, rushing down from its faraway Alpine heights, the Swiss mountainscape that contributes to the sudden swell of water that bedevils the land and its people after the spring and autumn rains. From Lyon to the crossroads the elementals would come often, owing largely to the strong waters of the Rhône and its tributaries, which, I would learn, were suffering an early and suspect swelling. Indeed, we'd encounter flooding all through the South, starting just south of Lyon, where the Saône, a quieter river, nearly as wide as the Rhône, was flowing fast. A woman I over-heard in a market stall told how, farther north, the banks of the Saône had been pushed back; from a second-story room, said she, she'd watched the Saône spread out shallowly over the countryside, rendering the land a lake whose waters seemed to lap at the feet of the distant, blue-gray Juras.

I worried that the flooding would impede us. At Lyon I conferred first with Father Louis—no happier at being summoned this second time—and then with Étienne. We were agreed: after an early-morning rest in Lyon, we'd drive on, keeping a bit ahead of the floodwaters.

I did not take a room that damp and sunless morning in Lyon, as Étienne deservedly did. I took instead to the streets, determined to keep pace with the city, not let it overwhelm me, as had Nantes. I found a river mist overhanging the place, hazing its every outline. The low sky was the color of soot; clouds threatened to let fall torrents of rain to spur the river waters, yet never did. That terribly humid day every wall seemed to weep, the pavers were slick and the balustrades of the staircases clung to one's palm, leaving it clammy as a cow's tongue. The Lyonnais, too, seemed imbued with a gray humidity. Their sleepy eyes brightened only when I passed in my . . . my rather extravagant attire. Finally, having my fill of stares in the street, I determined to find a tai-lor of the city who might put its famed silks to purpose and re-suit me.

Sweating beneath his dancing hands and tape, I ordered from a kindly sartor two pairs of the plainest trousers fashion would allow and several full blouses, the better to hide my . . . my silhouette. I asked the man the price of having him abandon all other work. He stated it. I doubled it, and said I would return in two hours' time. (I was growing ever more confident in such transactions.)

Lyon, I would see, serves as a portal between differing climates and cultures. Behind me I would leave the reserve of the northern gentleman, taking up instead the openness of the southerner. This, of course, complicated my charade, for it contradicted my own nature: shy, not sunny; water rather than wine.

The roads from Lyon were good. They mimed the river's course and carried us through its verdant valleys and mulberry landscape, the trees of which feed the silk manufacturers. (Those silks, yes. . . . The tailor had done well; and I left his city happily suited and in possession of several simple-cut batiste blouses, a waistcoat of gray silk and two pairs of black trousers that buttoned at the knee, just inside my high boots.)

The roads were good, yes, but some had already softened, run to mud in some places, mud into which the berlin sank too deeply down. In time the wheels would churn up mud enough to cover the entire coach, dulling its splendor somewhat, which was fine. Here and there the most ambitious floodwaters leapt to lap at, to suckle at the low belly of the berlin.

That day I'd peer from the rolling coach to see people of the country, in simple dress, standing along the riverbanks, on dikes and drays, on every raised surface. Further south I'd see them on the sills and roofs of their low-lying homes. Still, the people went about their ways. Fishermen fished, though they had to do so from atop stacked crates. Washerwomen washed, kneeling before those few rocks that were not yet submerged. It was the determined pursuit of *la vie quotidienne.* They'd look up from their labors as we passed; some waved, some pointed, others cursed or laughed as we rolled on; through the berlin's back window, I watched as they returned to their lives, to the watery work at hand.

Southward from Lyon, we were always a full half-day ahead of the worst flooding. Travelers told us repeatedly that conditions were worse to the east, or that the river rose high behind us, in a literal wake. Finally, I wondered: were the elementals somehow effecting this? Madeleine, agitated in Angers, and at Chambord, had caused the weather to turn. Was she, were *they* now affecting the river similarly? I shuddered to think what she might cause at the crossroads.

We were traveling through the rich plains beyond Vienne, along the willow-fringed banks of the river, where the North ceded to the South as vines were supplanted by cherries, apricots, and pears; farther on, the olive would commence its reign, overtaking all with its ageless and stunted gray-silver trees. Étienne had succeeded, deftly, in navigating Vienne's warren of medieval streets. Not knowing when the elementals would deign to come, I readied to rap at the roof and order him to stop, for the book I had in hand identified Vienne as nothing less than the cradle of Christianity in the West, and its Corinthian temple seemed to merit a tour. But just as I was about to direct Étienne to return to Vienne proper, I felt the cane slide from my fist, fast and slick. I hadn't to wonder long what had happened, for across from me I found Father Louis, cane in hand; beside him sat the succubus. "We haven't time to stop, witch. Are we not agreed: we will achieve the crossroads for *this* new moon and not the next?"

"Yes," I said, "of course. But . . ." and then, quite pathetically, as if to excuse myself, I pointed to the entry in the guide that featured a well-executed sketch of the temple.

Put your books aside, commanded Madeleine. *Let us speak of life!*

"Of life?" I asked.

Of life, said she. *And of the avenues unto death. . . . And let us do so before these damned waters rise any higher.*

And so, just beyond Vienne, they'd come—the elementals. To sit with me—mortal fashion—in the cab of the berlin, holding strongly to their own shapes. I was directed to draw the shades and light the two lamps that hung from their enameled hooks and swung with the coach. That light, far less constant than the sun's, rendered my companions quite changeable; at times whole hands and limbs would disappear, only to return when the shadows shifted. . . . I was unfazed: I had become accustomed to strangeness.

My memory of their speech is spotty. They told me extraordinary things; and as they spoke a tension descended like a great drape, and every word seemed weighted. After all, our southern progress was marked in hours now; and soon, if all went as "planned," Father Louis and Madeleine, together for centuries, in life and after, would separate. I knew little of said "plans," of course; but I knew, or *sensed* that we were dealing with the Great Mysteries. And so I was not surprised when, in the darkened cab, Madeleine set to speaking of the reincarnated soul.

Like you, said Madeleine to me, *on your last night at that convent school, when I knew that my life, or my death—call it what you will, but I refer of course to my present state— . . .*

when I knew that I was at the center of a mystery, I turned not to life for answers but to books. . . . You had those S-marked histories of the Burning Days, those trial transcripts and such.

Likewise, I read all I could find about the means of reaccessing life. Reincarnation, in general terms. And I read not out of mere curiosity, not just to exercise the mind; no, I sought direction, as a traveler does. I sought a way, an avenue unto death.

"A traveler?" I repeated, though the analogy was clear.

Yes, said Madeleine. *And why not? I'd traveled through a mortal life to a mortal death, and then on to this immortality; once there, of course, I knew the journey to be incomplete. My preferred destination was . . . was finitude. . . . How was it I ended up in the opposite place, a place of perpetuity?*

I understood that I'd been consigned by the Church—your most holy Church, whose rites are a mystery to their very practitioners!—to this . . . stasis, this unchangeable state. Realizing this, I sought a way out. Desperately. I would not be defeated! . . . Moreover, I wanted no part of life; I'd had quite enough.

"And you feel that way still?" I asked.

Defeated by the Church? Yes, there can be no question. That I want to die, to pass from this state? Yes, I feel that way still. The three of us sat staring at one another, and the unspoken was plain: Madeleine might soon have her wish.

When the succubus next spoke, her voice bore a lightness in its tone, almost of embarrassment. *Oh,* said she, *I read so very much, did I not?* She asked this of the priest, who did not respond. *Afraid, perhaps, of finding the answers I sought, I ignored my instincts, my hunches, and suspicions, and read far in the opposite direction.*

I read the kabbalah. . . . I read too in Arab and Muslim folklore. I read of the djinn, those demons ruled by Solomon with the aid of his ring, said to have been inscribed with the true and only name of God. Born of fire, the djinn were resident in the Kaf, a range of mountains carved of emerald and encircling the earth.

"A waste of time, all of it," spat the priest.

Well, did I not have time enough to waste? asked Madeleine. *I had an eternity,* mon vieux. Her speaking of these things annoyed the priest; it was clear. *He,* she said to me, with a nod toward the priest, *did not condone my research.*

Father Louis looked at me and asked, beseechingly, "You see, don't you, witch, how all of this is somehow . . . objectionable, *offensive* even?"

I did not have to respond, thankfully, for Madeleine did:

Ah, Louis, you remain marked by your mortal beliefs. You defend your silly——. She hesitated before continuing, and turning to me to say, *He's a priest of his Church, and he always will be.*

"And so let us speak of that Church, then," said the priest. "She condemned you, no? Not some band of demons resident in a ring."

Yes, said Madeleine. *Yes; let us speak of your Church.*

"It is your Church too, until you escape it." Silence then. Father Louis looked deeply at Madeleine—wordlessly, without apology for words that had seemed to me cruel. In time, he continued: "We believe that the Church, through the rites read over Madeleine, and owing to the disposition of her soul—that is, plainly, her burial at the crossroads in unconsecrated earth—we believe these things have stopped her soul whenever she's found a way, have barred her passage back into life, into a living being."

He paused. I said nothing. When again he spoke, it was to commence an explanation that only confused me more: "These are not tenets of Catholicism, or not solely. In fact, the Church anathematized the preexistence of the soul in 553, but prior to that—"

Prior to that, took up Madeleine, *the Egyptians believed in it. Zoroaster, the Persian prophet of the sixth century, believed in it. The Greeks Pythagoras and Plato believed in it. . . . Many in the East still believe. . . . And of course the Celts believed in it.*

"But a Celt," said Father Louis, "can convince himself of anything." They shared a smile at that: forgiveness, unsought, had come fast.

"Believed in 'it'?" I quoted. "By *it* you mean . . . ?"

"May I?" asked the priest of Madeleine.

Please do, said she, allowing the priest to speak thusly:

"The soul, you see, lives a series of lives in the flesh as part of a process of spiritual development; a process that ends only when perfection is achieved and the soul merges with . . . with the Divine Consciousness; in other words, the soul—the *essence* of a life—advances from human to god form; it aspires to, and sometimes achieves, another plane of existence."

"And . . ." I began, "is this . . . does this mean that . . . ?" I was overwhelmed.

Yes, affirmed Madeleine, before I could sputter to the end of my question.

"We've had some proof of it," concurred the priest. "Proof of the soul's many lives. Isn't that what you wanted to know—if the soul passes from host to host along its way?"

I nodded, and said, "Yet . . . yet you, Madeleine, have not been able to regain life even though you're able, apparently, to manipulate the souls, the wills, the essences of others."

I've tried, averred the succubus. *I've tried and failed innumerable times.*

"But that's not wholly true," amended the priest. "You have at times held to life."

Yes, well . . .

"You have?" I asked.

"She has indeed," said the priest. "But never for long."

"But . . . but how?" I asked.

Madeleine spoke of having hovered over copulating humans—"every variation thereof," qualified the priest—but those fornicating forms showed no entry to her, no "soul's door," as she put it, not even when coition resulted in the creation of a life.

In time—out of anger born, again, of disappointment; and, in Father Louis's case, "for fun"—the elementals began to *interfere* with coupling humans. And, finally, "attendance at ten thousand fucks," as Father Louis put it, rather indelicately, did finally show Madeleine a way.

Once, in a mountain village of northern Italy, Madeleine entered a woman *exactly* at the moment of conception. *Then*, said Madeleine, *when I did that, or when that happened—for it was serendipitous— I thought I'd found a way.* Madeleine, as pure soul—for want of a better word—was resident in that woman, in her womb, for a full term.

When I gained her womb, I was, at first, myself. That is, I knew all I'd known when first I'd entered her, before I married myself to the water of her being. Intact were my mind, my memories, my senses; I had the ability to speak, *though not the means, of course. It was a soundless world, a world of water, silent but for the muted drumming of two hearts. And I'll tell you, that existence was very much like ours when we, Louis and I, forsake all shapes, all semblance of* being. *When we do that, ours too is a water world.*

I was contained—the whole of me; my soul reduced—I was contained within that nascent being, that still-watery curl in her womb. But each day, each hour, I lost more and more of myself. Memories faded, thought slowed to a stop. Only instinct remained. Ah, but it was a joyous loss, for I knew it brought me nearer life.

"Were you . . . were you *born*, then?"

Madeleine did not answer me, not directly. Instead, she said this: *After nine months I knew nothing. I'd been reduced, distilled—by What, by Whom I've no idea—to life-matter, to human essence. I had a body and a consciousness, but to refer to that as me, to think of that as all that had once been Madeleine de la Mettrie, would be incorrect. Or so I believe.*

"Is it like that for others? Is it always the same, that . . . journey?"

I think not. I think that some are able to retain more memory, even some characteristics of a former form—eye color, mannerisms, temperament. . . . And so it is that some infants are born not with knowledge, per se, but knowing. *This, I believe, accounts for the range of wisdom among men. Some souls are born old, marked by lives already lived, lessons already learned.*

"Are all of us . . . ?" I began.

Are we all reincarnated, are we all comprised of residual soul?

"Yes," I said.

No, said the succubus, *I don't think so; some beings are newly born, products of mere, or rather pure Creation.*

"But tell me," I pressed, "tell me what happened when you were actually born?"

At parturition? . . . Ah, yes. Well, I saw a sight-obscuring light, the very same light I'd seen when I died. But mark me here: it was not a light that leads one toward it, that beckons; one hears the hysterics talk entirely too much about that sort of light. No, it was a light like . . . like shattering glass. A celestial fracture, if you will. And it was followed hard by an instant—an ineffable instant—of battling Chaos and calm—that, I believe, is common to every birth and death.

As that light faded I heard the slowing of first one heart and then the other. This was attended by a precipitous descent from warmth to coldness, a coldness like . . . like the ice at the earth's core. And then a recurring crash of light confirmed it: I, or rather my infant host, had died, and so too had its mother.

I rose then, again, ascended to the state I'd long known. Lifeless. Deathless. . . . This!

Madeleine hesitated. She mourned not those lost lives, but rather the lost opportunities; and this, strangely, did not seem callous to me. *After that particular disappointment,* she resumed, shyly, *I raged. I raged for decades and did things I will not speak of. . . . Vengeful, cacodemonic things.*

Father Louis sat expressionless and silent; if he knew what "things" the succubus spoke of, he'd not speak of them either.

"Did you ever try again?" I asked. "Try again to access or gain life in that way?"

I tried twice more, answered the succubus, *and with similar result. Once the fetus failed in the second month, and I rose up leaving the mother awash in blood. The second time I rode my host to term—and retained a great deal more wisdom as the birth date drew near—but the birth was complicated and again I ascended, having known less than a quarter hour of life.*

"That quarter hour, it was not enough to allow you to . . . to live and die, as you wished?"

Apparently not. The infant died, but I did not. I would have thought that span of life sufficient, but . . . But those rites read over my mortal remains, that curse cast over my immortal soul, those tricks of the Church, prevented my soul's escape. . . . Or so it seems.

"And those are the rites you seek to undo at the crossroads?"

Yes.

"You know," said I, quite suddenly, "I've no confidence I can *do* that. What if I do not have the power to—"

You do not need power, said the succubus; and she paused before adding, *Witch, you are power.*

37

The Carcass Waxer

SHOCK? WHAT *is* the word to describe what one feels upon hearing truths that man has sought for centuries?...Did I hear the elementals as certain saints are said to have heard the voice of God? Those saints heard the Word with neither shock nor surprise, for their faith had prepared them for it, led them to expect it; it seemed their reward. Might I say that I had faith, *have* faith of a kind? Might I say that I heard the words of the elementals as a sort of reward? Ah, but I indulge myself here. Certainly, I am no saint, no mystic. As we passed among the olive, the asphodel, the cypress, the laurel, and the vine—I peeked out from behind the drawn blind—it was Father Louis who turned our conversation from Madeleine's "avenues" to Paris, segueing with words similar to these:

"We tread the border of life and death," said he,

"and that is a place quite often marked by violence." And so it seemed he'd speak of ... of violence; but no: he spoke instead of meeting Sebastiana and Asmodei in Paris during the last decade of the last century. He'd gone on at length before I understood that he'd not changed his subject at all: speaking of Paris, he spoke still of violence.

The elementals told of events that transpired many years ago, some twenty years before my birth. Of course, to the elementals my lifespan was nothing, for they'd each endured ten such spans. To them life was a long unbroken line; and as their memories proved suspect in terms of dates and such, I augmented their tales with what I knew.

"I don't recall the year," said the priest at one point, rather characteristically, laughingly adding, "I haven't had recourse to a calendar for some time. In fact, the last one I saw was that of Fabre d'Églantine, that ridiculous Revolutionary calendar before which all were supposed to bow. How that amused me! Really, now: *Thermidor, Messidor ... Frimaire, Nivôse ...* How absurdly *arrogant* to rename time's component parts!" The priest referred, of course, to the short-lived calendar put forth in the first years after the Revolution—or *Années* I and II; it was held that a new day had dawned, a new day deserving of a new name.

"It was, I think," continued the priest, " '92, perhaps '93."

The King, of course, was newly dead, offered Madeleine.

"Yes, yes he was," said Father Louis, "but the Queen was not; she was not yet dead, was she?" They turned to me. The first date that came to mind was that of the King's execution:

"21 January," I said. "The King was killed on 21 January of '93."

"Ah, yes; so he was," mused Father Louis. He closed his eyes; when he opened them, he added, with a wry smile, "You, witch, may recall the date, but I recall the day."

"You were there?"

We were there, of course, said Madeleine. *All of Paris was there. Indeed, the Commune had to lock the city down, finally, to stop the flow of people into the capital. The city gates were shut, and the streets were lined with soldiers. It was said a thousand soldiers accompanied the King's coach to the scaffold.*

"Although, at that point no one dared call him King. Louis the Last, perhaps, or Citizen Capet, or the Pig of Varennes—most popularly, and finally, Louis the Shortened."

The "shortening" ended all sorts of other indignities, observed Madeleine. And then, rather sadly, she added, *I wonder if it wasn't in a way welcome?*

"My dear, you persist in thinking that everyone wishes to die!" chided

Father Louis. "I'm sure, given a choice, the Royals would have chosen to live out their fat and happy days in some gilded refuge, far from the rabble. . . . That said, it *is* true, the King was made to suffer all sorts of petty indignities in his final days."

I asked the priest what he meant, and he explained further: "Well, for example, while the King was imprisoned in the Temple, his jailers refused to do such things as remove their hats in his presence, and if they were seated when he passed they remained so. He was not allowed to wear his decorations when he went out for his daily walk . . . things like that—petty indignities, but bad enough in their way for a former King. Of course, those abuses progressed to verbal and finally physical abuse of"—here he smiled—"of the capital sort."

How it went from funny little nicknames and courtly slights to the lopping off of his head . . . I must confess, said Madeleine, *that road—the steep slope down to Revolution— remains a mystery to me. . . . But to return to the day in question . . .*

That day, with the King slated to go to the scaffold, Paris was a festival of death! All through the enormous crowd were little clearings in which the people danced the carmagnole. It seemed every second man had a drum, drums to mimic the quickening pulse of the people.

"So you were actually there, in the crowd, when the King was killed?"

No, not "in the crowd," as you put it—we were above the crowd, discarnate. Madeleine looked to the priest. *We were everywhere then,* said she, *everywhere life was likely to end suddenly and violently. But rarely did we take shape: a body would have been a hindrance, would have held us to one place at a time.*

"You can be in more than one place at a time?" I asked, knowing Madeleine's answer would call into question the very Trinity, the omnipresence of God and—

Well, said she, *not exactly.*

The priest elaborated: "Not like *that.* Not like you've been taught. What Madeleine means is that—discarnate, without the burden of a body—we could, rather we *can,* by means of the will, move quickly, very, *very* quickly, from place to place."

Indeed, laughed the succubus, *I once witnessed two executions at opposite ends of the city—one in the Place du Carrousel; the other I forget where—and the next day's paper held that both executions had happened at the very stroke of noon!* I'd never seen the succubus so animated; she was acting like a girl. *Ah yes, one of the executed was a boy, not yet twenty, court-martialed for kissing the embroidered fleur-de-lis on his old uniform. How the poor sot cried as he climbed up to the Blade.*

"Tell me more about the King," said I, straining to see Madeleine in the inconstant light of the cab, and leaving the landscape to roll by unadmired.

Well, let me see . . . he wore gray—gray stockings and gray culottes; and a pink waistcoat under a brown coat of silk. I remember that well. And his hair, it was coifed—

"And cut off in the back," added the priest, "so no braid would impede the Blade."

And he was calm, said Madeleine. Or appeared so at first. He ascended the scaffold and shook hands, as was customary, with Sanson and his son. But then an argument ensued.

"It was clear to the crowd," said Father Louis, "that Louis Capet did not want his hands tied behind his back. Sanson insisted. Finally, a priest intervened, whispering to the King, who relented. He hadn't much choice by then."

There was a moment when it seemed the mob might act.

"Yes."

Some shouted support for the King.

"Yes," said Father Louis, "though the law, posted everywhere, read something like this: 'Those applauding the King as he passes to the Timbers of Justice will be beaten; those cursing the King will be hanged.' I tell you: it was a time of great contradictions! There was a report in the journals the day after the King's execution that told of two men arrested along the King's route: the one had addressed the King as such, and the second had refused to do so."

And weren't both men killed? asked Madeleine. I believe they were—the monarchist by the Tribunal, sentenced without trial, and the insulter by his fellows in prison.

"Yes," said the priest, "I believe you are right."

"The prison massacres?" I asked reflexively.

"No, dear. That was a bit earlier, in '92," said the priest. He was amused. "But tell me, what do you know of the massacres?"

"I've read accounts of those atrocities. But surely you were witness to them. Tell me what you saw."

"Ah, but why, witch? If you know anything at all of those massacres you already know too much. And what's to say but that a band of fifteen or so citizens—far fewer than one imagines—riled by talk of the supposed sedition being stirred in the prisons, burst into several of them one late afternoon armed with blades. And the rest was butchery."

Don't let's speak of the prisons, pleaded Madeleine, not now. . . . The King, Louis; speak of the King.

"All that there is to say of the King, finally, is that they killed him. Sanson *fils* let fall the Blade at his father's order, and the head of the King of the French fell like a thousand others."

Can you believe, laughed Madeleine, that some expected the King's blood to be blue? There were bets, and a mad rush toward the scaffold to see it spurt from the neck. Some tasted it, even, and said that it was pré-salé, salted like the flesh of the livestock that grow fat on the salt marshes. After all, it was asked, hadn't the King lived off the land, too . . .

"Sanson held up the head; the crowd went still, silent. Then, slowly, rolling from the back of the crowd, washing forward to break like a wave on the scaffold, there came a dull and primal roar . . . It was quite eerie, that rumbling cheer . . .

"And so the people had killed their King."

Think of it, said Madeleine to me. Think of it! I knew the world had changed when I saw the schoolboys of the Quatre-Nations toss their hats in the air.

"The two parts of the King's corpse were carted off to a common burial," said the priest. "Sanson stayed behind to oversee the selling of souvenirs, handkerchiefs dipped in the King's blood, et cetera, for such was his right as Executioner."

And a lucrative right it was, added the succubus. Sanson, I tell you, was rich! He lived well. . . . He would sit fireside with his family at night—Gabriel, his eldest son, would later die of a broken neck: he'd fall from the scaffold while stretching to show the mob a head. And there was Henri, the second son, and the grandson, Henri-Clément, each of whom would become Monsieur Paris in his turn—they'd all sit fireside and Sanson père would draw a slow bow over his cello, or teach his parakeet the songs of his youth. And death—murder, really—was as common a topic of conversation as any other. I know: I visited Sanson several times.

"Visited?" I led. "You *visited* Sanson?"

No, no, no, said the succubus, not like that! No, I wanted just to watch him, see how it was he lived. And it was strange indeed to see Sanson kill the King, having watched him days earlier as he tended his tulip garden. Sanson, you see, was a dealer in death; and so I trailed him, convinced that if only I were present, and watching closely enough, I'd see, I'd discover . . . a rupture, some rent in the fabric of life, of death.

. . . And here I am these long years later, searching still.

The elementals told me more about the King, most of it, they said, they knew from Asmodei. It seems that for Asmodei, the King was something of a hobby. He would pose as a courtier; once, when the King went to the Temple, Asmodei was posted as a jailer, advancing in short order to the post of Shaver to the Former King. Yes, they said, Asmodei was often quite close to the King, whom Father Louis laughingly described as "inept, distracted at best, conniving at worst," and "led by his quite willful wife." He called the King a "mooncalf," and at this Madeleine joined him in laughter.

Louis, said she, I've not heard that word in a century! A moon-calf, indeed!

The priest, spurred by an admiring audience, spoke on: "Yes, imagine the bastard child of a god and a cow and . . . *voilà!* That's what he was—a moon-calf, a dolt!"

"Surely he wasn't as bad as all that," I began. "It is said that he had a way with numbers and riddles and—"

"It's true," opined the priest, "he was not stupid; and there's the true tragedy. He might have been, *could* have been, a good king. *Capable* of ruling, he was not *able* to rule, for he'd been far too disinterested for far too long; and so it was too late when crisis finally came."

The situation, or "crisis," at the time in question—that is, when my four saviors' paths crossed in Paris—was this:

The long habit of excess—Du Barry, Antoinette, the hundreds, the *thousands* of their privileged predecessors at Court—had brought the monarchy, and by extension the country, to the brink of ruin. France was bankrupt. And this situation, when finally it had to be recognized, was compounded by the dire effects of what I will call, rightly or not, Sebastiana's Winter.

The monarchy, spoiled by centuries of self-indulgence, epitomized now by a foreign-born Queen, was inert. It was a machine whose wheels were turned by money, as free-flowing water works a mill. There could be no monarchy without money. And was it *really* true that there was no money? That was the question on the pursed lips of the privileged—no matter that the starving poor of Paris ought to have been proof enough.

The King, when finally forced to act—and in what would be but the first of many tactical blunders—called together the Estates General in May of 1789. It was a legislative body that had been inactive for centuries and was all but forgotten. The first estate was comprised of the nobility; the second the clergy; and the third, in numbers far greater than the first two estates, the people. The King would leave it to them to somehow solve the state's financial crisis; they, eventually, would strive to do much, much more.

After days of debate the King was presented with nothing less than a new constitution.

"Capet," opined the priest, "ought to have kept his tiny mouth shut and just signed the blasted thing! Work around it if he wished, ignore it if he could—but if he'd just signed the thing he could have kept his crown, as well as a head to rest it on!" Instead, the King fought the people, slyly at first, denying them at every turn; and so, when finally he had no choice but to accede to "the People's will," his support was known to be insincere.

Meanwhile, said Madeleine, *the people grew hungrier and hungrier. They took the Bastille in an attempt to amass arms. The women of Paris, refusing to watch their children starve, marched on Versailles, and when they returned to Paris proper, muddy from the long day's march in the rain, they had with them the Royals, whom they forcibly installed in the old, unused palace of the Tuileries.*

"Where they could be watched," added the incubus. "By now a murderous hatred of the Queen had sprung up among the mob. And the people were actively working against the King, just as he worked against them." Of course, along with this internal unrest, France had also to contend with the advance of the Austro-Prussian armies.

In Paris, politics fast devolved to the cult of personality. The mob was swayed by men such as Danton (brusque, ugly, vulgar, and well-loved for a long while), Robespierre (brittle, bitter, and blood-thirsty) and Marat (who, in his *"L'Ami du Peuple,"* called repeatedly for the heads of all his enemies). Around these and other men there swirled storms of devotion, loyalty, hatred, and betrayal. Groups would rise—Danton's Cordeliers, Robespierre's Jacobins, the Girondins—and fall in their turn, losing first their influence, then their position, and finally their heads.

"Robespierre," said Father Louis, "somehow he'd last the longest. He'd not dance with the wooden widow till July of '94." Time enough, I knew, for him to orchestrate the Red Terror, in the final six weeks of which the papers of Paris listed no fewer than 1,400 executions. "It's true," said the priest, "I watched, *we* watched as men, women, and children were killed. Even a dog, taught to growl upon hearing the word 'Republican,' was guillotined along with his aged master."

And the corpses of suicides, offered Madeleine, reticently, *even they were subjected to the Blade, lest self-murder become too popular a means of avoiding justice.*

Through all this, of course, power was bounced about like a ball. From the Crown to the various Committees—of Vigilance, of General Security, et cetera—to the Commune, to the Tribunals; then, in '95, to the Directory; in '99, to the Consulate; and, in the early years of this century, to a tiny man from a faraway island, Corsica, the Emperor Napoleon Bonaparte. And I'll stop there, adding only that fifteen years ago, or thereabouts, there was installed, as we know, a king, Louis XVIII, brother of the executed Louis Capet. And so historians will debate, for centuries to come, what it was all worth. They will surely disagree, but none, I suspect, will conclude that it was *not* worth something.

. . . Ah, but I've spoken at length of things of concern to the world, perhaps, but not of concern to us here. For we are not *of* the world. Or are we? . . . *Though we may be peripheral,* said Sebastiana, *we are not insignificant.*

. . . I'll return now to the day in question, 21 January 1793. "A great day," said Father Louis.

"Why?" I countered. "Simply because the King was killed?"

"Mais non," said he, "that was the day we discovered Asmodei." He said they'd only had to follow the King's corpse to the Marguerite cemetery and there—

No, Louis, said the succubus, *it was the Madeleine cemetery—a name I'd remember. It was there they shoved the King's body into a too-small coffin and pitched the whole of it into a mass grave.* She added, disgustedly, *For a few sous, the sexton would let citizens toss a shovelful of lime down onto the King's coffin.*

"Perhaps you're right," said the priest.

I am. And it was not Capet's corpse that led us to Asmodei; it was his head, which took a quite different route, remember?

"Ah, yes," he said. "I remember now: Tussaud."

Yes, said Madeleine. *Tussaud.*

. . . Marie Grosholtz, by name; later, Madame Tussaud.

A mania for *des choses en cire* rose up during the Revolution. A medical man turned impresario, one Dr. Curtius, exhibited wax busts of celebrities and criminals at his Cabinet de Cire on the boulevard du Temple. His young assistant, not quite pretty but uncommonly ambitious, at first modeled for Curtius; she soon progressed to making casts. As Curtius was close to the Maestro—as Sanson was sometimes known—he received tips as to the who, what, and where of the executions. Upon receipt of such a tip, Curtius would dispatch Marie. She'd follow the tumbril from the scaffold to the Madeleine or some other cemetery, and there, working fast behind or sometimes *within* a tomb, sometimes *en plein air,* Marie would fashion the death masks on the heads themselves; from these would come the actual casts.

"La Tussaud was called the Carcass Waxer," said Father Louis, adding, admiringly, "and she was a hardworking girl!" Marie was commonly seen all during the Terror running after the tumbril, burdened with her baskets full of tongs, needles, linens, and wax, her dark cloak riding the wind behind her like wings. Securing the head, she'd carefully wipe the blood and reddened bran from it—bran lined the executioners' baskets to absorb the hot blood—smear the head with linseed oil and litharge, and wait for the mask to harden. The deed done, she'd toss the head back into its grave as though it were a fish too small to keep.

I believe it was in the very, very early hours of the morning, perhaps it was not yet light, when the elementals told me of Tussaud. I do not know where we were, though we must have been near Valence. I know only that our words were underscored by the murmur of water: everywhere the river rose.

"Asmodei," continued Father Louis, "saw profit in the Terror, as did so many others."

Yes, said Madeleine, *and he had connections. Owing to his formidable charms, or lies skillfully told, or brute force, there was nowhere off-limits to Asmodei. No one dared resist or refuse him.*

I didn't know what the elementals were getting at, and I said as much.

"Well," said the priest, slowly, "let us just say that had the King's coffin been opened that day at the cemetery . . ."

"No," said I. "Asmodei did not . . ."

"It was just the head, witch," said Father Louis, "and it was only for a few hours."

Just long enough for Marie to make her cast.

Hearing this, I was horrified, but not surprised; though in truth I had no difficulty imagining Asmodei absconding with the severed head of the King.

It seems Asmodei served as middleman, contracted to Curtius. For a fee, he'd somehow hand the desired heads over to Marie. This was no mean feat when the targeted head had so recently worn a crown.

"Sanson was in on the deal," said Father Louis. "So too was his driver. Just beyond the square, not far from the scaffold, the driver handed off to Asmodei a double-thick bag of burlap. Asmodei gave him, in exchange, a second head in an identical bag—heads, of course, were easily come by then—lest the sexton or the citizens waiting graveside grow suspicious, or want to see the royal head."

"But it would not be the head of Capet," I observed.

No, said Madeleine, *it would not. It would be an indistinguishable mass of blood and bran and matted hair. And no Christian or Citizen was then, that day, going to get too close to the severed head of the King, for there was still about it an aura of mystery and fear . . . Hadn't we all been taught that our kings were somehow linked to God, that they ruled by a right divinely accorded?*

"I see," said I.

Father Louis laughed. "Capet's head was pitched into its grave later that day, like a ball into its goal."

"Just thrown in?" I asked. "Beside the body and the false head?"

"Now there's a fine question, witch! For all I know the King of the French was buried with *two* heads!" The priest found this very funny; Madeleine less so. I found it not funny at all.

"And you witnessed all this?" I asked.

"Yes, and we were rather surprised by it, by the *bald* commerce of it all, if you will; and by the arrogance, the confidence of the man who brokered the deal: your Asmodei."

"*My* Asmodei?" I repeated. "Hardly."

True, said Madeleine. *I've never known a man who belonged so much to himself and so little to others. Sebastiana, try as she might, will never—*

"Yes," interrupted Father Louis, "that's when we first saw Asmodei. I knew immediately that he was a man worth watching."

And I knew right away he was no mere man, so beautiful he was, and so—

"Yes, well," said Father Louis, preempting Madeleine. ". . . We followed the corpse, its two parts; and when we saw Asmodei approach the driver and hand off the second head . . . Well, of course, we trailed the King's head, for the disposition of his corpse would offer up no secrets—there'd be no rites read, no ceremony; and that, of course, was the greatest insult of all!"

"You followed the head," I echoed. "To Tussaud?"

"Yes," said Father Louis, "but she was not yet Tussaud; she was still the gore-girl, Marie. In time, after the Terror, she'd head to England and I believe I've heard tell of some attraction of her own, her own Cabinet de Cire. But then, as I say, she was merely Marie."

It was not her we were interested in, said the succubus. *Nor was it the King's head.*

"No," agreed the priest. "It was Asmodei. We trailed him all over Paris for days after that. To countless executions. To brothels and pubs and various garrets, all repellent, which he kept throughout the city."

And eventually he led us to the Bal des Zephyrs, and to Sebastiana.

"*Et voilà*," said the satisfied priest, "here we all are."

38

Knights of the Dagger

S OME TIME LATER, the elementals gone, I had
Étienne stop at an open-air market near Montélimar,
and I treated myself to a block of the chocolate for
which that place is justly famed. There, I was also able
to procure nearly all I needed to concoct a batch of
the vinum sabbati according to a recipe rather loosely
recorded in Sebastiana's Book. Not only was the
recipe "loosely recorded," but it seemed every ingre-
dient was known by two, sometimes three names: the
familiar, the Latinate, and the Frenchified forms, say,
of some herb first discovered and named on the Italian peninsula. And yes, I knew that the slightest misstep in the making of the wine might render
poisonous what ought to have been potable. Regardless, in a day-lit room that rented hourly, entered
from the back of a roadside inn, in a riverside village

that had few sights to see, I set up a laboratory of sorts and set to work.

I was *dreadfully* tired now, and had to wheedle from the priest permission to stop—my goal was a nap, facilitated by the distillation of that wondrous brew that would take me from myself. Perhaps I ought not to admit that I desired to lose myself, for however long, let the wine relieve me of my thoughts and fears, but it is true: I wanted the peace of sleep, perhaps too the distraction of drunkenness, for I sought desperately to look away from certain facts:

This journey of mine, this "mission," was about to end. How or where, exactly, I'd no idea; but it would end very soon. On the morrow, I would work the Craft at the crossroads. Work it by the dark light of a new moon. To revivify and then let die a centuries-old succubus. And then what? I'd be on my own, setting sail for who knew where—and as a man, no less! Sailing to a new life across the sea. A new life lived in a new land . . . as a new man . . . with a new language.

Oui, I needed a drink.

And I had one all right. Truth to tell, I got terribly . . . inebriated; not on the *quantity* of drink I took, but rather, I think, on its low quality. (Witch, beware the wine! It is potent, and unpredictable; sometimes a salve, sometimes strong enough to envenom the very soul! It can slake thirsts you did not know you suffered, show you things you did not know you sought. . . . Still, I wonder just where I erred: I am suspicious of a certain mushroom I'd had to root for, pig-like, behind the inn.)

I would sleep for a short while on a narrow cot in the dark, dank room, my door locked against intruders. The place stank of risen water; and various bands around its mossy walls showed how high the river had risen in recent seasons. I would sleep surrounded by the residual roots and powders and yes, animal parts (I won't elaborate) that I'd used to distill the wine, not to mention the glass vials and pestles and shallow plates I'd had to procure for the practical aspects of the Craft. I would sleep several hours, but it would be a sleep beset with dreams. Dreadful dreams. Of death.

This dream was borne of a mind awash in images "shown" to me by the elementals, for as we'd ambled on, beyond Vienne, they'd spoken of Paris and the Terror, of events not recorded in any encyclopedia. . . . They spoke of things *macabre.*

Deep in the darkness of sleep I sensed . . . *motion.* A jaunty, bobbing motion. And then there came a slow, suffusing light: twilight, augmented by lit torches whose acrid smoke I could smell. My eyes burned, teared against that dreamed smoke and . . . Ah, but to say "my" eyes is inaccurate, for I *saw* with . . .

What I saw through were not "my" eyes at all but rather the eyes of a severed head raised high, a pike stuck into the hollow of its splintered spine.

Madeleine had told me, apropos of the massacres, that the soul remains
resident in the head much longer than in the body. Many were the people near
the scaffolds who witnessed severed heads speaking and screaming, which acts
calmed to the chattering of teeth, and death. She told me too that the vision of
a severed head—for they *can* see for a short while—is locked; it is a fixed vantage point, and so it was in the dream.

I, or rather *it* was on the march with the mob. By torchlight I saw other
heads atop other pikes. Right before me, dripping blood and flapping like a
fleshy bird on the wing, there was skewered the heart of a calf, or some such
animal; the sign appended to it read, "The Heart of an Aristocrat." . . . An
aristocrat. The head through which I saw was that of an aristocratic woman: I
knew it from the weight of the wig—intact, mockingly returned to its place
when the Blade had fallen—which I could *sense*.

There appeared before me in the dream the ill-lit, grimy, dirt-darkened
facade of a low building, its doors and windows grilled: a prison.

So it was the prison massacres I would witness, as the elementals had.
(Yes, the elementals had spoken of the massacres, at length and in gruesome
detail.) . . . I *knew* this, knew it even as I dreamed.

Summer's end, 1792. By then the Parisians were a population habituated to
gore. The guillotine had been in use since April, when Joseph-Ignace Guillotin,
doctor and deputy, would-be social reformer, had introduced the Great Blade
to ensure *égalité*, to balance the classes—albeit in death—when previously only
condemned nobles had been granted so expedient an end.

The doctor had demonstrated his device first on a bale of hay, then a
sheep, then a corpse, and finally a criminal. And oh what a hit it had been!
Soon fashionable women took to wearing tiny, jeweled guillotines in their
wigs, or pendant from their ears or necks, each complete with working blade.
Small guillotines of mahogany sat as centerpieces on one's dining table, with
blades used to slice cheese or fruit or dolls, the latter beheaded over dessert,
their raspberry blood let to drip over chocolate tortes. Every white handker-
chief *had* to show a crimson stain, testament to one's having witnessed at close
range the Blade's work.

Pamphlets were published daily, listing the day's schedule of executions, or
the winners in the "St. Guillotine lottery." As for the well-connected condemned, alone in their quite comfortable cells—one paid for one's keep and
was kept accordingly—they received amatory notes and gifts from unknown

suitors; bouquets were passed to them, bouquets of marguerites and, of course, *les immortelles*. Yes, the rich were spared the company of the masses and lived well in their decorated cells, their favorite furnishings from home arrayed about them. Many were allowed to come and go at will during daylight hours, careful always to grease the palms of their jailers as they did so. Visitors were received at all hours. And, not surprisingly, with so much of what remained of Society in jail, there was born a new species of salon. At Port-Libre (the former Port-Royal), for example, invited inmates gathered to hear recitations from imprisoned poets, improvisations by actors adaptable to any stage; at night's end, songs from the instruments of the skilled would wend their way through the vaulted corridors, lulling the condemned to sleep.

In the prisons, those who were deemed particularly dangerous, or who were otherwise reviled, rich or not, might find themselves in the close company of murderers, thieves, or, as was the case with Madame Roland, "fallen women." In addition to the constant attendance on death, which was everyone's lot, Madame Roland was made to witness certain scenes that were, due to its architecture, unique to her then home, the prison of St. Pélagie. That place, with its two wings running parallel to each other, the one housing women, the other men, saw enacted on its deep sills the most lewd theatricals imaginable, with the men doing to the men what the women might wish to do to them, and vice versa, with the women putting to purpose upon one another props quite crudely fashioned. It was a sort of inverted intercourse, and sex, its very *essence*, spread as a perfumed steam between the two cell blocks. . . . One imagines the Minister's wife standing by shamefaced while her cell mates "acted," or looked eagerly and excitedly on.

Clearly, few understood the political climate of the day; the politics of revolution were new to everyone. The least show of support or allegiance could, in time *would* be reason enough for condemnation, and summary dispatch to the scaffold.

There were *myriad* reasons to murder. It was sport disguised as justice. It was vengeance in the name of liberty. And liberty, it was said, was "a bitch that begged to be taken on a bed of cadavers." . . . Death's connoisseurs took their seats at the end of the Jardin des Tuileries—the best place to watch the Blade work in the Place de la Révolution—often picnicking with their families, their children curled at their feet or running about, stopping only to watch the heads fall. Of course, many of these connoisseurs would later find themselves atop the scaffold, watched in their turn.

All that long summer Paris had been awash in blood. Figuratively, but literally too, citizens complained of the stench, for in some faubourgs the gutters over-ran with gore. Many died of diseases borne on that slow scarlet stream.

It was all unaccountably base. Noble in its way—the Revolution—and yet unaccountably base.

That summer—'92—the prisons were overcrowded. More than one thou-sand citizens had been arrested on the flimsiest of warrants. Among this num-ber were the refractory, or nonjuring priests—those who would not swear an oath of loyalty to the Revolution above all else. Arrested too were those who'd served the Royals in any way, ranging from the most lowly servants in the royal household to the royal governess, Madame de Tourzel, and the Queen's confi-dante, the Princesse de Lamballe. Those nobles who stayed behind as their friends and relations fled became play pieces in a game the object of which was to arrest as many members of an *ancien régime* family as one could. The family members were then sent to separate prisons in an attempt to render all the more poignant their reunion atop the scaffold. These executions were much anticipated. Madeleine was present at one where Malesherbes was made to watch as the Blade took first his daughter, then his granddaughter, then his son-in-law, and finally his sister and her two secretaries; only then was the old man graced with the Blade.

. . . I've strayed. The dream, yes. . . .

I don't know which prison it was I saw in the dream. I saw it all as through a keyhole. I saw only what moved across my fixed field of vision, and so I could not turn this way or that to situate myself by signposts or landmarks. I saw . . .

I saw the mob draw itself tighter, to move more quickly through the prison's narrow entryway, which the warders had thrown open. Those with pikes were shoved to the fore. A horrid cast of heads came together. Some men, some women; the wigs of the women were powdered, the tall creations atilt, some tumbling down. None of these heads were *animate*, none of them saw as mine did. Besides these hideous heads there were also pikes topped with genitalia; one woman boasted that the red flaps atop her pike were the breasts of the Princesse de Lamballe. I'd learned from Father Louis that the Princesse had indeed met such an end; she was taken from her cell, hacked to pieces, and promenaded, on pike, before the windows of the Temple, where her friend the Queen was still imprisoned—the Queen, said to have recognized a certain piece of jewelry in the coiffure, had fainted away.

I saw raised arms bearing an assortment of weapons—mostly those sharp-ened iron rods favored by *les piquers*, but also pistols, bayonets, and, most frightful of all, the hand-crafted blades that would do butchers' work on behalf of . . .

It was the officials of the Commune, convinced that the prisons were hotbeds of conspiracy, who'd decided to turn over entire prison populations to the people. The courts of law, it was said, were too slow to act. And so there was sanctioned an orgy of slaughter that would last five days. In the end, hundreds of priests were dead, and the population of the Salpêtrière—which housed only women—was decimated.

It was not the Salpêtrière I saw, for with locked eyes I witnessed only the slaughter of men. Men pulled pleading from their open cells—opened, of course, by the jailers, who cooperated with the Commune's plan, for this "house cleaning" would empty cells that could be let again, at higher prices, at greater profit.... So indiscriminate were the slaughterers that they rarely stopped to see their work through: they'd swing their blades—here a limb lopped off, there a deep gash—and move on; few of the imprisoned died of their wounds directly: it was the steady exsanguination that brought death, and colored the prisons, colored the dream a deathly red. Every stone, every flat surface, was slick with blood. The slaughterers slipped on the stones as they escaped.

Sickening, the facility with which the people of Paris killed. Of course, they'd had occasion to hone their skills. The tenth of the preceding month, August, for example. It was then the people took the Tuileries, calling for the heads of the King and Queen. They'd first ransacked the *garde-meuble*, near the palace, taking from it antique halberds, knives, and a sword said to have belonged to Henri IV; most impractically, they took a cannon inlaid with silver, presented to Louis XIV by the King of Siam, and pushed it room to room, blowing out entire walls when they found thin, lacquered doors locked against them. The Royals fled under cover of the Swiss Guard. The King and Queen, the royal children and their governess, the Princesse de Lamballe, and several others hid for hours in a tiny closet in the chapel as the mob moved room to room, cracking mirrors as tall as three men, tossing gilded furniture from the windows, slashing tapestries and paintings. No one stole, for it was against the Revolution to covet the Royals' wealth. Destroy, and slaughter, but do not steal.

And slaughter they did, that day. The Swiss Guard, ill-equipped, quickly fell. So too did the band of the King's private protectors, a group of aged men known as the Knights of the Dagger. Slaughtered too, regardless of their sympathies, were the royal servants—cooks, grooms, seamstresses, page boys.

It was in September, their thirst for blood still not slaked, that the people passed through the prisons. October, November, and December came with more of the same; all the while, the Royals remained in the Temple, imprisoned and awaiting a fate that grew ever more certain.

Meanwhile, those in power—an ever-changing cast of characters—tried to determine how best to rid France of its Sovereigns. This, after all, was a lesson no European country of the day had learned. True, there was the American example; but they, the colonists, had simply sailed away from their King . . . sailed away to that vast country's eastern shore.

While debate raged, *la famille Capet* was kept in the Temple, a tower fortress on the grounds of an estate that had formerly belonged to the King's brother, Artois. The two floors accorded the family were comprised of tiny, airless rooms. The stony walls were slick with lichen. The ceilings were suffocatingly low. The floors were white-speckled with the droppings of vermin, still in residence despite "the royal infestation." No linens were allowed on the hard beds. The walls, which had long been painted with the pure white of the Bourbons, were bordered in insulting red, white, and blue bands; over this revolutionary pattern was scrawled the text of the Declaration of the Rights of Man and the Citizen.

Imprisoned, the royal children passed the days reciting Corneille, playing battledore and shuttlecock, bowling hoops and tossing balls. The Queen did needlework, which was confiscated and burned lest it conceal a secret message she sought to smuggle out to conspirators. As for the King, deprived of the intricate locks with which he'd passed countless hours, and too dispirited to keep up with his detailed lists—of his game, his riches, his courtiers—he suffered without distraction the insults, large and small, heaped upon him. As there'd been innumerable ways of honoring the King at Court, now, in prison, there were as many ways of insulting him: it was an inverted sort of protocol. And the family was never left alone: there was always a representative of the Commune present, even at their most intimate rituals. Indeed, a highlight of the day was the Queen's . . . evacuating; an alarm would rise, and all the guards would assemble to watch, to jeer, to cheer, and place grotesque bets.

The Queen found some solace in her dog, a gift from her lover, the Swedish envoy, Axel Fersen. (Only the King believed the dog was a gift from Madame de Guémenée.) Too, she shopped; for, even while their jailers were encouraged to heap all manner of abuse upon the Royals, even as their fate was being debated, the Legislative Assembly accorded the Capets a resident staff of thirteen, including a valet and the aforementioned shaver. (Imagine the particular thrill that Asmodei must have taken in holding to the multiple chins of the King, twice daily, a straight-edged razor.) . . . In keeping with this contradictory indulgence of the Royals, the Commune allowed the Queen to order a new wardrobe. Dressmakers came and went from the Temple, and seamstresses busied themselves outfitting a Queen they knew they would kill. She, in a typical act of vengeance, one particularly sweet, or *fragrant*, burdened the Commune with a bill for 100,000 francs—for perfumes.

Finally, early in the new year, the Convention, after thirty hours of debate, condemned the King to death.

Some months later, with the Revolutionary Army victorious over the allied forces at Hondschoote, it was determined that the Queen—known as "the first deputy's mother," a reference to her surviving son, whom only she referred to as Louis XVII—was expendable; her foreign affiliations, which had kept her alive, would no longer need to be called upon. She could be killed. But first there was the matter of a trial.

The Queen awaited her trial not in the Temple, but in the prison of La Conciergerie on the Île de la Cité, in a tiny room without windows. She was allowed no visitors; indeed, she never saw her children again. The charges against her—in general, Conspiring Against France—ranged in their particulars from her alleged complicity in various assassination plots to the counterfeiting of assignats to the disclosing of state secrets, and even, most absurdly, to incestuous relations with her son. This last charge the Queen fought vociferously; in her teary and strident defense, she nearly won over *les tricoteuses,* those old women who sat knitting through all the trials, looking up from their handiwork only to stab at the accused as they passed.

A jury of two carpenters, a musician, a hatter, a café-keeper, a wig-maker, and a printer unanimously convicted the Queen, and condemned her to death.

Such were the days—known now as the Reign of Terror, known then as the Reign of Virtue—during which the paths of my four saviors crossed.

Simply put, the elementals trailed Asmodei from the moment they discovered him in possession of the King's head. Eventually, he led them to the Bal des Zephyrs, held in the cemetery of St. Sulpice; and it was there they met Sebastiana.

Asmodei, said the elementals, was everywhere at once in the days of Blade and Blood; but Sebastiana's attendance at the ball was unusual—or so they'd learn—for she had long been living at a literal remove. Having thrown the Greek Supper and seen its consequences, having had her fill of Society and life itself, she'd retired to Chaillot. "Overwhelming was her remorse, her guilt," said Father Louis. "She'd sunk into a darkness of mood, an abyss from which she could not rise, abandoning her paints, poring over whatever *Books of Shadows* she could find, seeking a way to undo what she believed she had done."

In those early days, while still at Chaillot, Sebastiana would venture into Paris only to see what it was she'd wrought. She would load her coach with food, bags of coin, clothing; she'd go to where the poor were massed and give it all away. *Yes,* said Madeleine, *she gave away a great deal; but she'd earned such wealth, wealth unknown to any uncrowned woman.*

"She kept up with events in the aptly named capital," said Father Louis, "following every act of the Crown and the Clubs. And so it was she learned of the Victims' Balls, asking herself, 'Can it have come to *this*?' . . . She would go. To partake of Death, as the faithful do Holy Communion."

In order to attend these balls, said Madeleine, *one had to present documentation, proof that one had lost a close relation to the blade. It was a fine day for forgers; trade was brisk. And so it was Sebastiana attended the Bal des Zephyrs as the sister of one Madame Filleul, tried, convicted, and killed for "wasting the candles of the nation."*

"The Victims' Balls were *stylishly* grotesque," said Father Louis, "as death was fashionable then. To dress *à la victime* was all the rage. Women wore their hair up, and tied thin red ribbons round their necks; men too sported such 'blade marks.' At the end of each dance, one saluted one's partner with a sudden drop of the head, chin to chest, meant to mock the work of the blade."

Sebastiana came masked to the ball, said Madeleine; *otherwise she'd have been quickly recognized and associated with the Court or the Queen, and that was simply too risky. In Paris, then, one lived as one died: quickly.*

. . . She saw him standing far across the cemetery, tall and broad and pale as a Norse god. I remember his blond hair was untied, and he wore a scarlet domino and a half-mask of hardened black taffeta through which his emerald eyes burned. He approached her. He asked her to dance. And not a half-hour later she'd learned from him the latest German waltz. . . . And there the two of us stood, incarnate, watching as they traipsed over tombstones set flat in the ground.

Now doubtless she'd had a bit to drink. Doubtless too she was distracted by this strange man's attentions . . .

"*Oui,*" concurred the priest, "but by her own admission the act was rash." He explained: "The night nearly over, the moon opalescent overhead, the air thin and fine, Sebastiana showed Asmodei *l'oeil de crapaud.*"

And thusly did she win him to her side for life. This, with no little sarcasm, from the succubus. *Apparently, most men stare or scream or fall in a heap at the witch's feet when shown the eye. Not Asmodei. He simply threw back his blond mane and laughed that laugh of his. And they waltzed on. In their way, they are waltzing still.*

Within weeks, I learned, Asmodei was living in Sebastiana's cottage. Later, at the height of the Terror, when she decamped to the Breton coast, he followed. There they remain, living, according to the priest, "in an approximation of love, of family life . . . which satisfies, is enough."

Somehow, said Madeleine, *Asmodei roused her, finally. It was he who convinced her that it was not the literal climate she'd called down that had caused such catastrophe, but rather the climate of excess that had long been brewing. Why he, of all creatures, bothered with such an effort of kindness, I've no idea.*

"Love, I'd say," came the priest's response, which met with a sneer and silence from the succubus. (Sebastiana has written warmly, if discreetly, of that night; indeed, when first I discovered the entry, there fell from her Book a thin red ribbon, doubtless the very one she'd worn to tease or to appease the ghosts of the guillotined.)

Madeleine suspected Sebastiana was a witch when first she saw her; her showing Asmodei *l'oeil de crapaud* confirmed it. Not long after, though still not knowing what species of man Asmodei was, the elementals decided to ally themselves to those two beings, so fortuitously met. Their goal then was the same: Madeleine's end.

So, the elementals showed themselves to Asmodei and my Soror Mystica.

Father Louis visited Sebastiana in Chaillot. He considered going to her as the King (and he could have, for he had the Sovereign's gloves, stripped from the pudgy hands as they lay hardening in the tumbril), but in the end he decided on taking the more handsome shape of the Queen's lover, Fersen, the dashing Swede. (Of this encounter there is no mention in Sebastiana's Book.)

As for Asmodei, waking from a nap beneath a linden at the end of its seasonal turn, he encountered the Princesse de Lamballe, whom he'd seen several months earlier in . . . in several pieces. In this way his attention and admiration were won.

Years passed. And, as is the nature of a family, my four saviors were not always near one another, but neither were they ever far apart.

39

The Battle for a Single Soul

WE ARRIVED IN Orange. It was late in the day, for I'd whiled away some hours inducing the dream and recovering from same. The next night the new moon would rise. All was quiet in Orange, save for the rushing river, already on a level with its parapets and brilliantly blue under the last of the sun. The market was open but uncrowded. The houses were closed up tight, their northern faces devoid of windows or doors, owing, certainly, to the great winter mistral that blows down from Mount Ventoux, pulled by the warm Mediterranean and said to render the pale blue skies scar-white.

We drove on, out of Orange—past its copper and violet ruins, speaking so eloquently of the Roman era—toward Avignon. Along the way, rocky pine forests vied for precedence with orchards of almonds, olives, and cherries. Homes not so very far from the road sat up to their sills in brown water, and hay that had been harvested into cones poked up through the floodwaters, an archipelago of bristling, tiny islands.

We reached Avignon near dusk to find water in many of the streets of that ancient place. A rose-bronze moon was rising in the sky. I decided to sleep in Avignon, in a proper bed. From what little I understood of our mission and its map, we were near enough the crossroads. I did not consult the elementals, for they'd not shown themselves since Montélimar.

I let a room in the shadow of the Palace. And, ensuring that Étienne had money enough to see to his own amusement, I set off in search of mine.

In the still-settling, violet shadows of the Palace were encampments of gypsies, brightly clad. Stalls were established along the outer ramparts, giving the scene a fair-like aspect. Honeysuckle, eddying off the river, married the still air of a market square, infused with the aromas of saffron, thyme, fennel, sage, black pepper. In Avignon, as elsewhere in the South, I'd find the food wonderfully overrun by garlic and adrift in oil pressed from the olive; my tongue, accustomed to bland stews and overdone game, would suffer the concentration of spice.

As day gave over to night, and the streets grew cramped—with amusing abuse, bad language, and gesticulation the common tongue—I took refuge in a café off a secondary square, hard by the theater. I sat at a tiny table on the *terrasse*, beneath a pergola heavy with plumbago, and waited a long while for a waiter to come. When he did, I ordered *"un café, c'est tout,"* and when he stepped sniffingly away it was to reveal a woman seated two tables from mine whose beauty fell on me like a hammer-blow.

She was among a gaggle of women, all dressed similarly, in a garish fashion quite unfamiliar to me. Men lazed among them. Only when a call boy, tramping over my foot without apology, ran onto the *terrasse* to issue their common cue did the entire flock of actors rise up and run; and I saw by their strides and broad gestures that those whom I'd *supposed* to be women were costumed boys and men of slighter build. Coins were tossed onto the tables, which had been shoved together like game pieces. There were shouted protestations, and plans were made to meet at a later hour. The commotion caused several well-heeled ladies to look aghast at . . . at my mistress, seemingly the lone *true* woman, who stood, bowing to same with biting insincerity, and, abandoning a marble-topped table strewn with tiny white cups and distended snifters, proceeded to approach me. *Me!*

"Monsieur," said she, "are you the poet of Spain? I was to meet a poet of Spain here on the hour, just passed."

"No, Madame," I stammered. She stood before me in her merino skirt, dyed a deep orange, and a man's waistcoat of scarlet silk; into a pocket of the latter, and attached by a long gold chain, was tucked a pair of tortoise-shell spectacles. She was a tall woman. Her head was set squarely on her spine, thick and true. She had gray eyes that would go violet as the light died, a short, sculptural nose, and high-set cheekbones. Her black braids were wound into a tight bun, aromatically fixed with a rubbing of lemon oil. "You are not he?" she asked. I know now that she was waiting for me to stand, as a gentleman would have. When I, dumbstruck, failed to invite her to join me, she achieved the same end by saying, in a deeply accented French which I'd no hope of placing:

"I mistook you, Monsieur, for him. The South is chock-a-block with poets. But now you *must* buy me a chartreuse, as I'm far too embarrassed to take my leave."

"Certainly," said I. And when finally I stood, it was only to see her seat herself, as if we two were attached by a pulley system. "Chartreuse?" I led, recovering from these social gymnastics.

"Yes." She smiled. "The . . . *aqua vitae*, the very waters of life." And when the waiter returned, bearing my coffee, she waved both away, asking . . . no, *demanding* two of the sickly green liqueurs instead.

"Not a poet," said she, looking at me appraisingly and leaning nearer. "Are you then a white slaver? A crook of some kind come up from Marseilles to cool your scheming mind?"

Before I could answer, she went on: "*Don't* tell me. You are a heart-sick traveler. Provence, you know, is the recognized cure for northerners dying of broken hearts. You are a traveler, are you not?"

"I am. Yes."

"From where?" she asked. "And *to* where?"

"From the north . . . and I'm not quite sure to where." A breeze off the green river set to shimmering the flowered vines overhead. Pastel petals wafted down like confetti. The first chartreuse soon became a second.

"Ah," said she, wisely. "A vagabond of love." She looked at me so long, so hard, I had to look away; and with a flushed face I managed to say:

"Hardly. . . . Are you . . . are you from here, Madame?"

"I am better known in Arles, Monsieur, but best known in Greece. But *who* can resist dear Avignon. True: one must endure the gypsies." She then waved with both arms at a transvestite actor passing through the square, a skirt hiked up to his thin hips. Gesturing to same, she added, "One must endure too the traveling players." Yet she smiled broadly and offered her hand for a kiss as the player came to join us.

He did not sit; indeed, he addressed us both over a low fence of wrought iron that separated the *terrasse* from the square. "A friend of yours?" he asked, staring all the while at me. Though it seemed an impossibility—we'd only just met, and I'd not yet said a word!—it was clear I'd offended the man, who was frightfully thin and wore more rings than I knew a man might or could wear. Shaking his hand, which he offered grudgingly, was like taking up a bag of marbles.

"Acquaintances," said she, "proceeding fast toward friendship."

"Indeed," came the sniffling response. And then there was laughter, in which I did not share, for, not knowing *why* they laughed, it seemed foolish to join them. To judge by the actor's ongoing appraisal of my person, I was, I knew, the focus of the unspoken joke. "Are you," he asked, staring so hard at my . . . my various features as to make me shift in my seat, "are you in our play?" And turning to my companion, he added, "Certainly he *could* be. Among the chorines, *non?*" Now she turned to take me in as well; and, with a nod to the actor, her smile grew sly.

This last spoken insult was clear, and it cut deeper than either of them could have known. I was glad when my fast-friend said to the man, "Is that not your cue I hear? Go now. *Shoo!*" And she literally brushed him away; but not before he bent in too willowy a way to take my hand and kiss it, as he had my companion's some moments earlier. "Charmed," said he. And finally, with these words of the Bard's, he took a most welcome leave. " 'I will believe thou hast a mind that suits with this thy fair and outward character.' " Walking away, he turned back twice to look not at me but at my companion. Far away, he raised a thin arm overhead to wave, without turning, a jeweled hand; he seemed to me a sort of evil genie, and I willed him back into the bottle from which he'd come.

Immediately I worried that this woman, before whose beauty I was abashed, might find *me* rude—inexplicably, for it was the lean and snaky, overly lithe actor who'd intruded, who'd insinuated himself—and so I asked: "Are you an actress, then?"

"I was, formerly, and briefly," said she, seeming to appraise me still, ". . . and now I've *no* hope of regaining my former station in society." As she laughed at this, a cart was trundled past, laden with painted scenery. On the fractured canvas it seemed . . . yes, I discerned a shipwreck. "I've come for rehearsals, to *consult*, if you will. They open in two days; and the only thing that's a *wreck* is the leading '*lady*.'" She looked again at me, hard; sat back to take in my seated length. "*Twelfth Night*," said she, with a nod in the direction of the theater. "They're here with the Bard's cross-dressing caper. Sebastian, Viola, and the lot. . . . Do you know it?"

"I do indeed," said I, and now I knew the line the actor had thrown off. I swallowed hard and said, "I shall be sorry to miss it. I have never seen Shakespeare performed and I'd very much like—"

"Moving on, are you?"

"*Oui*, tomorrow. To Arles. To Marseilles, finally."

"And then? Overseas?"

"Yes." I was reacting bodily to her glance, which now was bold. When she took my hand in hers she no doubt found it clammy and slick. She offered a drawn-out "*Hmm*," as one might when tasting a new dish. Suddenly she let go my hand, sat back smiling, and changed her tack. "You must be *terribly* excited. About the sea voyage. Your first time?"

"Yes, it is. And, yes, I am, Madame. . . . In truth, I am more than excited: I am afraid, terribly so." Her eyes showed great sympathy, which ended when she, again, laid her hand on mine and I, foolishly, withdrew, so fast one would have thought she'd hurt me. "Worry not," said she, leaning so near I could smell the lemony scent of her shining hair. She added, "I bite only when invited." To this I failed to respond.

"Are you hungry?" she asked, not long after. I was, as was she. Within the quarter hour there sat before us a great fish stew, deeply spiced. We scooped it into our two bowls from the common one. Our chat during dinner—of her travels and light travails—was of little consequence, though her every word was a charm. Dessert involved my first taste of coconut, which I *very* much enjoyed. Finally, there came coffee and a final chartreuse. We raised the tiny glasses and my companion asked if she might make the toast. I shrugged, and she did so—and with words that nearly set me to choking, said, "To the memory of whoever you were."

"I . . . I . . ."

"Your hands will betray you," said she, with a conspirator's smile. "Beware them. . . . They are too graceful, too elegant to be the hands of a man. And your complexion is perfection." My hands? I'd always hated my hands, so huge, so . . .

"I . . . I . . ."

"There are laws, my dear, that's all. You must be aware of them." She sat back in her chair. "Do this," she commanded, crossing her legs as men do. "And this," drumming her fingers impatiently on the table and furrowing her brow. I aped her every move. ". . . It may have been easier for you in the North, for there, women are often mannish: such was the sacrifice of Catherine the Great, of Queen Elizabeth. But," she went on, "the southern woman triumphs as she is. . . . Théodora, Sémiramis, Cléopâtre." Surely my friend—I will call her Arlesienne, a Woman of Arles, for I never learned her name—*had* passed an hour or two upon the stage. She declaimed further: "Whether the southern woman is skirting the labyrinths of Crete, or walking dagger in hand along the bloody corridors of Mycenae, whether she poisons her man with ease befitting a Borgia or takes from the toreador's hand the still-beating trophy of the bull's heart . . ."

I coughed to reclaim her attentions, which had strayed in proportion to her rising voice. People were watching us. She concluded: "The southern woman has nothing to fear but her overwhelming sensuality. Now, Monsieur, pay our way from this place and follow me."

In a moonlit alley she critiqued my walk. She intentionally dropped a kerchief, and when I bent to retrieve it she judged that I'd done so all wrong. "At the *waist*, not at the knee!" Then that alley gave out onto another, and another; I was so turned around it was with great surprise, and crippling anticipation, that I soon found myself standing before my tiny inn, Arlesienne beside me. "Shall we, Monsieur?" she asked, slipping her arm through mine. I did not respond. I could not respond. Finally, she urged us forward, and into the inn we went.

I was some time under her . . . tutelage. It was fun, and yes, informative. That is, once she recovered from her initial surprise and learned the truth she'd only half-suspected.

"Mon Dieu!" said she, raising the back of her thin and elegant hand to her forehead and falling backward onto the bed, her vest and bodice undone. "Could it be the green faeries of the chartreuse have finally taken hold?" There I stood at the bed's end, my blouse open, my pants unbuttoned—not by me— and fallen to bunch at my knee, at the mouth of my boots. "I thought you were a simple woman, a woman a bit shy in the sapphic sense—of these I've known a few. But this! It's . . . it's . . . an embarrassment of riches!" And she fell then into a kind laughter that was the most welcome sound I'd ever heard. "Not to worry, lucky one," said she. "I've seen the same before, in Cairo. But I wonder, will I charge you double?" Again, that laughter. Only then did I under-

stand: here was that species of woman I'd long been warned against, a woman who charged for her . . . *intimacies*. And indeed, intimacies they were, for knowing what I knew it was as though a wall had crumbled and I could say what I had to say, ask what I had to ask, do what I had to do, all without fear of censure. It was as though some silly clock of shame had ticked to a stop. So it was I said, finally, summarily, "I know nothing," and she rose up into my arms, kissed me, and said, "That will all change in an hour's time."

There then recommenced that game of comparison that I, spurred by the succubus, had begun in the bath with Roméo. In Avignon, blessedly, there'd be no disruption.

Most marked in my memory is the weight of her breasts, so much fuller than mine. And the curve of her hips, so much more pronounced. But in truth, it was she who set to work with diligence, and without embarrassment—and she told me all she learned: "Ah, but it feels adequately deep and . . . and you've been with a man, haven't you? I can tell." There is intimacy, yes; but then there's *intimacy*—which is to say I did not tell Arlesienne about Father Louis and the night he'd come to me. Rather, writhing beneath and before and behind her, doing what I was told, I let her work on. "And this little devil is not little at all. I tell you because it's the question every man asks, and I suppose you're no different in *that* way." She asked if I was dry. "Do you bleed?" came the question a second time. And when finally I understood, I said, "Yes. On occasion. But not with what I understand to be regularity." This she thought interesting, but she said nothing more; instead, she lowered her mouth to my . . . offerings, and took them as a connoisseur would.

"Lucky, indeed," mused she as we lay, some time later, spent, in that narrow bed. I had so many questions to ask, so many things to say . . . and so I spoke not a word. Already I was recollecting events just passed, acts committed by and upon me. All I did manage to say—I admit it—is that I wanted more. "Perhaps some other time," laughed a tired Arlesienne, adding, "What you are, primarily, my friend, is young; and I am exhausted." She stood. She asked for my help in retrieving her clothes from the four corners of the room. She asked me to help her dress, and that was *not* the least erotic moment I spent in her company.

Finally, I followed her to the door, and there we stood, she dressed and me not. "Hear this," said she, fixing my gaze, "I find you beautiful. I do." I thanked her, for I believed her. And then, one hand on the door's latch, the other extended, palm up, she added, "And my advice to you is this: never do for free what it is you do best." I invited her to help herself to my money, and I cannot say how much she took. I will say only that I valued the lessons learned from Arlesienne far more than the coin they cost me.

At parting, I asked if I might see her again. "*Hélas*, no," said she. "I leave at dawn, or earlier, if *les acteurs*, whom I am due soon to meet, dissuade me from sleep altogether." And with a final kiss and the twin wishes of *"bonne chance"* and *"courage,"* Arlesienne left me.

From the window, I watched her. And glad I was when she turned to . . . No. It was not a wave she offered, not at first, but rather a salute of strength— a raised and clenched fist, teamed with the warmest of smiles. And then, only then, the gentlest of waves.

The last thing I remember of that night is looking down through the wavering glass of my second-story window, toward the square into which Arlesienne had disappeared, out over the full river, up the broad dark mass of the Palace; and up at the faintest of moons, wondering what powers it might possess and hoping—hope which I expressed aloud, in a godless prayer—that those powers might augment mine when finally we arrived at the crossroads. I did not sleep well, for I dreamed wakefully of Arlesienne.

The seventh day, the day of the deed, dawned sunny and bright.

I woke early, determined to see the sights. Surely we were near enough the crossroads that I could spend some time exploring? (In truth, I wanted to return to the café, wanted not so much to start a new day as to resume the night.) Apparently, it had rained quite heavily while I'd slept, and my hostess, at breakfast, upon learning of my intention to explore a bit, asked flatly, rudely, if I'd never seen mud before. Mud was all I was likely to see around Avignon, said she, as the river had risen in the night to meet the falling rain. ("The devil Rhône!" exclaimed she.) "Nevertheless," said I, "I shall have a walk," and at this she let go a snort and set three soft-boiled eggs before me.

The mountains of the Ardèche were sending torrents down their slopes to further raise the levels of the Rhône and its tributaries. I would learn from a traveler, present at breakfast, that river water had risen to the base of the city walls of nearby Vaucluse, where the quay was completely obscured and the surrounding country seemed but a vast lake of molten silver. Avignon, even after the night's rain, had fared a bit better. I could and did explore its streets, finding only the minority impassable.

Of course, I headed straight to the café. Waiters shoveled sand onto the rain-slickened pavers of the *terrasse*. In a corner, bent over a copy of *Le monde illustré*, sat a woman who was not Arlesienne. And though I took every turn in the expectation of suddenly seeing her before me—this despite what she'd told me of her plans—Arlesienne did not appear, and the sights of Avignon suffered her absence.

Indeed, I don't have many observations worth recording here, which is not to demean the place, but rather to attest to my distraction, which was extreme. . . . Finally, the day had come. The day of the deed. We were quite near the crossroads now and that very night the new moon would rise.

Among all that water—the risen water, the *worry* of water—it was my mind that skipped like a stone from thought to thought to thought. Arlesienne, of course, and lessons newly learned, but also . . . Well, I knew nothing of sailing, had never even been on a boat; yet soon I would take to the ocean. I was scared by all I'd read in novels of port cities and the nature of sailors. To me every sailor was a pirate. Surely I'd never pass among them as a man.

I was concerned most, that early morning in Avignon, about my practice of the Craft.

With these and other worries crowding my mind, I took to the still-empty streets and the role of tourist, which I'd play as best I could.

By the light of day the Palace was . . . was less impressive. Bald, plain, ugly, and so simply *defensive;* and built on a fourteenth-century platform of "principles that have not commended themselves to the esteem of posterity," as an Englishman, well-met in the shadows, put it. Indeed, what I remember most vividly of that, my matutinal visit to the Palace, is the Englishman, for with him I spoke English for the first time outside of a classroom or the privacy of my mind.

Indeed, from that morning in Avignon, much of what I'd see in the South took on a funereal cast, seemed but the deadened marriage of rock and ruin. . . . This, perhaps, is owing to the nature of our impending mission. . . . Funereal, indeed.

. . . I proceeded to cross the river and walk on for some while, muddy up to the knee, into Villeneuve-les-Avignon. Not much to commend that place either—again, the fault is mine—save for the huge round towers of its citadel and its long broken stretches of wall. Farther from the river, the place came to seem half-populated—and *that* half of the population comprised children, old women, and dogs lazing in the early sun. There were no streets to speak of. The unattractive houses seemed to have fallen here and there; they lay scattered about, crooked on the uneven ground, like the shriveled pits of fruits fallen from the vine, lifeless and hard. Lest I sound too harsh, let me add that as I walked through that place I saw beyond it an unflooded field of lavender, which cheered both Villeneuve and myself.

Crossing the river again, I encountered a flock of nuns in gray robes and red capes. They moved in procession. Each smiled at me in her turn, and those smiles—had I not been so anxious—might have been enough to render me melancholy for what remained of the day.

Back in Avignon before midday, I hired a much more agile conveyance and paid its driver well to take me out into the surrounding countryside. We headed into watery Vaucluse—I had to insist, and come up with more coin; I had also to suffer the constant sighing of my driver, whom I did not like, and who opined at one point that what I needed was not a driver but a gondolier.

Eventually we achieved higher ground, and I saw about me the famed landscape of Provence. It was odd to have risen from the sodden, if not flooded lowlands to this arid landscape, lacking the tall trees and hedgerows I'd known all my life. Here there bloomed only heath and scattered, scented shrubs, an occasional stand of cypress in the distance; and everything, including the almost painfully stunted, gnarled olive trees seemed to hunker low to the ground, as if crouched in fear of the sun or the sea or the coming mistral. Everywhere there rose up huge outcroppings of rock.

I had the driver stop and I stepped down from the two-wheeled rig that, behind a horse of suspect fitness, had carried me up, up to higher and drier ground. The driver seemed content to sit back, tip his hat against the lemony light of early afternoon, and wait for sleep to overtake him, which I've no doubt it quickly did. As for the old nag, well, it seemed a kindness on my part to let it stand still—and I hoped it would be standing, *still*, upon my return. I walked off, intent on exploring a bit on foot.

I walked in my new and ruined boots, soaked through, the drying mud like cake on the leather, over the uneven terrain, the gray-green slopes of stone and shrub.

I finally found myself in a sort of hollow, a sun-flooded dale. I sat beneath an olive tree, the branches fanning just overhead, and removed my boots. I lay back and listened to the silence, which ceded first to the close hum of bees and then, farther off, the whistling of an unseen shepherd and the bleating of his sheep. What a sweet lullaby it seemed.

And, nestled in a hillside hollow in Provence, on a late summer afternoon, recumbent under the shade-giving branches of an ancient olive tree, I wanted to sleep—for neither the night with Arlesienne nor the whole way south had been restful—but I could not. I did, however, lose myself, in thought if not sleep. I took to staring at one particular white rock, larger than those around it, one side of which seemed sculpted by wind, by rain, by sun, and by Time, and my thoughts soon veered off in a particular direction.

That rock reminded me of something I'd seen. A church. A church quickly visited, somewhere, as I'd made my way confusedly south. I'm almost, *almost* certain that it was the cathedral at Bourges that came to mind; I cannot swear to it. I was suffering a *confusion* of cathedrals. What I remembered then, on that hillside, the scents of thyme and rosemary released by the bruising hooves of those distant sheep, was this:

A tympanum I'd seen at a certain cathedral—I'd stood under it for some time, staring up at its arched, sculpted surface where it spread over the cathedral doors. I stood staring up as tourists and pilgrims and the everyday faithful of that city—again, I *think* it was Bourges; but it may have been Tours, where Madeleine startled me so—the faithful moved around me, into and out of the cathedral through three huge sets of wooden doors. I stood as still as those statues nestled into niches carved along the cathedral's inner walls. It struck me, that particular frieze.

Yes, I'd stood staring up a long while at that sculpted work—but only days later, hillside in Provence, the next moon the *new* moon . . . only then did I *understand* what it was I'd seen carved into that pale stone.

What I saw—as clearly as a stain spreading over that whiteness, rising up as sure as the river water—was a tympanum as wide as the outstretched arms of five men; at its arched center it stood as tall as two men. It depicted, simply, the battle for a single soul. But in its art there lay much, much more.

In my memory there are three bands of imagery: a center strip across the whole depicts a stern Christ with outstretched arms standing in Judgment; above Him an angel band whirls about; beneath Him, in a roiling mass, writhe the faithless and demonic.

The angels were winged, with sweet human faces. The lower band of the tympanum was crowded with men and beasts of the medievalists—indeed, most of the beings depicted were horrible hybrids, contorting in the flames to which the Judge of the Quick and the Dead had recently condemned them. (The sculpture seems a thing alive to me now, not static at all.) Among the damned I could discern representatives of the "faithless" races of man: Hebrews, Cappadocians, Arabs, Indians, Phrygians, Byzantines, Armenians, Scythians, Romans . . . all of them in stereotypical dress, and so easily identified. (There were others I did not know, of course.) Of greater interest, though, were the carved inhabitants of the medievals' imagined, *lower* worlds, their greater damnation evident in their consignment to the region beneath the faithless men, beneath the rings of flame. Here were centaurs: men to the navel, at which point they devolve into asses; Scylla, or women marked by the features of wolves, of she-bears, of dolphins; single-legged men all covered in hair; Cyclopses; Pygmies; men without mouths; headless beings with eyes on either shoulder and mouths atop their hearts; women with cows' tails and cloven feet and lips at the tips of their breasts. But what interested me most was the middle panel, the one wherein Christ was depicted at work, in Judgment.

On either side of the standing Christ—his arms outstretched, as though He *casts* souls this way and that—there were ranged three angels, each holding an instrument of the Passion. It was the angel nearest Christ who held a scale, lest the dim among the Faithful not understand the scene depicted. In powdery, cloud-like plumes, undetailed, the "good" were seen ascending en masse, a single swirling soul. Others descended into tall flames. But there, there at the center of the scene, kneeling between Christ and the angel holding the scale—...yes, there knelt a girl, her hands folded contritely, as if to attest to her powerlessness. Her face was beautiful, though without expression. It was clear: she awaited Judgment. And from behind Christ's stony robe there peered a lesser devil—horned head, hooked nose, with one hairy goat's leg creeping forth—intent on securing the girl's soul for Satan.

That was the moment depicted in stone: the Judgment. How much of that scene exists, in Bourges, in Tours, or elsewhere, and how much of it I imagined I cannot say. And again, as the elementals would say, that is not what matters....What seemed to me strange—I thought so then, and I think so now—is that the soul awaiting Judgment was that of a girl, not a man, not even a woman, but a *girl*. A girl knelt at the center of the world's oldest struggle. A girl like Madeleine.

There came over me then a feeling of...Well, how to describe what it was I felt as I sat suddenly upright—pricking my scalp on a branch of the olive tree—on that barren hill, hidden from the world in a hollow, the afternoon sun shafting down so golden, so pure on that great white rock? Dare I call it a revelation?

And so imagine what it was I felt that afternoon when suddenly I understood that come nightfall I was to be a player, an actor on the stage of the world, indeed in a drama that, to be simple, had only ever featured God and the Devil. I was to enter the great fray, to work the Craft among the forces of...call them what you will....Good and Evil, Chaos and Order. I was to do this! *Me!*

My pulse quickened. My eyes teared. I was conscious of the smile spreading over my face. And I heard in my head Sebastiana's words, written, in despair, at the end of her account of the Greek Supper. But I heard those words in a voice marked not by sadness, not by regret; what I heard then, in my Sister's voice, was an affirmation, words *triumphant*: "We are not insignificant. Though we may be peripheral, we are *not* insignificant."

Those words seemed to me a battle cry.

I ran back to that hired cab, tripping lightly over the rough terrain, boots in hand, as though I'd lived upon it all my life. I leapt rock to rock, stopping only to pick what seemed to me to be ripened olives. And *oh* that taste! I'd never eaten an olive off the vine before, and at first I nearly spat it out, so oily and bitter and sharp . . . But then the taste came around, and it seemed I . . . I *tasted* the very sun and the white rocks and the rough and low-growing herbs, redolent of salt and sea and. . . . *Enfin*, it seemed I tasted the world entire! Olives will always bring back that moment for me; they will be for me, always, the taste of joy. And it *was* joy I felt. Joy at knowing, at *believing* for the first time that I had a role in the world. Perhaps not clearly defined, not yet; and perhaps it will never be clearly defined, but I had a role to play. No one would ever tell me differently. (They will *not*.) . . . Oh yes, the world was mine, and I'd move differently through it regardless of what might happen that night under the new moon.

I snuck up on the sleeping driver, thinking should I . . . *Yes*, I should! I shouted in his ear and roughly shook his shoulder. He woke with a start to the sound of my laughter, full and unrestrained—had I *ever* laughed like that before? My laughter, *yes*, which resounded on that hill, ricocheted rock to rock, rolled over that rough landscape, overwhelming the silence, overwhelming the buzzing bees and the bleating sheep and the whistling shepherd.

It seems I hear it still, that laughter.

40

Gravedigger

THE DRIVER WAS a bit put off by me, by my having so woken him from his idyllic slumber. What did I care? I laughed full in his face. If he thought himself in the company of a lunatic, well, he would have been more right than he knew, for indeed I was crazed by the coming of the moon, still some hours off. Oh yes, I was *eager* for the new moon to rise, *eager* to work the Craft beneath it at the crossroads. A lunatic, indeed!

I directed the driver to hurry back to the inn in Avignon. As he was as eager to be rid of me as I was to achieve the city, we made excellent time. The sun had begun its descent: that ancient place seemed gold-cast . . . no, *candied*: awash in butterscotch and honey; with the river and the sun and the still air conspiring to set the scene to shimmering, as if beneath a rain of grated citrus rind and crystallized sugar.

I returned to my room, taking the stairs two at a time. I thought only of the brass bell. I wanted to ring it, wanted to summon the elementals.

And so I was at first surprised and then disappointed to discover a slip of paper under that bell, just where I'd left it on the sill. The heavy sheet was folded into quarters and in the instant it took to unfold it I thought back to that page I'd received from Madeleine at Ravndal, upon which she'd pled in blood, having dipped her pen in the font of her throat, *Help me.*

No blood this time. The words on the paper were in black ink, and it was a script I'd not seen before, excessively cursive, ornate. It was the hand of Father Louis: I knew this instantly, before I'd read a single word or trailed the train of words to its end in search of the nonexistent signature.

The note showed a sketched map, and cursory directions. It told what I was to do in the hours of the early evening. And it directed me to the crossroads, where the elementals would meet me at midnight.

I was not happy to read what else I read. Not at all.

For the note stated plainly that I was to enter a small cemetery near the papal palace, spade in hand, and there fill two burlap bags (which I found conveniently laid across my bed) with consecrated dirt dug from the freshest grave. *Mon Dieu!* It's too much! Add grave robber to the ever-lengthening list of what I was. *You are a man. You are a woman. You are a witch. . . . You are a ghoul digging dirt in the dark from atop the dead! . . .* No, I wasn't happy about this directive, not happy at all. But what was I to do?

The note went on: I was to pile the bags of dirt into the berlin and drive it—by myself, mind you, *sans* Étienne—to the crossroads, as marked on the map. Fortunately, my day's excursion had familiarized me a bit with the land beyond Avignon, and so I had a rough idea of where I was to go. (The crossroads—I cannot give the exact location—lay beyond Les Baux, north of Arles, amid the hills of the Alpilles.) Given the unknown roads and the darkness and the great weight of the berlin, which I'd have to drive slowly over the narrow and often steep roads, I'd leave myself two hours of traveling time. That seemed sufficient. Figuring back from midnight, I calculated that I'd a great deal to do in the coming hours. Night cover was needed. And, blessedly, a dark night it would be, for a new moon—aligned as it is with the sun— shows the earth its dark side.

And so there it was: the plan. Or the first part of it. I had my objections, yes, but it seemed to me simple enough. I had some questions too, primarily: why, if we were to disinter what remained of the mortal Madeleine, did I need to harvest two bags of blessed earth? I'd have an answer in time.

I got a bowl of stew from the innkeeper's son—no friendlier than she—
and returned with it to my room. I sat eating in silence. I felt so still, so
strangely still; at once eager and calm. I listened to the occasional comings and
goings of my fellow travelers, even eavesdropped at my door. I paced the room,
looking out my window on occasion to see people standing on the banks of
the river, gauging its level. A cart went slowly by beneath my window, laden
with sandbags. Children darted about like birds, excited by the occasion. For
them the flood was but a welcome break in the routine of their lives.

I sat on the edge of the bed. I was tired but sleep seemed out of the question. I banged the heels of my boots against the hearth, and let the loosened
mud fall into the fire. I located some playing cards and cheated terribly at soli-
taire. In short, I did this and that, waiting for the hour of action. And darkness. I waited for the moonrise, which finally did come to the accompaniment
of my own drumming heart. I thought often of the uncertain night to come,
the days to come, and then finally decided to sleep and chance the freight of
dreams; certainly, the thoughts conjured by my *conscious* mind were none too
pleasant. . . . But I could not sleep. I tossed and turned till the woolen blanket
was twisted around me.

All through those interminable hours, attendant upon the dark, I tried
without success to chase from my mind images of graves and splintered coffins
and putrid flesh; images of sea travel and sickness, red weather, and the salted
company of sailors—would they know what I was? *Who* I was? I fended off
thoughts of my coming life alone in a new land, homeless, friendless, struggling to speak a language not my own. I held to the promise of seeing Sebastiana again, for wasn't it said that a new witch had to host her Mystic Sister?
Surely Sebastiana would sail behind me, someday. But this happiness faded fast
as my thoughts turned to those witches I'd yet to meet, the coven I'd need to
convene—would it be a band frightful enough to scare the sisters present at
the Greek Supper? My thoughts grew dark as the night. . . . But I do not deign
to catalog such thoughts, for now—with that new land but a few hours off!—
they come again to taunt and tease me! It seems unwise to grant them stronger
shape through description. . . . But in truth—then as now—such thoughts
were, *are*, but the manifest flames of my fired excitement.

Finally, darkness. I gathered up all my things and quit the inn.

I easily found the berlin. I'd directed Étienne—who, presumably, was having his fun in Avignon: I'd not seen him since our arrival—I'd directed him to
park it on the darkest and least populous street he could find. He'd left a note
with the innkeeper, and she directed me to the street he named. He'd done a

good job with the team, too; I found them hayed and watered, and already hitched.

Rounding the corner of the street in question, there sat the berlin. Instantly, my cheeks flushed with embarrassment. Impossibly, it seemed even larger and more ornate. Two old women and a young man stood beside it, shining a lantern on its gilded and painted surfaces, wiping away the obscuring mud, climbing up to look in its windows; thankfully, Étienne had drawn all the shades, as directed. And then—quite cheeky, she was!—the heavier of the two women tried the door latch, first looking this way and that. It was locked, of course. (The key—or so I hoped—lay atop the back right wheel.) How I wanted then to scare that impudent cow like a sister of yore, send some vision to her, cause the door handle to come off in her hand as a length of bone or a writhing snake . . . (Someday, perhaps, I'll have greater facility with such spells.) Finally, the brazen bitch hopped thuddingly down from the runner, and the inquisitive trio tripped away. And I approached the berlin to the anxious snorts, the muffled welcome of my team.

I saw that the *necessaire* was still secure, strapped to the back of the berlin. Pity someone hadn't broken into *it*, relieved me of the remaining costumery I'd never wear, spare me the guilt I'd feel in ridding myself of those clothes. But then again I was fast filling the *necessaire* with books, books that I would not want to lose. (Only days later, at sea, would I realize just what treasures I'd left in that *necessaire*—secured only by a few worn-leather straps—there on that dark street.)

I sat in the berlin for some time, doors latched and shades drawn, but I cannot now account for a single moment of that time, tangled as I was in a skein of worries. I'd easily secured a spade, and I had the burlap bags. I'd changed into clothing suitably dark for grave robbing, or so it seemed to me; over this ensemble I wore a many-pocketed wagoner's coat, "borrowed" off a hook at the inn.

Finally, I forced myself from the confines of the cab to steal in the direction of the small cemetery, tools in hand. I slid from shadow to shadow, avoiding the light of posted torches as well as that which issued from the windows of the homes past which I practically *crawled*, so fearful was I of encountering someone curious, or worse, friendly. Eventually, I reached my goal—or so said the markings on the map—but there was no cemetery. *No cemetery!* I scanned the simple map again, and twice more. I turned it this way and that, turned *myself* this way and that till I was certain of my location. Yes, this is where it *should* be, I reasoned, but there *was* no cemetery! In fact, there was nothing at all.

The map had led me to the side door of a dilapidated cottage, dark as pitch and seemingly abandoned; and though there may well have been bodies buried in *its* yard, I doubted they lay in consecrated earth.

Not knowing what to do, I wandered a bit, keeping always to the deepest shadows. Imagine my relief when I stumbled upon, literally, a low fence of wrought iron that bounded a small yard *behind* said house—a cemetery! Or so said the tiny sign on its gate: actually, dark as it was, and not yet daring to light a lantern, I read the sign's raised cross with my fingers. I could not see very far into this yard. The sign said cemetery, or rather it bore a cross; but I was uncertain. It might have been a vegetable garden or a flower bed or a pitch for boules! I stepped over the low fence, cursing the priest when the wagoner's coat snagged a jagged upright. Then I saw the telltale signs: dull white tombstones poked crookedly up from the earth at all angles, like rows of rotted teeth. The cemetery was not more than forty paces wide, twenty deep. I worried that it was not the one I'd been directed to, but then I thought, What of it? This dirt is as consecrated as any other, no? Was that not a cross on the gate? I must say that there was planted in my mind, then, a seed of thought that soon sprouted terribly: what if this was *not* consecrated earth, and what if, for that reason, our work at the crossroads failed? I put such worries out of mind as best I could, and I took up the silver-headed spade.

I drew from a pocket of the coat—an inspired idea, stealing . . . no *borrowing* that coat—a single white taper, thick as my wrist, and lit it with some phosphorous matches. By its light I went grave to grave, crouching to read the dates, for I'd been directed to dig dirt from a *fresh* grave.

The dates! *Mon Dieu!* Ages past. Here lie Avignon's ancient dead, many of whom shared their year of demise. Cholera, no doubt. Or invading armies. What to do? What to do? I stepped from rough, clotted grass to dirt, and looking down, kneeling down, I saw what seemed a recently dug grave, for it showed no grass at all. The headstone was as yet uncarved, and free of lichen or moss; this eased me somewhat as I drove the spade down into the mounded dirt. I directed myself to dig. I was due at the crossroads by midnight. So dig I did, filling both bags with the worm-writhing soil. Begging pardon of its resident, I leveled the grave as best I could.

I tied the two bags together with a length of rope—I'm embarrassed now to say that I'd foreseen *every* possible need, and that the pockets of the coat were chock full of rope and a hundred such sundries. I slung the bags over my shoulders, so that one hung before me and the other behind. I held the spade too, assuming I'd need it again at the crossroads. Snuffing the taper between two spit-wet fingertips—the same fingers with which I then sketched the sign of the cross on the air—I stole from the cemetery the way I'd come. I made my way back to the berlin and hurled the burlap bags into it. A clock tower of the town showed I'd less than two hours in which to make my way from Avignon to the crossroads.

Soon I was on the road south, headed toward Les Baux.

Now it was time to worry about the floodwaters. What if they rendered the roads impassable? What if...? But I soon saw that the road I was to take out of Avignon *ascended* toward Les Baux, and so it seemed to me safe. In fact, the road leading to Les Baux winds around the foot of the hills atop which that city sits, the whole rocky ruin of it seemingly ready to slip from the summit to which it clings. The road then passes into a sort of valley, from which the approach up to the city proper is easily made, even by a carriage as large as ours.

In a day now centuries-past, Les Baux had been a great city. Indeed, more than a city: an empire. Then, the islanders of Sardinia and those nearer still—in Arles, in Marseilles—paid homage to the lords of Les Baux. These men, feudal proprietors all, never more than several hundred in number, and lords of fewer than five thousand subjects, were seneschals and captains-general of Piedmont, of Lombardy, and grand admirals of the kingdom of Naples; their daughters were coveted by the first princes of Europe.

But *that* was a long time ago.

How it all fell to ruin I've no idea. Doubtless the Revolution took its toll on whatever remained of the place years ago; but the fall of so great a place I cannot explain, can only date to the middle years of the seventeenth century (this according to Father Louis, who told me that much and no more later that night. "No questions now," said he. "The hour has come." As indeed it had). But I did learn this: Father Louis and Madeleine had lived and died in another city that sat at no great distance from Les Baux and is now so changed, so consumed by ruin as to be unrecognizable. On that place the mighty sculptor Time has had his way. What was once a city is now but a shade on the Map of Ages; it is not marked on the maps of our time. Neither will I locate it precisely here, other than to say again that it sits, or *sat* in a valley south of Les Baux and north of Arles.

As I rode up into Les Baux that night I saw few signs of its former glory. I saw, by the lights of my outer lanterns, the stony shells of its houses, and walls that rose and fell like stilled waves. There was what appeared to be the foundation of a castle, on a sort of promontory, and in my mind's eye the castle walls rose up gloriously and I could see their very windows and the sills on which prized ladies and honored men had once leaned, taking in the view of a world that belonged to them, or so it must have seemed. The streets were rough, narrow, and precipitous, and so my progress in the berlin was slow. This suited me. I wanted to see what I could, but I hadn't the time to explore on foot: according to the map, I still had to turn here, turn there, descending first into one valley and then another, deep within which lay Madeleine's grave.

And so, I drove slowly past what remained of Les Baux—a few houses still standing, empty, absent of doors, their unshuttered windows gaping like the mouths of the dumb. It was . . . *morbid,* and only heightened that melancholia that seems my lot. So I was glad when, at the first sign of the road's descent, the berlin sped up a bit beneath its own weight.

41

At the Crossroads

By MIDNIGHT I was where I needed to be: at the southernmost edge of that valley beyond Les Baux, beyond the fallen walls of a ruined city I cannot name, at the confluence of not two roads (as I'd imagined) but three. The crossroads.

But where was the grave? *How would I find the grave?* Wild lilac overgrew the whole, and the air was sweet from the gorse that would have shone like gold under the sun; yes, though it was dark and I saw no true colors, I will always envision that crossroads as a place of purple and gold. My question regarding the grave was soon answered.

Beside the road that headed due south there'd recently been cleared a rectangle of ground. Shaped as it was, even in that faint, faint moonlight, less strong than the lantern's light, the clearing would have put anyone in mind of a grave, a coffin.

The horses were restless, agitated; I worried that they'd rear, and I was *not* prepared to deal with anything out of the ordinary as far as the horses were concerned. I stopped the berlin. I came down from the driver's box to feed the horses what scraps of carrot and radish I'd stuffed in a pocket of the wagoner's coat; this seemed to distract, if not calm them. I walked away from the horses backward; I wonder if I was wary of them, or wary of approaching the grave head-on.

Standing over it, I saw that low tangles of catbrier and heath had been cleared from the site, and the top layer of sandy soil had been turned, as if by hand. At the head of the grave lay a small crucifix of white stone, or stone that had once been white but was now pocked and filthy, its marble edges friable. Had it been upright—which it purposefully was not—it would have stood no higher than my shin; it bore no inscription. From long habit, I crossed myself.

I felt then a strange admixture of anger and hope, of eagerness, of Crusader-like righteousness coupled with a "vengeance-that-would-be-ours." I felt a burgeoning strength. I would return to the berlin and retrieve the spade and the consecrated soil and begin to— But I stopped and stood stock-still when I saw the elementals across that narrow road, beside the berlin. They shone far brighter than the light of the moon allowed; I cannot account for that. (At sea I have seen patches of phosphorescence caused by sea creatures that emit a light all their own; perhaps that is akin to what the watery elementals did that night, I don't know.) . . . Let me add that I've no idea what I would have done if I'd taken up that soil and spade, if I'd started to dig without direction. I shudder to think what I might have uncovered on my own, for what Father Louis and I unearthed was frightful enough.

Oddly, when first I saw the elementals, I looked up to the sky. I opened my hands and tilted my face, as one does when expecting rain. I gauged the wind. I listened for the oncoming storm I had expected. But all was still. Still as death. I hoped then that Madeleine had laid the river down, calmed it, if in fact it was she, was *they* who, intentionally or not, had hastened its rising.

We stood across the road from one another for a long while. The elementals stood hand in hand, their shapes quite strong and, yes, eerily bright— moon-fed, it seemed. The priest wore his standard black; his white collar showed silver in the light. Madeleine wore her cerecloth rags, and though I'd long seen her in them, only then did I understand that such were the gummed, waxen remains of the dress she'd worn when interred.

I realized, then, that I'd never seen the elementals touch each other. I'd assumed that they could not; this, I know, is illogical, for certainly they'd touched me. But there they stood, joined in an almost child-like innocence. They seemed as eager as I; scared and saddened too. Clearly, their thoughts were one, for together they said:

You've come. Their conjoined voice laid open the silence, split it like a blade.

"I have," said I.

Thank you.

"Do you have the . . . the Church's earth?" Father Louis seemed angered at having to ask the question. He was not angry at me, I knew; rather he resented needing that earth, resented the strength resident in the consecrated soil.

"I do." I pointed to the cab behind them, where the two bags lay.

"Good," said the priest. "Get it."

Please, added Madeleine, with a smile and a tug at the priest's hand.

"Please," repeated the priest. "You've done well, witch, to get the dirt and drive it here. I thank you." He looked at Madeleine. "We *both* thank you."

Soon we all three of us stood graveside, staring down. I held the spade. The bags lay at either end of the grave. No one spoke. I heard the distant barking of wild dogs; thankfully, it remained distant. I heard too the cry of the raven, much nearer, and from it I took both confidence and comfort.

Finally, directed to do so, I set to digging.

The earth was dry and light, sandy. This valley had escaped the floodwaters. It occurred to me that I'd not passed any river on the way to the crossroads, neither a lake nor a stream. So how was it that the elementals held such strong shapes, strong enough for them to stand graveside, hand in hand? I cannot say. They, no doubt, would attribute it to the strength of the will, and perhaps that is the truest answer. I think too that the moon played its part, and that it . . . Ah, but I must be careful here—witches, I have read, too easily attribute all strangeness to the moon. I revert to what it was I first heard at C——: *There exists the inexplicable.*

I worked fast. Soon the shallow grave lay open. I stood in it up to the knee. Mounds of rock-laden earth lay graveside. When suddenly I felt the spade strike and splinter the rotted wood of a casket, I stopped. I lowered the lantern into the grave. A casket. I looked up at—

Continue, said Madeleine. The priest nodded down to me.

I laid bare the whole coffin, digging the sandy soil from around its four sides. With a rag—actually, it was a blouse drawn from the *necessaire* earlier that night, when first I'd dirtied my hands digging in the cemetery—I wiped the dirt from atop the casket. The wood was rotted, yes, but intact and fairly smooth to the touch. The tapered shape of the casket betrayed the body's positioning within it, and so I stood looking down at where the head would be, half-expecting the casket to open of its own accord, some *other* Madeleine pushing up from within. But there'd be no surprises, no tricks; I knew this when I looked up at the elementals and saw that they were . . . what is the word: scared, awed, expectant? . . . As for me, well, I was all that and more.

Time passed. Moments—minutes, perhaps—in which I cleaned the coffin off, swept away the sand, the dirt that lay deeper down, the pebbles, and . . . And what we all knew, but no one said, was that the coffin did not *need* to be cleaned; but we were all of us hesitant to . . .

"Will you open it, witch?" asked the priest, deferentially; some odd table had turned and the elementals were reliant on me now, to do *what* I'd no idea. No idea at all.

I sat on the edge of the grave, digging the soft sandy dirt from the coffin with my bare hands. And before I *understood* my actions, I'd curled my fingers under the casket's lid and lifted. Expecting some resistance—nails, or pegs, or even rusted hinges—I perhaps pulled too hard; there was no resistance at all, and I nearly toppled back before hearing the priest:

"*No!*" It was a hiss, urgent. "No! Not yet! The bags . . ." he began, and I quickly replaced the lid. Rather I let fall the lid, and it settled into place as if it had not been disturbed. I'd seen nothing inside the casket, but a cold, fetid scent had escaped it, and from this I turned away.

The priest was pointing at the burlap bags, one at either end of the grave. "First have the bags open and ready!" he commanded.

I opened one bag and then the other, folding down the rough rims of each. I remember well the contrast of the two soils: the Church's earth dark and rich as ground coffee, and the lighter soil of the crossroads like browned sugar.

What happened next is a bit confused in my mind though it happened but days ago. I was at once participant and observer.

Father Louis produced a book, a book like the Bible but not; that is, it looked like a Bible and had about it that book's weighty aspect, but it was not the Bible. Just what it was I don't know, I cannot say. He handed it down to me where I sat on the grave's edge. It fell open across my two hands. Did I see the passage marked? I did, I said. I was to begin reading that passage backward, bottom to top, right to left, word by word, aloud; and when I'd read it through once, I was to begin again. While reading it I was to hold my right hand high, raised to the new moon; my fingers, he said, were to remain splayed. (This he stressed.) I was to read till he told me to stop, stringing those words—it was

Latin, of course—stringing them one by one onto a nonsensical chain. I cannot say what it was I read that night; nor could I cull the slightest sense from the recitation as I spoke it. They were merely, simply, purely words. All I can say for certain is that had they been read as written—that is, forward—they would have constituted some rite of the Roman Church. As I read them—widdershins—they were *mere* words, as I say; but words which worked themselves somehow into a spell. And oh, what I was to witness when that spell—

... It was Father Louis who opened the casket, slowly, the second time. The wood gave with a sound like breaking ice. All the while I read. Reading like that—in Latin, backward, keeping my right hand open to the moon—well, need I say that it took some doing, and fierce concentration? Thus occupied, I did not see the contents of the casket when first they were revealed. Neither did I see that event that happened simultaneously, or so I think: the succubus's disappearance, her fast descent into her mortal grave.

When finally I stole a glance down into the casket what I saw was this:

There lay a leathery corpse clad in those familiar rags. Its face was featureless. Its positioning in the narrow box of pine is best described as fetal: curled on its left side, its knees drawn up, its head bent down. ... It was not what I expected to see. I'd expected to see one of two things: Madeleine as I knew her, or an unrecognizable pile of bones—a common skeleton. What I saw was neither one nor the other; it was ... it was both. As I sat graveside, reading that rite, trying too to see into the casket ... I *saw* that the corpse was no longer a corpse! What had been dead when uncovered was now animate.

Madeleine, the Madeleine I knew, had somehow descended to claim her remains. Had I peered into the casket when first Father Louis had opened it, I believe I would have seen the simple remains of a mortal. Dust. Bones. Perhaps better preserved than most. But by the time I saw her, *it*, there in the grave, Madeleine had already begun the reclamation. What I witnessed, glancing back again and again to the page from which I read, was the full reclamation of her remains. The remains—that mortal mass of time-darkened skin stretched tautly over bone—became, once again, Madeleine. The *living*—or so it seemed—Madeleine de la Mettrie. It remained so for but a short while. A very short while.

I saw the leathery skin grow supple, saw the desiccated flesh fill out, saw bones reattach themselves at the joints. The skin regained its mortal hue. The hair and the nails began to ... to grow, to verily *flow* from the body at a rate unknown to mortals. And then ... then I saw the neck, which moments earlier had been but a notched bone, turn. Madeleine's profile ceded, slowly, to the whole of her face, and she lay staring up at the priest. I *saw* this! Was witness to it! I remember the last word of the spell I spoke—*Dominus*—before I saw Madeleine's eyelids open and there—so horribly!—was the viscid gel that then congealed into eyes, beautiful brown eyes. With those eyes Madeleine smiled, smiled at Father Louis a long while.

Looking up at the priest, I saw tears slide from his eyes, tears that iced on his cheeks as he struggled through rites of his own. He had a silver flacon of oil; with it he wet his thumb and, in a stunted wave, set to crossing and recrossing the air over the grave, all the while reciting the *Misereatur* and the *Indulgentiam*. Extreme unction, it was, said for her salvation. "... help you with the Grace of the Holy Spirit; and may the Lord who frees you from sin save you and raise you up."

Madeleine's reclamation was complete when I saw the corpse's hideously long nails, curled like the claws of an animal, rescind; and her hair, which had grown into a black tangle, shrink back to the length it had been, presumably, when she died; ... but not before Father Louis reached down and claimed a fistful of hair and two, perhaps three whole nails, which came from the fingers easily. And there she lay, flat on her back, looking much as she'd looked the day of her death, beautiful but for the torn-away throat.

Father Louis now busied himself with a rite of a different sort. I saw him take from the folds of his shift a cast-iron kettle, ovoid, not much longer than his hand; and in it he placed the tangled hair, the slivers of nail, and the rest of the oil from his silver flacon. He muttered all the while, and the only words I distinguished were these: *lavende et miel*—lavender and honey—which he then added to the kettle, and, holding it tightly, he ... he caused the kettle to heat—I cannot say how—till finally steam hissed from a hole in its top.

Still I read on. It might have been the tenth, the twentieth time I read that passage.

... That state to which Madeleine had aspired for centuries was short-lived. Her beauty began to turn, and putrefaction began.

"Quickly!" said the priest. "Quickly, now!" Not knowing what it was he meant me to do, I could only mimic his actions. He dragged one of the bags nearer Madeleine's head; I dragged the other to the end of the casket. I resumed reading, but with a wave of his hand the priest stopped me. "It's done," he said. The spell had been cast. Or perhaps the Church's spell had been broken. ... The priest said nothing. His eyes were trained on Madeleine, who turned from life to death's processes. Again, all I could do was follow the priest: so I took up fistfuls of dirt and I too dropped them into the grave, onto

Madeleine where she lay, *alive*, still, the slightest smile discernible on her face and in her wide open eyes.

"The right hand only," said Father Louis to me. "Use your *right* hand, the moon-blessed hand only! Push it down into the dirt as a fist," he said, "open it in the dirt and close it again; draw it up and scatter the dirt, scatter it over . . . over her. . . . Take care, witch, to do it the same, *exactly* the same each time." He, I noticed, did not do it this way: he used two hands and worked hurriedly, sloppily, covering the upper body of the succubus as fast as he could. But I did as I was told.

Though the priest slowed, I kept the pace he'd set. Twenty, thirty, forty times I dipped my fist into the dirt, drew it up to scatter it over the body of the . . . the girl, the succubus, over the spirit, the eudemon . . . over Madeleine. My hand ached. Neither I nor the incubus spoke. I wonder, could Madeleine have spoken? I believe that yes, she could have. I believe she did *not* speak because there were no words but good-bye; and *that* she did not wish to say.

In time we'd emptied the two bags. It seemed too that I'd done all that was expected of me as regarded the moon and the reverse-ritual. Soon I *knew* I'd done my duty. Freed from action, I was a simple witness to what happened then.

Seeing that Father Louis had nearly emptied his bag, I'd hurried to empty mine, careful to work with only my "moon-blessed" hand. Madeleine, still well-fleshed, still full, was coated in consecrated soil. All through this bewitched burial, I focused my efforts on Madeleine's lower half: I scattered my bag of earth over her feet and legs, over her lower body. In this I was fortunate for I could never have done what Father Louis had then to do: scatter the consecrated earth over Madeleine's wide-eyed stare and beatific smile. She did not blink as the dirt fell onto her face. I very nearly turned from this, for her *welcoming* of the dirt disturbed me. But it was then Father Louis finally spoke his good-bye: "*Sit tibi terra levis,* my Madeleine." He said it again and again, said it each time he lowered a fistful of the Church's earth onto her face. *May this earth lie lightly upon you.* Again and again he said it. *May this earth lie lightly upon you.*

Finally, Madeleine lay covered in consecrated earth. I thought then that it was over. I thought we'd replace the casket's lid, perhaps read a second rite, utter some inconceivable good-bye. But no.

How to describe what I witnessed then? See, I haven't much time, for above me I hear trunks being dragged to and fro, the captain is shouting orders, and all is being readied for our entrance into the harbor, not an hour from now.

(Richmond is our port. Richmond, in the state of Virginia.) . . . So then: ordinary words to take us to the extraordinary end of this tale:

I saw Madeleine move beneath her blanket of earth. While we'd scattered the consecrated earth over her she'd stared unblinkingly up at us—at the priest, really—and she'd not moved other than to turn from that fetal position. She lay prone and perfectly still while we worked. But now it seemed she was . . . yes, she was returning to that fetal curl. Slowly, and with absolute grace . . . like the coursing of water, the easy rise of fire, a breath of wind . . . And there she lay: curled like a nascent being in the womb. It was then I knew we'd succeeded. And as that position speaks so eloquently of immortality, I could not help but wonder if Madeleine would return to live in another shape. I wonder still. If she will, if she does . . . if she *lives,* I hope she does so peaceably.

If only we'd replaced the casket's lid right then, but no. . . . Instead, we sat in silence on either side of the grave. Finally, the priest reached down to take up Madeleine's hand; her right hand, for she faced him, curled on her left side. I was surprised to see him withdraw his hand so suddenly, but surprise ceded to revulsion when I saw that he'd not withdrawn his hand at all. Rather, Madeleine's arm had fallen from her shoulder, and the hand had fallen from the wrist. Father Louis sat holding the succubus's hand in his, cupping it, for the hand had fast broken into a hundred tiny bones.

It was then I saw Madeleine's hair grow fuller, too full; soon it was the dark and writhing mass we'd first unearthed. Strands of hair turned with the worms in the soil, nearly obscuring Madeleine's face; and would that the hair *had* obscured that once-beautiful face, now thinning fast, for what I saw. . . . I'll say it fast and straight: I saw the pearlescent jelly of her eyes run from their sockets and dribble down over her face, the brown irises like broken yolks. The downflow of the right eye took with it the flesh of the nose; there remained then but a jagged socket in the skull. The cheeks and the lips fell away. The nails of the toes grew too, fast as the hair; they seemed like silver-blue shards of moon, growing backward into the soft flesh of the foot till that too fell away.

Flesh. And bone. Flesh and bone.

Yes, beneath that thin coat of consecrated earth I saw Madeleine's flesh putrefy and fall like stewed meat from the bone. Her breasts slid from her chest. Then fell the flanks of her thighs. She collapsed, right side onto left; it seemed the curled corpse settled again and again, shifted over the scraps of scarlet satin that remained to line the coffin. The ribs broke from their barrel-like curve. As for her innards? They devolved to ash, ash just barely discernible from the dark earth of the Church. Blood? There was none.

Madeleine was no more. Father Louis spilled the cup of his hands: the bones of Madeleine's hand fell into the dark dirt whitely, like stars; and then the priest cradled his crying face in hands dark with ash. I reached to his cold, shuddering shoulder and sought words that might comfort him. None came. But soon he lifted his face to me; as he licked the ash from his lips they curved into a smile that seemed at first perverse, and then, somehow, complete. Yes, complete. It was then he took up a pinch of tear-heavy ash, took it up between forefinger and thumb, and, wordlessly, let it fall into the tiny kettle at his side, whispering of the river Lethe in Hades, on whose waters one sailed toward Oblivion.

What had I done? I sat back, graveside. *What had I done?* I fairly folded in two, cradling my face in my filthy hands. Tears fell and turned to mud. *What had I done?* I must have asked the question aloud, for Father Louis offered this in response: "You drew down the moon. You worked the Craft as only a new witch can. For this, I thank you. *We* thank you." Then the priest said he needed my help still.

He raised high the kettle. Its dull iron shone beneath the starlight, the meager moonlight. "Take this," he said; and I did. It was warm, quite warm, though the hands from which it came were as cold as ever. Though I knew the hideous stew he'd made in it, from the kettle there came the sweetest aroma, and so I did not hesitate . . . rather I did not hesitate overlong when he directed me to drink its contents, saying, "I take her from my Church, and I give her over to the Church within you." . . . And while the incubus wept I drank down the mix, which was inexplicably soothing and smooth. "Contain her for all time," came the priest's choked words, "contain her as I could not."

Father Louis moved too fast for me to follow him. When next I saw him he stood again beside the grave. Beside me he placed a round wicker basket lined with black satin; it showed a sort of cowl that could be drawn up over it by means of a black ribbon. Wordlessly, he sat beside me. He leaned forward. He smoothed the earth and ash in the coffin. Sifted it, mixed it. And then, bone by bone, he took Madeleine up from where she lay. He placed the larger bones in the basket first. And—though it seemed to me a sad perversion of a child's game, skittles or jacks—I joined him, and soon the grave was empty of all but earth and ash.

42

South to the Sea

FATHER LOUIS AND I walked from the grave. We
did not take great pains to hide it, though we did
shovel the graveside dirt back into it, of course; and I
did take pains—literally!—to rearrange the stiff and
prickly bouquet of catbrier. It was early morning, perhaps three or four hours past midnight, three or four
hours before sunrise, and what little light there was at
that hour—starlight, or the faint light of the new and
shy moon—lit the grave a ghostly blue. It was but a
slit in the surface of the earth. Walking from the
grave, I did not look back. I looked only at the berlin;
caked with mud, still it glistened in that scarce light
like some wheeled and painted pearl, or some other
impossible thing. It shone with a light all its own, as
did the incubus, still.

Father Louis ascended to the berlin's box, quick as
a cat. I entered the cab. I don't know if the priest

held to his shape up there or if he merely guided the horses and let the berlin roll on, no driver visible to any mortal we might have met on the road. As I did not see, I cannot say. But at that hour, as we drove up out of the desolate valley, it didn't seem to matter.

We did not return to Avignon, as I've said. We drove on, and by break of day we were in Arles.

Seated in the cab that early morning, I was wide awake. The silence was broken only by the horses' hooves, the turning of the berlin's wheels, and the hard song sung by the basket of shifting bones beside me. It, that basket—of dark wicker, with its black satin lining—was what a woman of fashion might have used to transport a treasured hat; and it had that cowl, that excess of satin run through with ribbon, that one could draw to close the thing up, which, of course, I'd done. I went so far as to knot the ribbon. And finally I pushed the whole thing as far from me as possible, till it sat across the cab on the opposite banquette. With each turn in the road, with each dip of this wheel or that, it moved; and the least movement caused the skull—I was *sure* it was the skull— to roll within the basket and set the whole wicker mass to shifting, lurching like a thing alive.

Ah, but it was no living thing. I sat across from it some while before coming to understand this: it was *not* Madeleine, indeed had little to do with Madeleine. It was a mere basket of bones. A simple skeleton. Or was it? I confess: I did talk to it, did address it as I would have the succubus. I did so to assuage my fears, or perhaps to check my hopes. But Madeleine was gone. I'd no idea *where* she'd gone, but I was certain she was gone from those bones. She, like a cloud, those pure formations of *things* elemental, had coalesced and clung to the blue, the Infinite Blue, only to dissipate, dissolve into that same background of blue, Oblivion.

Soon the bones no longer disturbed me. Indeed, I gathered the basket to my side, quieted its contents by holding tightly to it.

We rolled into Arles—a dusty little town graced with an extraordinary palette; which I haven't the time to describe, for I am told that we are but a few hours from port (not *one* hour, as I'd heard earlier); yes, we are closing quickly on the American continent, its eastern seaboard; and I just heard someone shout that we are already in sight of land, but I dare not look, not yet.... We rolled into Arles under a rising sun and were, presumably, unseen. As was our habit, we secreted the berlin on as secluded, as dark and quiet a street as we could find. I'd already resolved to be rid of the thing by nightfall.

Descending, with the berlin barely having rocked to a stop, I saw that

Father Louis was gone. I worried that he was gone for good, now that our "work" was done. He stopped in Arles, I assume, because he knew I had things to do there, simple errands to see to before going on to Marseilles, before setting off to sea. Perhaps he had some spectral errands of his own, I don't know. He would mourn, certainly; and though I pitied the unsuspecting women of Arles, I did not care to consider just *how* the incubus might mourn.

I walked the streets of the city as the sun rose higher. I asked five people the name of their city's best inn—ah, those slow accents of the South, the singsong elision of words!—and made my way to the place named by three of the five. I paid the innkeeper twice the standard rate for her best room, on the top floor of a whitewashed, narrow stand of stone, and for that price she evicted its present tenant, for whom I'd a fast-fading sympathy. For I was feeling . . . *grand*. Hadn't I achieved a grand aspect of the Craft, something my Soror Mystica had been unable to do? Hadn't I drawn down the moon . . . whatever that meant? Hadn't I . . . in truth, I was newly taken with myself, indeed I was not acting like *myself* at all. . . . But who was I? That was a question I did not care to consider. Not just then.

I paid yet again so that my room—actually two rooms, with gritty stone floors and a view of the ruins of the Roman theater, albeit seen through greasy windows—might be made up quickly. This same payment, which I suppose *was* rather generous, secured for me a sizable breakfast of three boiled eggs, some black bread smeared with apricot paste, and a bowl of coffee, delivered to my room by the innkeeper herself; I could not eat it all, but I was buoyed to see that this *experienced* woman—this I assumed based on the evidence of an ample bosom, proudly shown—took me to be a ravenous man of the roads.

I instructed the innkeeper to wake me at two; and finally, as the Arlesiens rose that day, I sank, contentedly, into hours of uninterrupted, dreamless sleep.

I walked around Arles a bit that afternoon, but so distracted was I by events of the night before, and by the imagined events of the days to come, well . . . I did not make much of a tourist. Indeed, and in truth, it was my Arlesienne I sought; and so my eyes were trained on every passing face, every distant figure, and I saw not much of the city. What comes first to mind when I recall the place are those sharp tiny stones in the streets, like tacks, which too often made their way through the soles of my boots. With each pinprick of pain, I grew more and more determined to rid myself of that wardrobe Sebastiana had sent me off with. Of course, those boots had nothing to do with the contents of the *necessaire*; it was simply that their thin, impractical soles reminded me of the clothes' greater impracticality.

In Arles, and later in Marseilles, I augmented my wardrobe, choosing from shops and stalls that sold preworn clothes. (In exchange for what I chose, I left behind *fripperies* drawn from the *necessaire*.) I chose my clothes carefully, not because I cared about them, their cut or color; rather, it seemed to me I'd a thin line to tread. Overdressed, I'd be out of place in the port and aboard whatever ship would have me. Underdressed, I'd perhaps find it difficult to secure any passage at all. Overdressed, I might be taken advantage of, even robbed. Underdressed, I might be expected to... *Enfin*, after a spot of shopping I had a wardrobe that suited me, literally.

What clothes I could not trade—"Monsieur," asked the shopkeeper, "*who* would wear such a thing?"—I later gave away at the port of Marseilles. Simply, I set a pile of clothes down on the quay and invited passersby to pick through them. I confess, it was jarring to see a man of Africa, bound home to Alexandria, via Messina, take up an embroidered blouse of white silk, only slightly yellow with age, and rip from it its full sleeves; said he—in French I could barely understand; indeed his meaning was better conveyed by his gestures— such sleeves would surely get caught up in his ship's rigging and cause him all manner of grief, if not outright catastrophe.

Seated streetside in a café, still hoping to see again Arlesienne, I met a man. Rather, he met me.

Having carefully calculated the cost of two coffees, I was about to place coin enough on the marble table and take my leave when I was arrested by the corpulence of a man standing too close behind me. "Monsieur," said I, pushing past him, "*pardonnez-moi*." As if his stomach, girdled in a waistcoat of fine gray silk, stretched dangerously tight, its buttons about to bullet off at me, if not *through* me... as if his stomach were not obstacle enough, this man then extended his hand for me to take.

"Théophile Libaudet," said he, and, by dint of a social choreography I cannot describe, I soon found myself seated again at that same table, this stranger beside me.

His hands, I recall, were horribly fat, with whisker-like hairs on the dimpled knuckles. (I, remembering Arlesienne's admonition, had traded for a pair of men's traveling gloves, which, too awkward to wear at table, sat in my lap like a pet.) So malodorous was he of tobacco, I half expected a whole rolled leaf to appear in the stead of his tongue; but no... he simply drew from his vest pocket a cigar. "Cuban," said he, offering me a puff, which I declined. From another pocket came a silver flask. Emptying into their saucers the dregs of the coffees I'd had, and wiping out the cups with a silk kerchief, he poured from the flask. "The darkest of rums," said he. "From Jamaica, don't you know?" Smoke and drink arrayed, the fat man sat back; it seemed only then did he stop. Previously, he'd been a blur of motion, of bluster and pomp. "Now," said he, spreading his wide hand flat on the table and drumming his gouty thumb—his intention, I saw, was to show me two rings, which were, indeed, impressive— "Now," he resumed, "I stand at a loss: you know *my* name and I—"

I made up a name. Rather, I offered the name of a former Minister of Finance; if my forceful friend knew it, perhaps he was not as . . . as self-involved and stupid as he seemed. He did not know it. Indeed, I might have introduced myself as Jean Racine and told him the tale of Phèdre. I might have said I was Mirabeau, or Pope Leo XII, for I saw that he'd forgotten my name as soon as I'd spoken it. Nevertheless, I had to shake his hand a second time: it was like squeezing a skinless rat, and perhaps I withdrew too fast, rudely fast.

A waiter approached and Monsieur Libaudet, saying we had all we needed, gave him money enough to keep him away for the duration. Our cups he refilled with the pleasant, if strong, rum. "You are a traveler, *mon ami*?" he asked; in response, I turned the same question back on him, for I knew that to be his aim.

"Ah, yes, indeed. Around the world, around the world. . . . A man's duty, I always say. To see the world." He puffed and sipped. A procession of children passed then, in fabulous costume, and were tossed sweets and flowers and coin as they made their way to some ceremony in the not too distant bullring. My companion paid them no mind. "Just back from six months out, you know. The African continent. Pains and pleasures, it was; pains and pleasures. And you, young sir?"

"America," I said. And that was the first I knew of my own intentions. Sebastiana had said to cross the sea, she'd not said which sea. It was I who assumed the Atlantic; though, of course, much still depended on events in Marseilles.

"Ah, yes, indeed. America," mused the man. "Been there. Some years back. Not long after that messy business of 1812." I assumed he meant the war of that year. "America, eh?" said he, training his tiny eyes on mine, and then drawing from his waistcoat pocket, with great show, a golden watch, pendant from a braided chain of auburn hair. ". . . *Tempus fugit*, my young friend. But tell me—do you seek to make your name or secure your fortune?" Before I could conceive of an answer, he offered his own: "Of course, in a young country the two are often linked." He asked did I have a final destination. "New York, will it be? Boston, perhaps?" I said I did not. "My advice is this: make your name in the North, but seek your money in the South." He sat back smiling—the oracle had spoken—with his short-seeming arms crossed over the silk-wrapped barrel that he was. (I did not like him; at first this seemed to me unfortunate, but soon it would ease the transaction we would make, in which I'd gouge him good.)

The objective of my fellow's African travels was this: he'd great pride in what he called his *"cabinet de curiosités,"* long established at his home outside Lyon. In a salon "of fine decoration" he showed—"for contributions only"— such *objets* as "the pickled remains of two green monkeys, fully grown and dead of natural causes, of course." He continued his catalog: he'd a mummified child from the reign of the Ptolemies—". . . everything there has its price, if one knows the right native"; a lacquered crocodile standing "long as a log"; whales' teeth with seascapes scratched into them; several stuffed wolverines arranged in "a lifelike display." He went on, and I listened with revulsion and decreasing interest until he came to what seemed a particularly prized item: "I have," said he, as if in the greatest confidence, "the weighted dice of the Duc d'Orléans!"

"Non!" I enthused. (Instantly I had my idea.)

"Oui!" said he. And I, conspiring in turn, leaned in to ask the man this:

"Monsieur," I asked, "have you an interest in souvenirs of . . . of *l'ancien régime?"* His eyes went wide. As I hurried him from that café he panted like a dog; soon his bulk settled into its habitual gait—a wavelike motion, side to side, aided by the deft use of an ivory-topped cane—and we achieved the berlin in short order. Soon I'd sold it to him, bidding both him and it *adieu.* I thought to warn him of the flooding, but I did not; I reasoned that perhaps the Rhône had receded now, without the succubus to stir it. . . . It was a fair price I got, nearly twice what the man first offered, and the banking was easily seen to. In the course of that transaction, I discovered something of a taste for commerce—it was *fun,* as long as one knew how to read the coins and bills, and I did, finally. (My actual thought was this: Can a meretricious fool such as he *truly* become rich in this world? . . . If *he* could, perhaps I . . .)

Quickly now . . . (For I've just taken up this pen again, having risen from my tiny table to spy, through my cabin's sole, rounded window, that distant shore that we are fast approaching: it is, yes, the port of Richmond, in the state of Virginia. Of this city I know nothing, and of the state I know only that Th. Jefferson calls it home.)

. . . Without the berlin, I'd have to find another way to Marseilles. And I did so without difficulty, securing passage on a diligence that would leave Arles proper at nine the next morning. Its route would not be direct, but no matter. The new moon come and gone, my calendar was clear.

I returned to my two rooms in the early evening, flush with success, having dealt with the fat man, and despairing at not coming across Arlesienne. I was loaded down with booty culled from that city's booksellers. Two new suits were to be delivered that very night by the son of a most amenable tailor I'd discovered down an alley; he, at that very moment, was working double-quick for double-pay. I was tired, but excited too. Blood *rushed* through my veins, and I doubted sleep would come that night. I had still to make the morning trip to Marseilles and, again, the thought of sailors and sea travel chilled my rushing blood. (Strange that now, with the crossing nearly over, I know it to be nothing. Indeed, I enjoyed it, the rhythm and the roll of it, the silence of the sea . . . But still I sympathize with my former self, the sea-wary one.)

That night in Arles I sent the innkeeper's boy out for some brandy; and I was most appreciative when the hostess herself brought the bottle up to my room along with a crystal snifter that was almost clean. Less delectable was the slab of salt pork she proffered, along with a chunk of black bread that I had to soak in a cup of broth before I could bite it unreservedly, without fear of losing a tooth or two in its crust. I opened my windows to the quieting sounds of the city. The waxing crescent of moon shone none too brightly. I heard shutters closing against the night and its coming chill.

I ate. And I breathed deeply, for this can sometimes calm me. Tired as I was, that night in Arles, I could not resist thumbing through some of the books I'd bought—histories and random tracts, most of them touching in some way on our "dark arts." I'm glad I haven't the time, for I'd be embarrassed to account for the pleasure I took in those books . . . cutting the unread pages with a silver blade I bought for that purpose, fanning the thick, stiff pages so that the aroma of knowledge rose up to rival that of the brandy. . . .

Finally, and I've no idea what hour it was, my eyes grew tired; they teared as I tried to read. My eyelids were impossibly heavy; sleep would have its way, no matter the interest I took in the books before me, no matter my ceaseless wondering and worrying.

I left the books piled on that room's small table, which I'd pushed nearer the open window, and I left there too the remains of my supper—a tableau, it occurs to me now, very like the one in that lesser library at C———. I rose from the table and went to ready the bed, to fluff the flat pillow, and turn the coarse linen down over the thin mattress.

It was then I discovered, under that pillow, a dirtied pair of short pants, dyed indigo blue. I knew instantly whose they were; and in that same instant there came the chill I knew well.

I turned and there he stood, before the open window, his beauty defined by the lambent light rising from the lanterns just lit in the street, falling from the stars and the moon. . . . Roméo. It was Roméo.

An instant passed—and if only there'd been a way to hold to that instant, so fleet, so fine—and then I knew it all to be illusory.

"Why?" said I to Father Louis; for it was, of course, the incubus who stood before me in the shape of my Roméo. My eyes welled with tears that would not fall, so stubborn, as though refusing the truth in favor of the illusion. "Why?" I asked of the incubus. "I've told you, Louis, I've no interest in—"

"To thank you," said the priest, borrowing the boy's voice, Roméo's voice. Naked, he came to me and held me in Roméo's arms and kissed me with purloined lips and. . . . And I could not help but respond.

"I should have known you would not give up," I breathed. His thick neck was cold, yet the coldness seemed to fire my lips as I whispered, as I kissed and playfully bit his ear. . . . "Use his voice," I whispered, with a measure of shame.

"Yes," said Roméo, "you should have known."

There'd be no refusing his favors.

We made love. Or, as the priest would indelicately put it, "we fucked."

But the very nature of the elementals, succubus and incubus alike, was such that . . . well, I imagine loving sex with a mortal is rather more *tender*. If Madeleine had been mischievous, directing Roméo and me in the bath, now Father Louis, as Roméo, was flatly fiendish; for sex was but the means to an end, and the end was control, simply. Again—and was it not the priest himself who told me this?—one cannot fault one for doing what it is in one's nature to do. And so . . . his every touch fell upon me either icy or aflame, so that I lurched down that dark and unknown lane of pleasure as a drunk stumbles from the tavern, unsure of the way that might open before him. I would revel in the cold touch—far more accustomed was I to the cold than the hot—I would revel in his cold touching of my breasts, only to recoil, or try to recoil—in truth, he held me fast—when his kneading, rough touch turned hot, so very hot, and his lips, like pincers—the fire-red pincers for which every sister must bear an ancestral fear—fell upon my blood-thickened nipples. I cried out. Muffling me with his icy clamp of a hand, he laughed, and drove into me deeper. . . . But I could not get angry, for in his way he *was* sincere, this I knew; too, the pleasure was never far behind the pain. Worse, I trusted him, trusted him to lead me safely home to my self when his show of pleasure and pain was through; and, yes, still I clung to the illusion of Roméo, Roméo before me, atop me, within me. But I took care to not show too much pleasure, too much pain, for then, certainly, the incubus would change tack; again, it is control that such a one seeks, *control*. But my wiles were no match for his; and so soon I abandoned myself to him, as a marionette might to its master. And not long after, he was done; and I was spent in every way, *every* way, with little but welts, spiderish bites, and welling bruises to show for my efforts. And indeed I did make an effort, for after the elementals, and Roméo, and Arlesienne, I can love ... rather, I can take to the act of sex with some measure of confidence. Love eludes me still. . . . Ah, what I mean to say is this: that with Father Louis, in Arles, it was not love at all.

It was, at once, everything and nothing. Splendid and sad. It was and was not *my* Roméo. The essence of the boy, that very thing that, like the much sought philosopher's stone of the alchemists, might have made golden the relative dross of our ... our acrobatics, that *essential* Roméo the incubus could never contain, never control. . . . And so, if the question is this: Was my love for Roméo requited that night?—the answer is, emphatically, sadly, no. . . . But I am thankful at least that I had not wanted the boy so very long, for that wanting, and the waiting, would have grown richer with time, like wine; and then the taste I took from the incubus would have disappointed all the more.

But I say again, the priest was sincere in his effort to thank me; sincere, yes, and therefore ardent in his ... *attentions*, the receipt of which I do not regret. And I believe it was *not* the demon I knew that night, not truly, just as it was not my Roméo; it was, I believe, the essential, long-dead Father Louis. It was the sweet priest Madeleine had known in life. It was the one-time man of God; and the act, that night, seemed to me ... sacramental, *graceful* in the truest sense.

. . . As we lay some time later on that mattress, uncovered, my arms linked around the weighty cold of the incubus's, he spoke. He held still to Roméo's shape, though when he spoke the voice was his own. He was answering the question that had slipped from my lips. "What will you do?" I'd asked.

The incubus whispered his response, his lips to my ear; there was no discernible exhalation as he spoke and I could not but remark the absence, the *utter* absence of warmth when, sadly, he said: " 'Her lips suck forth my soul; see where it flies.' "

I knew the line. It is, appropriately enough, from Marlowe's *Dr. Faustus*. I knew too, instantly, as soon as the words were spoken, that Father Louis was saying good-bye. I'd known the moment would come, and I thought it was what I wanted. (Never once did I imagine him sailing with me. Never did I see him beside me in my New World.) But once the words were said, and the good-bye implied, well, it seemed my very self was rent: part of me was sad, terribly sad, and part of me grew fearful, for I was finally and undeniably alone.

The incubus rose off me. Only then, naked but for the blue shorts with which I demurely, foolishly, and ineffectively tried to cover myself, only then did I grow bone-chillingly cold. I maneuvered on the mattress, desperate to get beneath the one woolen blanket. . . . When last I saw the incubus he was walking toward the open window, Roméo's shape growing ever fainter, fainter . . . At the window he turned and bent double in a deep and courtly bow; and then he vanished, and I lay smiling at the air. My hand was raised as though to wave, but I found I could not execute that simple act, and my hand fell fast to my side.

. . . The next morning I boarded the diligence at the appointed hour. I had only the half-filled *nécessaire*, which the trap's two drivers—brothers, or cousins, to judge by their excessive and changeable familiarity—loaded. There were three other passengers from Arles, in whose company I pleasured.

As had happened near the crossroads, I was struck again by the moribund aspects of the secondary cities of the Rhône, the names of which escape me. (I've packed away the map: I haven't recourse to it right now.) We stopped in one such nameless place, its market crowded with the silks of Lyon, leatherware, and baled hemp; the bound wheat of Toulouse; wines of the Languedoc; sea salt from the Camargue; soaps of Marseilles; and casks of olive oil.

. . . Yes, after Arles the weary Rhône slows and eventually splits into *les deux Rhônes morts*, the "dead rivers," which crawl across the Camargue Delta. As we made our way thusly, slowly, to Marseilles, I took from my companions all they offered of the area. They laughed when I shrieked at the sight of flocked flamingos rising up in a roseate wave; of course, I said nothing when I saw what had occasioned their sudden movement: Maluenda, as raven, flew among them, black among the red and the blushing pink, ever watchful of me. Wild geese abounded, too. By the bright light, eagles and buzzards and pelicans patrolled the ivory sands. It was a herd of swift white horses—of the Saracen strain, I was told, useful in bullfighting—it was the horses, pale among the paler dunes, that occasioned my tears. The beauty of the land, its corn- and vine-covered plains crawling to the sea, its marshes spotted with half-wild cattle . . . the land affected me bodily. The beauty of it. I hadn't known Nature to be capable of such.

Later in the day we reached Marseilles. The calm of the Camargue only heightened my instinctive dislike and distrust of cities. And so, quickly, I secured passage on the *Ceremaju*, a smallish clipper owned by the Liverpudlian firm of Lloyd and Vredenburgh, slated to sail the next day and arrive in America some four or five weeks later—depending, of course, on conditions, which, thankfully, were good: easy seas and steady wind.

The *Ceremaju*—due to quarantining—sat still off the coast of "Dead Marseilles." (Sometime in the last century, a plague of the city claimed fifty thousand of its inhabitants in just two years; fully half the population. These days the fear is of yellow fever, said to be ravaging Spain. . . . *Enfin*, all ships are made to anchor in the quarantine harbor, Dieudonné, off the isle of Pomègues.) The *Ceremaju* would sail from Marseilles as soon as her hold could be emptied of its store of tea, tobacco, and corn and reloaded, I was happy to hear, with empty oil casks; it was owing to this buoyant cargo that the *Ceremaju* was, according to its captain, unsinkable.

Now I've considered not adding here, to this Book, to *my* Book, the following fact—but I will add it; it may amuse you, Reader, as it did *not* amuse me. See, the *Ceremaju* was, indeed *is* what's known as a hermaphrodite brig; that is, it is a two-masted vessel, square-rigged forward and schooner-rigged aft. Imagine my state when, acting my manly best to secure passage on said ship, it was so described to me by its captain, who, I was certain, was enjoying himself at my expense. But then he spoke of money, and I knew he was serious. And when he spoke of money, of the price of passage—there, amid the bustling crowd, with men of every description speaking all the world's languages, engaged in their dangerous work—I was greatly relieved; so relieved and eager I made the mistake of drawing out my money far too early in our negotiations. The ship was full-up, said its captain; my passage on it was an impossibility. ("We aren't fitted out for fine travelers," said my first American.) But he baldly stared at the wadded notes in my hand. Then again, said he . . . just maybe. . . . Finally, though this and that law and custom would require circumvention, which in turn required cash, he took me on. I paid a price that I will not record here, for on that occasion my bargaining skills, which I thought I'd honed on the man with the pickled green monkeys, quite deserted me, and I handed over to the captain . . . well, allow me to say it was "an excess of coin," little of which, I'm sure, will clink into the coffers of the Messieurs Lloyd and Vredenburgh.

I did receive, in return, the brig's most comfortable quarters: a room twice as long as it was wide, wide enough for a single berth; it has a starboard porthole, this table and chair, which I am eager to surrender, a bank of glass-enclosed bookshelves that I have sampled (reading all I ever care to read of adventures in the South Seas, of mythic sea beasts and islands where the women go about bare-breasted in skirts of grass), and a sort of pantry, which was, when I boarded, rather generously stocked with jugs of fresh water, a keg of sea biscuit, several Bologna sausages, a bowl of citrus, a ham, roast mutton, and bottles of assorted cordials and liqueurs, none of which I've failed to taste. All that was left for me to procure was a store of candles, some phosphorous matches, ink, and pens. This I had time enough to do in Marseilles that evening, before letting a room in a quayside inn, the common room of which I was afraid of entering, as it seemed home to the fearful sailor and the even more fearful woman who keeps his company. . . . I was wrong to think one might actually *sleep* in such a place. Having secured a map of America, I retired with it to my room, against the door of which I propped the only chair. On the bed, with torn cloth stuffed in my ears against the ceaseless singing from belowstairs, I studied the map. Hungry, I fell asleep. Hungrier still, I woke at first light. Famished, I was the first to board the *Ceremaju.* . . . So fast did I tear into that larder that I failed to bid *adieu* to the fading coast of France.

Happily, I can record here that our crossing was without incident, and that we—that is, the captain, a mate, a cook, four seamen, myself, and one Mr. Hunt, who is returning to Richmond in the company of a Negro girl whom he quite preposterously says he *owns,* and whom he has named Melody, for she sings beautifully—indeed much of what I've written above has been set down to her accompaniment. . . . *Enfin,* we are all about to arrive in Richmond in fine shape. To be accurate, I should say that I've a sore left shoulder owing to the swollen seas of three nights back which tossed me from my bunk not once, but twice; and sure there's been a bit of *le mal de mer,* but I'm told that is to be expected. A bit of *le mal du pays,* too; also to be expected, for who sails from their homeland without some measure of sadness?

So it's here, in sight of the seaboard—and I'm thrilled to see it, and to *smell* it too, for it is not the open sea that smells but rather the sea's edge—it is here that this tale ends. For now. Certainly, there's much more to come, all of it still a mystery to me. Perhaps I'll sail on. (I have enjoyed the sailing.) The captain has invited me to do so, and has told me of the brig's itinerary: more tobacco to be loaded on at Richmond, then it's off to the far tip of the Floridas for salt, which he'll carry to La Havane, Cuba, there loading up with coffee and hemp, which he'll relay to *La Nouvelle Orléans* . . . There, at least the language would be familiar. . . . *Alors, qui sait?*

From the scratchings and goings-on above deck one would think some wild animals had been loosed to run about. The mate is shouting this and that, none of which I understand—a new language, this, the *spoken* English of America. Melody, I notice, has stopped singing. I have written on and on, but now I must put this pen down, indeed pack it and all else I own into the *necessaire*. . . . Ah yes, the *necessaire*. That trunk with which I left Ravndal, that trunk I eventually emptied of Sebastiana's *musée des modes*, emptied of all but the black velvet bag, which I shoved this way and that as I repacked the trunk with new clothes and books, et cetera, never once thinking to open it and examine its contents.

In that black velvet bag, you see, I made a discovery. Two nights ago, when first it occurred to me that I ought to begin organizing my things and readying to disembark. Only then did I come across that sack Sebastiana had given me, pressed upon me at Ravndal. Only then did I open it, long after tossing it into the trunk without a thought. And what I found was enough to . . .

No, I cannot go on. There *simply* isn't time! The mate has knocked three times on my door. And there is confusion above deck, an excitement I am eager to join.

. . . So instead I will insert here those few words, those pages I scribbled that very night, two nights ago, seated topside with the deed already done, an inkwell steady in my left hand, a sharpened quill in my right. The sea was wonderfully steady. I wrote what follows by the high and bright light of the moon, of course.

Read on.

Epilogue

THIS SEA-NIGHT is sublime—wind enough to fill the sails, not enough to roil the black water.

Two, maybe three days from landfall, they say. I am ready.

I am a ship sailing out of my life. To a new life.

I am ready.

Topside now.

Had to move carefully, step lightly: winches like the hands of the greedy, pinching pulleys, sudden-swinging masts, and ropes coiled to strike like snakes . . . This brig is a thing alive, that much I've learned. And it sings—sings constantly—mimics the sea—the sucking wind, the high whine of the wind, the whisper of the waves . . . Dances too, dances its sea dance day and night.

———

I left the Books to come topside. To do what I had to do. To the accompaniment of these songs: the ship's, the sea's.

I came with hands full—the basket, the bag—to this, my spot, in a corner of the stern. (Men about, but none notice me. Some are asleep, swinging in hammocks.)

I have it all with me. No—I *had* it all with me.

I've already done what I had to do. Done it, yes.

Bone by bone from the soft basket went Madeleine into the sea.

The bag . . . Sebastiana's full black bag, full, full . . .

Forgotten till this night.

Packing that trunk—with books, new books—I saw again the soft black bag, curled like a cat in the canvas-lined corner. I touched it, to move it just so and . . . And I knew. Knew as soon as I touched it. Knew too what I would do.

I opened it. There, there like loot risen from the sea—belched up from the bloated belly of a long-gone galleon—there it all lay.

I spread the bag wide. Rolled its lips down. Both hands dipping, diving down birdlike, lifting the loot to let it rain back into the bag, again and again. My smile as bright as the silver and the gold and the gemstones.

Yes, there it all was:

Skavronsky's diamond heavy as an egg in my fist.

Rings from the Italian witches—Renata, Giuliana—rings of sea-green jasper and pale quirin.

The sapphire-set, golden ankh given by Luchina—it was Luchina, no? who gave the Egyptian gift of life to Sebastiana at the Greek Supper, sealing it with a kiss . . .

Bangles—one of them—of hammered gold—a cuff to cover the whole forearm. Rings to weight the witches' hand. Ropes of pearl—black, white, and gray—all entwined. Clusters of jeweled and filigreed silver and wrought gold and. . . .

The black bag full of jewels. The soft basket full of bones.

———

To decide. What to keep of all we are given, all we receive, all we seek out and take. To decide.

Too, the bracelet from the Prince of Nassau. *Ornez celle qui orne son siècle.* Adorn she who adorns her century.

   That and that alone I have kept. I wear it pushed high up onto my left forearm, as high as it will go, beneath a full sleeve.

   Ornez celle. Adorn she.

   All the rest of it into the sea, stone by stone into the sea, into the moonlit opaline churning of the sea, broken by the on-sailing brig.

Stones and bones. Jewels. All of it into the shadowed sea. The sea.

What I see—the deed done—is a chain: jewel to bone to jewel to bone . . . trailing this brig . . . sinking down, down into the Deep. . . . A necklace. . . . A bridge.

   Yes, a bridge of jewels and bones.

   . . . *Adorn she.*

My way must be my own, no? I will *make* my way my own. As you must make yours.

We all of us travel alone over bridges made of jewels and bones.

Acknowledgments

Thank you to my family for allowing me an avocation; and to my agent, Suzanne Gluck, and my editor, Trish Grader, for providing me with a profession. Thanks also to Ben Short for his generosity, and to the late Joe Jenner for his abiding guidance.